Lily Fairchild

Lily Fairchild

Don Gutteridge

Published by Tablo

For Colm O'Sullivan

Teacher, Scholar, Friend

In Memoriam

BOOK ONE

St. Vitus Dance

PART ONE

Lily

1

Moore Township, 1845

Something stirred in the darkness ahead. It made no sound, but it was present and alive. For as long as she could remember, she knew. The breath from a fawn's cough could tease her skin – like this ripple of shaded wind against her cheek – long before her ear caught the sound and identified it.

Lily was glad to be in the comfort of the trees' canopy. It was cozy here, like the cabin with Papa's fire blazing, when Mama was not in her bed. Lily wasn't afraid of the dark, though Mama sometimes shivered fearfully at night, especially those nights when Papa had "gone off" and Lily was beckoned to press her child's body against her mother's clenched form. She dreamt she was a moth spinning a warm cocoon around them both, full of charms to drive the uncertainty from Mama's eyes. While outside, heard only by her, the snow sang to the wind and no one in the world was lonely.

It was never lonesome in the bush. Here living things emerged and endured in the dappled undergrowth – ferns and worts and fungi and mosses, and, in the few random spots freckled by sun, surprised violets. Lily could sense the creatures' presence even as she took short quick steps towards the back bush, a place forbidden by Mama. She stopped to acknowledge them: a thrush untangled his song; a snakeskin combed the grass; a deermouse scuttled and froze.

"You stay away from the Indians, you hear?" Mama said so often. She seemed to hate them: they never did a lick of work; they drank whiskey, then went crazy and hurt people; they went hunting god-knows-where, taking good men with them, so the farms were neglected. And their women, they're wicked too, and dance and do bad things.... Lily wanted to ask, not about the bad things, but about the dancing, though she never did.

Lily knew where the Indians lived. Many nights, curled in the straw of her loft, she heard the drumbeats come across the tree-tops from miles away and settle into their clearing as if aimed there. They were not like her soft heartbeat, nor like the sprightly songs Mama sang at her spinning wheel. Theirs was a pounding, repetitive music that set her heart ajar, that made her long to know what words could be sung to such a rhythm, what dances would find their feet in such a frenzy. She wanted to see those women, how they moved in the firelight that twisted above the black roof of the bush, what their eyes said when they danced in the smoky, burnished, mosquito-riven dark.

An axe rang against a tree-trunk, clear as a church bell. *Papa's back.* Lily recognized the signature of his chopping: two vicious slashes, the second slightly more terrifying than the first, followed by two diminished, tentative "chunks." Maybe Mama would hear them too and leave her sick bed. Papa was in the North Field; that was good. He'd only "gone off" as far as the Frenchman's. Sometimes one of the LaRouche boys came back with him to help with the stumps or the burning. All three boys watched her with the edges of their eyes until Papa shouted at her to go away.

Papa had returned and that was enough to deter her from the bush and the forbidden terrain beyond the East Field, carefully planted now with wheat. She turned towards the North Field, five acres of newly cleared and fire-ravaged land where the Indians were not allowed to camp or hunt. Papa might be in a good mood. She listened carefully to the determined repetition of Papa's axe against the grained flesh of the tree. He was at one of the hardwoods again. Abruptly the axe fell silent. Lily held her breath. Then she heard the thunderous, sustained shriek as a two-hundred-year-old walnut came crashing through the forest to stun the ground with its sudden goodbye. She paused and listened to the tree's dying reverberate through the earth.

She would surprise Papa at his work, celebrate another tree felled, and laugh when he swept her up and twirled her around, saying . "Lady Fair Child, may I have the pleasure of this dance?"

2

Mama was in her bed again. Yesterday she had smiled at Lily and proposed they venture out to pick some raspberries for a pie. But they were too late for the berries, shriveled weeks before, and Mama had one of her coughing spells before they were back at the cabin. Papa as usual took some day-old soup in to her. Lily listened, as she always did, to catch the slightest hint of conversation between them. There was none, though Papa stayed a long while, until the haze of evening settled like a moss along the sills and Mama's breathing became regular, heavy with exhaustion.

This morning he left again. "Gotta have meat for that soup," he used to say to Lily, taking down his gun and putting on the buckskin he'd gotten from Old Samuels, the blind Indian who was an exception to Mama's suspicions. Lately Papa simply departed without a word. "Probably," Mama said, her voice shaking with effort, "with that Acorn fellow." Acorn, *Metagomin*, was one of Old Samuels' nephews; the other was *Pwau-na-shig*or Sounder.

But Lily was a help now; she was all of seven. If Papa set the pot on the irons and started the fire, she could cut up the turnips and toss them in, and stir the soup until its tiny rabbit bones surrendered their meat. There was a stone oven at one side of the fireplace; Lily would take the sourdough prepared by Madame LaRouche, and follow her instructions to make bread for Papa's supper. Next spring Papa was going to get them a pig. Already he'd built a pen for it against the east wall.

"Plenty pigs in the bush," Old Samuels would chortle. "Only White Mens builds him a house and grows him food." Then he would shake his head in mock bewilderment at the folly of his white neighbours. Nonetheless, he would wait with the patience of his seventy-odd years till Lily or Papa reached into the pot and offered a respectfully large morsel. Sometimes Lily would be working over the fire, humming one of Mama's songs, and when she turned, Old Samuels would be no more than five feet behind her, the black pennies where his eyes should have been giving nothing away. "You gonna be a good cook, like the Frenchman's woman."

Mama didn't like Old Samuels' habit of entering their cabin without announcing his arrival. Occasionally he would stay all day, sitting on his knees to the left of the fire where he could detect any cool draft from the curtained doorway, saying nothing. Sometimes he would talk to Lily, raising his thin voice just enough to include Mama, willing or no, in the one-way conversation. Old Samuels told long stories, most of which began, "Wasn't like that here in the olden days" and ending with, "and that's the truth, and I know 'cause I seen it, I seen it before these eyes of mine withered up." When Papa made the slightest demurral, he'd say, "Blind men don't lie."

"Before the White Mens come, this was a magic place," he would tell them. "The gods of the Mohawk and the gods of the Huron fought their great battles here among the spirits of my own people, the Attawandaron. In them days, the bears were as big as hickory trees." Pause for the power of that image to take root. "When the foreign gods left, they took all of the Hurons and most of my brothers with them. But the souls of my ancestors stayed right here where they been for a thousand generations. Attawandaron don't run; they hang round, like Old Samuels and Sounder and Acorn. Even when them Ojibwa sells this land they don't own to the White Mens, Old Samuels just laugh. And smoke his pipe – with White Mens' tobacco stolen from our gods who gave it as a gift to all men."

"He's got the manners of a ghost," Mama often said, but not once did she ask him to leave.

"How does he get here if he can't see?" Lily asked Papa.

"He's lived here so long he knows every bush and beetle in the territory," Papa said. And it seemed to be true, as Lily would watch him enter their property at the far corner of the East Field just past the Brown Creek, the stream that flowed, they said, all the way to the Indian camp in the back bush, and then thread his way through the maze of stumps and ash-heaps, never once stepping on the haphazard swirls of wheat between.

"Redmen smells his way in the bush," he told Lily. "Don't need eyes. Redmen sniffs the air currents like the white-tail." He demonstrated. "Raspberry jam," he announced, "from the Frenchman's woman."

"Yes," said Lily, duly amazed.

Last week, though, after LaRouche and his three eldest sons, Luc, Jean-Pierre and Anatole, had finished piling and burning the last log in the North Field, and after some firewater had been consumed by all, Lily saw Old Samuels weave his way towards the back bush, teetering and righting himself as he went. At the corner of the East Field, he paused. The sounds of the men parting in the other direction diminished and died. Old Samuels appeared to look towards the east. Then a small brown boy slipped from the bush and touched Old Samuels' hand. He shook it off. The boy turned, and Old Samuels followed, exactly two paces behind until the woods reclaimed them.

"Your Papa's got a nose for the wind," he said whenever Papa went off with Acorn or Sounder. "Hunting's no good here now. Not like the olden days. They go all the way to Chatham, I guess, to find the bucks this time of year."

Lily wanted to know more about Chatham but Mama began coughing in her bed and Lily rose to attend to her. By the time she returned, Old Samuels had lit up his pipe, stuffed with aromatic tobacco. When he got to smoking, he didn't talk.

Lily may not have known much about Chatham or any other nearby town – Port Sarnia, Sandwich, or London – but she had travelled some miles into the bush with Papa when he trapped in the winter. She had seen the other farms along the line north of them. She could read the trail-marking blazes on the trees and find the faint paths through the bush that would open suddenly upon sun-lit beaver meadows, some of them as wide as the East Field. Beyond the Millars' farm she had seen the crude road that was said to meander all the way to Port Sarnia, and from there to London, immeasurable miles to the east. She knew too that a great river swept by them no more than half-a-day's walk from their own doorstep. Someday Papa would show it to her.

Lily was not prepared for the Frenchman's farm, the home of LaRouche, his wife, and their brood of children. The usual procedure for a homesteader in the new territory was to clear room for a cabin near the front "line" of the property, then proceed in a systematic fashion to open up fields to the north, east and south. When at last Lily was allowed to accompany Anatole back to his place to fetch some garden greens for Mama, she was surprised to find their house set near the centre of several haphazard plots of no particular shape. Several nut trees had been left standing amidst the fledgling wheat and undisciplined vegetable garden. All trees were to be cut down: that was the unspoken code here, one of the necessities that drove the homesteaders to the mutual service and support they required to survive.

LaRouche's cabin had begun life as a log structure of typical rectangular design, but time, weather, and exigency had added their influences to the original. Rooms of planks and split logs, packed with mortar and straw, jutted, sagged, or lay half-built where the Frenchman's imagination or optimism had failed him. No windows looked in or out. Against the east wall, a lean-to of sorts had been erected wherein the ox-team of Bessie and Bert found comfort at day's end among the resident pigs and visiting barred rocks.

Much of the cooking and indeed family life took place outside the murky interior of the homestead. Using the trade he had abandoned for farming after the war against the States, LaRouche built a fine stone oven-and-fireplace protected from the rain by a canvas affair of army tenting, deer-hides and one old sail salvaged, according to its owner, from the Battle of Put-In Bay. Here Madame LaRouche – referred to as Maman by her brood of eleven and as Fluffy by her husband in undisguised admiration for her three hundred pounds of flesh, sturdiness and good health – presided over hearth and oven with a temper that alternated between wheezing cheeriness and tongue-biting pique.

Lily could not take her eyes off Maman. She watched in awe as the woman punched and tormented the sourdough as if she were beating the belly of an obdurate husband, her heavy bosom rolling beneath the homespun smock she wore night and day. Lily shuddered whenever Maman's hand shot out to stun the cheek of a child who ventured too close or dared too much. Later, she would see that same youngster comfortably housed in Maman's lap, drifting into secure sleep.

In return for offerings from Papa's hunting expeditions, Madame LaRouche provided welcome staples during the times when Mama was in bed: preserves, jams, greens from her garden in season, salt-port and "bully beef" from the venison Papa brought home. While the Frenchman himself did not hunt, having given up guns and wars following his service, he usually went along on the shorter excursions to supply encouragement, advice, and refreshments from his still in the bush. The older boys did not share their father's pacifism.

When her own mother slept or rested, Lily was left to spend hours with Maman and her youngest children, all boys except for Madeleine who was just six. Maman happily schooled Lily in cooking and sewing, all of which Lily had a talent for, though not as much persistence and application as Maman would have hoped. But then Lily was not French, Maman teased.

She sang while she baked – wistful melodies in her Norman tongue that seemed all the more serene because they sailed out of such an unnavigable source. Although Maman did not tell conventional stories, she had opinions on everyone and everything.

"Those Millars," she said with the hushed stridency reserved for such remarks, "they're gonna be trouble, wait and see. Scotch, the both of 'em. Give me the Irish any day, even your kind."

"An' you keep away from that Ol' Sams," she said in a more sinister tone. "That carrot of his may be shrivelled up but it's still got juice in the root. You mind them hands too, little chickadee; believe-you-me, Maman knows all about them kind of paws."

Lily of course paid little serious heed to any of this, but she smiled and nodded and did all she could to encourage Maman's chatter. "A pretty, fair thing like you oughta get away from this place as soon as you can. That's Maman's advice. Go to the city. Go to Chatham or Sandwich. They're real nice places. Lots of people."

Then Maman would launch on a description of her brief but dazzling courtship with Corporal LaRouche of Malden, of the clapboard house they'd lived in, the dances they attended, the clothes they wore, the times they had before the Yankees came and the world collapsed. "I said to Gaston, I'll go with you to the bush, I'll have your babies, I'll clean your house, but I'm not about to die out there without a priest at my side, prayin' in my ear and rubbin' my head with holy oil an' smoothin' my slide into Heaven."

Lily swallowed her gooseberry tart.

"I told him I don't care if he has to hop to Sandwich on one snowshoe in a blizzard – a promise is a promise." Maman surprised the pastry dough with a punch to the gut.

"What's a priest?" Lily ventured, at last.

A priest, it turned out, was a kind of preacher. Papa didn't like preachers. Once, last summer, when Lily had been hoeing on her own in the garden near the "line", she heard the crack of a twig along the path to the LaRouches'. She looked up in time to see a large florid man dressed all in black, still panting from the exertion of his trek through the bush. His blue eyes bounced like agates in his puffed face before they came to rest on the rims of his cheeks. His smile was as broad as his belly.

"Good afternoon, little elf," his voice boomed. "I am a man of God. I've come all the way from London. Just to see you."

Lily stared.

"Do you know who God is, little one?"

No response.

"Would you kindly tell your pa that the Methodist man is here."

Lily did not have to tell Papa. He had heard, even in the North Field, and had come striding past the cabin towards them. Lily knew enough to leave. She heard Papa's voice raised the way it was when he cursed Bert and Bessie or the trunk of a stubborn ironwood. His axe flashed in the sun. The preacher was already scuttling like a duck into the safety of the Lord's bush.

Lily wanted to ask Papa who God was; Mama tried to tell her.

Sometimes, after being in her bed for several days, when some colour had come back into her cheeks, Mama would reach under the bed and pull out the large, dark book she called the Bible. Lily watched, poised and alert, as Mama's fingers made the pages, thin as bee's wings, flutter and settle.

"These are the words God gave us."

"Read me some of them, Mama."

"Not today, my sweet. Mama's just a bit too tired. Tomorrow."

"Promise?"

"Promise."

Then, seeing the longing in her child's eyes, she would close the book and in a reedy quaver begin to sing the spinning song,

Hi diddle dum, hi diddle dare-o

Hi diddly iddly, hi diddle air-o

Hi diddle diddly, hi diddle um

At first Lily would hum along, then gradually pick up the tongue-tumbling syllables one at a time, like stitches, giving to them whatever meaning the emotions of the moment allowed.

As sometimes happened, Papa did not return by day's end. Lily had been able to find enough small logs to keep the fire alive overnight, though it was not banked properly and the cabin became suffocating in the late August heat. She made some tea, warmed up the soup, and went into Mama's room. Lily held her hand to guide the tin cup to her lips. After a few reluctant sips, Mama closed her eyes.

The morning outside was beautiful and Lily bent to her chores in the garden and yard. High in the pines and arching elms, cicadas soon announced noon. By then, Mama was sitting in the rocker Papa had fashioned for her out of cedar. She gave Lily a wan smile and asked: "Would you help Mama with her hair?" As her mother watched in wordless encouragement, Lily managed to heat a wide kettle of water and get it foaming with soap. Mama leaned over, her brow resting on the arm of the chair, her long hair reaching almost to the floor. For a moment she seemed to be asleep, but when Lily began to pour the soft warm water over her, letting it fall gently back into the kettle, she murmured and her hand reached out to squeeze Lily's. How beautiful Mama's hair was, its former glory regained as she sat back in the rocker and let the afternoon sun scatter praise where it could. Lily took her mother's bone-brush and stroked and stroked. A while later she said, "Let's have tea, little one."

Lily, excited, brought out the china pot and two tiny cups with matching blue saucers. She stirred the slumbering fire and prepared the tea just as she remembered Mama doing, then fetched the last of the blueberry cakes Maman LaRouche had given them. Mama began to speak softly, but insistently. "The place we come from, your Papa and me, is a long ways across the biggest ocean in the world. We were married there. We were very happy. But it wasn't a happy land. The priests and the preachers didn't get along. The crops failed, many times. We were hungry. Papa decided we should leave. You were already tucked inside my belly. We went on a sailing ship three times bigger than this house. Everything we owned was packed into two trunks they put in the hold."

The odour of hot ash hung in the air outside the cabin and in the room itself, blue-bottles buzzed, unappeased.

"I figured we'd die on that ship, but we didn't. We made it because we loved one another, we wanted happiness or death. At Quebec Papa bought tools and we got onto another ship, a smaller one, and sailed along the big lake just south of here. There a storm struck us down. The ship came apart in the waves near the long point. Dozens of people drowned. Papa and me were in the only boat that got to shore. We lost everything but our lives."

The room darkened steeply, the sun eclipsed by the high horizon of the trees. Lily carefully unwound Mama's fingers from the tea-cup, hearing her shallow breathing. How Lily wished that Old Samuels would arrive just now, slip in unnoticed, and be in the mood to tell a long story. Mama could just rock there and listen.

But Old Samuels did not come. The dusk of early evening drifted in, adhered. Lily decided to let the fire go out; the air was already too warm. Leaving her mother asleep in the chair, she started up the ladder to the loft.

"Don't go up, Lily. Sleep with Mama tonight."

Eagerly, Lily scrambled back down and then helped Mama towards her curtained cubicle. Her arms were thin as willow, the flesh draped over the bones. Lily slipped out of her cotton dress and under the sheet.

"Open this, please," Mama said. In her hand was a small box made of in-laid woods. It was the most beautiful object Lily had ever seen. With her nimble fingers she tripped the slim gold latch and the lid lifted. Mama brought out a cameo pendant with a silver chain that shimmered in the gloaming. Fortuitously the last log in the fire burst into brief flame, and Lily was able to see that there was, beneath the cameo's glaze, the merest sketch of a woman's head: two or three quick but telling strokes. With a start, Lily recognized her own eyes.

"Your grandmother."

Mama's eyes filled with tears. She reached into the box again. "I saved this, out of the storm." She held up a gold chain on the end of which dangled a slender cross no more than half an inch long. Instinctively Lily leaned forward and the crucifix settled on her throat as if it had always expected to be there. Then Mama fell back against her pillow. She crooked her left arm and Lily, as she had seen Maman LaRouche's little ones do so often, slid into the embrace and held herself there as if the world would end if she blinked.

Lily had left the bed curtain open. In the dark, the embers of the fire glowed, then succumbed without a murmur. The night-air, remembering that it was almost September, turned as chill and sharp as the sabre-shaped moon guiding it. When Lily woke, the sun was already above the tree-line, sifting through the east window. She had been kept warm through the night by the final, fierce heat of her mother's will. Beside her now, that flesh lay as cold as the ice that clenched the streams of mid-winter.

3

Maman LaRouche sent everyone out of the house while she dressed Mama's body. Papa, Gaston LaRouche, and Luc had sat in the lean-to shed sipping from a jug, murmuring occasionally in low voices, but mostly staring straight ahead into the bush. Once Lily thought she heard her mother's name spoken–"Kathleen"– like an exhalation of breath, but she wasn't sure. They put Mama's body, carefully wrapped in a white sheet of the softest cotton from Maman's cedar chest, in the ground on a slight knoll where the East Field joined the North. Jean-Pierre and Anatole had dug the hole.

Old Samuels came to the grave with his nephews, Sounder and Acorn; to Lily's astonishment, a tribe of wives and children followed behind them with heads down, though still resplendent in their furs and black-and white featherage. The Millars and the two new families from the North section arrived. Lily had never before seen so many people gathered in one place. She held Papa's hand tightly, and he squeezed back, almost hurting. Her heart reared through its sadness. Mr. Millar stepped forward, opened a black book, and read some words from it that the wind caught with ease and almost carried off. Maman LaRouche suddenly burst into sobs which she made no effort to staunch, fully drowning his eulogy. Lily understood even then that Maman was weeping for them all.

Old Samuels began to hum from somewhere deep in his body, letting the music of it find its own course and pace. The gravesite became quiet; the wind fell. His lamentation found syllables and sounds that might have been words, though no one present had ever heard the language they made. His blank eyes, like death's pennies, began to flutter in time with the rising and falling cadences of his song. He turned his ancient face upward, and his whole frame tensed, expectant, as if he had been asking some question over and over. He looked towards Papa and Lily. He smiled as only a man without eyes can smile, with every other feature of his face. In English he said: "The gods are listening; that is all we can ask."

Many times during the long winter following, when Papa was away trapping or hunting, Lily asked Maman who God was, thinking of Mama lying unattended in that cold grave under the snow. But Maman used the question to launch into another rant about priests and the promises of faithless husbands. Papa, who was always too tired to talk after his excursions, would just grunt in a dismissive tone, "Go ask Millar, he knows all about those things." Then he would go silent or out the door.

"Off to Chatham," Old Samuels would shake his head sadly. "Plenty bad people in Chatham, for sure." Or when Papa sometimes pointedly picked up his gun, leather pouches and haversack, and said to Lily, "Better tell them lady deer to stay back in the bush, darlin', your Papa's comin'," Old Samuels would whisper after him, "Your Papa's gone to Chatham to hunt *bucks*," and chortle.

On the subject of God, though, Old Samuels was eager and loquacious. "White Mens has the silliest ideas about the gods. It takes us Indians a day to stop laughin' when we hear about it. First they say there's only one god. If that's true then the white god must fight with himself. Anybody with ears and eyes –" he'd always pause here for a tiny ironic smile –"knows about the god in the thundercloud whose voice speaks blackly to the quiet gods in the lake and the summer creeks. And the god of the gentle winds has no love for the god of the blizzard that tears the trees in half and buries the earth. Anybody knows there's the good gods and the wicked gods, the guardian spirits and the demons. We must listen to the good gods to keep them on our side: they will help those who listen for them. Remember that, little one. But we must also help the gods. Sometimes the demons are too strong and the good gods go into hiding. That is a sad time for the world."

"What about heaven?" Lily asked, remembering Maman's assurance that her mother dwelled there.

"Your Mama, who was the dearest White Womens in this world, is not in heaven, little one. That Millar, he tells me heaven is a pretty house with beads and ornaments on it, up over the moon and the stars. That is silliness. The good gods would not build their house up there; they live here in the green world and in the stars themselves. Your Mama's body is under the earth, but the guardian gods have taken her spirit with them. Wherever they are, she will be also. If your eyes and ears are listening to the good gods, you will hear her voice among theirs. In that way she will always be near you."

"How do you know the good gods will speak to me?"

"Ah, that is easy. Because you sing their song, and you dance, and you are happy even when you're sad. And you make Old Samuels happy."

"I can't dance," said Lily.

Old Samuels paused to light his pipe. Lily thought he was finished talking for the day. "But you can. I hear dancing in your voice every day."

Lily did not like to be teased. For a while she sulked and avoided Old Samuels. She waited in the woods by the gravesite for a demon to whisper something outrageous to her. The old man took no notice. He stayed his usual time and without saying goodbye made his way across the field towards his great-nephew at the edge of the bush.

One night, alone in her loft, Lil woke to the harvest moon igniting the straw at her feet. She caught herself humming:

Hi diddle dum, hi diddle dare-o

Hi diddly iddly, hi diddle air-o

Hi diddle diddly, hi diddle um

Soon she felt the presence of a second part in flawless harmony with her own. She stopped. Her mother's voice continued, as clear and crystal as the moon's.

Lily was often alone, and had been as long as she could remember, even when Mama was alive. She was not lonely though. She could sit close by her father for hours while he chopped wood or repaired tools without the need to speak. Often she hummed, sang songs or made them up as she watched whatever scenes were played out before her. By herself in the fields she would lie on her back and dream the clouds into shapes of her wishing, or follow, minute by minute, the extravagant exit of the sun as it boiled and dissolved or tossed itself on the antlered tree-line and gave up its its blood in sunset. The few acres that defined her world pulsated with sights, sounds, smells, with the dramas of birth, struggle and demise. And now there were the guardians and the demons to listen for, the good gods in their hiding to be heeded and helped.

"This bush don't go on forever," Old Samuels said that spring, sensing restlessness in the girl. "Half a day's walk towards the sunset and you'll come to the River of Light that's been flowin' there since the last time the wild gods stirred the earth and created it over again. Two days walk towards the North Star where that river begins and there's the Freshwater Sea of the Hurons, bigger than the lakes on the moon." Lily had been dreaming of water ever since the first snow had widened the woods in October. In the midst of the bush, beyond the last blazed trail, she would suddenly imagine before her a stretch of blue, unrippled water, without edges or end, clear as cadmium. Then a crow would caw and the snow-bound trees pop back into view. In the early spring the bubbling of Brown Creek below the East Field would unexpectedly become magnified in her mind as if it were a torrent ripping out the throat of a narrows, roaring until Lily stopped her ears, fearing that she had somehow transgressed, that the demons had indeed inherited part of the earth.

"You're like Old Samuels, little one. Sometimes you know."

"I'll ask the guardians to bring back your eyes," Lily said.

"So I can see all the wickedness and foolishness again? It's not like olden times any more. Two days walk south of here and they say you'll come to roads chopped through the bush, and White Mens drives his wagons on roads made of dead trees, and Chatham is bigger than ten Ojibwa villages"

"Why does Papa go to Chatham?"

"I like your Papa. He's a good White Mens. I tell him my name is *Uhessemau*, but he says 'I can't say that so I'll just call you Old Samuels.' I like the name Old Samuels, so I keep it. Redmen don't fuss about names; we have many names before we die. If I die with Old Samuels, well that's okay with me." The old man puffed on his pipe, but he didn't answer Lily's question.

One evening Papa returned at dusk, his haversack full of store-bought bacon and sausages. The fresh provisions were not for storing though. "Start packin,' Lily. We're goin' up to Port Sarnia to watch the ceremonies."

It was Indian summer. The leaves had turned but not fallen. No wind disturbed their glow in a sun that blazed with more hope than heat. Along the forest track, purged of summer's mosquitoes, autumnal shadows stretched and stilled. Air in the lungs was claret, bracing. Papa measured his practiced stride to hers, and she floated gratefully in his wake.

They had left home while the sun was still a promise in the east, following the line that linked the four farms to the north. Lily had never been north of Millars' farm, never seen the River. The beaten path, so familiar to their feet, soon disappeared. There was just enough light to see the blazes, newly slashed, that marked the bush-trail ahead. They were going north, through nowhere to somewhere, at last.

Just as the sun bested the tree-line far to their right, they were joined by Acorn and Sounder. The young men slipped behind Lily without a word. Only when they stopped much later for a drink from a shallow spring and a brief rest did she notice that they were not in hunting attire. Their red and blue sashes against the white calico of their *capots*were dazzling, even amongst the maples and elms. Like Papa they carried haversacks stuffed with supplies. Sounder, as usual, grinned broadly at Lily, giving her a glimpse of the merriment that must have once quickened the eyes of Old Samuel himself. Acorn, according to his custom, nodded at her impassively, with no change of expression. Lily stared at the grimace of the black squirrel peering out of the fur on Acorn's shoulder.

To Papa they spoke in Pottawatomie, the language their parents had adopted when, according to Old Samuels, to utter a word in Attawandaron or Petun meant death. There was no one alive now who remembered those sweet, sharp sounds. Lily thought sadly of her mother's forgotten lullaby tongue. While they rested, Sounder chattered away to Papa like a jay. Already Lily could pick out some words; the pitch of rising excitement was plain. She detected "presents,""white soldier", "big river" and "village". Papa replied laconically, half listening as he did with Lily. But he was happy. His large hands cradled the back of his head, his eyes glowed with something remembered and anticipated. Lily found herself beside him and put her hand on his knee.

Sounder switched to English. "Little-maiden-with-the-goldenrod-hair is a brave walker, no?"

The ghost of a hand bent over hers…

"Big white general only give presents to womans with black hair. White generals plenty fussy 'bout presents."

…brushed and settled.

"Sounder like all womans; give presents to everybody." His eyes danced at the thought. "Even Acorn," he laughed, and did a little jig around his unimpressed cousin. "Ready to move?" Papa asked, in Acorn's direction.

Sometime after noon, they turned north-west, still following the blazed trail. To the west lay the River. Lily strained to hear its voice. The odd crow, unmated, cawed in complaint; a bear crumpled the dry brush nearby, seeking the late berries; a crab-apple dropped its sour fruit. Increasingly they passed through large natural clearings, beaver meadows or sandy patches where the hundred-foot oaks and pines had given way to clans of cherry, snow-apple, and sumac.

Mostly, though, they heard their own footfalls. Sounder, impatient with Papa's considered pace, scooted off into the semi-dark and popped up in front of them with a red squirrel in his hand, kicking out the last of its life.

"For supper," he explained, setting off again, guided by his own compass.

They came not to the River but to a well-established road, a fifteen-foot swath cut through the bush, the stumps pulled and the surface smoothed over with sand. Across the myriad streams trickling west towards the River, bridges of demi-logs had been crudely constructed. Lily realized that a horse and cart could travel here, though no vehicle approached them. They followed the road due north until the sun began to tilt sharply to their left. It will sink soon, right into the River, Lily thought.

"Are we near the water?" she asked, no longer able to contain her curiosity. How she wished she were Sounder, able to dance ahead and explore unfettered. Papa increased his pace; Acorn muttered his disapproval. After a while Sounder said quietly to Lily: "River of Light is just through the trees there. We been following it, but no path, even for a brave walker." Lily looked longingly to her left but saw only the black silhouettes of trees, fluted by the sun behind them. Her disappointment was interrupted by Sounder's cry, "Here's the farms!"

Before them was an immense expanse of open space unimpeded by trees. To the east of the road the bush had been denuded of all timber, all brush, in typical pioneer fashion, Not even a windbreak separated one farm from another. The stumps of the slain trees had been piled lengthwise to create makeshift fences, demarcating properties, fields, gardens, and dooryards. At first such angularity seemed alien to Lily, even painful to look at. But the sight of cabins, several of them larger than any in her settlement and ranged neatly back from the road in neighbourly view of one another, was overwhelming.

The others were apparently impervious to grandeur, for they had moved well ahead and were stopped, waiting for her, in front of the third cabin. The smoke from its fieldstone chimney lingered in welcome in the still air. It was only when Lily joined them that she glanced away from the farms to the west again and discovered that the bush had been cleared for a stretch of two or three hundred yards, all the way down to what could only be the River. "This way," Papa commanded, ushering her into the home of the Partridges.

Mrs. Partridge was surprisingly kind. She bathed Lily's blistered feet in soda water, rubbed them with ewe's grease, and put into her moccasins little pads of the softest cotton. "Store-bought at Cameron's," she said with restrained pride, "up at Port Sarnia." After a meal of quail roasted in a genuine iron stove, potatoes, squash, corn-bread with molasses, tart apple pie and mugs of warm goat's milk, the men slouched together by the fire, lit up their pipes, and conversed partly in English and partly in Pottawatomie. They were soon joined by two sturdy neighbours with buff red cheeks and flaming hair. Mrs. Partridge and her two elder daughters sat near the stove in the kitchen, one carding wool, the other preparing to "full" several man-sized macintoshes. Lily had many questions to ask but no words with which to express them. She listened, though, her eye never leaving the printed calico dresses of the elder daughters and the rounded bodies so restless beneath them.

The Partridges had a small shed that served as an outhouse. Lily left the door ajar, allowing the moon to pour its amber warmth through a wedge in the tree-line. She did not return to the cabin right away, instead walking past it and straight across the moon's carpet. She heard the River just ahead in the darkness behind the beam of light. Strange sand-grasses caressed her bare legs. At last she came to the water's edge and the voice of the River filled her ears. It roared with a hoarse breath, and in it, Lily thought she detected longing, anticipation, and the ache of seeking what always lay ahead, just out of sight. Under the circling stars, Lily listened for the language it used, but it was no tongue she had ever heard.

Later, from her cot near the board wall that separated the sleeping area from the main room, Lily tried to catch the scattered words of the men.

"Them surveyors was through here again last week, Michael."

"I heard," said Papa's voice. "Rumours floatin' about, up an' down the line. Talk of makin' this territory a county."

"White fella draws lines in the bush," said Sounder, making no attempt to disguise his disdain for the folly of the intruders.

Lily dozed, dreaming of water bigger than counties, borderless and infinitely serene.

"Went to the meetin' down at Chatham. Things is gettin' worse, we hear tell. Some new law comin' in over there about returnin' the poor devils. All legal-like, too."

"Sun-in-bitch Yankees," Sounder added.

"Over a hundred come across since August. We're lookin' for a new route, Harry. Them raiders is gettin' smarter by the hour. Reckon things could get real bad by summer."

"The committee can count on us."

"Damn right. None of us forgets what it was like to be a Highlander under George's boot. What do you want us to do?"

"Sun-in-bitch English!"

Lily was swimming, her hair fanned out like a parasol in a blue river.

Next day they rose and were well on their way before sunrise. But this time Lily knew more about what lay ahead. From various overheard conversations at the Partridges she learned that the village of Port Sarnia sat less than two hours' walk along River Road to the north, and that one was not to be surprised by periodic farms in lee of the road, though the spread of a dozen at what the locals called Bloomfield was the largest group below the Port itself. Here and there slash-roads were cut eastward through the woods so that one could imagine not merely strips of settlement, but successive waves challenging the hidden heart at the centre of the territory, known only to the natives and the hibernating bears who were said to rule there unmolested. At the end of River Road the bush would relent and they would come to a huge clearing where the river eased into a wide bay, the site of the new town, and behind it to the south and east the Ojibwa, or Chippewa, Reserve where several thousand Indians lived in scattered equanimity. What they were there to witness, what Sounder couldn't stop dancing about, was the arrival of the government ship for the annual dispersal of gifts given in exchange for land – territory of which the native owners had already been dispossessed.

Just moments before Lily and the others emerged from the bush into the misty dawn-light, the steamer *Hastings* weighed anchor and slipped from its overnight mooring in the bay towards the river bank below the town. On board was Major John Richardson, who had joined the official expedition at Windsor on October 9, 1948, and who was carefully recording the events surrounding the gift-giving ceremonies at the Reserves on Walpole Island and at Port Sarnia. The weather was flawless: the sky unscarred by cloud, the sun brilliant as a rubbed coin, the wind at ease in the sea-grasses along the shoreline. As if the whole enterprise had been choreographed, dozens of parties of Indians, large and small, materialized from the forest of their Reserve at various spots along the two-mile curve that formed the natural bend of the bay. Most walked, single file, with the women and children behind. Others, more resplendent, rode the motley ponies bred on the Island.

At some undetectable signal, the Government contingent marched down a single plank to the shore, a sort of colour guard, dazzling in blue, red and white, breaking off and standing crisply at attention while a larger platoon of regulars from the Canadian Rifles wheeled southerly just ahead of the navvies freighted with the Queen's largesse. At the same moment, five dignified Indians, obviously chiefs, moved towards the colour guard, stopped dead-still, and waited. Major Richardson, wan and aged beyond his years but impeccably turned out, stepped forward with Captain Rooke. While Her Majesty's gifts, neatly bound in fleece-white blankets tied at the four corners, were being carefully laid out in predetermined rows, White Man and Indian exchanged formal greetings, then sat down at the entrance to a huge skin tent and passed the ceremonial pipe. Major Richardson was seen to talk animatedly in Ojibwa to several of the chiefs whose smiles were all-encompassing. Meanwhile the more than one thousand natives who had now reached the plain began to select their presents. The bundles were not marked in any way, but each individual or group knew, from custom and tradition, which kind of bundle was intended, and deserved. There was no rush, no confusion even though the actions of the several families and tribes appeared to be spontaneous. Bundles were carried off to the edges of the plain where families had set up their cooking apparatus and blankets for the events ahead. Fires sprang up, cards and dice appeared, fresh calico paraded, Cavendish proffered and puffed. The Great White Mother had wafted her attention and grace across the world-sea and blessed them with this day.

Only one element seemed out of place on a morning described later by Richardson as having "all of the softness of mellowed autumn." One of the chiefs, a wrinkled and scarred veteran of the Battle of the Thames who had stood beside Tecumseh when the Yankee bullets ruptured the great man's heart, did not smile, did not sip peace with his brothers, did not take the gifts offered, did not bend his gaze from the badges and brass before him. He was *Shaw-wah-wan-noo*, the Shawnee or Southener, the only one of his race known to still inhabit these grounds so long after those cataclysmic events. Richardson, at an age when romanticizing is either foolish or profound, wrote in his account that this man, "notwithstanding five and thirty years had elapsed since Tecumseh's fall, during which he had mixed much with the whites, suffered not a word of English to come from his lips. He looked the dignified Indian and the conscious warrior, whom no intercourse with the white man could rob of his native independence of character."

Lily was made dizzy by the colour and the crowds. The Indians' regalia took two forms: the outlandish harlequin suits of many of the younger Chippewa – complete with scarlet sashes, blue leggings, black and white

ostrich feathers, and an English-made beaver hat – and the traditional
deerskins, rabbit furs and eagle feathers of the older males and of most of the
Pottawatomies. At first Lily could observe only the natives since, when she
had stepped out of the bush that morning, the plain was dotted with them.
Later she followed the slow-paced Acorn towards the bay and the ceremonial
party. There she saw the soldiers she had heard about from Gaston
LaRouche and his war stories. Their scarlet uniforms caught the mid-
morning sun, imprisoning it; the bright steel and gilt of their swords dazzled
all who dared look their way. Never had she seen men uniformly attired,
prancing in step, swinging their arms high in unison, marching to the
panicked hammering of drums. She saw too their sleek rifles and the
bayonets thin as a wish-bone: these weapons, she knew, were not for
hunting.

There were a few white women in the throng too, whose tailored jackets
and fancy bonnets she could only gawk at. Since observing the Partridges,
mother and daughters, she was all too aware of her sack-cloth chemise, her
improvised leggings, and her unadorned reddish-blond hair. She sat down by
the fire-pit, the better to hide from notice. She did not hear Acorn squat
beside her in the commotion, but then became aware of his presence. He
held out an offering.

"For you, little fawn," he said, averting his eyes. It was a gift, a buckskin
pouch bearing an intricate configuration of beading that might have been
inspired by the stars.

About noon-time, Lily ventured down to the River. The paddle-wheel
steamer blocked her view until, from its iron stack, clots of soot shot
upwards, smudging the sky. Several men tossed whole logs into a square
stove-like affair and the flame inside blew white and venomous. Suddenly a
man in a dirty uniform gave a shout. A metallic rod whined, the wooden
sides of the boat shivered, and the wheel beat frantically at the calm water,
sending the steamer northward towards the townsite.

The River was now hers. She could see the other side, but the trees there
were faded and shapeless, so vast was the blue torrent flowing past them. To
the south she could trace its surge for miles as it swept through the bush.
This was no creek, however magnified in imagination. No shadow touched
its translucent face save that of the herring-gull or fish-hawk; it was forever
open to the sun and the stars. There was an eternal earth-light in that blue
tidal twisting, even in the depths. It rejoiced in its flowing.

To the north, beyond this brief inlet, the near-bank bent slightly west, and Lily strained to see through the autumn haze the place where the Freshwater Sea of the Hurons fed its own waters into the River. She felt its mammoth presence behind the mist.

Papa spent much time talking with the officers and other white men from the steamer and Port Sarnia. Many times he laughed out loud; other times, his eyes clouded over, the way they did when he talked about Mama. Twice his gaze had searched out Lily among the throngs, looked relieved to find her, and then twinkled. Sounder hopped and skittered, threw dice and horse-traded, and finally snoozed beside her in the afternoon grass.

"I'll give you a half-dollar for it, ancient one." The officer held the coin up to the sun as if it were a jewel or a talisman. The old Pottawatomie chief eyed it, tempted. His hands unconsciously rubbed the black walnut war club they had polished with their affection these many years since the wars ended.

"This club belong to my father," he said, more to himself than to the pot-bellied military man before him.

"Two half-dollars, then."

The old one looked momentarily puzzled, then hurt. Finally he said, "One half-dollar," letting the officer reach across and lift the club from its accustomed grip.

Papa was about to step forward when something in the Indian's expression made him pause. Papa watched him put the silver coin into his pouch without examining it, and turn towards the river. Lily saw the look on Papa's face; it was the same he wore just before he swung the hatchet at the beaver or muskrat not drowned by the trap.

"Sun-in-bitch soldier," said Sounder behind them. Then, after a decent interval: "They start dancing now."

Against the tangerine sun, the Indian dancers were silhouettes freed from gravity, moving at the will of the drum. Their feet struck the ground as if beating the stretched hide of the earth itself. The air above shook with their cries. They danced towards enchantment, expiation, communion. Lily was drawn into the melee and felt her feet take off, seeking out the cadence, finding it with astonished ease, letting her body swing free. She danced until exhaustion overtook her and she moved to the edge of the circle to sit and watch once again.

After a while a small group of Pottawatomies approached the central fire.

They appeared to be members of a single family, a mother and father, some grown sons and a slender girl perhaps a few years older than Lily. The drum dance had stopped, but at a sign from the father it started again, subdued but insistent. His daughter knelt before him as he placed a garland of some sort on her head and began a long incantatory song in Pottawatomie. Lily could catch none of the words, but she knew it was a joyous chant, full of affection and hope.

"She has changed her name, little dancer." It was the voice of Southener, the Shawnee, seated beside her. "Her name was White Blossom. Tonight she becomes Seed-of-the-Snow-Apple. It has been proclaimed before all of the tribe. Now she must strive to live up to the name bestowed upon her."

Southener said nothing else, as the ceremony ended and the fire grew smoky and fickle.

Suddenly very tired, Lily dropped her head to his soft shoulder. Papa would find her there, safe and sleeping beside the old Shawnee.

4

In honour of Lily's eleventh birthday, Papa had installed a glass window in her loft sanctuary. From there she could see the quarter moon, the black rampart of trees, the outlines of the new road to the west, and the figures of two men walking purposefully towards the cabin. They knocked, doffed their hats at Papa's greeting, and entered, the candlelight catching their red hair, slick lapels, and polished boots.

As soon as Lily heard them speak she knew they were Scots. One spoke smoothly, the other with a sort of hitch, a kink somewhere in every sentence.

"Yes, thank you very much, but just a thimbleful if you don't mind. Good for the gout my doctor says."

A gurgle of whisky escaping.

"I'll join you as well. I haven't got the gout, but of course I'm anticipatin' it."

They both laughed.

"Bein' a gentleman who gets out and around, you'll know all about our new county status and the marvelous – could I say miraculous – changes it's bringin' to our citizens, whatever their race or beliefs."

"Or, uh, colour," added Kinky.

"Citizenship in Her Majesty's kingdom is colour-blind, I thank the Good Lord."

"To Her Majesty!"

"What sorta changes do you have in mind for me?" Papa asked, evenly.

"Well now, they aren't really, they don't exactly apply to you, specifically or –"

"What my cousin is sayin' is that we are merely servants, appendages of the council who in turn must carry out the laws duly passed by the Legislative Assembly to which – may I remind you – we all sent the Honourable Mr. MacLachlan."

"We got snowed in," said Papa.

"Precisely why the new road is bein' expedited."

"No citizen will be disenfranchised by a…by the weather."

"What laws?"

"You'll recall that the survey of '43, lamentable though it was, served us well enough, but a new one has been made necessary by certain *irregularities*discovered in the original."

"They had, after all, only the, ah, crudest of instruments and the Indians, we are told, ah, pulled up the markers as fast as they could be laid."

"Done, I'm assured, in all innocence."

"This ain't my land, then?"

"Dear sir, please, uh, please –"

"– don't leap to such dire conclusions. We're here on a mission of mercy, as it were. To be blunt, and to allay any apprehension on your part, let me say straightaway that I have been authorized by the duly elected council of Lambton County to inform you that several small errors were made, back in '43, in the lot alignments along this particular section of Moore Township."

"Very small errors, I assure you."

Papa's chair emitted a sudden groan.

"Infinitesimal."

"Tell me the truth."

After a pause, Smoothie said: "Your property is too far east, sir. That is why the road out there runs so far from your cabin-line. Your farm should front almost on the road."

"Five yards from it accordin' to the, ah, lawful survey."

"But that still leaves more than thirty yards –"

"Thirty-three to be precise. Ninety-nine feet, three inches."

"More than half my East Field!"

"That's correct."

"What does this mean?"

"Calm yourself, sir."

"In technical terms it means that you do not own a half of your East Field. And, correspondingly, you own a hundred feet of land to the west –"

"Covered in bush!"

"There's no need for, uh, that sort of tone."

"Donald is right. You'll have every opportunity to buy that improved field. No plans exist for a second line of farms behind this in the immediate future. We're movin' south with the new road, and the crossroad will continue from Millar's farm to the east."

"I'd say you have four – even five – years to buy that field."

"What with?" Papa's question went unanswered.

"There is, I'm afraid, one more point to be made."

"A very wee one," Kinky said.

"But pertinent. Accordin' to your contract you were to make a specific number of improvements within ten years, excludin' your first winter here."

"I've met them, every one of 'em."

"In a sense, yes.

But with the technical loss of your East Field, you have, uh, technically –" Smoothie's smoothness began to fail him.

"You'll need, sir, to clear another ten acres."

"But not by fall. That's why we've been sent here. The council is quite willin' to accept either solution: the immediate purchase of the cleared field –"

"On reasonable terms you may, uh, be certain."

"Or the clearing of ten acres by a year from September."

"No one wants to see you lose this farm or be cheated of the, uh, fruits of your labour. All of us are here to build a better country than the one we've known, in a spirit of, uh, co-operation."

"And love and harmony, free from prejudice."

"I ain't got the cash. You know that. So does MacLachlan. And I'd need money to hire help to clear a new field. I owe everybody in the district – time and dollars. I got no sons, you know. I got no wife."

Papa drank. "I'm no goddam squatter!"

The Scotch gentlemen's fancy clothes brushed restlessly against the coarse deal of the chairs.

"Perhaps the Lord will help you, sir."

"God damn the Lord!"

Gasps, scraping of chairs, rustle of coats, quick double-steps to the door.

In a quiet voice that came from a different, darker part of the soul, Smoothie said: "We both know where you can get cash, anytime you want it. Your comings an' doings have not gone unobserved. Good night, sir."

Papa did not reply, bidding goodbye with a sharp slam of the door. Though Lily could not see below, his agitation was palpable. She should go down to him, but hesitated. He had no son, he had no wife. As the night visitors passed beneath her window towards the county road, she heard their parting exchange.

"The man's a – a republican!"

"He's a fuckin' Irishman, that's what he is!"

By that summer of 1851, while the hand-axe still challenged every oak and ash, and the crops surprised themselves by flourishing, the machinery that would transform the countenance of Lambton County was well in motion. Road-gangs of disenchanted rustics and dispossessed natives hacked their way east to London and south to Wallaceburg. Surveyors bearing sextants roamed the back bush like spies, their chiseling eyes straightening bog and bend. To the east and south, barely out of earshot, the first locomotives would soon chuff and clang through morning mists undisturbed since the granite and peat and leafage rose triumphant from the retreating glaciers. And in Port Sarnia, the politicos, dreaming their mercantilist dream, strained to hear the chorus.

In the midsummer heat, the sudden lustiness of a cooling breeze felt good on the calves, arms, and neck. Lily watched the wind coax ripples out of the wheat as it rolled, resisted and sighed into acquiescence. It was at such moments that she tried hard to remember Mama as she had been before she took to her bed and left them. Yet summer days left little time for reminiscence. When the East Field turned golden brown, the LaRouche boys would be over the help them cut and thresh it. Luc and Jean-Pierre watched her as they worked, but when she turned her open gaze on them, they looked away sharply. In the vegetable garden, her own labour never ceased, with planting, weeding, staking and harvesting imposing a regimen from May until October.

"Your Papa now, he's gone and surprised us all," Maman LaRouche said, showing Lily how to pick a potato bug off its perch and squeeze it between thumb and forefinger just enough to split its seam. "Everybody said, 'he'll run off to the bush for sure now', or 'can't run a farm without a woman and a crop of kids,' an' so forth an' so on. Your Papa, he ain't no ordinary Joe. Ow!" One of the victims had bitten back. "Goddam *maudit*bugs! I don't blame anybody for wanting out of this this hell-hole."

Papa had indeed surprised his neighbours, possibly even disappointed the Millars with their thirty cleared acres, their crossroad and their planked façade. Following the trip to Port Sarnia, Papa had thrown himself into work. The North and East Fields were both fully cultivated. The garden was protected from wild pigs by a split-rail fence; a small shed housed the oxen, Bessie and Bert, when they were visiting; and, wonder of wonders, a root cellar was dug on the north side of the house. Papa took special care with this. He and the elder LaRouche boys spent several days excavating a cavernous hole in the ground, then covered it over with low planking and an angled roof. A door set in the roof at knee level lead to a set of narrow, crudely constructed stairs. Lily was the first to try them out. They led down to a platform of sorts and, to its right, an earthen floor cave with shelving. There the canning and the potatoes and turnips would find a cozy berth, summer and winter. Lily felt the dampness exuded by the violated ground and the faint warmth of sunlight caroming through the planks of the roof and side walls.

Old Samuels attended the christening of the "new room," politely declining the proffered drink, feeling the marvel of the deal planks and the cold metal eyes of the spikes that secured them. But he refused to enter the cellar itself.

"Bad spirits in there," he muttered theatrically.

"In here, ya' means," said Gaston LaRouche, shaking the jug and winking at the others.

"White Mens always tries to fix Nature," he persevered, searching the planking with his fingers for those icy arrowheads.

Papa continued to be away a great deal of the time. Fewer were the occasions when he returned with a deer or a bear to share among the neighbours. Some mornings Sounder and Acorn would be standing before the dead fire when Lily came down, guns in their hands, waiting patiently. "Your Papa not hunt today?" Sounder would say. "Got too many venisons already, I guess."

"Off to Chatham if you ask me," Maman would announce, asked or not. But despite any disapproval, she would invariably send little Marcel along to help Lily with the hoeing.

Sometimes when Papa came home from Chatham he would be tired but whistling, his eyes aglow. Other times he would brood; she couldn't talk to him for hours or look him straight in the eye. "It's a hell of a world out there, little one. We're better off right here."

Once she saw a letter on the table. "Can you read, Papa?"

He looked stung, as if she'd thrown a stone. "Yes, a little."

"Can you write?"

"Not too good."

"Can you teach me?" He looked at her, momentarily confused. "You'll get to read an' write , real soon. When you're a little older."

Lily sensed it would be some time yet. But the thought of it, the mere promise, was enough.

"Little White-Women's smart," Old Samuels said, "up here," pointing to a spot just above the shutters of his eyes. "And here," he added, indicating his ears. He meant of course that she had picked up, from him and his chattering nephew, quite a bit of the Pottawatomie tongue. At first she would attempt full conversations only with Sounder, grilling him for new words. Then Old Samuels took over her education, correcting the errors of his nephew, and delighting in his increasingly lengthy exchanges with this orphan of the forests.

"There's hope, maybe, for White Mens," he would say to his ancestors when she had mastered some grammatical intricacy that he would have thought incomprehensible to the simple mind of the intruders.

Papa, it seemed, had heeded Maman's advice, for in the winter that Lily was nine, he brought home a woman. Lily knew who she was. She had seen the Indians' camp in the back bush, not nearly so far away as she had imagined and much dirtier and sadder than she'd ever expected. No wonder Old Samuels liked to spend his day along 'the line'. Squalling papooses, yapping dogs, and quarrelling women amid the habitation of makeshift wigwams possessed none of the dignities she had witnessed at Port Sarnia. Among the inhabitants was a pretty young woman with eyes like polished chestnuts, whose sinewy beauty was already softening towards sumptuousness. Her name was *Penaseweushig*, or Birdsky, and she brought with her a four-or-five-year-old son of mixed blood (his hair was brown and curly), the incidental offspring of some heated, casual lust between the girl and any one of a dozen drifters happy to oblige and vanish. Birdsky, being a Chippewa, gave him the name *Waupoore*or Rabbit. From Birdsky and Rabbit, Lily learned, among other things, to speak yet another tongue.

The first time they came they stayed only a couple of months, until the snows melted, when mother and child simply disappeared one morning. Papa said nothing. Indeed, even though they could converse haltingly in English or fluently in Ojibwa, Papa and Birdsky spoke little, in the manner of the Indians themselves. Birdsky was easy to like. She did much of the cooking and cleaning, careful to defer to Lily if the moment demanded. When she returned later that summer, she willingly pitched in to help harvest the vegetables, and "do down" Maman's pickles and jams. Maman clucked a great deal about Birdsky's presence, but was kind to her and, Lily began to suspect, was genuinely fond of her company. In December one of her relatives from the camp came by and she went off with him. Papa was away and when he got back he looked immediately for her, but said nothing to Lily, nor could she read anything in his face. He's getting to be like Old Samuels on his quiet days, she thought. Birdsky returned again, unremarked, in the spring.

Rabbit was put in the small bed that Mama had used before she passed on. That bothered Lily for a while. But she enjoyed Rabbit: he laughed at her antics, he believed everything she told him, and he kept the prowling Luc off-guard and at bay. Papa and Birdsky shared the big bed almost below her.

She never tried, through the flimsy partition, to watch what they did at night. She could not help hearing though. Not once did Birdsky ever cry full-out, either in anguish or jubilation. Her hushed thrashings were pitted with mewling, aborted sighs, ambiguous gasps, and the hiss of air through teeth desperate for release. Papa's heavy plunging was accomplished with a grim silence that was broken, near the end, only by a staccato wheeze of relief accompanied on rare occasions by a lurching, crippled soprano cry that never took flight fully into pleasure or despair. That, and Maman's ribald asides, fed her imagination.

The first winter with Birdsky in residence, Lily cried herself to sleep most nights, though she had no idea why. She was happy that Papa had someone to hold and whisper to. She liked to watch Rabbit molding his myth-creatures out of blue clay from the dug cellar. She knew that being an adult meant coming together like that in pleasure and pain. Still, she cried, as quietly as she could.

By the second winter, some things had changed. She felt strange stirrings in her own body, as if invisible limbs were stretching in preparation. On her chest she watched in consternation as her breasts swelled around the blossom-heads she'd always known. Her leg-bones ached with growth. Luc's eyes fastened like beads on hooks to the bumps on her chest as she whirled and gambolled at the edges of his wretchedness. After, she would feel contrite, though furious at her own innocence and her inability to read what lay behind Luc's glances. As she lay above Papa and Birdsky, she took their muted, ambivalent passion and made her own translations in all the languages she had learned. She hoped they were as happy as the lovers in her dreams.

Lily was watching the bees in the basswood near the house. Birdsky's mama was sick so she and Rabbit were gone for a while. Old Samuels had not come around for days. Maman had asked her to stay over while Papa was off, but she was ashamed to be too near Luc. Here she wasn't lonely, but with the chores done, she was a little bored. The bees, however, were up to something. They were gathered into a single, swarming cloud that rolled and oozed, then miraculously began to lift itself into the air. It staggered, gained momentum and rose against the sky. Lily followed the swarm with her eyes, and was about to move to see where its new home might be when she heard a twig crack behind her.

A bear? No, the tread was too light, too cautious. Curious, she turned to the tree-line in front of the cabin, saw nothing, and waited. She was about to set off after the homing swarm when, quite distinctly, she heard a human sigh – the exhalation of someone either utterly exhausted or stunned by despair. She scanned the underbrush, more than curious now. Nothing moved. "Who's there?"

Silence. Breathing, then, constricted but deep. A man's.

"You hurt in there? You want me to come in after you?"

Panic, very clear, to the left, behind the wild raspberries picked clean by the starlings. Lily walked in that direction. She was not afraid, though the fixed intensity of her stare might have suggested so.

"I won't hurt you…"

She heard the body turn over. It was down in the twitch-grass, and struggling to rise. Lily moved quickly through the raspberries into the afternoon shadow of the tree-line. The figure had collapsed face-down, its head in the shade, its shoulders and body in the sunny grass. The body was motionless except for the steep breathing.

No sign of injury or wounds, no blood. The man, for so he definitely was, was clothed in rags, mere strips of cloth that might have been a shirt and trousers. No shoes at all; the feet were blistered and scarred. And the fellow was incredibly dirty; he must have slept in ploughed fields. Through the holes in his shirt Lily saw what appeared to be more scars on the back, like livid vipers twisted in some foul congregation.

His entire body began to tremble, the way a child's lower lip might quiver just before it bursts into tears. Maybe he had some terrible disease, cholera or fever. She saw the sweat bead on his almost bare shoulders. Holding her breath, she gently touched his arm to bid him turn over. "Please, sir, let me help you."

"I'se past help," came the voice, fatigued yet vivid and deep. Wearily, one limb at a time, the man rolled over in the grass. He was not dirty. He was black.

"His name is Solomon Johnson," Papa told her later. "He run away from us soon as we touched shore." Papa shook his head slowly. "Wouldn't believe he was in Canada; he thought we meant to trick him." He was talking more to himself than to Lily, who sat rigid beside him. "Poor bugger..."

Papa had not explained much that afternoon when he came home to find the black man in his bed being tended to by Lily. But it was more than she had ever heard before about what he had been doing on all those hunting trips. Papa and some men from the township had rowed Mr. Johnson across the River in the moonless dark. Solomon was a slave in the United States, Papa said, a life to be pitied. But once safe in Chatham, he would be free forever. Right now some bad men were chasing him, trying to take him back to his chains. Lily tried to imagine chains that could bind a human limb; all she could picture were the teeth on the muskrat trap, like a skeleton's smile.

After talking a long time with the black man, Papa helped him to his feet and led him outside and around the cabin to the root cellar. Lily followed, at Papa's prompting. They descended the little steps. Papa held up his hand. They stopped. Then he reached down and pulled the platform that served as a floor up on its hidden hinges. Lily gasped at the revelation of an even deeper pit below. Without hesitating, the black man stepped down into the dark and disappeared. A matched flared, then a flickering candle revealed a miniature bedroom about five-by-six and six-feet high. A pallet of blankets served as a bed. There was a stool and a bench to hold the candle or other necessities.

The black man looked up at them, exposing his huge, sad eyes. Then he smiled the widest smile Lily had ever seen. "How c'n I thank yo'all?" he said.

"Lily will bring you your food. You can stay up here long's nobody comes 'round. You need somethin', you just tap on this wall," Papa said, demonstrating.

"If'n you doan mind, suh, I prefers to stay down here. Down here I feels safe."

Papa didn't reply. He turned to leave. "I got a sturdy lock on this shed door," he said. "Lily's gonna lock it every time she brings you what you need. Nobody'll get in here. You'll be safe. I gotta go to Chatham, to the Committee. Won't be more than a day or so. We'll work out a safe route once we know where those Yankee bastards are or if they've gone back where they belong."

"I'se gon' stay right here, Mistuh Cor'cran, suh. I'se gon' be all right now. I be no more trouble, no suh."

"I'll be back in two or three days. You just keep your hopes up, Mr. Johnson. My Lily will take good care of you."

Papa showed Lily how to fit the key in the lock and open it. She felt trusted, like a grown-up, and charged with excitement. She wanted to learn more about the black men they brought across the River, about slavery, and these Yankee bastards who were chasing Solomon. But now was not the time, it seemed. While she prepared some cold beef, greens, and biscuits for Solomon's supper, Papa prepared to leave again.

Lily watched him reach the road that lead south, but instead of wheeling left he paused and looked up the line as if he were waiting for someone to catch up. Even from this distance Lily could tell that the jauntiness and intensity of purpose that had earlier quickened his gait and given an edge to every action, was now completely gone.

The voices hailing Papa were recognizable long before the figures emerged against the fading light. This time, though, the Scotch cousins were accompanied by a third man who, despite his powerful, squarish slope, trod a respectful distance behind his betters. An official of some kind, Lily thought. Old Smoothie greeted Papa, and together the entourage continued at a ruminative pace towards Chatham.

I'll never tell anyone he's down there, thought Lily. Ever.

Two days passed with no sign of Papa. Lily rehearsed what she would say when Old Samuels or one of the LaRouche boys came over. No one appeared. The sun shone, and the bees settled nicely in their new hive. Lily and Solomon had the homestead to themselves.

The first two or three times that Lily brought around his food, Solomon said nothing except "Thank yuh, Miz Lil, ma'am," his eyes downcast or averted.

"Why don't you eat up here? The sun's comin' through."

Solomon, below, devoured his food noisily.

"I can fetch a chair from the house, with a back on it."

The empty tin plate and clean spoon rose through the trap-door. "Thank yuh, Miz Lil, ma'am."

"Did you like the pickles, Solomon? Maman and me made them last fall."

A hand, seemingly detached, reached up and pulled the trap-door down like a mouth snapping shut. Reluctantly Lily gathered the utensils and with difficulty locked the outside door. She could feel him waiting to hear the comfort of its click.

"Tell me what it's like in the United States."

"Well, Miz Lil," Solomon replied, finishing the last of the dills from his noon dinner and settling back a little on Papa's chair. "Yuh wouldn' wanna go dere, no ma'am. It's an evil place, a wicked, wicked place –'da devil hisself don't wanna dere."

"Is that why you left?"

"Cain't talk 'boud dat, Miz Lil. Jus' cain't." He looked at the cellar floor.

"It's nice in Chatham. Maman says they got brick houses there. And board sidewalks. And schools for little children."

"Long's they ain't got no slaveholders, Ol' Solomon be happy."

Lily was accustomed to posing many questions in exchange for few answers, but she barely noticed that as the afternoon eased westward and Solomon showed no inclination to escape, she was doing more talking than she ever had. It appeared Solomon was a good listener, unfailingly alert and eager for her words. So attentive an audience was entirely new to her; even Solomon's sadness and hair-trigger jumpiness seemed to abate.

She told him all the things she knew that were interesting and that he might need to know when he got his freedom down in Chatham. He got an earful about the LaRouches and the war against the Yankees, about Old Samuels and his miraculous all-day pipe; about the quilting bee at Maman's last summer when the Frenchman drank too much hooch and dressed up like a priest in one of his wife's black slips and scared the ladies out of their wits; about Maman then going after him with the skillet, ruining a whole pan of perch. "Now you tell me a story," she said with gentle urgency.

"Solomon jus' like to listen, Miz Lily, ma'am. I'se accustomed ta jus' listenin'. A body get used to it, he do." She thought she caught the hint of jest in his eye.

"But how am I to know a person if they don't tell about themselves," Lily said.

"Nothin' ta tell. My life ahead of me, missy. Got nothin' behind me 'tall."

"But you were born. You had a mama and a papa. You lived

somewheres."

"Had no papa, no ma'am; had me a wonderful mama, but no papa ever come round us."

"Why'd your mama give you a funny name like Solomon?" she said.

"T'ain't funny," he said. "Come right from da Bible. Doan yo'all know da Lord's Book in dese parts? What kinda place I come to?"

"What kind of place did you come *from*?"

"Hertford County, North Carolina, nigh Murfreesboro," he said as if responding to an interrogator. "Work fer Mastah Cartwright. In da fields. I'se his slave, all da time."

Lily ached to know more, but prod as she would, she could get nothing further out of him. Indeed his original suspicion poured back into his face and demeanour as soon as she switched from telling to questioning.

Later that day, after a shared but quiet supper, Lily reached over to pick up the plate and mug. Solomon's left hand lay on the stool beside them. Lily let the petal of her right hand whisper to the ebony of his. Solomon jerked his entire body back as if he'd been lashed. The plate and cup clattered on the platform.

When Lily recovered from her surprise, she said "Are you hurtin' there, Solomon?"

Solomon could not reply. He was trembling head to toe, a cottontail before the weasel struck blood.

"I'll let you be," Lily said.

As she turned the key in the lock, she heard him squeeze into his ground-hole.

On the third morning he took his breakfast only after Lily had retreated. But at noon with the bright midsummer sun lancing into the upper cell, she found him seated in Papa's chair. She stood watch as he went into the woods to relieve himself. On the way back he scuttled like a crab across the twenty feet of open space, not knowing whether to look ahead or behind or everywhere at once. Lily wanted to leave the cellar door ajar to catch as much light as possible, but she closed it as soon as he squeezed past her. He sat down – embarrassed, ashamed, seething with irresolvable passions. Sweat sizzled on his brow until he got his desperate breathing under control. Lily did not leave. Nor did Solomon retreat to his burrow.

They ate together. The tea was cold but refreshing in the heat. When the black man lifted the mug to his lips and tossed his head back, he seemed to drown the room with his presence, his substance and shadow. In contrast, Lily's porcelain arms seemed to float free from their trim body like swan's wings. Lily's hair was for a moment indistinguishable from the sun's rays.

"Where's your wife?" Lily heard herself say.

Solomon looked up in disbelief. Terror and wonder passed simultaneously over his face. Lily could see plainly that he wanted to tell her the story of his wife and their grief, that he was overwhelmed with the need of someone to confide in and share the full horror of his ordeal. But he did not. Tears washed out of his doe's eyes, yet nothing could erase the anguish harboured behind them. There was no need to tell. Lily looked straight through Solomon's pain and saw in a single moment, the entire narrative of his travail. Whether she fell into a trance and dreamed it whole, or whether Solomon himself entered that dream to reveal his story, she never knew. She only knew what she saw, and would never forget.

She saw the master, that worthy of Hertford County who gloried in his notoriety as a 'nigger-breaker', challenged by the very presence of a young man named Solomon whose stamina and courage were a threat to God's ordained order. She saw Solomon stripped and lashed a hundred times, roped to stanchions like a steer, his skin flayed to make him cry out his submission. When the master could not break the black man's spirit, he had him measured by the smith for fetters that tore open his flesh till scars multiplied over scars. Out of desperation, longing for some kind of ending, Solomon fled into the woods, dragging his chains with him, only to be tracked by hounds and returned to his master, who, counting his losses, sent him off to the auction block. Solomon landed in Memphis, Tennessee, where he suffered two years of ordinary slavery: no beatings, no starvation, just dawn-to-dusk labour, nights of unrelieved muscle-ache, and the absence of hope.

Lily felt the momentary joy of union when Solomon gathered Mary to him and together they struggled to keep their love private and aimed, somehow, towards a better day. Then one morning in March he was hauled away without warning to the slave-pen in mid-town to be groomed again for auction. Filled with a rage beyond even his own imagining, he battered his way to an escape, returned for Mary, and together they ran. Lily saw then the six-week trek to the North, a hundred and thirty miles through swamp and bush, Mary having to be carried much of the way, food running out, the bounty hunters alerted. With spring dawning on the Ohio, they crossed into

Cairo and were found dazed and despairing in a field by a white man who said, 'Come with me.' And so they were fed, rested, and pointed to the next village up the line, the string of safe houses that would eventually end in a sanctuary known as Canada.

Between each town, though, lay the bush of southern Ohio and Illinois, and when the night skies clouded over, North was elusive. They staggered off-course, slept by day in caves or hollow logs, spent nights guessing where the safe house could be found. Many times they were too terrified to knock on the first door, too starved to head back into the bush, till at last Solomon would walk up to the kindest-looking white gentleman he could find and say, 'I'se lookin' fer mas' so-and-so livin' on such-and-such street,' and wait, heart hammering for the response that spelled life or death. 'You a runaway? Come with me.'

Until that day in Centralia when they collapsed at the doorstep of their safe house. To find two children there who seemed kind and well accustomed to such occurrences, giving them food and salves for their scrapes and bites and telling them to rest until their father returned. Lily shuddered as she saw the boy slip out of the house, the reward notice in his hand. Mary's screams woke Solomon but by the time he got to the window, Mary was already being carried by a posse of bounty-men towards the railroad station where she was bound and slung aboard a south-bound train like a piece of stray baggage. Solomon, out of instinct, was into the bush in a minute, lost his pursuers easily and eventually made his way to Chicago where he once again he had to put his trust in strangers. They were good to him there, consoling, holding out the bitter promise of freedom only two or three days away. It was decided to send Solomon by the lesser-used northern route, by rail through Schoolcraft, Lansing, almost to Port Huron where he was smuggled off, numb and submissive, and led through the forest to a secret point on the St. Clair River. Once delivered to the far shore, he bolted straight into the bush, beyond hope or memory or self-preservation, and gave himself up to the dark at the heart of the world.

As Lily was leaving, she snapped the lock shut but did not loop it through the hasp on the door-frame. How could she imprison him again?

Lily was half-way across the dooryard towards the road before she stopped to stare at the pedlar. It was not Lame Peter, from the north, as she expected.

"Afternoon!" he called jauntily, tying the donkey's halter-rope to a nearby birch and ambling towards her.

Lily waited, uncertain. He was a wiry man, all legs and arms with a long neck and a tiny bobbing head that made him look a bit like a tom-turkey combing gravel for tidbits. His blue trousers, scarlet shirt and smudged yellow bandana shone in the hot, high sun. A cherry-wood valise dangled from two fingers of his right hand. When he saw that Lily was not about to move, he stopped a few feet away and set the case down.

"A mighty fine July afternoon it is, young lady."

Lily waited, feeling she should say something customary.

"You the lady of the house?" he asked with a smile that was all teeth. She saw that though his skin was leathery and his brown beard unkempt, he was not an old man at all. The eyes were as black and lively as two tadpoles. They looked through her and beyond, taking in, in a single cast, the cabin, garden and distant fields.

"Yes," said Lily finally.

"Mama home?"

"Mama's up there," said Lil waving in the direction of the mounded gravesite.

"Mighty sorry to hear that. The Lord's will. So be it."

After a pause he grinned with his enthusiastic teeth and said, "You sure appear to be a young lady could look after her Papa, all right."

Lily looked at the ground.

"Papa home?" he asked, bending down to his case.

She was about to say 'no' when something made her tell an outright lie. "He's over to the Frenchman's, just past the North Field there, a-helpin' with a stump. Be back home any minute. I was just fixin' some coffee for him."

The pedlar didn't even glance up. "Name's Jones," he said. "Spartan Jones." He was fidgeting with the clasp on his case.

"You're not regular," Lily said. She'd caught a strange twang in his accent, not one she could place right off. "Nope. Come up from the south. Chatham way. Me and Bobby"– indicating the donkey –"tramped over the bush trail to the new road. Fresh territory, eh?"

Lily glanced over at Bobby who was chomping contentedly at the twitch-grass near the edge of the woods.

"Say now, I got here, just for a pretty young lady of the house like yourself, a whole boxful of tiny wonders: needles and coloured thread, and baubles and barrettes."

"I couldn't look at them unless Papa was here," Lily said. "Besides, we ain't got cash for that kind of foolishness," she added in her best Madame LaRouche tone.

"But you ain't seen it yet," he said, lifting the lid on his treasure trove. "Can't hurt nothin' just to have a peek, can it now? Tools for the industrious, cosmetics for the hopeful, temptations for the bold!" he said with another over-rehearsed flourish."

Lily looked hard at his face. He was smiling, the beads of his eyes danced and held her but gave nothing away. He was not much taller than Lily. Still, she steeled herself and said nothing.

"Jumpin' Judas but it's hot here!" said the pedlar, mopping his brow. "Got a cool cup of water inside?"

Lily was relieved to break his gaze and hurried around the corner to retrieve a dipper of water from the bucket she always kept in the shade of the cabin's west wall.

"Fresh outta the spring, 'bout an hour ago," she said.

For a second he looked hard at her, not changing his ever-friendly expression but focussing it in a slightly different way. It was as if the temperature had dropped a degree or so. Noisily and with obvious relish he drank from the dipper and then splashed the remainder of the water over his face. His beard went limp. Lily saw the scar just below the cheek at the line of the beard, like a stretched maggot.

"I hav'ta go now. Hate to leave off conversin' with a young lady as pretty as you, all grown-up an' lookin' after her Papa and, I'll bet, fendin' off the boys 'round here – but Bobby's gettin' anxious."

"Thank you for comin'" Lily heard her grown-up voice say.

He was only three steps away from her when he turned very casually and said, off-hand, "Will you let me give you a present, lass?"

"Papa wouldn't –"

"Just a trifle. Got me some bolt ends of cloth on Bobby there, no good to me now. I reckon, though, they'd make a pretty scarf or two. In the hands of a young lady that could sew," he added, with a wink as big as a rooster's swallowing corn.

Lily waited for the pedlar to turn towards the donkey but he stayed where he was, unsure of himself for the first time since his arrival. Lily noticed that he was staring over her right shoulder towards the north-west corner of the house. Could he see the root-cellar shed from that angle? Why would he be interested? She knew she must not glance in that direction. She had to get him to leave. "Perhaps Papa wouldn't mind, if they're real small pieces," Lily said, starting towards Bobby.

"Trifles," the pedlar grinned. "But on you –"

Lily was ahead of him, half-skipping towards the donkey whose indifference seemed absolute. The pedlar came at a bow-legged trot close behind. Lil stopped a few feet from Bobby, leaving ample room for the pedlar to sidle up to the beast and unpack his special wares. Lily was closest to the cabin, and she was fleet of foot.

"I reckon the scarlet would go nicest against that lily-white skin of yours, girl," he said, flipping the swatch of cloth from its pouch and letting it alight across Lily's shoulder only partly covered by the sack-cloth smock she wore all summer. His voice seemed suddenly to have dropped an octave, and it was full of razors. Lily was already bent to flee when his left hand grabbed her wrist and wrenched it with such unexpected force that she felt herself twist and collapse into the weeds, her skirt flung up over her thighs.

"No use a-cryin' out, sweetheart, nobody's gonna hear ya. Your pa's a long ways from here, and besides, you're about to get the surprise of yer life if I ain't mistaken, an' if I am, then we'll both enjoy ourselves."

Lily did not cry out, though she was sure her arm was broken. She was simply stunned for the moment, unable to comprehend the sudden vitriol from the pedlar.

"Quit squirmin', ya little snake, I'll bust yer other arm. Now let's see what we got 'neath all this cotton."

He was tearing at her underwear and trying at the same time to get his braces over his elbows –contradictory tasks that gave Lily a few seconds to catch her breath and think.

"Fuckin' nigger-lovin' hoo-ers, the lot of ya!" The underpants came apart with a shriek of their own, jerking Lily forward and up, a motion which she merely continued with accelerated determination. Thanks either to deep instincts or good fortune, she rammed her head like a ballpeen into his crotch.

With an explosion of wind resembling a death-rattle, he folded and fell into the grass. Lily was up in a wince and headed on a line towards the cabin where, under the big bed, a loaded fowling piece was kept at the ready. Clutching his wounded parts, the pedlar came after her in a wobbly trot, his lust consumed temporarily by rage. Lily would have made it easily to the gun and shot the pedlar without compunction, had she not stumbled and fallen no more than a dozen feet from the cabin. When she tried to get up, she cried out sharply and toppled back to the grass. Her right ankle was sprained, and this time the pain swept unfettered through her whole body.

The pedlar, seeing this, slowed his agonized pace. "I'll soon have ya whimperin' again," he seethed, pulling his braces, somewhat belatedly, all the way off. "A bit of buckle across the arse'll do it all right," he muttered while Lily sat bolt-upright, swallowing her pain, forcing her eyes open.

He came around behind her, his back to the cabin, expecting her to squirm away or at least try to protect herself. She did neither.

"I'm gonna whip yer butt an' then feed it somethin' it'll never forget."

The pedlar's braces came down randomly like a loose flail, metal slicing into her shoulders and arms, leather burning two diagonal strips across her back. The pain was just about to register from the first blow when she heard the whistle of leather drawn back for the second. It never came. Lily heard another sound and turned in time to see the water bucket bounce back from the pedlar's head with a crunch of flesh, maple and angle-iron. The pedlar's eyes popped skyward, his tongue flopped out of the gasp his mouth made, and he pitched forward onto the dooryard in a tangle of blood and grass.

"I'se killed him! I'se killed a white man!" Solomon was in a sorry state. He was pacing in circles, trying not to see the motionless body with its bloodied head, sprawled in plain daylight at the cabin door.

"Nobody saw, nobody saw nothin'," Lily kept saying, trying to catch the whirligig of his hand and stand on her one good foot. When she touched him, he stopped moving as if lightning had singled him out. He collapsed on the stool, staring away from the corpse towards the bush now deepening with late-day shadow.

"I jus' hears ya call out, jus' like... an' I comes runnin' through dat door an' I sees de man with de whips an' I jus' go crazy. Doan even 'member pickin' up dat bucket, I doan." He shook his head, then stared again at the bush beyond. "You hurt, Miz Lil?"

"No," Lil said. "He didn't hurt me." The stout flour-bag cotton of her smock had absorbed some of the lashing, though the buckles had left two stinging but superficial cuts. Her arm was sore but undamaged, and though her ankle was swelling, she found she could hobble satisfactorily.

"Well, I'se sho' glad he dead, if'n I have to go hang an' to hell for it. Guess I was wishin' to do dat to somebody fo' a long time now. A long, long time," he said.

"Papa'll be home soon, everything'll be fine," Lil said without much conviction, trying to stop her body from shaking head-to-toe and make her voice do what it was told.

Solomon heard her teeth start to chatter. "You best lock me up in de shed, missy. You best lock me in dere good."

Leaning on his arm, Lily led him to the cellar. Holding onto his hand a second longer than necessary, she watched him ease down into whatever comfort darkness afforded him. "Everything'll be all right," she said, suppressing the quiver in her tongue, "I promise."

"Jus' bolt up dat door," he said. "Please, Miz Lil, ma'am."

Reluctantly, Lily closed the door to the cellar, almost overcome by a second wave of shakes. As she clicked the lock into place she noted that both the hinges had been knocked more than half-way out of their moorings. In his frenzy to save her, the black man, thinking the door locked, had hurled his body almost through it. She pushed the screws back into place. If he wants to go, Lily thought, nothing will keep him there.

She knew exactly what she ought to do. Papa often got home just before dark. The sun was just about to sink below the tree-line, which left about two hours of hazy daylight. Lily ought to act the full measure of her eleven years and drag that man's body into the brush. She ought to throw dirt on the blood and mess to hide it. She ought to bring the donkey to the empty hut reserved for Bert and Bessie. She ought to fetch the fowling gun and have it ready for use. She ought to be able to stop the treachery of her own body which would not cease its shivering.

She did none of these. What if Papa did not come home? She hobbled, hopped and crawled into the undergrowth where the new South Field would be someday be planted, and hid herself. Against what, she could not imagine; perhaps only to sooth her ankle and regain her level head. There was just enough light left for her to see the outline of the cabin. From that direction came a sudden intermittent moaning. Terrified, she strained to check the corner of the cellar shed on the north side of the cabin. The moan grew louder, but it wasn't coming from the cellar. Lily turned in time to see the pedlar raise his head a few inches off the ground, groaning piteously all the while. In a moment he propped himself up to his elbows so that he could peer about him. Lily didn't breathe. He flopped to the left, turning over so that he could sit up and get his bearings. Then he put two fingers to his lips and whistled softly. To Lily's surprise, Bobby pulled free from his loose tether and stepped unhurriedly over to the pedlar, now evidently returned from the dead. The pedlar pulled on the halter, Bobby sank shakily to his knees, and his injured master rolled onto his stout back. Then donkey and burden moved into the near-dark where the north road lay. They turned neither north nor south, however; instead they continued due west, following the ancient deer-trail that wound its way eventually to the River.

Lily waited until the mosquitoes had become unbearable before she limped to the cabin. She no longer shook, but she was consumed by a dread that was worse, an apprehension that would not name itself. The image she carried across the clearing at that moment was a strange one: Maman LaRouche's strong grip ripping turnips out of the ground, her sickle slicing green from root before the plant could gasp, as Maman's sturdy foot, surging forward, buried itself cosily in the unresisting gash.

All that night Lily sat at the table facing the window and door on the south side, the fowling piece lying before her, cocked and expectant. When she had first entered the cabin, she rapped in code on the far wall and heard, after a while, the mutually reassuring response from Solomon somewhere below. Determined to remain awake to face whatever grim retribution might appear, Lily – fast asleep – dreamed she was awake, and very brave.

She awoke with a start to the sound of horses. The gun jumped too but held its peace. Forgetting the weapon, she ran to the door and flung it open. In the disfiguring light of the false-dawn, Lily saw three mounted men, two of them already in the dooryard, the third stopped behind them in the opening before the road. The horses snorted and jangled, sweating from exertion. Their heat washed over her.

The two men dismounted with a certain practised grace. Behind them, the third arrival remained on his steed, the swath of bandages on his head beaming like a Turk's turban across the clearing.

"Mornin', ma'am," said the taller of the two in a strange accent, mellifluous as honey. "Beggin'your pardon for disturbin' you this early in the day, but we're-all here on pressin' business."

The other one nodded but said nothing, glancing nervously around.

"What's your business with us," Lily said, trying to shake the sleep out of her voice. She wished she'd picked up the gun.

"Your Papa and me's made a certain transaction, ma'am."

"What kind of...transaction?" Shorty was edging towards the north-east corner of the cabin, holding his hat in his hand, nodding and trying to look casual.

The tall one brought out a leather purse; Lily heard the clink of coins inside. Her heart froze.

"My job is to bring you this here payment in return for certain goods you have in hand."

"This ain't a store," Lily said. Shorty had slipped around the corner.

The tall one put the purse into Lily's hand and as he did so grasped her gently but firmly by the wrist. "No need to get riled up, missy. We ain't in the habit of hurtin' decent folk. Beauregard and me are businessmen, that's all."

Lily was about to attempt a knee to the groin when Shorty's voice pierced the quiet of the pre-dawn. "The son-of-a-bitch's gone! He's flown the coop!" Breathless, he reappeared from the rear of the cabin.

"You sure?" snapped his partner, tightening his grip.

"Goddam right. The door's busted half off. They had him holed up like a polecat back there, but he's done beat it to the bush!"

"You let him out, gal?"

"Fuck no, I tell ya, Sherm, the door's lyin' in pieces. That big buck just blew outta there!"

"Cut the cursin'," Sherm said, more calmly. He loosened his hold on Lily's arm. "No call for that. Either your Daddy's cooked up this little treachery or that nigger's lit out on his own. Either way, we're gonna get him." He pulled the purse from their mutual grip. "You won't have need of this no more."

"We goin' into the bush after him?"

"Yes, we are. Tell that pedlar to vamoose. We don't need him any more." He turned to Lily. "You tell your Daddy to stay out of our way. Nobody need be hurt so long's we get our hands on the nigger. Good mornin' to you."

They mounted and cantered as far as their waiting accomplice. Sherm spoke sharply to him, and Bobby wheeled and loped southward, towards Chatham. They watched him for fully ten minutes, then circled and headed north in the direction they assumed Solomon had fled.

It must have been mid-morning when Papa came home. Lily had returned to her vigil at the table, the gun an inch away but untouched. She was no longer scared. Her ankle no longer throbbed. The dread which had so possessed her had finally divulged its name, and her soul longed for some relief beyond dreaming.

Lily didn't know how long Papa had been standing in the doorway when at last she looked up and saw him there. He turned his face away wearily and slumped on the stool before the spent fire. His flesh appeared to be too heavy for his bones.

"He got away," Lily said.

"They hurt you any?" he asked, rising and taking the hunting rifle from its place, not looking at her.

"None."

"An' that pedlar?" His sudden stare burned through her.

"Solomon, he run him off. Then he went, too."

Bullets clicked coldly in Papa's pouch.

"Keep an eye out," Papa said. "I'll be back before dark."

After him, in a voice that made her skull-bones hum, Lily shouted *Why? Why?*Papa of course did not respond. He had turned south towards Chatham.

It was dusk when he came home. Lily opened her eyes to catch Papa's face bending towards hers. It was sad; she saw her Mama in it.

"I'm sorry, princess. We're gonna have to leave this place."

5

Seven days later they were packed and ready to go. Papa had planned to get away at dawn, but he hadn't counted on the goodbyes that needed to be said. Maman surprised everyone by not weeping openly. Instead she braved a smile for Lily, hugging her fiercely as if she might transfer to those sapling limbs some of the bruised strength from her own decades of travail. Gaston and his boys touched their caps and mumbled *au voir* with exaggerated politeness, except for Luc whose heart was irreparably broken and shamed itself with silent, unconcealed tears.

Lily knew it was pointless to ask Papa why they had to leave, but she was certain it was due to more than their troubles with the Scotsmen and the pedlar. Papa would not give up the homestead, would not abandon Mama's grave to the winds and seasons, would not tear his little girl from the only world, the only people she had ever known – not for a mere Scotsman or a pedlar with a cracked head. Somehow it had more to do with Solomon and the look Papa gave her when she woke to find him staring from the doorway, the shed door in back of them protesting as it swung on one precarious hinge.

"We're goin' to live near Port Sarnia," was all he said, "with your Aunt Bridie."

Whose existence was news to Lily. From Mama she had gleaned a little about her relatives – enough to know that Papa came from a large family, that Mama's was mostly dead – but never had she had names to attach to any of them. Instead Mama told stories only about long-ago ancestors, all of whom apparently were squires or gawains or beauties of the first order. Mama's stories were like her songs, a kind of lullaby. But Bridie was no lullaby. She was a real, living aunt with a name as durable as a fieldstone. "I wrote Bridie a letter a while back," Papa said some days later, seeing Lily seated near the ripening wheat of the East Field and staring across to the red-blue granite on which one of Old Samuels' nephews had chipped the name 'Kathleen'.

"Chester and her been wantin' us to come up there ever since your

Mama passed on."

Chester?

"Land's mostly cleared up there. We'll help 'em out at first. Then get our own place." Lily wanted so badly to believe the enthusiasm now in his voice.

"We'll bring your Mama up there, too, some day," he added with effort, his hands trying to be light and consoling on her shoulders.

Mama wasn't *up there*, Lily knew, but could find no words to help Papa understand. She's here – in these trees, in the undug stones, in the birdsong and the wind, in that part of the sky she shared with us and that brings such joy to the guardian gods. Lily's quiet weeping made Papa's hands shake, and he turned back to the cabin.

It was a regular road now running abreast of the line of a dozen farms north of theirs. The new neighbours, above Millar's, came out to watch them leave, whole families lined up at the edge of their land waving curiously, uncertain of the meaning of what they were witnessing. When Lily and Papa passed the last farm, with only its entrance cleared, and stumps and tree branches smoking behind the log hut, the new road abruptly became a slashed trail again. Lily could not help but glance back. Standing in the middle of the road a hundred feet behind them were the unmistakable silhouettes of Old Samuels, Acorn and Sounder.

A few days before all three had materialized one morning, unannounced, and stayed the entire day, helping Papa with some of the packing and dismantling, but never once mentioning the fact of their leaving. Old Samuels puffed his pipe and talked exclusively to Lily in Pottawatomie. "White Mens always coming and going," he said several times, unprompted, "Attawandaron stays." Once he added, not without charity, "'Course, White Mens still young, got a lot to learn before this world ends." At dusk they left, saying no formal goodbyes but carrying Papa's sow in their arms as graciously as they could manage. Lily did not expect to see them again.

Papa and Lily followed the well-tramped trail north for several hours. The sun warmed them with its mid-day welcome. Wild phlox and amber columbine nodded jauntily from the verges. In the pines, tanagers and siskins tumbled and irridesced. A fox snake yawned his whole length in the heat kept cozy by the trail.

They were travelling light, of course. Papa had a backpack with food and overnight utensils, a water bottle, rifle and hatchet. In a harness neatly rigged by Acorn, Lily carried two blankets and some tarts slipped to her at the last moment by Maman. In the beaded pouch given her by Acorn and belted to her waist, she had carefully placed Mama's cameo pendant, the gold cross, and the rabbit's foot Old Samuels had rubbed almost smooth in thirty years of not worrying. There was no need for anything more: they had packed their few belongings – clothing, trappings, utensils, tools – in two large wooden cases about the size of a child's coffin. Luc, in a rush of altruism, had promised to hitch Bert and Bessie to Mr. Millar's cart as soon as they were free from their summer stumping, and deliver the trunks to Port Sarnia.

So it was only the weight of the day itself that bore heavily on them as they trudged away from all they had become a part of. Indeed whenever the little eddy of excitement which Lily had been suppressing all morning bubbled up on its own, she felt an acute sense of having betrayed something precious. I will hate Bridie, I will, was her less-than-comforting antidote.

There were now two routes to Port Sarnia. The lumber trail they were on led north-east to a junction with the main road running south-east from the town towards Enniskillen, the undisturbed heart of the Lambton bush. Twenty miles to the west, hugging the River, a trunk road – parts of it already planked – took the circuit rider and carpetbagger all the way to Wallaceburg and thence to Chatham. A number of Indian trails – blazed only – would take them to this latter marvel of the age. En route, they would stop at Corunna and visit with Mrs Partridge. Sometime during the mid-afternoon, Papa veered left into the bush, leaving the sun above them.

That season there was frenetic surveying and road-building through the undeveloped townships of Plympton, Enniskillen and Brooke, prompted in part by recent upheavals in Europe and their cataclysmic fallout. In half-a-dozen countries, upstart peasants and workers and a few middle-class dreamers had attempted – without consulting their betters – to make a home of the lands they had laboured on for generations. They failed, and paid the price exacted by their oppressors in the ritual rapine and domestic terrorism indigenous to the race. Thousands more were added daily to the earth's dispossessed. In Ireland, potato blight deposited its indelible pennies on the summer's crop, and hunger happily joined the scourge. A hundred thousand starving Irish crammed themselves into stinking cargo-ships and sailed for the world's end where, some of them believed, a plot of arable ground lay unspoiled by human greed.

Lily was annoyed with herself; she was slowing them down. Her head was spinning, probably from too much sun on the open road. She lingered behind a bit to vomit quietly in the underbrush, but Papa's hand was soon on her arm. He wiped her mouth with his flannel hanky and offered the last of the water. He sat down and in the healing shade they rested a while. Lily needed water, so Papa went off in search of a good spring. When they started up again, moving carefully from blaze to blaze under Papa's practiced eye, they stopped every half-hour or so. Lily felt better but very weak. When she rose to signal she was ready to go, Papa touched her shoulder with one finger, and sat down. Just before their midday meal she shamed herself utterly by drifting off to sleep. A trek of four hours stretched much longer. The shadows around them thickened and grew aggressive. So did the mosquitoes. Papa paused to examine a configuration of blazes on a huge hickory tree.

"The river road's only a half-mile away," Papa said. "But it's too late an' we're too tired to walk the five miles after that to the Partridges," he continued. "We'll make camp right here on the high ground."

Lily was sure she could hear the River tuning up for its nightsong.

With his swift, sharp hatchet Papa cut down several saplings, bent them into a frame and covered it with cedar boughs. The lean-to was just big enough for two, with a sturdy elm-bole to rest their backs against. More boughs were spread on the ground to serve as a bed when they were ready for sleep. But not just yet. In the opening of the lean-to, Papa built three small fires ringed by stones, two of which he smudged with damp evergreens, leaving the middle one to flicker brightly below the steaming tea. Papa and Lily were scrunched inside with the blanket over their shoulders, the smoke keeping the mosquitoes at bay and Maman's raspberry tarts sweetening on their tongues. Papa's left arm was raised and Lily snuggled in against him, relishing the muskiness of his rough shirt. She was about to slide down into sleep when she realized that Papa was talking.

"Bridie was the eldest. Eighteen and a local beauty. To us, she was a second mother. Then one day, just like that, Pa announces she's gonna be married up with an older man, a crony of his. Bridie says *no* in that iron-willed way she had. There was a terrible row, I can tell you. Ma hid in the stairwell cupboard. Next day without sayin' good-day-to-you or by-your-leave, she's gone. 'She'll come back,' I said to Ma, 'she loves us.' Pa ranted and raved for three days, 'Let the harridan be and be damned! She's no kin of mine.' The case is closed. He refuses to say her name an' forbids us to. She's drummed out of the tribe. Dead."

Papa lit his pipe. "I felt terrible," he said in a lower, different kind of voice. "I felt she'd abandoned me. When you're only twelve, somethin' like that seems like a betrayal. You put all your trust in a person an' then, like that, they're gone."

Papa drew the blanket around Lily's head. She snuggled close again, gripping his left hand with both of hers.

"It was two years later, Ma was quite sick, an' this letter arrived addressed to her. We all recognized Birdie's writing. She was a beautiful writer. She taught me to read, as best she could. So I read the letter, after Pa had headed for one of his meetins', of course. Bridie was in a place called Toronto, Upper Canada. She was well. She was goin' off to a town somewheres in the bush to work as a domestic.. She didn't name the town. She said we wasn't to bother tryin' to find out, she loved all of us dearly but she just had to do things this way as it was the only way for her. When I grew up, I knew what she meant. Back then, I hated her even more."

The moon slipped out from behind one of the high, breezy clouds feigning interest in the world's affairs.

"When your Mama an' me come out here some years later, we made no attempt at findin' her. As you're gonna see soon, this is a big country. But nobody ever put one over on Bridie, not even Pa with all his political shenanigans and bluster. Just after you was born we got a letter hand-delivered from Port Sarnia. From Bridie. She welcomed us to the county an' said the door was open to her house anytime. We always intended to go up there but your Mama was never well enough. We thought it best, for a while, not to get your hopes up."

He poked at the smudges, scattering the swarms.

"'Course that'll all be rectified soon. You're gonna see your Aunt Bridie and Uncle Chester at last, you are." Papa gave her an extra squeeze. "Yes, my Lady Fair Child, you're gonna have the time of your life up there. Before you know it we'll have a chunk of that cleared land and a white clapboard house to live in. We'll only be a mile from the town, too, with stores and mills and meetin' halls. First thing I'm gonna do is take you into town to Cameron's emporium and buy you your first store-bought dress – calico or lawn or kendall, take your pick, you'll be as pretty as a butterfly in a flax field in August."

Papa squeezed again. Lily gripped his hand to let him know she was still awake. The main fire was in its mellow, amber phase.

"Naturally your Aunt Bridie, bein' an' educated woman herself, will want you to have some proper schoolin'. They've got a school in Port Sarnia. You're gonna grow into a genuine young lady, I reckon: there'll be no stoppin' you once you reach that town."

Papa took his arm from her shoulder, shook the fire vigorously until the flames jumped again, and then reached into his pack. In his hands he held something small and leather-covered, a book.

"I don't want your Aunt Bridie thinkin' your Mama an' me didn't bring you up properly," he said, as Lily looked directly up into his face. "This here's a New Testament, a Bible. It was a gift, long ago, from my mother. I wrote an inscription to you in the front cover. My spellin's not too good so I had Mr. Millar write down the actual words. Someday real soon you'll be able to read it, an' the Bible, too. I want you to keep it an' treasure it, no matter what happens to you in this awful, tryin' world."

Papa had to stop to clear his throat. Lily reached out and took the Testament, its covers carrying the warmth of Papa's hands into hers.

"I'll tell you what it says, for now," he went on. Once again he cleared his throat. "To my dearest princess, the Lady Fair Child, from your Papa who loves you forever."

Lily tucked the precious book into her pouch, and slipped drowsily into the care of Papa's arms. He rocked her, gently, to sleep.

The sun, well above the tree-tops, woke Lily with a start. She was not in the least surprised to look over and see that she was alone. Papa had left her the food, water and utensils. And a note, on folded, thick, yellow-white paper. Lily did not open it. *I can't read.* It must be for Bridie.

Another voice said: the new road is a twenty-minute walk across a blazed trail; there will be travellers on that road; they will help. Mrs. Partridge is five miles up that road; she will remember me and everyone in Port Sarnia will know who Bridie is. I have nothing to fear. Papa loves me; he expects me to go to Bridie's.

But then maybe he's gone to scout the new road? Besides good folk, there are pedlars and bounty-hunters to beware of. It would be terrible if I wandered off and Papa came back to find me gone. He'd be so worried. I'll stay here till he comes for me. That's why he left the food and water. He thinks I'm sick. He loves me. It says so in this little book, it's written there, forever.

When she finished the last of the water, Lily began to worry. It was past five o'clock. Papa was not coming. He expected her to get to that road and find the Partridges. Still feeling dizzy and very weak (what was wrong with her? she thought), Lily gathered their belongings and looked westward for the next blaze. The shadows were massing even now, and it was not easy to pick out the year-old slashes from trunk to trunk or the modest impressions left on the trail by its mocassined patrons. An hour or so later Lily admitted reluctantly that she was lost. She was not scared of being alone in the woods; she never had been. The mosquitoes were bad but she had matches, she could make a camp of sorts. What concerned her was that she didn't know where she was. Nor would she be able to find her bearings in a terrain bereft of familiar landmarks. Desperately she tried to keep to the westward by the sun but it disappeared for minutes at a time in the closed canopy one hundred and fifty feet overhead.

When she stumbled into a beaver meadow, she looked up and saw in despair that it was now fully night-time. The stars winked invitations at her. Then she saw the dipper – the Silver Gourd – shining clear in its northern berth. She turned due left into the darkness. Ten minutes later she emerged from the dense forest onto the roadway. The fresh planking hummed beneath her feet. Inside she hummed too and did a little jig. She looked northward up the forty-foot width of the highway. She was exhausted. A sort of numbness was starting to spread up the calves of her legs. She couldn't make it to the Partridges. She was also very thirsty. She knew she shouldn't sleep without drinking. Then she remembered: this was the River Road. To her left she saw that the bush was thin and intermittent, smallish pines in a sandy soil that glittered in the starlight. She listened, forcing her breath in. Though the night was still, her River poured its restless energy onward. What a wonderful sound, Lily said aloud. Slowly but with more certainty than she had felt all day, Lily eased her way through the pine grove towards the beckoning music of the great waterway. There would be some breeze there, and open space: she could sleep undisturbed in the sandy bank. In the morning everything would be all right. Papa would be proud of her.

Just as the muted roar of the River was beginning to build in her ears, Lily came to a tiny feeder stream. Bending, she scooped the fresh, chill water to her face, drinking and cleansing simultaneously. The breeze off the water ahead was cool on her cheeks. She could see the moon plainly through the last trees between her and her goal. She was about to step out onto the sandy bank when she froze. The first warning she had of danger was the waver of firelight above the shoreline; then came the smell of burnt meat; then the voices and their unmistakable accents.

In the shimmering glow around her, Lily saw that she was standing, still hidden by the pines, slightly above a cove where the stream entered the River, a gravelly indent that formed a beach four or five feet below the main line of the bank. A pit-fire was in full bloom; two figures were seated on stumps, roasting something that might have been rabbit. A longish bundle lay rumpled in the shadows behind them. On the point formed by the cove, tied to a boulder, a row-boat rocked and complained.

"Goddammit, I figure we oughta haul his black arse across while the gettin's good."

"I'm hungry. So are you."

"Hungry for two thousand dollars, I am."

"Besides, I don't like that moon. It's gonna cloud over afore midnight. Eat."

"This shit's all burnt."

"Suits you then, don't it."

Lily backed off so that she was fully shielded by a tall pine. Neither man was looking in her direction; they faced the south-west where the moon sat, unclouded. Something icy and alien gripped her. She could not flee; she could not even close her eyes. Hence, she was the first to see the rumpled bundle flinch, stretch, and assemble itself. Solomon was sitting up, his hands bound behind him with rope. Another rope dangled loosely from an ankle. Somehow he had worked his legs free. Without taking his eyes off the backs of his captors, he rose to his full height without the slightest sound and edged towards the boat fifteen feet away.

"Sometimes, Sherm, you talk to me as if I was no better'n that nigger."

Sherm let the opportunity pass.

"Matter-of-fact, think I'll feed some of this here charcoal to him right now. Can't have him lookin' too lean, can we?" Beau turned. "Christ! He's after the boat."

Both men leapt toward the boat, but Solomon was already there. He placed one foot over the gunwale, the other on the rock next to the painter, and gave a tremendous shove. The painter rope popped free and the boat shot out into the swift current. Solomon fell face-down into the aft section with a clatter of wood and bone. Unruddered, the boat spun slowly, caught in a momentary eddy.

"What the fuck you doin', you stupid nigger! You can't row that thing with your hands tied up. Come on back here!"

"We'll get him downstream," Sherm said, already heading back for his gun. "If not, he'll end up on the other side. They always do."

But Beau wasn't listening. *"Jesus!"* he screamed as if his soul had been seared. "He's goin' over!"

Solomon was standing upright, his powerful six-foot frame black against the pre-harvest moon behind him. He was standing on one of the thwarts staring down into the current that was just catching the boat and swinging it, it seemed, southward to safety, and freedom. But Solomon jumped high and northward, as if his fugitive eye lay still upon the gourd of the North Star. His body, abandoned by the boat, arced across the horizon and entered the water face-first. The eddy of bubbles, which was all that marked his exit, was soon swept away.

"I never seen the like o' that, *never*. Did ya see the stupid fucker, Sherm? Jumps right in there an' takes our two thousand bucks with him."

Sherm was throwing water on the fire and gathering their things together. "We better get lookin' for another boat. This ain't exactly friendly territory, you know."

Beau continued to stare out over the foaming torrent, reluctant to leave.

"Maybe we can get the body," Sherm said.

Long after the bounty-hunters had left – their fire doused, the sky clouded over and menacing, the wind rushing to keep up with the river's urgency – Lily stood where she was and wrestled with the dark angels of her imagination. Once again she saw Solomon hunted through the unending nights, fleeing further and further into the forest.

Or did he welcome those River waters, she wondered, the tender descent, the soft bottom-sands sifted and cleansed by centuries of seeking, the icy currents that would carry his bones seaward over time.

She must get to Corunna as soon as possible; the night wind was up; the sky, threatening. How long had she been staring at the River? She was shivering with fright or worse, fever. There was no feeling in her feet as she turned north, stumbling in the dark on debris and branches. Then the rain came, lashing and cold.

She fell and rolled onto her side, partly screened by some underbrush. Too numbed to rise, she could only peer curiously at the silver imbedded in her right hand. No dream forestalled her slow falling away.

Even though she had not yet opened her eyes, Lily was awake. She was warm, a wooly shawl curled around her shoulders, and her shivering had subsided. Someone had found her and brought her to a safe place. Nearby a dampened fire radiated heat and welcome. *Papa?*She opened her eyes and looked to the crouched figure across from her.

"Ah, the little one wakes up."

"Where is Papa?" she asked, faintly, in Pottawatomie.

Southener, his kindly eyes scrutinizing her, said: "I made you drink the tamarack tea; I am sorry if I frightened you. You were shaking with swamp fever."

Lily felt too weak to move, but Southener noted her anxious glances about the campsite, which was deep in one of the pine groves.

"Your possessions are safe, little one," he smiled, his skin as rough as hickory bark, his sable hair flecked with gray and tied back with a leather thong. "I found them when I picked you up, soaking and hot, on that pitiful roadway." He reached down and produced Lily's drenched pack and the beaded pouch. "Thank you," Lily whispered. "You're young and very strong," he said, stirring the fire a little to give more light to their conversation. "Already the fever is gone. By morning you'll be ready to go north."

Did he know?

"When I started to dry out your things, I found this map," he said unfolding for her Papa's unread note. "It will tell you where to go."

So Papa had not left her a letter after all. Lily tried to think what that meant, but she could not think at all, she was drifting into sleep again. After another short rest, she took some of the tea Southener has prepared and allowed him wash the cuts on her legs and treat them with tiny leaves. The stinging was not unpleasant.

"As soon as the sun comes up, I must leave you. There's meat in your pack; eat it if you can. You're safe here. When you feel like walking, the road is directly east of us; the morning sun over the tree-line will take you right there."

"I remember you, Southener," Lily said.

"You were the best dancer," Southener said. "I watched you all day. You let the spirits loose in your legs. Now your tongue tells the true story."

"Old Samuels taught me," Lily said, wide awake now, every nerve alert.

"You have made me happy in my age," he went on in a hushed tone that

Lily had already come to recognize and revere. "I am almost at the end of my exile. I have no use for the magic amulet that has shielded me from my enemies and rescued me from my own folly many a time."

From a pocket he drew a pebble of blood-red jasper that glowed even in the dull dawn-light. In his palm, it seemed to pulse as if quickened by the fire's flame, alive with hope and memory. Its irregular oval shape suggested a living infant's heart.

"This will bring you luck all your days," he said. "Not happiness, as you already know, for they do not wear the same colour. But it will make your life a good one, with enough joy to keep you from despair, enough hurt to keep you loving. It will help you find a home, here and in the hereafter. It has done all of these things for me, fivefold.

"I received this magic stone on a sacred ground, long known as such by generation of tribes who have dwelt in these woods and passed on, as we all do. I ask only two things in return. The days of its guardianship are almost over; there is little magic left in the forests and the streams. So, when you have no more use for the stone's powers, I ask that you return it to the sacred grove whence it came, to the gods of that place who lent their spirit to it. I have looked at the map your Papa left, and I know when the proper time comes, you will be close to it. There is no way of marking such a place on a map, for the penitent must feel its presence before he can see it. You will know when you are standing on it, though, because it resides beneath the protecting branches of a giant hickory on a knoll just where the forest begins, and when you look west and north you will be able to see, at the commencement of summer, the joining of the Lake and the River set perfectly on a line to the North Star, whom we call the Eye of Wendigo."

"Second, I am nearing my own end. My people have been scattered like chaff before the flail. There is no home for us to rest our souls in. Save one. North of the town your father has chosen for you lies the military reserve, a boggy swampland no one, not even the rapacious whites, will ever want. Above the main bay, just past the point where lake and river meet, is a small cove among the sand dunes, and here, unseen among the grasses and snakeweed, is an ancient Indian cemetery which bears the remains of hundreds of souls who could find no burial place with their own people. It's a graveyard for wanderers, for the lost, and for the permanently dispossessed. If the military knew it was there they would perhaps allow the spirits to remain undisturbed, but certainly they would let no new dead be interred there. So it is that we few remaining outcasts must have our corpses carried there in the dark and secretly buried in that sacred earth. My request to you is to keep that ground holy in your mind, protect it with your life, and once in a while honour it with your presence and prayers. If you see a freshly-turned mound among the milkweed and rustling poplar, know that I lie under it, wanting, like all of us, to be remembered."

With that he placed the talisman in Lily's left hand and rolled her fingers gently over it.

The map's instructions were sharp and ineluctable. With her pendant, crucifix, rabbit's foot, Testament and Southener's amulet tucked lovingly in their leather sachet, Lily began the long walk north moments after sunrise.

She did not stop at the Partridges, but walked steadily, almost serenely, through the booming hamlet of Froomfield. Through the Reserve, six miles long, the road meandered and invited rest, but Lily kept her pace, noticed but unaccosted, until just before noon she walked into Port Sarnia.

Her boots, worn thin, cracked on the town's singular macadam. Lily was tempted neither left nor right, indifferent to Cameron's Emporium with its checker-glass windows a-glitter with frill and frumpery; undistracted by the fragrances of two bakeries and a tannery, undeterred by no less than seven churches. A mile up this high road Lily noticed the break in the forest wall. For the first time in many hours her heart jumped in its stirrups. The map was real. She could read it. Something vital with a future waited for her at the end of this lane.

There, set in two pockets of cleared pine, lay the farms. A small one to the left with a log hut and sheds; a larger one to the right with a whitewashed, split-log house, sideboard barns, and a pond with Sunday-white geese on it.

At the last moment Lily remembered to knock on the firmly latched, blue-trimmed door set in the exact centre of the white-washed cottage. She felt the shadow of the overhanging eave cool her cheek. She pulled tightly the bridle on her heart, and waited.

The door was pulled inward slowly, guardedly. Lily saw the strong woman's-hand, brown from the sun, gripping the sash before the face and figure were disclosed.

"Yes?"

"Aunt Bridie?"

"An' who might you be?"

"I'm...Lily."

"What do you want here, girl? State your business or leave a body in peace."

"Papa sent me."

Sensing the bewilderment in the woman's face, Lil's heart sank. She fought against the faintness and vertigo as best she could, but it felt as if her bones had melted outright in a treacherous sun. As she slumped onto the doorstep, she was certain she heard herself say, "I'm Lily." And, thinking of her father, added, "Lily Fairchild."

6

Saturday was Lily's favourite day. Summer and winter, spring and fall, Saturday was the day of deliverance. Even though the mid-summer sun had lifted barely half a brow over the forest rim in the distant east, Lily felt liberated; and she conveyed her excitement to Benjamin, the Walpole 'paint' who jogged happily over the rough road towards the village of Part Sarnia. This June Saturday was particularly magical.

Aunt Bridie had rejected Uncle Chester's plea for a genuine birthday cake –"You'll spoil the child silly, you old coot"– but she had baked a strawberry pie special for the occasion and even wrapped the newly-made linen blouse and plain calico skirt in tissue as if it were a real surprise. Chester applauded when Lily opened it; Bridie gave him one of her quartering glances but said nothing. Later, as they sat outside on wicker chairs in a garden perfumed with wild hedge roses, their widower neighbour Bill walked over, and through his shy grin – made more prominent by the absence of all but two mismatching front teeth – presented Lily with a blue hair ribbon that might have been made of silk.

"Ma bought it for my daughter, Violet, way back, but she don't wear it," he explained. Lily kissed him on the cheek, which either frightened or scandalized him into a hasty departure. When he had gone, Bridie mumbled about such "fool things" as hair ribbons, so Lily, though tempted by the encouragement in Chester's eye, hid the gift away with her other precious mementoes. In the weeks after her arrival, she had thought she ought to reveal to Bridie the sacred objects in her treasure-pouch, but even then something told her to hold back, that a lady as angular and opinionated as Aunt Bridie would not likely be impressed by a native talisman or even one of God's Testaments. So they remained secreted in her room to be taken out on those few occasions when she had felt unhappy here, or homesick for what she'd left behind.

Which was not often. And certainly never on Saturdays. She reined in Benjamin as they neared Exmouth Street, the edge of the cleared plain that was soon to be an official town, a county seat. It was a new split-log road and dangerously rough. She glanced back at her cargo of eggs and fresh raspberries – so neatly packed in the boxwood containers Chester had tacked together with guarded precision. They rested in a market wagon he had customized with double-leather springs and straw padding, and fitted with snug compartments for Bridie's eggs and seasonal specialties.

Lily had no reason in this world to be sad. She loved her aunt and uncle and she was loved by them. Bridie, her flame-red hair so earnestly harnessed during the day, would come to Lily at bedtime, her hair loose and haphazard, her ice-blue eyes weakened by fatigue, and bending over, bless Lily's cheek with a dry, well-meant kiss. "Thank your maker for makin' you and givin' you such a day," she would invariably murmur before snuffing the candle. It was the only religious sentiment that ever passed her lips. Bridie did not, it seemed, believe in "all this churchin'." Chester, if he held an opinion on the subject, did not offer it.

Over the previous three years, Bridie had taught Lily much about "how to get along in this world", starting in the fields where, in the rich humus of the cleared pine-woods, they grew vegetables and fruits of every tint and texture. Bridie adamantly did not grow wheat, unlike the farmers in the townships east along the London Road or north along the Errol Road, who had to haul their crop to the grist mills where they "left half their profits," or who had to accept that far-off wars would determine their prices.

"Turnips are slow-growin' but they eat easy and winter over," Bridie cautioned more than once during their back-bending weeding marathons. Bridie's bonnet framed her sharp features like a sapper's helmet and a long linen shawl was covered her arms to her wrists. Her skin was not allowed to tan, even in August's humidity when perspiration poured down her back and chest. Lily, wanting to cry out sometimes at her rebellious muscles, swallowed her aches and grew strong.

Their produce and the eggs from a hundred Rhode Island reds, were taken to town each Saturday where they found a ready market. Although most villagers had gardens of their own, the three hotels and five boarding houses that served an army of bachelor workers at the new factories and on the right-of-way clearance out to Enniskillen, along with stopover sailors and excursion passengers, needed a ceaseless supply of provisions in season. Bridie had been the first to seize this opportunity, and though she suffered periodic competition from the local farmer's market, her reliability, home-delivery service, and unfailingly superior produce had won her a steady and profitable business.

"Take care of the pennies an' the pounds'll take care of themselves," Bridie had coached Lily on the day she first took her niece with her into town to "learn the business" and "see for yourself how the other-half lives."

"Your Auntie's the smartest woman in this township," Chester said, helping her stake the beans that summer. "When we came lookin' up here from London, she sees this pine-bush an' she says here's the best spot for what we want. I says, no, it's a mile from town an' nowhere near the cleared lots on the London Road. But she says the soil'll be better here, and of course she was right, includin' that sandy stretch towards the lakeside where the berries grow big as plums, an' includin' the pine itself, some of which we sold the first year and every year since."

Chester had lost his rhythm and a section of the bean plants toppled to the ground.

"Mind you now, it was cuttin' them pines that give me the crick in my back, so's I ain't been too good at weedin' or any heavy work ever since, which along with my fluctuatin' ticker don't make me the hardiest farmer."

"Then your Auntie decides to go in for eggs, so we buys the hens an' I build the two coops and we're in business." Lily looked at the east field next to Bill's makeshift barn where their only field-crop – feed corn – was greening in the sun. "Yessir, it's your Auntie's got the head for business."

The sun was fully up when Benjamin trotted past the London Road crossing and kept southerly on Front Street. To her right, Lily could see the cobalt of the River – the St, Clair River, she'd been told to call it – its beauty only slightly dimmed by familiarity. She had not yet seen the Lake, though every day steamers left the bay for distant points north, and its untouched beaches lay less than a mile through the pines behind her house. The muffled thunder of its breakers was audible below the wind on stormy nights in April or November. "Nothin' to see up there but a lot of water," Bridie admonished her, though Chester's look said otherwise.

Past the London Road lay the town itself, boasting more than a thousand souls. Already a second thoroughfare back from the River, Christina Street, was filling up with clapboard and split-log houses, with shops and a second tannery. Benjamin, unaided, drew driver and cart straight down Front Street to the Western Hotel opposite the Ferry Dock, no more than half a mile from the site of the last gift-giving ceremony. She always started with the hotels since their staffs were up at dawn and happy to welcome her wide-awake greeting. Then she did the boarding-houses on the five east-west intersecting streets that stretched, houseless, into cleared land for more than a mile. By then it was usually after seven and she moved on to the fifteen or twenty private homes on the route, abodes of the well-to-do who, though they could afford gardens and gardeners, preferred to be known to pay for their produce.

Lily thought fleetingly of her first encounters, clinging to a straight-backed Bridie on the wagon seat, intimidated by these well-dressed women and their eccentric town accents. If introductions could not be avoided, she was Lily Ramsbottom, given Chester's name. Mostly, she was allowed to stay silent, handing Bridie the proper boxes, rearranging those left in the cart, and feeding, watering and soothing Benjamin excessively. All the while she kept her ears and a curious eye open.

"Good morning, Bridie," said Mrs. McWhinney, the clothier's wife, in an off-hand way from her watch at the rose bush. "Just take them right through the shed there and leave them on the bench by the sink, that's a good dear," she added, as if addressing her Sunday school class at the Church of England.

Bridie set the eggs and a clutch of rhubarb on a table by the shed door. "No need to stir, Maggie," she called out, "I'll collect next time."

Maggie caught sight of the figure of a child in the cart and inadvertently cut the throat of a prize rose.

"Morning, Miz Ramsbottom," said the Reverend McHarg's missus from the back door of the red-fronted brick manse, her voice carrying to the far pews.

"Three dozen today, Clara?"

"Who's the little bundle you brung with you?" Pince-nez poking around Bridie, glinting towards the cart on the street.

"Got some late raspberries I think the reverend would appreciate. Like to see 'em?"

"I'll come out and have a look, I will," burbled Mrs. McHarg, brushing past a startled Bridie, who recovered in time to insert her body between the pince-nez and the cowering child on the cart-seat.

"Oh what a dear little orphling! Where *did*you pick up such a precious thing?"

Bridie reached into the cart, drew out a quart of enticing berries, and said evenly: "These are free, for my best customer."

Mrs. McHarg, a Presbyterian inured to temptation, hesitated just long enough before accepting the offering in both hands, then quickly regained the offensive. "A foundling?" she asked, raising the tip of her Calvinist nose.

Bridie touched the reins smartly and Benjamin lurched forward. Looking straight ahead she said, "My daughter," and was already moving too resolutely for any exclamation to be heard. Lily thought she heard a berry-box crack open as it struck the ground.

"My gracious, you're early! Barely got my bonnet on! But ain't you a sight for sore eyes; an' you brought the wee one along for company. How's my Lily Blossom doin' today? Cat got your tongue?" Mrs. Salter was constitutionally cheerful despite her husband being a Methodist lay preacher who could, according to Auntie "rant and roll with the best of them hell-an-damnationers."

"Heard a box of your tomatoes went bad on you last week," Bridie said from the side porch of the St. Clair Inn. "Here's an extra two boxes of the best. Guaranteed."

The good lady blushed. "Goodness me, but it's that big-mouth girl of mine blabbin' an' exaggeratin' all over town. I'll take the switch to her, I reckon." She also took the berries.

Vines of ivy and other exotica climbed about a third of the way up the walls of the stone cottage belonging to the Misses Baines-Powell, plump Caroline and fat Charlotte. The sign in front announced "Baines-Powell: Musical Instruction, By Arrangement." Bridie tried to explain what that meant. Only one of the instructresses ever came to the back door, though not always the same one. The other hovered in the draped shadows of the sitting room beyond.

"Found a slug in my cabbage," said Miss Charlotte, peering past Bridie at Lily, who was holding a rack of berry-boxes, as if there were some direct but unnamable connection between slugs and girl-helpers of questionable kin.

"Boil them like I told you?" Bridie asked.

"Of course. Made no difference. Ugly thing popped out onto Miss Baines-Powell's plate an' she almost 'et it, didn't you, dear?"

Muffled assent from within.

"Get a rollin' boil, Charlotte, an' keep at it for five to seven minutes. Nothin' else can be done."

Bridie took three boxes of berries from the rack and set them beside the eggs and carrots on the porch step. "There you are, Charlotte. That'll be ninety-six cents. Any changes for next week? The corn'll be in most likely."

Charlotte surrendered the money and stood watching them leave. Lily always lingered behind a bit, ears pricked.

"Scruffy little ragamuffin, ain't she?"

"You think with the prices Bridie charges she'd be able to put a decent dress on the girl."

"Might even be pretty, don't you think, Lottie?"

"It'd take some scrubbin', I'm afraid."

Bridie always walked steadily forward; she was not a lingerer. Once she turned and said, "Don't let those two old maids go puttin' a lot of tom-fool notions in your head."

The Templeton house was the most attractive of their stops, though by no means the most ostentatious in town. It wasn't even brick, but the siding was lovingly lapped and painted a shade of blue that resembled the River when the ice leaves it in March. The gardens here flourished, invariably dazzling Lily with their lush variety: delphinium, giant poppies, sunflowers, peonies, arboured roses, and marigolds and lilies with the tang of marsh still in them.

Mrs. Alice Templeton almost always intercepted them at the side door. Trim, silver-haired, neatly attired, smiling with both eyes, she invariably asked them to come into the front den, to cool or warm or dry themselves, depending on the season. Sometimes Maurice Templeton, a prominent lawyer, was discovered snoozing there into a gray volume on his lap. Lily feasted on the sight of book-lined walls, porcelain figurines and blue chinaware displayed in an adjoining dining room. The odour of pipe-tobacco lingered and stirred the memory.

On a lucky day there was Ceylon tea and tarts, and talk.

"Your brother's daughter, you say? I can certainly see your eyes there, no question about that."

"She's had no upbringin', mind you, but she's a good worker."

"Another cake, Lily?"

"No, ma'am. Thank you."

"Go ahead, looks like it'd do you good."

Lily glanced at Aunt Bridie. "No, thank you, ma'am."

"Say, Bridie, my girls are both at boarding school in London, as you know, and I've never thrown away any of their dresses or slips. God knows, there's a pile of bonnets too in a trunk –"

Bridie rose suddenly to her full height. "Thank you for the tea, missus, but we really must be gettin' along. Got a schedule to keep." In fact, the Templetons were always their last stop.

"But I haven't paid you yet."

"Next time," Bridie replied; they were already at the door. Once away, Bridie tried to make light of their hasty departure. "We'd never get away from the old gabbler. Never did hear anyone like to carry on so and fritter away so much time. Besides, your uncle'd wear his shoes to bed if we left him alone too long."

Then, more seriously, she added, "They're all the same, Lily. You remember that. Can't leave off interferin' with people's lives."

Lily was not sure. Was it "interferin" to offer unused dresses and bonnets? And that triggered another thought: why had Luc never delivered father's trunks? And why had she not heard from her father? She was sure he loved her and she thought often of his kindly face.

Come winter, the physical labour of planting, weeding and harvesting was exchanged for equally arduous indoor tasks. Bridie made quilts and candles and soon discovered that Lily's fingers were more nimble than her own. Her chores in the barn and coops never ended, nor her share of the cooking, regular mending and wood chopping when Chester's back acted up, as it did more often of late. Lily found the fine needlework as fatiguing as hoeing lettuce; but she loved arranging the harlequin swatches of the quilts, composing their colours into prescribed patterns. By April Bridie and Lily had stitched eight quilts that would bring ready cash to tide them over the lean spring months. With candle sales, there was sufficient to buy them each a pair of new leather boots from McWhinney's Haberdashery.

By the third summer, after her fourteenth birthday, Lily Ramsbottom was making half of their deliveries alone. More and more, Bridie left the egg-and-vegetable side of the business to her, while she herself drummed up further trade in the expanding sections back of Christina Street or scouted the competition's prices at the Saturday market beside the St. Clair Inn. As far as Lily could tell, Bridie was never tempted by the displays of finery in the shops along Front Street.

"Tell me, Lily dear, what Church is your aunt raisin' you in?" asked Mrs. McHarg, sweetly, for her husband's sake.

"The green peppers're good today, ma'am. Crisp as ice."

"You *are* attendin' a church of some kind, aren't you?"

"No, ma'am." Lily felt her eyes drop, a flush of red staining her cheeks.

"You poor, poor thing, you." The woman's voice trembled with delicious shock. "An' why not?" she ventured.

"We work on Sundays," Lily said, looking up proudly.

Mrs. McHarg was speechless. Lily was already giving Benjamin a nudge when she heard faintly from the back doorway: "That woman oughta be hanged!" Then: "Lily, you tell that so-called aunt of yours not to bother comin' round here again!"

Lily did no such thing.

Lily loved the boarding houses, especially the rambling clapboard establishment on Lochiel Street run by Char Hazelberry. If she wished, which was often, Lily stepped right inside the cozy kitchens where aproned servants cooked and scrubbed and gossiped; where some of the resident working men – dilatory, hungover or recuperative – lingered about to tease them. When Lily questioned the landlady's name, Badger McCovey whispered breezily in her ear: "Short for Charity, but she ain't got none, get it?" Walleye Watson, his good peeper next to hers, declared, "It's the way she cooks the food!" He tried to wink, with absurd results, and she laughed with the rest of the room.

"Hi, toots, gonna take me to the shindig, Saird'y?"

"I get first dance, promise?"

"Not me, I'll take the last one, eh Lily gal?"

"Don't you pay them geezers no mind," Char would tell Lily. "Most of them's well past it anyways! They couldn't raise dust in a hen-house."

Lily usually left Char's place feeling faintly wicked but welcomed and cheered, – and humming all the way to Exmouth.

Lily carried the last order of the day to the back of the Templeton's blue cottage, under the rose arbour in primary bloom and into the meadow of the Templeton's dooryard. She was delighted to see the cedar table covered with a linen cloth and set for tea. The missus must be planning a garden party, she thought. And by the looks of the fancy cakes and scones and the silver tea-set, the company expected must be the hoity-toity. Mrs. Templeton popped from her shed, brushing back her uncovered hair, and swept across the lawn to Lily.

"Well, young lady, don't just stand there lookin', *sit down.*"

Mrs. Templeton showed Lily the proper way to pour tea and how to hold a scone with three digits and some dignity. She smiled sideways and whispered, "Wouldn't want to upset the good ladies of the town, now would we?" She took Lily's arm and escorted her about the garden, explaining carefully how one nursed and groomed such unruly beauty, prompting Lily to recall and speak about the wild blossoms of the townships.

"Well, Lily my sweet," she said with a sigh, "I mustn't keep you. Bridie will soon be frettin'." She tied Lily's bonnet snugly below her chin. "I just hope your auntie knows what a prize she's got."

Lily blushed. Bridie, she knew, would not approve of such "spoilin'" that could "turn a girl's head" in a direction that would eventually – one had to assume – prove regrettable.

As Lily was leaving, Mrs. Templeton turned suddenly and called after her. She had a piece of paper in her hand. "I almost forgot: Maurice and I are holding meeting here in a week, we'll need a few extras, delivered early in the morning if that's all right."

"Yes, ma'am." Lily's eyes were fastened on the fluttering note.

"There's so many things, I wrote them all down for you. Here, take this along."

Lily took the paper, turned and was almost under the rose arbour when Mrs. Templeton said, a bit too quickly, "Oh Lily, would you mind checking, do I have cucumbers on that list?"

Lily froze. She felt the confiding coziness of the morning ebb away.

"Just take a quick glance at the list, love." Mrs. Templeton prompted, but kindly

Lily looked sideways then directly to Mrs. Templeton. "I can't," she said tonelessly.

"Well then, it's high time we did something about that!"

Lily desperately wanted to be present when Bridie and Mrs. Templeton had their *tête à tête*. A letter in an engraved envelope had been delivered right to their door by a suborned errand-boy. Bridie read it, her brow furrowing, her lips mouthing the words. "Some nerve!" But next morning she and Lily scoured the house and, to Lily's amazement, a pewter tea-service materialized from the steamer-trunk to be set upon a crocheted tablecloth of ancient but unblemished vintage. Then she and Uncle Chester – only one of them protesting – were banished to the barn.

Bridie was a good reader, Chester said so many times. But there were no books in evidence in their home. Lily did see her aunt reading, though, for each week she picked up *The Canadian Observer* and brought it home, taking special pains to read it on the Sabbath. Chester would peek at it occasionally but would say to Lily, "It's full of radical ranting, girl, an' bad politics that'll come to no good end." He sigh with the feigned resignation he used whenever Bridie's behavior frustrated him. "It's beyond me why she takes in that stuff. 'Course, you gotta remember where she come from."

Lily couldn't remember what she didn't know. Bridie wouldn't talk about the old country. Chester would, after a slug or two from his cache in Benjamin's stall, about the Ramsbottom tribe in Lancashire, the innumerable cousins he'd never met, his own history as the only child of a shipwright attached to the military command during the Simcoe regime, the premature deaths of his parents from cholera. The Ramsbottoms, however legendary, were not blood.

"Don't ask," Auntie would say, seeing the tilt of Lily's chin. "The Old Country's old, it's only good for forgettin'. This is the here and now and that's what's important."

Seeing Lily's disappointment, Chester slipped into his bedroom, opened the trunk with a squeal that arched Bridie's's eyebrows, and returned with a large leather-bound book. "I'll just read her the story parts," he said in Bridie's direction. "It's her right, you know," he added vehemently though his voice didn't sound fully confident until Samson had pushed both columns aside and brought the wicked temple down upon himself.

The next winter Chester grew bolder and brought out a calf-covered novel called *The Last of the Mohicans*, from which he read aloud to Lily, curled up on his lap in the armchair, all through that dark, cold season. Last winter, when *The Deerslayer* made its debut, Lily perched on the ample arm of the chair and followed the words on the page. Soon she was able to point to some of the words and repeat them back. "See, Bridie love, the young lady can read. Smart as a whip, she is."

Bridie, who appeared not to be listening, snapped, "Don't be turnin' her head, you old fool. She can't read. Soon as I get some time, soon as everybody around here pulls their weight, I'm gonna teach the child to read properly."

"Don't blame the girl," he said petulantly. "After all, she's had no educatin' to speak of."

"An' never *will* with the likes of you around her." The reading was over for that evening.

When Lily ventured in to see if Bridie and Mrs Templeton were still talking, she found Mrs. Templeton adjusting her Sunday hat and looking quite pleased with herself. "Thanks for the tea, Bridie. You really must let me return the hospitality soon."

In her working smock, Lily felt smudged and unworthy, but Mrs. Templeton kissed her warmly on the cheek. Bridie smoothed her skirt and said to Lily: "It's all fixed. You'll start in at the Common School first thing next Monday."

Lily turned her shining face to Mrs. Templeton. "Don't thank me, young lady. Thank your Aunt; she's givin' up the best helper she's got."

Bridie wanted to be severe but couldn't manage it.

Her aunt had argued for starting in September when the new term began. After all, only one week remained in the current school year. "This way," Mrs. Templeton had insisted, "she can try it out, introduce herself to Miss Pringle, and get set up for the fall term." What she really meant was that it would be cruel to let a girl of Lily's temperament wait in uncertainty over a whole summer.

"Only if Chester'll help out with the weedin'," Bridie had countered. Fortunately Chester's troublesome back took a turn for the better, and dressed in a brown-and-tan gingham especially cut down by Bridie and with a lunch-pail in hand, Lily set off for Port Sarnia.

The Monday-morning sun had risen full of hope, then retreated. An east wind brought dark clouds prophesying thunder, and worse. The rain gusted sideways at Lily, who was torn between sheltering in the bush by the road or being late for school. Mrs. Templeton had made the arrangements; Lily was expected. Using her thin broadcloth shawl as deftly as she could, Lily manoeuvred her way through the squalls and mud into the open streets of the town. She was soaked through to the skin. Even her petticoat, improvised from a plain calico skirt, was sodden. Her boots were wet and plastered with grime that splashed up to her ankles and soiled the hem of her dress. Lily gritted her teeth and wedged her right cheek into the rain.

When she got to the schoolhouse on George Street, the sun was making a comeback. No children skipped or cavorted in the grounds. Lily paused at the door about to knock when a large boy with a pimple on his nose opened it, and called back: "It's the new girl, Miss Pringle! Looks like she's fallen in Durand's Pond!"

A gale of laughter greeted Lily as she entered the room, her shawl dripping. Standing at the front behind a table, Miss Pringle – frightfully tall, angular, eyes overly brilliant like a starved cat's – slammed her fuller down.

"Behave yourselves, class," she shouted an octave above normal. "Remember, you're young ladies and gentlemen."

The ragtaggles and strays among this motley group of ages and sexes were not taken in: ladies-and-gentlemen-to-be went to the Grammar School on Christina Street. When the hubbub had died of its own weight, Miss Pringle said, "Please hang your cloak on the nail to your right, and take a seat. Class, say hello to our new pupil, Miss Lily Ramsbottom."

The surname had barely left Miss Pringle's lips when three or four unsynchronized snorts were heard, followed by girlish giggles. "That's enough!" bellowed Miss Pringle. "We don't make fun of people's names no matter how odd they may be."

Lily sat down at an empty place on the bench that held three other girls who might have been her age. Her gingham, still sopping, clung to her. The dark-haired girl next to her edged away.

"Have you attended school elsewhere?" Miss Pringle asked sweetly, not leaving her post.

"No, ma'am. This is my first time."

Miss Pringle paused, her gasp communicated instantly to the class. "Then what on earth are you doing sitting with the Fourth Book?" she snapped with more satisfaction than the situation warranted. Her ruler pointed left like a claw. "You'll have to sit with the First Book, over there."

Lily saw a spot at the end of the back-left bench beside an oversized boy who swivelled and beamed at her. Lily hesitated.

"There's a Reading Primer waiting for you," Miss Pringle said, indicating the gray-backed tome on the desk. Lily rose to take her appointed place, now studied more carefully by the teacher.

"Good heavens!" sputtered Miss Pringle, as she took in Lily's thin but drenched gingham. The class reeled as one and swung to the point of Miss Pringle's scandalized glare. "You can't sit there... like that!" she sputtered, unconsciously lifting her hands towards her own well-harnessed bosom. "Please retrieve your cloak!"

Beside her, not unkindly, the boy in Book One whispered: "Your bubs are peekin'."

Chester was all for driving into town and taking his buggy-whip to Miss Pringle, even after hearing Lily's abbreviated account of her humiliation.

"Don't you fret about it, child," Bridie soothed. "Not much learnin' goes on in schools anyway. Come September, we'll teach you to read proper." She was looking at Lily now. "Remember this: We're not gonna spend all our life chewin' dirt."

The summer of Lily's fifteenth year was not as uneventful as she had feared. Bridie, ever eager for new business, opened a stall at the farmer's market on Saturday mornings during the growing season, giving over the house-to-house deliveries completely to Lily. Their neighbor Bill, content to let his wheat ripen unaided, was brought over to help with the added weeding, picking and preparations for marketing. Uncle's back seemed baulkier than usual. In mid-July Bridie astonished them by announcing that she was leaving for a few days to cook for the road-clearance workers who had set up a tent city near the Reserve. Rumours in the town suggested that some of the clearing was in anticipation of a railway line, but no confirmation was available.

"Your auntie ain't worked for nobody, cookin' or cleanin', since her days in Toronto. She don't believe in it. Got her pride, that woman." Lily nodded.

"We need the money," was all Bridie would say. "I'm gonna hire a man to cut pine again. They're a cash crop like anything else. Besides, we should try to clear another two acres for planting next year."

Bridie was so exhausted when she came home from her three-day stint at the camp that she went straight to bed and slept right through Bill's Saturday visit and harmonica serenade. Lily was even persuaded to attempt a jig. The two men sipped from Bill's flask and tapped in time.

"Why don't you ever bring Violet with you?" Lily asked, flushed and sweating. "I could teach her to dance."

"Oh, she don't dance none," Bill said in a drawl that was as lethargic as his music was sprightly. "She's a bit tetched in the head, you know. Been like that since she were a babe. No sir, she don't like to come outta the house at all."

Chester asked Lily if she'd like to try a "wee drop", and was so persistent that Lily made a show of tilting the flask against her teeth, wincing and gasping in feigned pleasure. They seemed satisfied with her performance. To deflect their further hopes she called for a hornpipe and flung her body into the music's coil. The two men applauded in appreciation as Lily came to a stop in the middle of the room. The last filament of Bill's music quavered in the coal-oil light when Lily caught sight of a face in the window above the sink, staring at her with wide innocent eyes full of longing. For a second Lily thought she was looking at herself.

Then Violet let out the whirring, wordless cry she used for delight or despair, and vanished into the night.

It was August. Bridie was off to the camp once more "just to help out." At Chester's insistence, she agreed to deposit their savings in the Bank of Upper Canada in Port Sarnia. At the beginning of the month a hired hand arrived to cut timber and be generally useful around the place. Chester was made to give up his workshop in the barn wherein a pallet and table were installed for the new arrival. Uncle's back "did a dip" and he was laid up with lumbago for several days. Lily did the chores by herself. She might have been a little resentful but then watching the hired man proved to be adequate compensation.

Lily expected the fellow to be old, grizzled, and down-on-his-luck. Instead, Cam was twenty, as sleek and muscled as a muskellunge, with an open smile and black Scotch eyes that were curious and bold. "A bit too bold if you ask me," said Bridie. To Bridie, Cam was unfailingly polite and deferential, and he certainly was a good worker. In ninety-degree heat he stripped to his waist, confronted the four-foot girth of a pine, and slung his executioner's axe. Sweat raced in rivulets down the small of his back, staining his trousers to the thighs. Positioning herself perfectly between the vegetable rows, Lily was able to keep a close watch on his performance.

The feelings she was experiencing were new, and puzzling. She knew what animals suffered to procreate and what men and women, for inscrutable reasons, accomplished in their midnight chambers. That such acts might be accompanied by the most exquisite configuration of emotion, titillation and ecstasy had not occurred to her outside the vague intimations of her dreams. Until now. Her legs, made sturdy with farm work, went to jelly in his presence; her heart, thoroughly sound, pounded as if in distress. Always he was polite, solicitous: "Can I help you with that, Lily? Looks too heavy for you, that pail." But his gaze clung to her, and she wondered frantically if he too could see her breasts, if even the extra band of muslin she tied around herself were not enough to bridle them.

"That young man's got to go," Bridie said near month's end. "He never stops leerin' at Lily."

"But the girl's fifteen," said Chester. "She's bound to attract the boys."

"I'll stay out of his way, Auntie."

"He's a real good worker, woman. You know how bad my back's been lately."

"I know how bad your medicine's been," she shot back. Then full of weariness she said, "All right. He stays. But just till the next section's done. Then out he goes, bag and baggage."

As if he had overheard the threat, Cam took his glistening biceps and shoulders to the farthest corner of the timber stand, out of sight and harm's way. He ate his lunch in the woods. At supper he wore a clean shirt and got Bridie talking about her business, the growth in town, even radical politics. Bridie was amazed to learn that one so young could understand the imperatives of George Brown's 'true grit' policies. Lily, naturally, had expected such genius from the outset. Chester swung between envy and relief. September came. The muggy weather remained. So did Cam. Bridie left for the camp "one last time, I swear by all the snakes in Scotland!"

Lily felt undone by Cam's sudden distance. With Bridie away, he returned to the bush after supper, swinging his axe against the yielding pine until twilight. I'll go to him, Lily decided. And why not? Something inevitable and foregone has already happened; it's only the working out that's left.

Leaving Chester slumped in a doze, Lily slipped out into the gloaming. It was a perfect night. Even Bill had gone off to town in his buggy. She and Cam would be alone under a consenting moon. With no particular stratagem in mind, Lily hastened towards the barn. A sound, like the cry of a creature struck by talons, came from Lily's left. She stopped. Now it was a soft mewling. Old Bill's tabby birthing kittens again? Lily sidled through the beanstalks and came up behind the Indian corn that bordered on Bill's property. His log barn was illuminated in the moonlight as war the source of the sounds.

Violet was half-sitting with her back against the wall, her loose dress open to expose her breasts, which Cam was kneading with both hands as if he were stretching dough. Violet's own hands were busy in Cam's lap, coaxing his flabby member as they would the Guernsey's teat. Violet uttered a wail of pain, release or frustration – Lily could not discern which.

"Shut up, ya fuckin' bitch! Shut the hell up!" He slapped her so hard her head snapped back and hit the logs behind her. Then he was shoving his instrument into his trousers and stomping away into the dark. Violet's sobs pursued him, inarticulate and discordant. But, at the first nicker of Bill's pony in the lane, she stopped, pulled her dress together, and scuttled towards the unlit cabin.

Lily stood in the corn, bereft, empty, then furious. Above her the jib of the quartering moon luffed, and went out.

"Three of 'em, city-biddies," Bill warned Bridie at the doorstep "All dolled up for christenin' by the look of it." And he winked mysteriously towards Lily. "They've already made the turn, I reckon."

Aunt Bridie never panicked, especially on Saturday afternoons in September with the weather clement and the week's market done. "If God hadn't been Presbyterian," she would say, "he'd've made his Sabbath on Saturday afternoons so's all of us could rest together." Nonetheless, she went indoors at a trot, signaling for Lily to follow.

"It's the Ladies Aid for sure," she mumbled. Wordlessly they hurried about "straightening up" the living area. Bridie covered the table, set it for tea and put the kettle on. She turned to Lily. "This is about you, you can be sure."

No doubt they were coming to drag her away to Miss Pringle's school. "Go an' see that uncle of yours is safe in his stall," Bridie said, removing her apron but otherwise making no further concessions to the visitors. Lily raced to the barn. Chester was in his workshop, now fully restored to him since Cam's sudden departure. He hadn't bothered to remove the pallet, finding it a more convenient spot to rest between stints at the workbench. That is where Lily found him.

Meanwhile, the delegation had arrived: the missuses McHarg, Salter and McWhinney. After tea and niceties, Mrs. McWhinney took the lead. "I'll come right to the point," she said with mercantilist efficiency, draining her cup.

"The point," interrupted Reverend McHarg's representative, "is Lily."

Bridie poured Mrs. McWhinney another cup of tea.

"The point is the baptism of this innocent child."

"We know how good you been to her an' all," added Josephine Salter hastily. "Nobody can take that away from you. You been a wonderful momma to this dear little foundlin' here. Just the other night I says to Mr. Salter –"

"What Josie means, is that it may be all right for you to reject your Maker, to live out here in a state of sin and run the risk of eternal damnation –"

"You're a bright woman, Bridie," said Mrs McWhinney. "Nobody denies you that. You work hard an' you keep your own counsel. Well an' good. But we're talkin' here about the girl. Now we all might come from different churches, an' we have our set-to's from time to time, but we all agree on this – the girl deserves a chance to save her own soul."

"It don't even matter who baptizes her," added Mrs. Salter with Methodist charity. "It's just gotta be done, that's all."

No one had looked directly at Lily during this exchange though she was occasionally acknowledged with a flutter of fingers or a glancing nod. Bridie sat straight-backed, following each of the speakers with intense interest.

"Do you intend to toss a coin?" she asked.

"Bridie, this is serious. We're just askin' you to think about the girl, about her future."

"In Heaven or Port Sarnia?"

The sudden edge to Aunt Bridie's voice silenced Mrs. Salter and Mrs. McWhinney. They hadn't expected it to come to this. Mrs. McHarg, being Orange, had more ancient claim on self-righteousness.

"Both," she said.

Bridie leaned forward and looked over at Lily, who could not read the emotions held in check by that awesome will. "Well then," she said. "We'll let the girl decide. Lily, dear, what do you say?"

Lily, concluding it was time to find out once and for all who this God was, answered, "Yes."

It was agreed that Lily Ramsbottom's religious education would begin a week Sunday with an interview with the Reverend McHarg himself at the Manse. He would determine the status of the girl's 'natural' inclinations to religious sentiment, after which she would be placed exclusively in the hands of Mrs. McHarg for special tutoring before being released to the general influence of Sunday School and Service.

On the day of the interview, Chester took Lily by horse and cart to the door of the imposing red-brick Manse. He held her hand, squeezed it, and tried to say something encouraging, but couldn't. Lily watched the rig move west down George Street and stop in front of the Anglican Church whose spire glinted above the horizon. Uncle Chester got out and, a bit like a thief entering a shop, went in.

"Come in, come in, my child!" boomed the Reverend Clarion McHarg, swivelling in his desk chair and waving the deaf housekeeper away.

Lily obeyed. The woman had taken her shawl somewhere. She peered around the dimly-lit room embroidered with walnut and cherrywood and leather-skinned tomes of impressive dimension.

"Sit," said the Reverend, pointing to a padded, armless chair across from the littered secretary. "My, don't we look pretty, today," he added, finishing up a sentence and blotting it. Adjusted now to the poor light, Lily saw that his features were all crags and cliffs, with spiky eyebrows that bunched like a pair of singed caterpillars. Despite the eager teeth of his smile, his eyes burned. "You're the...young lady from the township my wife was telling me about?"

"Yes, your reverence." Chester had instructed her in the appropriate form of address.

"I ain't been baptized," Lily ventured.

"*Haven't*been," he said automatically.

"Yes, sir. My aunt says I haven't had a proper upbringin'.."

"Do you know what being baptized in the Lord means?"

"No, sir."

"Well, then, let's find out, shall we, how much you *do*know." The caterpillars arched expectantly. "God will be pleased, I'm sure, to have you join His congregation of the Saved."

"Yes," Lily said. "I come here to find out about him. I do have questions."

"Such as?"

"Can I talk to him?"

The good Reverend smiled as if charmed by the naiveté of such a remark. "You may *pray*to Him."

"How do I do that?" Lily wanted to hear it from the source.

My word, the ignorance of some of these country folks was appalling! "You get down on your knees, close your eyes, and tell God about your sins and ask Him to offer you strength and succor."

"What sins?"

The Reverend stared at Lily as if trying to catch her out at some trick. "You don't know?"

"No, sir."

"Well, I can see that Mrs. McHarg has some tough cloth to cut here."

"Can I speak to God, like this, like we are?" Lily said.

"Of course not," he snapped. "The Lord will answer your prayers if and when He decides."

"When he does answer, will it be in English?"

"Are you being blasphemous, child?"

"What's blasphemous, sir?"

"God speaks to each man in his own tongue; He hears, sees and knows everything."

"Uncle Chester says that according to his Bible, God talks in Hebrew."

"Damnation to Uncle Chester! Excuse me, child. You see why we must all pray."

Lily didn't. She straightened up, charily. McHarg did the same. "Would God, if I prayed to him real hard, talk to me in Pottawatomie?"

The caterpillars jumped in agitation. "Who put you up to this? That heathen aunt of yours?" He had both of her shoulders in his grip.

"No, sir. I just thought if your god can talk in every tongue, then he could if he wants talk to me in Pottawatomie. Or Chippewa or Attawan –"

"Cease this sacrilege! *Now!*"

Lily quaked before Reverend McHarg's temper. His hands had slipped down so that they were squeezing her exposed forearms. Suddenly he let go of her as if she were contagious. He sat down again, gathering the frayed ends of his composure. Lily didn't move. He seemed surprised, even discomfited, by the fact that she had fled his study. He felt her presence– the Lord's anteroom, as it were – as something indefinably threatening and darkly tempting.

"Mrs. Beecroft will show you out," he said at last. When she reached the study door, though, he shouted desperately. "Whatever becomes of you, Miss, just remember this: God is not a Pottawatomie!"

As best she could, Lily told Bridie what had trespassed at the Manse. Bridie listened with interest, not once interrupting.

"God's not there," Lily said. "I know it."

Bridie's face clouded. "I don't deny it. But if you turn away from all the churchin' these folk 'round here can't do without, they'll never ever forgive you. You'll have to pay for that rebel streak all your life."

"But you –"

"Yes, I did it, I know. As far as I'm concerned, the god they pray to was invented by landlords and greengrocers. An' now that I look at you, I see somethin' in your face, somethin' from that mad father of yours or the wild bush you was let roam in –." She didn't finish, as if she'd already said too much. Then: "Well, don't just stand there with your legs in a knot, get that frumpery off, we got corn to shuck!"

When they were again working side by side, Lily said, "Will you teach me how to read?"

"Yes, honey, real soon. That's a solemn promise." And she tore at the stubborn shocks in a frenzy.

Contrary to her own declarations, Bridie was off to cook at the camp yet again. As many of the workers brought their families into the area and moved to more permanent quarters, Bridie's business followed them. Already she was plotting the use of the new acres cleared, cut and sold by Cam before he left, not even taking his last week's pay. Orders were left with her subordinates: Lily was to bake two dozen pumpkin pies for a special Thanksgiving celebration at the camp, courtesy of the soon-to-be-announced candidate for mayor of the newly incorporated town: Maurice Templeton, Esquire. "I'm trustin' you to do as I've showed you; somethin' big could come outta this," Bridie said. Second, Chester was to give the north coop a thorough scrubbing and white-washing as several hens had recently died from some mysterious cause.

Lily was delighted, but Chester's back went on leave. Lately Bridie had been more than usually stern and grumpy, snapping at her and Chester with little or no provocation. Most of her wrath was directed towards him, though Lily failed to see why. Seldom would he talk back, and even then the argument always collapsed after a single strike. Sometimes he would look over at Lily, aggrieved and helpless, as if to say, "See, this is what it's really like." Once she had seen Chester, unaware he was being observed, pick up Bridie's pince-nez – which she needed to read *The Observer*and "do the books"– and hid them under the mattress. Bridie searched high and low for them, more than routinely disturbed that she had been so careless as to mislay them. Chester meantime made a great fuss about helping her locate them: "Thought they might've fallen off in the fruit cellar when you was labellin' the jars, but not so, I'm afraid," he said solicitously. "Not like you to be so careless with your valuables." Three days later when the spectacles turned up magically between two butter-boxes on the kitchen shelf, Bridie gave her husband the oddest look, then went about her business.

Grumbling about his lumbago, Chester went off to the north chicken coop, tools in hand. Lily went to the pumpkin patch and started the laborious task of loading the ripest ones into the barrow and pushing them through the loose soil to the dooryard. On the very first load Lily saw she had been too ambitious: the wheel buried itself in the ground, and when Lily got angry with it, it lurched sideways and sent the pumpkins thumping overboard. Uncle Chester was suddenly beside her. "I'll help you with that," he said. "Damn woman oughta know better'n to make you push a thing like this. There's times I think she just forgets you're a girl...a young lady," he said, puffing and huffing a huge pumpkin into the barrow.

"Be careful of your heart, now," Lily said, but she was happy to have help. Together they managed to get three loads of the unwieldy fruit safely to a pile beside the stoop.

"There now, my lass, you can go on with your woman's work," said Chester.

Lily leaned over and kissed him on the cheek. "Maybe I can get this done an' come help with the coop."

He sighed: "That's a dog's work," and trudged off.

Lily split the pumpkins and removed the pulp, then cooked and strained it in large kettles supplied by Mrs Templeton before setting it in the cool of the back shed. She would have to build a hot, sustaining fire in the stove for the pies; in the meantime, she and Chester would eat a cold supper.

After getting a good blaze started, she set out to fetch him home. The first place she looked was the barn. He wasn't in his workshop; nor were there any signs that he had been there. Puzzled, she walked over to the north coop. Inside she was greeted by a spray of chicken feathers and dust; when it settled in the fading light, she saw Chester sprawled on his back, his clay jug overturned and empty beside him. He was awake, but his eyes were half-lidded as if he were just waking or about to drop off. His face glowed as if sunburned. The place was a mess, and Uncle Chester lay fully in it; bits of cast-off straw and chicken droppings, hen-pecked dirt and disembowelled seed-husks. "Uncle?"

"Ah, is it you, Lily? You see what she's done now, you see what she's driven us to?"

"Come on, Uncle. Your supper's ready."

"You're the loyal one, though. Chester can always count on his little Lily." She had him by the arm, and he made a half-hearted effort to get up. "You wouldn't drive a man to this, would you, my sweet?"

He was up, but when she let go, his eyes rolled and he slumped back into the muck. "Where'd the room go?" he said, trying to laugh through his coughing jag. Lily was able to wrap one of his arms around her shoulder and with great difficulty manoeuvre him out of the coop and onto the path that led to the house. The odours of whiskey and offal contended in the evening air.

"You always thought she was so damn smart, didn't you, pickin' this spot out. Well, you're old enough now to be told the truth," he said, guiding his slurs. He stopped to retch into the last of the cucumbers.

"I'll put some tea on," Lily said.

"Picked this hell-hole in a pine-bush 'cause it was next to the army reserve. They're gonna build a fort an' barracks right there, she says, an' we'll be right next to them. Some fort, eh? Nothin' but pine trees an' always will be! Some smart, eh?"

They were at the house. Uncle Chester dropped to his knees and vomited copiously on the flagstones, spraying Lily in the process. Then he looked up at her as if he had just wakened from a messy dream and was wondering where he was: "Your Auntie's a good woman," he said softly. "An' don't you ever forget it."

"I'll get out the tub," Lily said. "You can just sit right here." Lily hurried inside, got him a cup of clear tea, and then proceeded to prepare a bath. Using the extra kettles from the Templetons, she boiled enough water to almost fill the shiny metal tub they'd bought last winter to help "straighten out" his unreliable backbone. Not once had Bridie used it, nor had Lily – both of them continuing to wash at the outside pump in the sheltering dusk or once-a-week with a pail and warm water and soap in the dank kitchen.

Lily went out to Chester with a flannel sheet, and after managing to slurp half-a-cup of tea, he wobbled to his feet and let Lily pull off his reeking shirt and trousers under cover. Somehow, with Lily keeping the sheet in place, he succeeded in removing his undervest and linens. Through the sheet Lily could see how thin his arms and legs had become in the last year, He held her hand like a little boy as he stepped into the tub, cupping his private parts in an automatic gesture. But Lily had already turned away, leaving the warm steamy room and walking wearily to the well-pump through the cloudless afterglow of twilight. Her arm ached as she primed and pumped, and her skin recoiled at the icy touch of the water. Nonetheless, she stripped naked and scoured herself with lye-soap, letting it sting and purge. The chill air soon dried her, and she slipped her nightshirt over the gooseflesh. Suddenly she was famished, and very thirsty. She felt the moon's weight on her back as she headed for the house.

Chester was out of the tub, sitting in his wingback chair with the flannel towel wrapped around him, toga-like. He was clean, but the fatigue and strain of the day's excess was etched into his face. He's an old man, thought Lily. He forced a sheepish smile.

"What would I do without you, Lily?" he said wanly.

7

Much had happened to the world since 1855. The boom of the mid-fifties gave way to the bust of '57 and '58. In the wake of the depression, few if any in Lambton County would have anticipated or paid attention to the publication of Darwin's *On the Origin of the Species* and if they had, they would have been outraged by its apostasy while simultaneously appropriating it to explain – despite temporary recessions – the inevitability of progress, North American style. The word "progress" itself was in the air, on the tongues of Tory and Reformer alike, and its principal articulation was in the chug of the locomotive.

The Great Western Railway had hammered its cross-ties through the startled forests of Kent all the way to Chatham and Windsor, eclipsing villages and fathering towns, its patrimony as ineluctable as a mutant gene in biological ascendancy. Its managing director, Charles John Brydges, had already dreamt a horizontal line through the maze between London and Port Sarnia. Unbeknownst to the good burghers of either town, the Grand Trunk had hatched a scheme to drive a second line, slightly north, from Stratford to the military reserve at the junction of Lake Huron and the St. Clair River, denoted on the official maps as Point Edward though known locally as "the ordnance lands" or "the rapids" or just plain "Slocum's fishery". At the stroke of a pen, the hamlets of Forest and Thedford were declared to have a future. The future also looked brighter for John A. Macdonald who, having purchased a leasehold on said lands, stood to make a handsome profit.

Important as these latter developments were, the most pressing concern for the Lambtonians of 1858 was the poor weather and the resultant general crop failure. It rained all spring, followed by weeks of summer drought. Every imaginable variety of blight and pestilence – taking their cue from Darwin – took full advantage of the situation and ravaged those inferior species to near extinction. Whilst some of the cereal crops fared reasonably well, Bridie's garden plot suffered most cruelly. They watched it mildew in the wet and wither in the heat, while slugs and mites and chiggers and rusts flourished. In August, a paralytic bacterium swept through one of the coops;

the birds' corpses had to be burned like stubble.

For a time Chester forgot about his weak ticker and bad back, and pitched in to salvage part of the potato crop and most of the hardy turnip. Lily flailed at bugs, pinched worms and popped caterpillars till exhaustion overtook her each night that summer. They could not deny the inevitable; their business was in ruins.

"We'll start over next spring," Bridie said after each disaster. "That's why we got cash in the bank." In desperation she would mention the recent survey of the pine-bush and swamps of the ordnance grounds. Uncle Chester would sigh knowingly.

But there was more to it than the accidents of weather. Unable to keep up deliveries except for a few eggs to the old customers, Bridie was compelled to sell what produce her garden did yield to jobbers, who collected it at the farm gate with their great wagons and took it off to the expanding markets in town and to the wharfs where lake-steamers whisked it daily to the hostels of Detroit and Cleveland. Within months the stock-cars and hoppers of the Great Western would be shunting produce between towns within hours, not days. The era of large-scale cash cropping had been launched.

"We'll lick them," Bridie said. "We'll get by. We always have, haven't we, Chester?" Uncle had succumbed to sleep.

One stroke of good fortune was that Bill, with his own farm in disarray, had abandoned it and become more or less their hired man. Without him they could not have managed to salvage anything of that season. On the twenty-first of June he brought over a bottle of mulberry wine and they all toasted Lily's eighteenth birthday. There was no society coming out for Lily, however, unless she counted waltzing with her uncle in the kitchen.

A few days later, Lily found Bridie at the kitchen table with her head in her hands. She was ashen; the perpetual glint in her eyes was glazed with disappointment and something worse, despair. With her intrinsic strength and constitutional optimism, Bridie had faced any number of temporary calamities in the past. She would suffer any physical discomfort, any mental anguish, and take any risks demanded by Fate so long as there was hope that she could escape the one thing in life she feared the most: the drudgery of a labour which has no end, no gain, beyond mere survival. Even the meaning of seasons would be lost. In the pleading of those eyes Lily saw the fear of a life lived without a future and a glimpse of a woman's lot in such times.

Bridie looked up. "The worst of it, Lily, the very worst of it is somethin'

I've dreaded like the plague itself. You'll have to go out to service."

Lily could think of nothing to say.

"We'll need the money. I got plans to rearrange this place, I have. Next spring. When things are better. But we'll have to have money."

By now Lily had found a voice to reply. "Who wants me?" she said.

"I dread to tell you," Auntie said. "Lord knows what'll become of you in that town."

Lily tried as best she could to look concerned.

"But she'll pay well, no doubt, Mrs. Templeton will."

"Weepin' just blinds you to what is right in front of you," Old Samuels used to say. Lily never saw him cry, despite the anguish he must have felt when telling his stories of the diaspora of the Attawandarons and the disappearance of their ancient tongue. Sitting in her new room at the Templetons, couched for the first time in her life with luxury, she examined her tiny chest of accumulated treasures – the rabbit's foot, pendant, crucifix, Testament, and jasper talisman – and simply wept for all the lost benefactors these objects recalled.

Later when she was able to stop and present a decent, grateful face to Mr and Mrs Templeton, she realized how utterly fatigued she had been on her arrival here at the end of September. From pre-dawn till deep dusk, Bernie, Chester and Lily had toiled in the devastated fields to salvage what they could of the harvest, to garner seed and cuttings for a doubtful spring, to pickle and can and store what they could to tide them over the winter and, most important for Bridie, to conserve their depleted reserve of cash. By ten o'clock each night, barely able to swallow some cold mutton and sourdough, they collapsed into a dreamless sleep. In such circumstances conversation seemed not only redundant but threatening. Relying as she did on day-dreams and the spontaneous hum of music inside her, Lily soon found herself laboring without the solace of fancy or song.

It was almost a week before she was able to leave this pink and papered boudoir – young Pamela's room before she left for school – and join her new household. Mrs. Templeton came in several times a day to talk to her, to listen with patience and near-understanding, and divert her with family news or a display of Pamela's "old" frocks for which she assumed Lily would be a "perfect match". Gradually the numbness of mental and physical exhaustion wore off, and Lily felt the re-emergence of her familiar self. She fell asleep in the feather tick with the talisman in her clutch, and that night she dreamed of a fine-boned young man with loose, sandy hair and a radium stare that held her in its power till he dissolved in an ambiguous mist.

"You're certainly not going to be a servant in my house!" Mrs. Templeton exclaimed when Lily appeared on a Saturday morning attired in her own housedress and a maid's apron she had found in the upstairs hall closet. "Gracious, what would Bridie think of me, then?"

She marched Lily back up the carpeted stairs to Pamela's bedroom and with commendable briskness re-attired her for her new role. Pulling Lily in front of a long mirror on the inside of the door of the black-walnut wardrobe, she said with satisfaction, "There, now. What do you think?"

Lily was sure what Bridie would think. Since no mirror ever graced her aunt's house –"greatest time-waster and corrupter of good intentions ever devised"– Lily had little experience in physical self-assessment. On occasion she had peered at her rippled face in the goose-pond and watched fascinated as that other visage – fay, unmoored, incomplete – yearned back at her from the depths. But she had appreciation of her whole body or the sudden shape it had taken.

"The dress is beautiful," Lily said. "But how can I work in these petticoats?"

"The dress is not beautiful, pet, *you are*. It's high time you realized that. Walk around for me. See? You have no idea how graceful you really are. Bridie tried to take it out of you, no doubt, putting calluses on your hands and letting the sun burn and freckle that glorious Irish skin of yours."

Lily was abashed. She felt she ought to defend Bridie but couldn't find ready words to do so. Mrs. Templeton was not looking for commentary.

"I've got Iris to do the housework, pet," she explained, "and Bonnie comes in to serve and scull at parties. But I do my own cooking and you'll be a big help to me. Other times, like now, I want you to be my 'companion', to sit with me at teas, to talk to me when you feel like it, and to let me make a lady out of you."

Lily looked dubious.

"I'll send your wages to Bridie every month," she said, picking up one of Pamela's cloth-and-china dolls and caressing it fondly.

Lily relaxed a little; Aunt Bridie was counting on her for that. "Will you teach me to read?"

"Of course, pet," said Mrs. Templeton, suddenly as serious as Lily. "Why do you think I arranged your rescue?"

They began with recipes, just the two of them working in the kitchen. Mrs. Templeton was amazingly patient. She sounded out the recipe words slowly and repeatedly with Lily at her shoulder. They would say them together, Lily's alto voice melding with the older woman's soprano.

After the second week Lily was reading the familiar recipes haltingly to Mrs. Templeton who matched her actions to Lily's words. "Remember now, pet, read the words clearly, 'cause I'm doing exactly what you say. If the pie wins a prize, then we'll know you can read!" she giggled.

Towards the end of October, Mrs. Templeton would sit with Lily before a blazing fire in the parlour and read from *The Arabian Nights*, a book that Bridie would have found scandalous not because of its racy tales but rather for its utter "silliness". Lily began to 'read' parts of these stories aloud, easy sections carefully picked out by Mrs. Templeton and abetted by repetition and memory. One evening she was allowed to take the book to her room where she struggled once again through the early paragraphs of Aladdin and his magic lamp. There was some imperative in this story that drove her to try to decipher the exotic words, to grasp at the central thread of events whose import she sensed but could not pin down. Suddenly the aura of meaning faded and went out like the genie himself. In frustration she threw the book across the room and sat shaking for five minutes before she hurried over in panic to see if she had damaged it. Only her pride was bruised.

Even Mr Templeton – now His Worship the Mayor – got into the game. He would call Lily into his den, detonate a cigar, wave her to a plump chair, and begin to read aloud from one of his legal tomes. "Know what *that*word means, Lily?" he'd say with mock-sternness, rolling off his tongue some arcane polysyllable. Lily would shake her head. "Neither does Judge Maitland!" he'd rumble. "And I doubt if the dolt who thought it up does either!" Then he'd go dead-serious again. "But that's the law, Lily dear. Men have been hanged on it!" Lily soon realized that this was a game he had played with both his daughters before they left for school in London and marriage in Toronto. And some of the words she would remember.

Lily found herself doing little domestic work. The calluses on her hands shrank and faded. Bonnet and parasol soon whitened her skin, though the freckles remained as permanent record of a different past. Lily even attended church – the Anglican church – with the Templetons, though no word was ever said about baptism nor question raised about her not taking communion. The Church of England seemed to be quite accommodating after all. Lily watched, listened, and learned.

After Church she would be given the pony-and-surrey and allowed to drive out to visit her Bridie and Chester. Chester was always overjoyed to see her, though he would sometimes embarrass the women – for different reasons – by bursting into tears without apparent reason. Bridie's assessment of Lily's gradual transformation to citified lady was not discernible in her talk or her manner. She continued to refer to Lily's "work" and as the girl prepared to leave each Sunday, she would grasp her hand and say, "Thank you, lass. You're a good girl."

Lily's duties consisted mainly of being at Mrs. Templeton's side during her frequent 'At Homes', given in deference to her role as the wife of the mayor. "Sweet but dreadfully quiet," Lily overheard one of the dowagers remark to another. "Might be pretty, in time, though Lord knows where she comes from." Her days as a tactful delivery girl and easy conversationalist served her well with the women when at tea. The surprise and challenge came from the gentlemen and grandees who frequented the bi-weekly political 'socials' (salons was a word not infrequently heard) held by the mayor. As hostesses, Lily and Mrs. Templeton engineered the distribution of food and drink and were expected to provide casual divertissement for those gentlemen who found the strain of political discussion too hard on a thinning intellect.

The political chatter in late 1858 concerned the coming of the Great Western and the machinations of its rival, the Grand Trunk. Much bitterness, not fully assuaged by the good brandy and home-made chocolates, was expressed over the shabby treatment of the town's noblest citizen, Malcolm "Coon" Cameron, whose moderate reformers had been outflanked by the chicanery of the Clear Grits. Lily was exposed to the intemperate talk of radicals as well as the lamentations of old-compact Tories and the hollow bellicosities of the local Orangemen, Although His Worship would soon depart Port Sarnia and later join the coalition as a repentant reformer, his hospitality was so generous that the warring factions in town not only answered all invitations to attend, but often broke protocol by appearing unannounced. The result was a series of spirited and spirit-fuelled soirees which furthered Lily's education in unexpected ways.

Regardless of party affiliation or ideological bent, Lily learned there were four elements common to a politician's life: food, liquor, gossip and sex. Indeed, she soon became adept at identifying parliamentary loyalties not by the swagger and fire of the rhetoric but by the method through which the fourth element was realized. The very first evening she attended one of these salons – radiant in Pamela's 'best', her eyes alight with intelligence – Lily was standing suitably aloof from a heated exchange about the abomination of separate school rights, intent on following the swing of the argument, when she felt a hand slink its way across the stretched silk at her lower back.

"Don't let those Orangemen put ideas into your pretty head," whispered the owner of the errant appendage into her ear. Lily turned to see Dr. Michaelmas, the ardent Reformer, smiling behind his trimmed moustaches.

"It's not my head concerns me at the moment," Lily said, slipping to one side and casting him an ambivalent smile.

Without a doubt, she concluded, you could tell a Reformer because they were all sly touch, accidental nudge, a fleshy press in tight corners. The Old Tories, on the other hand, because of their advanced infirmities or belief in divine right, were the boldest. Judge Maitland, for example, stalked her in the den on the pretext of discussing recipes and tried to pinch her bum through two layers of crinoline. "My God, you're a little beauty," he drooled, aiming a paw at her décolletage, his lust positively aquiline. Lily knew she could cry for help, but instead she curled up her fingers and delivered a muted rebuff to the old scarecrow's lower abdomen – not hard enough to cripple his intent outright yet insistent enough to make him wheeze, double, and hobble towards the parlour. She watched him trying to straighten his stride as he headed for the brandy. "Got your limp again?" said McWhinney, the clothier. "Touch of the gout," whistled his Honour.

The radicals, or Clear Grits as they styled themselves, so loved the buzz of their own perorations that they made their passes at her in verbal terms only- innuendo, *double entendre*, a *sotto voce* vulgarism when desire overwhelmed – though she had little doubt that, were their sundry propositions to be accepted, they might have flashed the genuine metal. However, they soon discovered that this waif from the sticks was unconscionably swift at rejoinder and not as accustomed to acquiescence as a real lady might be.

"That orphling brat of Templeton's got a wicked tongue in her head," one guest told a consoling judge later. "She needs to be taken in hand." But of course they had already tried that.

Not once was she accosted by any of the Orangemen. They were either uninterested in anything but the eradication of popery or were put off by the gold cross she wore on these occasions.

Lily's rebuffs and inventive parries did not escape the notice of Alice Templeton. "You're learning fast and well," she said with undisguised admiration.

"Are they all like that?"

"Most of them, I'm afraid. It's the climate."

Lily laughed but then said soberly, "Why do we put up with it?"

Mrs. Templeton sighed deeply. "There's an awful lot we have to put with," she said.

Not me, Lily thought.

3

When Mrs. Templeton heard that Lily had never seen the Lake, she was shocked, and set about to remedy the situation. Lily politely refused her offer of a cruise on the *Michigan*or one of the other steamers now plying the water routes on a regular basis.

"You mean you wish to walk down there and just look at it?" she said, swivelling on the piano bench to face Lily.

"Yes, that's all."

"But, pet, why didn't you do so when you lived at Bridie's? The sand beach is no more than half-a-mile through the pinery back of your place."

"Auntie was strict about that," Lily said defensively. "She was always worried about the fishermen. Besides, she never liked me just traipsin' off on my own. Could you blame her?"

"Not at all," said Mrs. Templeton, closing the sheet music. "Goodness knows a number of the town girls have been accosted by the riff raff down there cutting brush for the railway. Fishermen, I hear tell, are even worse." Her tone was less-than-serious.

"May I go, then?"

"Of course. Follow Front Street until it turns into the trail the Slocum people sometimes use to get down to the fishery. Just before it comes out at the swamp below the beach, veer right – you'll see an Indian trail that'll take you over the dunes to Canatara beach. Of course, you could also walk up the coast past the fisherman's shanties, but I wouldn't advise it."

"I'll go right now, if I may?"

"Well, all right. But I *was* tuning up here to start your dancing lessons," she said. "We mustn't wait too long. Never know when a big fancy-ball might be upcoming."

Though it had been seven years since she had walked through thick brush, Lily felt at home on the fishery trail with the pines flaring overhead, the undergrowth spare, and shadowed, with shafts of brilliant light where the sun fitfully penetrated. This trail was worn and clear. Ten minutes or so into it, she heard the shouts of the men with their nets along the river bank sweeping for pickerel. Just ahead the woods brightened, so Lily, her instincts sharp, peered to the right and spotted the crossed-blaze – perhaps ten years or more in age – that signaled a Pottawatomie trail. She moved from mark to mark towards the sound of waves breaking in the near distance. Scanning the trunks at eye-level, she found herself abruptly in the full glare of early afternoon sun. The roaring of the waves was much louder, but when she looked ahead expecting to see the Lake, she saw only a series of sand-dunes about twelve feet in height.

Lily took off her shoes and stockings, dashed barefoot through the hot sand, fell scampering up the nearest dune, got up, her palms burning, her legs scything, until she stood on top and caught her first glimpse of the Freshwater Sea of the Hurons. What she saw initially was an uninterrupted blue stretching to the north and west so far that it became indistinguishable from the sky. The sun's light and the heat were lost in a greater immensity: the vast, tense energy of water on the move – homeward. When Lily was able to pull her gaze from the vanishing point directly to the north-west, she saw and heard at last the reach of the wavelets on the shore. Their sound was the intermittent, quiescent breath of a hibernating bear. Below the brassy surface that lay so placidly before her, Lily could feel the pulse of a cobalt heart whose energies charged the secret and vital parts of the earth's anatomy. There was here the sign of some pilgrimage whose spirit she shared.

Then, a girl again, she dashed across the crystalline beach and splashed and paddled and strutted and planted her footprints in the permeable sands. It was Indian summer: the air was warm and thin as new wine, the water icy, the sand purging. She did not want to leave.

When she did, she mounted the highest dune north from the trail and looked back towards the town-site. The houses of Port Sarnia were not yet visible. But she could see – where the Lake poured into the chasm of the St.

Clair only half-a-mile across – the shanties where Slocum's people kept their nets and cleaned their catch. Between the edge of the pinery and the River lay a quarter-mile of swamps full of disheveled cattails and yellowing milkweed. Could they ever build a railroad over that? To the far south-west Lily saw also the palisades of Fort Gratiot, the Stars and Stripes saluting self-importantly above it. Overhead, herring gulls whirled and rehearsed their mating dance.

Looking to retrace her route by the blazed trail, Lily noticed that to the north the sand-dunes were thicker, reaching far back into a low brush of runt alders and hawthorn. Something drew her that way, away from the marked trail. The dunes gradually subsided, giving way to a small, rolling field dotted with dwarf trees. The pinery enclosed it on three sides. Though there was nothing visible to the unpractised eye, Lily sensed immediately that she was in a burial ground. The Lake breeze did not penetrate this far but Lily felt the eddies and parabolas of moving, sentient beings occupying space. She stepped carefully ahead. The grave plots were barely discernible; obscured by knot-grass and hoarhound and sand-burs. Yet Lily could see that the ground had sunk almost imperceptibly, marking the modest dimensions of each site.

After a while, Lily spotted a new grave, its sand piled two inches above ground to accommodate the later natural sinking. Clusters of grass had been replanted to root and flourish and to camouflage in the coming spring. Winter would soon provide its own disguise.

You are here at last, Southener, Lily thought. You came under cover of dark and they laid you to rest among the other nameless wanderers and refugees, the outcasts and pariahs and survivors, the renegades and the prophets like you. I haven't forgotten the jasper heart. Already it has brought me more luck that I ever hoped for. And I won't forget your request. Somehow I'll find the sacred place in these woods and return the magic to it. I'll come here every time I can, and honour your grave. Surely here, with swamps and dunes all around, you'll be safe.

She thought then of her mother's headstone, alone in an unfrequented corner of some stranger's field, the script of her name chipped out so crudely no one would recall whose soul sought refuge below it. I must go back there. I will.

"Lily, pet, you're back at last," an excited Mrs. Templeton greeted her.

"I hope you weren't worried," Lily said, embarrassed by the state of her attire.

"Heavens no, I just couldn't wait to tell you. It's all been settled. The new railway station will be ready in a week and the first train is coming in on the nineteenth. There'll be a dinner and a ball."

"Are we invited?" Lily said.

"Invited? We're hosting it! And you've got exactly two weeks to learn how to dance!"

And in two weeks, the feat was accomplished. As Mrs. Templeton never tired of saying, "the girl's a natural!" Natural or not, it took some practice to disentangle the intricacies of the quadrille, galop, valse, polka and inevitable lancers. While Mrs. Templeton played a suitable tune on the piano, Mayor Templeton would serve as Lily's partner, then hop to one side and quickly demonstrate what the other couples of the quadrille would be up to – often forgetting where he was or two-stepping inadvertently into the galop. In the waltz, His Worship was superb, guiding Lily and his ample paunch around the parlour in mutual three-quarter delight. Lily could not help humming, though it was apparently a form of impoliteness.

"Let your *feet* feel the music," Mrs. Templeton said, pouncing on the keys.

"But she is, sweet, she is; her whole body is," puffed the Mayor, sensing the triphammer pulse of the tune through Lily's right hand and the small of her back, and marveling at the weightless power of her presence. She will do well, this one, he thought. Suddenly, he loved his wife more than ever.

A few minutes before the appointed hour, the crowd lining both sides of the cleared right-of-way that cradled the tracks heard the approaching sound of the first locomotive in Lambton.

A low thunder of iron-on-iron gained volume and pitch, scattering wildlife through the shuddering swamps and fernshaws. Trunk and bole and root quivered like tuning forks in its wake. Just before the track's curve at the edge of town, the engine whistle shrieked steam to announce its imminent arrival. Two thousand waiting citizens responded as one: a raucous, antiphonal cheer went up, followed by a second when the first smoke was spotted above the bush, then the chuffing stack. A whoop of self-congratulatory joy rose when the entire juggernaut hove into full view and, at speeds only dreamt of, roared past their applause and braked towards a stop. The assembled dignitaries dropped all pretense of disinterest.

Before the station – an imposing, pseudo-gothic structure of stone, red brick and elm – #52 engine, bearing the name *Prospero* in gold against a fern-green skin, skidded to a halt with a hiss and a screech that stunned the worshippers: a keening skirl of a cry like that of a disembowelled recruit at Culloden. The Great Western Railway had arrived.

The passenger coaches debouched onto the freshly planked platform several squads of V.I.P.'s, some genuine, many self-appointed. The forward platoon consisted of Sir Oliver Steele, vice-president of the Great Western, with Lady Marigold Steele, and the Mayor of London, trailed by four councilors and their wives. Behind them, with a scandalously blonde female anchored to his right arm, came a handsome figure soon identified as the notorious roué of London and Toronto, Stanley R. Dowling, known abroad as "Mad Cap." Not only had he debauched a succession of willing virgins, but it was rumoured he had been drummed out of the militia. For reasons no respectable person could understand or commend, he had, from obscure origins, made his way up in the world and in a society whose standards were obviously rotting at the core. He was said to have been made a director of the Great Western and to have speculated recklessly on local railway ventures that left *him* rich and the *towns* bankrupt.

Lady Steele held Lily's fascination as the official party slow-marched towards Mayor Templeton's group, behind which the lady folk of the town were expectantly assembled. She was several decades younger than her be-knighted husband, with fresh-scrubbed skin and sloe eyes bearing a look of distant, wry amusement. Dowling, Lily noted, smiling publicly at his tow-haired escort, but cast sidelong glances at Lady Steele, who absorbed them, unreturned. It was clear that Dowling would be lord of any domain he chose to occupy: with his jet-black hair, brows and side-whiskers, eyes bitumous and smouldering; carriage regal and never without purpose. He was a man in his prime, with poise and presence. His dowry: the future.

As His Worship shook hands with the worthies from London and Toronto, the band struck up a martial air and the crowd, crushing in around the train and dignitaries, applauded wildly. If they had any doubts about the intrusion of railways into their lives, they did not express them on this occasion. As the formal introductions and exchange of greetings were taking place, Lily looked anxiously at the throng of faces about her. Finally, she spotted them. Chester grinned and waved excessively; Bridie, apparently, did not see her.

A dinner was served at six o'clock for the more than one hundred and fifty well-wishers and their guests – all men. In 1858 and for some years to come, the wives and darlings of celebrities did not grace the tables of such public colloquies. Hence, the intelligence emanating from the event had to be derived from second-hand sources. Fortunately the ladies had access to a number of impeccable, though not coincident, accounts of what transpired. Since this was the largest dinner ever held in Port Sarnia, the only room big enough to accommodate the guests and their appetites was in the Orange Lodge near the St. Clair Inn. Thus it was that Mrs. Josephine Salter, whose kitchen was called upon to cater the meal, was able to store up enough gossip to feed her habit for a year; likewise, at a lower level, for Char Hazelberry whose own kitchen provided the tarts and trifle, and who luckily was required to bring along her best girls, Betsy and Winnie, to aid in the service thereof and in the dissemination of news thereafter.

No less than eighteen toasts were proposed and replied to, with claret for the elect and water for the saved. His Worship led the way with one to the Queen Herself, followed rapidly by those to the president of the Great Western, his board of directors, his English backers and the British Parliament. A toast was even offered to the president of the United States of America and responded to at length by the mayor of Port Huron, Michigan, whose country also had a stake in these enterprises. According to the report in *The Observer* his American Worship emphasized that two things were held in common by both republicans and monarchists: a tradition of fair play and justice as well as an unshakeable belief in progress, a progress rendered visible and measurable by the march of iron through the untracked wastes of the continent. Indeed, he concluded, the password of both great nations was identical: *onward*. The applause was deafening. Lily heard it, sitting in her room with Bonnie and Mrs. Templeton fussing over her with pins and thread, and thinking only of Bridie there at the station in the midst of such commotion, staring at nothing.

The ball, held in the concourse of the new station, began at nine in the evening and through its twenty-two dances endured until almost three in the morning. The town band of Goderich, which had come down by steamer in the afternoon, provided a passable imitation of its betters at Osgoode in Toronto. The gentlemen of Port Sarnia – attired in the severe, black formality of the period – offered a striking contrast to the uninhibited extravagance of the wives and young ladies. All agreed that it was a heaven-blessed sight to see against the drab umbers of late autumn such butterfly hues as danced in the gowns of the weaker sex. The only exceptions, on the stronger side, were a handful of elder townsmen who had dusted off their faded militia uniforms from the time of the rebellion, and five young gentlemen from London, three of them in the scarlet-gold-and-white of the British regular and the other two in the blue tunics of the new militia unit just formed in Middlesex.

Mrs. Templeton, flush with excitement and her first sip of French champagne, taxied up to Lily and said, "It's filled already, pet. They saw you in the promenade and near trampled me to death to sign up." She was waving Lily's dance-card which was already two-thirds filled with local worthies and beaux and, as she called them, "regrettable necessaries," plus "several of the nicest catches from London."

Lily, too, had been keeping a watch for desirable partners. She saw Lady Marigold in earnest conversation with Sir Oliver; nearby, Mad-Cap Dowling was chatting animatedly with one of the smooth-cheeked young soldiers, but managing all the same to cast little semaphores of affection towards the dark lady. She inclined her ringlets only slightly in his direction. It was during such an exchange that Lily noticed for the first time one of the two militiamen standing beside Dowling. Next to the regulars and to Dowling himself, the young corporal certainly seemed nondescript: he was of medium height, his hair a sandy tint the face beardless but for a thin moustache, fine-boned, housing two eyes that darted about like curious bluebirds avid for the high air. She could see him straining to fill out his tunic, to accommodate its projection of power, but there was an insecurity and a restlessness in the very way he stood with his weight on one foot and his hands fretting for a place to light. When he turned in her direction, Lily felt the intensity of his appraisal, and realized with a start that she had been staring at him far longer than propriety permitted. He gave her a polite across-the-room smile and rejoined the conversation at hand. No matter. The cause was already won. That strange sense of certainty, of seeing the thing before its shadow came back with a rush of blood to her cheeks and a swelling in her heart.

The band from Goderich had just struck up a quadrille.

"Here comes your first admirer," said Mrs. Templeton. Gratefully Lily let herself be swept into the square by His Worship. Once the dancing actually began, Lily found herself completely absorbed by it. She couldn't think of anything else when there was music in her, she could only feel, and mime that feeling with her feet and arms and the bow of her body. She galloped and polka-ed and waltzed and quadrilled. Her black-suited partners – so cordial, so deferential in their requests – became faceless instruments of her need to surrender to the discipline of the rhythm.

Between dances, however, when couples chatted, sipped, and nibbled sandwiches for solace, Lily felt anxious and drained. With only two dances left, the object of her desires had not appeared in the same set nor had he been among her partners. Delicately, she asked Mrs. Templeton if she knew the names of any of the military gentlemen from London. "Well, Mr. Carleton and Mr. James are both lieutenants in the fusiliers, she said, nodding a head in the direction of faces Lily did not recognize. "The others I don't know." That's that, then, Lily thought, turning to her card to see "Mr. Marshall" next in the list.

She looked up in expectation of a "regrettable necessary," when there he was, not a foot from her. "I believe I have the honour of this dance. My name is Tom Marshall. I'm from London."

The penultimate dance was the fast-paced *lancers* with eight couples challenging the military complexity of its steps. There was little opportunity to converse in the midst of such manoeuvres. Nonetheless, she felt Tom's arms momentarily about her waist, her hand clasped in his, and confirmed her premonition of his vulnerability, his erratic energy, his need for safe harbour. She placed her face naked before his gaze, released a locked part of herself to him for scrutiny and care. He smiled at her when they were apart and possessed her with his grasp when they sashayed or twirled in linked curves. He wafted words to her and she nodded as if they were comprehensible.

When the lancers ended, he ferried her towards the table where the punch was wilting in the heat. Now they would talk and it would begin. He placed a crystal goblet in her hands. She drank thirstily.

"Lily, you're the best dancer of the lot. Surely you can't be from Port Sarnia," he said with a twinkle.

She was about to reply when his eye was caught by a beckoning gesture to their left. "Damn," he muttered to himself. "Would you please excuse me, Miss Ramsbottom; I'm wanted by my party. It's been a pleasure meeting you. I hope we'll meet again."

She could only murmur thanks and watch him walk over to the Dowling group. Lady Marigold and her husband had joined them. When the music started for the last dance, a Strauss waltz, she saw His Nibs take the withered fingertips of the judge's wife. Dowling put his arm about the waist of the dark lady and they strolled with utmost ease to the centre of the floor. So engrossed was Lily in this minor melodrama that she almost missed seeing Corporal Marshall offer his arm to Miss Platinum and, when the music began, clasp her pliant body to his own.

Lily was in a deep, daylight sleep following a night of restless dreams and near-dreams, when she was awakened by Mrs. Templeton gently shaking her shoulder. She blinked at the invading light. "What's wrong?" she said.

"It's your Auntie," Mrs. Templeton said.

Lily saw Bridie hovering behind Mrs. Templeton, her face sombre.

"Are you all right, Auntie?"

"Yes, love. It's your Uncle Chester." Her voice was close to breaking. "His heart give out."

8

The year 1860 was born in hope. For the county's farmers, victims of the 'black frost' of 1859, there was not much else left. Those who tilled the soil were left with shrivelled roots and wizened leafage to mock them through the hot summer of '59 with little chance that they could afford even to buy seed for next year's planting and some chance in the back townships that they might starve or chew their way through a winter of turnip, chicory and hazelnut.

Typhus, cholera and diphtheria trimmed the infant population with regular and reliable horror, and struck down among the adults those who were weak or unwary. Moreover, the high cost of progress – of living up to the county's adopted motto, *Ongoing*– appeared to be routinely accepted by the populace. Certainly the 440 shipping disasters listed for 1859, at a cost of $668,565.00 and 105 lives, offered no deterrent to the expansion of water commerce. Nor did they discourage excursionists and pleasure-seekers from boarding hundreds of cruiser-craft and heading out 'into the blue'. In September 1860, the excursion boat *Lady Elgin* went down with a loss of 287 lives. The disasters on the new, often jerry-built, railroads, though not as calamitous, were as frequent and as cavalier. Notwithstanding, the Great Western moved more than 800,000 passengers per annum in Upper Canada in these years. And the Grand Trunk had designs of its own on the landscape. Elsewhere, bridges were being flung across the St. Lawrence at Quebec and at Lewiston, swing ferries wobbled over the St. Clair rapids, and canals were deepened and widened – each leap forward taking its routine toll in killed and maimed.

But the spring of 1860 seemed blessed by that same Providence whose hand was ever on the tiller and the throttle. Sun and rain collaborated so that the wheat grew and the fruit trees blossomed on cue. Even Bridie began once again to entertain the notion of a future. She had become resigned to the fact that all of their efforts had now to be put into maintaining a few cash crops to be sold, at outrageously low prices, at the farm gate. Nonetheless, she persevered through two long winters with her quilting despite the onset of arthritis, which she mocked as "a little twinge or two to remind me I'm gettin' old an' to keep me honest." Only their cash reserves had allowed them to survive the ravages of the black frost, but as Bridie often said, "We're holdin' our own with our heads up, lass, don't ever forget that." Still, Lily sensed a hollowness to Bridie's aphorisms and more than a little world-weariness.

With Chester a virtual invalid, there was no talk of Lily's going back into service even though the income would have helped them a great deal. Someone had to nurse the man night and day, summer and winter. His heart attack had been real, and he was fortunate enough to have the doctor arrive from town too late to be of immediate harm, and thus managed to survive. For months he lay on Lily's bed (she now slept on a cot in the kitchen) barely able to express his thanks as she fed him with a spoon, emptied his festering bedpan, or bathed his bleached flesh. By the spring of 1859 his voice was a guttural rasp, like a wraith calling from some shallow part of purgatory.

"I don't pray much, Lily," Bridie said. "But if I did, I'd ask my maker to take Chester back. Nobody oughta suffer like that."

However, early in the summer of '59, even as the black frost's legacy lingered, Chester stirred himself, sat up, smiled, and became impossible. Bridie stared at him as if he had, for a second and more unforgivable time, betrayed her. But she did her duty. They bought a wicker chair with feather pillows and wheels so that he could sit by the stove or out on the flagstones in the sun or be ferried about on short excursions through the garden and woodlot. Alas, his appreciation was in short supply. He whined and wheedled, threw tantrums and dinner plates, cried like a baby and grumbled like an ogre, and generally wallowed in self-pity.

"I should've gone," he'd say, "the world'd be a better place without old Chester in it." Bridie would glare, then relent and say without conviction, "But you'll be up an' walkin' soon. Is there anythin' special Lily can fix you for supper?"

"Well, rhubarb tart'd be nice, but I expect it's too late for that." It invariably was, and he then had to be mollified with whatever second-best alternative could be offered.

If it hadn't been for Bill, the farm itself would have collapsed. When his wheat crop was wiped out by the black frost, he came to Bridie and asked her to buy his fields, leaving him only his shanty and garden, and hoping for continuing employment as her hired hand. Sniffing the scent of an opportunity, Bridie went into town that very day, withdrew most of her savings from the Bank of Upper Canada, and doubled her land holdings when everyone else was retrenching or going under. More and more, Bridie seemed to be placing her hopes not on their crops or cash from the woodlot but on the sounds now ringing through the pinery that lay between their fields and the waters to the north and west. The long-rumoured arrival of the second and most ambitious of the great railway networks, was happening. And less than half-a-mile from their property.

"I told you, didn't I, Chester, they'd build somethin' big on that land. That's why we moved out here in the first place, Lily. Mayn't be soldiers over there, but there's gonna be trains," she said wistfully, "an' people, too. We're gonna have neighbours, lass, a real town of our own right next door. Didn't I say so, Chester?"

July was sweltering, but Bridie, Bill and Lily had no choice but to sweat in the fields. Lily burned, freckled, peeled and then burned anew. Chester took his first convalescent steps, tottered, fell, sprained his wrist, setting him back once again.

About the middle of the month, Violet ran off. Work was halted so that a search could begin. Lily went first to the pond where she'd spotted Violet peering into its coppery mirror on several recent occasions. Only the gander and his harem were there, looking on in bemusement. Throughout the afternoon they combed the pinery, and Bridie even walked as far as the oak ridge and Little Lake to the north-east, pausing to contemplate the future as she crossed the freshly-laid imprint of the Grand Trunk.

But it was Lily who found Violet sitting in a daze in a field near the railway worker's shanties, down by the construction site for the new wharf and station. It was dusk, and Violet must have become alarmed enough to start crying. When Lily arrived, Violet was sobbing incoherently; Lily could make out no word. She put her arm about the wretched girl and half-carried her home. Bridie intercepted them near the house and together they took Violet into the tallow-lit gloom of the log hut. Bill, sitting with his head buried in his hands, looked up with mixed rage and relief, but said nothing. He glared at Violet as Bridie and Lily calmed the girl's sobbing, washed her streaked face, helped her into a clean nightdress. Finally they rose and with reluctance left the house. Outside they paused, waiting for the explosion within and ready to intervene if necessary.

From the hut came the unmistakable sound of Bill's harmonica: thin strains of an old-country air, reedy and elegiac. The women went home.

For a year they had heard the distant din of railway construction, the saws, axes, hammers and navvies' curses of a brutal work-in-progress. By the fall, Bridie walked over every day she could to watch the ties straighten the landscape, foot by foot, amazed that such delicate calligraphy had printed its message from here to London and beyond, to the edge of the ocean itself they were told. During the search for Violet, Lily had glimpsed the havoc wrought there and felt an irresistible urge to return in the daylight to see it for herself.

A few hundred yards north of their woodlot the destruction began. Lily had imagined a neat swath cut through the bush; there was no bush left. Every pine within a mile's radius of the wharf-site, on the River just below the Lake, had been haphazardly hacked away. The areas near the right-of-way were efficiently trim, but the so-called town-site was a wasteland of split trunks, charred branches and smouldering stumps. The sprawling, unpainted wharfs and freight-sheds were almost completed, and to the south at the periphery of the remaining stand of trees, Lily spied the brick station-and-hotel towering three stories above the shoreline. Its several dozen glazed windows beamed 'progress' across a clearing that, it seemed, must inevitably yield houses and people to inhabit them. But why would they come here? Why would they want to? For now, only a handful of workers' shanties, which had served the fisherman before them, gave any promise of settlement.

Though she was curious, Lily didn't approach the station-hotel. Something told her she would see the inside of it soon enough. Instead she walked across the tracks to the point where the Lake and River joined, and stared out at the generous beauty of the blue waters flowing out of the north-sky itself and condescending to the south. She glanced anxiously towards the scrub bush and dunes along the lakeshore, noting with relief that progress had by-passed the sleeping graves of the lost. You are safe, Southener, she thought.

"She's gone again," said Bridie sternly when Lily entered the garden.

This time they did not find her. Not that evening, nor the next morning. At noon several men on horseback rode up the lane and stopped in front of the shanty. Bill was with them. Lily and Bridie hurried over, leaving Chester to fend for himself. They found Bill utterly distraught. "They say she's crazy an' they have to take her away, an' they just picks her up an' her eyes is beggin' me, an' they just cart her off to London. They're gonna lock her up, Bridie, they're gonna lock her up somewheres."

Bridie took control, and got the whole story. But nothing could be done, they said. Three or four of the railway workmen had pulled Violet into a field where they raped her repeatedly, and then left her there bleeding and babbling in her alien speech. The incident had been witnessed by a minor official of the Grand Trunk who was inspecting one of the fancy new rooms on the third floor of the hotel. He couldn't exactly see who the men were from such a distance, and didn't report the incident till the next morning because he saw the girl get up on her own and wander towards Sarnia. Naturally he reckoned that it wasn't really rape after all.

In the end, no one was ever charged with the crime. No reliable witnesses could be found. Violet, her terror and pain locked forever inside her, "went crazy", and the constable and the magistrate decided she would be better off "getting proper treatment". was inconsolable. Bridie ranted against all officialdom and grew grim. Lily felt bereft of something irreplaceable. She got a taste of what despair would be like.

3

Sometime towards dawn Lily was awakened by a blaze of lightning, followed seconds later by a hard crack of thunder. Then the rain came, first slashing at the dry woods and vulnerable gardens, then easing off to a steady, sustaining downpour. When she arose with the sun, the air was sweet with growth, the earth slaked and grateful.

Hearing Bridie stir restlessly in her room, Lily sat on the cot for a long while letting the infant light brush over her, quicksilvering her skin. She reached into the applewood box below the cot and drew out the leather pouch. The jasper talisman felt cold in her cupped palms. She pressed it tightly, squeezing her eyes shut, and begging the driven thoughts in her mind to seek some shape, some release, some reconciliation. It occurred to her that she might be praying. The talisman grew warm, incarnadine, then seemed to pulse in her grip. "Are you up, dear?"

"Yes, Auntie. You stay put a while. It's a bit wet for weedin' right off."

She heard the creak and shuffle of her aunt rigging her body for the day ahead.

Later, Lily glanced up from her hoeing. Bridie was waving from the yard, something white and fluttering in her hand. When Lily came up to her, she recognized Silas, the butcher's son.

"He's brung a note from Alice Templeton," said Bridie evenly. "Do you want me to read it?"

"Please."

In a halting voice, Bridie read: "Dear Lily: You are cordially invited to attend the official luncheon for His Royal Highness, Albert Edward, Prince of Wales, to be held at the Grand Trunk Hotel at twelve noon, September 13, 1860. Please say you'll come. Affectionately, Alice Templeton."

Bridie looked at Lily expectantly. "Sounds like Mrs Templeton would like you there," she said to fill the silence. Silas nodded.

"Tell her, thanks. But no."

"You want me to write that?"

"Yes."

"Lily, love, I think you oughta go. What else *is* there?" Bridie said pointedly.

"We got weedin' to do," Lily said, and started for the potato patch.

Silas came back two hours later with a second missive. Again Bridie prepared to read the note aloud. Chester, who despite his infirmaties was walking now with two canes, came out to listen.

"This is queer," Aunt Bridie said. "It says only: 'Lily dearest: there will be a military escort from London.' Now what's that supposed to mean?"

"It means he's the Prince of Wales," Chester said. "The heir to the throne."

"The *English* throne," Bridie snapped.

"Now don't start again, woman, with them radical ideas. I got a bum ticker, you know."

"An' how could the world ever forget it?"

"Tell her *yes*," Lily said to the startled trio.

9

The visit of Queen Victoria's firstborn son to Her Majesty's dominions in August and September of 1860 was the greatest public event yet in British North America's fledgling existence. No fewer than four books were published to commemorate the events of the pretender's 'progress,' one of them in Boston, no less. Newspapers everywhere devoted their column-inches to tracking every royal move and the public's response. Even the Prince's dance cards were faithfully reproduced as if they were imperishable poems.

The hour-by-hour sweep of H.R.H. through the County of Lambton on September 13 was likewise exhaustively recorded for posterity. The Royal Party and a regiment of well-wishers and hopefuls boarded the Great Western in London at 9:00 a.m. (The Prince's special car, however, belonged to the Grand Trunk: the rival railways had declared a truce to demonstrate their unshakeable faith in the Empire.) At 11:00 a.m. they touched down in Sarnia where H.R.H. stepped from his mobile drawing room, flanked by railway moguls, hastily promoted lieutenant-colonels, and the young scion's guardian, the unflappable Duke of Newcastle. The waiting scarlet carpet was variously reported to be either one hundred or three hundred yards in length, the latter being a local estimate. More than five thousand subjects were said to be gathered at the Great Western depot and wharf – almost the county's total population. The succession of toasts and responses which followed managed to delay the schedule by almost an hour. The only speech worth the space given to it was that of Chief Kan-was-ga-shi, Great Bear of the North, one of the several hundred Ojibwas who had come down from the wilds of Manitoulin for the occasion:

Brother, Great Brother, the sky is beautiful. It was the wish of the Great Spirit that we should meet in this place. I hope the sky will continue to look fine, to give happiness to both the whites and to the Indians. You see the Indians who are around you. It is their earnest desire that you will always remember them.

It is not recorded whether any of those assembled caught the ironies either in the words themselves or the circumstances in which they were delivered.

After presenting the chiefs with silver medallions, the Prince led a cavalcade of carriages, mounted citizenry and rearguard foot-soldiers to the magnificent station-hotel of the Grand Trunk, showpiece of the new town-site already being referred to as Point Edward. Therein, the pooh-bahs received their luncheon and basked in the reflected glory and unabashed good humour of the young and future king. With no coaching whatsoever, the Prince proposed a toast to the "Prosperity of the Grand Trunk Railway." Its regional vice-president, Dunbar Cruickshank, responded with unforced enthusiasm.

After the meal H.R.H. and a very select group of dignitaries boarded the Grand Trunk steamer *Michigan*and sailed up the St. Clair and onto Lake Huron. By 3:30 p.m. the Royal Cortege was back at the Great Western depot and entrained for London where the Prince gave a levee that same evening which outshone even the shameless extravagance of the one given at Toronto's Osgoode Hall two nights earlier. The entire episode, emblazoned forever in local annals, had lasted a mere four-and-a-half hours.

Only Lily's affection for the Templetons and her deep sense of gratitude towards them gave her the strength to submit to their fawning attentions. Certainly Mrs. Templeton had done her best with a sow's ear. It was Bridie who'd insisted she come into stay with her benefactress for a full week before the event: "We'll manage. Besides, you'll have to get used to city ways all over," she said. "Won't be easy gettin' them feet of yours into shoes again."

Lily's outfit had been made by Mrs. Templeton's dressmaker "from the ground up this time", complete with a parasol, white gloves and linen handkerchiefs.

"My word, Lily, what a figure you've got! Not even the farm can spoil you, though it's tryin'," said Mrs. Templeton, examining Lily's calloused work hands.

Lily tolerated all the fuss, and tried to be joyful when His Worship whirled her about the parlour to the thump of the piano for old times' sake. She knew how much they missed their daughters. From the maid she learned that both daughters had promised to come down from Toronto for the Prince's visit but at the last minute received invitations, through their prominent husbands, to attend the Royal Ball at Osgoode. Lily understood the obligation placed upon her by the Templeton's expectations, but she anticipated and hoped for more personal desires to be met.

When the royal train pulled into the station, Lily was standing beside Mrs. Templeton just behind the mayor and his officials. She had a clear view of the Prince as he approached them gingerly across the red carpet, his chaperone at his elbow, both of them aglitter in military regalia. The next rank brought the railroad bosses, among them the successor to Sir Oliver Steele (dead of a mysterious stroke), the fiercely ambitious Dunbar Cruickshank, and a recently appointed t vice-president of the Grand Trunk, Cap Dowling. Lily was not perturbed to see Lady Marigold Steele, the dark lady, at his elbow and out of her widow's weeds for the occasion. Fanned out behind were several scarlet-coated regular officers and blue-clad militiamen. Tom Marshall was not among them.

By the conclusion of the luncheon, Lily was as puzzled as she was hurt. Why didn't you come, Tom? she thought, listening to the last of the toasts. The talisman had surely pulsed as she held it; its augury was as clear as a proclamation. Was she mistaken?

"Great news, pet! I knew the Prince had his eye on you! We've been invited aboard the *Michigan*! And –" Mrs. Templeton lowered her voice theatrically, "that old snoop of a Duke isn't coming."

But Lily knew whom the royal glance had favoured whenever discretion permitted. Seated two chairs from her at the woman's table, the dark lady occupied her own kind of throne.

Alice Templeton and Lily sat apart from the others on red-striped deck chairs letting the warm September breeze ruffle their parasols and watching their fellow passengers preen and promenade before the royal presence. The ladies coasted by like bevies of sea-birds looking for land. The men gathered for serious gossip around a ring of cigars. The Prince himself had changed into a smart blue tunic of only faintly military character with gilded epaulettes and splendid brass buttons. He stood on the foredeck of the ship like Nelson staring down the French, as the conversation of Cap Dowling and his party of monopolizers drifted insubstantially around him. Undaunted, the young ladies, made valiant by their finery, tacked and jibbed past the Commodore in hope that he might cast a mariner's eye upon an unguarded throat, a careless ankle, a shameless *coup d'oeil*. The Prince hove to his duty.

Ahead of them Lily could see only a vague horizon of mixed blue, sky and water, as if the elements were permitted to blend their irreconcilable properties. Behind them and to the west the shoreline grew faint. She left off staring out at the water and turned back to catch Dowling engaged in an animated monologue with His Highness. A few feet away Lady Marigold, her luxuriant sensuality limned by a white hat and dress, observed his gestures with cunning impassivity. While the debutantes and duennas fought against dishevelling lake-breeze, Lady Marigold removed her hat and hairpins and let the wind have its way. Lily remarked with some satisfaction that the Prince took every opportunity to glance over at the bereaved widow, though she gave no signal to either man.

Dowling suddenly turned away from the Royal Guest and came over to the Templeton clique. "His Highness has had a long day," he proclaimed. He's going to rest in his quarters."

No one would have been terribly surprised if Cap had trailed His Royal Highness and joined him in his nap, but he did not. The Prince moved alone but briskly towards the cabin deck. There was a flutter and rearranging of plumage among the ladies, fresh cigars and configurations appeared amongst the men, and the ship – almost beyond landfall – circled and headed southeast towards civilization. Mrs. Templeton took the opportunity to excuse herself to the ladies facilities.

Lily stayed back to see if Lady Marigold would make her move, when someone touched her sleeve. She turned round to find the Prince's valet: "His Highness would like to see you in his suite," he said as if announcing supper. It took a few seconds for the import of the message to dawn. When it did, she glanced about, saw that Mayor Templeton was engaged and Mrs. Templeton nowhere in sight, and she made a decision.

She followed the valet's trails to the royal rooms, actually the captain's quarters hastily re-tailored in Detroit to fit the Royal Personage. When the man-servant opened a diminutive varnished door with brass knobs, Lily entered what would normally have served the skipper as office and sitting room. A large desk, brocade settee and purplish Queen Anne chair struck Lily's eye immediately.

"This way, miss," the valet said, using his usher's voice.

Lily stepped through a second door and entered a small chamber. The Prince was seated on an undersized, embroidered chair before an escritoire. Smoky light poured through a porthole window, falling across a twin to the Prince's chair. an oval Oriental rug, and a vermillion-and-white scrolled quilt which made no pretense of hiding the silk sheets beneath it. This was, incontestably, a bedroom.

Set up on the escritoire was a table cloth on which had been placed a silver bucket sprouting a bottle of champagne and two crystal glasses that would sing at the merest hint of a fingernail. A black cigar, cut but unlit, lurked in a gold ashtray.

"Please, come in," said the Prince rising and extending his hand casually towards the unoccupied chair. "It's Lily, is it not?"

Lily was so struck with the English orotundity of his voice, at once formal, distant and ingratiating, that she did not immediately reply. "Yes, Your Highness," she said. Then: "Lily Fairchild." As she said it, her father's face came into view.

The Prince hesitated for a moment. "Please, sit down. Let me take your gloves and hat."

Lily sat on the edge of the chair. When she peeled off her elbow-length gloves, she tried to keep her palms down. In removing her bonnet, she pulled out not only the hat-pin but the barrettes that held her hair in check. It tumbled forward. She heard the royal breath indrawn. She didn't look up again until he said, "Will you join me in a glass of champagne?"

"Yes, please, Your –"

"Call me Albert," he said. "My mother does."

Lily laughed. "I don't think I could," she said.

"Please forgive my informality," he said, referring, Lily assumed, to the fact that he had removed his tunic, vest, collar and ties, and was seated in evident comfort in his trousers and open shirt. "Uniforms, I'm afraid, offer more pleasure to the adulating crowds than to the objects of their worship."

Lily smiled, quite aware that this was a quip used on many an occasion. Though his practised delivery disguised shyness, perhaps even uncertainty, she was sure she detected in his demeanour when she herself grew brave enough to look directly at him. He was popping the champagne cork efficiently, but when he came to pour, Lily saw his hand shake a little.

"Damn!" he said when the bubbly slopped over the glass, fizzing and exuberant. He was about to apologize for the *damn* when Lily's giggle cut him off. He grinned boyishly, then stared at her, puzzled but powerfully attracted.

"What do we toast?" Lily said.

"Well, that Dowling fellow told me they're going to name the village where the station is after me: Point Edward. In my honour."

"Some honour, since it's not even your first name," Lily said risking boldness but lifting her glass.

He laughed in delight. "To Point Albert, regardless!" he said merrily.

They clinked glasses and drank deeply. The Prince, a bit hastily perhaps, filled the glasses again. Lily rose and took a step towards the door.

"Please don't go," he said. "I just wanted to talk," he added. "I get so sick of all that polite chatter, all that hypocritical handshaking and endless palaver about the weather and the crops and the engines of progress, and –"

Lily made a decision before he could finish his sentence.

"Will you help me?" Lily asked quietly, lifting her arms slightly.

She took a step backwards and the Prince, summoning all eighteen and three quarters of his years to maintain his composure, began to unhook her dress. "Thank you," she said when he had finished. She drew her arms out of the liberated sleeves, then let the vast folds descend gratefully over the layered crinolines. "Help me get these cages off," she laughed, and he eagerly hoisted them over her head and let them clatter to the floor where they rolled away like lopsided tankards.

"I hope you don't mind the informality, Your Highness," she said, allowing him to take in her full-length muslin slip, stockings and camisole. The Prince was obviously unaccustomed to such unbridled beauty – the burned-flaxen hair irreconciled to ringlets, the rough-tender hands, the freckled buff of cheek, the flecked hazel-green eyes, the unawakened wonder of poised womanhood. He reached for the cigar. "Shall I open the window?" he offered.

"No, please. Smoke don't bother me none. I like it." He puffed and temporized, casting sideways glances in her direction, like a puritan at a peep show. Lily finished her champagne, and poured herself a third glass, emptying the bottle. The second the valet had touched her arm she had known what was expected of her. She had followed him in full knowledge.

She put down her empty glass, rose, and pulled the cigar from between the Prince's teeth. She dropped it in its gold ash tray, the live end white-hot. Grasping the young man's hands in her own, she lead him to the bed where she stretched languidly across the comforter.

Lily closed her eyes. Yes, she thought, it's time to act, to make something happen, *anything*. She heard the rustle and clink of His Highness at the extreme edge of dishabillement. She reached down and drew her slip, then her camisole over her head, feeling the rush of air on her nakedness like a lover's breath.

The Prince was arched over her, pale and trembling, his muscled alabaster flesh as vulnerable and as omnipotent as a Lancelot stripped of armour. Lily assessed the reticence and the lust in his eyes, and blessed them both.

10

Lily was cleaning out the stalls of Benjamin and the Guernsey, as well as that of Gert, the little Jersey they'd acquired from Bill. Both cows had been bred to an itinerant bull who showed up at their gate one day with his master in tow, but it appeared as if only the Jersey was about to bear the fruits of that brief, awesome encounter. Lily poked at the mess in front of her. At least in January there was little smell, and the frozen manure and straw could be forked rather than shovelled. Bridie and Bill were in the woodlot, sawing the stiff pine logs into portable lengths and finding the packed snow and solid earth a convenient, almost hospitable, environment in which to labour. Chester, walking unaided now, would be keeping himself useful by replenishing the wood in both stove and fireplace.

As Lily heaved a forkful of manure onto the sled, she felt a twinge in her lower abdomen. She stood stock-still as the wavelets of pain worked themselves ashore, then leaned on her fork, catching her breath and waiting for worse. Something fibrous and alien cramped in her, seeking expulsion. I'm going to faint, she thought, but the sharp air in her lungs brought her upright again. Well, she thought, I'll have to tell Aunt Bridie now. The question is no longer when, but how much?

Lily waited until Bill had tucked Chester into his robes and set off in the cutter with him for a leisurely ride through the oak ridge to Little Lake, where the town's best mingled with the township hopefuls on the ice-pond.

Not having spent long enough in polite society to become practiced in its subtle arts, Lily could think of no indirect way to convey her news. "I got somethin' I have to tell you," she said when they had settled at opposite ends of a half-finished quilt.

"I figured so. You ain't stopped fidgetin' since this morning. A body'd think you'd contracted St. Vitus' Dance or somethin'."

"I'm pregnant," Lily said. "Four months and three days."

Whatever revelation Bridie had braced herself for, this was not it. "That's not possible! What on earth do you know of such things?"

Then, following the succinct disclosure of certain irrefutable biological facts: "My lord, child! Do you know what you've done? Do you have any idea what this means for you?"

Lily said she assumed she was going to be a mother, in June.

Bridie sighed in exasperation, but quickly softened. "Are you feelin' all right?"

"I'm fine."

"Don't you go shovellin' manure now, you promise me?"

"I can't work in the barn any more. I'm sorry."

"I knew I never should've let you go with that woman. I told you the city ways'd destroy you, didn't I? But I don't blame you, child, I really don't. I put the blame onto the shoulders of Alice Templeton, I do. And the man responsible, of course. Who *was* the scoundrel, then?"

As simply as she could, Lily suggested that no one had seduced or deceived her.

"You can't tell me a girl of your age an' your innocence wasn't abused by some blackguard who likely lied to get his way. You forget, child, I lived in Toronto an' London, I went out to service with no family to back me up. There's nothin' you can tell me about 'gentlemen' I don't already know twice over. An' I trusted that woman, calls herself a Christian to watch out for you, to protect you from this, this–."

Lily refused to divulge the name of the father.

"Every girl who's ever been in your position – an' I saw plenty in Toronto – has said the same thing, at first," Bridie said with surprising gentleness. "But there's no other way out of the mess, lass. He'll have to make amends. We've got the law, such as it is, on our side. You are still a minor after all. If you can stand him, then he must marry you. If not, then other arrangements can be made."

"I won't tell, ever," Lily said. "No one'd believe me anyways."

"Not the *Mayor*?" Bridie went white.

"Not anybody you know.

"He's gone, Auntie," Lily said firmly. Then: "I don't want to see him again."

Bridie knew better than to try to change her mind, but she had to at least prepare Lily for the consequences.

"Look me straight in the eye. You are an unmarried girl, and in another month your belly will swell up for all the world to see. An' when it's seen, the tongues of the town will start waggin'. They'll say that your Uncle is the father or old Bill or worse, they'll say you've been seen down by the railroad shacks just like Violet, hangin' round them navvies an' deservin' everythin' you get from your sinnin'."

Lily had no reply.

"Now you know I don't give a sweet fig for the opinion of such people, but will *you* ever get used to them church ladies thinkin' an' callin' your child a bastard an' keepin' it out of school an' makin' it an outcast. What I'm tellin' you is as long as we stay right here on this plot of land, our lives are our own, but as soon as we step off, they belong to those people out there."

For a moment Bridie looked weary, beyond recovery. "We are women, Lily, an' poor; the world's not ours to make."

Lily didn't argue the point, but waited a moment to let Bridie know she respected all that she'd said. Then, simply, "I want to have the baby here. At home."

Bridie studied the girl's face closely and recognized the innocent naivete and resolute strength that had coalesced early in her own life and led to rebellion, flight, and independence. She could do nothing less than support this young woman in her determination.

"*We'll* keep the babe," she said. "No one, not even Bill will know it's yours. We'll move you into the kitchen for the winter, make you some large housedresses, keep Chester in the dark as long as we can. An' after it's born, we'll say the child belongs to my cousin, an' I'll...go off to London an' pretend to come back with it an'–"

Auntie's eyes glinted with intrigue.

"Oh, Lily, we'll manage," she said. "We always have."

Two days later as Lily was preparing a mustard plaster for the cold Chester had caught while visiting the ice-pond, the patient whispered to her: "Love, if you have anythin' you need to tell your Uncle, go right ahead. You can trust me. And if I need to, I can handle your Auntie." The last remark was qualified somewhat by a spasm of coughing, but the import of his commentary was clear. That evening when Bridie shuffled in wearily from the woodlot, Chester was sworn to secrecy and taken into the conspiracy. He beamed for days.

The plot went well throughout the winter. The ruse of having Lily work exclusively indoors was quite plausible and Bill simply had no curiosity in the matter. Ever since Violet had been taken away, he had become even more taciturn and withdrawn, though his work for Bridie was accomplished with a conscientious concern. Occasionally he would consent to take Sunday dinner with them, but most of the time he ate on the job or took Bridie's offerings back to his hermitage. Two or three times that winter they heard the discordant strains of the mouth-organ seeking some elusive harmonies, and would know that he had 'fallen off the wagon' again. Mostly though he slept off his excesses and popped up a day later at dawn ready for work as if nothing had happened.

An excuse was always found to explain her absence from errands into Port Sarnia and occasional travellers, brought to their door by a January squall or one of February's ice-storms, only smiled their gratitude for the warmth of Lily's hospitality.

In fact the only visitors to arrive with a predetermined purpose were three gentlemen who said they were from "the railway" and asked to see Bridie alone. Lily and Chester went for a slow walk through the arbours of snow, holding each other upright and sending their laughter skyward. When they got back, Bridie forced a smile to acknowledge their return, but Lily recognized the subtle signs that the news was grim.

"They wanted to buy us out," she scoffed. "I told them where to go, and it ain't cool there."

By now, the woodlot was cleared on the north-east side right back to the Grand Trunk property. Only a windbreak of pines on the north-west side separated them from the village-to-be. Bridie could cut and saw and haul and also keep an appraiser's eye on the phantom town-site wherein so many of her hopes now lay.

What surprised Lily about the baby taking shape in her body was how disconnected its existence seemed from the event that initiated it. Certainly the Prince's pleasure in of that lusty and extraordinary encounter did not have *this*end in view. Nor did Lily's own surrender have any purpose but the immediacy of its joy and pain, the need to feel that she was the agent, not just a passive observer, of her own life. But the child inside her proclaimed its separate existence almost from the start, impudent and demanding.

Her abdomen, as Bridie predicted, swelled outward and inward as well, pressing against her back. Her belly felt like a rind or a casing that might harden and burst without warning in the night. The babe cared little that she could neither walk nor sit nor lie with ease. Moreover, when she wanted to sleep, it decided it wanted to swim. Huffing and panting at the end of a day's work, she could feel it sucking on her flagging energies, pulling the best of her blood into its own. Yet she felt no resentment. I will bear you, she thought often, then I will name you, and love you. Forever.

By mid-April the snows had vanished. The crocuses and stove-pipes dotted the lawns and gardens of the town by the River and the Lake. The rains fell, gentle and inevitable. Surveyors arrived to lay out the streets and lots of yet another village destined to germinate and bloom within a single season. Bridie looked on this event and at the unswaddled belly of her niece, and permitted her heart to leap in expectation.

No one at the Great Western station that April evening took any particular notice of an impeccably attired gentleman, accompanied by his valet, as he disembarked from the first-class Toronto car and crossed to the livery at the east end of the building. Sarnia was an important town now: politicians and businessmen and pretenders of all sorts stepped off the 6:40 almost every day of the week. Such anonymity seemed to suit this visitor's liking for the exchange which resulted in the rental of a democrat –*sans* local driver – was done with despatch and discretion. The valet took the reins while the Honourable Charles Gunther Murchison settled down into leather and velvet, and studiously ignored the regional scenery. They turned north-east up the Errol Road and drove into the dusk of early spring. It was almost dark when the driver, following some route previously committed to memory, veered into the lane of the Ramsbottom farm.

Having made introductions, Murchison dispatched his valet to the rig and turned to address Bridie, clearly the head of the household, directly. Chester perched on the edge of his chair, a spectator. Lily was in her bedroom, just waking from a restless doze.

"I have come on the most urgent of matters, Mrs. Ramsbottom, straight from the office of Governor Head himself. I apologize again for the suddenness of our appearance so late in the day, but when you hear what news I bring, you will understand our need for covert action. Several lives are at stake."

Chester leaned forward; Bridie blinked but gave no ground. "Whose lives?" she asked evenly.

"Before I am permitted to offer detailed explanations, I must talk with your...niece." He was like an eagle at home in this strange eyrie, his bronze pate feathered at the sides with silvery whiskers, his aquiline beak and assayer's eyes piercing every shadow in the coal-oil gloom, his bearing regal as befitting a man who has twice been a cabinet minister, who stared down a dozen rebel guns in 1837 and prevailed.

"My niece isn't well," Bridie said. "She's not available to you, sir, nor to the governor."

Murchison took no offense. "I'm afraid she must be. The orders I am under, you see, come from Her Majesty."

Uncle Chester fell part-way off his chair and barely recovered in time to abort the crick in his back. Lily opened her eyes.

"The Queen?"

"Yes. Directly from the palace, through His Excellency in Quebec. I have been asked to seek out and speak with your niece on a matter of the utmost delicacy and urgency."

A glimmer of insight reached Bridie's eyes, then faded in disbelief.

"With all respect, sir, my niece is ill and can't be disturbed. If you tell me what you need, of me or her, I'll talk to her in the morning. Surely even our Queen would understand the need not to upset a sick child."

Lily raised her head, the better to catch Murchison's words. "I appreciate your desire to protect your niece, Mrs. Ramsbottom, and I know His Excellency and Her Majesty would applaud your loyalty and solicitude. But it is imperative that I at least *see* your niece. If she is ill, I can return to speak with her tomorrow."

"It's all right, Auntie," Lily said stepping slowly into the room's light.

Twenty minutes later, Aunt Bridie was sitting in the straightback chair by the stove. Her face was ashen.

"You see," Murchison was explaining in lower but no-less-formal tones, "I had no idea whether the girl had informed you of the possible paternity of the child. Indeed, we did not know for sure that the girl was 'enceinte', though one of our sources, a young man disguised as a lost traveller and sitting now in my carriage, reported the possibility to us two months ago. All this was carried out, you understand, at the request of Her Majesty after a belated confession on the part of His Highness. Then, of course, we had to use the utmost discretion possible to ascertain the moral character of the girl. It proved, as I'm sure you know, ma'am, to be unimpeachably stainless." He was speaking directly to the stunned Bridie, averting his eagle gaze from the Lily's heavy-laden figure seated to his right.

"It is the Prince's babe," Lily said again.

Murchison shifted tone and stance, as if he were a lawyer changing from defense to prosecution. "Now that these most difficult and delicate matters are clear, I have the awful duty to inform you of the decisions taken, as I have said, at the highest levels of state. I have been commanded to explain to you that these decisions have been reached after full consideration of the best and just interests of all parties concerned. The Prince, you will be pleased to know, is contrite and eager to make amends for his youthful indiscretion." He looked about for some confirmation, but only Chester was nodding, unconsciously.

"Now that we know the baby will have royal blood in its veins, we are under the strictest obligation, as citizens and subjects of the Empire, to treat that fact with the awe and respect it deserves. Her Majesty expressly wishes the child to be born in circumstances most conducive to its general health, including the utmost care of the mother during the crucial days of her lying-in. The best doctors and midwives are to be consulted; a hospital or surgery must be close at hand in case of emergencies."

"We got no hospital here," Bridie said.

"Precisely. You take my very point," the solicitor said, wheeling to face the invisible jury. "We have come to take Lily to a place where all of these conditions obtain, where both her well-being and that of the child will be assured. Moreover, we are not insensible of the social difficulties associated with a child born out of wedlock; the Prince himself was particularly concerned about this point. Hence, the immediate and secret removal of the girl to a house we have arranged in London will be of benefit to all concerned."

"And after the babe is born?" Bridie said coldly into the ensuing silence.

"Mother and child can be returned here, of course. Not right away naturally. Perhaps a husband can be found for her, or a reasonable story concocted to account for the exceptional circumstances. Whatever arrangements are decided *post partum*," he said relishing the Latin, "Her Majesty has commanded Her viceroy here in the dominion to disburse appropriate funds for the maintenance of the child till it comes of age. Furthermore –"

"We don't want any of your money," Bridie cut him off.

"Now, sweetie –" Chester said, but was silenced by a stare.

"Would you kindly get the girl's things together as soon as possible? There's a train leaving here in an hour; we've arranged a special car to be attached."

Aunt Bridie stood up. "The girl, as you call her, only goes if she wants to.

Please tell Her Majesty that we are quite capable of taking care of our own, royal blood or not. An' we don't take charity."

"May I see Lily alone, then?"

Lily nodded to her Aunt.

"If you must."

The privy-councillor and ex-Grenadier was disconcerted by the way the girl gazed directly at him while he lectured her, with just the slightest hint of disapproval. Moreover, the thumping of the baby on the drum of her abdomen was disturbingly audible.

"We understand your reluctance to leave home, but we ask that you reflect on all the advantages that will accrue to a positive decision to go to London. The lady who has agreed to care for you is a woman of the highest quality and discretion. We also recognize that you are part of a working family and that your loss over the next three months or so will impose serious hardships on your Aunt and Uncle. Thus, though your Aunt sees it as charity, His Excellency will, with or without her consent, deposit a hundred dollars in her account at the Bank of Upper Canada for each month you are away, for as long as it takes to resolve matters in a satisfactory manner."

When Aunt Bridie and Uncle Chester were waved back in, they found Lily standing by the stove, her eyes brimming with tears.

11

Mrs. Edgeworth's walled garden in May was as beautiful as the East Gate to Eden, as that lady iterated often when the ladies of London gathered there, as they did each Thursday afternoon during the warm season. , Lily was obliged to observe the ritual teas from her room on the second floor of the red-brick mansion. She was not to be seen in public and particularly *en silhouette*. Those were the principal terms of her confinement. But when it was not Thursday afternoon, Lily was free to roam the gardens at will, protected from prurient view by its fieldstone walls, rampant privet and gothic elms. Hedges of honeysuckle and wild lilac marked out avenues for the eye, arrested by arbours of budded rose, beds of thrusting tulips, and the prodigality of peony and rose-of-sharon. Here Lily whiled away the weeks and hours of her twenty-first spring.

Of London itself she had seen little since that night in mid-April when she had been lifted from a private railway car and placed gently in a closed carriage to be driven through the dark to the Edgeworth home. The full moon allowed her to catch glimpses in outline of the largest, most imposing buildings she had ever seen. The gas-lamps along Richmond Street glittered like amethyst and cast across their path the shadows of railings, newel-posts, pitched gables, and spires. There appeared to be no trees except for occasional decorative saplings of maple or elm on the steep lawns of the palaces along North Street. As they wheeled onto the latter to head east, Lily drew in her breath at the sight of two cathedrals whose grand martellos carved the night-sky into Protestant and Catholic halves.

So this is civilization, Lily thought. This is what the Millars and the Partridges dreamed of as they hacked their trees to death, slashed, burned, pulverized and ground the very ash of them back into the resisting earth. This is what the burghers of Sarnia, with their muddy streets and clanging foundries and clapboard shells, yearned towards?

"You can't *read*? My gracious Godfrey, what *have*they done to you in that dreadful bush-town?" Mrs. Anthony Edgeworth's questions were usually pointed comments on the deteriorating human condition. "Well, we'll soon rectify *that*! We shan't have a son of the aristocracy grow up in a family of illiterates now, shall we?" She blushed then, as she did easily and often.

"Oh, I am sorry, dear-heart. I am expressly forbidden to mention things like that. Walls have ears, you know.""I had no upbringin'," Lily said helpfully.

"Well now, that isn't *your*fault. We'll just see what we can do in the few weeks at our disposal," she said with determined cheeriness. Then she released a bosomy sigh. "If only the Colonel were alive, he'd take you in hand."

So it was that just as the first lilacs sprang into bloom, drenching the air with the sweet phrases of their perfume, Mrs. Edgeworth donned her best brocade and ushered the freshly attired Lily into the grotto where Lamb's *Tales From Shakespeare* could be suitably worshipped.

"She's very quick," Mrs. Edgeworth said consolingly to the vicar, after another of his less-than-successful exchanges of catechism with the unlettered and unrepentant girl. "She took an instant fancy to Portia and Rosalind. Isn't that intriguing?" The vicar thought not. "She can tell you right back, quick as a wink, the whole story of *The Tempest*, or *The Winter's Tale*." His reverence thought perhaps *Pilgrim's Progress* would be more suitable fodder.

To Dr. Hackney, taking his leave after his bi-weekly check of the patient, she said, "And yesterday I decided to read her some of the Bard himself. Of course, as you remember, I don't read nearly as well as the Colonel, but do you know that wisp of a girl understood those speeches!" How she wished she could confide in the vicar and the doctor, but only *she* knew that the father of the child was some important figure-of-state from Toronto and that secrecy was imperative. The doctor, the vicar and Lucille, her servant, were told only that the girl was the daughter of a friend from the country, and that discretion was requested. Lucille was, alas, "dumb as a post but ever so sweet" and fully devoted to her mistress.

Lily soon discovered that Lucille was not at all dumb, only French, and that a great deal of the French she had learned from Maman LaRouche came back to her easily. The two girls, barely a year apart, chatted amiably in both tongues during the drowsy afternoons of early spring with the earth greening around them and the air as clear as claret.

When not reading to her, Mrs. Edgeworth took full advantage of her captive pupil to give her a singular history of England from the narrow but no-less-illuminating perspective of her own family and, where verisimilitude demanded, that of the late Colonel's. "Oh how my Aunt Fanny laughs when I tell her in letters that I live in London on the Thames in Middlesex County. She's of the opinion that we all live in log cabins and spend most of our days swatting flies." Then she would sweep the garden and environs with her Canterbury gaze: "Ridiculous, isn't it? But the Colonel, bless his memory, helped to make it what it is today. My only worry is that my dear nephew, Tippy, the Colonel's sister's boy, whom I've raised since he was a tot of ten, will not be the kind of man his father and uncle were."

And on she would go about Tippy's modest indiscretions – his poor grades in school, his truancy, his current "escapade" in Toronto, where he was supposed to be learning the law in a respectable firm, but was more often seen elsewhere in unmentionable establishments. Lily listened, quite content to nod assent or demurral as the moment dictated, watching the concern and vulnerable kindness play across the face of this affectionate stranger woman.

Is this the way it is, the way it's going to be? Lily thought. These sudden, powerful, random bondings followed by the wrenching of separation, bleak rides in the night towards dawnings we have not even had time or the wonder to dream of?

Finally, a month after her arrival, Lily received a letter from Bridie. She spotted her own name in capital letters on the envelope, and could make out the name of the street and city, but Mrs. Edgeworth had a little difficulty following her aunt's scrawl.

Port Sarnia, C.W.

May 2, 1861

Dear Lily:

Sorry to be so long in writing to you. Word has been got to us that you are doing fine. Things are so confused here that I ought to wait until the news is good before sending it along to you. Uncle Chester is getting stronger by the day. Old Bill is about the same. We all miss you terrible. Just after you left, some bigwigs from the railroad came over here and made an offer to buy our property. I told them no, this land was our living, we would never leave it. Then they said the railroad needed the land for the town-site of Point Edward. They now own all of it but our section. They said they would expropriate it; that's a two-dollar word for taking it and paying us as little as they can get away with. If they take the farm, I don't know what we'll do. A friend of Uncle Chester's has written from London with a business proposition but nothing is about to happen very soon you can rest assured. So we don't want you to worry, just stay healthy and bring us back the babe. We'll be here waiting. We've always got by and we always will.

Love,

Aunt Bridie

xoxoxo Uncle Chester

But Lily did worry. Bridie's hopes, pinned so precariously to the railway's expansion, were about to be dashed by the very instrument expected to fulfill them. Whatever happened with the farm, she knew it would not fatten itself at the expense of the Grand Trunk.

No more letters came. June arrived and with it the time for her lying-in.

Lily did not lack for either care or advice. Lucille's household duties were lightened so that she could play the role of nursemaid, a part she relished, though her ministrations in the stuffy, darkened room where the patient was forcibly detained, were more colloquial than therapeutic. Mrs. Edgeworth herself supervised the serving of the meals and spent part of each afternoon and evening reading to or regaling her "dear-heart." Dr. Hackney now came once a week to take her pulse, depress her tongue and poke or stroke the protuberance that used to be her belly. Giving it a farewell pat he turned, on his last visit, to Mrs. Edgeworth and proclaimed: "It will come on time, Elspeth. Of course it's no great accomplishment to predict the exit day when the entry point, so to speak, has been so accurately documented." Being a woman of the world, Elspeth did not blush, much. Then seeing the entreaty in Lily's eyes, he said for all to hear: "A son: one week: on the fourteenth most probably."

Unbeknownst to Dr. Hackney, his visits were invariably followed by the arrival, through the back-garden gate, of Elsie Crampton, the regional midwife. Elsie's examination was more probing, inquisitive and jovial than the good physician's. Lucille and Elspeth followed her in, trailed by her assistant, a buxom, overblown Irish girl named Maureen, who had recently delivered a son to the skeptical world. The midwife's smile was lop-sided (she had teeth only on the left side) but generous, and Lily felt strangely comforted in her presence, even though her confinement in this canopied, velveteened chamber seemed out of tune with the raw germination inside her. Mrs. Crampton held her hand, talked to her, and gave her instructions for the ordeal of the birthing day.

"It's gonna be a bit late, I think," she announced to the curious assembly.

"About the twenty-first or twenty-second, I'd say. Which means she's gonna be a stubborn little cuss, but a genuine beauty."

The women of the chorus agreed.

"On my birthday?" Lily said, looking at Lucille "Could be, dearie, but I wouldn't pray too hard for it, 'cause the longer you stay penned up here the paler and weaker you get. I don't believe in all this lying-in stuff."

Lily didn't pray but she hoped, all the same. The fifteenth passed with no signs of the contractions she'd been alerted to. Dr. Hackney arrived for his weekly check, feigned puzzlement, let his fingers linger affectionately on Lily's pumpkin bulge, and muttered to Mrs. Edgeworth at the door: "No question: I'll be back before the night's over."

In the early hours of the morning of June 21, the first spasm struck. Lily was startled by its severity, and not a little frightened. She had been well-prepared for the sequence of calamities to follow: Lucille was the middle child of a family of thirteen and reported graphically upon the numerous, horrific births she claimed to have witnessed. Mrs. Crampton had described to her in clinical terms the necessity of these discomforts and added the assurance that "when you see the babe you'll have already forgotten the pain." Cold comfort that was here in a stranger's house in a foreign town with her belly squeezing her stomach into her throat and her bowels into her spine. She gritted her teeth and let the aftershocks knit their way through her flesh; she would not cry out. When the third contraction gripped and held, Lily reached over to pull the bell-cord.

In the blackness of her pain, Lily was aware that she was surrounded by women. Their faces, their detached, consoling hands floated intermittently above her: Mrs. Edgeworth trying to mask her anguish, Mrs. Crampton too busy to register feeling, Maureen impassively efficient, Lucille agog with fright and devotion. Just after sunrise her body, now totally outside her control, gave one last convulsive heave and banished the little beast forever to the far outports of air, space, time and consanguinity. The pain was now bearable; she released her grip on Lucille's hand and could feel instead the midwife's fingers stretching, pulling, yielding.

There was a smack like the crack of a stick, followed by a stuttering wawl that rose to a series of well-defined shrieks before settling into the regular breathing and occasional gurglings of a healthy newborn. "It's a girl," said Mrs. Crampton between commands.

"How   wonderful!"   said   Mrs.   Edgeworth,   almost   hiding   her disappointment.

Moments later, the baby – wiped clean, its umbilical cord neatly knotted – was laid beside Lily on the linen sheet. On the canopy overhead she noted the cherubs and the lambs and the crenellated walls in the distance. Then she gazed across at the child curling in the arch of her shoulder and breast. The eyes peering back were her own.

You've given me great pain, she thought, as its miniature mouth nudged towards the expectant nipple, but you needed the pain to separate yourself from me, to put something between us, to be yourself. Now I can hold you, love you, and give you your name. And she did, saying the syllables in a low murmur over and over as sleep closed in. Soon after, she did not feel her daughter being gently extracted from a mother's grip.

When Lily woke it was afternoon, of what day she didn't know. She was fevered and ached all over. She reached for the baby. It wasn't there. In the hazy light allowed by the curtain, she could make the form of Maureen seated in the armchair across the room. Her blouse was open with one puffed breast shining and stiff-nippled and the other hidden behind the head of the suckling child. The noise of its feeding filled the room.

"Now don't you worry, dear-heart," Mrs. Edgeworth soothed a few minutes later, her brow creased with worry. "Everything's going to be fine. Dr. Hackney says you've got a slight infection. I must say he wasn't too happy arriving late and finding Mrs. Crampton on her way out, but he's been a dear anyway. He's left this medicine for you and –"

At last she noticed Lily's nod towards the baby and its nurse. "Oh, *that*. Dr. Hackney says with your fever and all, you wouldn't have enough milk, so Maureen, who God be thanked has more than enough for her own and yours, is helping out, *aren't you, dear?*"

Maureen responded by changing breasts and sighing with satisfaction.

"Believe me, love, it's all for the best."

"What day is it?"

"You've been in and out of a doze for three days now. But you *are* looking real good today. Shall I get you something to eat?"

"Could I hold the babe, afterwards?"

Lily *was* feeling better. She ate some soup, then her daughter was laid beside her, and when the women left for a moment, she eased a nipple into the nuzzling lips. She felt their pull upon her, amazed by the strength and depth of the need there, the compulsion of bonding it brought. Together they drifted to their separate sleep.

When she woke the next morning, feeling ravenous and fully alert, the room was empty. Moments later the door opened and Mrs. Edgeworth entered, trailed by a strange man who strode to her bedside and sat down on Lucille's chair as if it had been set out there especially for him.

"This is Mr. Clayton Thackeray, .," she said to Lily with a tremor in her voice. "He's come all the way from Toronto, from the government, to see you, *if* you're feeling up to it."

"I'm feelin' all right," Lily said, staring at the intruder from the city. He was formally attired in spats and morning coat and stiff collar; his face was obsessively whiskered with a pair of hooded eyes like two chips of anthracite. No amount of girdling could control the overbite of his belly.

"I'm glad to hear it, child," said the member of the Legislature, as if to the Opposition benches. "We have important business to discuss, *vital* business."

Mrs. Edgeworth closed the door to mute as best as possible the booming rhetoric of his delivery, then stood leaning against it and watching.

"I would like you to listen carefully to what I have to say. While you may find parts of it distasteful, I want you to remember that my communication to you comes from the highest authority in the land, that the decisions which have been taken have been thoroughly and humanely considered, and that the best interests of all concerned will be served by ready obedience." Lily studied him, conceding nothing, offering nothing. She recognized the official timbre of the voice and braced herself. When he turned slightly to Mrs. Edgeworth for support, she was staring at the carpet.

"Well, then," he began again, "I've been asked by the Honourable Mr. Murchison to convey to you the following information. We have it from the *highest authority,*" "that the father of the child, a man of pre-eminence as you know, wishes to it raised in the most congenial and appropriate circumstances. With the welfare of the child uppermost in mind, certain investigations, shall we say, were carried out in Port Sarnia. Alas, the results were not favourable. I'm sure I do not need to tell you that the financial and particularly the, ah, *moral* circumstances of the Ramsbottom household leave much to be desired."

Lily looked questioning.

"What the gentleman means, dear-heart, is that your Uncle and Aunt don't go to church regularly," said Mrs. Edgeworth.

"What the gentleman means, child, is that the *mother* of the babe's father insists that it be raised in the Church of England, a not unreasonable request, you will agree."

Only Mrs. Edgeworth, faintly, agreed.

"And in this instance the *grandmother's* wishes are paramount, as only you know," he said to Lily. "Hence these decisions have been taken in the best interests of all concerned. The child will go to Toronto with its nurse to be adopted by a prominent family there who know *generally* about the circumstances of its conception and birth and, in spite of such, have, in the most magnanimous and humanitarian of gestures, offered to give this poor creature life and hope."

Lily flinched. "It is all for the best, Lily, I believe that," said Mrs. Edgeworth near tears.

"Indeed so," said Thackeray. "The wet-nurse is packed and ready to go, as is the infant itself. Mrs. Edgeworth will have the satisfaction of knowing that she not only saved the reputation of a wayward girl but that the illegitimate offspring of the unfortunate union will be given a second chance at life. You, my child, will suffer briefly at the loss of an infant not yet dear to you, but may return to your own family purified and renewed. As a bonus for any inconvenience, I am also authorized to tell you that a cash settlement in compensation has already been deposited in your Aunt's account in a Port Sarnia bank."

Clayton Thackeray sat back waiting for some response , be it tears, rage, or thanks. He got nothing. Finally rising, he said to Mrs. Edgeworth, "Not a soul in Port Sarnia has gained a whiff of this. It's been handled with the utmost discretion and concern for the feelings of those involved. The girl will return with not a single blot upon her character." With that, he swept out, Mrs Thackeray following behind to see him properly away.

A moment later Mrs. Edgeworth returned. Lily had not moved.

"Oh, Lily. Mr. Thackeray asked me to find out something important for him. It seems the lady in Toronto who's going to adopt the babe wants to know, just for herself, the last name of the babe's mother. I'm to write it down on this card."

Apparently Lily didn't hear, her mind far away.

"It will all work out, dear-heart," Mrs. Edgeworth said, dropping all pretense. "We'll work it out together." She took Lily's hand, its calluses grown smooth, its flesh pink again. "Can you tell me your name? Not Ramsbottom, but the one you had before you were taken in."

"Fair Child..." Lily said distractedly

Mrs. Edgeworth wrote it down.

It was July 4. If she were home now Lily would be watching the fireworks display across the River as the Yankees celebrated the seizing of their liberty. Many people took the ferry over and stood in the grounds of Fort Gratiot to view the skyrockets soared independently starward, hear the army band strike up a victory march and the guns that had driven the British back where they belonged boom over the non-partisan blue of the fresh-water sea to the north.

According to all observers, Lily was "recuperating nicely." She left her room for daily walks about the garden. She let Lucille chatter on at will. The colour flowed back into her cheeks; the freckles reappeared with it.

Lily knew this hurt was permanent, like many others before it. It seemed safer, she thought, to stay inside the ache, to let it be continually numbing, and build whatever remained of her life around it. But, as before, the sun rose each day with impudent optimism, the rosebushes stretched and infected the garden with their ungirded profligacy. The wind sweetened her chamber each morning. She ate and grew lithe again. At night she held the jasper talisman in her fist, and waited for a sign of its magic to re-enter the world.

In the meantime, she realized she must write to Bridie. Mrs. Edgeworth helped her, the day after the baby's swift departure, by writing down Lily's words and mailing off the letter immediately.

"Dear Aunt Bridie: I love you and Uncle very much. I am fine. The babe was born dead. I will be coming home as soon as I get strong enough. Soon. Love, Lily."

Despite her careful monitoring Mrs. Edgeworth detected Lily crying only once: the evening after the letter was sent. She was left alone.

Two weeks then passed with no reply from Bridie. She understood why her Aunt had chosen not to write before the birth of the child, but fully expected a response to her terrible news. Lily began to feel that something momentous was about to happen, though she was uncertain whether it would be happy or sad. The talisman was strangely silent, as if it had already spoken on the subject and was surprised that Lily was not able to interpret the obvious.

Lily was about to suggest to Mrs. Edgeworth that she ought to return home as soon as possible when she experienced a slight haemorrhage and was put back to bed with stern warnings. However, in the late afternoon she persuaded Lucille to help her into the wicker wheelchair and push her into the garden, where she sat by the rose arbour in the westering sun, pondering her predicament. What am I doing here? she thought. I want only to belong to some place, to someone besides myself. The young man inside the Prince's suit was not the one, clearly, but they had created a child together. And what has it come to? What did it bring? "My word, look who it is!" Mrs. Edgeworth's voice cracked with some of its former zest. "Lucille, come here quick! Tippy's coming up the walk!"

There was a scurry in the household behind Lily. She turned away, letting the sun warm the nape of her neck. Between female greetings and excited exclamations came the rumble of a man's response. For a while all was quiet within. Lily grew strangely tense, the hairs on her neck rose. Her heart pitched without reason. She heard the slap of the screen door, the steady step, the coolness of the shadow blotting out the light behind her. She turned in her chair to face the silhouette framed by the setting sun.

"Tom," she said, steadying her voice.

12

Lily learned Tom Marshall's history in disjointed conversations over the remaining weeks of her recovering. While Elspeth Edgeworth hovered in the background, alternately heartened and worried by the obvious attraction between the two dearest young people in her life, she nonetheless allowed Tom to escort Lily on walks beyond the house, knowing he would not permit her take the physical risks she seemed all too eager to chance.

Lily was likewise ambivalent, hungry to be in Tom's company, but abashed at the circumstances of their second encounter. She let him talk, encouraged his honesty, hoped to find the answers to her uncertainties in his confessions. At the same time, she knew he was disturbed by her independence but she could not hide her nature.

"I don't remember much about my parents except my mother was beautiful and my father tall and stern in his uniform. It was he who got sick first, consumption according to my Aunt, then mother went down with it and I was torn away from them. For my own good, of course. I remember my mother's face, , too weak to smile or cry or comfort me. Weeks later I was taken by the Colonel and Aunt Elspeth to their funeral. All of London was there, she said. My parents are over there." He pointed vaguely southwest to where the pink spire of St. Paul's glinted through the trees.

"I guess you could say I was spoiled. Aunt Elspeth finally got the child the Colonel was too busy to provide her with, and she made the most of it. She had an ensign's uniform made for me to prance about in when I was barely eleven. But rich, no. My father left me a small sum to be given out as an annuity from my eighteenth to my twenty-sixth year. That ends this fall."

Lily squeezed his arm to get a firmer grip as they started north on Colborne Street, on this her first excursion around the block.

"Take it easy," Tom said. "Nurse's orders."

"Your Auntie bought you the wrong costume," she said lightly.

"I was a real rebel; I must've come close to breaking my Aunt's heart many times. Especially after the Colonel died in '50. I hated Latin. I hated Greek. I hated school. I played hooky to go fishing or help the boys build

huts and forts and kites. I was pretty good with my hands then. I liked those
scruffy, bad-mouthed kids… It's funny, don't you think, that even though I
loved to scuffle and carry on mock battles with the ruffians down by river,
my Aunt decided I was too undisciplined to follow my father and uncle into
the military. She decided I was to be a scholar, she had an eye on the new
university in Toronto, maybe a future in law. She kept me in school, one way
or another, mostly through bribes or long bouts of weeping and sighing and
calling up the ghost of the Colonel."

In the field before the Thames where they were walking for the first time,
wild daisies with single-eyed resolve contended with the twitch grass and
still-stemmed blue devil.

"But I was stubborn, I guess."

"You joined the militia," Lily said, holding a daisy under her chin as if it
were a dandelion.

"Yes," he said after a pause. "Major Bruce's Volunteer Corps."

"We drilled every other Saturday over there in Cricket Square," Tom
said. "I was determined to show the world I could make it as a soldier on my
own talents, not claim it because of my upbringing."

"I had no upbringin'," Lily said, almost automatically.

Tom released her arm. "Why do you say things like that?" he said with a
mixture of hurt and anger. She wasn't sure herself, except that it might be she
was testing him. "Because they're true," Lily told him instead, walking ahead
with a steadiness that was only partly feigned. She leaned back against the
fence for support, waiting for him to catch up.

At last he came up to her, but when they resumed their stroll, he kept
rigidly to her left.

"Why do you want to be a soldier?" she asked.

"Well, I guess I started out just wanting to prove something to my Aunt
and her friends. I was never too good at it, even then. By the time I was
eighteen I was running around with Mad-Cap Dowling and that fast crowd,
drinking and carrying on."

"With fallen women," Lily added.

"Scarlet women is the term used in polite society," Tom said, scanning
her face. "I had my own money at last and spent it as fast as it came in. So
when my Aunt suggested I go off to Toronto, not to the University but to
clerk in a law firm, I said yes. I wanted to travel, to see the country and the
big city. I discovered that the Dowlings of this world are not confined to

London."

"An' then?"

"Then I decided one morning last fall that with my income about to end this year, I had to look at my life, my future. And I did. I joined the Canadian Rifles volunteer brigade the next day. I attended all the drills, read the manuals, bought my own uniform and was made a corporal. Then I heard that the British Army was going to allow Canadians to join regular units to serve here and abroad."

Overhead, cicadas announced August with a reedy voluntary. In the meadow grasshoppers dozed in the heat.

"What do soldiers do," Lily asked, "besides killing people?"

Tom was taken aback. Her directness was something he could find no antidote for. Had she just asked a question or made a cutting appraisal? Nothing in her steady gaze could help him. He gathered his dignity and said overly loud: "The British Army and our militia do not kill people. Our job is to protect the lands and homes and lives of our citizens – ordinary people like your Uncle and Aunt who would be prey to thieves, murderers and foreigners. None of us would be safe without them. None of us would be *here*without them. Surely you've heard of the Rebellion? The Patriot's War?"

"I had no schoolin'," Lily said.

He pretended to ignore this remark. "Even now there's rumblings of a war between the states over there, a big fight over slavery. We've been put on alert at all the border points. There's a good chance I'll get into the regulars by September. That's what I want. To defend my country. That's what putting on the uniform is about." His eyes were glistening, and in spite of herself Lily was held by the earnest, frightened power in them. "The army's about the things that are most important to any man anywhere: honour, duty, loyalty, service and patriotism."

He sought the confirmation of Lily's hand; she allowed him to take it, but said after a bit: "I've heard of them words."

He gave her a grateful, if uneasy smile.

Another day they set out for the river bank below Westminster Bridge, Tom solicitous as they made their way to the water's edge.

"I'm not as fragile as you think," she teased.

"Actually, I don't know *anything*about you," Tom said, suddenly serious as they sat down in the grass.

"You know I had a baby," Lily said in that tone which left him puzzled and annoyed. "And I got no husband. And I'm your Aunt's charity case."

"For God's sake, stop talking like that! It's... it's –"

"True?"

"– disgusting and reeking of self-pity."

Lily stared at her face in the shimmering water, prepared to believe he might be right.

"I'm sorry," he said.

"You're in my care," Tom said feebly. "My Aunt, she's trusted me, she's –"

Tom's arms were around her then, gripping her fiercely. She let him pull both her softness and her strength against his rigidity. His lips brushed her eyelids, her cheeks, then met her own rising. They simply held each other for a long time, as if there were a question to be raised and no one to utter the first syllable of the answer.

"Lily," he said, "I can't live without you. I have every reason to believe you have strong feelings for me."

Lily gave him no help, but even in his turmoil he could see that she was alert and listening. "I love you. I don't pity you. How can anyone pity a person who is twice as strong as they are? I may not know what love is, but I can still say I love you and know I'm telling the truth."

"Yes," Lily said.

"Here is a token of what I feel," he said shyly, opening his fist – his sword hand – and letting the sun catch the facets of the ruby stone set in a gold ring. "My mother's," he said. "For you. For us."

Lily made no gesture towards the words or the gift.

"I'm asking you to marry me right away, to go off to Toronto with me. I've got word that the Regulars will take me; that'll mean a salary, a home for us, perhaps by the lake or on the island."

Lily looked as if she were struggling to interpret the speech of an earnest but thick-tongued foreigner. Surprise, wonder, doubt –all contended there as Tom talked on.

"I'm almost certain to be stationed at Fort York, unless some foreign war broke out, but there's little chance of that. Lily, I'm asking you to take a chance on me. I'll love you like no other man will ever love you."

Lily had no doubts about that.

"I do love you, Tom."

"Then you'll marry me?"

Lily looked away, then back. "I can't," she said.

"But *why?*"

She felt the full weight of his hurt and her own.

"I can't marry a soldier."

The next day, Tom's absence from the house was palpable.

"Where's Tom?" Lily said to Mrs. Edgeworth at breakfast.

"Tippy's been called away to Toronto," said the good lady, somewhat evasively. She had no idea when he might be back, but sincerely hoped it would be soon.

Lily could not sleep. Two nightmare scenes recurred and competed to keep her edgy and restless. One concerned her infant daughter, drowned and lying at the bottom of an ebony stream, her eyes wide open. The other put her and Tom on a train, not in a passenger coach but on top of the tender. They were roaring through a night-blizzard with the engine's boiler red-hot. The train lifted up off the tracks, driving skyward into the throat of the maelstrom that could only end in catastrophe.

Mrs. Edgeworth changed the sweat-soaked sheets each morning, and thought of calling the doctor. She feared that Lily was having a relapse.

And why was there no word from Bridie and Chester? Mrs. Edgeworth had persuaded her to send a telegram to Port Sarnia, but it was returned with the curt message: "No response".

On the third day of Tom's unexplained disappearance – even his Aunt looked anxious – Lily announced that she was better and would leave for home the next day, the fifteenth of August. She had been away for over three months.

Mrs. Edgeworth teetered on the brink of indecision, then abandoned her well-bred propriety. "He'll be back," she said, dropping all pretense. "I know him, dear-heart."

"I've got to see my Aunt and uncle," Lily said.

"Oh, I know, Lily, I know I can't keep you. I've been too selfish already."

"Can you buy a ticket for me?" Lily asked.

"Of course, I can. You can have all the money you need."

"Just the ticket, please. And I'd like to send another telegram if I could, asking them to meet me at the station."

"Of course, of course."

Lily reached for her hands, and the two women hugged each other in consolation, rocking gently back and forth in the midst of their mutual helplessness.

In less than ten minutes the train had left the city and plunged straight into the bush. Lily sat by herself on a bench and gazed blankly at the landscape fleeing past her. In two hours she would be in Port Sarnia, a journey that only three years before would have taken a full day in ideal weather. She thought of her own two-day's trek up the River so long ago.

Here and there, as the coach rocked and swayed, Lily noted the gaps in the trees where a farm had been cleared up to the right-of-way, an occasional cabin in the distance with its chimney-smoke rising, the flash of an apron or a quilt signalling life, and hope. Beyond the thick border of woods on either side of the track lay hundreds of partially cleared farms like these. The bush had been broken.

Lily soon found herself drowsy. The repetition of tree-line and the rocking monotony of the wheels below her made her heavy-lidded. Though she was certain she was not asleep, the images of sleep rose up and fell away. She was in the cabin brushing her mother's hair, pulling the livid sun through it with every stroke.. Then Maman LaRouche appeared, her cheeks buffed by oven-heat, bending down to wrap a sprite of a girl and in the great loaves of her arms. Behind her at the verge of the North Field, Old Samuels waved at her, the smoke from his calumet whitening around him. Then Papa comes to launch her upon his shoulder and they stride through the umber dawn towards a sun rising in the east, towards the rhythm of skin-drums and a ululating chant. The train jogged, bucked, shuddered and squealed to a halt. Lily looked out. They were not in Port Sarnia.

"What are we doing here?" she heard a male voice ask the conductor farther down the coach. She could hear the confusion of people collecting their belongings and shuffling to the exits.

"Wyoming Station," said a deeper voice. "We stop here now. It's the oil boom south of here. Dozens of people every day, carryin' their life on their backs. Diggin' for oil. Crazy, the whole bunch of them."

When Lily opened her eyes again, they were moving cautiously through the environs of Port Sarnia, now referred to by the inhabitants as plain Sarnia. She picked up her carpetbag crammed with the gifts she could find no way to refuse, and walked through the stifling air to the end of the coach where she waited quietly until the train stopped. The conductor took her bag as she stepped down, and held her arm.

"Watch your step, ma'am," he said, following her with his practiced eye.

Lily stood in the bracing air of the open platform, looking into the dispersing crowd. In a few minutes she was almost alone. No one was waiting for her. She went over to the baggage-man and asked if he could find her a taxi. He took all of her in – slowly – then said , "Yes, ma'am. Just here for a visit, are you?" He whistled towards the livery area.

Lily smiled her gratitude. Moments later Pig-Eye Poland, who had driven cart and cab for two decades, pulled up with his pair of bays. Lily gave him the instructions.

"You from London?" he asked when they were underway.

"Just arrived," Lily said to the man who had waved to her every Saturday as she trotted Benjamin up to the back door of the St. Clair Inn.

•

Pig-Eye's steady chatter ceased by the time they left Exmouth Street and headed north-east up the Errol Road. He sensed the tension in Lily's laconic replies, and respected her need for silence. At the gate she paid him twenty cents from the silver coins Mrs. Edgeworth had pressed on her "for emergencies, dear-heart". It was late afternoon and the August sun still burned hazily over the western sky. Lily looked at her home.

The fields had been planted, but instead of the neat rows of beans and potatoes, Lily saw ragweed and wild mustard and Scotch thistle choking in their own glut. The little barn and south coop struck her with their old familiarity, but not a sound came from them. Only the flap of a stunted corn-leaf in the wind reached across the waste of Aunt Bridie's prized garden. No smoke in the chimney. Well, it was afternoon and very hot. As she approached she saw that the door was shut tight, and the windows pressed against the sashes. She listened. Behind the woodshed a groundhog rubbed its back against the rim of its burrow; a garter snake sawed through the grass. *"They ain't there!"*

Bill had emerged from his hut and was calling to her as he hobbled across the cucumber patch. She waited for him to come to her before she said, "Are they in town?"

"Then you ain't heard," Bill said, suddenly looking at the ground and smacking his gums together nervously.

Lily waited.

"Bridie wrote you a letter about it," Bill said.

"It never arrived. Where've they gone?"

"Packed up an' went off to the oil fields down there Petrolia way," he added, seeing her puzzlement.

"Left the farm?"

"Yup. After fifteen years they just up an' left. God-damnedest thing I ever seen," he said, "For good?"

"Yup. Had their bags packed by noon an' just left the house an' the doo-dads and all standin' pat, an' hitched up Benjamin an' headed for the oil."

Gradually Lily got the whole story from him. She took him inside where she found virtually all of their possessions still in place Lily started a small fire, made some tea, and tried to keep Bill settled long enough to achieve some kind of coherence.

Bridie and Chester had gone to the Petrolia area about the time the baby was born. Bridie had put all the details in a letter which Lily didn't receive. The Grand Trunk had served the expropriation papers on them in early June. Bill's hut and yard were exempted, as were the house, barn, coop, shed, pond and kitchen garden of the Ramsbottom property, about an acre and a half in total. The rest – the fields, woodlot, cleared fallow, planted gardens – were needed, they said, for the sprawling company town already starting to unfold on the ordnance grounds of Point Edward. The Ramsbottoms would be permitted to harvest this year's crop or take a small sum in lieu thereof. A "reasonable – even generous –" offer was made for the seized acreage and pinery. That such money was of little value to a couple who had depended on developed land for their continuing livelihood was an argument considered by the directorate to be almost seditious in nature and intent.

Chester had told Bill about the business proposal of his friend from London, who had written during the winter to say that he had put capital into an oil-drilling company under the command of a fast-talking, knowledgeable New Yorker, and that they were looking for another partner. Bridie began quizzing Chester closely on the matter, and within a day the decision had been made. Bill was to sell off the Guernsey and the remaining chickens and take what he could use or sell from the garden, They left him some money, but he had hidden it so well he could no longer find it.

"But why did they do it?" Lily said.

"Dunno, little one. Never seen the like of it. Woman like that farms all her days, then just up an' leaves it all. I saw her walk out to them cabbages that mornin', an' she mumbled somethin' at them, an' then kicked one of 'em square in the head."

"She hated it," Lily said.

"All she said to me was: 'I can't let Lily an' the babe come back to this patch of ground.'"

"But the baby died," Lily said. "She knew that."

After a while Bill said, "They're stayin' in a fancy hotel somewhere – it's wrote down for you – an' you're to go there soon's you get back. They'll send a buggy to Wyomin' to take you an' the babe down. You're to live with them there."

"The baby died." she repeated.

Bill went to the cupboard and pulled out some rumpled papers. "Here. You're to send a telegram the minute you arrive."

Lily looked around at all that was familiar, at nine years of her life spent in this kitchen with its seasons of disappointment and delight, of love and its absence.

"This here paper's specially for you," Bill said, flogging his memory for some gist of its significance.

Lily took it. She recognized her name in print and Bridie's signature, and a bit of the date.

"What does it say?" she asked.

"It's a deed," Bill said, showing the purple of his gums as he stuttered over the legal script: "It gives you – Lily Ramsbottom – what's left of the farm when the railroad is done."

Lily stared at the official stamp.

"Your Aunt says to me, Bill, she says, you tell her the patch is hers, so's she'll always have a home to come back to no matter what happens to us down there."

Bill downed the last of his tea. The kettle was humming again, but Lily made no move to tend it.

"I can go to the telegraph first thing in the mornin'," Bill said at the door.

"Not yet, Bill. I want to wait a bit. To think."

"Okay." He was about to leave when he pretended to remember something. "By-the-by," he said, "when you was down to London way, did ya happen to see anythin' of my Violet?"

The hoe in her hands felt good again: sturdy, righteous. She worked without rest in the steaming humidity. Familiar blisters formed on her palms; her back ached like a loosened tooth; her hair was a frazzled rope. Still, the weeds were uprooted and the vegetables took hold. She herself ate what she could find in their larders, scraping off the mould with a jack-knife.

By the third morning she smelled worse than Bill and could hardly get out of bed. She shuffled through the shed to the back door where she eased herself down on the bench so that the morning sun would catch and soften the seizure in her back. If anyone saw me like this, she thought, they'd think I was a crone three times my age.

She heard Bill coming faithfully up the path to the front door, as he had each morning only to see in her face the answer to his offer to send that the telegram. She poked her head around the shed corner to intercept him. The sunlight rolled in a horizontal wave across the frayed garden and struck the approaching figure with indelible illumination.

Lily saw the carpenter's tool-kit first, then the overalls, bib, and navvy's cap.

"Good mornin', ma'am," Tom said. "I'm lookin' for work."

PART TWO

Tom

13

Besides the wedding of Thomas Marshall and Lily Ramsbottom, *née* Corcoran, the year 1861 produced several events of moment in what was known throughout the province as the "Lambton swamps." Alexander Mackenzie had succeeded in overthrowing the old reformer, "Coon" Cameron, and delivering the counties of the West into the political jaws of the Clear Grits. The gum-beds of Enniskillen ceased harassing wayward oxen and began oozing oil, in commercial quantities plump enough to be noticed in Chicago and New York. Twenty thousand barrels – each one constructed on-the-spot of the finest, most perishable oak – were hauled through bogs and sloughs up to Wyoming Station. Within a year the town of Oil Springs was confected to match the expectations of the drillers, dreamers, and exploiters of the human condition.

Less ostentatious but no less bumptious was the village that rose around the railway terminus on the old ordnance grounds, stretching towards Bridie and Chester's former holdings. What boundless optimism it was to lay out a town site crammed with streets, without the ghost of a house to grace them, and each one meridian-straight, square to the intangible North, and named for royalty: Emma, Maud, Alice, Alexandra, Albert, Alfred and, of course, Victoria –*regina and imperatrix*. By the summer of 1861, besides the makeshift workers' shanties sprawled around the sheds and yards, several clapboard houses and one less doubting brick establishment had aligned themselves with that confident future. Some attempt was made by outsiders to call the new municipality Huron Village, but the Point it had been and so remained.

The nuptial ceremony did not take place until early September. Lily herself didn't know why, but she set up a room for Tom in Benjamin's barn, where Chester had so often hibernated, and to the amazement of Bill who watched till his eyes glazed and he fell asleep propped up on the sill each night, the lovers parted half-way down the garden path just before dark, each to a cold bed.

Tom had proposed for the second time on the day of his arrival, and Lily had said yes.

"Tomorrow?"

"Soon."

The groom-to-be then bedded down in the straw, grateful that the pony had moved to new quarters in town a month before. While Lily pondered the precise date, a daily routine was established. In the morning they worked side by side to save what they could of the garden and to prepare for a more productive season of their own next spring. Lily tried not to laugh at Tom's ungainliness in the field, where he would attack all growth in a frenzy, then retreat exhausted, with his hands blistered and rebellious. Working at the steady pace she had learned so long ago, Lily would outlast him in the noontime heat, then invite him to rest alongside her when they took a break for a simple midday meal. In the afternoon Tom would take up his tool-kit, fling it like a haversack over his shoulder and, whistling a grenadier's march, head for the rail-yards through the parapet of pines separating them from the town-site. Lily watched him till his sandy hair was no longer distinguishable from the goldenrod in full bloom. Most days he came back at dusk, telegraphing the coins in his pocket: the Grand Trunk in its benevolence had found some occasional task for his limited skills.

"Almost got enough to pay the preacher," he'd say each time, going through a mock counting-ceremony till she laughed and made a grab for the half-dollars, whereupon he would seize her wrists, pull her to him and give Bill, watching from his cabin, a quick seizure by kissing her full on the lips.

"What do you charge, mam'selle?"

"More 'n you earn in a year, laddie."

"Then I'm off to seek my fortune in the big, bad world!"

"I'll be waitin', if you ain't too long."

The railway expropriation left them with so little land that they dismantled what was left of the hen-houses to make room for a larger garden. A make-shift coop was rigged up near the barn, but no chickens were to be installed until after the wedding. In the meantime, Booster the gander was made a gift of three lubricious females, whom he trod regularly and flamboyantly near the pond below Lily's window.

On the last day of August she heard Tom's step in the field; he wasn't whistling. She came out to meet him, apprehensive. He stopped just where the stunted sunflowers grimaced in the thinning light.

"What's happened?"

"Nothing much. They've finished the new freight-shed."

She brightened.

His smile was genuine but guarded. "They're taking on stevedores. Full time. I'm one of them."

After supper they set the date.

The ceremony itself took place on a warm Saturday morning in September on the porch of the Anglican church, the site resorted to as the best compromise, considering the lapsed faith of the groom and the apostasy of the bride. "It would mean a great deal to Auntie," Tom had said. Lily replied, "Well, one of our aunts anyway," and smiled in the hope that Bridie herself might savour the ironies.

Mrs. Edgeworth was too ill to travel, and so it fell to Alice and Maurice Templeton to serve as witnesses and as family for the occasion. Mrs. Templeton was deliciously horrified at the thought of a semi-sanctified union under some shady portico in the far reaches of the nave. She insisted that Lily wear the dress she had worn to the Great Western Ball three years before, and though it needed some alterations, Lily was happy with the results and the appropriateness. He won't remember, she thought, but I will.

A small reception followed, just tea, cakes and chilled champagne among the rusting flowers, with the Templetons' daughters and their prospering husbands down from Toronto to supervise the move of their parents. For Mrs. Templeton, and Lily, too, that was the only sad aspect of an otherwise happy event. Maurice had at last been persuaded that his business and political fortunes lay ahead of him in the provincial capital, and his wife – eager to be near her first grandchild – overcame her reluctance. The decision had been made. Both Lily and her benefactress well knew though that, despite the miracle of railroads, a separation of two hundred miles and a full social stratum meant it could be many years before they were likely to meet again.

Bridie and Chester did not come. Lily had dictated a letter which Tom penned, telling them of the impending marriage, and several days later a long letter arrived from "Oil Springs, Enniskillen Township." Needless to say, Bridie was relieved to learn that Lily was all right, and delighted with the proposed union. No mention was made of the baby's death.

"We are doing fine," she went on. "Please don't worry. When you come to us I'll explain why we did what we did, though I'm not sure I even understand it myself. Anyway, I reckon you won't believe this but Chester and me took all the money from the sale – the robbery, that is – of the farm and the savings in the bank we all helped to earn, and we packed up in one day and moved down here. Your Uncle's friend in London said we should join up with his friend from New York and form a company to search for oil. I didn't know anything about oil but I'm learning fast. Mr. Armbruster is a wonderful man. We're living for a while here in the Lucky Derrick Hotel. We have a huge piece of land out by Black Creek. Uncle Chester is back making things like barrels and rigs. Mr. Armbruster and I look after the business end. We are doing very well. We may be rich someday. But you know, Lily, your happiness means so much to us. We want you and Tom to come and stay with us as soon as you can."

Because of their enterprise, it seemed, Bridie and Chester were unable to attend the wedding, but Tom and Lily were to go to Oil Springs for their honeymoon, and then on to London for a week with Mrs. Edgeworth.

After the morning vows and the afternoon champagne and the extended goodbyes, Mr. and Mrs. Thomas Marshall were carried off by the Great Western Railway as far as Wyoming Station, where they disembarked in preparation for the fifteen-mile journey south to Enniskillen.

"At least we don't have trunks to lug about," Tom said, looking around in bewilderment at the prospectors and their families as they dragged steam-trunks, suitcases, haversacks, tool-boxes and assorted bundles of blankets and clothing along the plank platform and down the improvised alleys of the shantytown. Babies squalled, draymen cursed, women fretted, husbands railed and cuffed. Somehow bag and baggage managed to find their way onto the waiting carts. Driven by the fearsome oaths of the teamsters, the horses lurched southward on what appeared to be a road through the bush.

"Plank road all the way to Oil Springs," a grizzled veteran of these wars yelled into Tom's face. "Just built her last month. A joy to ride on!"

Lily squeezed Tom's arm in a reassuring gesture. It struck her forcefully how much of an urban man he was. She wondered if he knew or would be upset to know how much at home she felt here, looking beyond this chaotic scene and seeing the rows of farms backing sleepily onto the right-of-way, a team of oxen currying the earth with slow patience, the distant chime of an axe in some field-to-be, the curl of woodsmoke from homesteads secure among the trees.

"There's our coach," Lily shouted.

Tom was speechless at the sight of a sort of haywagon, drawn by four horses, on which five backless benches had been set in rows, sheltered by a wooden roof supported by stilts. An orange fringe adorned the perimeter of the roof, below hand-printed lettering identifying "Enniskillen Coach Lines: the Road to Oil."

Ten minutes after the coach and its ten passengers left the depot at Wyoming, they were swallowed by the bush so thoroughly that the effronteries of the makeshift town were instantly forgotten. The hardwood stands, festering swamps, treacherous sloughs, and oozing gumbo of petroleum – none were sympathetic to road construction. Three times the Road-to-Oil express had to be assisted by the passengers themselves. On the first two occasions, where sloughs had simply swallowed both planks and supporting logs, the three women passengers were implored to remain aboard while the combined animus of the seven gentlemen and the verbal efforts of the owner-operator succeeded in disgorging the wheels long enough for the horses to reach secure ground. On the third occasion, when a ruptured plank caused one of the front wheels to snap off, flinging the coach and all into the muck beside the road, even the ladies had to descend and pitch in.

"Damn your aunt anyway!" Tom said, grabbing at a strut to steady himself.

Lily held her laughter firmly in check. Half-an-hour later she was snoozing on his broad shoulder.

"I don't believe it," Tom was saying in her left ear. "Civilization. Of a sort."

"That there's Petroli-a!" shouted the driver in his best tour-guide voice. "Don't blink now or you'll miss 'er!"

To their left they could see a broad clearing, the steeple of a church, several brave storefronts, and a scattering of shanties, tents and open-air camps. But what caught every eye in the carriage was the huge brick refinery with its sixteen stills and chimney towering above the highest elm or pine. In the distance the passengers saw their first three-poled oil-rig, the jerker-lines pecking away at the earth below like robins after a rain.

"My God," Tom said as they plunged again into the bush, "where *are* we going? Three hours ago we were sipping champagne in a garden."

"Bridie says it's a grand place for a honeymoon."

"If you're a toad," Tom said.

It appeared Aunt Bridie may have been right. Towards the end of their third hour of jouncing, with the sun beginning to weaken over the western rim, they saw the unmistakable signs of human habitation. No farms of any kind, but rugged clearings, large and small, had been hacked out of the wilderness. Pines lay rotting where they had been slaughtered, stumps protruded and tilted every which way, while still other trees – giant ash or ironwood – remained afoot, though horribly gashed and left to cure themselves. Tents or shacks were the only visible dwellings, usually squatting right beside a tri-pod log-derrick or a mound of greasy clay or occasionally near a drilling-rig pounding into the rock below. Everywhere the odour of oil hung in the air.

Gazing upon the mud-spattered beauty of his bride, Tom felt his heart sink even lower, beyond anger. Lily brushed his cheek with her lips for consolation.

"Look," she said.

The rutted road had mysteriously flattened and smoothed to the gritty bounce of gravel. In the midst of the outlying shantytown, they now beheld a self-contained one-street town. The silvery dusk-glow may have lent it more allure than it deserved, but it was a wondrous sight to the travel-weary arrivals.

King Street, so declared by the black-and-white signs on either side and repeated at the two crossroads interrupting its quarter-mile length, was a freshly planked broadway, surmounted by sidewalks of finer board and trim railings, and overlooked by posts carrying a telegraph wire and the largest kerosene lamps in the known world. The shops, taverns and offices, many more than two storeys high, faced one another, proud of their false fronts. Ladies with long dresses and parasols strolled along the walkways, gathered at corners, or sat happily on benches surrounded by flowerboxes. Men in dress coats buzzed in front of the taverns, while tradesmen rushed here and there with purpose, and the twilight air shook with the cries of draymen. At the northern end of the street, an overhead arch announced the "Oil Capital of the World."

"Six hotels, five gambling dens and a dozen oil companies!" proclaimed their indefatigable guide. "An' this here's the one we stop at."

Lily looked up and guessed that this was the Lucky Derrick Hotel, the second-to-last building on the broadway. Next to it at a little distance lay the livery stable, bustling with activity. Beyond that, the bush reasserted its hegemony.

"Well now, here's the honeymooners!" boomed a voice with a twang as clear as the Liberty Bell. "You must be young Tom," said a florid-faced man, thrusting out a hand to pull Tom onto the boardwalk.

"And by golly this has to be the blushing bride. We've been waiting for you, sweetheart. Now don't you look a beauty." Lily felt the pulp of his grip on her fingers and hopped down, as gracefully as she could manage, beside Tom.

"I'm Melville Armbruster. Just call me Mel." His grin was as brisk as a shoeshine.

Standing under the porch roof of the hotel were Uncle Chester and Aunt Bridie. Lily went to them, the four months' separation feeling like four years. Chester stepped forward and without a glance at her despoiled dress, hugged her with arms that said, "we're not letting you get away again."

Lily turned to Bridie, who met her extended hands, and they held one another at elbow's length, letting their eyes speak both greetings and questions. Too soon Lily had to disengage, not fully satisfied with the brief tenderness she glimpsed in Bridie beneath a new layer of toughness that reflected the latest calamities. More than that, Lily was puzzled by the presence of some eccentric note of hope, barely disguised. Does she really believe in all this? Lily could not help wondering. Had Bridie let her guard down after so much straightening experience? Surrendered to some final, lethal euphoric?

Bridie cast a speculative eye across the handsome form of Tom Marshall, then took in Lily as she stood beside him.

"I'm afraid we're a bit of a mess, Mrs. Ramsbottom," Tom said, releasing her hand.

"Aunt Bridie will do," she said firmly.

"Now don't fuss about the mud, folks," said Melville Armbruster. "We got rooms and a bath and as soon as you're changed, we're all going to sit down and have us a king-size family dinner."

Lily saw his gold tooth flash like a fang.

Armbruster's boasting about their accommodation was not much exaggerated. The company formed by their unlikely trio, New York and Upper Canadian Oil Explorations Ltd., had leased the back quarter of the Lucky Derrick – two floors that included a sitting room, dining area and huge bathroom downstairs, plus three bedrooms upstairs with a water-closet at the end of the hall. They had their own entrance. "Twenty dollars a day," the New York partner informed them before they could ask.

Bridie had smiled ever so slightly at that with a quick lilt of the brow, and
Lily had caught the signal though she could not decipher it. What was even
more curious, possibly distressing, was the way in which she sat so close to
Chester, spooning sugar into his coffee, turning to him for confirmation of a
point not in dispute, and once even patting him on the hand affectionately
when he described for Lily's benefit the especially efficient method he had
devised out at "the works" for making barrels on the spot.

"Your uncle's workin' on a new kind of jerker-line," she said.

"He's the king-pin in this operation," said Armbruster, jiggling the
champagne glasses.

Chester blushed, then beamed. Lily felt the stanchions give way under
some part of the world she had deemed substantial. I'm being foolish, she
thought. I want my own happiness to be so perfect I can't rejoice in theirs.

"We're not exactly rich *yet*," Armbruster was saying, steak sauce a-drool
on his chin, "but as you can see, we ain't precisely starving either. We're
scooping up the surface oil quite regular and shipping it out to London and
even to Boston, thanks to the railways. Greatest invention since the Lord
pulled the rib out of Adam and gave us the fair sex." He included Bridie and
Lily in his generous assessment and no doubt the ample serving-girl who
brought in silver tureens and bulging platters of food for their conspicuous
consumption.

"To the railways!" Chester blurted out, glass raised foolishly before he
realized his blunder.

"To the Great Western for bringing us together," Tom said quickly into
the embarrassed silence. Bridie gave him a look bordering on approval.

After an interminable day that had been given over to others, the bride
and groom at last found themselves alone and unencumbered in a room they
could make their own. For a moment, drained by the shock of departure, the
travails of the journey, the puzzlement of abrupt reunion, Lily wondered if
she could recover that part of herself she had saved for her new husband. But
as Tom, naked, slipped under the covers beside her, the feather mattress
offering no resistance to whatever shapes they might wish to compose, all
doubts vanished. Even the thought that this whole episode might be a
charade, a girl's doll-house dream of a rescued princess and her toy soldier.
Tom, too, might well be wondering what he was doing here, miles from the
nearest parade ground, in a room overwhelmed by Persian carpets, rococo
wainscoting, and Venetian wallpaper, pledged to a woman whose allure was

still a mystery to him and whose history he dare not mention.

So, like many others before and after them, hoping to escape the past for an unknown future, Lily and Tom gave themselves up to love. They let their bodies articulate what they felt, hoped, and craved, yet had no words to say. They sought in the other's flesh the pulse of their own. In the aftermath they clung together, even in sleep, like sole survivors.

After breakfast the next morning, they all drove out to Black Creek to examine the oil-drilling operations of the new company. "There's a bit of walking to do out there; hope the kids have some energy left!" declared Armbruster with a leering wink.

But it was Chester who had to stop every hundred yards or so as they hiked from the edge of the bush-trail towards the drilling site. "You go ahead, I'll be okay," he gasped, but Bridie said with genuine warmth, "Don't be silly, Chester, we're in no hurry. That oil's been there a long time before we come lookin' for it."

"Yessiree," Armbruster chimed in on cue, and began explaining to Tom the geological formations and glacial events that had miraculously convened to produce the very petroleum they could smell seeping out of the earth around them. Chester caught his breath, took his wife's hand and strode forward. Bridie, Lily noted, turned briefly to Armbruster as if to say thanks.

A half-mile or so into the dense bush brought them to a ten-acre clearing, the property of New York and Upper Canadian Oil Explorations. Here Armbruster took full control of matters, guiding Tom firmly away from Lily and leading him from one piece of machinery to another, certain that his exposition was both fascinating and necessary. To Lily's surprise, Bridie followed them, listening intently to the details and even offering one or two comments herself – which seemed to please Armbruster. If Tom were bored he gave no sign of it, relying on the engrained courtesies of his upbringing. Lily felt a twinge of something close to envy. "Show me your woodworkin' place, Uncle," she said more loudly than necessary.

Having got his second wind, Chester smiled freely at her. "Lily," he said, "I want to tell you, while I have the chance, that I'm very, very happy for you. An' no one in this world deserves happiness more than you."

"What's this?" Lily said, pointing to a metal contraption off to the north.

"That, my girl, is a little invention I'm workin' on. To speed up the barrel makin'. Come on over and I'll tell you more about it than you'll ever wanna hear." He offered his arm.

They crossed the litter of broken trees, gouged roots and scorched pits towards a series of shacks and wooden benches that formed the cooperage section of the operations. To the south, where the others had gone, lay the three jerker-lines perpetually pumping the thick oil from shallow wells that had been dug out several months before. A single steam-engine, shrouded somewhat by the nearby trees, provided power for the pumps and for Chester's carpentry works. Lily could see several men in the bush, cutting and preparing firewood.

"We got five young men workin' for us," Chester explained. "Two of them help me with the barrels an' shippin'. Nice lads, they are, from over Moore township way."

Lily could see the pleasure, so long absent, in her uncle's face, some sense that the world was not only still evolving but that it still held a place for him. But she knew him too well to be totally taken in. As he hopped about the area showing off, as modestly as he dare, the intricacies of his efforts and his plans for the coming winter, Lily was faintly aware that his eyes reflected the hysterical hope of an orphaned child who's found a home as perfect as it is temporary.

"You gonna stay on that land, with Tom?" he asked in a sudden shift of tone.

"Maybe," Lily said. "It's not that far away."

"Oh," Chester said, "I didn't mean it that way at all. It's just that your young man, well, he –"

"– don't look like a farmer."

"I wouldn't've said it quite like that," he said, smiling as she did.

"He was a lawyer's clerk and a militia man," said Lily with as much pride as regret. "He can be whatever he sets out to be."

Chester paused at that remark but said amiably, "I don't doubt that for a minute."

Just then the door to one of the shacks opened and a young man about Lily's age emerged, blinking and then blushing.

"Don't be shy now, Jimmy," Chester said to him. "This here's my favourite niece Lily come to see whether we're doin' a decent job. Lily, this is Jimmy Miller."

"From Moore Township?" Lily asked in surprise.

"They got a lumber trail now goes from Black Creek here straight west to the big river," said Chester as if to answer her question.

Jimmy Millar had recognized Lily at once, even remembered the day when she and Papa had left their home for the last time. Though he was only eight years old and hiding behind his mother's apron as his family watched them pass, he recalled his envy of father-and-daughter as they headed north to cities and roads and talk of railways. Urged on by Lily's soft but insistent questioning, Jimmy related what news he could of those left behind.

The winter of their departure, Maman LaRouche had fallen ill, then progressively weaker until finally she begged her husband to go for the priest, just as he'd promised. LaRouche dutifully set out for Port Sarnia on snowshoes, taking three days to reach St. Joseph's and persuade a priest to return with him by horse and cutter. A mishap on the journey home snapped the Frenchman's leg very near the Millars' farm, and while an itinerant quack attended to his injuries, it was left to the Millars' eldest son and the priest to discover that Maman was already dead. Her body was wrapped in the linen shroud she had brought with her from Sandwich, then packed in ice in the ox-shed, where it remained until spring.

Not surprisingly, LaRouche's leg did not set properly. By March and the first signs of break-up, it was clear that gangrene had set in. Millar sent his eldest boy for a legitimate doctor from Port Sarnia. When he arrived a week later, frost-bitten and muddy, he confirmed gangrene and offered either amputation (in the town, of course, after a jaunt across the spring "roads") or opium. LaRouche cursed him in English and *joual*, and had him escorted to Millar's corner.

He was saved from the final agonies of a gangrenous death when, in the midst of the first warm rain of the season, he contracted tetanus, which pursued him faster than the venom in his leg. As luck would have it, a preacher on his quarterly circuit happened to be in the area scouting converts. At the LaRouche childrens' behest, he lingered long enough to preside over the double interment, offering Methodist homilies to the dead and scant comfort to the surviving. Later on, proper headstones were erected. They rested not more than forty feet from the granite stone of their neighbour.

"Some of the LaRouche boys are still there," Jimmy went on. "But the place is a mess. They mostly hire out for booze money. None of 'em got married. Luc sometimes lives with an Indian woman. Madeleine died."

For a moment Jimmy did not understand Lily's next question. "Oh, *them*," he said, as light flooded in. "That squatters' camp broke up right after you left. The government opened up those back lots and Old Samuels an' his brood just disappeared into the trees. Nobody's seen or heard of 'em since."

Lily didn't respond.

"What about you," Jimmy said. "How's your Pa doin'?"

"He's dead," Lily said, surprising herself with the quick conviction in her voice. Deep down, she had to acknowledge this was not a lie. Loss upon loss.

Just then, Tom and the others came into view. Armbruster's voice reached her. "And this is just the part that pays the bills, Tom, my boy. The real bonanza's in the deep-drilling rig we're moving in next week. Yessir, we're going as far down into that rock as we can 'cause there's an ocean of oil just waiting there to make us all millionaires. If I was you, I'd talk turkey to that aunt of yours in London. A little capital's all you need."

Tom was nodding his head politely. Bridie was walking between them. She seemed so much smaller than the men.

"What's the matter?" Tom said, rolling into the feathery shadows of their afternoon bed.

"Nothin'," Lily said, leaning over him and planting a series of frantic little kisses along his great chest and massive shoulders. "Nothin' you can't cure."

And she sighed extravagantly as he gripped her breasts and eased her towards acceptance. Nothing you *can* cure, she thought sadly, her loving of him trebled by that awful knowledge.

Aunt Bridie looked straight at her and said, "You want to know why we up and left the farm. Well, you've got a right to."

They were alone in the sitting room, the men having gone off to try their luck at the casino two doors down.

"Not really," Lily replied, "if you don't want to tell –" She waited for her aunt to move away from the window and sit down on the divan beside her. "As long as you're happy. Besides, I left you, remember."

Aunt Bridie fiddled with the tassel on a sofa cushion. "We never felt that," she said softly. "We knew why you went. It came near to breakin' Chester's heart when he found out the baby had died. But it saved him, too, in a way. All through that horrible business with the railroad, he was a great strength to me. Imagine that. 'Lily's comin' back,' he'd say. 'She'll need a home more than ever now.' But I was mad at the railway people, madder than I've been for a long time." She peeked over at Lily and forced a thin smile.

"When they took what all of us built up with our sweat an' bones for ten years, I must tell you, Lily dearest, I was about ready to call it quits. That

Grand Trunk man driving those red stakes into our land felt like stakes driven into my heart. If it hadn't been for Chester an' the thought of you sufferin' down there in London, I don't know what I'd have done." Her voice, usually so strong and clear, broke with the memory of those weeks.

"So when Chester's friend in London suggested we pack our bags an' take all our savings an' make the craziest gamble of our lives, it took about thirty seconds to make up my mind. Chester's still shakin', as you can see."

"But all this," Lily said carefully, "is so new an' different from what you're used to. This place, these people...."

Aunt Bridie smiled. "You mean Mel," she said. "Lily, you're almost as smart as your auntie. And as dumb naive, thank the Lord. I know it looks like phoniness an' sin an' greed. But it's just another version of livin'. Remember, before I was a farmer an' fruit vendor, I was a housemaid, an' before that a rebel daughter who gave up her family an' her country with barely a night's thought. When I married your Uncle Chester, I knew less about him than you do about Tom."

The mellowing late-afternoon sun flowed into the room around them. "When you see Fate comin' down on you, there's nothin' you can do but get out of its way before it crushes you. A body can only fight so long; after a while you're not a fighter, you're a fool."

Birdie paused then brightened.

"Tell me you'll come an' live with us again."

"Here?"

"Not right here, of course. As soon as the big well comes in, your uncle an' me will build a cottage on the outskirts, with trees and a garden. A flower garden."

"We ain't made any real plans yet," Lily said.

"Don't you worry about Mel now," Aunt Bridie said. "There's a good man under all that blarney. I know. I'm Irish, remember?"

"I'm sure there is," Lily said.

"All I'm askin' is for you to talk it over with Tom. There's plenty of work. Lots of opportunity for a young man with ambition."

"I'll talk to him," Lily said, catching yearning in her aunt's eyes.

"Tell him you gotta take chances in this world," Bridie said in the same encouraging tone.

Lily crossed the room and took her hands in her own. "But you left me the deed," Lily said.

Bridie gave a wry smile full of tenderness and doubt. Then she stared out at the setting sun. "It wasn't for you alone," she whispered.

"Oh –" Lily said. Then she put her arms around her aunt and held her as she might her own mother. Bridie's body shrank, then the tears came, irregular and fugitive.

"There'll be another one soon," Lily said. "I promise."

14

Although they lived on the far edge of the new village, shielded from it by the last rows of primeval forest, Lily and Tom felt their lives growing in parallel with it. Very soon after their return from a week with Mrs. Edgeworth, now officially Aunt Elspeth, Tom took up his job with the Grand Trunk and settled into a daily routine that Lily hoped might go on forever. Bridie's proposition that they move to Petrolia seemed less and less plausible.

Each morning just as the sun reached the tree-line and their cockerel announced his lustiness, Lily detached herself carefully and reluctantly from the cocoon of warmth she helped create with her lover's body, and started a brisk fire in the stove. The kindling she had chopped the previous afternoon snapped and thirsted after air. She would then pump the kettle full and place it over the open flame, before slipping into the bedroom again to watch her husband's face in sleep. She had to be quick, of course, or the day's schedule would be set ajar. Tom, pawing his way out of some dream or other, might ring her with his powerful arms – now thickened by the hauling of hundred-pound kegs and sacks – and pull her back into his reverie. Beyond an initial cry of mock protest, she made no resistance, for Tom's loving would be slow and dream-like, and she was glad she'd had no one to tell her exactly what love could or shouldn't be. If Tom were somewhat taken aback by her aggressiveness at night, he very soon adjusted to it, and here in these improvised and illicit mornings they found a mutual pace that left them both adrift, awash in desire without appetite. It was during one of these sessions late in September, on a misty Sunday morning, that Lily unexpectedly broke the spell and thrashed her way to a first, shuddering, climax.

"Good morning," Tom said when he'd caught his breath and found his voice.

Lily shut her eyes and clung to his shoulders, letting the last wavelets of pleasure fend for themselves. "Nobody told me about this," she breathed against him.

"Me neither," Tom said. "And on a Sunday at that."

She felt the laughter rumble through his chest, and she hugged him, and marvelled at the mystery of the world's working.

Except for Sundays, she had learned to discipline herself to the point where Tom would have to dissemble sleep as she started breakfast and then spring like a lynx at her when she bent to watch him wake. She soon learned, also, that a sudden giggle or a quick tickle under the arms deflated his desires or the fancies that fed them, after which they would tussle and cavort like a couple of cubs until one of them toppled onto the cold floor and breakfast and work reasserted their sober priorities.

Tom liked a hearty breakfast, so Lily cooked him back-bacon and eggs (provided by their own hens now), then joined him for toast, jam and tea. She didn't mind in the least that he could be grumpy in the morning; she was accustomed to rising at dawn and found herself unable to contain her humming and good cheer. Besides, she wasn't eager to talk too much over breakfast since one of her recurring fears was that they would run out of things to say to each another, though barely a month had passed since the wedding.

Once, walking through the oak-and-maple bush east of the house with the leaves crackling underfoot, Tom had turned to her and said: "Lily, darling, if you and another just like you inherited the earth, there'd soon be no talking left at all." But she was sure Tom loved her precisely because she was such a good listener. After supper or a stroll through the woods on Sundays, he loved to tell stories about his wild school-days, his escapades with Mad-Cap Dowling, or the absurdities of the characters he'd encountered in the practice of law in Toronto. Not that he wouldn't try to prompt Lily herself to open up: "Why don't you ever talk about yourself? You don't have to tell me all," he would laugh. "I just want to know as much of you as I can."

So, on well- spaced occasions, Lily would take up the burden of story-telling, selecting the happy nostalgia of her trips to Port Sarnia to peddle her fruits and vegetables, the eccentricities of the Misses Baines-Powell, the boozy warmth of Char Hazelberry and her girls Betsy and Winnie, Mrs. Templeton's kindness, old Bill's antics. But she did not have Tom's ease of his delivery or confidence. Even now she had an intimation of the difficulty she would experience in the community – particularly the community of women where the comforting reciprocity of small-talk was the principal means of social connection.

Here at home, though, during the honeymoon of their love, Lily discovered that while their conversation was light, there was also a much richer kind of communication, one at which she had always excelled. Over breakfast, Tom might raise his left eyebrow and Lily would know to fill his cup with tea. When he left for work they no longer said "goodbye." Tom would simply embrace her with one arm, his lunch-box in the other, as if to say "It's all right, I'll be back soon." And she would briefly detain his outstretched hand and give it a single pat, intimating, "I know you work hard, and I'll be here when you return." So subtle had these gestures become that any variation from the norm could be devastating. One day Tom seemed particularly testy over breakfast, and later when he put his arm around her on the stoop, he pulled back too quickly. Her caress ended in mid-air. Lily felt it like a slap to the face. But when he returned at dusk, he hugged her till he felt her forgiveness.

Being a man of easy words, Tom was also more easily stung by them than she was. Lily was more hurt by an unthinking shrug of the shoulder than by any direct complaint Tom might make about her cooking or her not dressing up when Aunt Elspeth was "good enough to give you that trousseau of beautiful things." *Salvaged from the outcasts of her daughters,* Lily might have replied but bit her tongue. I've spent my life listening to words, she thought, but not necessarily reacting to them. Better to absorb them, consider them, find out what lies under them.

For Lily, much of that first autumn was spent in waiting of one kind or another. Tom would trudge off in the early dawn, and she would stand in the partly redeemed garden and watch until he disappeared through the trees. There was plenty of work for her during the day, cleaning the house, tending the last of their meagre harvest, "doing down"' some of the cucumbers, baking bread, and then, in the afternoon hours, chopping wood, mending, sewing, and preparing the robust suppers Tom expected. Several times a week she went over to see that Bill was all right, taking him baked goods and vegetables, and checking that his cupboard was stocked with staples. He was growing worse, it appeared. Increasingly he seemed distracted and forgetful. Lily often had to remind him that he had promised so-and-so up the line a day's chopping, or even point him in the right direction.

Every hour was filled with chores and anticipation. Tom was everywhere: in the sock she was darning, a sweater she was knitting him for winter, the sheets as she changed them. The memory of his lovemaking, his stark worship of her body and its unpredictable release, rippled through her all morning long or ambushed her at odd moments. Occasionally some imagined slight would fester until she would see his figure rise in front of the setting sun and bring with it the kind of healing possible only at the end of day. At least the waiting-out of his absence was over.

But there were other, more shaded types of waiting: waiting to see what sort of toll the labour of the day had taken on his body: sore back, bruised arms, or crushed fingers. And on his spirit: fatigue, anger, or rebellion. For her these meant myriad adjustments to be made and tolerated and woven into the harmony of a home. If Tom were watching her in the same way, she could not detect it, nor, she guessed, would he ever know how much giving – beyond the visible – she was offering him each day. I have made him my life, she thought. Even though I ought to, I seem to have no regrets.

One day late in November, a week before the ice froze over the river but long after Tom's nightly treks homeward were made in the autumnal dark, Lily sat beside her lamp and waited for her husband. Overtime again, she thought resentfully. For two nights in a row he had arrived at eight o'clock, too exhausted by a twelve-hour shift to eat a proper supper or do anything else but fall comatose on the bed.

On the third night, it was well past eight o'clock. The fire was almost out beneath the congealing stew. Never had Tom worked this late. Even the Grand Trunk admitted the limits of exhaustion. Her only comfort was that after one more week of this, Tom would be transferred to the new car-shops beside the round-house. Here he would ply his carpenter's trade, replacing broken boards in box-cars and other rolling stock. Lily had seen the glaze of defeat in his eyes these past few weeks. The labouring job had been at best a mixed blessing. Early on, it had put muscle on his fine frame and brought a proud smile to his face as he counted out the dollars on the table every payday. But that body and that power came with a cost, she soon found out. Many an evening during October she had rubbed liniment into his aches, applied plasters to his cuts and scrapes.

But tonight he was not here to be tended. It was at least ten o'clock by the moon's position in the southern sky. Perhaps he had been seriously hurt; barrels and cartons were forever toppling and injuring the men. Already two workers had suffered broken arms and dismissal – without compensation, of course. An incapacitated man was a threat to the health of the company.

What will we do if Tom can't work? Lily thought. What we've always done: get by. I'm as strong as any man in my own way. He wonders why I don't wear those London ladies' dresses, but I've no flesh to fill them out. My hips are as lean as a boy's, my breasts small and unwomanly. My skin is sun-burned, my hair dull as straw. How could a man as handsome as Tom feel so passionate about me? I don't intend to ask him. I only want him to come home safely, now, in one piece.

As if on cue, Tom came noisily up the path and flung open the door.

"Hullo, Lily love," he grinned broadly. "Think I might be a wee bit late."

Lily smelled the whiskey before she could rise to face him. She brushed by him to the stove, where she began poking paper into the corpse of the fire.

"Ah, the little woman's saved supper for me. Thank you, darling. Thank you very much," he slurred. He stumbled, righted himself, and managed to land one buttock on a chair.

"We worked some overtime," he said, "then Gimpy and Bruce and me went down to the bunk house to toast our good fortune at being dray-horses for the Grand Trunk Railway."

The kindling had caught, and Lily shook the flaccid stew across the stove-lids.

"Stop that infernal racket, woman!" Tom yelled. "I don't need anything to eat, can't you see that? Are you deaf and blind? I'm *drunk*. Glorious, stupid, falling-down drunk!"

Lily headed for the bedroom.

"Where in hell are you going now?"

"To get the bed-warmer," Lily said in a neutral voice. "And the liniment."

"Come over here!"

Lily stood her ground.

"For Christ's sake, woman, come over here before I puke in your stewpot!"

Lily edged towards Tom. He was sitting with his head between his hands, shivering no doubt from the cold and false embrace of the alcohol. Lily stopped near the stove, but she made no move towards the simmering stew. Tom coughed in a series of ghastly spasms, but when she made to assist, he raised a warning hand.

Finally, taking a deep breath, he looked up at his wife, the one soul on this earth he would give his life for, and said through the press of tears, "For

God's sake, Lily, why can't you get mad or scream or curse me or hit me with a frying pan. I'm no damn saint, you know. I'm a human being." And to prove it, he sobbed into his hands and could not be consoled.

Tom's winter job repairing the Grand Trunk's rolling stock was secure and lucrative. Indeed, the car-shops, as they were called, became a stable source of employment for the Point's inhabitants for decades to come. The great highballs from the American mid-west thundered up from Chicago laden with corn and wheat and roared back with over-priced implements and calico from the factories of the eastern seaboard and, thanks to the Grand Trunk, from the fledgling foundries of Montreal, Toronto and London. In the winter of 1861-62, there was no tunnel under the St. Clair River or bridge over it. Situated on the narrowest neck of the mighty waterway, Point Edward's destiny was already appointed: it was to be the gateway to a westering continent.

However, by mid-December the river was jammed with ice, silencing the freight-sheds with steamers, paddle-wheelers, sloops and yawls alike out for the season. The huge barges and ferries that wheeled up to a hundred box-cars a day back and forth between the two nations were stuck fast at the wharf. Occasionally, during a January thaw or a freak contortion of the ice-pack, the fierce current would surge in the sunlight and a wild dash would be made across the divide – box-cars, deck hands and ferry-boat tilting, skidding and slewing in the northerly gales. All the company's employees were pressed into service, including the carpenters and joiners. The box-cars, many of them fully loaded, had to be pinioned to the ferry's deck with ropes and blocks. Often several of them pulled loose in the lurching swells, and the desperate crew would try to jerk the lines back into place, sometimes improvising an ingenious brace but mostly using the brute strength of their backs, while icy spray broke over them and jagged floes crashed by. That winter they didn't lose a single box-car. Three men were crippled and let go.

Tom insisted that Lily come down to watch one of these spectacles. Finally, she agreed. As it turned out, the crossing was relatively uneventful except for one stock-car full of chilled cattle that tore loose from its moorings and slid part-way into the water before it could be winched back into place. Lily could see the commotion and hear the cries of the terrified beasts, but she lost sight of Tom, and when one of the men flipped into the water, her heart stopped. Seconds later the fellow was hauled back in on a safety rope, striking the deck with the thud of a frozen seal. In a minute he was up, and

Lily was sure she could hear laughter; then the man who had engineered the rescue peered towards the wharf, towards Lily, and, she was certain, waved at her.

A few hours later, Tom escorted her to the little tea-room in the grand concourse of the railway station. Lily made no mention of the luncheon she had shared with royalty in the adjoining ballroom, and certainly no one present on that occasion would have recognized her today as the object of a prince's attention. Lily was not thinking of such things, of course. She was trying to understand the gleam in her husband's eye, the sureness of his stride beside her, the jauntiness in his voice. He paid no heed to the rope-burns on his hands as he sat across from her, his tea cooling, and recounted every detail of the crossing and the rescue.

"We did it again," he said. "You see why I wanted you to come down and watch. I only wish I could bring you on board. You can't imagine what it feels like out there with the wind howling in your ears and the ice bouncing all around you, and the ropes stretching and everybody holding their breath waiting for something to break loose, knowing that one slip and you'll either be crushed to death or dumped into the drink and frozen like a brick. Did you see me yank ol' Mason out of the pond? He's not thawed out yet!"

Too quickly, Lily said something she immediately regretted.

"How many of them cows died?"

By mid-January winter had settled in for a long stay. No ferries challenged the ice. The snow bloomed and foliated the hardwoods behind the house and plumped the pines along the lane towards the Errol Road. It was a soft, blanched world that threw into sharp relief those few surviving angularities of landscape.

Lily found Bridie's quilting frame in the shed and, near it, a bundle of remnants collected from the cast-offs of Sarnia's *petite-bourgeoisie*.

"What's that contraption?" Tom said that Sunday afternoon, glancing up from his labours over a broken chair.

"It's Aunt Bridie's," Lily said. "I'm gonna make quilts. And sell them," she added.

Tom went back to his repairs, but soon he was seated behind Lily as her hands played with the myriad shapes and hues of cloth scattered on the floor, out of which she was improvising patterns later to be sewn into their own kind of landscape.

"How do you know what goes where?" Tom asked quietly. Lily shrugged and continued. She didn't know herself what prompted her to select one piece and place it a certain way over another. She fiddled and nudged and tested, until bits of colour and cotton became half-cast suns, ovular moons, a tree's boughs arched, a slice of fern reaching for light. The afternoon was gone. Tom was still there.

Christmas was one of those familial interludes appreciated in retrospect more for its happy interruption of daily routine than for its own special ambience. A few days before the holiday, two train-tickets arrived from Aunt Elspeth along with a touching invitation and word that Bridie and Chester were in London on business. Thus, Christmas day – its religious significance noted only, it seemed, by Mrs. Edgeworth and that "fine American gentleman," Melville Armbruster – was spent in feasting, toasting and voluble good cheer.

Lily found herself tingling with pride at the sight of Bridie holding her own in such a household: her new clothes, serviceable yet carrying a hint of fashion (a bow at the waist, a tiny yellow hanky at the sleeve, a violet hidden among the folds); her upright bearing; her country speech undercut with wit and calculated humour; the ease with which the topics of the day were discussed and dissected. Mrs. Edgeworth was in awe, while Armbruster was enthralled, kissing Bridie's hand with Yankee extravagance, sliding her chair in at the strategic moment. Lily reminded herself that, after all, her aunt had once been an urban woman in service to what passed for high society in the provinces. Notwithstanding, Lily was puzzled by the nameless resentment that welled up at such thoughts. Bridie, in turn, waited for news that Lily could not deliver.

Chester looked pale but happy and full of enthusiasm for his projects, as their drilling was to continue even through these winter months. Tom seemed in his element also, and after Christmas dinner he went up to his old room and came down in uniform to entertain the guests with hilarious stories about the Battle of Montgomery's Tavern and other escapades of the province's military past. Lily did not join in the laughter.

With river traffic once again at a standstill, Tom was unable to disguise his frustration. Lily could pick up every tic of irritation, but she was careful not to overcompensate with excess cheeriness or solicitude. She did kill one of the hens for a Sunday dinner and stuffed it with Tom's favourite dressing, an offering that brought a brief spate of good humour.

One day in early February, Tom came home late and slightly drunk. He seemed cheerful enough, however, and beyond banging a pot or two for effect and serving supper in its lukewarm state, Lily did nothing out of the ordinary. Tom seemed amused by her performance, and later his love-making was as playful as it was prolonged. For two days thereafter he arrived home on time in spite of the near-blizzard that buried the hen-house.

"The men are organizing a sleigh-ride for the families and girl-friends," he announced. "Next week. Be a good chance for you to meet some people."

Lily feigned interest, watching for signs.

The following evening he was drunk again and decidedly uncheerful. He uttered nothing decipherable, fumbled with his supper, and finally vomited all over the floor. By the time she got it cleaned up and dampened down the two fires, Tom was snoring, fully-clothed and stinking on the bed. Lily slipped into her former bedroom. Her dreams were not happy ones. At breakfast she said, "I'd like to go on that sleigh-ride."

The weather would be perfect for the "tallyho," as the locals called it. The blizzard had been followed by five days of clear, below-zero skies; the snows had settled in the bush and tramped smooth on the village paths. The night before the planned festivities was beautiful. The stars shone with such clarity even prophecy seemed possible and the completed moon sailed alone, serene and sibylline. Seated on a stool near the west window, putting the last stitches into a quilt piece, Lily was hardly aware that the evening had passed and her husband was not yet home.

It might have been midnight when she saw two figures staggering through the drifts of the garden towards the house. The moon sketched their antic silhouettes. They were singing a bawdy shanty of some sort, and laughing heartily as they pitched and yawed through the yard. The stranger, she guessed, would have to be Gimpy Fitchett: there was an extra stammer in his swagger. As they navigated in the general direction of the door, arms interlinked, voices joined in the hunt for harmony, Tom changed the tune, bellowing moonward in a mock-heroic Irishman's lilt:

In Dublin's fair city

Lived a maiden so pretty

Her name was sweet Lily

Lil-lee my love!

At least they're happy, Lily thought, poking the fire into life and hoping for the best.

Greetings made and a bottle produced, the men took their place at the table while Lily held dinner.

"Come on, duckling, come over here and say hello to Gimpy," Tom said as he tipped another dollop of whiskey into the coffee Lily had prepared.

"I said hello to Gimpy," Lily said. "Five times."

"It's okay, Tommy. Just take it easy, eh?" Gimpy, more sober than when he'd first arrived, put a soothing hand on his buddy's shoulder.

"Don't tell me what to do," Tom said. "I get enough of that at the shop all day long."

"Maybe some more coffee, missus," Gimpy said with deliberate kindness.

"Are you gonna come over and say a nice proper hello to ol' Gimp or aren't you?"

"You oughta have some supper," Lily said. She stared at the lukewarm pots on the stove.

"Ain't that sweet now, Gimp ol' boy, the little lady wants me to have some supper. I think maybe she don't like me drinking coffee, eh?" He winked with the wrong eye.

"You go ahead, Tommy. But if it ain't too much trouble, I'd like a bit of that grub, ma'am. Smells real nice." He grinned, exposing crooked teeth, and adjusted his stiffened leg, the result of an accident during his glory days as a trainman.

"If you like horseshit," Tom said, and started in with a barrack's version of Molly Malone:

Oh her blooms were so ample

The lads love to sample

The sweetmeats of –

The grub to which Gimpy alluded – a potato-and-roast-beef hash – abruptly left the stove and struck the would-be balladeer flush on the tonsils. Tom blinked in disbelief as the concoction fell onto his work shirt. Before he could recover, Lily had her boots and coat on and was slamming the door behind her with resolute finality. She marched towards the north-east woods, their voices rising and then waning.

"Goddammit, you come back here, woman! You hear me?"

"Now, Tommy, Tommy. It don't matter none."

"You get your carcass back here or I'll –"

"Let it go. Come on now."

"Lil-eee!"

Lily let a deer-trail lead her into the woods, into the silk oblivion of silence and deep snow. The wind-chill anesthetized the blood under her skin and she walked and walked till she found again some part of her being she could inhabit with dignity.

She found herself sitting in a tiny cove of snow along the frozen creek. Underneath the camouflage she was sure she could hear the water still moving, its voice faint, tinsel-like, a dolphin's song from a distant sea. She heard the weasel's ermine belly dragging at the burrow's edge, felt his ferret's glare on her heart. Then he was gone, scrambling underground, his ears picking up the same sound that made Lily leap straight up and freeze.

It was the crashing of masculine boots against the snow, punctuated by the snap of brittle twigs. Lily swung round in time to see a black figure staggering through the trees, its exaggerated shadow slashing and dissolving into the chiaroscuro of the moon-lit forest. Quickly Lily picked up the deer-trail to her right and fled as quietly as she dare. Against the hammering of her heart she heard the attacking footfalls fade, and when she stopped, the silence of the bush had reasserted itself. Who could it have been? Not Tom, that was certain. She took her bearings, concluding with relief that she had ended up less than a quarter-of-a-mile from the house. What time it was she could only guess. She headed south-west towards the remains of the pinery.

A few minutes later she could see the opening in the trees ahead. She was almost home. The figure surprised her completely when it leaped out of the shadows to her left, flung its arms out like wings and stumbled towards her with a cry that was not threatening as expected, but pleading. She stepped to one side, catching one of its wing-arms and tipped the creature into the snow, where it lay crumpled and still. Gently, Lily drew back the fur flap of the Russian helmet.

"I been lookin' everywhere for Violet. She's run off again. I been lookin' all over and I can't find her no place. You seen my Violet?"

"Violet's safe in London," Lily said, trying to get Bill to his feet. "Let's go home now."

"I can't go home without my Violet."

Lily ignored his desperate objections. She dragged him to his feet, and forced his arm over her shoulder. He was not much taller than she but he was still muscled and a dead-weight. She gasped as the stench of his breath struck her: something besides his teeth had died in there. One step at a time, through drifts and over felled trunks with the cold icing her sweat and stiffening muscle against bone, Lily carried Bill the four hundred yards to the edge of their property. The sudden illumination of moonlight-on-snow in the clearing seemed to jar something in Bill's brain, and he said softly to Lily, standing on both feet, "You're Lily. Are we home now?" And they tramped together towards his darkened hut. Lily saw a dim glow in the window of her own house as they passed it, but no sound carried outward. The chimney was smokeless.

In the candlelight, Bill's kitchen was dank, cold and stinking of rotted food, mould, and urine. Her teeth chattering and her fingers numb, Lily found some bits of wood and paper, enough to get a smudged fire going in the ancient stove. She removed Bill's outer clothing, shielding herself from his asthmatic breathing with one forearm. From a pile in a corner she retrieved a wool sweater and pulled it around him like a shawl. He leaned towards the heat as Lily rubbed his stiff hands in her own. The flesh on his face drooped, sallow and cadaverous.

"When did you last eat?" Lily said, casting about for any signs of recent cooking. "Didn't you cook up that bacon I brung you Tuesday? You like bacon a lot."

"Violet always cooks the bacon," he said warily, his head slumping onto one shoulder.

Lily managed to get enough of a fire going to warm the pathetic little room and start a kettle boiling. She made some tea and then threw a handful of oatmeal into a pot. Both she attempted to feed to the barely conscious man in careful spoonfuls. Time and again she raised the spoon to his lips, but he wouldn't or couldn't take it. Why she began to hum she didn't know, but she felt Bill's neck muscles relax under her grip, and then heard her own voice, deep and instinctive. At first there were no words, no need for them, but they surfaced on their own and bore no meaning beyond the memories of the time and place they evoked.

Hi diddle dum, hi diddle dare-o

Hi diddly idly, hi diddle air-o

Hi diddle diddly, hi diddle um

Bill settled into a profound, restorative sleep, snoring like an exhausted horse, with his fingers, softened by the heat, curled in his lap like a baby's.

Lily didn't leave. She sat in that befouled and moribund room and thought of Maman LaRouche baking bread in the open-air oven; of Mama's hair unfolding in its last sunlight; of Old Samuel's flow of words as smooth as hickory smoke; of Southener's face as the sea-sands gently settled over it; of

Papa's grief as he stood fixed behind a tree, watching his child dissolve into the distance.

When Lily came in at last, Tom was sitting in the glow of a single coal-oil lamp. He had heard her step in the yard and was fully awake to face her. He had plotted both an offense and a defense, but when her eyes came into the light, all premeditation was swept away. Sober now and contrite, he wrapped her in his arms, even as he knew that her forgiveness would never be enough.

As for Lily, she was spent of all anger and instead of resentment felt only gratitude for the husband who was with her still. Half-way between midnight and dawn, Lily spoke of the things she had kept hidden, of the dreams that haunted her, her words unspooling as smoothly as spider's silk towards a web. But even as the old pain eased with each successive event, she sensed that she was passing the private burden of her past to the unpredictable mercies of her husband. From this moment onward, her history, with its attendant joys and griefs, would become part of the *materiel*of their relationship, available to interpretation and amendment. By the time she'd finished talking, the fire was a low smouldering, the light in the room radiant.

Tom held her close again, but his voice was steely. "God damn me to hell, but if I ever get these hands on any one of the bastards that hurt you, I'll squeeze the life right out of him."

On February 19, 1862, Hugh Nixon Shaw's drilling crew struck oil hundreds of feet below the gumbo surface of Enniskillen Township. It was to be the world's first recorded gusher and the world's first uncapped wildcat. History does not record what the near-penniless Nixon expected, but it was certainly not the gas-propelled blowout that shook the early-morning chill and sent a plume of hot, black syrup as high as the treetops and as wide as the snowscape around it. While the well remained uncapped, oil escaped in sticky rivulets towards Black Creek, where it slithered a ways in the ice and congealed. Someone from Pennsylvania arrived to improvise a method of staunching the wound, but not before an estimated thirty thousand gallons of oil had been lost. In the spring, an exotic sheen was observed on Black Creek and on the Sydenham River, and by early summer vast surfaces of Lakes St. Clair and Erie glistened eerily. The world's first oil slick had also been achieved.

The echo of that February blast reverberated far and wide, and the oil boom took on the intensity and surreality of a California gold rush. The town of Oil Springs would boast two thousand greedy souls by the year 1864 – a year or so before all boasting became bravado, the wells died of superfluity, and the rich and the broken departed on the same trains. Ten years after that particular Oil Springs boom, the last board of the last saloon was consumed in some anonymous hobo's bonfire among the twitch-grass and scrub hawthorn that had consumed the town site. Hugh Nixon Shaw saw none of this. He was asphyxiated in his own well on February 11, 1863.

On the morning of February 20, 1862, Chester Ramsbottom shook the sleep out of his eyes and stepped out of his warm shanty into the winter air. He liked staying out here alone even though Bridie worried about his occasional blackouts. Here he could think and dream and conjure his modest plans for the days and weeks ahead.

The boys had already arrived; he could hear the steam-engine starting up in the drilling area, a cacophony he could never quite get accustomed to. Bridie and Armbruster had gone over to the Shaw site yesterday afternoon and not returned. A loud blast had been heard from that direction and already rumours were flying. He could hear the excited buzz of the drillers under the relentless slamming of the bit into the rock fathoms below.

Chester decided to take it easy. He was a bit short of breath this morning and besides, he was well ahead of schedule: they would have more barrels than oil to fill them by spring. The Millar brothers had been sent home to attend the funeral of their youngest sister, felled suddenly by diphtheria. He thought of Lily.

Near the lean-to which he had rigged up with boughs and furs, Chester built a slow fire, fried some bacon, found he couldn't eat it, and lay down with his head against the supporting tree with a buffalo robe across his knees. Despite the nipping air and the thudding monotony of the drill, he drifted into sleep.

Sometime about noon on that day, New York and Upper Canadian Oil Explorations also struck oil, at a hundred and fifty-two feet, a well only half the size of the Shaw strike, but a bonanza nonetheless. It too came with mere seconds' warning, the crew scattering at the hoarse roar of underground breath released after eons of capture, and falling stunned into the brush as the top blew off with a volcanic crack and thunderous remonstration.

Uncle Chester popped upright as if he had been awakened suddenly by a dinner-gong, his eyes sprung from their dream, as wide and as vacant as a doll's, and blue as ball-bearings.

The funeral was held quite sensibly in the village of Petrolia where the Wesleyan Methodists has already erected a six-hundred-seat edifice to the glory of their version of the Divine Creator. Chester's mother had once been converted to this church. The good Reverend Kilreath reminded the tiny, shivering band of mourners of that fact, though he could think of few others to include in a necessarily abbreviated eulogy. The wind was cold enough to make a trespasser confess.

Lily stood beside Bridie and gazed at the casket ("shipped straight from London by express," Armbruster said in the husky shout he had concocted for solemn moments), set over a pit excavated out of the frozen earth. Tom was a step behind her, ready to take her arm. Nearby she could feel the bewildered, estranged presence of the Millar lads, three members of the crew, and the owner-operator of the Lucky Derrick. Bill had sobbed like a baby when Tom told him the news, but an hour later his mind failed him again. "When did you say young Chester was comin' back?" Bridie as usual contained her grief; she did not weep. Lily saw pain in her aunt's eyes only when she looked at her niece, her lips opening to say something, but then closing again in reluctant resignation. Then, as the minister drew the cross of sand over the coffin-lid and murmured the final words "dust to dust," Bridie went faint, slumping against Lily's grip. Armbruster stepped forward and steadied her, and Bridie let her head fall gratefully against his shoulder. Lily scarcely noticed. She was staring at the only other gravestones in the newly consecrated grounds: three white tablets in a neat row, each bearing the same family name: "Morton: Elijah, age 6; Sarah, age 3; Joshua, age 1; taken into the bosom of Our Lord in September of the year 1861." Last fall's scarlet fever epidemic. Behind her, Jimmy Millar sobbed without shame.

After the others had walked down to the carriages, Lily remained for a moment over her uncle's grave. Here, alone with whatever remained of his spirit, she tried to find some meaning in these windfall happenings. Old Samuels' words came back to her, about how the soul leaves its earthly housing only to seek some finer refuge out there in the spaces and seasons and harmonies that all along gave it nurture and definition. What spaces or seasons were there for Chester? What sense did his flesh make of this ground, this earth that was forest only a year before, now spouting oil from its slaughtered heart? Chester's hands, she thought, were a shopkeeper's hands, a woodcarver's hands at home with a doll's cradle or a toy gismo.

What sort of place has been reserved for him here?

Finally, she was able to weep, but not before she heard herself say – to Old Samuels or to the benign divinities wherever they were skulking on such a macabre afternoon –"Does all loving end like this?"

It was the kind of spring that made prolonged grieving seem an unwarranted indulgence. Crocuses and trilliums festooned the walkways in the woods. Winter wheat tossed its maiden-fuzz in the fields along the Errol Road. The earth turned easily under the spade. The air smelled of lilacs and orange blossom and wild crab.

Nonetheless, Lily encountered reminders every day – dust settling on Chester's workbench, his tools untouched, *Last of the Mohicans* under the washstand with its marker still in place – of her loss and her grief. In the evenings with Tom she was able to share some of these feelings, not always by talking about them specifically – though she noted how Tom contrived to raise Uncle Chester's name as often as he thought appropriate – but by simply having him in the room, close and companionably beside her. It was a comfort she could not recall ever having experienced before, and even as she allowed herself to soften into its consolation, she was only too aware of the evanescence of all things cherished.

On one of their long Sunday walks, Tom steered her gently through the windbreak and across the wide meadow towards the town-site. Though the only sounds were the cries of killdeer over the grass and the clarinet rasp of redwing blackbirds among the reeds of the marsh, Lily could see from the skeletons of half-built houses ahead that on weekdays the air must have clanged with the sounds of progress. The transformation of the ordnance grounds was well under way. Almost four blocks of homes were completed or under construction, mostly single-storey frame cottages set in civilized rows along the premeditated streets named for Queen and empire. Along Michigan Avenue, the only anomalous face among the royal suite, several brick buildings announced the arrival of commerce: a post office, Redmond's grocery, the Black Bass Inn and Tavern. Along Prince Street, facing the fields below the river, the first of the Grand Trunk hotels was rising brick by yellow brick.

"Three stories and thirty rooms," Tom said as they strolled by it. "The bigwigs will stay here, not overnight like they do in the Grand Station, but when they're assigned here for a lengthier stint." He grasped her hand tightly. "Come on over this way, I've got something to show you."

They walked east along Victoria where a block of cottages had been completed late last fall. Already the window boxes sprouted petunias and they found several families out on their shaded verandahs, digesting Sunday dinner. Tom stopped beside a cottage lovingly painted white, with a well-dug garden in back and a rose arbour in front.

"My boss's house," said Tom. "He rents it from the company."

"Are all these company houses?"

"More or less. It owns all the land, but if and when you can afford it, you can buy your house and property from them. They don't care as long as they make money."

He paused to let that thought settle.

"Well," Tom said, "do you like it?"

From somewhere inside they heard a baby squall and subside.

Though no pact was formally acknowledged, the accumulation of cash for an eventual move to the new village became their mutual project. Tom worked as much overtime as he could get. Lily sold her quilts at the Methodist bazaar and accepted occasional requests for mind-numbing seamstress work. She extended the garden as far as their shrunken acre would allow, and set up a stand at the end of the lane on Errol Road, now busy with traffic to the northern counties. She arranged for two township farmers to take some of their produce to Saturday market, though the profit was miniscule. Their lovemaking suffered somewhat when their enthusiasm was tempered by common fatigue. Yet Lily felt their love strengthening. All around them things were greening, lives were changing, and civilities multiplied. It seemed improbable that they too should not be swept along on such an irresistible tide of progress.

One evening early in September Tom did not come home for supper. He had assured her that there was no overtime work to be had for several weeks to come. At first Lily was worried, then annoyed, then anxious. There was still a little daylight when she saw Gimpy's unmistakable silhouette crossing the fields towards the windbreak. The pace and tilt of his stride told her that something was wrong. His expression confirmed it.

"He's been hurt?" she asked, trying to remember if the stove were okay to abandon as is.

Gimpy nodded, out of breath, his eyes casting about for some place safe to rest.

"How bad?"

"Real bad, ma'am. We can't wake him up."

"Please take me to him," Lily said, tightening her shawl.

"You got a Bible?" Gimpy rasped, trying to be helpful.

Tom was lying on the dock in the open where a barrel of nails had fallen on his head more than two hours before. Someone had covered him with dusty sacks. His eyes were seized shut, a dried trickle of blood in his hair and over his left eye, his breathing shallow but regular.

"We tried, tried everythin'," Bags Starkey, the foreman, said to Lily as she bent over her husband. "Cold cloths, ice from the barn, slappin' his face, pinchin' his cheeks, everythin'. He's been lyin' just like that ever since it happened."

"Where's the doctor?" Lily said.

"The one on Front Street, he's drunk an' can't be rolled over. The other one's out in the township somewhere on a call." He turned to the others for confirmation. Lily leaned over the death-mask of Tom's face and spoke softly but clearly into his ear. "It's me, Tom. It's Lily. I need to talk to you."

The onlookers were startled, even more so when Lily put her arms around her husband and pulled him into her embrace, kneeling beside him and holding his dead-weight with her own litheness. Several looked away. Lily continued to murmur sharply into Tom's ear until all of the men had averted their gaze, not knowing what to do or where to direct their pity.

Moments later, Tom's eyelids fluttered. He let out a huge, purging breath that sent chills up the spines of the men. Then a low groan as some particular pain was identified.

"Tom, listen to me. I got somethin' important to tell you." She pulled his limp hand across her belly. "I've got your baby in here," she said as loudly as she dare.

A month later, when a scar on his temple and a crackling good yarn were all that remained of Tom's brush with death, Lily was no longer lying.

Tom took the letter to Bridie, announcing the happy news, down to the post office in Sarnia so it would reach her more quickly. When he came home from work that same evening, he had a different letter in his hand. "It's from your aunt," he said. "I picked it up at our own post office not a few minutes ago."

Bridie's familiar script graced the envelope. He opened it eagerly and began reading aloud.

London, Canada West

October 20, 1862

Dear Tom and Lily:

Just a short note to let you know that Melville and I were married today at the Middlesex Court House. We leave tonight for New York. We've sold everything at Oil Springs. I'll send details from the City when we get there. Take care, Lily.

Love,

Bridie Armbruster

15

By the winter of 1862-63 it was accepted that both the Great Western and the Grand Trunk railways had come to stay in Lambton County. Each was foreordained to establish in its wake a settled and hopeful community. Port Sarnia, later Sarnia, had begun its economic life as a deep-water harbour on the Great Lakes system, but the welcome arrival of the Great Western had opened up the hinterlands behind it and guaranteed its fate as county town. Point Edward, by contrast, was an afterthought of the Grand Trunk, a place where the workers and their burdensome families might live while temporarily serving the cause of British mercantilist expansion. Where houses were necessary, so were streets – of a sort. Greater priority was assigned to the station-hotel itself, the construction of a chain of subsidiary inns of lesser comfort and repute along Michigan Avenue and Prince Street nearest the rail-yards, and the erection – in the spirit of free enterprise – of several capacious, rambling three-storey clapboard houses to serve as warrens for dozens of itinerant navvies and stevedores. The spring of 1863 saw such facilities well established, along with several stores, two taverns, a post office and a barber shop. Point Edward was a motley, uncoordinated, boyish hamlet, mere appendage to a grinding dynamo. Unlike its ambitious neighbour, puffed with Scots' bravado and cunning, it had no sense at all of itself, of what it might become, of the pain it would eventually suffer merely to be born.

"You must stop working so hard," Tom said.

Lily remembered that hard work hadn't done her harm the last time, but she thought it best not to express the sentiment.

"I'll let you know when I'm not up to it." And she pushed him out into the overnight snowfall – the first of the season – and watched him plant his boot prints all the way up to the windbreak. Inside, she could feel the child clinging to her with both of its tiny hands.

Humming, doing a shy two-step, she cleared up the breakfast dishes, banked both fires, ate an extra slice of bread-and-molasses, and settled in beside her quilting frame. This one's for you, she said aloud, whatever your name shall be. When her eyes grew strained and her leg cramped, she got up, put her coat and boots on, and walked across to Bill's.

"You gotta eat, Bill," she shouted in his ear, the steam of her breath filling the hutch. She wrapped his shoulders with one of his stinking shawls and got a bit of a fire going.

Bill grunted something, but she was unable now to understand any of his words, if indeed any were intended. At times she thought he might be trying to sing or to recite some faded chant from his boyhood, his mouth producing a wavering note as if an errant breeze had blown over a castaway fiddle. Then it was her turn to hum a tune from her own childhood – sweet, reminiscent, lullaby-low – until his face softened and he would lie back in his chair by the window. Sometimes, then, he would eat.

Twice a week Lily walked into the village to do some shopping at Redmond's store at Durham's Dry Goods. The storekeepers nodded pleasantly to her, often called her by name, sometimes chatted about the weather or the progress being made down "at the yard." Lily smiled and gradually, as she assured Tom over supper, she was learning how to chat idly and even enjoy it. Twice the Grand Trunk had allowed the round-house and car-shop gang use one of the small rooms in the station complex for a Saturday night gathering, and Lily and Tom attended both parties. The men drank whiskey by the cup from a barrel while the wives and lady-friends bunched in the corners gossiping. Tom kept himself free from the whiskey and danced with Lily most of the night, at the cost of much barbed teasing from his mates. Between numbers, Lily talked to the other young wives. They seemed to like her. She was invited to tea. She surprised herself and Tom by accepting.

"Well, how did you like Maudie Bacon?" Tom asked, after one such social outing.

"She's very nice. She was raised on a farm in Moore township near Froomfield. She remembers the Millars and she was friends with the Partridge girls."

"So you did more than chank cakes and cheese?" he said, reaching for one of Lily's own muffins. "This time next year we should be thinking about picking out a place of our own. Maybe in the same block as Maudie's. You'd like that, eh?"

Lily nodded. "First things first, though," she said, glancing down.

Lily went again to Maudie's house, a neat white cottage with a brick chimney and a fancy metal stove to keep it cozy through the winter. Maudie was friendly and incurably chatty; she quizzed Lily on every aspect of her history in Moore township, and to her surprise Lily found herself not only answering but volunteering extra detail, embellishment, even. The ladies – farm girls everyone who had married young and willingly trailed their husbands to the excitement of the new towns – seemed particularly titillated by her stories about Old Samuels, Sounder and Acorn. Afterwards she felt vaguely guilty and if Tom asked her how her "hen session" went, she would snap at him or keep a morose silence as long as she could bear to. He put her moods down to the delicacy of her condition.

Lily recognized that Tom was genuinely happier than before. He liked the winter work, in part because he hated the slave-labour of the summers in the freight-sheds. But also because in the car-shops he could use his hands and his brains. He could work in concert with a select crew assessing problems and improvising solutions as the rolling stock limped or was dragged into their repair depot with all manner of fracture and trauma, casualties of rough stints on the open rails that now stretched from Portland, Maine, to Chicago. And even though Tom might never be a master carpenter, he liked the challenge, the camaraderie and the unpredictability of their daily routine. Early in March, after Lily had complained of unusually severe cramps in her stomach, Tom arrived home from work with a brisk little man in tow.

"This is Dr. Dollard from Sarnia," Tom said, unwrapping their guest from a black beaten-lambswool coat.

"How do you do, Mrs. Marshall," the doctor intoned absently, waving her to a nearby cot.

"I've had some crampin', doctor. Maybe somethin' I ate."

Dr. Dollard ignored this and all subsequent remarks from Lily or Tom, who was determined to be helpful. Primly he drew Lily's skirt and half-slip away to expose the stretched skin beneath. He tapped, tamped, and plumbed, giving out every once in a while untranslated "ahs" and "hmms."

He wheeled around to Tom.

"Your wife is at least seven months pregnant," he announced. "She is not eating enough to sustain two life-systems, hence the stomach cramps. She is getting too much exercise, hence the general faintness and wan complexion. I recommend a bottle of *Ayer's Sarsaparilla* for the stomach. That'll be sixty-three cents for the medicine and a dollar for the visit."

Tom blanched.

"Pay me when you can," Dr. Dollard flashed an avuncular smile at Lily. "The young lady's health is the main thing. When she goes into labour, send a message for me, day or night, and I'll come straightaway. You know where I am." He put a bottle of patent medicine on the table, shook Tom's hand, rescued his coat and decamped.

"Tom," Lily said, waving off the *Sarsasparilla*, "I want you to promise me one thing."

"Anything," he said.

"I want a midwife for this baby."

By the next day Lily was feeling fine. She got some food into Bill and walked him out to his privy and back. When he spotted the medicine bottle in her apron pocket, he grunted avidly. She left it beside him on the arm of his chair and by the time she got the door jammed shut, he had consumed it all. I hope he's not pregnant, she thought, skipping through the snow to get the baby's attention. It responded with a surly kick. No sense of humour, she laughed, and stretched her lungs against the brisk late-winter air.

Tom was waiting. "Your informants are correct," he said. "There *is* a local midwife. I went to see her. She said she knows where we live. In fact, she seemed to know all about us. She'll come when you need her."

"Thank you," Lily said. "But you look worried. Somethin' wrong with her?"

"She's got a terrific reputation around here," Tom said slowly, selecting his words with care, "but she lives down past Prince Street, towards the dunes, where the squatters are."

"You don't think she oughta come?"

"I didn't say that," Tom said and his glance told her: *I know, I promised.*

No more was said on the subject.

On the first day of spring the screw-prop grain-carrier *Lake Erie* nudged its bulk through the scattered ice-floes of the St. Clair River and docked at the Point Edward elevator. A day later Tom was moved from the car-shops to his summer job in the freight-sheds: lugging crates from ship to box-car and box-car to ship. The new regional manager, Warden Hargreaves, who set up temporary personal quarters in the luxury suite of the Queen's Hotel on Prince Street, promised Tom that there was a good chance he could be made part of the permanent repair crew by the following spring. That hope and the more certain promise of a child to carry on his name buoyed his spirits considerably. So much so that only Lily could detect the minute signs of tension and strain that habitually afflicted him at this time of year. Although her own back had begun to throb, especially after a full day over her quilting – she'd sold two to Mrs. Salter, and Tom had put the cash in the Sarnia bank – she spent the evenings of early April rubbing liniment into Tom's back and arms. Outside, the snow-flushed creek and sudden freshets chattered their way across the wakened landscape.

"We oughta start diggin' the garden," Lily said.

"We don't need a garden this year," Tom said. "And next year somebody else can worry about this place. Don't you go near it, you hear?"

Lily heard. Nonetheless, she did slip out as soon as the sun was up and burning through the green gauze of the trees and bushes. But the baby had dropped and she felt as wobbly as a pear, so she merely pruned the perennials as best she could and scraped away the detritus from the fall harvest. No spading, she thought, I've got to be very careful. Unless I can rouse Bill to some work. She could tell by the sun that it was barely mid-afternoon. She turned and started over to Bill's hut when her eye caught a movement near the windbreak. It was Tom, coming at full tilt across the field which lay between them and the village proper. She met him, breathless, at the tree-line.

"It's Bags Starkey," Tom said. "A crate carrying half a locomotive boiler fell on his legs. Crushed both his feet. He's bleeding real bad. They don't want to move him too far. They need sheets for bandages."

Lily ran towards the house without a moment's hesitation. "For God's sake, Lil!" Tom yelled, but he fell to his knees, panting helplessly.

That evening, Tom relayed the terrible details of Bags' accident.

"He's alive, but that's about all you can say. He wasn't supposed to be in there lifting, but the crate was badly built and it got stuck, and ol' Bags must've thought he was still a spring chicken the way he tore into it and swore away at us till the damn thing came loose, and buried him. We had to get it off with a block and tackle, and not once did the man cry out."

She didn't encourage him, but he had to let it out.

"Both feet crushed like tomato pulp, blood was squirting everywhere. Gimpy was sick all over himself. But Bags is a tough bugger. And the doctor says he'll likely have both his feet, though the bones won't ever set straight and there's still a chance of gangrene. His cousin came down from London; they're holed up in a little rooming house on George Street. We went to see him today. The company's gonna dock our pay, but we went anyway."

"We could take up a collection or somethin'," Lily said very quietly. "I got lots of preserves left."

"He's got no job, Lily. They told him yesterday. He begged for an office job, swore he'd be better in a month, he'd be able to get 'round on crutches. He knows the operation, he's been with them for six years, from the very beginning. Warden Hargreaves said he was sorry but he was only carrying out company policy, orders given way over his head and all that shit. You know the line."

Lily nodded, then a sliver of fear shot through her.

"I've made up my mind," he said. "I'm going to see Hargreaves tomorrow. In his office. I'm going to get Bags Starkey's job back."

"Don't do it," Lily said.

"I've got to. If I don't try, I won't be able to live with myself."

"I understand that," Lily said. "And I know what'll happen. I'm only askin' for the baby's sake, not my own."

"Nothing will ever happen in this world," Tom said angrily, "unless somebody is willing to stand up and be counted. Somebody has to fight."

Lily wanted to reply, but she held her peace.

The next day, Tom reported the results. "Well," he said to her, his fury undiminished, "I got the satisfaction of telling that cowardly bastard what I thought of him." His hands shook as he poured himself a mug of cold tea. Lily was knitting in the rocker by the south window. She felt Tom's stare on her, keen as an accusation.

"An' he fired you," Lily said without emotion.

"He certainly did not." Tom pounced on her presumption. "He only had the guts to suspend me," Tom announced triumphantly.

Lily heard him scrabbling under the sink for the big jug.

"I got a free holiday till October," he laughed. She heard the gurgle of raw whiskey. "Can't do without me in the car-shops. What do you think of that, eh?"

What Lily thought of it mattered little. What it meant was that without a garden and at best a bit of casual work for Tom over the summer, they would have to spend every cent of their savings just to survive. There would be no white-walled cottage in the new village.

Gimpy arrived to console his friend through the bleak evening ahead. Lily went to the bedroom and lay down. Even with the comforter wrapped around her, she found herself shivering. She caught no conversation from the other room, only low mutterings and occasional curses accompanied by the steady clink of crockery. With her teeth chattering she rose in the darkness, fumbled under the bed till she felt the leather sachet in her grasp, opened it and drew into her hand the familiar talisman. Its allusive warmth spread through her whole body and beckoned sleep her way. When she woke in the morning, the magic jasper lay on her chest, beating there like a hummingbird's ruby heart.

She stepped into the quick heat of the big room. The kitchen stove throbbed jovially. Tom was standing by the door, fully dressed, his walking boots agleam. In the crook of his arm lay the twelve-gauge double-barrel.

"Where're you goin'?" Lily asked.

"You all right? You had a lot of covers on you."

"Where're you goin' with that?"

He grinned, and she saw with relief the blend of daring and reserve she so loved and trusted. "I'm going hunting," he said. "Rabbits. Got to put food on the table, now don't we?"

With the baby due in a few weeks, Tom tried hard to adjust to the situation he had put himself in. He was positively heroic in his attempts to keep himself busy and useful. He went hunting up in First Bush almost every morning. He helped Gimpy and Maudie's husband, Garth, trap a few tardy muskrats down along the verges of the swamp. Their skins hung stretched and reeking in the little barn beside the latest slaughtered cottontail. He walked over to Sarnia to hang around the boiler works or one of the sawmills in hope of picking up some casual labour. In these ways he managed to keep out of the house till suppertime and arrive home with his signature grin in place. Sometimes she would stretch out on the cot after supper, and Tom would run a caressing hand over her belly for what seemed like hours on end, neither of them saying a word, the slow sunset easing darkness into the spaces around them like a spell. They marvelled at the baby's energy, throwing tantrums of fist-and-feet in several directions and at times of its own choosing. Lily's back ached with the weight. It's all right, she kept telling it – him – you just keep kicking. I want you big and strong and alive.

While they were eating supper one evening early in May, Gimpy arrived with a telegram clutched in his hand. "Come in on the telegraph 'bout an hour ago. I told Farley I'd bring it on up here, thought I'd better."

From the anxiety on his face and his reluctance to hand over the fretful paper, Lily was certain he had seen the news and that it was dreadful.

"It's your auntie," he said, looking away.

Tom snatched the envelope from Gimpy's hand and tore it open.

Seven months and not a word from Bridie. No further explanation of the hasty marriage and departure from Oil Springs; no acknowledgment of their letter with what should have been the most welcome news for her. *I don't even know where you are, Bridie, Lily thought not without bitterness; I can't comfort you if you need me, I can't give you a better reason for living. I don't know what to do with this stored-up, useless love.*

Tom was mumbling over the words of the telegram as he read. She saw him go pale, and while her heart sank, she knew perfectly well that Bridie was not dead. All winter long, she'd heard her voice in the hollows of sleep, in the dream below dreams – not as it used to be, brave and clear and certain, but very faint, a voice calling out yet too weary or bewildered to compose a full cry for help. *You are alive, Bridie:what are you trying to tell me?*

"It's Elspeth," Tom said. "She's had some kind of attack. She wants me in London, as soon as possible."

Tom's letter from London, which Gimpy helped her decipher, said that he would be away at least a week. But she was not to worry: Aunt Elspeth had merely suffered a faint one morning and fallen down against her bedstead. She had a nasty bruise on her temple, but was as cheery as ever, and she and Lucille were determined to spoil him. Elspeth was wildly excited about the expected arrival and bent on living long enough to see Tom's son heading a regiment someday. The doctor reported that she may have had a mild stroke but he did not see any cause for alarm. In the last sentence – delivered with a wondrous blush from Gimpy – Tom urged her to cross her legs tight till he could get home.

Meanwhile, Gimpy came by every afternoon and Maudie brought her some baking and helped with the housework. Lily had occasional trouble getting to sleep, and when she did, the dreams that assailed her from the deep part of night left her sweating and exhausted in the morning. She remembered she didn't even know the midwife's last name.

The night before she expected Tom home, Lily surprised herself by falling into a dreamless sleep. The evening had been very warm for mid-May, the air suffused with lilac and wild-apple blossom. She lay down on top of the comforter with only a cotton nightshirt on, gazing at the swell of her flesh until sleep relieved her of all speculation. Sometime towards dawn the wind shifted to the east and blew with the abandon of a spring storm. When Lily woke, the sun was up but smothered by a skyful of nimbus cloud bullying its way westward. The wind roared through the pinery and fern-leafed hardwoods with the hoarse clamour of a doomsday horn. She sat bolt upright, and before she was certain she was even awake, Lily found herself outside.

Soaked, shivering, fearful with dread, she made for the battered door of Bill's hut. She stood there until her breathing steadied and a resolute calm took hold. It's happened, she thought. She pushed the door aside and went in.

Bill was dead, though she had to walk over and touch him to confirm it. He was sitting where he always did, in his chair by the only window, with a clear view of the lane, his neighbour's cottage and the rising sun over the tree-line. His eyes were wide open, full of arrested anticipation, and seemed focussed down the lane that ended at the Errol Road, as if he were at any moment expecting the arrival of someone dear to his heart.

Hours later, Lily was still sitting by her stove, wrapped in a shawl and wondering if she could walk all the way to the village for assistance with Bill, when she heard Tom's call from the road. She went out to greet him, embarrassed by the flush of joy she felt but driven by the urgency of Bill's demise. What she saw stopped her breath. Tom was striding down the lane waving to her, and behind him, skipping to keep pace, bounced a slight female figure, also waving. Lily waited until they were almost upon her before she allowed herself to believe it was Lucille.

Old Bill, as they were always to remember him, was buried in the public cemetery of Sarnia less than half-a-mile from the property he had occupied for as long as anyone could recall. Tom sent a telegram to the asylum in London, hoping they could find some way to tell Violet. In the meantime the sheriff's bailiffs arrived to claim the valuables. It appeared that Bill had not paid his taxes with the money Tom gave him and the Grand Trunk bought him out for the sums owed. Warden Hargreaves, it was said, had personally intervened to keep the acquisition quiet and permit the man to live out his days in security and dignity. The day after the funeral Tom received word back from the authorities in London.

"Violet's gone," Tom said. "It says here she ran off three days ago and they haven't found a trace of her anywhere."

Lucille's arrival was a welcome distraction from fresh sorrows. Tom explained her availability: Aunt Elspeth had recovered sufficiently to travel to Toronto for an extended visit with the Colonel's sister, long a widow and now quite frail and in need of companionship. Hence, Lucille was to be despatched, at some personal sacrifice, to assist the baby's entry into the world, after which she was to come to Toronto and escort Aunt Elspeth back to Lambton to inspect and approve.

Lucille was a joy and a wonder. Freed from the supervisory affection of Mrs. Edgeworth, she became a volatile blend of wood-nymph and street-urchin. She never walked where she could flit, saunter, glide or dart. She assaulted the objects in a room with her flung glances: "Oh, Lily, what a *beautiful* quilt!" "What a sweet little tea-pot!" "Where on *earth* did you get calico with them colours!" She filled the kitchen and big room with a quarter-acre of lilacs stripped from every lane within a mile's radius. When she was excited, which was a good deal of the time, she lapsed into a headlong patter where French and English vied for supremacy, to the detriment of sense but the sheer delight of any listener. Lily and Lucille told each other the stories they had rehearsed back in London, but now with more flair, more dazzle, and a lot less crippling veracity. They spoke endlessly about the baby, its restless energy and demanding requirements, even before birth.

"My *Maman* had a lot of kids, you know. She swell out like a pumpkin every spring and *woosh*, down she go every September. But Maman always wear a big dress, like a tent, an' so we never got to see what shape the pumpkin take under all that. Always I wonder, eh?"

Since the baby was late – it was already the first week in June – and Lily seemed to spend much of her day with Lucille, Tom took more and more time away from home. He hounded the numerous small factories in Sarnia but got precious little work for the hours he put in to the search. Though he refused to admit it openly, Lily knew that somehow the word had been passed from above and was being obeyed. Even the Great Western, competitor of the Grand Trunk, could find no spot for an experienced hand. When Tom took up the spade and headed into their garden, she knew for certain that he too had given up.

But he was still her Tom, a man of spirit, and she loved him till her heart ached whenever he came into the kitchen smiling and teasing "his girls."

"Gimpy and the fellas think I got a harem up here!" he'd say, leering at Lucille.

"Well, ain't ya'?" she'd say right back.

Or he'd come across to Lily at the stove, wheel her about for a kiss, give her belly a lustful bunt and say, "You'll have to lean forward, missus, there's somebody standing between us."

Later, in the gloom of dusk, Lily would watch him hacking at the clods in the garden, harrowing his hands twice as badly as the tough earth, trying as always to overwhelm it, or cow it with a quixotic show of force. On the fifteenth of June he walked up the Errol Road and hired on with the first farmer he saw behind a team of plough-horses. Two days later she saw him sneak into Benjamin's stall where he kept a jug of soul-restorer poorly hidden. When he came to bed in the middle of the night, he curled his body behind hers as close as he could fit it, and slid his scarred hands around her breasts. "I do love you," he whispered.

After breakfast that Sunday, while Lucille was helping Lily with the dishes, Tom poked his head into the room and said, "There's horses in the lane." Still wiping their hands on their aprons, they got outside in time to see a matched team of Belgians hauling behind them an over-sized buckboard very like the one used to deliver beer barrels from the new brewery. The driver, swatting occasionally at the reins, and his assistant, with both hands grappling the bench beneath them, managed to steer the vehicle

sedately up to the gate of the Marshall place.

"Where in sam hell did you learn to drive horses?" Tom hollered as he dashed across to the visitors.

"I worked for a week in an abattoir," Gimpy said. "Good mornin', ladies. I hope you'll pardon the intrudin', but me gentleman friend here felt the need of a little airin'."

The gentleman was Bags Starkey. Thin, wan, shivering despite the gathering heat of the day, he unhooked his hands and flashed a huge smile at Lucille and Lily as they came over to the buckboard.

"Mornin', Mrs. Marshall, Tom. I don't believe I've had the honour of –"

"Lucille Verchères," Tom said.

"Ah, ça va bien, ma'amselle? "

While Lucille blushed and attempted to find a dry hand to offer, Lily and Tom tried not to look at his feet, or rather the yards of white bandage that had been wrapped around them and that, except for the stipple of dried blood, might have been mistaken for giant baby booties.

"This here's Robert Starkey," Gimpy said. "He speaks English, too."

"Just call me Bags, everybody does except my mother," Bags said. "Could we interest anyone in a drive through the countryside? Best of accommodations."

"We got Barney and Sue here for the whole day," Gimpy said, never taking his eyes off Lucille. "We're tryin' to dry 'em out."

"Might even rouse the interest of someone we're all waitin' to meet," Bags said, gripping the bench with his left hand so he could teeter over to wink in Lily's direction.

"Why don't we take *you*for a ride," Lily said.

Tom was staring grimly at Bags' swaddled feet.

Bags fitted very nicely into Uncle Chester's wicker wheelchair, retrieved from the woodshed and padded out with pillows. With Gimpy pushing and Tom stationed at the vehicle's left wheel, Bags, his lady companion and her duenna promenaded past the garden, where they admired the early radish. They whirled at the barn and headed back by an even more circuitous route. "Quite splendid! Simply charming!" Bags shouted, "And only the servants live there, you say!"

"*Oui, capitaine-le*" Lucille giggled, skipping to keep up with the postilion's pace.

Bags pulled a mouth-organ from his back pocket, wincing a bit as one of his legs hit bottom, and began to play a jig, sprightly and yet ever so delicate. Lily and Lucille joined hands and performed on the lawn of their dooryard a somewhat Gallic version of the Irish national ditty, ending with panting and laughter.

Bags began to play again, a soft, melodious air that sang of something lost and green and never-again-to-be-possessed. Part-way through a tiny voice joined in and made the morning complete:

Un Canadien errant
Banni des foyers
Un Canadien errant
Banni des foyers
Parcourait en pleurant
Des pays étrangers

After a convivial lunch served out of doors, the two visitors prepared to take their leave. Bags smiled again at the ladies, winked at Tom, and then waved one brave hand from his perch on the buckboard. Gimpy whipped the horses to life, Lucille's farewell kiss still burning on his cheek. The rig clattered down the lane and muffled all farewells. Just before it disappeared into the trees at the big bend, Bags hunched over, as if he'd taken a cramp, and let his head hang helplessly between his knees.

Lily squeezed Lucille's hand. Then she looked for Tom. He had turned resolutely in the direction of the barn.

"You better fetch Tom," Lily said.

Lucille went white. *"Le bébé?"*

"Yes. Tell Tom to get the midwife. It's not gonna be long."

"He's gone, Lily. I didn't want to wake you up for supper, you looked so peaceful –"

"Where'd he go?"

"Off to the town, I think. Oh, Lily he was –"

"Don't start cryin' on me," Lily said. "Please listen. Stoke up that stove real good. Fill the water tank all the way up. Get out the clean flannels I put in the hamper. Then go into the village. Ask around for Tom. If you can't find him, see if you can find the midwife."

Lily let out a wrenching cry that caused the saucepan to leap right out of Lucille's hands. "What the matter? *Mon Dieu, mon Dieu!*"

"It's just a labour pain," Lily said when she could feel her heart again. "The little bugger wants out."

Lucille didn't laugh, and Lily saw at once that the girl was terrified – and not at all familiar with childbirth.

"I'll tend to the fire," Lily said. "You go for Tom and the midwife."

"But how do I find this – this *sage-femme?*" she said.

"Just *ask*, you silly girl," Lily snapped. Lily waved her over to the cot, put her arm around her, and then holding her chin gently, said to her: "Don't worry, *ma petite*. We've done this all before, haven't we? Just go to Mr. Redmond's place, the grocery on the main street. He'll still be there. Ask him to fetch the midwife for you. Then bring her here. Okay?"

"Okay."

"Her name's Sophie. She lives where the squatters stay down by the dunes. That's all I know."

As Lucille reached the door, Lily let out another cry, and Lucille started back.

"Go! And hurry," Lily gasped out. "Please."

Lucille disappeared into the withered sunset.

The pains were coming about seven or eight minutes apart as far as Lily could judge. They were as raw and frightening as the last time, perhaps more so because she knew how long they would continue, and how much more frequently they would come to remind her how cowardly and insignificant and dispensable she really was, a mere web of nerve and muscle. Like millions of child-bearers before her, she knew she would cry out for relief and expiation, would curse the universe that could look on with such indifference while the pain wracked from within as if it were rending the body apart with a single, whittled fingernail.

Why did you leave me? she heard a voice like hers shout from the underworld of her pain. *I need you, Bridie. I do.*

An hour later, only the glow from the stove-pipes offered any light to the room when the door burst open and a burly figure strode to stage-centre and stalled, as if wondering in which direction the audience lay.

"Jesus-Christ-in-a-butter-box! Where in hell's the light?"

Lucille, a trembling silhouette in the wake of this overbearing presence, flitted across to where she had left Lily. "It's *la sage-femme*, she's come with me."

"So I hear," Lily whispered weakly. The midwife was already at the stove, taking charge with ferocious efficiency. Flames shot through the grate and smoke retreated up the chimney-flue. Wielding a lighted chip, the woman broached several lamps and within seconds every object in the room softened into view.

"Well now, ain't that a damn sight better? You must be the victim," she said, ambling over to Lily who was struggling to sit up, a cautionary hand on her abdomen. "I'm Sophie Potts."

"I'm Lily. And I think you've come just in time."

"I've heard all about you," Sophie said, and she bent over Lily, easing her gently down with a fleshy hand that looked as if it could milk a herd of Holsteins. "My, my, you got a live one in there, my girl."

Without turning from Lily she barked directions at Lucille: "Get fresh wood on that fire. I want that water hot enough to boil a baker's bowlin' balls. Then haul the oil-cloth off of that table an' throw it across the bed back there. Then bring all the pillows an' sheets you can find. We gotta make this young'un as comfortable as we can. Right, dearie?"

Lily cried out and her body thrashed. Quickly both of Sophie's hands were laid on Lily's convulsing muscles, like a phrenologist divining truth from a skull's topology. "Wonderful...wonderful...Such power for a pretty little sunfish like you." She kneaded and soothed. Her milkmaid's fingers seemed to communicate directly with the rolling musculature under them.

"We got about half an hour, I'd say," Sophie said, "so let's get you off of this cadet cot and on to somethin' soft an' motherly."

She reached down, wrapped both arms around Lily, and lifted her into the air. Sophie's arms were plump and pink, but their strength gave Lily immediate reassurance . When Sophie breathed extravagantly on her, Lily caught the echoes of garlic, herring-smelt and improvised whiskey.

While Sophie held Lily aloft, Lucille covered the bed with the oil-cloth and several layers of clean sheets. She fluffed two feather pillows. Sophie laid Lily down as carefully as she would a bruised bird.

"Hang on," she said, clasping Lily's right hand just as the convulsion struck and struck again. Lily's scream brought Lucille to her toes with a snap.

"It's okay," Sophie said in a different voice. "It's Nature's way. You gotta holler or you'll bust open like a milkweed pod. Now you bring Sophie in her medicine kit." The cramp had eased off, but Lily kept her grip on Sophie's hand.

Suddenly there was a clatter and a thump outside the house.

"Shit," Sophie hissed, "I forgot all about the bastard."

She rumbled past Lucille to the door, then returned with her catch. "I found him pissed to the gills in Car-teer's pig-sty," Sophie said, pulling Tom's stumbling figure into the light. "Carted the silly-ass as far as the back-garden an' plunked him down in the compost heap where I figured he'd feel more at home. Some sight, eh?" And she released a laugh like a trumpet-blast that made the baby lurch in its nest. "I reckoned he belonged to you!"

Tom moaned and tried to sit up, in which position he hoped that his eyes might actually open to something familiar.

Lily came right off the sheets, her nightshirt flung as wide as her cry.

"Oh *Maman, Maman*," Lucille sobbed.

Sophie put one paw on Lucille and the other on Tom. "Go put some coffee on," she said to Lucille with such force that the girl stiffened with more resolve than fear, "stick a funnel down his throat an' start pourin'." With that she jerked Tom out of the room and dumped him onto the cot.

"I'm sorry, Lily, real sorry," Tom called with great effort, attempting to overcome his slur.

"You stay put," Sophie shouted back to him from the doorway. "We don't need you. You done your damage about nine months ago, though I'm damned if I know how you managed it."

Lucille got the coffee boiling in a saucepan and somehow managed to administer it to Tom, who was jolted out of his fog by the staccato of cries from the other room. Tom winced, then shuddered as each one nicked him like a sniper's bullet. He barely recognized them as his wife's voice.

At last, Sophie came out of the bedroom with the baby in her arms, Lucille at her side. Tom was seated almost upright at the kitchen table. "It's a boy!" Lucille announced.

"How's Lily?"

"Lily's fine," Sophie affirmed.

"Thank God," Tom said, rising.

"Thank me an' Mother Nature," Sophie said, opening her treasure to display a bawling, blood-smeared being with its knotted umbilical raffishly displayed.

Tom peered into its bluish eyes, astonished that already they were staring back at him, perhaps some primitive, fearful thought about the world even now collecting in its tiny brain. "How can I ever thank you," Tom said.

Sophie gave him a steady, mocking appraisal. "First, I charge five bucks," she said with a sort of sly cackle as she turned to lead them all back into Lily's room. "An' second, I'd like a nip of that hair-straightener you tore into this evenin'."

Lily, pale as the flower of her name, held the child close to her. Her eyes drooped with exhaustion, but she refused to give up consciousness, wanting to seal the baby's arrival with her unceasing adoration.

"He'll be here when you wake up," Lucille whispered tenderly in her ear. "So will we, *certain.*"

Sophie took several jars from a knapsack and put them on the dresser. "Now Lucille dear, you soak them cloths in this here linseed oil, then put on plenty of this powder, then put the whole shebang onto your lady's injured parts – three times a day. An' throw out the rags when you're done."

"What's this bottle for?"

"That's nerve tonic. Special recipe. Good for just about everythin' bad."

"How often do Lily have to take it?"

Sophie snorted. "It's not for Lily," she said. "It's for the perpetrator."

Tom lay beside Lily. In the kitchen Lucille hummed a Norman ditty. The kettle steamed. Young Robert had both chubby hands on his mother's breast, sucking nourishment into his sturdy body with abandon and no particular thanks. Lily was quite happy to have their firstborn named for Bags Starkey. It seemed right, in so many ways.

"You get to name the girl," Tom said.

I already have, Lily thought.

"And isn't that Potts woman the most foul-mouthed creature you ever laid eyes on?"

Lily changed breasts, and smiled. "She *was* nice, wasn't she?"

16

Robert Marshall was born into the pastoral world of Canada West on June 19, 1863. He suckled lustily and his tiny limbs grew apace.

The Grand Trunk, inspired by a government loan, took on extra help, including past miscreants, so Tom went back to his part-time labour with a light and willing step.

Lucille stayed on, her good cheer interrupted only by those moments when she would stop in the midst of a chore – scrubbing a pot, feeding the stove – and stare across at mother-and-child, overcome by a sense of wonder, pure and inexplicable.

Lily allowed little separation between herself and her baby. He was never more than an elbow's length from her, day or night. She could not yet bring herself to call him Robert; he was just "baby," then "Nubbins"– a miraculous miniature she and Tom had created out of their own ecstasies and who, for the moment, served only to extend and refine the sensual tips of her body: lips, nipples, grazing fingertips, nuzzling nose. Thus it was that sometime about the middle of July, Tom lifted the sleeping babe from between them, laid it in its bassinet, and reclaimed the warmth of that space, draping his angular, urgent length along her own. Lily was astonished to find her legs opening, as of old, to accommodate her husband's desire and equally strange, when the climax shook her sideways and brought her upright with gazelle's eyes. Lucille moaned in her sleep, and hung on.

Only two things brought a ripple of discontent to Lily's perfect summer. Lucille was asked by Aunt Elspeth to accompany her back to Toronto, where they would take up permanent residence. That good woman had made the train trip unescorted in the end, on the Grand Trunk day-express, which she was convinced, with all its shaking and clatter, had designs on her sanity. Nevertheless, she arrived safely at the Point Edward station, where she was greeted by her "dear Tippy" who had at last settled down and made a man of himself. If she needed further proof of his conversion, it was evident on her arrival at the Marshall homestead, where she was introduced to Robert, the spitting image of the dead Colonel, and to whom she offered her blessing.

She was also discreet enough not to ask if the babe had been christened: not knowing was, in this particular case only, the more bearable of the alternatives.

In almost every way Aunt Elspeth seemed her usual, vital self. She showered Lily, Lucille and the infant with small, lovingly selected gifts. Her unaffected warmth spread through the household and the neighbourhood. During her week's stay, she left her mark (and money) in every store and establishment along Michigan Avenue. She had taken rooms in the Grand Trunk station-hotel, insisted on dining lavishly there with Lily and Tom, then Lily and Lucille, and finally Tom alone. She left a trunkful of clothes for Lily.

"Use them for rugs or your quilts if you find them too old-fashioned, but I don't need them anymore, a woman of my age and advanced reputation," and she laughed in that wonderful way she had of including herself in the joke.

On the day of her departure she spent a long, quiet minute alone in the bedroom with Robert while Lucille fidgeted by the door and Tom held the horses of the buggy he'd rented for the occasion. Aunt Elspeth had insisted that she sleep at least one night "in the abode of the people I love the dearest." They put her in Lily's old bedroom with Lucille. Everyone, it seemed, had spent most of the night listening to the baby's soft breathing. Aunt Elspeth smiled bravely through Lucille's weeping as the goodbyes were said. "Buck up, girl, we'll be back for Christmas, that's a promise. And as soon as the little tyke's old enough, we'll have him on the train to Toronto to see us."

Lily felt in Elspeth's desperate farewell hug that there was more to tell. Tom revealed it at noon when he returned from his half-day's work in the sheds.

"Her health's all right. The stroke left her weak but you can see she's capable of exerting herself when she has a will, and a reason."

"What's wrong, then?"

"She's utterly broke. Bankrupt."

"But how?"

"She had to sell the house and everything in it last month. The sheriff and bailiffs did it all. That's why she moved to Toronto, I think. She didn't want to be there when it happened. The Colonel left her little but the property. She should have sold half of it and lived off the money, but she had no head for business. She just mortgaged the place twice over till it was time to go.

Her sister-in-law's taken her in. Elspeth sold some jewellery to pay for this trip. I got it all out of her at lunch on Thursday. I'd been sworn to secrecy."

"What can we do?"

Tom shook his head in resignation. "She always detested my Aunt Sylvia."

One evening in September, Tom and Lily walked farther than usual. They turned north at the river to skirt the squatter's shacks and strolled along the beach below the dunes. It was an Indian summer evening, thin yet still mellow, the heat of day snoozing on the cool night-air drifting in from the placid lake. Herring-gulls hovered, letting their wings sing for them. Sandpipers skittered at their approach. Somewhere past the dunes, the last bluebirds gathered for a valedictory chorale. Lily and Tom continued to walk, while "Nubbins" slept –peaceful, free of colic and dream – in the papoose frame Tom had made and now wore strapped to his broad back.

Out on the lake several ships were visible in the middle and far distance, their funnels puffing smoke that barely smudged the vast ocean of sky overhead. As they reached the end of the curved beach at Canatara and turned to retrace their path, a large four-masted schooner hove into view around the bend at Sarnia Bay and entered the lake. Among the last of its breed, the old grain-carrier seemed cocky and defiant as it caught the southerly breeze square on its main-sails, its lacquered masts bent to the limit of their deep, ravelled grain, its rigging dotted with nimble creatures adjusting the jib. Slim, wind-sure, graceful as an aging eland, it angled into the open water and nosed its prow towards the unmapable horizon where it was said magnetic north linked up with a polar star.

Just then a spotted dog with floppy ears came skidding down a dune ahead of them, closely pursued by two young boys. Lily watched them tumble in the sand while the dog snapped at their heels. The more they shouted, the louder the dog barked. Lily felt her hand tighten in Tom's. She stopped, involuntarily turning with the pressure of her husband's grip until she was beside him once more. He had paused with his eyes on the schooner, and as it sailed into the hazy, westering sky, his gaze never left it till it was a faded dot indistinguishable from the horizon-line.

"I'm expectin'," Lily said.

"What?"

"Gonna have your baby, sailor."

The winter in its own way was as happy as the summer. The baby was weaned, answered happily to "Robbie," began to crawl over the floor and furniture – terrifying everyone but himself – and started crying for more than his food. He was a robust, healthy creature with his father's sandy hair and clear blue eyes. He rode his father's arms like a bronco, giggling hysterically as he was whirled through the high air and complaining only when he was let down. On hands and knees, he trailed Tom into the bedroom or into the forbidden territory of the woodshed. When the snow came, Tom built him a wooden sled, and only Tom was permitted to tuck him in before they all set out for Little Lake or to the village to be shown off. When he was tired, his sweet temper turned decidedly cranky, but Lily didn't mind. She let him thrash some in her arms, her breasts reminding him of what he had abandoned for these risky new pleasures, her lullaby as soothing as ever against the edges of his fatigue.

Tom went back to the job he liked in the car-shops. They had spent all their savings just to survive his lay-off and the summer's drought that sent food prices soaring. Neither of them mentioned a new house in the village; it would be a while, but it would come eventually.

For Lily this third pregnancy did not go as smoothly as the first two. She had morning sickness all fall, was intermittently nauseous and cramped thereafter, and did not seem to take any strength from the general state of well-being she felt. However, when Gimpy Fitchett announced in January that he was going to marry Clara Grocott, a farm-girl from up the Errol Road who worked in Redmond's grocery, Lily was overjoyed and for a while, happily distracted. Clara was added to the Wednesday teas at Maudie Bacon's, and Lily found that she liked the girl. She even joined in the many discussions about the wedding dress and the details of the reception afterwards in one of the parlours of the Grand Trunk station. She promised Clara a quilt for her wedding night and set about completing it with enthusiasm.

Aunt Elspeth, of course, did not come for Christmas but sent a lovely note and an heirloom silver cream-and-sugar set rescued from the bailiffs. Her letter informed them that Lucille was engaged to a British regular stationed at Fort York, but had promised to stay on as long as she was needed. Once January came, though, all attention was focussed on the Fitchett wedding. Particularly happy was the arrival of Bags Starkey with his cousin from London. He was manoeuvring quite well on his own with the aid of two crutches and a disarming grin. He marvelled at the vigour of his namesake. Unfortunately he had to return to London right after the service because there was a chance he might get a job there as a ticket agent for the Great Western.

The ceremony was held at the Methodist Church in Sarnia, where the Reverend Elmo Noseworthy managed to dull with his homiletic proclivities an otherwise colourful and spontaneously joyful occasion. After the formalities of a dinner at the Grand Trunk, where the toasts were charged with apple-juice, the older folk said their farewells and the younger ones, including the bride and groom, remained to continue the celebration. A cask of whiskey was discovered nearby, with a dozen bottles of iced champagne for the ladies. The working men and their wives sang, danced and caroused until they were kicked out at ten in the evening. The happy couple then repaired by cutter to the bride's home, left vacant for them, where they were to spend the night before setting out on the day-express for Toronto and a week's honeymoon.

Unknown to them, a charivari, or shivaree as it was called thereabouts, had been cooked up by several of Gimpy's crew and avidly agreed to by at least a dozen others, including Lily. As soon as the couple left the station, the participants pulled out the canvas bags containing their costumes and instruments. While two fellows hitched up a team and sleigh, the others donned their cloaks and masks and hopped aboard, singing badly enough to wake even the most unappreciative sleeper. Silver flasks returned the silver moonlight.

The party arrived at the Errol Road not more than fifteen minutes behind the lovers themselves. "Just time enough to get their nerve up!" some wag remarked to more laughter than he deserved. As they approached the isolated farmhouse, the revellers shushed each other repeatedly until only the comic jingle of the harness-bells could be heard. A wan light showed through the blind on an upstairs window. The buskers leapt soundlessly into the fresh snow and, as prearranged, formed a loose ring around the building. Lily, clad in a sort of bat's costume, carried an outsized tambourine. All I need is a broom, Lily thought, hoping the baby she carried would not complain too loudly about the night's ride. She'd had only one glass of champagne, hours ago, but her heart hammered with excitement and she longed for the signal to be given. Near her she could see Tom in a deerskin coat with a set of rusting antlers strapped to his brow and shoulders. Further down she spotted Maudie's husband dressed like *Bonhomme* with coal eyes, a carrot nose and a waxed turnip where his legs joined. Maudie herself, habilled like a milkmaid, raised the alarm with a single clang of her cowbell.

The din – sudden and unrelenting – would have stunned a deaf-mute: tuneless bell, soured horns of every ilk, tea-kettle drums, and underneath it all a thumping, manic tambourine. The window above shot open, and Gimpy, wrapped diagonally in a towel, blinked unbelievingly into the soft darkness, then staggered back as a chorus of chanting voices joined the accompaniment.

Gim-pee Fit-chett!

Gim-pee Fit-chett!

Give your all,

Limpy, Limpy

Ain't no ball!

Clar-ra Fit-chett!

Clar-ra Fit-chett!

Give him some

Limpy Gimpy

Ain't any fun!

Clara's ghost appeared beside her husband, and a further cheer went up from the troupe.

Come down! Come down!

Or we'll wind you up

And blow your house down!

At last the wretched couple, hastily clothed, opened the front door and the troubadours entered en masse. Some untapped champagne was produced, toasts and cheers rained down upon Gimpy and Clara, who responded with the remnants of their dignity and good will. Following traditions as old as the *habitant's* arrival, the well-wishers departed meekly soon after, then sat motionless in the woods for twenty minutes, and when the time seemed propitious, sent up a final, deflating barrage of congratulation.

At Robbie's birth the father was drunk and the attending midwife sober; at his sibling's arrival, it was the reverse. Which was only appropriate; nothing about this pregnancy had seemed normal. The baby would not kick, as the other two had. Even by the seventh month – the middle of March – Lily had to lie on her side and press her fingers firmly into her abdomen at a point where she figured his forehead ought to be and then repeat her invitation before she felt a faint "tunk" returned to her from within, like a single tap on a toy drum. At least it's alive, she thought, though it doesn't seem anxious to come into the world. "It's probably a girl," Tom would soothe, "as shy as her mother."

"It don't feel like a girl."

If by chance it should turn out to be another boy, Tom had already won Lily's approval to call him Bradley, Aunt Elspeth's family name.

Cramps and nausea struck Lily down at odd and inconvenient moments. She had missed two of the Wednesday teas because of it, and was beginning to feel quite isolated. But with Robbie now crawling about like a rambunctious baby-coon she was kept busy and alert and often laughing at his antics. He's a show-off, she concluded, and we're spoiling him rotten with attention. What else would they do? Her heart would skip a beat while she watched him climb Uncle Chester's chair, test the limits of his agility against gravity, then having breathlessly escaped, look up and laugh as if he had just played a joke on the universe. When he toppled, which wasn't often, he would lie stunned, waiting for the pain and trying out his arms and the air tentatively and then, reassured that the world's kick was not lethal, snap his head across to glare at his mother. Sometimes he cried, but always he let her know that this humiliation was, deep-down, *her*failure to govern the forces aligned against him. Only in the most extreme instances – when the terror inside was wild and formless – would he consent to collapse in her arms for consolation. If Tom were watching, he never cried.

Despite these daily joys and minor catastrophes, Lily found herself missing the company of Maudie Bacon, Clara Fitchett, Alice Bowls and the other workers' wives who visited one another, chatted on Michigan Avenue between shops, exchanged recipes and gossip, and generally provided some relief from the never-ending labour of their days and weeks. Like Lily, these women were young and new to town-life. On their family farms they had shared the work with siblings and cousins and spinster aunts. Here they had to rely on one another. Lily was accepted into their company cheerfully, but she found that most of the organized social events revolved around the church – its physical facility and the calendar it provided for the seasonal flow of Canadian life: christenings, weddings, and baptisms; concerts, temperance meetings, and bazaars.

"Oh, just come along, Lily," Maudie told her again and again. "We love you. And I don't believe *half*of what that old fart up there goes on about, nor do most of the girls."

"I can't," Lily told them, and she knew that after a while, when the village built its own churches and she kept on saying no, it would begin to matter all the more.

"You *do* believe in God?" Clara once asked, shocked at her own question. Lily could find no words to answer her, and was immensely relieved that whatever expression she was offering Clara was sufficient. "Well, then, come along, for heaven's sake!"

The day before All Fool's Day, Tom came in for supper looking grim. He waited impatiently until young Mary Bacon, who had been helping with the housework and minding Robbie while Lily napped, left for the village.

"I didn't want to get your hopes up," he began, "but before Christmas I wrote to the lawyers I used to work for in Toronto and asked them, as a favour to me, if they would check into the existence of an oil company controlled by Melville Armbruster in or around New York. I got a letter back this afternoon."

Lily flinched, one hand absently on her abdomen.

"Maybe I should save this for –"

"Go on," Lily said. "It's just the usual."

"They did find a company, a real estate company, registered in New York City, with Armbruster as president and majority owner. But it was sold – very suddenly and rather mysteriously – in the spring of last year. After that, there is no trace of him anywhere in the business world of that area, as far as they can tell. They also wrote to his solicitors, Van Diemen and Cruickshank, and they said that he had gotten out of business altogether, and if he had a forwarding address, they were not free to give it out."

Lily began clearing away the dishes.

"I'd like to go down there and thrash it out of them." Tom said.

Bridie's alive, I know it. I hear the underwater voice, pleading.

"Was that all?"

"That was it."

Lily flinched again, bent double by the pain.

"Oh God, I knew I should've kept this till after," Tom said, hurrying over to her. He got as far as one of the kitchen chairs.

She was smiling through her grimace. "In a few minutes it's gonna be after," she warned him.

"It can't be! You're only seven months –"

"Started earlier this afternoon. An' this ain't false labour," she said, suppressing a groan. "Feels funny, but it's real."

"Damn, we should've kept Mary here. Never mind. I'll get you set up in the bedroom. If Robbie wakes up, just let him cry. I'll be back in forty minutes flat. With Sophie."

About two hours later, well after the sun had set and the night-chill was settling in over the trees, Lily heard the sound of multiple footsteps along the back-garden path. Robbie was awake at her side, but restless and irritable. She felt numbed and disoriented by the pain. The sheets were soaked through with her sweat. She was terrified the boy would tumble off the bed, strike his head on the floor, and lie helplessly dying while she lay equally helpless above him. However, he seemed to sense that something was wrong, clinging to her damp fingers and complaining only fitfully. All this pain, Lily was thinking, and nothing is happening. The contractions seized her in fierce, expulsive knots, then hovered until the next nerve triggered them again. But the baby gave no sign of readiness to be dislodged; it seemed instead to be resisting, pounding the little battering ram of its brow against her stomach, her lungs, her heart. She screamed as loud as she could but no sound reached her ears. She heard a distant thump. The cramp eased and her mind let the room back in. Robbie was crying.

"Marlene, get the little tyke outta here! Hurry up or I'll give you another cuff." It was Sophie's voice. Lily began to weep quietly with relief.

"You go right ahead an' cry, sweetie, Sophie's here an' everything's gonna be all right." She had gotten the lamp lit and was leaning over Lily, resting a certain hand on her fevered head. Lily looked into the familiar but somewhat distorted face of the *sage femme*, swollen and lopsided, the colour of a fresh bruise.

"I brung Marlene with me to help out," she whispered to Lily. Her large frame, which, through Lily's blurred vision, seemed pudgier than ever, wobbled backwards towards a stool, landed crookedly on it, and slid with it at an acute angle to the floor. Her eyes bounced once, like a sturgeon's hitting bottom, and stuck open in permanent surprise. "*Jesus-Murphy!*" she hollered. "Marlene, get your arse in here."

Marlene was already at the door, quailing. She inched forward, held out a quivering hand, and when held fast, heaved back with all her fifteen-year-old might. Sophie came upright, wheezing and not overly grateful. Marlene scooted off to her duties. Lily could smell the alcohol breath that Sophie was spraying like weed-killer into the room.

"Don't worry none, Lily dear," Sophie said, trying to blink. "I've had a bit to drink today. Hubby left me for the boats. Kind of a sad affair, eh? Gone for the whole month, he has. Don't you worry none, I'm still the best midwife in this county."

"Where's Tom?" was all Lily could say.

Sophie snorted. "Ha! He's gone after that quack, Dollard. That makes two arseholes I gotta deal with."

Marlene appeared several times with mugs of coffee which Sophie swallowed at a gulp.

At last something turned over in Sophie's brain, roused no doubt by Lily's increasingly frequent cries. Sophie was accustomed to shrieks and could read their vocal code as easily as print on paper. She did not like what she was hearing. She put both hands over Lily's flinching abdomen and kept them there while the spasms continued.

"Damnation," she murmured, then a shout: "Marlene!"

Marlene was ready with the cloths and steaming kettles. Behind her came Tom.

"What's happening?" he said. He was gray from exertion and worry. He had run into the village and then all the way to Sarnia and then into the township in search of Dollard or McElroy or any professional medical assistance. No doctor could be found.

"We got trouble," Sophie said without turning to face him. She waved Marlene to the other side of the bed.

"You get her to drink some of this if you have to force it down her throat. Then keep the sweat outta her eyes, an' this towel between her teeth when she needs it."

To Tom, she said, "An' you, ya' dumb untrustin' bastard, get your butt over here an' hold a leg. I can't do this without you."

"You're drunk!" Tom shouted. "You're pissed! You think I'm gonna let you touch my wife?"

"Right now, I'm all you got. Hold her gently just behind the knee," Sophie said. She had to force his hand there and close it while Marlene administered the potion.

"It's a narcotic," Sophie said. "Old Indian recipe. Christ, I can't work up here. Come on, we'll put this mattress on the floor."

They lowered the mattress and its tender cargo as gently as they could, where Sophie then heaved her bulk between Lily's spread legs and set to work. "A breech birth," she said, "little bugger's tryin' to come out feet first."

Tom kept his eyes averted, occasionally peeking up from his station to read the agony on his wife's face, and worse: that glint of first terror when the mind begins to doubt the body's capability. He could not, however, block out the sounds that filled the room: Sophie's grunts and curses as she pushed and wheedled, and Lily's continuous whimper interrupted only by a stiletto cry that confirmed the depth of her agony.

"Come outta there, you little fucker!" Sophie commanded. "Marlene, get that towel between her teeth before she bites her tongue off! Tom Marshall, bring in hot water an' fresh towels. We're gonna need 'em."

When Tom came back in, Lily was arched fully and breathing like an asthmatic near the end. Sophie was hunched over with her arms stiffened and pulling back. Tom saw the child's legs in Sophie's grasp, covered in blood. "Gotta hurry, gotta hurry," she panted. She gave a wrench, Lily coughed and moaned, and a rump popped into view, followed immediately by a curved back and the rim of a skull.

"Holy Jesus," Sophie whispered.

"The fuckin' cord is wrapped around his neck. Help me!"

Tom's hand shook, and the sweat poured into his eyes, but somehow he managed to take hold of the eel-slippery, half-born creature while Sophie reached one finger through the flensed crevice and with a series of deft manoeuvres somehow coordinated with Lily's last spasms, slipped the cord over the baby's head as it propelled itself at last into the air above the ocean.

Dangling it upside down as the afterbirth gushed in a fetid pool at her feet, Sophie tapped on its heels and it howled triumphantly, as if it had made this journey, thank you, on its own merit. Bradley Marshall uttered a defiant if reluctant greeting to the world.

"I'm gonna leave Marlene here," Sophie said, after tending to the immediate needs of both mother and babe. "Lily's very weak an' ripped open a bit. She'll need the narcotic, too, and the tonic later on. Marlene knows what to do. I'll come back if you need me. Just send Marlene."

Tom poured himself another mug of coffee. He had no energy left to object or argue, but he did register the alarming appearance of the woman who had just saved the life of his wife and his son. Sophie looked utterly wasted, drained of all vitality. The left side of her face was swollen to twice its size, leaving only a puffed slit for the dark, gypsy's eye to gaze through.

The red badge of abuse he'd noticed there earlier was now a purpling tumour.

"Who did that to you?" Tom asked.

Sophie glared balefully at him, then smiled as best she could and said, "My hubbie, of course. With his stokin' fist."

The shock must have registered on Tom's face for Sophie said: "You don't think I'd let anybody else do this to me, do you?" She straightened up. "Now where do you keep the pain-killer around here?"

"The minute I'm feelin' up to it, I'm gonna walk over there an' thank that woman myself," Lily said.

Tom tossed Robbie into Uncle Chester's chair, then nuzzled into him till the boy screamed in delight.

"I may just take her the biggest pie I've ever baked," Lily said. Then, "*Ow*, I swear this little jigger's tryin' to bite me."

Tom came over. "She lives on squatter's row, remember," he said.

"Does that matter?" Lily said.

She'd heard Gimpy and others decry the whole population of that neighbourhood. "Bunch of hoo-ers an' pimps," Gimpy declared at one of the Saturday dances. "Railway oughta clean them gypsies right outta there."

"They squat on Grand Trunk land, an' just 'cause it ain't good for nothin' else don't mean they shouldn't kick their butts clean to London an' back," his pal had added.

"Marg's hubby slips over to Car-teer's come Saturday night," Maudie whispered, assuming Lily would recognize the name of the local bootlegger.

"Could be worse," Clara countered. "Hazel's ain't far away." Hazel's Heaven it was called – where the pimps and hooers committed their scandalous acts.

"When we get our own church here next year," Maudie said, "that'll be the end of all that filth. Then maybe honest folk won't have to lock their doors at night or keep an eye out on the boardwalk for the riff-raff that comes floatin' up from that sewer."

Lily herself had seen children – freckled, orange-headed, streaked with dirt – bounding over the tracks from that direction to be shooed and badgered by the neighbouring townsfolk as if they were chickens out of their run. "Them's the McCourt brood," Redmond sighed over his scales, "leastways the redheads is, the others are most likely bastards of dubious origin, if you know what I mean. Jess McCourt died under a hopper-wheel up in Camlachie two winters ago – cut him right in two, clean as a firelog. His old lady scrubs out toilets for the Grand Trunk; they don't care if she squats in that shack, long as she does the work."

A little over a month later, carrying an apple pie made from the first crop of green cookers out of Clara Fitchett's orchard, Lily turned off Michigan Avenue onto Prince Street. Several sailors lounged on the patio outside the Queen's Hotel; she let their whistles sail amiably by. Prince Street, named in honour of His Royal Highness, was less than a hundred yards long, ending its brief north-easterly path a few feet before the Grand Trunk main line. Beyond the tracks lay a screen of runt hawthorn, soft poplar and red-willow and beyond that, a patchy piece of open ground covered with sawgrass and sandburs that rolled northward until overtaken by the dunes and the beach below them. Lily spotted a walking path in the grass and went through the curtain of bush into what had already become known, inside and outside the community, as Mushroom Alley.

And there was a kind of lane or alley, about as broad as a dog-cart's track, that might have been labelled a street if it had not so flagrantly meandered and ox-bowed its way among the residences on either side. The first two dwellings Lily saw, partly hidden away among some poplars, were not luxurious enough even to be called shanties. They were confected out of the jetsam of the Grand Trunk: rusted corrugated iron, chipped packing cases and chewed-up boxcar doors. A stampede of copper-topped and black-haired children, boys and girls, hurtled past Lily without a nod, intent on some game more compelling than the arrival of a stranger. McCourts and McLeods, she thought. From the edge of a hog-wallow, Lily felt the cold eyes of a woman who did not acknowledge her wave but watched her until she had veered out of sight. She began to wonder how she would ever discover where Sophie Potts lived if no one here would speak to her.

She looked away towards the river mouth, whose contrary currents she could hear even from this distance. Where the grassy field sloped away towards the water, she could see the smoke from several campfires and the indistinct figures of the hobos and bums just off the trains. They slept down there in the open or in makeshift lean-to's; some of them, it was widely rumoured, were American deserters from the Union Army or spies from the Confederacy. None had ever been apprehended. Lily quickened her pace.

Around another bend she encountered what appeared to be a deserted shack on her right and a bit farther on the left a sizable-looking house with a verandah, glazed windows, several rambling sheds somewhat attached to the main structure, a barn behind, along with a coop and pig-pen. Some attempt had been made to grow vegetables in the thin, wind-bitter soil. The clapboard had long ago been painted, a sprightly blue perhaps. Seated on a wicker rocker on the verandah, Lily spied the unmistakeable profile of young Marlene.

Lily called to her and started through the burdocks, balancing her pie with its gauze cover. Marlene appeared surprised, squinted into the sunlight, then bolted off the porch and into the back yard where she disappeared behind one of the outhouses. Lily stopped. The grasshoppers see-sawed around her. No sound came from the house. Well, she'd come this far. Faintly came the echo of children's voices, the ebb and flow of their carefree play somewhere among the pliant dunes. She walked boldly up to the verandah, slipped on a wobbly step, righted herself noisily, and rapped on the screen door, an action which stirred up a harem of flies drowsing there.

"Anybody home?" Lily called softly. The flies had noticed the pie. As she turned to go, she heard the squeak of a chair, as if someone had just shifted their weight. "You there, Sophie?"

"Who is it?" It was a male voice, deep and threatening.

"I come to see Sophie. Is she here?"

A long pause. "An' who might you be?"

"Tell her Lily came to see her. I'll come back another time."

A shadow filled the doorway. Two black eyes, like chiselled coal set in a bearded face, peered out at her. White teeth flashed in a too-friendly grin.

"Hey, you don't go runnin' off, Miss Lily What's-her-name. Don't you know a joke when you hear one?"

Lily paused without turning back.

"Better brush them flies offa that pie," he said. "I like my sweets nice an' clean."

Lily looked back up at him. "Is Sophie home?"

"Why don't you come inside like a proper lady and I'll see if she might be."

He opened the door with a flourish and she saw him fully in the light. He was a large, well-proportioned man with a handsome face, arms that bulged with a surplus of muscle, and ape-size hands that were scarred with calluses as thick and layered as a toad's skin. His teeth were wonderfully even. The only thing to mar an otherwise striking impression was a slight crook of the spine, camouflaged by his loose work shirt, as if he had spent too long arched in one position.

"I said come in. I'm Morty Potts, Stoker to some."

"Sophie home?"

"You got a one-track mind, girl." She caught the blast of his whiskey breath. "Soph'll be real mad now if I don't invite you in to wait for her."

"Where is she?"

"She's down at the lake bathin' the kids. There's only me here."

"An' Marlene."

His stare darkened. Flies were pouring into the house as he held the door wide open. Lily caught a whiff of urine. "Marlene's gone off," he said. "Most likely she's fetchin' her momma right now, so why don't you just come on in an' have a drink ...of tea."

"I can't wait. Please tell Sophie I'll be back." She turned back down the stairs.

"Hey!" he called to her. "You gonna leave that pie?

She set it down on the step without a backwards glance.

As Lily made the first bend in the alley, out of the corner of her eye she saw Marlene emerge from the bushes and tiptoe up to the house. Lily sped up but she wasn't fast enough. The smack of hand to cheek resounded behind her. She heard the girl shriek once like a reflex. She thought of a stoker's hands, ferrying coal from bin to blast with Beelzebub's grip.

"Well," Tom said, grateful for her return. "Did she like the pie?"

"She wasn't home," Lily said.

"Oh. That's too bad." He looked away. "You going back?"

"Soon as I can," she said with conviction.

17

By 1866 the hastily arranged marriage of the two Canadas was heading, after twenty-five years of mutual incompatibility, towards certain divorce – unless some close relatives could be persuaded to share the misery in a more encompassing family unit dubbed by its proponents "confederation." The papers were full of little else but news of the scheme and of the tub-thumping Fenians – many of them Civil War veterans – just below the border, uttering the most horrible threats against the peace of not only Canadians but also and especially New Brunswickers, Nova Scotians and Prince Edward Islanders. The hue and cry went up everywhere, no more so than in those towns unfortunate enough to abut an American state bristling with Fenian brothers determined to liberate Ireland by decapitating the silos of every British barn between Fort Erie and Sarnia.

In the teeth of such threats, it is little wonder that scant attention was paid to local concerns: the ongoing rate wars between the Great Western and Grand Trunk; or the rumblings of discontent faintly heard from the New West where Canadians were already wearing out their welcome among the puzzled natives and Metis; or the visiting phrenologist from Boston who proclaimed in the town hall of Sarnia that man was a developmental creature and the earth around him eons old, only to be scientifically refuted, to general approbation, the next week by a learned doctor of Theology from Pittsburgh; or the death of Mrs. Elspeth Edgeworth, widow of the late Colonel Edgeworth of London, who passed away quietly in her sleep at the home of her sister-in-law in Toronto. The good woman was laid to rest beside her husband in their home city.

Lily insisted they could not afford train fare for both of them to attend the funeral in London. She even believed it as she said it, and was secretly hurt when Tom showed no inclination to accept her argument.

"Of course we can afford it," he snapped, "and we both know very well why you won't go."

She was about to say something in her defense when Brad's whimper from the boys' room sent her scurrying.

"You'll have to leave him some day, you know," he called after her.

From the moment of his unorthodox and premature arrival, Bradley Marshall was a difficult child, demanding Lily's service at any hour of the clock, suckling beyond his capacity, and then upchucking the lot. Whereupon he would cry with doubled hunger and indignation. When he did manage to feed satisfactorily, he would be wakened by colic, wailing his grief far into the night and early dawn. Where Robbie had been cherubic, Brad was wizened and irritable; where Robbie was robust and outgoing, Brad was sickly and withdrawn. After his colic subsided, he picked up a touch of whooping cough from his brother, then the chicken-pox, and most recently the red measles. Lily had two sick children to care for, and a husband with little sleep to sweeten his shortened temper.

Robbie suffered his maladies gallantly, lying in his bed (Tom had made them single bunks for their room) and letting Lily minister to him, smiling bleakly when she had to leave to attend Brad. In many ways, Lily often thought, these were their best moments together: Robbie knew for certain who she was, what she was for, why she couldn't be done without. As a result, Robbie responded easily to treatment and was soon over his afflictions, bruiting his appreciation to the wild woods and fields he loved to roam– within a mother's shout of the house.

Poor Brad never quite recovered from one malady before the next one struck; he suffered badly and without patience. He would shriek till his nose ran or fall into an unceasing whimpering that grated the nerves. Tom would plop the child into Lily's arms wherever she was and stomp off without a word. Usually she could hear him take his gun down and head off for First Bush, with Robbie trailing him ineffectually to the edge of the garden, then returning to Lily to cry out his resentment or, more likely, make certain that her attempts to soothe Brad were unsuccessful. When both boys were sick together, Tom would bring young Mary Bacon out from the village to help. Mary was always cheerful and efficient, and especially attentive to Robbie's show of acrobatics. Brad did not "take to" Mary, who happily failed to notice.

After Brad's second birthday, Lily detected a change in his behaviour and in their relationship. He had begun to talk early at sixteen months, but despite the facility of his speech, he used it mainly to establish the urgency of his desires. Lily cradled, hummed and sang to him often during these stressful periods, and he responded in a curious way: he consumed the lullaby syllables thirstily, drawing them into his discomfort like a tonic, giving nothing back but the grateful easing of his tense little body in the singer's arms. The songs Lily sang to him in those early months, born out of desperation and sometimes even panic, were those she remembered, however obliquely, from her own mother's lips. They did as much to soothe the mother as they did the child.

At age two, Brad could not only string sentences together, he could take a word or phrase, as Robbie might a rubber ball, and play with it – experimenting, examining, and testing its resilience against foreign objects – for his own endless amusement. One of those objects became Lily, who tossed the words right back in rhymes or songs or different sentences. While Robbie foraged out-of-doors, toy rifle at the ready to stun the first squirrel, Lily and Brad spent the mornings in perpetual conversation. Sometimes when Mary Bacon came out to help with the housework, she brought her little brother, Mitchell, and while the two older boys rampaged through the wilds out back, Mary hummed over the kitchen stove and Lily sat in Uncle Chester's chair and began to tell Brad all the stories she knew. Brad did not always listen silently. At a signal from Lily he would jump straight into the narrative and help her make it up, and when it broke down, as it must, in rambunctious nonsense, they would both laugh till even Mary would start giggling.

Tom was quick to notice Brad's ability with language. "Well, at last there seems to be a little human being under all that crying and carrying on," he remarked one day. Lily in turn tried to include Tom in the conversations. As first she had little success. Brad would simply clam up and sulk if Tom hung about too long on the fringes of their word games. "You're too big," Lily said to Tom, trying to make light of it. "Why don't you get down on your hands an' knees an' just peek over the table, like you did with Robbie." Tom went along and it worked. Gradually Tom was let into the play, where he did quite well, and occasionally Brad would say something his father found especially amusing. Whereupon Tom would fall backwards and laugh and kick like a tipsy mule, inspiring more giggles from Robbie than anyone else.

But Tom just wasn't around enough, Lily concluded. For the time being, Brad was unwilling to play his games with Tom alone, even though Lily looked for opportunities to leave them together.

"C'mon, Robbie," she'd say, "You an' me'll go down to the creek an' see if those trout are still there." Robbie would glance anxiously at Tom, torn between loyalty and desire, and then give in to the latter. The only way she could keep Robbie happy was to let him lead *her* to the secret pool and point out all its cumulative mysteries. Often they returned to a silent house.

In the realm of work, at least, Lily expected Tom to be more content. No longer would he have to switch over to the freight-sheds every April. He was made a permanent member of the car-shop, his specialty the repair of crippled stock cars. He would tear out the splintered sections and improvise replacement pieces at minimal cost to the Grand Trunk.

"I'll never be a cabinet-maker," he'd say, "but at least these hands are good for something."

The only sad news was that Gimpy and Clara had settled in Sarnia. Though they still saw them on special occasions, some of the old intimacy was lost. Tom had a number of acquaintances at work, some of whom he hunted and fished with, but with Bags' departure to London (no news) and Gimpy's defection, Tom had so far not found friends to replace them. Though he never said it aloud, with Gimpy gone to the Great Western, Tom had a better chance at becoming assistant foreman.

Soon, Lily thought, we'll start talking again about that cottage in the village.

It was late April. Brad was asleep inside; his glands were swollen. Lily was digging in the garden. Robbie was helping with his toy shovel. After a week's lay-off Tom was back at work. Lily's mind was full of plans for the coming season. She hummed a waltz tune, one she remembered dancing to long ago. Suddenly Robbie peeked up and said, "Ma, what's a Fee-neen?"

"Where'd you hear that word?"

"When me an' Da was fishin'."

"Did Mr. Bacon use that word?"

"Uh, uh. Da did. What is it? Da won't tell me."

"They're bad men, but they live a long way over the river. They can't hurt you none. So don't you go worryin' about them."

He paused, then brought his shovel to his shoulder and aimed it. "I ain't scared," he laughed and pulled the trigger; the weapon went off with an explosion of spittle. Lily said nothing. After a while the shovel resumed its more humble duties.

When Tom came in from work, Lily was bent over the rabbit stew. She listened for the familiar rattle of his lunch bucket and "thunk" of his cap on its peg, but none came. She turned to look, the hair on the nape of her neck rising.

He was all in green, tunic and breeches, with black polished boots. A bit of gold piping winked here and there. The rifle in his fist gleamed brightly.

"I joined up," he said.

The Fenian scare had reached its zenith. Enemy troop movements were being reported daily all the way from New Brunswick to the Niagara frontier. For several months the spanking new Canadian militia, side by side with British regulars, had been patrolling the borders of Canada East and Canada West. Point Edward was a critical spot, the nexus of two great transportation facilities. The Grand Trunk round-house and yards harboured at any given moment more than fifty locomotives. The economy of the united provinces could be crippled with a single surprise strike across the St. Clair River. Near the railyards stood an elevator crammed with last fall's wheat reserves. Beyond, the Lambton countryside was dotted with Irish Catholic farms whose inhabitants were rumoured to be seething with two hundred years' worth of resentment. Three militia groups with local commanders were formed as part of the 27th Battalion: the Sarnia Infantry and Artillery Brigade, plus two units from Point Edward known as the Grand Trunk Companies. Eventually they took on the name they had already chosen unofficially for themselves: the St. Clair Borderers.

To assist them in defending the vital installations of the region, the government sent several companies from elsewhere in the province, and these were billeted in what remained of the original ordnance grounds, the flat, grassy plain between Mushroom Alley and the lakeshore. There the spring breezes billowed the white tents and the sun shimmered on bayonet and buckle. Flocks of truant boys crouched breathless in the bushes nearby, then dashed off to the dunes to replicate the dress-parades and battle tactics they had been permitted to witness. The Borderers joined the outsiders for combined exercises, but they also rehearsed independently on the Sarnia parade-ground or among the dunes themselves, firing their rifles into the air, hurling imprecations into the wind blowing from Fort Gratiot, showing curious lads who longed to be a year older how to fix a bayonet without severing a finger. One rumour, widely believed, suggested that a Gatling gun had been smuggled in from the States and cached somewhere near Mushroom Alley. Ordinary folk bolted their doors and kept the curtains drawn.

With a logic known only to the Irish, the main Fenian assault of 1866 did not come against the vital, vulnerable Western region, but across the Niagara River against loyalist strongholds rooted in that countryside since the expulsions of the 1780s. Despite the advantages of familiar terrain and a spy system which informed them of every twitch made by the enemy, the Canadian militia, in their maiden engagement, set a standard for ineptitude that only the fiascos of the Great War would surpass. Heroism there was aplenty, even a victory of sorts at Ridgeway. But the soldiers weren't cheering. The Fenian raiders retreated across the border to bide their time.

"They're keeping up an alert till the end of the summer," Tom said. "We drill three times a week. The company is giving us a day-a-week off to go on sentry duty. With half-pay," he added with great emphasis.

Robbie was fiddling with the bolt on his father's rifle.

"Stop that, Robbie," Lily said.

Robbie looked at Tom for reinforcement and continued.

"You do what I say," Lily said to Robbie, slapping his fingers away from the gun.

Robbie's lips quivered but he didn't cry.

From the other room Brad whimpered in his sleep. Lily started towards him.

"Go ahead," Tom said, more in exasperation than anger. "But don't take it out on Robbie. I don't know what else you expect me to do; I was a soldier, remember?"

"I hate her! I hate her!" she heard Robbie say as she entered the room where Brad was thrashing in his bed, his jaws swollen shut by the mumps.

"You say that again," Tom said, "and I'll stuff your mouth with soap." Robbie wailed loudly. I know how you feel, Lily thought.

That night in bed Tom reached over, uncoiled her arms, softened her neck with his stroking, and when she was ready, made love to her with the only passion he was still certain they could share. He wasn't wrong. A long while after, he told her, "They're beautiful children. I love them both. Almost as much as I love their mother."

He expected no reply, but her fingers roamed the reaches and most sensitive places of his body, communicating her reciprocated commitment.

I love him, even now, like this, she thought, fighting her drowsiness. I love him even more. How can that be? Does love need a flare of anger, an edge of panic? She envied his dreamless slumber, his lying there as if the peace that had seized his body had been deserved or sanctioned by some force beyond the muscle pumping plasma into his imagination.

When she fell asleep she dreamed, as she feared she would, about soldiers dying in swamps and bloody quagmires, outflanked, outnumbered, and for no purpose that she could fathom.

18

It was spring again. Because it was unlikely they would be able to afford the move into the village for at least another year, Lily decided to spruce up their modest homestead. She had planted bulbs in the fall and their green spires now aimed at the sky. Tom had built a trellis beside the kitchen window and helped her transplant a budding rosebush from Maudie Bacon's garden. A white flowerbox set under the front window in the south sun would soon accommodate her geranium cuttings, nursed indoors through the winter. She and Brad made up a song about flowers. "Tu-lips, two-lips, do-lips" Brad sang, delighted at language's happy coincidences. Another year here, Lily thought, and none of us will want to move. Tom was taking Robbie on his shoulders down to the creek to fish every Sunday afternoon. Brad routinely trailed after her as she spaded and harrowed the garden, distracting her with his banter and shy teasing.

On a bright windless Sunday in May, Lily was sitting on the stoop cutting the roots out of the last of the winter potatoes when she heard Brad say with a sinking whine, "Some people comin', Ma."

She looked towards the lane. Trouble. She could tell from the way the two figures held themselves sturdy in the black carriage, as if they were brunting a stiff northerly. She could sniff rectitude at fifty paces. The horses, frothing against a strict rein, wheeled through the gateway and into the yard, where they stopped, much relieved.

"Good morning, missus," hallooed a large man holding the reins. He wrapped them firmly in place and proceeded to dismount. He waddled around in front of the horses, and stretched out a pudgy hand to his companion. She took it automatically, as if lifting a latch-key, and stepped onto the grass with a practiced swirl. Hand-in-glove, they trundelled towards Lily.

"I am the Reverend Dougall Hardman," the parson announced, "of the Wesleyan Methodist Church in Port Sarnia. And this is my good wife, Mrs. Hardman."

"Charity," said the good wife without dropping her smile.

"Yes, and you must be the young Mrs. Marshall we've heard so much about," the preacher said, reaching unsuccessfully for her hand and glancing past her towards the house.

Clara, thought Lily.

"Lily, isn't it?"

"Yes, how do you do."

"And who's this darling little creature?"

Brad ducked behind Lily's skirt.

The Reverend Hardman cleared his throat with pre-sermon vigour. "Ah, we've come on official business. Is your husband at home, missus?"

"No, he isn't." She hesitated, then said, "He an' Robbie are off fishin'."

The parson swallowed his astonishment long enough to say, "We'll come in and wait, if it isn't too much trouble."

"What a pretty little cottage," Mrs. Hardman said.

The Reverend Hardman was obese: his jowls jiggled contrapuntally with the jawbone, driving the bellows of his windy sentences. His cleric's collar lay buried in his neck-flesh so deeply that only a thin ring of it peeked through, like a band on a turkey. When he sat at his ease in Uncle Chester's chair, his great belly rested on two bony knees; his plump fingers fed on Lily's proffered macaroons and tea-cakes like loose mice. Notwithstanding, there was something different here from the usual parson fattened up by too many teas, bake-sales, and middle-age. From the slim leg, the curve of the shoulder and the quick feet came the hint of a once-muscular frame, leathered skin, and agility. A circuit-rider, Lily thought, the memory striking deep.

Charity Hardman was a bosomy but well-proportioned woman, trussed, corseted and handsomely turned out in a mauve dress whose flounces and lacy appendages might have been described by some as bounteous. She sipped her tea with white gloves intact, resisting all temptation to indulge further. From the edge of her chair she kept her wifely eye on her husband's converging chins, and nodded ritually on some cue from him which Lily was unable to detect.

Working from the general principle that anything he had to say was of riveting significance, Reverend Hardman proceeded to deliver the long history of his church in the country, winding his way eventually towards the good news that next autumn the Wesleyan Methodists were going to build a church in Point Edward that would rival the Anglican one now there in size, expense and depth of devotion. And in the true spirit of ecumenical

Christianity, the edifice would be open to Congregationalists and Presbyterians (no Baptists) until such times as they could afford their own houses of worship.

"You will agree that this is a signal achievement, indeed an honour for such a small and as yet unincorporated village?"

Mrs. Reverend nodded.

"Of course, I was quick to volunteer my services. As Mrs. Hardman can confirm, I have always been a man to take on a fresh challenge for the sake of Our Lord."

Mrs. Reverend tilted her petalled hat in Lily's direction.

"As minister to a new flock my duties are manifold," he said, crushing a macaroon on the downbeat. "First, we shall need commitment, real commitment from our doughty band of believers."

"Money," murmured his wife, delicately.

"True, true. We are looking for pledges, for tithing in the old-fashioned sense."

Lily brought out the last of the macaroons.

"Secondly, we'll need the use of all the talents, the combined gifts, as it were, of our supporters." He stared wistfully at his tea, dotted with crumbs.

"Men to assist with the stone-work and the roof," offered his help-mate.

"Precisely. And finally we shall need the love and spiritual wishes of the whole Christian community. We need their prayers for our success as we seek most humbly to establish a fellowship of adherents among the workers of the Grand Trunk and their loving families."

For once, Mrs. Hardman had nothing to add.

"As you can tell, missus, I am a blunt, straightforward man." Lily felt his gaze sharpen on her face. "We would like you and your husband to think seriously about how much you are prepared to give us in support of God's work. More important even, we are hoping to open a Sabbath school in September. It is our understanding that your eldest – the one now, ah, fishing with his father – will soon be four-years old."

So it *was* Clara, Lily decided.

"Mrs. Hardman has agreed, on top of all her other onerous duties, to take on the little ones, suffering them to come unto her, as it were."

Mrs. Hardman lengthened her smile a notch.

"He ain't been baptized," Lily said.

The parson showed no surprise. "Don't be ashamed, my dear girl," he said, glancing sideways at the vacant plate. "I've been a circuit rider, I know the country ways. Things get put off. Spiritual matters are often suspended by more pressing demands of the moment. We shall make arrangements for both your children to be baptized. Why, we could inaugurate the church with such a happy ceremony!" He smiled as if he'd just thought of the notion.

"Such a beautiful child," Mrs. Hardman said, looking about for Brad.

Lily stood up. "When Tom gets home, we'll talk over what you've said. It's been nice meetin' you."

The reverend was resettled in the carriage when Charity Hardman came back for her parasol.

The smile on her face had hardened to another purpose. She took Lily by the arm and whispered earnestly, "Clara's told me all about you, Lily. Won't you think seriously about comin' to the new church? It gets awful lonesome out here in the country. Besides, we got to stick together, you know. I mean us women."

"Mrs. Hardman!" from the carriage.

"Coming!" she shouted back. In a lower voice tinged with malice, she said to Lily, "An' you don't have to swallow all the malarkey you hear from *that*source!"

As the carriage disappeared, Lily heard the crack of the whip over the horses' heads.

The fathers of Confederation set aside July 1, 1867, as the day when the citizens of the new Dominion were to celebrate this historic act of collective paternity. That there may have been more cause for excitement in the boardrooms and on the front benches of the nation did not in any way diminish the general enthusiasm of the magic hour. Even before the ink was dry on the British North America Act, the yearning for a united land from sea to sea was being translated into affirmative action.

On June 28, 1867, *The Sarnia Observer* noted that a complaint had been received from German emigrants heading west for Manitoba; to wit, the cattle cars that had been rigged out for their comfort contained, they said, only one bucket of water to last five-dozen souls from Toronto to the Point Edward wharf. Naturally such ingratitude was dealt with curtly and correctly in the Grand Trunk's statement of denial. Thirsty or not, the movement westward had begun, and was inevitable: a new destiny was becoming manifest.

No town celebrated the nativity more avidly than Sarnia. The local press accounts told the whole story. "During the morning a large number of loyal yeoman from the neighbouring townships, accompanied in most cases by the members of their families, came into town by all the leading roads, until ultimately there was a larger influx of strangers than was ever before present, except on the occasion of the visit of His Royal Highness the Prince of Wales." Two infantry companies from Moore and Sarnia marched to the parade-grounds led by the Sarnia Cornet Band, bugles ablaze in the sun. Here they were joined by the Grand Trunk Rifle Companies from Point Edward under Major Riley.

"After going through a variety of evolutions, the Companies were formed into line, and fired the *feu-de-joie* at noon." A grand procession then made its way back through the town's thoroughfares, bedecked with bunting and spruce-boughs and lined with crowds cheering and waving flags, as if Wellington himself were marching home from Waterloo. Right behind the band came the volunteers – their combat dreams still warm – and then the town clerk with Queen Victoria's Proclamation and, wonder of wonders, "four young virgins in white, in a carriage and four, as representatives of the four Provinces." Following on the heels of the Fire Brigades of Port Huron and Sarnia were the Sabbath school children, skipping, scooting and tumbling in egregious disarray. Particularly impressive were the volunteer companies of the St. Clair Borderers, all in green, rifles erect, bayonets glinting, their synchronized strut signalling their martial pride and boasting of heroics certain to come.

When the soldiers fired their rifles at noon, Brad screamed and jumped into Lily's arms. Robbie hopped up and down, searching for a face among the uniforms. She had just got Brad settled down, standing with the boys at the corner of Christina and George, when the bugles struck up a battle hymn right in front of them. She could feel Robbie's body through his hand keeping time to the quick-step. The green tunics of the Borderers swept into view around the corner.

Robbie leapt up with a body-length salute and cried out, "Look, there's Da!"

Tom came in from work looking sombre. Since his promotion to assistant foreman (Warden Hargreaves had been transferred temporarily to Ottawa for strategic purposes), he was invariably all smiles.

"We got a letter, from New York," he announced.

Lily stood beside him as he read, seeing the words and hearing the strange voice of Melville Armbruster ricochet inside them.

Long Island, New York

August 5, 1867

Dear Lily:

I am writing to tell you that your Aunt Bridie passed away yesterday. She died peacefully in her sleep, and now rests in the arms of her Maker. Let me tell you what has happened since those happy days when we last saw you. I hope and pray that you will understand.

When Bridie and I got to New York after the wedding in London, we stayed only long enough to meet my family, and then we were off on a honeymoon and business trip that lasted three glorious months. We travelled first-class by train to Baltimore, Washington, St. Louis, Chicago and as far west as St. Cloud, Minnesota. We stayed at the best hotels, several of which we invested in, and I showed your Aunt the heart and soul of democratic America. She said it was the happiest time of her life. Certainly it was that, and more, for me. Let me say also that Bridie never forgot your Uncle Chester or you and Tom. Whenever we'd tour a lumber mill or carriage maker's, she'd say, 'now wouldn't Chester just love a set-up like this' or 'I wish young Tom could see all this, all the opportunities for a man with his talent and education'. Of course she never stopped talking about her Lily, and praying she'd hear news when we got back about a baby-on-the-way.

She never got back, though – at least not the Bridie we all knew and loved. In Buffalo, on our return trip, she caught some kind of influenza and by the time we reached home back in New York, she was gravely ill in a coma. I was about to send a telegram to you when she miraculously awakened and seemed to recover. A day later, however, she suffered what the doctors called a stroke. It left her paralyzed all down the left side. But ill as she was, she could still talk in a slurred voice only I could understand. When I suggested I ought to telegraph you people and send money for train tickets to New York, she indicated firmly, *no*. At first I refused to believe her, but I could see in her eyes and in the tortured twisting of her body every time she spoke that she really meant it. She did not want her Lily to see her like this, though she would never tell me why. I honoured her wish, though I've been wracked by guilt and unease every day and night since.

For almost five years now we have been living on my family's estate, Bridie and me. I've been taking care of her every need, and she has been as brave and wonderful in her dying as she was in her living. I have no regrets, save the fact that caring for her meant cutting us off from you. But her eyes never once said *yes*, not in all these months of pain and even in the last serene moments when we both knew the end was near. She is gone now, and I can tell the whole story. She was a remarkable woman.

She will be buried in the Armbruster mausoleum tomorrow. I sincerely hope you can come to visit the gravesite and I trust that I'll have the opportunity to learn from you more about this great woman I only got to know a little, so late in my life.

All my love,

Melville Armbruster

Something fell out of the envelope. Lily picked it up. It was an American one-hundred-dollar bill, a parting gift in one sense from Aunt Bridie.

Tom held Lily in his foreman's arms all that night. At breakfast she said to him, "I think it's time we moved."

"Soon," he said. "That's a promise."

From the outset, Point Edward was no ordinary or typical small community of Canada West or Ontario as it was now nominated in official circles and on the fresh maps of the new Dominion. By May of 1879, it numbered some seven hundred soul, and was growing weekly. But it would be some years before it incorporated as a self-governing village. The hegemony of the Grand Trunk still lay heavily upon it.

Though many of the properties and businesses had been purchased outright from the company, the railway still owned five boarding houses on St. Clair Street and most of the undeveloped, but appreciating, land to the east and south-east. Eighty percent of the men in the village worked for the Grand Trunk, the others ran businesses or supplied services directly dependent on it. Because the company's facilities were concentrated along the waterfront, the town grew around them in a horse-shoe shape. Here, there would be no village green flanked by churches, library or town hall with quaint cottages radiating in trim ranks to the outskirts where a tannery or mill or furniture factory might spill their pastoral smoke into the serene evenings of Middletown, Ontario.

There was nothing sleepy about Point Edward. Night and day three dozen locomotives ran their own version of the anvil chorus. Screw-prop freighters churned into the berths along the Grand Trunk wharf and hooted for attention. Twice a day, passenger trains – local and express – roared to a stop before the gothic grandeur of the station-hotel, discharging political hacks, carpetbaggers and commercial bashaws of every breed into the luxury and corruption that only a first-class colonial hotel can guarantee. Occasionally there arrived a cattle-train with Icelandic immigrants heading for the about-to-be-annexed New West. Surrounding the din and hubbub of the rail-yards were a dozen thriving but obstreperous enterprises linked to prosperity by rail and sail: smithies hammering out plates and spikes, welders scorching metal into submission, even a manufacturer of barrel-staves who preferred to labour at night. So it was that the town proper did not begin for half-a-mile from its commercial heart on Prince Street, which ran parallel to the river and was unique among small-village boulevards in having buildings only on its east side and each one of them a hotel or an establishment with pretentions in that direction.

While the Grand Trunk station-hotel accommodated those worthies staying overnight on business or waiting for water transportation, smaller hostels like The Queen's served the drummers, gamblers, mountebanks, beached sailors and low-brimmed capitalists seeking illicit pleasures of sundry kind. When the beverage rooms closed, one could drink one's way into a whiskey stupor in the sanctity of an upstairs boudoir complete with country courtesan and douche. If more daring (or desperate), one could slip over the tracks into Mushroom Alley where the gormandizing was as licorous as it was revulsive. At night all the decent burghers of the village clamped shut their shutters and their curiosity. On Sundays the parsons inveighed thunderously from three pulpits, but did not extend their pastorates quite as far as Prince Street itself.

Thanks to a continuous stream of itinerants of every class, Point Edward enjoyed an incongruous cosmopolitanism. Yet there existed alongside it – or within it – a typically ingrown, self-generating community of the Ontario variety. Amazingly, the two societies rarely blended, even at the edges, though they were materially responsible for each other's welfare. The "village" of Point Edward provided the Grand Trunk with a supply of respectable workers with families to ballast their commitment and a church to teach them their manners. The company ensured the permanent citizens a life of modest affluence and certain progress in divine concert with the Dominion itself.

Lily Marshall stood at her kitchen window and surveyed the wonders of her small world. The tulips she had planted along the garden path bloomed gaily in primary reds and yellows. Along the lane, the lilacs that old Bill helped Uncle Chester plant so long ago exploded a dozenfold in mauve and evening indigo, their underground runners popping up everywhere, stitching earth to air. At the edge of the spaded vegetable patch, Robbie, soon to be seven, roamed like a scout for King Arthur, nose to the ground, wooden sabre cocked and ready, and muttering *abracadabra* oaths to keep his courage charged. Tom had read a book of the Arthurian legends to him, indeed read to them all, around the winter fire. Robbie could hardly sit still long enough to hear the end of an adventure; he would be itching to act it out, to get outdoors and test his knightly skills.

Lily watched Brad during these storytelling sessions, saw him form the words in his mouth almost simultaneous with Tom's delivery, as if he were tasting them. Lily sat beside Tom on the arm of the big chair where she could follow the page, picking out recognizable words and sentences. She could read – not yet at Tom's pace but soon. When Robbie went off to school in the village in September, she would have him bring home the gray-covered primer, and they would learn together. And Brad too. Lily and her boys.

That's how people identified them along Michigan Avenue when she pulled the boys into town on the toboggan. "And how are the tow-heads this morning?" grocer Redmond would say, ruffling their hair under the tuques and slipping them an appeasing sweet. "Like two beans on a platter."

But of course they were as different as two boys could be. For Robbie the world around him was the gift of a benign games-master, made for him to explore or plunder. He could watch with dispassion as his father skinned a freshly-killed rabbit, not connecting the clouded eyes in the death-clench of that animal's face with the bright kinship of those that peered out at him from a brush pile or turned their tender curiosity upon him when he disturbed them over lunch at the lettuce patch. Brad, too, as his health improved, loved to be outdoors in the summer. When the family went walking together, Brad would lag or meander, sometimes stopping in mid-stride as something in the air struck him still: a thrush's sigh from the shadows, beads of dew along a leaf trapped by light, a crow raking the silence with his caw, the flick of a trout in a pool with no bottom. From this window she could, if she were careful, watch him out there, listening, touching, reaching for the roots of awe. At such moments she wished she could bring him – and Robbie as well – to Old Samuels and hear them talk together or not talk in those silences-between-souls she knew were gone now from her own life. Robbie would have bounced into the woods on Sounder's heels, Brad and Acorn would have been fast friends.

Naturally Tom found it easier to relate to Robbie, sometimes letting him come along while he hunted, the boy carrying the lumpy burlap with two dead cottontails on his back. Robbie worshipped Tom's presence and filled his absence with reverent re-enactments of their pleasures. Brad, horrified by the barn, the stench of carcasses and the accusing eyes of slain creatures, took to Tom slowly and obliquely. At last Tom seemed to understand and accept this, and gradually Brad caught sight of those parts of Tom she herself had loved outright from the moment of contact across a faraway dance-floor – his quick, warm smile, his vulnerability, his devotion. In late winter, Brad eased himself up onto Tom's knee, and Tom kept right on reading.

They are each an extension of one part of Tom, she thought. Does he know that? Is that why he can love them in such different ways? How much of me lies enfolded in them, I don't really know. I can't see such things because I think of my love for them as complete and whole – an unending ache when I fear for their safety, panic when their bodies shiver on the brink of fever, joy that swells out of my heart and leaves me without breath when I see them laughing all together. We are a family. I never hoped for more.

Tom was offered the foreman's job, starting in September. He felt vindicated. He wrote to Bags Starkey's cousin in London to offer Bags a job, but word came back that he had "gone off" without telling anyone where. On the first sunny Sunday in April, Tom had borrowed Gimpy's old buggy and taken the whole family for a drive in the country. On the way back home they detoured into the village, and Tom, going strangely quiet, pulled the horses up at the corner of Albert and Ernest. Tom pointed his whip towards a newly-built frame cottage covered with cedar-shakes, whose aroma sweetened the air for blocks around.

"It comes up for sale," Tom said, "at the end of the summer."

Lily took hold of his other hand. "The school's just down the street a ways," she said to the boys.

To the north Lily could hear the waves repeating their chant on Canatara.

What more could I want, Lily thought, watching Brad from her kitchen window as he sat on the oak-stump in the May sunshine staring past his brother's antics into the woods beyond. The move into the village would be the last link in the chain of connection Lily felt all around her these days. They would at last become part of some larger community, one in which, though she herself might never feel fully a citizen, the boys could grow up inside so naturally they would think later on they had invented it. For Tom, it meant committing himself more certainly to a life he had taken up in large measure because of his love for her; company and family and town would be his domain. But there was a part of him – as with her – that would always remain unreconciled to domesticity, to the predictable rhythms of civility, to a God who hurled brimstone one moment and puffed on a pipe the next. I loved that in him too, she thought, I must have – that perverse will to hazard, to ride the flux, to play truth-or-dare with the random deities of the universe.

Old Samuels was right: the gods don't disassemble when the hedgerows and the houses and walled gardens go up. When the white man cleared the forest of the great trees that were left in the wake of the fleeing ice, the demons who lived in them did not perish in their ash, they were released into the volatility of air where they still whirl and collide and howl like schizophrenics. Even now they ride the winds of pestilence over the corrupt earth, mocking and vengeful. Lily had heard their mocking laughter many times.

Gimpy and Clara had returned to Point Edward once more, the joy of their renewed friendship buoyed by the anticipation of the couple's first child. Then when Clara's boy was stillborn and she had come down with childbed fever, Lily had wrapped the fetus in a blanket and covered its drowned eyes and begged Clara not to look. She had sat beside her friend for weeks thereafter, watching her grimace with dreadful pain and dreams of the dead child's face.

During the winter there had been a diphtheria scare. Quarantine signs dotted the village doors. Lily didn't go into town for weeks. Word came that Maudie Bacon's youngest was stricken. "She's got Mary there to help," was all Tom said. A week later Maudie's little girl was dead, the first person to be buried in the cemetery grounds recently donated by the Grand Trunk to the three churches. She's near the woods and the shy trilliums, Lily thought, blotting out the nasal sentiments of Reverend Hardman. Old Samuels would approve. But what would he say about Aunt Bridie encased in knickerbocker granite lintelled with a family name that would have shrivelled a leprechaun's laugh. Or Uncle Chester buttoned up in the chaste Methodist grave of a sometime oil town, the name on the headstone a perpetual puzzlement to the locals ever after. Where were their spirits now?

A few weeks later, Lily caught Robbie in her room with the leather pouch wide open on the floor and one of its objects in his hand. "Ugh!" he snorted, "a dead rabbit's foot." Lily scolded him more severely than he thought necessary, and then gently replaced the cross, pendant, stone and Testament. The rabbit's foot she kept in her hand till it warmed. "Did Da shoot that?" Robbie asked hesitantly.

Lily slipped the token into her apron pocket, and when Tom took the boys off to watch the ice break up on the creek, she put on her coat and scarf and headed towards town. She went around the northern perimeter, avoiding the streets, walked along the tracks a ways till she could see the smoke from the shacks in Mushroom Alley, then veered north through the brush, coming out after a while into the windswept clearing she knew so well. She sat down and caught her breath. Soon the voices began, one by one, to detach themselves from the wind. She heard Acorn say something to Sounder and caught Sounder's shrill laughter. Southener repeated words to her she had almost forgotten. She saw the outlines of his grave, now sunken below ground level with the weight of a dozen years. But where was Old Samuels? Slowly she felt her head turn to the north-east, and perhaps ten minutes later she was able to discern a slight rectangular hump in the sand, well disguised by grass and young aldershoots. She approached the grave, knelt down, spoke reverential words in an ancient tongue, then scooped up a little sand, placed the rabbit's foot in the hollow, and covered it. *Goodbye, Old Samuels.*

Lily had just started to prepare Tom's supper when he surprised her, standing in the doorway the way he always did when there was news.

"It's all right," he said, seeing her reaction. "We've been called up, but it's nothing to worry about."

Lily found herself sitting on the arm of the big chair, a kettle steaming in her hand.

"We're going west. There's been some trouble with the half-breeds out there, but nobody expects we'll have to do much shooting."

Lily felt the kettle brush the floor.

"Say something, Lily. Don't just sit there looking at me like that."

"You're a volunteer."

"Even so, you know I've got to go."

Yes, I do know, she wanted to say. And I've tried to understand all these years, I really have. Maybe it's partly my fault for loving that unknowable darkness in you, for being afraid of it, for wanting to bring it too close to the sunlight and tame it with familiarity, yet all along secretly cherishing it, as I do those kinds of things in myself I keep hidden from you. I *do* know. And I know also that I could reach out at this moment and touch you in a way that would make you want to stay. If I do, I may regret it for the rest of my life. If I don't...

"We're going to sail into the north," Tom was saying, settling her into the chair, "all the way to the lakehead, then cross the Rainy River system in canoes like the old voyageurs. Then we march over the prairie to Fort Garry where we stay for a while to make sure the new province gets off to a proper start. No fighting, no war. Monsieur Riel won't be there to greet us."

"Think of the boys," she said.

"I am," Tom said. "With the money I'll earn, we'll be able to buy furniture for the new house, clothes and books for the boys when they go to school. You'll be able to throw away that wretched quilting frame forever. We'll come back here and put a torch to this old place and make sure it stays a part of our past. Lily, I've got to do this."

Yes, it may be the last chance.

"I'm gonna come back, you know."

"I ain't goin' down to the boat."

Lily said her goodbyes at the gate. Gimpy came with his buggy to take Tom and his gear to the troop-ship waiting at the wharf, and to supervise Robbie who was being allowed to cheer the soldiers off with his hanky-sized Union Jack. Lily waited until the horses had almost reached the bend before she began to tremble. Tom turned in his seat and waved back to her, his figure caught for a second in a burst of lilac-spray. It was an image she would hold in her heart for a long, long time. A few weeks after Tom left, Lily missed her second period.

Early in May of 1870 the new Dominion under the stewardship of Sir John A. Macdonald undertook its first large-scale mobilization and transfer of troops to a distant war zone. Railroad, lake-steamer, bateaux and forced march were splendidly coordinated so that in a mere ninety-six days Colonel Wolseley's army of twelve-hundred volunteers and regulars arrived at the outskirts of Fort Garry, Manitoba, to claim the province for Canada. No resistance was met, not a soul opposed them.

But the getting-there was itself a triumph of Canadian ingenuity. Troop-trains left Montreal and Toronto, picked up volunteer units along the main-line and deposited them on the wharfs of Collingwood and Point Edward, where troop-ships – refitted freighters – whisked the battalions northeastward along the ancient fur-trading routes of Champlain, Radisson and Groseilliers, and the mighty LaSalle. At Fort William they disembarked, seasick but singing, and clambered into hastily constructed bateaux which were part canoe and part sailboat. In mid-May they disappeared into the bush and did not emerge again until August 23. Occasional scouts, of hardy native stock, returned to Fort William to report on morale and on progress made to a tense and bored populace. These messengers also brought out mail destined for the home front.

So it was that Lily received five letters from Tom written over a span of six weeks, the last one dated "August 7, 1870, near Rat Portage." Gimpy and Clara, who was pregnant again, came over, and they read through them. Though Lily found she could follow much of Tom's elegant script, she preferred to let Gimpy read aloud so that she could close her eyes and picture every scene and savour the words Tom chose. His account was all the more vivid in her nighttime dreams.

Tom was attached to a forward unit, his company the only volunteer group to be so honoured. The first few days were jolly ones while the recruits stretched out the muscles cramped by several days in steerage. The sun warmed them by day and the crisp stars overhead at night seemed to bless their enterprise. Then the rains came during a forty-two-mile portage up to Lake Shebandowan. Fire and torrential spring storms had destroyed the primitive right-of-way. Tom's crew headed into the bush with axe and whip-saw. "I felt like one of the pioneers out there, hacking and cursing and blistering in places I didn't know I owned." It took three weeks to clear a path wide enough for the rearguard to dismantle and carry their boats through, along with two-hundred-pound barrels of salt-pork, cannon, cannonballs, rifles and cases of ammunition. The bulkier craft had to be pushed ahead on rollers which disappeared into the muskeg as fast as Tom's crew could cut them.

Now did the muscles rebel in the wet bivouacs of a chilling night, the mosquitoes take up the flies' leavings and the rain wash entire tents away from their frail moorings. Exhausted but undaunted, the raw troops reached for fresh inspiration and found it on the smooth straits of Lac des Mille Lacs and the resurgence of July's best sun. While the paddling arms had strengthened and spirits brightened again, the jolting pattern of shooting rapids, driving hullward into stiff winds on open lakes, making sharp, brutal portages, and searching hopelessly for a dry bivouac soon took their toll. The food worsened. Dysentery and the grippe left dozens of men to languish in the rear, slumped among the supplies, moaning to keep each other company. But Tom miraculously felt stronger, healthier, more alive. He was placed in the vanguard of the paddlers, in the slick canoes manned by Iroquois and Métis scouts. He sang with them. He seemed to forget where they were going and why. He did not wonder at the arrival of Métis scouts sent by the "rebel" Riel to welcome and guide them in. He revelled in the challenge of the white water, the muskeg like quicksand, the raw cold of the rivers lit by sun but never warmed even in the sweltering heat of early August. Lily could almost hear him singing, she could see the reddish-blond beard circling the elementary blue of his eyes, she could yearn to be with him anywhere, always, below the altar of the stars.

On August 8 the expedition neared Rat Portage, passing through an uncharted narrows in the Winnipeg River. Tom's lead canoe was tossed dangerously by the frantic rapids, then dextrously righted by a dozen experienced paddles, battered sideways by a furtive boulder to an edge of balance, only to be slung straight by the current itself as it hurtled blindly westward. All at once the canoe pitched left as if a sail had been punched by a gust. It yawed, skidded rudderless along a flat patch in the eye of something sinister, spun counter-clockwise like the earth itself, then threw off its burden, tipping its paddlers one by one into the gorge below. Tom struck the surface, leaned on its buoyancy for a long second, waved his arms at some invisible rope in the air and went under. His head bobbed up again farther down the roiling half-mile narrows, amidst rocks that had broached the skin of many a birch-bark canoe or the drum of a man's belly. He made no sound at all and after a while his eyes quit looking anywhere. When his body was hauled ashore, floating serenely in a trout-pool miles away, the underwater rocks had battered it almost beyond recognition. There was no bleeding because his body was near frozen; the cold had killed him, they said, before he could be drowned or bludgeoned to death. Just as well.

Still, there on shore it was August with a brutal sun overhead. Nothing to do but bury the soldier with as much dignity as possible, with due acknowledgment of his valour, his patriotism. They gouged a shallow grave

out of the muskeg and laid him there in a spruce coffin girdled by a Union
Jack. The men shivered as the Last Post rang hollow over the Barrens,
haunted by stunted cedars, wreaths of sphagnum, and brackish moss-water.

Two months later, after many of the troops had been quietly returned
home by rail through St. Cloud and Chicago, Major Bolton came to the
house to tell Lily the story of Tom's heroic death. The details he provided
her – in a kind and fatherly manner that genuinely touched her – added little
to what she had already seen in her own way.

After he left, Lily stood for some time, staring out of the kitchen window
she had for so long used to measure the ebb and flow of her earthly
existence. She tried not to imagine a world that could no longer acknowledge
the absence of Aunt Bridie or Uncle Chester, of Bill and the moon-sad face of
his Violet, of Old Samuels and all his kind, and Mama and Maman and Aunt
Elspeth, and Papa wherever the woods was hiding him. She tried not to
imagine a life without Tom, without the kind of love engendered in the
dream-songs of the young for whom the future is as real as a moment of
touch-and-surrender. She tried not to think of the gods mad enough to have
contrived it. No deity – whatever its hue or cry – could have invented this,
she thought. I cannot accept it. What do you think of that, old Shaman? Do
you hear me calling out, shouting *I am Lily Marshall, I am Lily Marshall, I am
Lily Marshall.* And who is there to care?

Something urgent was poking itself into her ribs.

"Mama," Brad said at her side, still prodding.

"Not now."

"Tell me a story, Mama, the one about Sir Galahad. Please."

And somehow, she did.

PART THREE

Sophie

19

1

In the middle of October 1870 Maudie Bacon's husband, Garth, returned home from the wars to a hero's welcome. Riel and his Métis hooligans had been routed without a shot fired. Manitoba was salvaged for the Confederation and the federalist cause materially advanced. The Grand Trunk, rumoured to be vying with some upstart pomposity calling itself the Canadian Pacific for the rights to extend their brand of capitalism to the salmon basins of British Columbia, honoured Corporal Bacon and four other local boys at a banquet held at the Point Edward wharf. Major Bolton, representing Colonel Wolseley, toasted the valiant and spoke reverently of Tom Marshall, the fallen comrade no one more than he, his commanding officer, could wish to have been present amongst them. His sentiments echoed all round. The hero's widow, alas, was not there to acknowledge them.

•

As Lily feared, Robbie took Tom's death hard. He seemed pleased with the notion that his father had died in uniform while leading his men through impenetrable bush and over raging torrents and across waste marshes, every thicket treacherous with Indians who could will their shadows into the shapes of monsters and trolls. From her place at the window, Lily watched him slash his way into the underbrush, heard his bullying ululations, then waited, heart in mouth. Her brave warrior tramped out of the woodlot, weapon trailing in the dirt. Buoyancy vanished from the large eyes that rolled from side to side in a vain attempt to identify the enemy who would not show himself. She had explained to him that his father's body had stopped being, like the frozen sparrow's on the window-ledge, or like Bachelor Bill under the earth a mile away. The things they loved most about him, the way he smiled and listened and spoke, had flown back into the air. But five minutes later he would scowl at her with innocent ferocity. "When's Da comin' home?"

Lily suggested he was seven going on eight, and that his Da would be proud if he walked into town each morning to the big school and learned to read and write and start to become a man.

"I want Da to take me." That was that.

When she propped him up on the chair arm and began to read the story of Ali Baba (she'd memorized it word for word and detail for detail, but still felt the letters crystallizing on the page, having their miraculous say), he kicked the book out of her hands and stomped off. Later, he allowed himself to be held while he cried out at the trolls and ogres whose deaths he had marked in black on his avenging scroll. She knew these compulsory tears were a tiny portion of the huge rage that shook him. This would become for him the unanswerable anger of his life. When she wept – for herself, for Tom, for the deep absence no accumulation of days would fill – most of her tears were for her son, for the life he had dreamed, for the consolation she would be forever called upon to give and be rebuked for. Perhaps I am better off, she thought. I never learned to dream too far ahead. Old Samuels taught us how to dream backwards and be content. Teach me to be lucky, she begged him one terrible November night as she sat in the dark, swaddling her son's fury

Brad was different. He accepted her account of body and spirit, though she could tell it had no more reality for him than the rhymes bouncing in his head at night or as he lay among the clover of the meadowlands above the village. Avid for company, the boys often played side by side, but only rarely did their discrete fantasies intersect, and when they did, the outcome was usually swift and violent. Brad accepted Robbie's sudden unprovoked fists as part of his lot in the scheme of things, even his due. But when the latter added, "I hate you", Brad would stop crying and grow still. This seemed to please Robbie as much as the tears, for he could then carry on his own game without the background annoyance of his brother's silliness. As a result, Brad drew even closer to her. He ventured out less. He begged her to read to him, and as soon as she had got beyond her repertoire of memorized pieces, slowing to a near halt at the balking print, he would throw a tantrum, yelling with impudent mockery the meaning of a word that would not come off her tongue. Later, in bed, he would nuzzle against her and sing "A froggie came a-wooing" till she relented and joined him partway through and they finished up with a harmonious roar. I'm spoiling him, she thought, but she couldn't think how else she could love him. Once when he called to her from his sleep, she came across to the boys' room in time to hear him say, "I saw Da, in my dream. He talked to me." Robbie awakened too. "Da's dead." She held them both. When she woke up in the morning, they were still there.

"Ah, there goes Lily and her boys," grocer Redmond remarked to a customer during one of Lily's infrequent visits to town. Lily and her boys. That would be it – her life – at least as far as she could see.

•

There seemed little time to think about the pregnancy, now in its eighth month. Fortunately, it felt like the first one, lively and healthful. She had no discomfort except for the weight of the girl herself – she knew it would be a girl and addressed it as 'she'. This one will be mine, my private treasure, she thought, tasting the bitter sweetness of the notion. I shall try to give her father to her – when she's ready – but by then she'll be bonded to me. You have your Papa's smile, I'll say to her, and we'll hug one another, feeling your absence, Tom, in our separate ways. Stop it, stop this, remember Old Samuels – dream backwards, dream of your lover blessing your flesh with the fire you stirred and vanquished with your own desire, his seed tucked away already bequeathed.

November of 1870 turned out to be a cold and nasty month. Sleet storms roared in off the Lake freezing the last leaves to their branches while gusting after-winds snapped them free again. Every morning Lily got a fire going early in order to boil gallons of water to unlock the ice choking the well line under the sink and the one in the yard. Robbie and Brad carted wood in from the shed – several of Garth Bacons pals had come out in September and cut four cords – but she had used too much kindling trying to get hot fires going. . Young Mary Bacon was sent out by Maudie every Saturday but had to return weekdays to go to school. "A whim she'll get over soon enough," Maudie promised. Mary helped to clean and prepare food ahead, but she was less proficient with an axe. One day she walked Robbie in and out of the village several times – once in the dark – to make sure he could find his way to Maudie's house at any hour, should the baby decide to make an impromptu entrance. From Bacon's a buggy would be despatched to pick up

Dr. Dollard in Sarnia. "Sophie's out of business," Maudie said through Mary, "too drunk to deliver." Robbie was delighted with his role as scout and forerunner. Lily was sure he rehearsed it during the afternoons when she had to lie down to rest and he was ordered not to leave the yard. At any rate, Lily could see that life was going to be no easier after the baby came. She would need help. Help would cost money, even if one of Clara's sisters could be persuaded to give up school for a while and come. And money there was little of. They had saved almost a hundred dollars towards the cottage in town, and the Government had promised some compensation whenever they could find time to pass the necessary legislation. She could live for a year or more on that. Perhaps longer if the boys didn't go to school, an option she had never considered. What then? The whole acreage could be turned over and made productive, provided she was strong enough in the spring. But prices were uncertain as the new Confederation sorted out its priorities.; The weather was fickle and the competition fierce.

"You see now," Maudie would say, not ungenerously, " why so many of us cling to the church. What else've we got to protect us when we're down, when our men desert us?"

Late one afternoon, when she was out in the garden area looking for Robbie, she saw his tiny figure zigzagging through the withered bull thistle of the meadow. Her eye caught the pines on either side of the opening she stood in. The windbreak: Uncle Chester's barrier against the encroaching world, Aunt Bridie's signal to the Grand Trunk of defiance and separateness, Lily's beloved evergreens that sang softly in the summer and held the stars aloft in black winter skies. The last of the ancient horizons, old sagamore, she whispered to his presence somewhere beside her. Say yes. Robbie's death shriek shook her awake. A bull thistle toppled. Another. He waved to the sentry.

They must go. This winter, white-pine would still be fetching a good price before the peninsula was opened up for systematic slaughter. Also, she realized, it was time. The smoke from the cottages was less than half a mile away. Some of the timber she could take back as sawn boards; she'd get someone, perhaps the timber-cutter, to put up two chicken coops. Chickens she knew. Eggs were a sure living. She'd trade vegetables for grain. Her thoughts raced, full of figures, schemes, possibilities. She barely felt Robbie's petulant tug on her sleeve.

When Mary Bacon came that last Saturday in November, Lily was still excited, and some of her enthusiasm had rubbed off on the boys. "I'm gonna help cut the trees down!" Robbie announced, "an' Brad an' me's gonna collect the eggs every mornin', ain't we, Brad?" He demonstrated his technique for terrorizing any hen who harboured thoughts of saving an egg for her own pleasure. Lily came out with Tom's writing pad, his quill pen and a bottle of thickened ink. "I'd like a message to be put up in the post office," she said, and Mary, wide-eyed, picked up the pen, eager to display her newly-achieved skills. She left, skipping through the wet snow.

"When the hens get too old to give eggs," Brad said, "what'll we do with them?"

"Chop off their heads an' eat 'em!" Robbie said. "Eh, Mama?"

Lily didn't hear. She was clutching her abdomen with both hands.

"The baby kick you?" Brad said, open-mouthed.

"You okay, Mama?" Robbie clasped her arm and steadied her.

"Yes," she hissed, sitting down, dredging up a thin smile.

That was no contraction, she thought.

2

Whatever fears pursued him, Robbie Marshall acted with a courage and sense of purpose that would have made his father whistle with pride. Despite the galling pain that stabbed spitefully at her body, Lily found time to worry about her seven-year-old melting into the snowy dark, lamp in hand, the map of his voyage floating a foot beyond its glow, her life in his care. As each scream jolted through her clenched teeth, Brad jumped in the invisible ring that pinned him to this one spot. Between jolts she was at last able to ask him for water and another blanket. A long time later, hours it seemed, he meandered back in, humming to himself. He put the blanket on and began tucking her in, one fold at a time. There was no water. Her throat burned. The pain no longer sliced into her in slender arcs; it scoured at the entire abdominal cavity, as if some drunken ploughman were dragging a harrow-disc cornerwise across it. Then the air around her went numb. She dreamt of Maman LaRouche in her ice-house, the soothing cool of ice on the skin, a sunny room shorn of flies.

Dr. Dollard arrived with a rush and a clatter that woke Brad out of his dazed sleep. He started to cry as if he would die were he to stop. Mary went straight to him, forgetting that Robbie was still in her arms dreaming he was awake and strong and not lost. Maudie and the doctor headed for the bedroom. Garth Bacon tethered the horse and sat in the democrat shivering between 'belts' from his flask. He was only thirty but looked fifty – he'd seen too much of this. Nothing could ever brace him against the kind of screams that came, undeflected by wood or grass or muffling snow or alcohol. He thought of a pig being gutted alive by a deaf-and-dumb butcher. She'll die, he thought. We'll all die.

Dr. Dollard, puffing and sweating like a lumberjack, swore at Maudie, the fickleness of chloroform, at God's indifference – wishing to Christ the woman would stop rising out of her death drowse just long enough to disembowel him with an accusing shriek. "I said give me the forceps, you stupid girl. Quick! I might be able to save the child!"

Maudie stood frozen. She couldn't understand what was holding her upright. She could see nothing but a brace of female thighs wrenched apart. A small, bloody skull was driven back and up and in by some bellicose, furred sphincter the doctor's paws plunged into with fury and disgust. Around her the air stank, like an outhouse in Hell. Mary caught hold of her sister-in-law just as she gave up the ghost. Then Mary herself handed Dr. Dollard his forceps and positioned the lamp so he could see. She saw the dried blood on their pincering grip. She wondered how she had been born, then forgiven, then loved.

"Gotcha by the ears, you little bugger," the doctor gasped, pulling back as if he were rowing a coal-barge upstream. Lily made no sound to interrupt the whooshing blast of blood and pus that greased the baby's slide into the air. The force of it knocked the doctor back onto his rump. The foetus dripped onto the bed. Maudie was awake now. All was in motion. The age-old rituals. Garth had come in and was stoking the fire. He listened for the signal, the all-clear. It didn't come.

Lily opened her eyes to see the tears in those of the women. "Thank God, you're alive," Maudie said. "It's a miracle."

"The baby's gone," said Dr. Dollard wearily. "Probably died yesterday."

Lily whispered something in Maudie's ear. "She wants to know if it was a girl," Maudie said.

The doctor appeared puzzled. "As a matter of fact, it was," he said. "But it was all for the best, Mrs. Marshall. Your little girl was hydrocephalic, a Mongolian idiot."

Maudie and Mary both shuddered. The Lord moved in mysterious ways His wonders to perform.

"Come on, ladies," barked the doctor, "we've got work to do."

•

Three weeks later Lily, always a marvel to the skeptics of the medical profession, felt well enough to send Mary back to her studies. Brad had slept with Mary every night since the stillbirth of little Kathleen. When Mary left he crawled in beside his mother. Robbie announced he was ready to trek into the village to give school a try. After the holiday, Lily promised, and he dashed out into the snow to re-enact the legend of his pilgrimage he was longing to find an audience for.

Lily was sound asleep on the kitchen cot when Brad shook her awake. His eyes directed her towards the doorway. She felt the draft over her bare legs, the thinness of her shift under the blanket. The door closed and before it, filling most of the space, stood a tall, dark-skinned young man whose moustache rubbed against his smile. He pulled the tuque off his head and held it in front of him.

"Your boy," he said with a grin that was both sheepish and bold, "he tell me to come in." Robbie popped out from behind one of the powerful legs; he had an axe in his hands.

Lily sat up, still blinking.

The accent was familiar. "I come about the notice in the post office," he said and ruffled Robbie's hair.

3

Ti-Jean Thériault swung his big axe and another of the great pines crashed to the ground right where it was supposed to. The boys, well out of the way, jumped up and sprinted through the snow towards Ti-Jean, who posed for them, one foot on the fallen tree like a hunter beaming over a bull moose. He grinned wickedly and flung Robbie through the air, laughing at his squeals of terror and glee. Brad laughed, too, seated as usual about three feet away from Ti-Jean in a place where he could observe him, secure and rapt. Often Ti-Jean would make teasing lunges his way but he always stopped just short, just in time. Robbie grabbed his father's hatchet and under Ti-Jean's tutelage soon became proficient at stripping away the small branches of a felled tree. Brad would follow behind, trailing his fingers along the bark and stubs, humming to himself, keeping an eye on Ti-Jean in hope that he would burst into his strange, loud, off-beat singing. Once, while they sat on a log sharing jam sandwiches, Lily saw Brad lean over and press his face into Ti-Jean's rough Hudson's Bay shirt; Ti-Jean kept right on talking to Robbie.

Voici l'hiver arrivé

Les rivières sont gelées

C'est le temps d'aller aux bois

Dans les chantiers nous hivernerons

Dans les chantiers nous hivernerons

Brad, dawdling behind Robbie and his chattering hatchet, repeated the music with his high, boyish flute, the backwoodsy accent flawless. Soon he drifted off into the shelter of the hardwoods while Robbie kept hacking dutifully and Ti-Jean lit his clay-pipe, uttering puffs of smoke through his frozen breath. Later on Brad circled back, coming up unnoticed behind the busy labourers – the song still singing in his head.

Every morning now the boys were up before Lily. Robbie got a smoky fire going in the stove while Brad discomfited the embers into the fireplace. Moments after sunrise they headed out to the windbreak to watch for the jaunty figure of Ti-Jean cutting across the fields from the village. Lily could hear them arguing about who had seen him first. Robbie always won. Ti-Jean was boarding at Green House, a dingy hostel run by the Grand Trunk. He came every morning, Monday to Saturday – whistling, singing, puffing on his pipe, wool shirt open at the throat. He worked until four o'clock, when he waved the boys goodbye across the fields and disappeared. Lily made him and the boys a lunch, and brought hot tea out to the worksite from time to time. Robbie insisted on drinking out of a tin mug.

Lily assumed that Ti-Jean would be returning home to his family in Woodston up in Huron County for the Christmas holiday. She was surprised when he asked, in the diffident manner he used when talking to her, if he might join them for the occasion. "Yes! Yes!" Robbie said before Brad could get in. Lily, who could deny her boys little, said yes. Tom had always maintained the traditions of Christmas he had inherited from Aunt Elspeth and insisted they keep them up 'for Auntie's sake'.

When Ti-Jean asked her to come with them to select a tree, she said no, that she wasn't feeling up to a walk in the woods yet. He understood perfectly and the three men tramped off, axe and hatchets aloft, into the bush. Lily watched them for a bit but had to sit down shortly. She felt dizzy; her heart fluttered and slammed. Get up, woman, she said aloud, you've got work to do and a life to lead.

Somewhat later she put on her macintosh and boots and went out to wait for them. She noted that Ti-Jean was more than half-way through his work. He had cleared an opening in the windbreak almost fifty feet wide. She could see straight across to the village. When the job was finished, she realized that she would be able to stand in her kitchen window and view the entire sweep of the town from the rail-yards and docks in the south-west to the dunes and First Bush in the north and north-east. Between these extremes lay the cottages of the labouring folk, already four-streets square with hearth-fires aglow, smoke from their chimneys welcoming and insular, the cries of their children carrying over the fields. She thought she could see the tall brick chimney of the new two-room school on Victoria Street. Above the low snow-covered landscape before her, the winter sun burned without solace.

•

At Ti-Jean's behest Lily brought out the little Testament with Papa's writing on it. "I read in English almost as good as French," he announced after dinner. "That's what my Maman say, an' she's never wrong, eh?" He winked at the boys and grinned shyly in Lily's direction. "Always my job to read the Christmas story."

"After mass?"

He laughed, went red in the face. "*Ah, non, nous sommes Hugenots.*"

He read the St. Luke version of the nativity in a halting cadence that soon established its own authenticity, its own sort of flawed beauty – at least in the mind of one of the listeners. Though Lily had heard it before, she never lost her sense of the story's magic, of its having happened in a long-ago time when such mysteries were radiant with possibility. She glanced at Brad and was not disappointed.

Some small presents were exchanged. Robbie's eyes lit up at the sight of a bone-handled knife in its own leather case. Brad clutched the wooden carving of a Gryphon as if it were greased and likely to slip away. Lily blushed when she saw the Irish linen handkerchief. She went back into the shed and came out with a quilt under her arm. Ti-Jean stopped smiling. He took it in his hands, and she saw them shake a little. "Maman makes these," he said. "But not like this."

"Not that one," Lily said. "You can keep that one for now, but I'll make you a proper one in the new year, when I'm feelin' better."

Ti-Jean jumped up and went over to his haversack he'd pulled the presents out of. He had a leather case in his hand. He drew out a fiddle, perched on a stool and began to play. And sing.

Quand tu retourn' chez son père
Aussi pour revoir ta mère
Le bonhomme est a la porte
La bonn'femme fête la gargotte
Dans le chantiers, ah ! n'hivernerons plus!
Dans le chantiers, ah ! n'hivernerons plus!

They all joined in on the chorus.

•

With both children asleep on the rug in front of the fire, Ti-Jean held the Testament in his hands for a moment, stared at Lily and said, "Who is Lady Fairchild?"

"Somebody who lived a long time ago," Lily said.

•

Just after New Year's when Lily arrived one morning with a jug of tea, Robbie looked up with a smug smile on his face. "Ti-Jean's in the barn, ain't he, Brad?" Brad's smile confirmed the conspiracy.

"There's an old stove in there," Ti-Jean said when he came up to them.

"And a sleepin' cot," Robbie said.

"We moved it there when Bachelor Bill's place was torn down by the railroad," Lily said.

Ti-Jean looked at the broken window. "A bit of glass an' it could be fixed up real nice."

"Nice an' warm," Robbie said.

"But you'll be through cuttin' in two weeks," Lily said.

"Not if I rent a team an' haul these logs to the mill before the break-up."

"I couldn't afford to pay you."

"We'll help, won't we, Brad?"

"After the mill pays you, that's okay with me."

"It'd be cheaper in the long run," said Lily slowly.

"I could get some boards sawn," he said, nodding to the boys.

"To build the coops," said Robbie.

"For the chickens," said Brad.

"I'm real good with my hands."

Lily smiled. "Accordin' to Maman."

•

Robbie promised to give school a try as soon as Ti-Jean no longer needed him in the woodlot. It was nearing the end of January and Lily felt much stronger. She accompanied Ti-Jean and the boys to Little Lake but did not join them on the ice. Brad cried because he fell and couldn't keep up but settled down when Ti-Jean sat and whittled a sea-monster out of a piece of frozen driftwood then told him a story about it. Robbie found some older boys and showed them how good he was on skates. In a week or so the horses were due to arrive and both boys would get to drive them. Ti-Jean fixed up Uncle Chester's hideaway so that it was indeed warm and cozy. He loved the rope rug Lily gave him and the curtains she adapted for the window over the bunk. He even had a little shelf where he kept some French books.

Lily began to get herself organized for the spring. She hauled out of the shed Uncle Chester's boxes and containers, still bearing the stamp of his patient hand. She set up the quilting frame, hoping to get four or five completed by April. With the boys out of her hair, even on Sundays, she could work miracles. However, she discovered she was short of rags and swatches. She knew she should go over to see Clara, who would supply her ten times over, but she hesitated. Later, when I'm ready, she thought. Then she noticed the trunk where she'd tossed all of Tom's clothes last August. She opened it quietly as one eases open a closet where some ghost has slept undisturbed. She lifted them, squeezed them, smelled them, let their hues and textures become vivid again. Then she took her scissors and one by one cut the shirts, trousers, underclothes, socks and his navvy's cap into neat geometric shapes she would weave into remembrance.

Ti-Jean did not stay every evening after their supper was done, though the boys made his periodic escape difficult. He had young friends in town ("a *girl* friend," Robbie breathed) or he had a book to finish reading in his refurbished quarters. But sometimes he stayed for a few moments after the boys were ordered to bed to have a quiet cup of coffee with Lily. As soon as they were alone, he became very shy, and only by gentle questioning could Lily – knitting or sifting patches for her quilts – get him to talk about himself. It wasn't long before she learned to their mutual surprise that although he was born and raised in Woodston, his mother had come there from Sandwich in 1835. As a girl she had known Maman LaRouche, a LaPeche like her and a second cousin. Lily found it fascinating to hear of the Frenchman's exploits in the War of 1812 narrated once again, but this time through a different set of filters. Maman herself came through as lively and as special as she had been in real life. Lily added some of her own favourite 'Maman' stories to the legend, the happier ones, the ones she cherished. Lily and Ti-Jean lapsed so easily into French that she was often unaware of it until some exotic phrase jolted the flow of their evening soliloquies. It was much later – and sandwiched between longer, more reminiscent narratives – that she was able to piece together fragments of his own story. His father had come to the Huron Tract with John Galt and Tiger Dunlop. He was a lusty primitive who lived for cutting trees and trekking miles into the snowbound bushlands of the county. Ti-Jean was the oldest of eleven children. His mother wanted him to stay in school, and he had wanted to stay, but at thirteen he was side by side with his father in a pinery. His father roughed him up on a whim or in a whiskey rage. He slapped his wife when she dared to intervene, and Ti-Jean, who was almost twenty and no longer *petit*, blackened both of his father's eyes, keeping him out of the bush for a week. His mother cried over her son and said she was ashamed of him, so he left to seek his fortune out of the bush, on the docks or the railroad or in a factory. He didn't write and didn't go home for Christmas. He would never go home again.

•

"It's a beautiful baby girl with the sweetest big blue eyes I've ever seen," Maudie said.

"When was it born?" Lily asked.

"Just before Christmas. A few weeks late."

"Clara was never one for bein' on time," Lily said and saw the puzzlement in Maudie's face. "I'm kiddin'," she added. Maudie appeared to be thrown into worse confusion, but after a strong dose of fresh tea she recovered.

"You need to get into town more," she said.

"Sarnia's a long ways for me."

"You know I mean the Point. Us. Our Wednesday afternoons."

"I know. I don't want you to ever feel I'm ungrateful. You an' Garth saved my life. I'll come. Soon."

"Clara wants desperately to see you, but she's shy about bringin' the baby out here. She'd like you to come to the Christenin' next Sunday."

Lily listened for a while to Robbie barking his hopeless commands at Dick and Diamond, the team of Belgians with a mind of their own. "I just can't, Maudie. Not yet."

"We understand, we honestly do. But will you think about comin' to the wedding in March, then? We're cookin' up a shivaree." Lily smiled on cue. "You know Steve, Garth's younger brother, an' his girl Elaine is just the sweetest thing you'd ever wanna meet."

Lily waited for the codicil.

"'Course, she's Baptist, but still an' all –"

Ti-Jean let out an oak-rattling whoop and the horses, chained logs, master and apprentices could be heard moving through the woods towards the winding road that led all the way to Sarnia.

Maudie dropped her voice into a deeper, minor key, full of inescapable regret. Lily leaned back. "You know, of course, it don't mean nothin' to me, or Garth for that matter, but I wouldn't be much of a friend if I didn't tell you what kind of ugly, disgustin' gossip is goin' around town."

"Folks don't like me cuttin' down the windbreak?"

Maudie skidded a bit but got right back on the rails: "It's about...*him*."

"Who?"

"You know who, the Frenchie."

"Ti-Jean Thériault?"

"Lily, I'm serious. I'm worried about your welfare even if you ain't. You gotta remember your boys're gonna be in school next fall. Think of them, for God's sake."

"They like the Frenchie."

"That ain't the point an' you know it. Folks are sayin' that he's livin' out here. That he used to be seen comin' home from here every afternoon at a respectable hour, but after New Year's he's only been back to town three or four times." She cast a furtive glance towards the bedrooms, blushed, and plunged into the mire. "People are wonderin' just where he's hangin' up his socks, if you get my meanin'."

"In the barn," Lily said. She followed Maudie's gaze around to the window and out across the drifts to where the smoke hung above the chimney pipe Ti-Jean had rigged up. "Ain't that where Frenchies usually live?"

"Thank the Lord," sighed Maudie, depleted and relieved. "I'll spread the word." She finished her tea, took Lily by the hand and just squeezed it. For some occasions even Maudie had no words.

"I *will* think about the weddin'," Lily said and brushed her friend's forehead with a kiss. "By the way," she added, handing Maudie a package wrapped in tissue, "I made this little quilt for the baby."

•

The windbreak was down. The west wind that blew over the village continued across the open fields and ruffled the shingles on the house where Lily and her boys lived. All the logs had been taken to the mill on Sarnia Bay. Ti-Jean received his pay. A wagonload of sawn boards and joists arrived in the last week of February and were stored in Benjamin's stall until the first crack in the winter weather. A few days later it thawed a bit, and Ti-Jean and his helpers cleared the ground and drew the outlines of two coops in the softening earth. The boys begged to go with Ti-Jean into Sarnia to buy nails and two tack-hammers. But Brad came down with a hacking cough, and despite having made up his mind to sulk all day, he was delighted to discover his mother could sing in French as well as that other weird tongue. He fell asleep and when he woke she was sitting on his bed.

Just as Ti-Jean and Robbie came up the lane, the wind changed direction, slicing down unopposed from the north-west. By the time they had their boots off, the snow had started in earnest.

Robbie was exhausted. Lily managed to get a little soup into Brad before he fell into a deep slumber beside his brother. She drew the comforter over them. Ti-Jean was behind her in the doorway, watching. She kissed each of her sons, and when she turned to slip out, Ti-Jean was no longer there.

She found him in front of the fire, propped on one elbow and staring into the flames, enlivened by the storm swirling above them. The room drew itself inward. Lily sat down on the sheepskin next to Ti-Jean, then lay back, succumbing to the languorous heat of the fire already beginning to wane. He slipped his sweater over his head – his skin rubbed copper in the ebb of light. Behind her, the kitchen lamp sputtered, and she felt the darkness against the calves of her legs, her bare arms, the nape of her neck. Outside, the snow ceased, as if touched by a wizard's wand.

Ti-Jean rose up slowly, – his torso bent like a paladin's shield, burnished and rippled from splendid use. He leaned over, captured her wrist and drew her up with him so they stood together, only the fold of their hands fluttering between the reach and yearn of their bodies. His open hand folded around her waist, and he eased her breast against his. He was moving his legs against hers, nudging, urging, coaxing them into sensual motion. Hesitant, anapest , with no music but the song they were singing separately in their loneliness. They were dancing in a circle no rounder than the moon's on All Hallow's Eve. His teeth crushed her lips; she nipped his tongue with her own. A wave of chilling air shot between them.

"I got to go home," he said. "For a little while."

Lily gathered her breath. "Of course, you must. They been waitin' a long time for you."

"I'll come back."

"Don't promise."

●

Lily helped him pack his few belongings. She was surprised to note that it was only eight o'clock. The wind had eased off and fresh snow glittered as the moon sailed in and out of the thick clouds. Ti-Jean said there was a way freight leaving for the north from the railyards in about an hour. He knew the engineer; he could be home by midnight. He was a long time in the boys' bedroom, though he did not wake them up to say goodbye. He held Lily again at the door, and for a second neither of them was willing to admit the impossibility of what they both desired. Then he turned and left. He didn't stop to wave as he did with the boys.

Lily fell exhausted into Uncle Chester's chair. Only the feeble glow from the spent fire gave any relief to the gathering gloom. Before she lit the lamp beside the quilting frame, she spoke into the darkness: "See what you've done? See what you've brought me to? Why did you leave me, Tom?"

20

When the snow stopped falling early in the evening, it seemed providential to the roisterers at the wedding of young Stevie Bacon and Elaine. The Richmond House dining room had scarcely been able to contain such lengthy toasts and the exuberant dancing that followed. Several carolers toppled out of doors into the alleys behind where they butted and boasted, making repeated use of the goose-down drifts. There was a hearty cheer when the wind died and the moon guided their way again. It was nearing ten o'clock, almost time for the bride and groom to board the royal carriage and be whisked away to reconsummate their passion. Conspiracy had been afoot for days, led by the groom's sibling, who had selected only the brightest and the best to take part in his shivaree. "Just give 'em fifteen minutes," Garth commanded with a fratricidal leer, "I know my brother!" A special 'theme' had been chosen for the costumes and musical score: wild creatures of the wood and tundra, a great notion somewhere confounded. Ten of the fifteen elect arrived wearing the ceremonial outfits of Blackfoot Indian Chiefs – the kind of natives invented to meet the expectations of the first Europeans. But several pygmy-like trolls, a diaphanous jinn (female class), and a brownish bear of indistinct origins served to give the troupe as a whole a more representative cast. Tom-toms abounded as well as horns to simulate the sounds of Arcady gone berserk.

The wedding sleigh had no sooner turned the corner at Edward Street when the revellers emptied out of a dozen secret places of the Richmond House into the vacant lot next door. They hooted, admired, tested and tumbled towards assembly. The bear ambled after one of the squaws, licking her chin as if it were a honeycomb until she was, alas, rescued. From The Queen's livery stable across the street a beer wagon, devoid of barrels, came skidding behind the bit-chomping fury of matched Percherons. The coachman had some difficulty in checking their devotion long enough for the carousing tribesmen to board, but even the bear was pulled, rump first, into this racing, four-masted schooner of delight. The runners over the snow sang in sibilants; the wassailers tipped their flasks starward and hugged and rehearsed the ages-old scenes of *carnivale.*

As prearranged, the sled was brought to a halt a block away from the victim's house. Garth Bacon, straightening his eagle's feathers, called for silence.He looked at the ground in a puzzling manner that sent an icy shiver through the crowd. "No tracks." The news was passed along in a sinking whisper. Garth came back from his inspection of the house and peered disconsolately into the faces agleam with war paint and blazing, expectant eyes.

"They sure didn't come here," he said. "There's no sign of horses and no footprints anywhere near the place. We've been hoodwinked. Where in hell'd they go?" There was much fruitless speculation. Harvey Shawyer spoke up. "No wonder my Bess was actin' queer all day."

"Queerer than usual, you mean."

"Shut up, Digger." Harvey was the bride's uncle by marriage. "She blushed every time I mentioned Woodston for the last two weeks."

"Woodston?"

"Bess's sister lives up there. An' her husband's the engineer on the way freight!"

"An' the way-freight was sittin' there, an hour late, waitin' for them!"

"Hoodwinked," Garth said, his regalia adroop. "C'mon, Mose, turn 'em around, we still got a bit of the night left."

Most of the revellers clambered back onto the wagon and let it carry them at a forlorn trot back to the Richmond House, where a few would try to revamp their gaiety. The bona fide roisterers, however, remained, half-a-dozen strong: male, thwarted and bearish. They sat down on a snowbank outside the dark house and drank from a common flask. Digger Smythe stood up. His eyes ballooned in the moonlight like Bacchus before a binge.

"Fellas, we might've missed some cozy bundlin' in this here house, but I know where there's some fresh snugglin' takin' place right this minute. And it ain't been blessed by no minister and it ain't been properly shivareed!"

A chorus of whoops confirmed the righteousness of the suggestion, and the motley band of make-believe savages set out to the southeast across the fields in pursuit of pleasure. They were not a third of the way when the wind began to gust through their merriment. Then the snow came back in broken flurries, periodically blotting out the orange glow on the horizon ahead of them.

The chieftain halted his troop with a raised palm. He bent over and out of his ample quiver many cattails fell into anxious hands. A match flared. The flames from the kerosene-soaked torches leapt in the dark. A tom-tom began to search for a stag's heartbeat. On the faces of the war-dancers slashes of chrome and ochre shimmered like harlequin masks under gaslight. The roisterers – fired by whiskey and ineradicable envy – swarmed the isolated cottage, waving their flambeaux like flags from purgatory. They chanted over and over till syllables separated one from the other and smote the air like incendiaries:

Shame, shame, double shame
Shame, shame upon your name

In their zeal several harrowers broke ranks and dashed up to the windows of the seraglio, thrusting their torches against the tainted glass and grinning hideously, as if to deliver the devil a blow in kind. In their haste, two of them bumped into one another, stumbled, left their torches where they dropped, and began slugging it out. Around them the litany of mortification continued.

•

At first Lily was not frightened. When she heard the shouting, she got up from her quilting in time to see the torches flare up then watched them approach raggedly through the snow. She recalled that Stevie Bacon was to have been married earlier in the day and guessed this was the spillover from the customary shivaree. The bizarre costumery and derisive, taunting chant merely reinforced her suspicions. She decided to douse the lamp, slide the bar across both doors and wait them out: whiskey valour, she knew, had a short life. And the boys were in a deep, safe sleep. But when the wild, uncoordinated whooping started and several of the savages made daring charges at the house, Lily decided it might be better to waken the boys and tell them what was going on. Tom's shotgun hung where it always did near the main door.

She started towards the boys' room when she heard Brad shriek. Fumbling with the lamp, she ran in to find him paralyzed with fright in front of the tiny window over the bed. The afterimage of the demon's visage still glimmered in the glass – a distorted grimace so real it could have been the bogeyman stepped right out of an innocent's nightmare. Then the torch flames rose up and incinerated it. Brad leapt across the bed and grabbed Lily around the waist and buried his face in her skirt.

"Mama, Mama, Mama," he screamed. Lily picked him up and carried him into the big room; Robbie trailed them with a lamp.

"It's all right, it's all right," she murmured, cradling him on the cot, "it's only the men from the wedding, come to give us a little scare, like Hallowe'en. They'll go away soon. Shh...shh..."

Suddenly, Robbie yelped as if he'd been stepped on. "There's another one!" he cried. Across the kitchen window, Carcajou flashed through a gauntlet of fire and perforated shadow. A rabid coyote's grin swallowed his eyes, and his mouth became a wolverine's howl, hovering and thinning. Robbie began to sob with fear, reaching for his mother's hand and jerking it away from Brad's shoulder.

"Make them go away, make them go away." Brad's screams connected and became one hysterical plea. Lily jumped when something thudded against the shed wall behind her. They're coming in, she thought. Where are the shells?

Shame, shame, double shame
Shame, shame upon your name
Marshall, Marshall, Marshall, Marshall
Shame, shame –

The chant stopped. Soft but urgent footfalls in the snow. Silence. They were gone. Brad was now blubbering contently in her lap. Robbie had let go.

"Mama!" he shouted. "The shed's on fire!"

Lily whirled around. Smoke poured under the door to the shed. She ran across and flung back the bar. When she looked into the back room she saw the woodpile ablaze, as was the outside wall behind it. She watched the hopping blue flames take hold of the cottage roof.

"Robbie, get your boots an' your coats. We gotta get out right now." She slammed the door and raced across to the bedroom, fighting the panic that clutched at her throat and paralyzed her thoughts. Blankets, she muttered, it's freezing out there and half a mile to the nearest house. She grabbed whatever was nearby, stuffed mittens and scarves into her pockets and rushed back to the boys, neither of whom had moved an inch. The room was full of smoke and the roof over them seemed to be melting. Struggling with her own fear as best she could, she dragged her boys through the front door and out into the night. She did not know in which direction they ran, but they kept running until she found herself winded and kneeling in a huge drift.

"Mama, we're freezin'," Robbie sobbed with his arm around Brad, who was speechless, and coughing.

Lily found two blankets still tangled in her arms. She wrapped the boys up and squeezed them against her. They had no boots, but only their thick night-socks on. She was barefoot. She looked back and could hear the crackling of wood ablaze but saw nothing except the wild blizzard raging around them. The barn, she thought. We should have gone to the barn. Ti-Jean's stove might still have been warm. Where was it? A charred beam crashed noisily, but she could not tell which direction the sound had come from. The wind-driven snow muffled and warped. We'll freeze out here, she thought.

"Come on," she said to the boys, "let's start walkin'; we gotta get to town."

"I know the way," Robbie said, "even in the dark."

There was no darkness to be seen, not a jot. They walked in what Lily prayed was a straight line. She picked up Brad and carried him swaddled in her arms. All the feeling left her feet. Robbie dissolved in front of her. She cried out his name. The wind blew it back. He rematerialized in her hand. "I saw a light," he said, "I *think*I did. Over that way." Her legs were gone, she couldn't tell if they were moving or not. "Come on, Mama, come *on!*" She allowed herself to be dragged along. Suddenly, all the feeling and power returned to her legs and she was running swift as a deer towards an obliterating white light as big as the sun. It had a halo shimmering around it; she called out words of welcome. "Get up, Mama, get up! *Please.*"

•

She was being carried bumpily, head dangling, the snow melting and seeping down into her eyes. But the arm around her was powerful, and the stride under her was sure and unrelenting. Her feet were burning. She heard Robbie's breathing somewhere behind her. Where was Brad? They were slowing down. Light pierced the snow-haze, then a wavelet of warm air as gentle as that from a baker's oven. Kitchen smells. Feet on fire.

•

Lily had been looking at Robbie and Brad for several moments before she realized she was awake. They smiled warily at her. They were alive. She peered around. They were sitting on a mattress on the floor of a shanty. She recognized the smells, the drafts, the excessive heat. Someone had rubbed her feet and slathered them with grease. She could feel the blisters rising against it. She looked for their saviour. He emerged from behind the stove, his arms loaded with elm. He smiled at her.

At first she thought it was a trick of the candlelight or a result of the dizziness following her blackout but in a moment realized what she saw was real. The man – grizzled, in his sixties, hair askew as if in a state of permanent fright – had only one arm. It was an elongated ape-like appendage grown in strength and bulk since losing its coordinate. He had taken off his musty sweater, leaving only a sweat-creased undershirt that exposed the socket where the left arm had once joined his torso. A pouch of flesh as puckered as the grin of a toothless crone. His face was animated by wrinkles and gesticulating eyes unchecked by brows. A thin scar wriggled over one side of his grin.

He gestured with his fingers and arm like a mime drawing a map of his words with his body. Lily felt the tension and frustration in his eyes as she shook her head and tried to find her own voice. Suddenly, with a magician's celerity he was out of the door and gone. Lily leaned over and drew Brad into her embrace. He was silent and still – deep in shock. Robbie crawled next to her and hung on, crying softly to himself. Wherever they were, they were safe, and together. She gritted her teeth against the searing pain in her feet, closed her eyes, and waited.

Minutes, hours later, the door swung open. Lily felt the breeze of a great bustle and flurry against her eyelids but could not persuade them to open. The door rattled shut with resolution. She smelled garlic, whiskey, fresh sweat—a huge presence in the room.

"Christ take me ridin' in a teacup, it's Lily Marshall, an' the two bairns I brung into the world!"

Lily opened her eyes and saw the familiar face beaming down at her. "Sophie," she whispered.

"Spartacus here tells me your house burned down an' he found you an' your lads wanderin' up Michigan Ave."

"He saved our lives," Lily said.

"Only Spartacus is dumb enough to be out in a storm like this, eh? But thank the Lord he was. My, my, look at those feet. C'mon, you old fart," she snapped, "help me carry them across to my place."

Spartacus peered over Sophie's shoulder like a genie waiting to be recognized. Lily saw his eyes clearly in the light. She knew them. He hopped to one side and swept Robbie up onto his gnome's shoulder. Brad clung to his mother.

"We better get a sled," Sophie said. "Don't worry, Lily. We got lots of room at our place. You're safe now. You're in the Alley."

Spartacus went out carrying Robbie. Lily tried to get up.

"Don't worry about him, he looks queer but he's okay. Can't talk a word to strangers. Used to be a pedlar south of here years ago until some mark he was skinnin' ripped his arm right outta the socket an' beat him over the head with it like a Chinaman's gong. Ain't been right since."

Brad moaned in his dreams. Lily was shaking all over.

"Just a little fright," Sophie soothed as she turned Lily's feet over in her soft palms. "And a twinge of frostbite." She reached up and unhooked Brad from his mother's death-grip. The child settled against her bosom – cradled by two sturdy, rocking arms.

"He'll be all right. One of my boys'll be along in a minute with a sled."

"Thank you," Lily murmured drowsily.

"What's that you got there?" Sophie said.

Lily had pulled something out of the large pocket in her skirt. It lay clamped in her left hand. She looked down at the leather sachet bearing its treasure. As she slipped into unconsciousness, she was sure she could feel the pulsing of the jasper heart.

21

1

Sophie Potts was something else. Everybody in Mushroom Alley said so in one odd way or another, and Lily wasn't about to deny one dram of the praise due her. From the moment she entered Spartacus' hovel and saw Lily's boys shivering with dazed refugee's eyes, she took charge of the situation. "Bein' a midwife, as I used to be, you kinda get used to fear an' confusion." "Some women used to think I was an angel an' some tried to spit in my face like it was all *my* fault. Either way, I just plunged in an' did my job. You don't expect thanks in this world or you'll wait a long time for the train to come in." The next day Sophie sent her older boys, Stewie and John, to see what had happened. In the meantime, she put salve on Lily's burns, lay her down in her own bed and fed her broth a teaspoonful at a time "My Peg's takin' care of your boys," she said, "they ain't got a scratch on them." The smell of bacon frying and singed toast floated through the house and lingered; Lily heard the skirl of children's laughter and Robbie's voice, low and brave. "It's all right, Brad, everythin's gonna be all right." John and Stewie reported back, out of breath and saucer-eyed. Sophie came in and sat down heavily beside Lily on the bed. "Nothin' left of the house. Just charcoal. Even the stove melted. The snow stopped it from spreadin'. Your little barn wasn't touched."

Lily tried to take this in. Robbie suddenly peeked around the curtained doorway, half wrestling with two black-haired male replicas of Sophie Potts, and grinning. "We could set up in the barn for now," she said. "Then…"

"You could stay here, too," Sophie said.

And they did.

•

As soon as Lily was able to walk, Sophie led her across the cart path that served as a road towards a barnboard shack squatting forlornly among the scrub alders. For a big woman Sophie moved adroitly in an ambling trot. When they came up to the shack, she eyed it with the zeal of a horse-trader, kicked the door open and seemed delighted that it stayed upright on its rusty hinges. "Solid wood," she said, entering and motioning Lily in after her. "Christ knows where them Icelanders hooked it from." To emphasize her point she slapped both palms down upon a thick table that dominated the large main room. Dust skittered into the thin sunlight offered by two narrow windows. Sophie pointed to a misshapen stone hearth unadorned by andiron or grate. "Only place in the Alley, except the hooerhouse, that's got one of these. I don't think the poor buggars knew what a stove was. Most of 'em live in igloos back home, I'm told." She tested the resistance of a doorless cupboard over the washstand, loosening one shelf but otherwise seeming to approve. "For your best china," she winked. Then she flung back a curtain that once might have been a velveteen skirt, and when the dust cleared she said, "*Voilà*, they left the beds! See, you could put a screen down the middle an' have yourself two bedrooms, one for the boys." Lily's eyes were casting slowly about the room.

"Back there?" she asked.

"Ah, that's what I really brung you over for," Sophie said. She pushed open the back door and squeezed herself through. "Them Icelanders, there was two of them, brothers we reckoned, sneaked off the train headin' for Manitoba an' set up house in the shanty that used to sit right here. Then they built this place. Didn't talk to a soul, but I liked them. We could hear them jabberin' away in their crazy lingo – either laughin' to bust a gut or arguin' fit to murder – and as the Alleyfolk usually do, we left them food an' essentials when they wasn't lookin'. We figured they was plannin' on becomin' fishermen 'cause they went down to the shore every day an' stood watchin' the pickerel netters. One day they started buildin' a boat, just back of here then added on this big shed. An icehouse, we thought. One day soon after, some official lookin' gentleman come up the Alley an' before anybody could figure out a way of warnin' them, the two brothers was hauled away in irons, lookin' awful sad. We never did find out what crime they committed." The shed had no floor but it was spacious, had windows on the east side, and boasted several homemade tables and benches and two enormous cast-iron pots.

"You can set up in here. It's perfect."

•

What Lily set up, with a lot of help from Sophie and others, was a laundering room. After the Icelanders had been taken off to the wilds of the Manitoba Interlake, a woman named Mabel Trout had moved in with her two daughters and established herself as a washerwoman. She had five customers from the 'big houses' up on Victoria Street, and sometimes handled the overflow from the Queen's after a ship or two had debouched its crews upon the lower town. "A hard-workin' woman, I'll give her due," Sophie said. "She deserved better than those sluts of hers – lazy as sows in the sun, they'd sit an' watch her scrubbin' her hands raw an' never lift a finger. Had fancy ideas, they did, till one got the clap workin' part-time up at Hazel's an' the other got herself knocked up an' dumped by her so-called respectable gentleman friend from Charles Street. Went bonkers, dear old Mabel did – scrubbin' shit off too many nappies, I reckon. Anyways they had to cart her off to London, screamin' all the way. And I'm tellin' you, you gotta be far gone to be taken for crazy in *this* part of town!"

Mabel's place had subsequently been taken up by a number of transients and hopefuls over the course of the winter. "None of 'em lasted much longer than a pig's fart," Sophie said. "People see these empty shacks an' they think all they got to do is move in an' settle down free of charge. Ain't that easy. I seen a hundred come an' go. It takes a special breed to live here for very long." She paused, then grinned: "We got rules, you know."

Although it seemed obvious to Lily that Sophie felt some special affection for her, the latter made no effort to explain the intricate code of behaviour that governed the lives of the permanent residents of Mushroom Alley. "You gotta learn them on your own, so you'll know for sure whether you can stay," Sophie told her. Lily learned some of them every day during those first few weeks in which, though no overt decision was made, she began to clean up and repair the Icelanders' shack for habitation. Sophie was able to supply Lily and her boys with clothing to keep warm, drawing upon her vast, motley stock of wretched hand-me-downs. "When you got eight kids, nothin' gets wasted." Lily wore a moth-eaten sweater of Marlene's, wondering where Marlene herself was and why Sophie, who gabbed on relentlessly about her children, never mentioned her. Robbie and Brad were well supplied with assorted tuques, mittens and piebald macintoshes. Spring was only weeks away.

There was no furniture and not a single utensil. But the day after Lily began sweeping the filth out of the main room, she found several pots and pans and a kettle, well weathered but intact, sitting on the table. Next day there was a chipped chamber pot and accessories. Then four shell-shocked wicker chairs. Finally, a sofa desperately in need of a good home. When queried, Sophie just shook her head and jammed a spoonful of porridge into Bricky's clenched jaws (Bricky was short for Baby Ricky, Sophie's five-year-old, loudly proclaimed 'love child'). "Maybe it was the good fairy," said nine-year-old Wee Sue, who still persisted in believing in such things. However, the moment the gifts stopped arriving, Sophie said, "Spartacus brung them over. If you don't like them you can go over to his junkyard an' pick out better ones. He likes to choose things himself for the first time. He won't be hurt if you take them back for tradin'. He likes to trade. Got little use for money."

"I got money," Lily said. "How much do I pay him?"

"He likes coins best," was all Sophie would say.

When Sophie suggested that Lily take over Mabel's defunct business, Lily agreed.She could think of no other course of action to pursue. She could not bring herself to return to her own property and gaze on the ruins of the house where she had spent nineteen of her thirty years. Nor could she stay in the barn where Uncle Chester had gone to escape from himself, where Benjamin had waited all those years, where the jersey had died giving birth, where Ti-Jean had lain awake nights dreaming of her hurt eyes. It would be a long time before she went back there.

Right now they needed a stove to heat water; they needed firewood, mangles and scrub boards and irons (Mabel's had been looted. "Here, we call it re-usin'," Sophie explained). Lily had some money left in the bank but she was afraid to spend it. As soon as she could, she and Robbie walked down to McHale's General Store and loaded up a sled with groceries. When Sophie was out, she stocked her shelves and pantry. Nothing was said.

"Don't buy a stove," Sophie said. "Stewie says there's a good one in your barn. We'll haveta get it here before all the snow melts."

As far as Lily could see, no plans were made for moving the stove. She

continued to fix up the Icelanders' shack. The boys helped, still somewhat
dazed by the sudden changes, but like most children, unable to cope with
being inactive. Without any advance warning, the stove arrived on top of a
large sled. "You Lily?" asked the grizzled driver from his bench. In the keen
air his odour preceded him by several rods. "Yes." He put two fingers in
between his toothless gums and sent an icy whistle up the Alley. Then he
dropped his chin on his chest and appeared to doze off. The boys ogled the
horses, easing up to them and venturing a pat or two. A quarter of an hour
later several bulky young men – McLeods, McCourts and Shawyers from
their genetic trademarks – trudged in from sundry directions, Bachelor Bill's
stove was carried into the workroom and its pipes set up and adjusted to fit
the hole already in the roof. When Lily came out to thank the driver, he was
gone. "Belcher, the honeyman," Sophie said later. "An off sod, that one."

"How can I thank him?"

"Leave him alone."

By the time spring came and the earth around her heaved with tendril,
bulb and root, Lily was ready to leave the rambling comforts of Sophie's
house. At first she thought there should be some ceremony to mark the
occasion, but it soon became clear that none was called for. Sophie went off
with Peg and Stewie in search of morels, and when she came home hours
later, Lily and her boys were gone.

Lily got a rousing fire started and baked some extra biscuits in Bachelor
Bill's stove, whose whims she knew intimately. She sat on the boys' bed
singing softly to them and keeping one ear tuned to the outdoors. When
Brad fell asleep at last, she sat at the table looking into the dark towards the
river. No one came, that day or the next. Finally she walked over to Sophie's
house, knocked, and getting no response, eased the door open and sat down
to wait. The kitchen felt queer. The objects in it began to sway. She grabbed
the tabletop to steady herself. A great emptiness swelled up inside her. She
was a little girl afloat on her own body, a wafer of ice on a steaming,
featureless sea. The tears, copious and scalding, assuaged nothing, purged
nothing, not even the rage she aimed at her own heart.

When she looked up again, Sophie was standing off to one side; she had
been there for some time, it seemed, from the stillness of her pose and the
resolute composure of her face. "Cryin' won't help," she said gently. "But
not cryin's worse. I done my share." She went over to the stove, thrashed the
grates and put a kettle on for tea. "When you're ready, love, we'll sit down

an' talk about the launderin' business. An' anything else you care to tell."

2

Peg used to collect and deliver the laundry from the 'fancy houses' on Victoria Street, taking John or Stewie along to help pull the wagon over the tracks or through the mud of the Alley. Crazy Mabel gave them a nickel apiece. But according to Sophie, Peg was now too old for such a menial task. She was seventeen and ready to go out 'into service' if she wanted to. Although Sophie nattered and swore at all her kids indiscriminately and cuffed them whenever they were unwitting enough to loiter within range, she seemed to have almost no impact on the direction of their behaviour or their lives. "My Peg's got the kinda boobies gentleman wanta use for doorknobs," she'd sigh. But when Peg announced she intended to go to work as a maid for a bigwig at the refinery in Sarnia ("a notorious rake" who had "sprinkled the county with his bastards"), Sophie ranted and huffed like a storm warning, threatened to "set your Pa on you", sighed, and let her go. She even helped her pack her bags, and said to Lily, "Jesus, I envy her." Thus it was that Fred – or Blubber as he was affectionately called – with Robbie dragged along 'for training', became the delivery boy for the Alley's newest washerwoman. Lily didn't ask how Sophie managed to regain the interrupted business, but all five customers returned to the fold. "I know more about them ladies than their priests," was all Sophie had to say on the matter. It was more than enough. Spring arrived in full force. I may not be alive yet, Lily thought, but I'm living. That's something. On April first they celebrated Brad's seventh birthday.

•

Whenever Stoker came home Sophie was a different person. The changes in her, which Lily came to know intimately in the months ahead, began a week or so before he actually made his appearance. Blubber or Wee Sue would detect more sting in her glancing blows and glare back with lips aquiver. Sophie, rarely quiet for more than twenty seconds, carrying on a marathon gossipy tale while giving Lily a cooking lesson, boxing the ears of the nearest 'brat', or breaking up a skirmish in the yard outside with a lash of her trumpet tongue, now fell into pockets of silence. Her good humour, as indigenous to her as the jowls that telegraphed it, began to fail her, and she would sting the handiest victim – child, neighbour, kettle – with a fearsome, Bible-shaking curse.

"I lost forty pounds since I brought your Brad into the world," she said one day when Lily came into the kitchen and found her settled and steaming in a tin vat formerly used to nurture beer. Now filled with an endless supply of hot water by Peg and Wee Sue, Sophie plopped a sponged into Lily's hand, and she automatically began to scrub the great dame's back. Sophie released an elephantine sigh and then lay back among the cleansing suds. Her voluptuous breasts, liberated from their natural function, floated before her like plump, spiced offerings. She was very vain about her skin; at the beach she had John and Stewie erect a portable sunshade over her, and when she bathed in the Lake, she donned a bonnet bigger than most parasols.

"Stoker's comin' down from the bush," she said languidly, probably not even aware that her fingers had reached up to imprison her engorged nipples. "Gonna be here five days before the boat leaves. Five whole – goddamn you, girl, that's *hot*, you wanna *scald* my skin, you want your daddy to warm your ass so's you won't be able to sit down from here to next week!" Wee Sue, already well out of range and on her way for more healing water, ignored the comment.

"Stoker's real fussy about my skin. After all, the man's had nothin' to rub his hands over but the bark of a tamarack for almost three months." At this point several mammoth towels – once white – were brought in by the servant girls and held theatrically along one side of the tub. Lily offered her hand and Sophie rose out of the petal-scented waters – all pink curves and mahogany thatch and acres of scrubbed skin inviting touch.

"Get outta here, Stewie! You some kinda *pervert* or somethin'?"

•

Stoker Potts came home the next day, hopping off the way-freight as it slowed down for the curve behind his house. He sprinted across the flats towards what appeared to be a flag-sized Chinese poppy waving to him from his verandah.

•

Lily was not introduced to any of the Alleyfolk. "They know you're here," Sophie said. "You'll get to meet most of them, if they want to be met, and on their own good time." In the early weeks, Lily could not be sure that anyone in the Alley knew anyone else. One day a gangling black man, decked out in tie and tails three sizes too small for him, walked by and waved as if he knew her. An hour later, he walked back up the Alley and studiously ignored her, even though she was pulling weeds right beside the path. Nobody was actually seen visiting anyone else; but information – fact, rumour, gossip – travelled quickly. A woman, vaguely familiar, in a purple-flowered dress and unmatched sunbonnet strolled past and smiled broadly at Robbie.

"You must be Lily's eldest" she was heard to say and kept on walking.

"They'll let you know when they're ready," Sophie said. "'Round here we give people whatever privacy they want. But that don't mean we ain't friendly."

Sometimes Lily could see Sophie herself in her back yard feeding Duchess, her sow, or urging on Stewie and John in their labours. She would come up to the fence and stand there, waiting, till finally she could wait no longer and called out "Good mornin'!" Many seconds later Sophie might glance over and give the intruder the meagrest nod of acknowledgement and then continue on with her own work. Even the children –dozens of McLeods, McCourts, Shawyers – when they roved over the whole of the Alley in the dusk playing hide and seek, never hid out in Lily's yard, nor did she ever see the catcher venture across the invisible boundaries of her 'property'.

"Don't ask me why," Sophie said, "*why* is a question we don't have to ask in the Alley."

•

Stoker stayed for a week, as the ship on which he was chief fireman, the *Princess of Wales*, had been delayed in dry dock at Collingwood. Lily knew enough to stay put; besides, she was busy setting up the laundry equipment in the Icelanders' shed. John and Stewie soon arrived and proved to be of great assistance. They came every day and helped Lily move the two cords of wood into the shelter. The arrival of wood she purchased from the local supplier was a cause for much amusement along the Alley, as Sophie told her later. No one could ever remember an Alley person actually *buying* fuel before this.

"How do you get it?"

"We swipe it," Sophie replied, "but only what we can use."

They made two spacious windows for her in the south wall and did the glazing perfectly. They walked out to the old property and hauled back some lumber out of which they constructed benches and tables. They promised to add a wooden floor before winter – "when we can pick up enough lumber," they said. Robbie and Brad watched every move they made.

"I'm goin' up to the bush with Dad come next fall," John told them.

Robbie asked him if he'd found a little hatchet when he went through the house that got burnt. Then he looked at his mother and said, "When's Ti-Jean comin' back?"

The day before he left, Stoker came over to say hello. Lily was in the workroom when John and Stewie came in looking irritated.

"Dad wants to meet you," Stewie said. Lily put down the pot she was holding and brushed her apron. "He's out on the road."

"Oh." Lily walked through the house and waved him in from the front door. He had no recollection of their earlier meeting. On Lily's side, she was seeing a different man. He was still bearded, a bit more angular than muscular, with rugged handsome features and a bluff, engaging manner of speaking that seemed out of tune with long months spent isolated in the bush or hunched alone in front of a blazing furnace. His eyes danced lasciviously, like coal dust in the fractured sunlight.

"Glad ta meet ya, Lily," he boomed. "When I come back from my layover in a couple of weeks, we'll have ourselves a drink together, eh? In the meantime, anythin' you need these lads for, you just whistle. They're good boys, they are."

There was no expression of any kind on the boys' faces.

•

That evening as she lay in the semi-sleep she was getting used to, Lily heard a commotion from the Potts' house across the way: escalating laughter as raucous as it was hollow. Male shouts followed, and a series of haranguing shrieks carried their own brand of venom, taunting and mocking. Then silence. Lily dozed, grateful. The crashing of glass, as loud and as ominous as if Orion had burst overhead brought her wide awake. Brad stirred beside her and she put a hand on his fevered head. Sometimes he coughed all night.

"I'll kill you, you fat bitch!"

The words sailed clear and free down the whole of the Alley. Then a sort of muffled scuffling, as if heavy furniture were being abused and feet reluctantly dragged. A low pleading voice against the grim music. Nothing more – though Lily waited till the sun trembled over the window-sill and exhaustion claimed her.

Two days later when Lily came in to fix the boys' dinner, Sophie was sitting at the table. This was a custom Lily was just beginning to understand. Though no one asked after anybody's business or initiated a conversation without invitation, it was all right among genuine friends – indeed it may have been a symbol of such – to simply enter their homes or yards and 'sit a spell'. It put the host under no particular obligation; you could keep on about your business if you chose without jeopardizing the friendship, and sooner or later the visitor would leave. Like Old Samuels, she thought, in some ways. But it was also clear that such special intrusions often indicated a desire to talk. She sat down and squeezed out a smile. Sophie, the smudges of fatigue below her eyes almost completely faded, grinned.

"I hate to brag but that Stoker's *some* man. If Christ was hung like that, there wouldn't be a female heathen left upon God's earth." She stropped the nearest thigh and then snorted with the force of a crushed walnut.

Later, after tea and a few nibbled biscuits, Sophie sighed and said, "Burton didn't come back from the bush with Stoker."

"Who's Burton?"

"Our oldest boy," Sophie said.

3

During those first few traumatic weeks Lily kept a close watch on her sons. In some ways the shock of their loss and removal was easier for Brad than Robbie. Brad developed a bad cold and an asthmatic cough that made him continually fretful and in need of constant mothering. He clung to Lily's skirts everywhere she went during the day and slept beside her at night. He cherished her attention so much that it seemed to compensate, at least momentarily, for all the privations and physical discomforts. Robbie, on the other hand, would not stay put. He wandered beyond the margins of her supervision, his eyes fixed on the exotic rituals of the boy herds and girl flocks who yahooed, frisked and caromed among the bushes and dunes for much of the day ("Don't none of them go to school?" "Some of them, sometimes," Sophie said) and all evening till the moon went down or got swallowed by cloud. When a gang of boys about his own age roared by on their way to the beach or the grassy flats, Robbie would stand in front of the house and watch them pass, his feet longing simply to follow and take their own chances with rejection. Occasionally Lily would see one or two of the lads – dirt-streaked, barefoot ragamuffins – glance over at the motionless creature by the wayside, and then carry on as if impelled by the demands of some game they had never learned the rules of.

A few days before his eighth birthday, Robbie edged out to the road at the first yip of the approaching horde, so that when they swept by – spears poised for some imminent slaughter – he was naturally drawn into the irresistible current of their energy. So intent was this tribe upon the annihilation of its enemy that not one soul noted the addition of a whooping, fleet-footed brave whose heart soared with joy and the gratitude of those forever to be included. From that moment on, Lily's main concern was the whereabouts of her eldest.

"Don't fuss," Sophie soothed, "they always come back sooner or later."

Neither boy was able yet to sleep without violent dreams that shook them in their beds like scarlet fever or St. Vitus' Dance. Often, just before bed, Brad would see behind the lamp-lit window some configuration of shadow – severed, truncated, bloating ogre-flesh – and shriek. He would continue whimpering, even when Lily turned the lamp down so that only the blunt shadow of the night was visible anywhere. Even Robbie was susceptible to these sudden incursions from 'out there', and so it was not uncommon for Lily to have to sit with an arm around each boy, singing and murmuring them towards sleep. Even so, she thought as she watched them fret, they're lucky; the gremlins they're scared of are the only ones that will do them no harm.

Robbie, unused to sharing his exploits and triumphs, had some difficulty adjusting to the inviolable rules of the Alley games. Three times in one week he came home with a bloody nose and scuffed knuckles. For hours he would sulk, never telling the horrid details of whatever humiliation he had suffered and glared at his mother as if it were all her fault. But he always went back, grim lipped. Lily felt proud of him and yet somehow betrayed, left out, found unworthy. She thought of Sophie's Burton, and was ashamed.

When Brad finally recovered from his cough, and when Lily herself felt comfortable enough, she and her boys walked up Victoria Street to the Edward Street Common School. Until this time Lily had not ventured out of the Alley except to go briefly along Prince Street past the Queen's Hotel to the General Store for supplies or to walk along the cinder road to the rail-yards where she bought the firewood to get her business launched. For some reason she could not bring herself to go up Michigan Ave. to the familiar shops – Redmond's, Durham's Dry Goods Emporium – where she knew she would meet a dozen friendly, and perhaps even anxious, faces. Soon, she promised herself. Victoria was the last east-west street running parallel to Michigan Avenue and to the railroad tracks a hundred yards to the north. It boasted the largest private houses in the village. Robbie proudly pointed out the residences of their customers. "That's Mrs. Saltman's, the baker's wife, she give me a penny for myself!" They came to the frame building that served as the public school – three teachers and eight grades. They stood on the boardwalk in the early morning sun. The windows were wide open, a breeze billowed the blinds. They could hear the scratch of chalk on slates. "There's nobody in there," Brad whispered. "Stewie won't go to school," Robbie said, "Mr. Grindly whips him."

"Shush," Lily said. "Stewie's just tryin' to spook you. Come September, you boys're gonna walk up here every mornin'. You're gonna learn to read and write." And that's the only thing I know for sure, she thought.

•

Lily decided it was time to walk up Michigan Ave. She picked a sunny July day and in the glare of noon came up from Prince Street all the way to Redmond's.

"Sorry to hear about your place burnin' down," the grocer said. "No insurance, I take it." Lily nodded and gave him her order. "Bring the boys along," he said. "I always got a licorice or two for my favourite tow-heads."

Lily promised she would, said goodbye to Mrs. Redmond and started home. Standing in front of Durham's Dry Goods, chatting with three of the women from the Wednesday tea group, was Maudie Bacon. Shaking a little inside, Lily walked towards them so that she could be face-to-face with Maudie. A few feet away, she opened her lips to say 'hello' just as Maudie's eyes cornered her own for a telling second. The word froze in its frame. Maudie turned back to her friends with a snap of her head that conveyed to Lily so much more than the simple, lethal snub intended.

Lily kept on walking down to the docks. At the coal company she ordered enough coke to last her the winter.

22

1

Sophie was right. By the time the boys started school in September, Lily had met in one way or another most of the regular denizens of Mushroom Alley. One bright morning in early June while hanging out Mrs. Christie's washing, Lily heard someone calling. The sound came from a clump of trees to the north of her yard: a high-pitched, plaintive call that could have been a command or a cry for help. That's odd, Lily thought, there's nothing between me and Hazel's Heaven up on the dunes. Maybe somebody's caught up in the short-cut running down to the beach. She craned her neck, and the call came again, a man's voice echoing thinly in the empty morning of the Alley. He must be in a tree, Lily thought as she dropped her work and started through to the scrub, watching out for the sudden hawthorns.

"Ship ahoy!"

Lily came out into a little clearing which she was surprised to discover. A wretched hovel not much bigger than a pup-tent sat between two hummocks of sand. An open fire smouldering in front of the entrance. There were no windows. Lily's gaze was drawn upward to what appeared to be scaffolding erected on a steep hummock a few rods away but turned out to be the frame of a barn or coop that some previous tenant had begun in earnest and abandoned.

"Reverse engines! Reverse engines! Three points to the starboard, Mr. Collins. Steady now, steady on."

Perched on the upper rafters, with his feet on a crosspiece and his arms on the top joist, was a tiny gnome of a man with snow-white hair frothing about his face like the first foam of a breaker. He wore a captain's hat and a uniform whose brass buttons glinted with authority and pride. One hand was on his brow shielding his eyes from the fierce sea sun, the other steady as a rock on the bridge rail. His knees swayed with the pitch of the waves, leaving his upper body resolute and unshakable.

"Funnel off the port bow! All hands on deck. Prepare for May Day, Mr. Collins. No panic, please. No panic."

Suddenly his horizon burst apart with a dozen howling children who dashed out of the bushes as if on cue, washed past Lily and swarmed over the scaffolding like tars littering a mainsail. Of indeterminate sex, they scrambled, hurled threats and boasts aloft, enacted duels to the death, sent pirates to their graves, and steadfastly ignored their captain's call to abandon ship. Neither the old man nor the children fully acknowledged the presence or legitimacy of the other, but they seemed intricately bound up in a similar game, never quite out of the other's reach. Pirate kings lunged and skewered the old man countless times, and he in turn pleaded in vain with the blackguards to let the women and children enter the lifeboats first. It seemed to Lily – watching, ignored – that they had stumbled into each other's dream.

"Batty as a bull with three balls," Sophie wheezed, "but harmless. Nice old guy, really. Billy Whittle's his name, but everybody here just calls him Cap. That's what he was. Used to pilot the *Erie Shore* till she cracked up in a tornado back in 'sixty-five. He got everybody off an' then lashed him an' his wife to the mast. He begged her to get into the last lifeboat but she wouldn't. The storm broke them up. They were both washed ashore up near Port Franks. He was still breathin'. She wasn't."

•

It was at the Dominion Day festivities that Lily formally met the three women whose celebrated fecundity had produced almost three-dozen offspring incontrovertibly identifiable by their hair. It was a genetic miracle that might have delighted Mendel – red-headed McCourts (actually a hybrid orange shade unremarked anywhere else), tow-headed Shawyers (with characteristic cowlick) and black-haired/whey-faced McLeods (with pointed snotty noses that made them resemble starlings on the run). Until puberty, which attacked them disgracefully early, the sexes were indistinguishable by manner, instinct or dress. By age twelve, nature decided to have its way with them: the girls willowed and billowed shamelessly through the village, sending one kind of shudder through every respectable father and another kind through their curious sons. The boys toughened and grew lusty, and decent mothers everywhere locked up their puzzled daughters.

Though Lily did not get to know them well – they were clannish, exhausted from day labour and childbearing, and not quite ready to admit they were stuck in the Alley for a lifetime – she admired and felt sorry for them. Later, when she herself felt more settled, she was able to help them in the small, unobtrusive ways allowed her. She had tea and chatted with Mrs. McLeod on many occasions and once or twice with Mrs. Shawyer and Mrs. McCourt, but never with all three together. In that regard they formed an exclusive club, sharing their common miseries, shrivelled hopes and the need to exchange petty, emancipating spites. To these ends Lily was, in their limited view, a washout. Miseries they had aplenty: each had husbands who were unemployable because they were alcoholic or alcoholic because they were unemployable. Their men were rarely at home, eternally seeking odd jobs 'digging ditches' up north or down in Kent or in the States, coming home long enough to terrorize the kids, quench their abbreviated lusts, and contribute to the steady advance of progress through procreation. The older boys would get work, help support the brood for a bit, then take up with some girl and move off. The older girls went into service and helped feed the younger ones until they found a spouse or let their master get them pregnant. Then they returned home to bear the bastard and take up permanent residence among their own kind.

These few families proved to be an endless drain on the charity of the three churches whose auxiliaries competed mightily in fruitless attempts at reform and repudiation. "Even typhoid wouldn't wipe them out," an exasperated elder was heard to say one Sunday morning in the vestry. Nonetheless, it was generally conceded that the girls were good workers. There were at least seven of them serving as maids or scullions throughout the village and the town.

•

Lily's business was almost more than she could handle. She needed a much larger tub for soaking the huge bloodied sheets sent down to her from The Queen's. She mentioned this to Sophie. Several days later she heard Honeyman's wagon stop in the road near her front door, and when she went around to see what was up, Belcher waved to her and pointed at a shiny, coppery object behind him. Spartacus was already trying to wrest it loose, and soon three boys materialized to help carry it into the workroom. It was a brewer's vat, somewhat tarnished and battered but otherwise serviceable.

"Where'd he pick this up?" Lily asked Honeyman, who chewed his tobacco and looked at his toeless boots whenever he talked to a 'lady'.

"In the brewery junkpile down on Front Street. Surprisin', ain't it, what a sane man will throw out." Nothing in Mushroom Alley surprised Lily. "Old Spartacus here, he's got a keen eye for junk."

Lily got her cookie-box and counted out two dollars in change. "That's too much, Lily," Spartacus said in a clear and slightly accented voice.

Honeyman was so startled he swallowed his cud.

•

When Lily went to the beach, as she often did that sultry summer of 'seventy-one, she took the shortcut that ran from the road past her place through the scrub and curved below the back-yards of the last two houses before the Lake – Hazel's Heaven and Baptiste Cartier's blind-pig. The boys were curious about the faded clapboard house with the mauve trim, the only house of unnatural tint in the Alley. They were equally puzzled by the flounces and underclothing that curtsied in the breeze off the water. Pinkish corsets drooped like parboiled lobsters, and pennant-sized pantaloons fluttering in cerise, marigold and Kelly green. The slightest kiss of wind sensuously fanned innumerable pairs of silky stockings. The boys kept their distance, though, because they were afraid of the bootlegger's pig, Aquinas, kept in a pen near the path. He was a gargantuan Polish China boar, who snorted and pawed the muck with his cleft trotters, ramming his malodorous snout into a trough of slime. He cast the baleful glare of his blood-puffed eyes at the white morsel of little boys who might venture too near and be eaten in a wink.

As far as Lily could learn, John the Baptist (as he was known here) kept Aquinas as his pet, throwing the most dreadful tantrums whenever anyone – denizen or stranger – came too close or made some drunken slighting remark about its potency or suggested it might be of singular service to certain females along the lane. Often he could be heard talking to it – in French or some private *joual* they shared to keep mankind at bay. He was a morose man, utterly taciturn except when conversing with his pet or cursing trespassers. But he made the best and safest hooch in town, and try as they might, neither man nor boy inside or outside the Alley was able to trail him long enough to discover the whereabouts of his still. Once, a gang of toughs had set watch on his place day and night for a week. As far as they could tell, he never left his yard, coming out only to feed Aquinas or sit gabbing with him in the middle of a moonless night. Yet, fresh supplies appeared for the weekend crowd of sailors and the overspill from Hazel's.

On the way back from the beach, Lily often walked the long way around, up the little cliff and onto the lane itself, where the boys could gawk at the big windows beside the verandah on the whorehouse, hoping for a peek at the exotic plumage inside. The girls never came out in daylight, and Lily had warned them away from here after dusk. Across from Hazel's and next to Honeyman's place was another gray shack remarkable only for the five or six sheds behind it, several of them lean-to's, and an old army tent that looked as if it had been recently shelled. "Stumpy lives there," Sophie had said. "He thinks God was a fish."

One day in July just as Lily and the boys climbed up the slope onto the lane, she spied a strange man coming towards them. He obviously saw no one ahead for he swung onto the path that led up to Stumpy's shack. It was his way of walking that alerted Lily: an ambling, rolling, almost bouncing gait that a deckhand might use in a high sea but only if his legs had been frozen from the shins down. Stumpy, Lily thought. He was dressed in overalls and a wool shirt, his beard and gray hair as tangled and forlorn as fishnets on some deserted tidal flat. She never would have recognized him from that face so completely altered in seven short years, but the walk was unforgettable. She told the boys to go on home, and then broke all the rules by trailing Stumpy into his house. When he looked in astonishment at her intrusion, she smiled sadly and said, "Hello, Bags."

•

"It's Stumpy now," he said with both resignation and pride. He sat out on a bench overlooking the beach below and told Lily his story, but only after she had told him as much of her own as she could bear. He had got a job in London as an office clerk in a stagecoach line, but he had been too miserable at being cooped up or just too ornery, because he was soon fired. He took straight to drink and got so bad even his cousin threw him out onto the street. Some preacher found him in the gutter, taught him to see God in all His glory, and sent him abroad to bear witness and teach the world how to overcome the accidents of fate. He cared nothing for material goods now; he lived only for God and to serve the outcasts of mankind. So he worked in the fish plant in the warm seasons to get enough money to aid the down-trodden all year long. He showed Lily the shelters he'd erected in his yard to accommodate the hoboes and unemployed and outlawed who jumped train at the end of the line and wandered in dazed, cold, crippled, without hope or the will to hope. Here he fed them, talked a little religion, listened to their woeful tales, and showed them the stumps that God had blessed him with as proof of his own temptation, apostasy and resurrection.

"We all need God, Lily. I do hope you've found Him. Is there anythin' I can do to help you? If so, you just holler an' Stump'll be there."

Lily touched the back of his hand, felt how benevolent the sun was, recalled the cool clasp of the waves on her legs, the soaring delight of her boys at play. "I'd like a little music," she whispered.

2

About a week before school was to open, Robbie came panting up behind her in the workroom. "Come quick, Mama, there's a naked lady gettin' beat up over in the dunes! She's cryin' an' blubberin'. We heard her, didn't we, Brad?" Lily looked at Brad who'd come running in after his brother. "A big black man's beatin' her up," he said. "Beatin' her to death!" Robbie added, and Lily knew she must go.

The two boys dragged her along through the scrub to the edge of the dunes behind Hazel's place. Robbie was about to point triumphantly to the exact spot of the murder when Brad yelled, "Up there!" They all turned and looked towards Hazel's just in time to see a flash of leg, buttock and arm. Black and white blurred together as they disappeared hastily beyond the flapping bedsheets.

"She looks quite alive to me," Lily said, pulling her hand free of Robbie's.

"He took all her clothes away," Robbie said, "an' I heard her cryin'."

Lily was about to drag her boys home and find some way to explain what they had seen, when she was stopped by a rasping female voice.

"Goddam you, Shad, I told you to keep that black pecker in your pants and I meant it. Betsy Riley, I'm ashamed of you, runnin' around starkers where anybody from the town could see you plain as porridge. I'm ashamed to know you, girl. Now get in there, both of you, before I take the rug beater to your butts." A door slammed amid less-than-contrite giggling, and the woman with a voice like a claw hammer emerged at the top of the rise and began jerking pegs out of the sheets as if they were hairs on the head of her victims. Her quick eye spotted the strangers below. Lily saw the sun ricochet from a gold tooth. The woman's arm was waving them a welcome.

"You boys go on ahead to Sophie's; don't forget the carnival's on this aft," she said.

But the boys slipped into the bushes and watched from below as long as they dare. When Lily came up to the woman, they both stood stock still for a second then spoke almost simultaneously.

"Lily Ramsbottom!"

"Char?"

Char Hazelberry, now known as Hazel, reached out with her scullion's grip and pulled Lily to her bosom. "It *is* you, I can't believe it, you ain't changed a bit. Winnie said she was sure it was you but I didn't believe her. Now I got to believe my own eyes, don't I? Come on in an*-' meet the girls."

•

Hazel added a dollop of whiskey to her coffee and sighed across her bosom. "We was all doin' just fine, thank you. Winnie's sister took the babe – real cute little fella, wasn't he, Win – and our business was goin' great guns. Then I decided to accept the job at the St. Clair Inn when the new owner took over. I was chief cook with my own staff – naturally I carted Winnie an' Betsy along with me an' for a time we run the best cookery in town. We heard that from the drummers an' regulars, didn't we, Bet. But that owner an' his snooty lady was somethin' else! Remember that wart on his nose?" She glanced at Winnie and Betsy and was rewarded with reminiscent snickers. "Well, to make a long story longer, the old geezer – he must've been *sixty* – corners me in the pantry on St. Patrick's day an' tries to lift my skirt, pretty as you please. Naturally I resisted an' even threatened to tell his Bible-thumpin' wife. That backed him up real quick. But not for long. I discover he's been pesterin' both Win an' Bet, poor dears, an' them not havin' the wherewithal to resist, an' so I goes straight to his office to have it out, an' the very mention of his sin must've set his gong a-clappin', 'cause he reaches over an' flips both my bosoms right outta their harness. Well, I let out a screech that would've shook grandpa outta eternity, and in rushes the wife. Naturally I appeal to her as a woman and a believer, but you'll never in a hundred years guess what happened. She sided with the old goat! She called me a slut and a hooer and a panderer, an' she told me to take my girls an' depart on the instant. An' the last I see of them hypocrites, she's soothin' an' cooin' up to him an' we're out on the street without a pot to pee in. And, can you beat this, she blabs it all over Sarnia that we're bawds an' harlots, an' we have no hope ever again of gettin' work in a respectable place."

"So we come here," Winnie said with the bubbling giggle she'd had since she turned fifteen. Now, in the tired and creased flesh of her forties, it seemed eccentric, as if she had adopted such a youthful mannerism for effect. "What's *your* excuse!" she laughed.

It took almost two hours to exchange histories, but in this strange, enclosed space, time seemed even of less importance than it did on the lane outside. The parlour where they sat might have graced the seraglio of a second-rate sultan, with its faded Armenian carpets overlapping on the floor; damask curtains with gold tassels to repudiate the prying sun; sofas all curve and cushion and invitation; a myriad of tiny lamps with Oriental shades; the afterburn of incense still in the air. A black-skinned, white-shirted Dahomey sat cross-legged, with hookah, on the albino bearskin spread before the portico, which led to purdah and its languorous, mediterranean pleasures.

"This here's Mr. Lincoln – I understand you met briefly out back. Mr. Shadrack Lincoln—we call him Shad."

"And a few other things," said Betsy. She was unable to take her eyes off Lily, whom she found to be the same and yet so much different and wondering if Lily were thinking the same thing about her.

"Shad might look dumb, but he's quite smart, ain't you, Shad?" Shad smiled dreamily, but Lily felt his eyes scan and appraise her. "He don't talk, so folks around here think he's stupid. But back in Philadelphia he used to be a lawyer's clerk, readin' law books an' writin' out lawyer's briefs. He was a regular black gentleman. He's still got some of his master's suits given to him when he was set free."

"What happened to him?" Lily asked, looking his way. Their glances locked for a second, then peering through the opium daze, the mute pose of the face, she knew full well what she might find in the dark history unreleased behind those eyes.

"After the kafuffle at Harper's Ferry back in 'fifty-nine, you know—when the niggers took a run at the federal army an' got butchered, there was hell to

pay among the slaves everywhere. Some vigilantes come in the night an'
drug poor Shad outta his bed an' hauled him kickin' an' screamin' off to the
nearest woods." She paused and checked out the victim. He lay on his back
upon the rug, the pipe beside him, breathing deeply.

"I think he's left us," Winnie whispered.

"Well, Lily dear, shame to say but them vigilantes went an' cut his
tongue out an' they smashed all the fingers on his right hand so's he couldn't
write no more an' left him on his master's doorstep, bleedin' an' sobbin' his
heart out."

"But they didn't know Shad was left-handed –"

"I'll tell it, if you don't mind," Hazel said sharply, not quite ready to
forget the recent transgression on the dunes. "Anyways, Shad recovered an'
was able to write but he couldn't talk no more an' from time to time, as he
do now, he went a bit crazy in the head. So his master set him free an' sent
him up to Canada to work on the farm of a friend. We're glad to have him.
He's a dear man, smart as a whip, an' when them sailors get rambunctious in
here on a Saturday night, all he has to do is roll them eyes, froth a bit at the
mouth and start gargling out his dumb-language an' they head outta here in
a hurry. He does all our shoppin' in town, too." She sighed. "Poor Shad; he's
got to listen to Win an' Bet chatter all day an' night an' he don't get to say a
word!"

When Lily got up to go, Hazel hugged her again and said, "We have tea
up here every Monday – our day off – so why don't you come? Sophie
usually does. You can meet the other three girls – they're still young an' need
their sleep – and of course our housekeeper an' chief pot-scrubber."

"That's Vi," Betsy said.

"She's down at the beach for a swim," Winnie said.

"*Always* down there, it seems to me," Hazel added.

"Talkin' to the waves."

"*They* can understand her," Winnie tittered.

"Hush up," Hazel said to her. "Vi's a sweet thing an' you know it. You'll
come an' see us, then, Lily?"

Lily nodded and waved goodbye several times before she came down to
the path behind the brothel. Something urged her to turn towards the Lake.

•

The beach was deserted. Though it was a sweltering August afternoon, all the children were off to a travelling carnival and freak show down in Bayview Park. The immaculate sand glittered under a Grecian sun. Lily took off her shoes and stood wriggling her toes until they touched the cool damp granules below the surface. For a few moments she stood perfectly still and listened to the waves, scarcely nudged by a westerly breeze as they broke idly on the shale of pebbles and seashell that ringed the water's edge as far as the eye could follow. Farther out the lake was calm, without current or direction, indifferent to the winds, an abiding blue beyond the reach of any sun or season. Lily closed hers eyes.

When she opened them she saw something move across the plane of the water's dominion about twenty yards out where the bottom sailed from underfoot. A swimmer – made elegant by buoyancy, the arms lifting in slowed sequence closer to the blood's own beat, with a leg kick like the silver spray of a mermaid's fin, hair fanned out in winged ebony, the body aimed with the grace of a dolphin's dance. For a second Lily herself felt that wondrous free-fall moment between stroking and surrender. The swimmer touched down reluctantly then stood upright among the taffeta froth of the rollers near shore.

It was a plain, female body clearly visible below the homemade bathing costume pressed wetly against the outlines underneath: lumpish curves, knob knees, a slack belly, masculine feet. Thick black hair was matted against the face, browned unevenly by the sun, the large eyes darkly innocent, the right side of the jaw crooked where it had grown accustomed to the hare-lip above it.

"Hello, Lily. They said it was you livin' down there in the Icelanders' shack, but I didn't believe 'em. I ain't allowed to go down that way."

The words, distorted only by the narrow wheeze of the cleft palate, came out as clear and as natural as a gossip's whisper. As Lily walked towards Violet she shed her outer clothing – skirt and blouse – and covered only by her shift, she took the swimmer's hand and together they turned back into the waves. When the first breaker foamed against her thighs, Lily jumped and giggled and Violet let go of her hand and laughed and then began to run across the lake lifting one foot out of the water and splashing it down just as the other one broke the surface. Lily came skitter-splashing behind her, laughter bubbling in her throat. Moments later, the lake had them, and they capitulated with a wild, surrendering dive into the green looking-glass dream of its depths: the cold, total possession of its grip on the nippled breast, the silenced ear-drum and the pinioned arms. They rose again to the icy-hot surface. They were amphibian and swam in unison as whale and dolphin do. They rolled dorsally, lolled weightless on their backs facing the firmament, turned in their own time and swam with slow, synchronous ease back to the dry island of the beach. Linking hands again they walked up onto the white sand and lay down to contemplate the sky and bask in the body's long thaw.

Why here, why now? What is it we do to deserve or not deserve such fitful collisions of joy? What is the sun seeing now, gazing down at us? Can it care the way we do? Do we make *anything* happen? Lily reached over and touched Violet's hand. "I love you, Lily," Violet whispered. "I always did."

Yes, we do. We must.

23

1

Robbie and Brad started school in September. Lily felt she ought to accompany them on the first day but Sophie warned her away from such foolishness. Robbie was delighted to be able to walk ahead with the older boys, while Brad took hold of Wee Sue's hand and headed up Victoria Street humming out loud. All summer long Wee Sue had taken Brad under wing – except for the two weeks he was quarantined with chicken-pox – and taught him how to read. They were both excited about the possibility of startling Miss Timmins into a moment's silence. Wee Sue squeezed his hand possessively and smiled at the envy in the eyes of the other nine-year-old girls who flocked about them from the adjoining side streets and lanes. "I'm to take care of him," she announced at every opportunity.

If Miss Timmins, the maiden lady who taught Primer and Book One were startled, she did her best to conceal the fact. Still, it was clear that Brad could read the second primer-book with ease by the end of the month while others, like Robbie, were still stumbling through the recitation of the ABCs. When his printing improved in October, Brad was moved into the front seat of the second row, a bona fide member of Book One. Brad loved school. He loved Miss Timmins. He stayed in at recess and helped her clean the blackboards. Wee Sue rejoined her own troop. On the way home from school he had to be saved from the fists and taunts of the other boys by his older brother, who returned him to his mother, shaking but unscathed. While Lily could sooth Brad's feelings, she could not explain away the bewilderment in his eyes; the child's hurt questioning of the unjust order of things, of secret burdens already inherited without understanding or consent. A few feet away, she could hear Robbie running cold water from the pump over the cuts on his knuckles, and the other chamber of her heart contracted. She knew better than to go to him now – to say one word of praise or consolation.

Though Wee Sue no longer dared to befriend Brad at school, she continued her affection guiltily at home. She smuggled over to his house a bundle of books, mostly readers and texts which the older Potts had 'forgotten' to return to the school following their various unorthodox departures. They had been locked in a trunk in Sophie's room because no books of any kind were to be exposed in Sophie's presence, on pain of death. Lily wanted to ask Sophie why, but could not find the opportunity to do so.

"Mama hated school," Wee Sue said. "Her teachers were mean to her."

This grievance notwithstanding, Sophie never complained when Principal Grindly took the strap to any of her charges, and she advised Lily to do likewise.

"I got a simple rule: for every whack on the calluses they get there, I give 'em two on the backside when they get home. And if that don't do the trick, I threaten to tell Stoker."

Lily sat beside Brad on the battered settee Spartacus had picked up for them, and together they read their way through the first two primers. At first, Brad was faster than she was, guessing the words quickly and triumphantly, running his finger under the magic letters a second in front of his nimble tongue, never forgetting a word once he had sounded it out. After Christmas, though, Wee Sue brought over a large tome called *McGuffey's Fourth Eclectic Reader*, and the stories and poems in there frustrated even Brad's obsessive efforts. Lily herself found it hard to believe, but she began to get the sense of such pieces as "The Wreck of the Hesperus," Mrs. Moodie's "Burning of the Fallow" and "Little Daffydowndilly" by Mr. Hawthorne, even without knowing all the words. Brad became dazed, then numbed, then furious as the indecipherable phrases accumulated and mocked him. He went back to his own Reader and after a while, when he settled down, they would take turns again, reciting and listening, giving and accepting, till he fell asleep on her shoulder. Then she could open the big book silently and astonish herself once more by reading it – on her own, unaided. The ancient stories and fables came off the page at her as if the bards themselves were sequestered among the shadows. I am thirty-one years old, she thought, and something magical is just beginning. She shivered but made no attempt to pull the shawl around her.

•

Robbie's first season at school was not only difficult but a foreshadowing of the troublesome years to follow. In some ways he was as bright as Brad; by the end of the first grade he could read, print his letters, and do the simple sums required. But in temperament he was too much like his father – headstrong, impetuous and fiercely proud. In vain Lily searched for the first signs – any portent – of Tom's redeeming qualities: his good humour, his trusting affection, his courage. Only the latter was visible as Robbie continued to defend his brother, risking not only the inevitable bruises and scrapes but much more: the fellowship of the ruffians and outcasts he needed unconditionally as companions. Somehow he managed to maintain their fickle admiration even while he punched out the bullies among them whenever he had to. They were a strange lot. Lily made no pretense of understanding the contradictory laws of their code, and she had no doubt about the claims it made upon Robbie's loyalties. Unfortunately, in defending his brother for reasons, which to him, grew more obscure and untenable each time an enemy was silenced, Robbie's feelings for Brad began to swing from blinding love to intermittent revulsion. When there was affection it was no longer of the open, trusting kind. Strangely, Robbie did not seem in the least jealous of Brad's brilliant progress in reading and writing, almost as if he didn't consider achievements of that kind worthy of any response. They existed in a world he had no desire to enter.

"He's just like all my boys," Sophie consoled. "Not one of them ever liked school. An' why should they? They went there long enough to learn to read an' write their names an' count up to a hundred – just enough so's the bigwigs an' bosses won't be able to cheat them outta their drawers. What else do you need to know to dig ditches or sling flour sacks on the docks, eh? My John's gone off to the sheds this year, an' Stewie'll go next. For the girls it's even sillier. How is book learnin' gonna help you be a parlour maid or save you from gettin' knocked up by your mistress's hubbie or son or stable boy?" She spoke this latter sentence with some bitterness.

"Peg?" Lily said.

"You guessed it, an' the silly bitch didn't have enough brains to go for the top, where there's some money at least. A stable hand she tells me, who says he's gonna make an honest woman outta her as soon as he can find another job. She can't come back here, Stoker don't approve of them kind of shenanigans. He's got his pride."

One day in the spring Robbie came home from school in the middle of the morning. She stood up from her steaming wash and saw him standing forlornly in the open doorway of the laundry shed, his chin on his chest, his hands – always active, poised to clench or welcome – drooped at his side. She heard him swallowing his tears.

"He sent me home. I ain't goin' back." It was not a boast nor a threat nor a defence; it was spoken as an inevitable, regrettable truth. The pathos of it struck Lily so forcefully that she had to busy herself with taking off his sweater and getting him some tea and a cake before she could bring herself to get the whole story. Apparently he had used blasphemous language in the presence of several girls and within earshot of Miss Timmins. Mr. Grindly subsequently interrogated the blasphemer in his office and declared him, in official tones, to be a "little heathen devoid of any sense of the Christian religion." He had been sent home to learn the Lord's Prayer, after which he was to recite it ten times for Miss Timmins as punishment – a gesture of mercy since the alternative was the strap, and even Mr. Grindly did not recommend such extreme retribution for those in the first form, even if it was almost June.

"Robbie, you must go back," Lily said, and in words she hoped he would understand, she told him about her own brief career in school and the drastic effects it had had upon her life ever since. He nodded – dumbly, faithfully, letting his trust open up once again to her. While he watched her every move, Lily went to her bed and from under it drew the leather pouch. She took out Papa's Testament and found printed in the front section 'The Lord's Prayer'. She read it through, puzzled. "I'll teach it to you,"She was at a loss to explain the words to her son. They defeated her. She sensed some power under them, in their oracular cadence, but it was the potency of a charm, felt yet untranslatable. She exhorted Robbie just to commit the phrases to memory like learning a nonsense rhyme or a skipping song. It didn't work. He tried, not because he wanted to return to the schoolroom but because he still had faith in the woman who was always at home when he came back, who had not gone away and died on him, and because the underworld of masculine loyalties and camaraderie associated with school had put its brand on him. He tried but he could not do it. He couldn't memorize the meaningless words and he couldn't yet read them himself.

The next morning Lily persuaded Wee Sue to walk Brad to school. She was abrupt with him, and he left in a sulk. Then she sat once more with Robbie and together they failed again the test before them. Lily took his hand in hers. Very quietly she said, "Robbie, you gotta go back to school. Your life depends on it. Do you follow me?"

Bewildered by his mother's tears, he said, "If you want me to. I ain't afraid."

Lily walked beside him half-way up Victoria Street. He let her hold his hand until they were within sight of the school. Then he broke away and strode ahead, his stiffening posture warning her off. She watched him hesitate before the large door marked in stone 'BOYS', and then enter. She followed after until she stood in the schoolyard a few feet away from the building, but on the side without windows – unobserved, listening. Long moments later, the crack of pebbled leather on stretched skin resounded down the hallway, through the senior and junior rooms, out the wide-open windows and over the spring gardens of the neighbouring houses. The cruelty of the sound stunned a robin in full flight. Lily let her heart disintegrate.

2

Lily worked hard to make her business a success. "I get exhausted just watchin'," Sophie would say, settled in her captain's chair by the south window of the shed. Lily had added two more customers farther up Victoria Street, and the new owner of The Queen's, Kevin Malloney, doubled the number of items she had been assigned under the former management. However, he did insist that she herself pick up and deliver them as he didn't trust his property to wayward boys. Lily knew quite well why he preferred her to come in person.

"He just looks," Lily said in her own defence.

"No man only looks," Sophie shot back.

In the summertime, the work was hard because the stove always had to be on, heat wave or no. The steaming water boiled your hands as well as the clothes and reddened your cheeks permanently. The iron skidded into palm and fingertip; the bulk of wet sheets hung out to dry bent the back into spasms and left the shoulders burning with aftershock. Sophie recommended brandy, then reluctantly some Indian herb tea she happened to have around.

The surest cure was a trek to the beach with her boys, with Sophie and her trailing ménage, or sometimes alone with only Violet to talk to and swim with. After the boys were in school, she got Hazel's permission to walk with Violet to the Sarnia Cemetery where they lay white chrysanthemums on Bachelor Bill's grave. On the way home they swung back through the woods and came out into the clearing where they had first met. No trace of the shanty remained, but Violet stood and stared at the rusting gate and at the mutilated tree line behind it. Lily's house was charred rubble. She was tempted to go through it, searching for *what* she had no idea, but resisted. Instead, like Violet, she stood watching the ruins and waiting in vain for some definable feeling to take shape out of the general numbness. They held hands as they hiked across the fields towards their village.

In the winter months Lily found that the front half of her got steamed and scorched while the back half froze. No amount of heat could warm the laundry room itself. The constant fog from the hot water rose and stiffened into rivulets of ice along the north wall, and over the course of the winter they became stalactites perfectly suited to the dark, cavernous atmosphere of the place. Lily developed chilblains, rashes and a continuous cold. So it was with as much relief as pleasure that she began to accompany Sophie up to Hazel's on most Monday afternoons for a long, gossipy, hearth-cozy tea. Often, she was too weary to say much or even be a good listener. At Hazel's no one seemed to notice.

On his own or occasionally with Brad, Robbie continued to pick up and deliver the laundry, collecting the money and presenting it to his mother. He now chopped all of the wood. Some of his cronies began to tease him about being a 'washerwoman's suck', and he often returned in a black pout. But whatever standing he might have lost during the week, he made up for on Saturday when he used the nickel Lily gave him to buy it back. He needs a friend, Lily thought, not companions.

In June, Robbie was promoted to Book One and Brad all the way to Senior Book Two. With her winter cough completely gone, Lily put up fresh gingham curtains and wondered who she might offend by trying a little paint on the outside of her house. Already bored by the forced vacation, Brad looked up from his reading one July day and said, as if he had thought the question out carefully, "Mama, are we really Alleyfolk?"

24

1

In the early hours of Wednesday, August 23, 1872, the gunboat *Prince Alfred* slipped unnoticed from its berth in Goderich Harbour and steamed southward through the summer darkness. As the sun rose over east Lambton, the ship and its precious cargo eased into the first down currents of the St. Clair River and docked at the Point Edward wharf. The sun lifted into the sky, sizzling and solitary. Nothing stirred on the *Prince Alfred* until about nine o'clock when stewards in white suits fluttered from cabin to galley and back. As the morning advanced, movements aboard seemed to take on a greater urgency. Dark marine uniforms trailed or led the stewards, and always at double match. Several doors slammed in undisguised anger. Stevedores on the dayshift stopped to watch. Something momentous was at hand.

This latter suspicion was confirmed around eleven o'clock when a private coach and four were spotted coming down Michigan Ave. with as much haste as was compatible with the decorum of its occupants and the occasion. The vehicle wheeled onto the wharf, clattered to a standstill before the gangplank (just lowered), and debouched two distinguished gentlemen already sweating in their morning coats and stiff collars. They brushed past the paid help with the unmistakable briskness of the provincial politician. They entered the captain's quarters on the rear deck. Fifteen minutes later they re-emerged, blinking into the sun and sweating more profoundly than before. A crowd of thirty people had gathered on the wharf as rumour continued to sweep through the village. The local hosts now moved along the deck in a deferential manner, Uriah-Heaping their way towards the gangplank in the van of the very-important-person, who, upon espying an audience, tipped his hat and uttered an automatic smile. Several persons cheered as Sir John A. Macdonald, the Prime Minister of the five-year-old Dominion and the first Father of Confederation, stepped shakily towards their approbation.

●

August twenty-first had been designated as nomination day for Lambton
County in the federal elections of 1872. Candidates for both parties, the
Conservatives and the Reformers, would take the stand, make their pitch and
be judged by the members of their own group. The hustings had been
erected only the day before in the middle of Market Square in Sarnia, and in
the heat of midday, sawdust and pine tar perfumed the air. The rumour that
Sir John A. himself would attend to speak on behalf of Mr. Vidal and
confront, in his own riding, the man he feared and disliked most, had been
disseminated by the local Conservatives. They had learned of its legitimacy
only moments before the *Prince Alfred* had departed Goderich. After all, Sir
John A. was not well. The weather was semi-tropical, the County was a
bastion of Brownite Reformism, and not much could be gained by
contending with Alex Mackenzie, Sarnia stonemason and Leader of the
Opposition, on his home ground. But then, the story went, Sir John A. had
never been a conventional politician. Mr. Vidal and his Tory colleagues did
their best to swallow their astonishment wen the great man stepped out of
the coach onto the soil of Market Square for the first time. He glared at the
raw hustings in the way an exhausted tragedian might glower at the bare,
unlit stage before him.

Sir John A. was not well. Although recovered from the kidney stone that
had almost killed him two years before, he had been drinking and travelling
and speaking and drinking for six weeks as the election dragged through that
wretchedly hot summer. At fifty-nine, he was already old, a grizzled veteran
with a long record of victories and defeats. But he had one last mission: to get
the railway built to the Pacific and consolidate the nation's grip on the
continent and its vast resources. Re-election was necessary by all means if the
country were to survive. Sir Hugh Allen's support – bribe money as later
called by the impious – was not to be eschewed.

Burdens upon his conscience made sleep impossible: the revelation that
the Montreal financier's consortium for constructing the C.P.R. was two-
thirds American; the presence of a condescending, bullying Yankees in the
Premier's office at three in the morning. A telegram from Sir Hugh had
reached him *en train* between London and Goderich, threatening to expose

the whole sordid mess. Now, his eldest enemy sat across from him, composed, plebeian in his open shirt, his probity rigid and unyielding. When several hundred participants and onlookers had gathered by one o'clock, Sir John was already in need of a drink. Mr. Vidal passed him a crystal goblet brimming with ice-water.

•

Mr. Gemmil of *The Sarnia Observer* has recorded the details of the political square dance that ensued. Sir John, with obsequious humility and a clear sense of occasion, deferred to his rival, begging that he of local prominence should speak first. The stonemason conceded, beginning to feel the heat himself, and the proceedings got underway. Alex Mackenzie was duly nominated by a regional worthy, Peter Graham, Esq. of Warwick, who pointed out the virtues of the candidate. He was a genuine, not a self-dubbed member of the working class who required no well-stocked purse to win elections. Nor did he need, as Mr. Vidal apparently did, the support of outsiders like the Knight of Kingston and his posse of political hacks. Mr. Vidal himself was then nominated in yet another lengthy speech.

More interest was shown at Sir John A.'s nomination (a ploy to allow him to speak later) along with a half-dozen other nominal candidates with a thirst for rudimentary oratory. Thus it was almost three o'clock when Alex Mackenzie rose to accept the nomination of his enthusiasts still able to cheer despite the heat and the petrifying boredom of the speeches to date.

The stonecutter stood to thunderous applause. His angular features forewarned the weak at heart that here was a man of little compromise when truth and honesty were at risk. His eyes were as sharp as a jeweller's chisel. He said he felt flattered to have the Premier of the Dominion, who had so often supped with the gods, among them. He, a common mortal, might indeed feel abashed in his presence. His tone then darkened as he attacked Sir John's pretense of a coalition government. He ridiculed the Tories' attempts to pass as 'progressive', and excoriated the Government's ruinously generous terms for British Columbia's entry into Confederation. This resounded especially in light of Ontarians having had to give their land gratis to the railroads besides a million dollars a year from the public trencher forever after. It was quarter to four when he sat down to prolonged cheers. In the eaves of the Town Hall behind them even the pigeons had wilted, dreaming of cool breezes and evening dews.

No one left the square. Marketeers and strays had entered the drama to see the outcome. All eyes were on the Prime Minister. If his supporters had not known better, he might have been thought dozing through some of the lesser encomiums. Fireworks erupted as the arch-Tory, Mr. Vidal, popped up to read a damning letter discrediting Alex Mackenzie on a local drainage issue. The crowd, ninety percent Reformers, roared disapproval, and just as fisticuffs were about to be deployed, Mr. Vidal finished reading the last half of the letter, which, coincidentally happened to exonerate his opponent. *The Observer* reported that 'a scene of uproar and confusion ensued that beggars description'.

It was the figure of Sir John rising and assuming the podium that calmed both the outraged and the outrageous. At four o'clock, the heat had reached its zenith; in the far southwest, convection clouds were building. Sweat, unthinned by alcohol, thickened on the statesman's upper lip, dribbled down his pale face and hung in parchment nodules from his chin like cast-off syllables from old speeches. He tucked his left hand in his waistband to keep it from quivering, and with his right sawed the air. In front of him, he heard a cacophony of rejoinders, putdowns, crippling witticisms, sentences in the old, clean, high style: a phrase (a word even) with some touch of the truth still unuttered in it. The shallow applause from a thousand previous masterful efforts hissed on the whiskey-drum of his skull. He needed a drink. The sun's heat congealed in his gut. He would open his mouth and vomit all over Mr. Vidal's handshake. From the left side of the platform, Mr. Mackenzie skewered him with his Presbyterian eye. He blinked, and began one more time.

The Observer comments on the speech: 'We regret that our limited space will not permit our giving a detailed report of Sir John's speech in this issue. We will merely say that for a gentleman of his fame, it was one of the most miserable attempts at public speaking we ever heard; while it was at the same time so full of misrepresentations and misstatements...that it has led to the conclusion that he was either so much *indisposed* as not to know what he was saying, or that he purposely occupied his position in the hustings in order that he might wickedly and maliciously traduce and slander a man infinitely his superior. Such reckless, unfounded and abominable charges...coming from the lips of the Crown in the Dominion of Canada is sufficient to cast a stigma on the whole population, in the eyes of every civilized people'.

When the token candidates had withdrawn, the preordained nominees were confirmed and the meeting disbanded. Partisans kicked their dogs and horses awake and set out to slake their thirst. Some stayed to watch the demi-royal party disappear into the Town Hall for a formal dinner and self-congratulatory toasts. There was spirited wagering as to whether His Highness would make it past the soup course, but he boarded a carriage under his own impetus about nine o'clock that evening and reached the safety of his gunboat at the Point Edward wharf.

2

The people of the Point were less interested in politics than one of those flash-floods that cuts through the brooding heat, cleanses the air for a precious hour or two, and leaves the browning grass refreshed. Along the lanes and alleys of the Point, it also left vast pools of murky water, child-size puddles and dizzying rivulets . The Alleykids filled the twilight with the dissonant song of their happiness. As darkness descended, more steeply now as September nighed, their voices dwindled. By ten-thirty, the Alley was silent except for the occasional hushed exchange of sailors approaching Hazel's Heaven in twos and threes. The moon rose unobserved.

Around midnight a pair of sailors, their thirst satisfied at John the Baptist's and their lust at Hazel's ersatz Eden, sloshed noisily down towards Michigan Ave. One of them slid into a slough, cursing and coughing up slime while his buddy sniggered in sympathy. Pressing a damp cloth against Brad's fevered brow, Lily heard them clearly somewhere below her front path. Brad moaned a little and turned over. In a while, his breathing became steady. Lily slipped back to her own bed. She was very tired, having washed and ironed the hotel's weekly quota of sheets in the intense heat of the day. Even the flies had capitulated. She peered out the side window and in the moonlight could see the puddles and sudden bogs glistening all the way along the lane. The two sailors had recovered and disappeared. Lily lay her head on the sash and sucked in the damp-cool air.

When she looked up much later, she was surprised to see a solitary figure making its way towards her. At first she thought it might be wounded because it was staggering and then stopping short, as if calculating the extent of pain, only to step out again and teeter its way forward. The man, for so it was from the cut of his gentleman's coat, grunted a curse every time a wayward foot deposited him in a puddle, but to no evident effect as the splashing and cursing continued at an accelerated pace. He'll never make it to John the Baptist's, Lily mused. It was not an uncommon sight, but she was a little puzzled by the clothes and by something unique in the gestures, something melancholy and alone. As she was about to blow out the night-candle, she heard a loud splash, then nothing.

Wrapping a shawl over her shift, she went out into the yard and looked down the lane. Grass and mud oozed between her toes. "You all right out there?" Nothing. Drunk and passed out, was her first thought. Well, he won't freeze out here tonight. Something urged her to continue, and a few yards farther down where the curve widened the path, she saw the man face-down and unmoving. He was not on the ground but in the middle of a small slough with his hands stretched out, feet splayed, and his face buried in the six-inch slime. He's drowned, she thought, racing over and grabbing him by the shoulders and flinging him on his back. His eyes were sealed shut with mud, his nostrils plugged, mouth gagged. On her knees in the water, she wetted her fingers and scooped the muck out of his mouth, at the same time splashing his face with handfuls of water. Then she struck him on the back with her balled fist as if he were a newborn resisting breath. A wheezing rattle started up from somewhere deep inside, and the man coughed once wrenchingly, as if scraping the catarrh from his lungs. His eyes popped open and welcomed the pain of the grit against them. For several minutes he gagged and spat, swinging between disgust and fury, it seemed. Then he began to weep softly before he slid into unconsciousness in the arms of his saviour.

One minute longer, Lily thought as she carried the frail victim up the path to her house, and he would have been a dead man. Maybe he wanted to be.

•

When Lily woke it was still dark. A fresh breeze fluffed the curtains beside her head. She uncrooked her neck and peered across the room. The fire she had set in the hearth glowed weakly; the clothes-horse she had brought in from the shed still held the suitcoat, trousers, socks and linen underthings she had removed from the soaked, comatose body of the stranger. He sat exactly where she had propped him up on the settee with pillows and a quilt. His eyes were wide open, staring at the last nugget of firelight, which in its turn kindled some flickering vitality in them. Lily saw at once that these eyes were intelligent, guarded, caring, and as alert and quick as a hare's in the open field. He had been awake for some time and seemed quite settled in the coziness of the room. His chin rested comfortably on his chest, his face pallid yet void of any real tension. He appeared to be a man accustomed to waking up in strange places with harmless hangovers and no memory of what indiscretions led him thence.

"Don't be alarmed, madam. I've just been watching you sleep."

She picked out his Scotch burr, somewhat undercut by the vowels of the countryside. Though softened to suit the room and the occasion, the voice was deep and resonant.

"You'll pardon my dishabillement, I trust, particularly because you appear to have taken a major role in effecting it." His eye twinkled and she sensed the effort behind his words. "I hope the sight of unaccommodated man has not discouraged you forever from respecting the species?" He pulled the quilt across the upper reaches of his hairy chest, and his lip curled towards a smile.

"You one of them politician fellas?"

The smile completed its trajectory. He was scrutinizing her through the semi-darkness. "Could we have some light?"

"Of course." Lily got up and lit the small lamp beside her. She glanced over at the curtained-off section where the boys slept. She realized she stood only in her shift, so she went into her cubicle and returned wearing the floral kimono Sophie had given her ("Don't worry, it's Marlene's, she don't need it no more."). She stirred the fire and put the kettle on for tea. For a moment she felt embarrassed to be standing with a man clothed only in a quilt, his most intimate apparel displayed on a rack like the severed parts of his body set out in the sun to be cured. Then she recalled she had dragged him through the mud of her own yard up the steps and into this room only hours before, and with no other recourse, had stripped away every shred of clothing and laid his unconscious form on the settee. She had proceeded to rub him dry with a thick towel from The Queen's, apply a vigorous sheen of liniment, and mummify him with blankets. When she had made him comfortable and was certain his breathing was normal, she took his clothes into the shed and by the light of a candle, scrubbed the mud and vomit off them. She lit a fire, and set them on the horse to dry. What a pathetic, withered creature had been revealed to her beneath the gentleman's disguise – hardly an ounce of flesh to float the brittling bones into old age. She handed him his tea and sat down in the chair near him. "You been up to that meetin' in Sarnia?"

"I confess that I have."

"Government man?"

"I must plead guilty to that also."

"How'd you get way down here?"

He chuckled grimly and sipped his tea with a greedy, unsteady hand. In the lamplight his complexion had the pallor of a gutted mullet. "That's a long story, only part of which I can recall. I'm staying on the big boat docked up by the station. One of my friends from the town was in the process of leading me to a local watering-hole with the refreshing name of John the Baptist's when his legs went numb and he retired to the wayside. Being the intrepid type, I continued apace." He held out his cup for more tea and when he had trapped her glance, he said, "You are definitely not John the Baptist."

"You give me a terrible fright, I thought you was dead for a minute."

"No doubt I was," he said..

•

The false dawn told her it must be close to four o'clock. "We lead a difficult life," he was saying. "Politicians are a greatly misunderstood breed, especially in this ill-informed country. It's one of the richest places in the Dominion. I see farms from the train and the shoreline, wealthy beyond description and owned by men like my own parents—slaves and vassals in their home country."

The clothes were dry now. Lily held the quilt as a screen behind which, labouring for breath, he donned his gentleman's vestments once more.

"They attribute their success to their own hard work. But they don't understand that the government and politicians negotiated the Reciprocity Treaty which kept the wheat flowing to the United States throughout the Civil War. Yet when that treaty is abrogated by the intransigence of the Yankees they are quick to blame *us* for their troubles, including, if you please, the foul weather and the bugs. We have done everything imaginable for the people of this county, and what is our reward? A hotbed of unrepentant

Reformers whose *laissez-faire* mumbo-jumbo would ruin every farmer in Lambton." He looked at Lily.

"Maybe they just want to have a little say in what's bein' done for them," she said.

He opened his mouth to say something profound but nothing came out. She went over to the clotheshorse where his morning coat still hung and began brushing the residual dried mud off it, one speck at a time.

He continued while she worked. "The railroads are an even more egregious example of ingratitude." "What was this town before the Grand Trunk? How did the farmers move their wheat to the markets of the whole continent or the lumbermen their timber to the mills of America? Would there be an oil boom without railcars to deliver crude to the refineries? They whine and complain about the loss of a few acres in a county with millions to squander, about a few tarnished hands in the till when there's enough in the larder to make us all rich. But everyone wants it *now*, wants it *cheap* and without *pain*.

"There will be no country from sea to sea without the Canadian Pacific to bind it into one. They laugh at a band of steel stretching across prairies occupied only by a scattering of aborigines, but I see those grasslands full of people and wheat and British towns and villages." He sighed, intermittent between exhaustion and the ignition of fresh fervour. He turned for sympathy.

Lily shook the suitcoat and held it up to the lamplight. "Did anybody ask them Indians what they wanted?" she said.

He looked aggrieved but soon recovered sufficiently to say "I take it you don't approve of railroads, either?"

Lily nodded.

"You have a personal grudge?"

Lily thought for a moment. "No." Something in the manner of her denial arrested his attention. He peered around the room at the shabby furniture, the cracks in the siding and the patchwork roof as if he were seeing it for the first time. "Why do you live here?" he asked softly.

"My husband died. Then our house burned down. We came here, me an' my two boys."

"I have a daughter," he said. "She's not well."

"Sorry to hear that."

"Your husband had no insurance? No pension?"

"No. He died up north." She hesitated as if contemplating some revelation which might alter the precarious feeling that now lay between them. Then she said, "But we get along here just fine. I got my own work, an' my boys are goin' to school. We're all right."

"Yes, I can see you are," he said. "And things will soon be better for us all. You have to believe that the sacrifices you've made are for the best, that life *will* get better. You are still young, you are a vigorous and attractive and kind woman. You will marry again."

He put out his arm and she slid the coat over it. He winced and clutched at his eyelid. "Damn, got something stuck in here," he said.

Lily bent over him with a damp cloth and gently rolled the upper lid back till the mote was revealed. "Just a piece of grit," she said, swabbing it away.

She felt the chuckle rumble all the way through him. "It's not *clear* grit, I hope?"

•

"You make sure you keep your boys in school," he said, letting her do up the buttons and straighten the lapels. "Right now, ignorance is our only enemy. We need an educated populace if we're to preserve this democracy from the corruption of Yankee republicanism and the excesses of our own greed. I want to see the schools of this county bulging with happy faces. Maybe then, long after I'm dead, they'll be able to understand what we've built out of a wilderness. I try to remember that few of our citizens have had time to learn much history or comprehend the difference between tyranny and constitutional freedom. When they get particularly vehement, I skewer them with my Scot's glare. 'You registered your opinion with your vote – a privilege shared by few in this irksome world – so kindly shut up till the next election'. Over half the people in this county don't bother to vote, and when they do, they haven't a clue what the issues are. Tell your boys to stay in school as long as they can. We'll need them. No democracy can long survive if its citizens don't inform themselves of the issues. Is that not an absolute truth?"

Lily handed him the leather case she had retrieved from the puddle beside him, carefully tucking the official-looking papers and letters back in. "Can't say," she said. "I don't get no vote. I'm a woman."

•

They stood on the wooden stoop. The sun was up, simmering and blood-shot over First Bush. Whorls of mist skittered above the vanishing pools along the grassy lanes of Mushroom Alley.

"Thank you, Lily Marshall. I shall never forget what you've done. I shall not forget *you*, either." He leaned back to take her in one more time. "You must believe in Fate," he said, "in your own personal destiny. It's the only way."

She watched him till the mist clothed him in its own kind of obscurity.

25

1

The five-year reign of the Reform government from 1873 to 1878 was not a happy one. In the winter of 1873 the Pacific Railway Scandal had broken over its authors' heads so resoundingly it has been capitalized ever since. The succeeding Liberals under Alex Mackenzie of Sarnia tried hard, but there seemed no quick cure for the economic ills of the fledgling nation. It had caught the world's disease, or the fallout from its ceaseless wars, famine, and all the human skulduggery that kept the maggots jigging in a carcass which could rot but not perish. Free trade or reciprocity, responsible government in a chastened monarchy, or the licensed chaos of republicanism, *laissez-faire* or the Temperance Act: the shibboleths that men shaped their existence to were falling all over the earth like the pillars of Sodom. The Great Depression that was to last the whole decade settled everywhere at once. The railroad to the Pacific inched ahead then rusted in the prairie rain. Tricked out of their inheritance in Red River, the Métis slipped through the shadows and reappeared a thousand miles from the nearest spike. No one noticed. Wheat, unsaleable, fermented in the field; factory workers were laid off; the employees of the Grand Trunk had their pay cut in half. In the township, Clara Fitchett's brother hanged himself in the family barn.

In the Point the depression was felt everywhere except in Mushroom Alley. The railway slump affected every respectable household and incidentally stalled the attempts of its most prominent citizens – storekeepers, foremen, civil servants and clergymen – to wrest the village from the benign paternity of the Grand Trunk. Though almost all the homes and shops were now owned outright, no one in such uncertain times wanted to ruffle the king's feathers. By mutual unspoken consent, all talk of incorporation ceased. Still, there was some excited buzzing when a distinguished gentleman recently retired from the railway wars arrived in town without prior notice one day in the summer of 1876. Within weeks, he

had established an independent industry not fifty yards from the roundhouse.
It turned out to be a factory of sorts, bigger than a hay barn and clanking
with impressive machinery. Ten local men were immediately employed; Hap
Withers was made foreman. By September, the facts were irrefutable: the
entrepreneur himself had purchased the Blakely home on Victoria Street and
was settling in to oversee his handiwork. Every morning at nine, Stanley R.
"Cap" Dowling, promenaded down Michigan Ave., offering his profile to the
shop windows on either side of the thoroughfare before disappearing down
the cinder path to his foundry. Independent industry, as he said at the
haberdashers', that's what we need at this moment in our history. The words
were repeated with annotation and gloss all over town. Just how
independent the industry was, was a matter of personal interpretation. The
welders and smithies inside Dowling Enterprises manufactured plates, spikes
and various latches used in coupling devices on box-cars. Most of these, it
was rumoured, were transhipped fifty yards or so to the Grand Trunk
Railway. Nevertheless, people kept an eye on Cap Dowling, entrepreneur.

Except the Alleyfolk. They were too busy to notice anything for long.
Depression or no, the necessity of the services they rendered remained
unchanged. There was no diminution in the number of clients demanding to
be inspired at Hazel's Heaven. Someone had to scrub off or bleach out the
weekly blood and semen splashed on the bedsheets of McHale's and The
Queen's. Respectable householders defecated at the customary rate and so
the talents of Honeyman Belcher were in steady demand. Not a single
McLeod, McCourt or Shawyer lost her job as maid, though the salaries were
attenuated and the after-hours requests somewhat more importunate.
Spartacus had to pick more judiciously through the corporate garbage for
gems, but with his magpie instinct and carrion's pride, he kept the boulevard
as impeccable as ever. The only businesses to increase their trade were those
of John the Baptist, whose inexhaustible still frothed away like Parnassus in
its secret bower. Stumpy's eleemosynary institute now overflowed with the
destitute and the dazed who dropped off the way freight every morning and
evening. Sophie Potts bred her sow every season and sold the suckling to
Duckface Malloney. She tended her chickens with the same smothering
carelessness she offered her children. "We always do okay for ourselves," she
would tell anyone within earshot. "After all, mushrooms come rosier in
manure, don't they?"

2

For Lily these would be remembered as good years. McHale's Hotel and two large boarding houses on St. Clair Street were added to her business. She asked Spartacus if he would act as her delivery man, and even though it meant a drop in his status, he smiled and shook his head yes. Then one Monday, when the afternoon session at Hazel's had been prorogued, she asked that good woman if Violet could come down several days a week and work for her. Hazel was almost too quick to agree, Violet was ecstatic, and the arrangements completed within the hour.

"You're putting the money you earn in a safe place?" Lily asked her a few weeks later. Violet nodded her head vigorously. Hazel's taking every cent, Lily thought. When she saw the panic in Violet's face, she patted her on the arm and said, "You can give some to Hazel, for your room an' board."

"Anythin' you say, Lily."

Violet was a wonderful, joyous companion to Lily's own labours, which continued every day of the week except Monday afternoons. The good part was that they could take an hour or two off whenever the weather or mood tempted them. While they worked side by side they hummed – to themselves or mysteriously in sudden, improvised concert – and sometimes they swapped stories. Violet's speech always tightened and splayed as the momentum of an anecdote increased. Whenever they were together, they felt the overpowering presence of the shared space between them – lending its shadow to the body needing it most. When the clothes could be hung out in the breeze, they sang the French song Lily had learned from Ti-Jean and taught with ease to the 'idiot' daughter of Bachelor Bill. They sang it lustily like an extravagant surrogate for joy and loud enough to shiver the testicles of Baptiste Cartier's bachelor boar.

•

With the profits she made from her work, Lily began to make the house more comfortable for her boys. What Spartacus couldn't salvage for her, he managed to purchase second-hand and deliver to her door. He loved a cup of tea but always drank it from a mug with one foot on the front stoop. Lily got proper beds and ticks for all of them, a plush chesterfield and chair, two large reading lamps, a set of dinner plants and cups that almost matched, a small cooking stove for the main room, and a handsome walnut bookcase with glass doors only one of which was cracked. Hap Withers supplied two of his many sons to rebuild her floor, partition the sleeping quarters, seal the windows and eaves to discourage mosquitoes and drafts, and put a slatted platform over the bare dirt of the laundry room. Lily tried knitting again but she was too exhausted, and she had to spend precious dollars on clothing for her sprouting, handsome schoolboys. After Violet came to help out, Lily tried putting in a garden, but nothing would grow in the sand on her property except burs and sawgrass. She gave up even though a few shrunken vegetables would have meant more money for important things. Like books for Brad.

Brad was a wizard at school. He did everything with absolute ease confidence, even arithmetic. But reading and writing were the things he loved most. Lily marvelled and worried. Miss Timmins kept him only two years before she passed him along to the senior teacher, Miss Constance Stockton, newly arrived in relief of the footsore Mr. Grindly. Miss Stockton had a First-Class Certificate from the Normal School and she came to them from one of the better academies in Toronto for reasons still being speculated upon. The village folk were honoured merely by her presence among them. Brad thrived under her aggressive tutelage. Though such preferment usually spelled disaster among one's peers as it had that first year, Brad's star was so high and bright that he became an object of wonder among them, a person wholly apart from them and, hence, immune from the cruel sanctions of their fraternity. In his second-last year – Junior Book Four – he wrote a play for the Christmas concert and the lesser breed of the senior school allowed themselves to be flattered and bullied by his direction. Lily sat in the back row with Sophie and watched in awe. "You better put the kibosh on this schoolin' business right now," Sophie said afterwards. "It starts to go to their heads an' then all hell breaks loose. There's nothin' you can do once they get too much of it in their blood. Like Marlene."

Sophie demonstrated her views by taking Wee Sue out of school in the middle of grade eight – a few months before her Entrance Exams – and shipping her off to keep house for a retired shed foreman on Alfred Street. "At least he's too old to get her in the family way," she laughed. "He might be able to get it half-way up on a good day but he sure as hell can't catch her." Wee Sue continued to read books despite her mother's embargo on them in the Potts' house, smuggling them in from her employer's surprisingly interesting collection and lending them in turn to Lily and Brad.

When in 1875 a proper street railway was opened to connect Sarnia and Point Edward with an hourly service, Lily could take Brad and Wee Sue with her to the new public library on Wellington Street. Brad loved fiction and poetry, devouring the romances of Scott and much of Palgrave's Golden Treasury. For a while Lily tried to read along with him, to feel vicariously some of the pleasure she could see in his eyes and the way his whole frail body bent towards the book he was reading. But she was just too tired; the print crumbled into meaningless alphabets. She would shake the book with rage, then resignation. Often she would come awake, still sitting with a book in her hand, the chimney-glass scorched, and discover Brad in the other chair with his eyes alert and tirelessly skimming page after page. Sometimes she would sit beside him and put her arm around his shoulder. He would snuggle against her, continuing to absorb the magic print before him but letting her take a full part in his own joy, acknowledging the primacy of her claim. When she prompted, he would recount the seven wonders of Midlothian or leave her breathless by reciting those poems about Lucy and the last green field. At other times he would stiffen the moment her hand touched his shoulder and she would be shut out, even if he relented later, as he often did, and included her in his re-enactment of the story. When typhoid fever struck the village in 'seventy-six and swept away two of the Sawyer children, Lily kept her boys at home. She wouldn't even let them out in the yard.

Brad didn't mind much, but Robbie did. He could never be cooped up for long. Maybe that was why he had so much trouble in school. He longed to be outdoors, and the stuffy, fly-ridden weather of Miss Timmins' room was more than he could bear. He never got out of the junior division, though he stuck it out, uncomplainingly, for almost six years. What he loved most was fishing and hunting with the older boys of the Alley, and Fred Potts in particular, now known simply as Blub. Robbie skinned the rabbits they shot (with Blub's twelve-gauge) over at Potts before he brought them home for Lily to cook. He was saving the furs for a jacket he hoped his mother would make him. Sometimes he and Blub would 'borrow' a boat from the fishery and head out into the Lake for the day. Fresh perch could be sold in town for cash; Robbie saved his money for a gun. When Lily expressed her concern about his truancy and his passion for hunting, Sophie gave a ruminative chuckle.

"He's just tryin' to wear a man's socks – a little bit too soon maybe but then Blub's almost three years older, ain't he? Why don't you just give in an' let the kid quit school? Let him get a job an' make his way in the world. We don't *own* them, you know."

I know, Lily thought, thinking of Sophie's own brood scattered and dissident all over the province.

"With John and Stewie off workin' for the Great Western in Sarnia an' Peg married to that nogoodnik *chauffeur*, I only got three left home myself. But if we don't let go of 'em, they let go of us."

Lily gave in. After driving the truant officer off her place with a broom and then sitting for an hour in the privy before she stopped shaking, Lily said yes, and in the spring of 1877, two months before his fourteenth birthday, Robbie left school for good. Mr. Redmond, true to his word, gave Robbie a part-time job on the delivery wagon. When Lily suggested he might rent the wagon to deliver laundry as well, he stared at her with a resentment that dumbfounded and then cut deeply. She saw the word of assent on his lips but recovered in time to say, "Never mind, really, it was a silly idea." Relief flooded his face but did not wash away the other, darker emotion. At least he has a friend, she thought, watching him dash off towards the Potts' house, trying not to resent in her own fragile way the hundreds of sleepless nights and restless afternoons she had already spent worrying, wondering when and if he would come home. What new bruise might he have to camouflage in the coming days. They spoke little now beyond the brief courtesies of the day. Moreover, Robbie and his brother seemed merely to coexist, chillingly polite in her presence. I am losing them, she thought one day in her desperation. The more I love them and want them to be themselves, the worse it gets. How can that be? If not love, then what?

When Brad came down with pneumonia in the terrible winter of 1877-78, she sat at his bedside night after night cooling him with iced cloths. She steadied with her own strength the terror that flickered in his eyes as he began to question his own immortality, to doubt the voices prophesying glory to the credulous. Often, when she fell into a doze in her chair, she would rouse to his soft moans and find Robbie across from her, cupping his brother's flaxen head in a hunter's hand and spooning fresh soup through those limp poet's lips. Lily closed her eyes and pretended to sleep. After a while she heard the low murmur of their little-boy voices. If not love, she thought, then nothing. That's all I know.

3

Like most relationships in the alley, the one that developed between Lily Marshall and Sophie Potts over the depression years was marked by both intimacy and independence. Whenever Lily felt down or in need of company, she would slip over to Sophie's place where, summer or winter, the iron stove crackled and the kettle whistled. Without knocking she would slide into the rambling kitchen where 'her chair' would be waiting. Likewise, Lily would often look up from her scrubbing, bathed in steam, and make out the ample silhouette of her neighbour fixed to the old rocker by the south window. If Sophie were busy – doing her own never-quite-finished laundry with a bare-bottomed Bricky hopping behind her, or hacking at her garden lathered in sweat – then Lily would make herself a cup of tea and talk to Wee Sue. Sometimes she would just sit and let the myriad dramas of the Potts' household absorb her interest and draw her away from herself. She needed to recuperate, to become aware once again that there existed other lives, other acts of caring and slight and needing more love than there was anywhere.

If Sophie were about to go out on an errand, she would nod at Lily and then disappear down the lane. No offense meant or taken. In the summer, Lily might hear the cries of Sophie's youngest ones, and pulling Brad out of his chair, drop her scrub board and head up the path towards the beach with towels and swimsuits in hand until they caught up with the Potts' clan, already augmented by several McLeods and Shawyers. Lily would fall in beside Sophie, and together they would lead the children down to the water. It was only on holidays and other rare occasions that they made formal plans to picnic or go skating on the flats or sledding over the dunes.

In the Alley, it was better to let things happen. Somehow, word was passed along as needed, movements were detected by some inner radar, random sound was read with the clarity of print. Here, a pact was signed without recourse to clause or declaration and rarely broken. Yet the independence of each participant was re-established as soon as the hour or afternoon or safari was complete. It was as if, not having any legal claim to their property, they chose to guard themselves – their time, feelings, rights, dreams – with double the zeal of any ratepayer.

For example, Lily knew that two days before Stoker came home for his three-day layover in the summer or week's rest and recreation in winter, she could not engage Sophie in anything but the most superficial conversation. Even then Sophie might lash out at her or cuff little Bricky without cause as her anticipation took full possession of her. And when Stoker did waltz up the lane, braying out some bawdy sailor's song loud enough to alert the entire Alley of his arrival, Lily knew enough to stay away and mind her own business no matter what concatenation of squeals, groans and leathery collisions breached the night air. In the Alley, no one interfered. Lily did not speak five words to Morton Potts in five years. She saw him only from a distance, bare-chested in the sun, sleeping off a hangover on his verandah, tilting after his little one as the ogre in some mock fable, roaring loudly as they squealed with laughter and scampered away.

As far as Lily could see, Stoker was either shaken by uncontrollable hilarity or he was comatose. What she knew of him she heard from Sophie who spoke of nothing else for three days after his departure – until she had exorcised whatever demons had driven them both through these furloughs of ecstasy and retribution. She would downplay the bruises on her arms and neck even though no one ever remarked upon them. "The tokens of love, Lil," she would sigh. "When you marry a lumberjack and a stoker, you gotta expect some rough lovin'." She would roll her eyes theatrically to mask any feelings she might let free. "As my old granny always said, you can't make a primrose out of a preacher's arse." Then she would manufacture a belly-laugh that Boadicea might have borrowed to stymie Caesar's waves.

Monday afternoons were reserved for tea at Hazel's, but of course there were no invitations and an absent guest was under no obligation to explain or justify. Most of the regulars arrived, feigned surprise at the sight of the pewter tea-service and sweetcakes, and stayed to chat. Sophie was almost always present – except when Stoker was at home – as was Lily. Yet they never walked up the lane together by design, and often returned according to their own schedule. When they did share the walk home, they might well continue a discussion begun earlier or simply stroll silently, happy in one another's company. Hazel had two favourite topics – local gossip and politics whenever it could be reconstrued as local gossip. With the constant comings and doings of many powerful but undertitillated gentlemen through her portals and bedsteads, the latter bit of legerdemain was not too difficult.

Shadrack Lincoln, the mute, was often seen reading the radical newspapers – abandoned by the clientele in their haste to pursue less intellectual delights. But he could not contribute to the debates except by grunting approval or disgust, or occasionally, when his frustration built to a point where no other release was possible, by scribbling upon the schoolboy's slate Lily had brought for him one day.

Sophie often dominated the political discussion though no one knew where she acquired her extensive knowledge of provincial and federal affairs. Her source of local 'intelligence' was well known. Every week or so, and never on the same day twice in a row, she waddled past the General Store in McHale's where most of the Alleyfolk shopped and headed straight up the street to the main concourse of stores and services, the hub of respectable gossip and social interchange. Dressed in her orange smock or her squirrel fur with the heads attached and chattering, Sophie paddled her way blithely upstream, deliberately fixing victims in her wicked sights and greeting them with boisterous familiarity. The ladies of the town had no choice but to respond. She was too large and garrulous, and besides she knew more about them and had seen more of their flesh and blood than they themselves had. It was in these brief, shell-shocked exchanges that vital information spilled into public view, or in the longer conversations that Sophie-the-Wise carried on with the storekeepers. They genuinely liked her and much appreciated the stir she made among the village hens and their imperturbable pecking order. It took days for the dust to settle.

Once, after Sophie had lampooned the Prime Minister for two-and-a-half acts ("He's got a voice like a crow with the palsy!"), Shadrack motioned Lily over to his corner and pointed at the words on his slate: 'I give her the papers every week'.

"No wonder this country's in a depression. Every one of you thought with old Alex up there in Ottawa we'd all be shittin' shamrocks. Now don't get me wrong, Alex's a good man, got a heart as big as a squash, but he's got the brains of a stonecutter and he's as straight-laced as they make 'em. Wouldn't say poop if his tongue got tangled in it." She paused for effect or breath. "Every muscle in that man's body is stiff as a steel poker,'ceptin' the one that oughta be!" Her cackle shook Hazel's hens out of their four-o'clock drowse.

When Lily got to know Sophie well enough, she asked her why she had given up being a midwife. Sophie gave various answers depending on her mood. "Too many of them damn quacks from the university tellin' me what I didn't need to know," or "All the women out there want the doctors anyway, why should I fight it," or "I gave it up in 'sixty-five just a little after your Brad was born. I could see the writin' on the wall, I was just a woman with not a shred of schoolin' to my name," or "Women feel safer with a man rummagin' around down there, they're used to it!" But one morning after Stoker had left, she sat bathing the cut on her cheek by the stove and confessed to Lily that Stoker had ordered her to give it up because he said it interrupted their brief times together and "he accused me of neglectin' my own kids for the sake of other people's. He said I was a piss-poor mother. What could I say, I was already pregnant with precious little Bricky, our love child. What could I say, Lil?"

So it was that the women of the village had to rely upon the distant charity of the Sarnia doctors several miles and sometimes desperate hours away. Mildred McLeod, the youngest of the McLeod servant girls, got herself pregnant, and one night near her time, Lily was awakened by a savage scream that sounded as if some cat was being flayed alive under her window. She hurried through the dark down to the source of the agony and met Sarie McLeod with her gray hair fanned around her face like a shriek and not one word in her wild eyes.

"Calm down, Sarie," Lily said, trembling all over. "Has the doctor been sent for?"

"Hours ago, hours ago," Sarie mumbled at last and could find nothing better to say for some time.

Lily was thinking these screams would wake the whole lane, that Sophie would hear them and come down. But she didn't. Lily went in to the stricken girl and before she realized what she was doing, she was giving orders to young Kathleen and Frieda and soothing Mildred who was suffering more from terror than pain. Lily whispered into her ear the things she remembered being told herself by the *sage-femme* who had brought her comfort in her own labour. She found her palm resting on the girl's spasming belly like a benediction of some sort, and though she had little idea of what she was supposed to feel there or actually do, she soon had Mildred relaxing between contractions, turning her fawn's gaze up at the visiting angel, and inhaling deeply when she was told. Behind her, preparations for the event itself fell into place as they would have if Sarie, exhausted by one too many of these melodramas, had not panicked and sent the household into chaos. Moments later Dr. Dollard arrived, exhausted from twenty hours on the road. Together, he and Lily gave nature a brief assist and the child nosed its way into the world. It had not occurred to Lily, or anyone else, to go up to

Sophie's. Sophie *had* heard, and once that fact was known, nothing else could be done. That was the way it was in Mushroom Alley.

Word spread beyond the Alley, however, and during the middle years of the Liberal regime, Lily was called out into the village proper to assist Dr. Dollard in the safe delivery of six or seven babies. Along her own lane she guided another McLeod, a McCourt and a brace of Shawyers into the waiting air, occasionally before the arrival of the harried doctor. She described each trauma in detail to Sophie, who felt not the least embarrassment in commenting and dealing out advice. Or in reminiscing about her own glory days.

"So there I am washin' the blood an' muck off the baby's bottom, an' Missus Christie perks up and says to me, 'do it look like it's Da?' and I says 'I can't tell, dearie, I ain't seen your hubbie with his pants all the way down yet!'"

When the baker's daughter, Fanny Saltman, gave birth to a foetus so deformed that Dr. Dollard didn't even try to smack breath into its misery, and when Fanny died later that day with her eyes open and the sunlight streaming over the bed, Lily told Dr. Dollard that she couldn't help out any more. And she didn't, though she lived in dread that some female scream would jolt her awake some night and she would have no choice. It never did.

"You got the brains for it an' the heart," Sophie had predicted, "but not the stomach." The closest Lily ever came to discovering what might have happened the night Sophie did not come down to McLeod's, was when she suggested that Sophie return to the service as it was obviously needed, even if she could only do it in the winter months when Stoker was away for six weeks at a stretch.

"Once I quit somethin', I quit it," she said with virtuous finality.

"Like you did with readin'?" Lily said.

4

"The kids wanna go to the circus," Sophie announced.

Robbie and even Brad had talked of little else since the posters went up on the fenceposts of the village. Darling Brothers Circus and Travelling Sideshow, they boasted in black capitals. The place and date were hand-stamped below the engraved horse with the mane like a mermaid's hair:

Bayview Park, Friday and Saturday. Most of the village was waiting in formation for the circus train when it pulled into the Grand Trunk station and then backed down a siding which took it past the grain elevator almost to the edge of the park that lay between the town and the village.

The Potts and the Marshalls climbed aboard the new Sarnia Street Railway that Saturday and rode in style 'on the rails', even if the smart leather-seated carriage was drawn along by a single dray who clumped over the fickle ties. Sophie had her two youngest in tow, Wee Sue and Bricky, and Brad sat with them imagining he was really older than Sue. Blub and Robbie had run on ahead of them, with their own well-rubbed coins jingling in their pockets.

"We'll be lucky if we get a 'hello' outta them two today," Sophie said, fluffing up the tired ruffles on her pink party dress. She sniffed at the toilet water she had spilled on the flanks of a partially exposed bosom. "Fred's been in a devil of a mood lately, ever since they laid him off at the sheds. I keep tellin' him his brothers'll get him into the Great Western, but he won't listen to me or anybody else. He oughta be more like your Robbie – content with his lot."

By the time the trolley stopped at the park and the bright minarets of the circus tents floated into view across the green green grass, Sophie had forgotten all about Blub and any other sorrows she may have been harbouring. Brad decided he wanted to see the show under the Big Top with the clowns, animals and acrobats. So did Wee Sue, but since the first performance was not due to start for an hour, it was decided that the mothers should escort Bricky through the kiddies' section – complete with roundabout, a pony-ride, and a corral full of exotic but harmless creatures deemed to be 'cute'. Brad and Wee Sue headed in the direction of the side-show tents with their striped cupolas and brass balls and grisly promise.

"I hope we're doin' the right thing – lettin' them two go off together on their own."

"Brad'll behave," Lily said.

"Ain't Brad I'm worried about," Sophie laughed, and jammed another taffy apple into Bricky's face. He was looking somewhat peaked after a mere four rides on the roundabout. "You want a meat-pie to settle your tummy?"

Lily loved the colours and sounds and odours around her. They stopped to admire the visible music of a steam-organ and then a leather-skinned man who played an Irish ditty on slender bottles bubbling with melodic dyes, and then a juggler who defied geometry with his dizzying blue triangles. Barkers and grifters called out to them to come win their fortunes, try their luck, take a chance, carry off the main prize – in a lingo as old as bazaars or gypsies. Hawkers from the shadow of awnings spread their walnut eyes over every patch of pink female flesh that passed them by.

Sophie sat Bricky down in the shade of a tree, jammed two fingers down his throat and ducked as he brought up the excess of her affection. Wee Sue and Brad came up, flushed and giggling. Sophie gave them a searching look then said to Wee Sue, "Why don't you an' Brad stay here with Bricky for ten minutes. We'll meet you at the entrance to the Big Top."

Before Lily could say anything, Sophie was trundling ahead of her towards the games of chance. She stopped to catch her breath, her great breasts flexing like independent bellows unsupported beneath the frumpery of her garish costume. "Did you get a gander at him on the first round?" she puffed, and without waiting for a response, aimed her slow-motion trot in the direction of a sign which said: *Guess Your Weight Within Five Pounds or You Win*. Standing below this standard near an impressive set of scales was a dark, muscular man with a Moroccan's moustache and Neanderthal eyes. They lit up with larceny and other lusts as soon as they spotted the two women approaching. Lily felt herself skewered and turning slowly on a spit.

"Ready to give away one of them kewpie dolls?" Sophie blared with the brass section of her voice.

"Haven't lost one today," said the grafter. "But you look like you could fool a man, even a man of great experience such as myself."

"How much is it gonna cost me?"

"Depends on what you're willin' to give, but a nickle'll do. For a start."

"I never start nothin' I can't finish."

Lily slipped back into the small crowd that had formed around the scene and its possibilities. Behind them she could hear the 'thunk' of a hammer and the clank of a rusty bell. Sophie turned just enough to acknowledge the claims of the spectators without actually looking at them, and then made a surprisingly nimble pirouette somewhere inside the gaze of the guess-your-weight man. The onlookers gasped as if they had just seen an elephant do a cartwheel. They applauded both the feat and its elegance.

"That's all of me," she beamed, "or almost all."

"Could there be more?" said the carny, winking to the front rows.

"You gonna frisk me for hidden objects?"

"An' where would you hide them, eh?" the carny said, brandishing a white card and ostentatiously writing down his educated guess. "Three hundred and ten pounds," he announced, "of the prettiest pink flesh this side of Chicago."

Sophie snorted and stepped onto the scales. "With or without my bonnet?" She flipped off her enormous hat and shook out her curling, chestnut hair. The contrast between it and her Irish skin, uncaressed by any sun, was dazzling. Several cheers went up. The carny slipped the weights along the scale as dextrously as if he were milking a cow, but the outcome had never been in doubt. He was more than twenty pounds out.

"Your lucky day, madam!" he cried to the 'marks' gawping at the prize-table, and he waved the biggest, rosiest kewpie past their avid stare and placed it gently on the upslope of Sophie's bosom.

"My lucky day," Sophie said. She wheeled to her supporters. "And I didn't even haveta put that brick between my tits!"

A grown man in the crowd blushed, but the carny laughed and said, "Honey, you couldn't get a toe-nail down there!"

Then he did an astonishing thing. He glanced at Sophie for a long second then pushed his way through the throng over to the sledge-hammer game, and yanked the ten-pound mallet out of a customer's hand. "Another kewpie for the great lady!" He raised the hammer as easily as a match to light his pipe and brought it crashing down on the button. The clapper shot up the stiff pole as if it were greased and slammed into the bell so vehemently the ringing shook the lions awake in their cages a hundred feet away.

•

Later in the afternoon Lily found Bricky asleep in her lap.

"Funny, we ain't seen Blub or Robbie all day," Brad said to Wee Sue.

"They went to the freak shows, I bet," said Wee Sue, reluctant to let go of Brad's hand.

"You take Bricky along with you on the trolley," Lily said. "I need to walk some. Sophie'll likely be home by now anyway."

"I never knew Ma to get sick to her stomach before," Wee Sue said. She picked up her brother and gave Brad a look that brought him trailing along after her, muttering. She's two years older than him, Lily thought.

With the music of the Flying Arabians still echoing inside her, Lily set out

across Bayview Park. Something more than music had made her
anxious—something to do with Brad or with Robbie who'd been depressed
lately, or with Sophie herself. If I walk it off, perhaps nothing will happen,
she told herself. The unlandscaped section of the park was very pleasant. She
avoided the stone bridge, took off her shoes and waded across the drain thick
with aging lily pads and young jack-in-the-pulpit. On the other side, she
veered off the path into the swale that wound its way through the scattered
maples and brought her out behind St. Clair Street.

Lily was upon them before she could stop herself. They sprawled in the
tender grass at the bottom of the swail. The carny man lay on top of her with
neither his hands nor feet touching the ground, his knees braced on the
promontories of her thighs. His torso nestled in the crevasse of her breasts,
the gnarled brown root of his back twisting and flinging the buttocks forward
in frantic spasms. He floated on flesh, abob on the blood-tinted acreage of
her skin like some scorched Casanova riding the cornucopia of Aphrodite's
thighs, the coral shell of her bedchamber and the resurrecting wave under it.
Against the heave of his paramour's breath, he exhaled a sequence of abrupt
barking sounds, like a dog being kicked repeatedly in the ribs. Sophie opened
her eyes and through the glazed lattice of her lust she looked up at Lily then
twirled the kewpie doll on one finger, like a trophy.

•

"Don't stare at me like that," Sophie said in the kitchen an hour or so later. "I
ain't pissed in the Holy Grail, you know."

"It's not that, really," Lily said. "It's just, I thought all them things you
said about Stoke, you know, whenever he –"

"I meant 'em, every word. Stoker's damn good to me—we been good
together for as long as I can remember. But how often is he here, eh? How
many times does he leave me high an' dry an' hangin' out there like a wash
in the wind? You think the bugger keeps it in his pants all those weeks in the
bush, or up in Fort William overflowin' with squaws an' hooers?" She was
slowed by a new look of amazement in Lily's face.

"Then the carny man..."

"Of course he wasn't the first, don't you listen to what a body tells you?
But I ain't no hooer like them floozies up at Hazel's or them harlots of Sarie
McLeod's. You ain't thinkin' that sort of thing?"

Lily touched her friend's arm. "I ain't thinkin' anythin', Soph, you know that. If you want to tell me, fine. It don't matter, really."

"I can't help myself," Sophie said. "I try real hard, but then some night a young sailor boy comes totterin' down from Hazel's lookin' sad an' lonesome, and I call over to him and ask him if he'd like a good cup of tea, an' sometimes he comes in, an' usually he's been disgusted by what he's seen up the hill or he got to the porch an' turned back while his buddies made fun of him, and I just settle him down an' we talk in the dark, real quiet like, an' once in a while I just take him into my bed, and it's as warm an' toasty an' nice as you could dream of."

"Does Stoker know?"

Sophie went white. "Stoker must never know. I'm no hooer. What's done in the Alley is never told."

"An' the park?"

"The only time, I swear it." She shivered. "Never again, not like that."

They sat in silence for a while, listening to Wee Sue's laughter and Bricky's squealing from the other room.

"Are you tellin' me you ain't been with a man since Tom?" Sophie said casually as if they had been in the middle of a conversation.

Lily nodded.

"Then you mean that devil's shivaree an' your house burnin' down was all for nothing?"

"Ti-Jean wasn't there, he left to see his mother."

"He was one handsome fella, eh?"

"Uh huh." For the first time Lily was able to smile, feeling once again the undefiled kinship between them.

"You need to take a lover," Sophie said quietly.

•

Lily was putting Brad's supper on his plate and beginning to wonder where Robbie had got to when Sophie pulled open the front door and stood on the stoop trying to catch her breath.

"What's wrong?"

"They've run away with the circus," she gasped. "Stumpy saw them gettin' on the train at the park."

"Who, Sophie, *who!*"

"Freddie, an' your Robbie. They're gone."

Lily grabbed Brad and pulled him past Sophie. "Run up to the station an' see if the circus train's left yet. Hurry." Brad was already off, his whippet legs flashing in the sunset over the river flats. Lily followed only yards behind him even though her heart, after the first convulsion, refused to make another move. Sophie rumbled after them, sobbing and thrashing her hands. The circus train with its purple and yellow-striped coaches and box-cars could be seen against the orange glow of the horizon ahead, moving slowly and inexorably around the curve that would take it north out of the country, out of all reach, beyond the range of forgiveness and regret. The derision of its chattering bogie wheels stunned the two women as they came to a foolish halt among the milkweed and the wild mustard and the evening swallows overhead.

"Stoker'll kill me," Sophie said.

Suddenly Brad shouted and the women turned to stare across the space cleared by the deserting train. A male figure, only a shadow against the perishing sun, trotted towards them, holding something aloft in its right hand like an offering. No one moved an inch until Robbie came up to them, the fishing rod over his shoulder and a string of perch thrust out for admiration and approval.

"Can we have them for supper, Ma?"

•

Sophie sat in the swelter of her kitchen wrapped in a shawl and sipping from a glass of brown liquor. "Go on, have some, it won't kill you. John the Baptist makes his pig try it first. Go on."

Lily let a drop of the hooch slither its way over her tongue.

"He'll kill me, you know. He never got over Burton stayin' up in Bruce County, an' he keeps askin' why Stewie an' John don't come home to see him no more, an' I tell him they're busy gettin' their lives started on the Great Western, an' he yells 'yeah, two fuckin' miles away!' I can't think of a thing to say back except that Peg brought her little one over here last month an' he was so happy with that baby I thought he'd cry. Then he an' Peg got to arguin' about religion an' how her husband insisted on havin' Peg dunked in Perch Creek an' gettin' the baby baptized too an' then Peg just up an' leaves, and I want to say, 'See, it ain't all my fault, you can't blame me for

Peg nor for Marlene, no sir. It ain't my fault Marlene won't ever come home or even see her own brothers an' sisters or tell anyone where she's livin'."

"I'll stay with you," Lily said. "I ain't afraid of Stoker."

"No. You mustn't do that, you mustn't ever think of doin' anythin' like that." She drained her glass, keeping her lips sealed to trap the afterwaves of the whiskey. "You promise me that."

"Why don't you leave him?"

Sophie flinched at the question. The long look she gave Lily ran the gamut through incomprehension to resentment, hurt, self-loathing and resignation. "You don't understand, Lil. I deserve it."

26

1

One Monday in June of 1877, Lily was a bit later than usual arriving at Hazel's.She and Sophie had been up most of the night sitting with Bricky who was down with the mumps and having a bad time of it. Sophie said she was too tired and too hot to come so Lily walked on by herself. As she went past Stumpy's and waved to Cap Whittle on his bridge, she felt a deep unease inside and quickened her pace. Violet had not been well, Winnie was thought to have got herself pregnant again and was very depressed. There was something waiting for her in the yellow and purple house at the top of the rise, of that she was certain. She leaned on the newel post, her head woozy, her breath staccato. I'm just tired, she thought, and went in.

•

Everyone was listening so intently to the newcomer that Lily was able to slip unnoticed into her usual chair in the corner by the southeast window. She noted with relief that both Violet and Winnie were hanging on each word being spoken by the tall, silver-haired man. He was like no other Negro she had ever seen with his gold-rimmed spectacles, his trim business suit, white shirt and cravat, his patent-leather shoes and the pearl-knobbed cane he leaned on from time to time for rhetorical effect. His voice was baritone, beautifully cadenced, and urban to the last vowel. He was a sixty-year-old American gentleman whose skin had been accidentally charcoaled. Lily caught the end of what had been a detailed story of hairbreadth escape and considerable pathos. The whisper of Hazel's taffeta could be heard across the room. A single gold tear rolled down the right cheek of Shadrack Lincoln, seated at the feet of the stranger and peering up with adoration and awe.

Winnie leaned over and spoke into Lily's ear: "He's Mr. Abraham Jackson, from *Philadelphia*." And, Lily learned later, come to the County in search of the long-lost cousin of a friend in Pennsylvania who turned out to be their own Shadrack Lincoln. The story, just completed, had been one of a series Mr. Jackson had been urged to tell about his days on the Underground Railroad.

"Those were exciting days, and they were dreadful days. But even now we have much work to do. Many of the committees we formed then are still in operation, but instead of helping people to escape to freedom, we're involved in a variety of Negro causes, including this one – searching for missing relatives and trying to put back together families broken up by the heinous institution of slavery. We're also helping many of the people who fled here to Canada without wives, children or parents to resettle back in their home counties if they wish to." He glanced at Shadrack.

"Tell us more about the Railroad, Mr. Jackson," Hazel said, as if she were coaxing a reluctant diva towards an encore. "Did you ever get up as far as Canada?" She looked about for support. Betsy filled his cup with alacrity for they all knew he had to catch the late-afternoon express for London.

"I worked out of Philadelphia. I worked for Stephen Smith, a wealthy lumberman of my own race. He financed much of the local operation, which centred on Mr. William Still, whom you've heard about. I was supposed to be an agent for the lumber company, but my travels in Pennsylvania were really designed to keep supplies and money flowing to key points along the line. We were the principal relay station on the main route from the Carolinas over what we called the Great Black Way of the Appalachians—and thence on to Ohio. No, I never did get to Canada myself, but I heard detailed accounts of the bravery and dedication of Canadians, and many of them came to work for us on the American side. In fact, it was through the Partridge family in Moore Township that we were able to get a line on the whereabouts of Shadrack here. Many of the old railroaders continue to help us out in any way they can. I talked with Harry Partridge before I came up to Sarnia, and we reminisced about the old days. In particular, we talked about the Canadians who'd served the cause so well back in the 'fifties when the Fugitive Slave Law made it a dangerous business. You may already have heard of the exploits of Bill Shepherd, Harold Flint, Michael Corcoran ...–"

"Quick, get the smellin' salts, Vi," Hazel cried, holding Lily in her arms.

•

Here in the Alley, no questions were asked. Hazel had given them her own sitting room where the curtains, carpet and plush chairs combined to soften voices and accentuate intimacy. Abraham Jackson sat no more than a yard from Lily and delivered his soliloquy in a hushed, elegiac tone, as if the theme itself might overwhelm the solitary listener or crush the fragility of the words.

"I knew your father long before I met him. He was an early organizer of the Railroad at the Michigan-Canadian border crossing, one of the most dangerous spots on the line. After the Fugitive Slave Law the bounty-hunters concentrated on these crossing points, and they didn't care who they killed to get their quarry. I heard of your father's courage from the great Harriet Tubman herself. So when he came over to our side of the border in 1851, he had many influential friends to help him. I met him that fall in William Still's living room in Philadelphia. We never asked him much about why he had to leave Canada, but I could see that he was suffering a great deal as a consequence. Later on, he confided to me that he had, in a vengeful rage, accidentally killed a man who had committed some crime against his family. He feared there was a warrant out for his arrest. Only a few years ago did I learn that there never had been any such warrant. The Lord saw fit to bring him to us, and we were grateful.

"Your father became the most important person in the human chain of ties, rails, siding and way stations that made up the Underground Road to Freedom during those grim years before the War. His job was to pick up refugees along the edges of the Carolinas and direct them or lead them himself over the Appalachian Way, with bounty-hunters and bears and renegade outlaw bands all looking for the same helpless prey. He was shot twice, frost-bitten many times, and cut his way out of a southern jail before a lynch mob could take its revenge. He was a legend among the Negros and Abolitionists everywhere—he was a man possessed."

He paused as if to let that much sink in, but Lily's querying, avid eyes urged him on.

"I met him often at Still's house during our many strategy sessions, and it was there that I saw him for the last time in March of 'fifty-eight, almost twenty years ago. I remember every detail of that evening because all the important people on the Railroad were there to meet and listen to another legendary figure of the day—John Brown, Old Brown of Ottawatomie. He was there with his son, John Jr., looking for money and recruits. That night he got both. I tried to talk your father out of it, but like so many others, he too had glimpsed the apocalyptic blaze in Old Brown's eye. I guess he felt the same frustrations that Brown did after a decade of danger, senseless death and no sign of victory anywhere. Only the trickle of lives they had redeemed with such expense of body and spirit, while the principal evil festered and gloated on every side. They were ready to chance Armageddon. We never saw him again."

He paused, swallowed thickly and continued. "He died at Harper's Ferry in the blood and horror of that wonderful *débâcle*. His name is not recorded among the official twenty-two, but his bravery there is well-known among the people he died trying to liberate. He was guarding the Potomac Bridge with Oliver Brown and others when the militia arrived and drove them off. Apparently your father refused to retreat and was shot on the bridge. Before the local troops, slavering for blood and souvenirs, could reach him, he jumped or fell into the river, where the current swept him towards the sea. The Virginia guardsmen stood on the bridge and used his body for target practice till it drifted out of their range of interest. But when the Federal Marines went looking for it later that evening, it was gone, spirited off by a group of free Negroes who carried it upstream to Chambersburg where they buried it secretly in their churchyard. It's still there under a plain white stone marked simply 'Mr. Corcoran'. Every year hundreds of people, black and white, slip quietly into the shade of that little cemetery to pay their respects."

Lily was about to speak but sensed there was more.

"Your father came back to Canada once. I learned this from Harriet Tubman, who told me about it only a few weeks before my trip up here. He had been present at the famous Constitutional Convention John Brown held in Chatham in April of 1858. Still afraid of being apprehended by the Canadian authorities, he dyed his hair black, shaved his beard and sneaked into the province for the two key days of the Convention. He told Brown he had to take part of a day to ride north to visit his sister and daughter in Port Sarnia. She recalled this because she said she had rarely seen him so agitated. When he got back late on the Friday, she took special pains to talk with him about the trip. He told her he had found his sister's farm easily enough. He walked up the lane till he heard voices in the garden beside the cottage, and then stopped. He said the two women were in the garden, working and humming and seemingly content despite the Black Frost that had ravaged both our countries that spring. He told Harriet that he watched them for a long time, hoping they might glance up and see him. But they didn't—he found he couldn't speak and then he left."

After a while Lily said, "Did he ever talk about us?"

"Ah, yes, Mrs. Marshall, all the time. He told me once that as soon as his mission was ended, he planned to go back and bring his daughter to live with him in the States. That thought was on his mind constantly."

From the sadness of his smile Lily knew he was lying.

2

When Lily came around the bend towards her house, her thoughts were so roiled she almost bumped into the woman standing patiently by the front stoop. A white glove shot out.

"I'm Miss Stockton." The voice was crisp but distant. "Bradley's teacher."

"How do you do," Lily said in a tone she herself didn't recognize.

"May I come in?"

Lily stood by the door, puzzled.

"I'd like to discuss your son's future with you." Miss Stockton avoided the railing as she lurched up beside her host.

Inside, Lily became aware of the lunch dishes piled in a basin where the flies were noisily congregating.

"I'll get a fire goin' for some tea."

"Thank you, no. I've got an appointment in a few minutes uptown."

"Please sit down, then."

Miss Stockton's reserve came close to failing her as she searched for a safe place to deposit her petal-pink, delicately flounced dress. She decided the middle cushion of the chesterfield was the least lethal of the available sites and perched on its edge. Lily sat opposite her on the easy chair and waited.

"You may not be aware of it, Mrs. Marshall, but your son is the brightest pupil I have seen in five years of teaching, here and in Toronto. Inspector Whitecastle was here last week and fully corroborated my own intuitions."

"He's a real good reader," Lily said to be helpful.

Miss Stockton flashed an ambiguous smile and continued. "What I'm saying in practical terms is that your son will undoubtedly score highly on all the papers of his entrance examination next week. He will be eligible to go to the high school in Sarnia, and it is my considered opinion that he will be a first-class candidate for the University of Toronto in whatever field he chooses."

Lily appeared to be absorbing this revelation.

"You *have* thought about sending Bradley to high school?"

"He's been askin' me about it, yes."

"Good, good. With the extra coaching I've been giving him in the evenings this month—and I do hope you don't mind his being away from home too much . . . " She chanced a more searching appraisal of the second-hand ambience of the room: blotched window-glass, marauding flies, the absence of a study or desk, the tilted bookcase in one corner. "But I fully expect him to get straight A's."

Lily gave no sign of being overwhelmed by this news.

"The main reason I've come is to discuss a delicate matter, and since I've always been a straightforward person, I'll get directly to the point. While there are no tuition fees for the high school, Bradley will have to buy his own books, mathematical instruments and supplies. He will have to take the trolley to Sarnia every day. He . . . "

"He'll need some money," Lily said.

"Precisely, Mrs. Marshall, how quickly you see my point. He'll also need—how shall I word it—more fashionable kind of clothing. Not to show off, mind you, or get a swelled head, but just so he won't stand out for the wrong reasons or be picked on by city pupils who can sometimes be quite cruel in these matters."

"I been puttin' money aside all along," Lily said.

"Splendid. And since we obviously see eye to eye on these critical matters, may I make one final suggestion. If you can see your way clear, perhaps not the first year since Bradley's just thirteen, but by the second year or so, you might consider letting him board at one of the many fine homes near the school."

Lily's eyes narrowed slightly.

"That way he won't have to spend an hour a day on the trolley, and more important, he'd be able to use the school library after hours or the public library down the street, and . . ." she aimed her pity towards the cubicle where the boys slept . . . "of course he could have a quiet room of his own in which to study. My purpose today, Mrs. Marshall, has been to relay

Inspector Whitecastle's enthusiasm for, and my own endorsement of, Bradley's genius to make these decisions more comfortable for you to consider."

Lily showed her visitor out.

Miss Stockton turned on the stoop and said in her own cabbagetown cadence: "You're gonna let him go, aren't you?"

Lily nodded, and touched her reassuringly on the arm.

•

Back inside the warm room, Lily felt woozy and sat down at the kitchen table. Must be the heat, she thought. Robbie clumped in from the back shed. "No supper?" he said.

"You seen Brad?"

"Yeah, he's up at Redmond's fussin' over that Potts girl. They were stuffin' their faces with chocolate the last I saw of 'em."

"Miss Stockton, his teacher, was just here. I thought he'd be home to find out what was goin' on."

Robbie went over to the tinderbox. "He knows, all right," he said bitterly. "But he won't come home till dark."

"Why not?"

"He's ashamed to."

27

1

Dominion Day that year marked the first decade of the new nation, and in Sarnia the opening of Lake Chipican and the surrounding Canatara Park. The new recreation facility was festooned with picnic benches, a bandstand and a mammoth open-air dance pavilion. The grand *debut* of the facility was celebrated with the usual political speech making, boosterism and fireworks. But by far the greatest attraction would be the regatta on Lake Chipican itself, starring no less a celebrity than Ned Hanlon, the legendary world-class punter. Sophie decided that Lily ought to go because she had been down in the dumps lately and needed a little music and dancing to cheer her up. When Lily protested that Lake Chipican was their own Little Lake with a fancy name attached to it to make it sound vaguely Indian, Sophie appealed directly to the boys seated nearby, and the day was carried.

Almost everyone from both the town of Sarnia and the unincorporated village of Point Edward came to watch the races and the mighty Ned Hanlon. His combination of strength and agility, power and grace, appealed to the ages and sexes that rimmed the pond seven deep that Saturday afternoon.

Sophie and Lily spent the day together. The young people went off by themselves in twos and threes, returning only for supper or an extra nickel. Wee Sue and Brad took Bricky swimming. The sun shone benevolently down upon the festivities, glistening on the muscular arms of the rowers. They pulled in furious unison, skimming the surface of the pond with the seeming ease of Argonauts, their rhythmic, guttural grunting muffled by the adulating crowd. Sophie was apparelled in a peach-yellow sundress and a billowing bonnet that gave her the appearance of a ruffled bobolink. She clasped Lily by the hand and pulled her here and there to improve their view of the racers and get a close-up gander at Ned Hanlon himself. Sophie's ken, however, soon narrowed to the hefty coxswain of one of the rowing eights, the largest of the shells in the competition, requiring men of fortitude and amplitude to propel her forward, stroke and counter-stroke. Lily preferred the scullers, the solitary racers whisking daft as dragonflies, commuting water to air.

During the picnic supper, the Sarnia Bugles entertained from the bandshell, and the husky athletes mingled with their worshippers. Several of them had volunteered to supervise the children's races. Robbie won a prize and was presented with a ribbon by Ned Hanlon himself. With the sun behind them making them mere silhouettes, Lily watched her son and the illustrious Torontonian during the brief ceremony. She knew much more was being exchanged than a mere ribbon. He's just like Tom, she was thinking; he can't live long on small rations of hope. The smile he flashed her way was like a reprieve. When Lily looked around for Sophie, she was gone. Bricky had been laid under an oak to sleep off his indigestion. The young folk had disappeared again, and in the distance, the orchestra struck its first chord in the new pavilion.

By the time Lily got over there, the hardwood dance-floor was already covered by couples enlinked in a Strauss Waltz, animated by the strings and muted horns of the Detroit City Orchestra just arrived by lake-steamer. The underside of the pagoda-like roof over the raised platform was hung with coloured lanterns and pastel ribbons even though the sun would provide all the illumination required for two hours yet. No one noticed the anomaly. The air of early evening was cool, the music exotic and seductive. Sophie danced with the 'eights' man, who was smartly attired in yachting white. Lily could see that he too was surprised, and not a little flushed and exhilarated, by the nimble ponderance of her step, the grand sway of her circling. She was so absorbed in observing this scene she hardly felt the pressure on her arm guiding her gently into the slipstream of music and dance. Did I say 'yes'? she thought, settling into the stranger's embrace.

He was one of the scullers, who had come second only to Ned Hanlon himself. In his oar's grip he held Lily as lightly as he would a falling rose petal. His sandy hair fluttered in the breeze of their own making. In the whirling fandango his fingers on her back praised and applauded; in the slow waltz, she put her brow against his bare chin. They navigated the shoals and eddies of the music with such mutual acuity Lily could feel no part of his motion but the point where brow and chin swivelled on a single bead of sweat. During the jigs she lifted her skirt above her knees and closed her eyes until she could hear, somewhere behind the fiddle's slither, the bounce of a breath-driven harmonica. When it stopped, she leaned against the railing to steady herself. Her *premier danseur,* Shamus O'Huguin from Burlington, was catechizing her with insatiable sea-green eyes.

As dusk descended and mosquitoes began rising from the swamps and pools, the music slowed to a last waltz. Young and old and many between clung together in pairs. They danced as if they believed such bonding of purpose and desire and hope were as permanent a part of the human condition as war and depression and the fading of fidelity. "We're all goin' over to the Grand Trunk for a party," he whispered. "You'll come?"

Jostling couples pushed towards the steps and illicit laughter percolated from the shadows. Sophie Potts was waving goodbye with her baby finger and ambling into the brush with her amiable paramour. Lily turned back to the young oarsman and she could tell from the smile on his face that she was about to say yes.

"You comin', Ma?"

It was Robbie, at the bottom of the steps, alone.

"Yes," she said, and released her lover's hand.

2

Next day the Sunday hush lay more heavily than usual upon the village. The church bells importuned as noisily as ever, but empty places were noted in several pews, even in the choir stall. Lily listened to their familiar, reassuring ring as she ironed a clean shirt for Brad. He was to go down to Sarnia tomorrow for his interview with Mr. Axelrod, the principal-designate of the recently constructed, independent high school. Brad lay on the chesterfield pretending to be absorbed by some verse-saga called *Don Juan,* a gift from Miss Stockton – daintily inscribed – in honour of his extraordinary performance on the entrance examination. Lily had taken some of the cash she had been putting away in a crockery jar under her bed and purchased her son his first store-bought oxfords, suit, vest and tie. Robbie was off by himself hunting cottontail in Second Bush.

It was a hot and humid July day without the relief of a breeze. Lily thought she should go over to Sophie's to see if the kids wanted to have a picnic and spend the day on the beach. If Wee Sue came along, then Brad would also. She was mulling these thoughts over sleepily – her dreams had been deep and disruptive for weeks now – when she was startled by a commotion in the back shed. A laundry pail clattered, pursued by a mutilated curse. Sophie.

Lily arrived in time to help her upright. Sophie glared at the offending pail then flashed a grin at Lily, catching her with a boozy gust of breath. Her eyes hovered, radium red. The look she gave Lily (just before the mask of her face closed over it) skidded on the edge that separated ecstasy from desperation.

"C'mon, Lil, we're gonna have us some fun, some *real* fun," she said in a voice amazingly unslurred.

Lily took her friend by the arm: "Let me get you home to bed, Soph. You ain't had much sleep, I bet."

"If you're suggestin' I been drink' an' screwin' all night, then you're absolutely right," she laughed, pulling away and grabbing Lily's hand. "C'mon, you an' me's gonna haul old Duchess's ass up the hill an' give that bachelor pig up there the thrill of his life!" She rocked back on her heels, sat down on the cushions of her rump, and let out a dry, rattling cackle.

Lily allowed herself to be dragged across the lane to the Potts' yard where it became clear that Sophie had already put her plan into action. Beside the pigpen sat the rickety trundle wagon Stoker used for hauling logs or vegetables up to the house. Duchess had been lured out of her shady retreat with a bucket of milk slops set near the gate to the sty.

"C'mon, Lil, I need a little help gettin' her up on the wagon. Mind you, if she knew where she was goin' she'd hop up there like a toad into poop, but she won't listen to a word I say to her." She flung open the barrier and called out in saccharine, seductive tones: "Soo-ee, soo-ee, soo-ee!"

Duchess pricked up her floppy ears and blinked but decided not to abandon the slop bucket in spite of its barrenness. She was a fine Chesterwhite sow with rosy-hued skin, a soft, lecherous snout, and fold upon fold of self-satisfied fat. Whenever she was in heat, like now, she lazed in the mud and dreamed of Farmer Holly's Yorkshire boar rearing up behind her, his cleft trotters flailing against her roused flanks. But Farmer Holly's boar was much overdue.

"Son-of-a-bitch up an' died on us," Sophie explained, circling the wary sow. "The old man, not the stud," she chuckled. "Now you put that there ramp up to the wagon while I push this barrel of grease shit from the rear."

"Soph, you're crazy. You can't get Duchess up on that contraption, an' you can't let her in with John the Baptist's boar. He'll kill you."

"He ain't home," Sophie said. "Gone perch fishin' with Hap Withers' boys, out on the *lake* for the *whole* day!"

"He ain't gonna like it; you know how he feels about Aquinas."

Sophie glared over at Lily. "Hey, you an Alleywoman or not?"

Lily grabbed the two planks and tried to make a ramp out of them. Sophie managed to get downwind of Duchess and plop a hand on each of the sow's haunches. She grunted and heaved the animal forward and was making headway when she decided to expedite its progress by twisting its tail three hundred degrees counterclockwise. Duchess squealed like a bruised bagpipe at the outrage and lurched sideways. Sophie lost her handhold, overcompensated and flopped flat on her back in the slime. Lily leaned forward and put a gentle arm lock on Duchess while Sophie yawed fitfully in the mire, gained a knee, and then let her jaw slacken like a hippo's yawn.

"You *blubber bucket! You bulb-bellied slop cunt of a pig's hooer! You fat-tit, slant-eyed son-of-a-boar's bitch!*" She hollered through her megaphone at the stunned sow – its eyes red as raspberries – and continued improvising her medley of curses, their foul effluence rising into the air above the Alley. By the time Lily had seduced Duchess to one of the trundle wagon's uprights and pulled Sophie to her feet, they were surrounded by McLeods, McCourts and Shawyers of every size and sex. All were eager to help.

Sophie, canary yellow from the front and mud umber from the back, re-established what she took to be her dignity by hurling commands into the chaos. Amid much laughter and several temporary setbacks, she somehow managed to assist the terrified sow up the plank and into the wagon. Lily hopped aboard and tried to sooth Duchess with nonsense patter she thought might approximate a porcine lullaby. While having little evident effect on the beast, it did succeed in reducing Lily and Sophie to a state of paralyzing mirth. Sophie leaned the mighty ballast of her body against the rear of the rig while a dozen ululating children pushed from the side and pursued some invisible Pied Piper up the dusty trail towards the bootlegger's shack. Other pleasure seekers, large and small, joined the procession en route. Cap Whittle was seen scrambling down a yardarm. Spartacus and Stumpy fell in behind, and Honeyman Belcher left his pony to graze where it stood.

As the tumbrel lumbered past Hazel's Heaven, the hoots and cries of the cavalcade awoke the drowsy concubines within. By the time it reached the stamping ground of John the Baptists's soul-mate, the afternoon was aflutter with petticoat and tinkling laughter. As the circus crowd gathered and jostled for the best view, Sophie halted the carriage with a toss of her head and waddled towards the abode of the victim. All commentary ceased. Wavelets could be heard stroking Canatara beach.

Aquinas had come out of his sanctuary to accost the intruders. In some ways his pen was the sturdiest and most impressive structure on the Alley. A commodious corral of stout split logs and deeply augured posts braided with chicken-wire allowed him freedom to exercise his bulk. He could loll in the soothing mud, or intimidate children and idling strangers by stamping his trotters on the gravel pad and grunting like a tusked peccary in the wild. Behind him stood a hutch-like affair constructed by his friend and helpmate. It was watertight, shingled with cedar shake, and the south side of it could be opened to the air by raising the two wall-size shutters on their hinges and laying them flat across the roof. This transformation occurred on warm sunny days when Aquinas preferred to lie in his manger, shaded and content, and peer out at the fevered world beyond. If his feed trough were less than a head loll away, and if he were hungry, as he often was, he might even nudge open the lid of the large grain box where the goodies were stored.

At this moment, though, with the afternoon sun blinding him, Aquinas was alone, surrounded by silent, gawking faces and under siege from a large female who had entered the gate beside the open hutch as if she were waltzing into church. Trying hard to ignore the presence of those arrayed behind her, he pawed the turf with his right trotter and stiffened his jowls. He belched volcanically and aimed a vicious snort in Sophie's direction. As he looked about, ready to mount a charge, his beady eye caught sight of Duchess, who was being escorted down the wagon ramp behind the invading force. His nostrils flared, appraised the available odours, and tightened. Sophie hauled Duchess by the ears into the pen and Lily slammed the gate in back of them. This acted as a signal for the silent chorus to erupt in a series of whoops, hollers, lewd anatomical suggestions and general merriment.

Aquinas froze, and waited in the middle of the sty as the dust from his terrible stomping settled in pools around him. Something in the aura about Duchess – with her pink plumpness, undulant softness, wobbling, fetid underparts – prevented him from outright retreat. He watched in rapt trepidation as Duchess, veteran breeder that she was, waddled into the muddy wallow a few feet away, tipped forward on her knuckles and presented herself for servicing.

A rasping cheer went up from the well-wishers. Sophie picked up its inspiration. "All right you black-balled son-of-a-bitch" she yelled at Aquinas. "Let's see what kinda stud you are!"

Aquinas, tempted and shivering, stumbled forward two steps, all caution overpowered by the incense of passion just beyond his nose. At the last possible second with Duchess braced for capture and rude entry, he lunged, splashed through the muck and headed for his manger. Sophie cantered after the spooked hog, cutting him off at the corner of the opening to his hutch where they collided with a blubbery thud. Both combatants went down but Sophie was up first, spitting sludge and umbrage. She flopped on top of Aquinas, who made no pretense of resistance. He had given up all emotion but fear, and as she threw a choke chain of flesh around his neck and jerked him vertical, he closed his eyes and howled as piteously as a barrow staring at his clipped testicles.

"Grab him by the handle!" someone offered.

"He ain't got one!"

Sophie dragged him stiff-legged across the wallow towards the puzzled sow. She might have succeeded in carrying out such a forced congress if Duchess herself had not decided she required more privacy to satisfy her procreative longing. She stood up, unstuck her front trotters from the mud and stumped towards the shelter.

"The other way! The other way!"

Sophie uttered an oath that sprung something inside the boar's head. All six hundred pounds of him went limp. Undaunted, Sophie gripped him by the knuckles and inched him back towards the sow now settled in the shade of the manger. The crowd whooped. Lily came to Sophie's side. Together they tugged Aquina's dead weight through the slough, tumbling into it themselves, and popping up again. Only their eyes and teeth signalled the manic delight of their laughter and fury. Finally, riding a crest of cheering, they pitched the wretched creature into the straw beside Duchess. Lily fell back against the stool John the Baptist used when conversing with his bachelor friend and let the tears wash over the mud on her cheeks. But Sophie, fuelled by some darker purpose, belly flopped between the dazed beasts and made a lunge for Aquinas's crotch. But in panic or dread or desire, the Polish China boar rose up and then down, and with a savage thrust, did his pedigree proud.

Before the crowd could confer its ultimate accolade on Sophie's daring, two more unexpected things happened. First, Cap Whittle, athwart an alder branch, cried out, *"Man ahoy!"* and John the Baptist was spotted tearing across the flats towards the *mêlée*. Second, the combined plentitude of sow, boar and human attendants caused the ground to give way under them. Straw, dirt, pig shit, rotting timbers, splintered floorboards—all caved inward and down and swept a cargo of flesh into the vortex. Moments later, through a maze of squeals, gasps and settling dust, first Lily, then Duchess, Aquinas, then Sophie, clambered up and rolled onto firm ground.

As the throng parted and drew back to allow for the entrance of the aggrieved party, whose French oaths and howl of desolation preceded him by two hundred yards, they gasped as one when the earth rumbled and exploded. A geyser of smoke and steam shot up no more than a handspan behind Sophie's rump. The shock of it bowled her over against Lily, and, arms enlinked, they followed the goose-white plume as it hissed skyward from its underground eruption. Moments later, Cap Whittle caught the first whiff of raw whiskey.

•

A few weeks later, Sophie stopped Lily on the lane. "Hey, I got news. Duchess is up the stump." She grinned her most wicked grin: "Must've been the holy water!"

28

1

In September of 1878, after flinging their slogans and exordia fruitlessly into the machinery of the universe, the Liberals lay down and let the Tories take up the torch with their cries of 'National Policy' and 'Reciprocity of Tariffs'. Hopes were raised much faster than the fallen economy. The North-West Mounted Police cantered onto the plains to save them from whiskey and Indians. The Métis retreated even farther up the North Saskatchewan to obscure enclaves with immemorable names like Duck Lake and Batoche. With Sir John A. – resuscitated and breathing fire – at the throttle, the Canadian Pacific Railway took lethal aim at the Rockies. Shockwaves of its revived thunder rolled into the Ontario boardrooms of the Great Western and the Grand Trunk. Talk of amalgamation was in the air that autumn. Retrenchment and consolidation were dusted off and re-presented as bywords of conventional wisdom. Whatever the reason, the Grand Trunk did decide it was no longer expedient to supervise the daily comings and doings of its foster-child, Point Edward. Incorporation was added to its list of bywords. After all, the company had more reserve land than it would ever need for future development. It had already sold off the choice commercial lots it could not use and even had a fine local candidate in mind to act as reeve and avuncular guide. The necessary legal trivia were arranged in the summer of 1878, elections for the first council announced for early October, and a proclamation date set for the transfer of power: January 1, 1879.

2

Hazel first raised the question, but it soon became general up and down the Alley: what would be the fate of squatters and outcasts in a village controlled by its own elders and *grandees*? This question took on more biting import

when it was learned that the Railway was ceding – gratis and as a gesture of
its good will – all such marginal territories to the corporation for 'future
recreational or industrial development'. The town council would own the
Alley outright. When the elections in October returned two clergymen, a
shop foreman and a druggist as councillors, and acclaimed Stanley R. 'Cap'
Dowling as reeve-elect, no doubt was left about the precariousness of the
Alley community. When they gathered at Hazel's on the Saturday following
the municipal election – more than two dozen of them, including old Angus
Shawyer sobered up for the day – they were not unaware of the irony of the
situation. A town meeting of people had settled here so they wouldn't ever
have to worry about politics, and they had never been called upon to confess
they were a community of *any* kind, even renegades.

Stump Starkey, Bible clamped akimbo, ascended the dais and accepted
the burden of explaining the legal details as far as they were known. When
each of these had been depreciated by argument and imprecation, he went
on to recite the actual words of the Reverend Clough, councillor-elect, who
had declared from the sanctity of his altar that the new village would be
'purged of that empustulated rot by spring'. Suggestions were made for
remediation, all indictable, and then the mood of anger changed to
frustration, and finally, to sullen resignation. At the point where the meeting
was about to break up, Sophie Potts was helped onto the makeshift platform
(Shadrack Lincoln's steamer trunk). The silence turned from sulky to
expectant. Braced on either arm by Stumpy and Spartacus, she began to
speak.

Sophie was now a gargantuan figure. The hummocks and drumlins and
foothills of her flesh were housed in a cerise-and-violet-striped awning which
Spartacus had filched from a Sarnia squire and Lily had fashioned into a
presentable container. Her cheeks, unbusked by sun, were nonetheless
puffed with scarlet striations from the effort of breathing. The spoor of her
sweat knocked dogs to their knees. Her chicory-dark hair sprouted up
anywhere in thicket and thew. When she spoke, her voice, though
unmistakably female, reminded listeners of hickory smoke, licorice and deep-
ground peppercorn.

"First of all, I'm sick an' tired of this whinin' an' gabble-gruntin'. Won't
do us no more good than a tinker's fart, an' it's not worthy of any one of you.
I know you all. I met you one at a time. I liked an' I hated you as I saw fit an'
you deserved. We all came here for our own special purpose, an' we don't

have to tell one another why. We like it here for our own peculiar reasons, an' most of us wanna keep it that way. Most of us won't do too good out there in the other world. We know too damn much about livin' to last long out there. The question for us is not 'do we want to stay?' but 'how can we swing it?' Well, I'm gonna tell you how, right now."

Stumpy and Spartacus got a firm double grip and eased Sophie forward till she caught her breath.

"You're all tryin' to dream up ways of defendin' your rights or gettin' back at the respectable folk or cuttin' your losses before you hightail it outta here like a jarful of spooked jackrabbits. Well, you don't need to. This town ain't gonna toss us out on our noses no matter how much hot air the Reverend One-Ball Clough bellows out his belfry. This town needs us, an' they know it. All we got to do is remind them a little bit."

No one present had ever heard Sophie Potts talk like this before. Her gossipy tales and deadly retorts, her mustard tongue and nettling glance, her Olympian profanity – these were legend on the lane, but not this. The Alleyfolk listened, not quite believing what they heard.

"Think about it. Them people out there may look on us as a cartful of cripples, ninnies, hooers and downright heathen, but they get a lot of pleasure out of thinkin' such things an' feelin' a tad better about themselves for thinkin' them. And all the time they know they can't do without us. If Honeyman left, who would clean the shithouses an' septic tanks? If they lost Spartacus, who would keep their boulevards clean an' give 'em a pile of cheap furniture from Sarnia to choose from? Who'd keep the tramps safe an' warm outta harm's way if Stumpy up an' left? And if Hazel were shut down, where would all them rutting sailors end up, eh? In the chaste beds of their precious little daughters! They may curse old Baptiste every mornin' before prayers, but half the town buys its hooch from that fine, unlicensed establishment. If they dump the Shawyers an' McLeods an' McCourts onto the streets, what maids will change the sheets on their beds, or wipe the snot off their kids' faces? An' think of the mountain of dirty laundry chokin' the closets an' hallways of the town's best houses if our dear Lily was given her walkin' papers?"

Sophie had struck the chord she had intended. Now she merely played the instrument with intervals for deep breathing. "Now, here's the plan," she said, when the cheering had almost ceased.

She had worked it out in her own mind, trying it out first on Lily, and together they shaped it for presentation. The Alleyfolk, each in the course of his self-appointed duties, would take a petition out among the populace. The gist of the petition, written out in legal fashion by Shadrack Lincoln, was this: for a fee to be negotiated, the squatters on the lane known as Mushroom Alley would have their properties surveyed, after which they would be given outright title. The lane itself would be attached to Prince Street at the south side of the tracks. The finished product looked impressive, and five copies were made. The strategy, as evolved by Sophie and Lily, was first to talk, in the natural course of business or social interchange, individually with storekeepers, a lady-of-the-house, a day-labourer resting at Baptiste's or exercising at Hazel's, a satisfied customer, a charitable heart – and when that individual seemed convinced by the justice or necessity of the cause, then and only then would the petition be proffered for a confirming signature. Moreover, only the petition for that designated interest-group would be shown. There were separate duplicate petitions for housewives, shopkeepers, Grand Trunk employees and other workers, tradesmen, and various self-appointed burghers of high standing. Discreetness, subterfuge, a touch of flim-flam – traits revered and practiced in the Alley – were thus to be used to telling effect.

The stratagem worked. On the five documents they amassed three hundred fifty signatures, more than half of the adult population of the village – though not all by any means were eligible voters. But the moral impetus of the suit was considerable. Few of the resident landowners could deny having a father or grandfather who had begun life in British North America as a squatter. Nor was the instinct to poach completely extinguished by the advance of civility.

A delegation was appointed to take the petition to Reeve-elect Dowling. Stumpy was chosen to present the suit and do all the talking, his chief qualification for the task being his gender. Dowling lived in a two-storey brick house on Victoria Street in a style appropriate to a factory owner, retired railway executive and budding politician. A maid, Carrie McCourt, answered the door and curtseyed before she recognized her neighbours. She lapsed into an incurable titter. Before she recovered, they were inside, past the vestibule and into the drawing room: Stumpy, Sophie, Maggie Shawyer, Hazel and, well in the background, Lily Marshall. Dowling, his tie askew and his shirt in a rumpus, was caught off guard and never regained his balance. He read through the papers at a muttering clip, glancing up from time to time at the odd components of the delegation, none of whom he recognized with any certainty. He said nothing for five minutes. Then he looked up at Stumpy.

"Well, I am the Reeve of all the people here. I'll present this to the council in January. Carrie will show you out."

Sophie brushed Stumpy back with a gentle flipper and rolled her bulk till it was planted in front of the reeve-elect, now trapped between his fireplace and divan. "Take it to them right now. We got to know your feelings on this right away. We don't propose to hang around an' wait for your mercy or neglect. We mean what we say here. All the services we provide are gonna vanish quicker than you can count your money. The people who signed there are tellin' you they want them services an' that they agree we got the same squatters' rights as was given to their parents an' to the lowliest of Negro slaves brung over the border from the States. We want an answer in a week, one way or another."

Dowling gave them all his best smile but there was no mirth in it. He promised a response within a week.

3

I'm thirty-eight years old, Lily thought. It's time I put down roots of my own. I'll take some of Brad's schooling money and turn the place into a cottage. I'll paint it blue. It'll be a place he'll want to come back to, the kind of place everybody needs once in a while – a sanctuary. For me, it will be home.

It was hard for Lily to believe that Brad was now in grade ten at the Sarnia High School, having completed grade nine with honours in every subject. He was studying literature and grammar and mathematics, even French. But when she attempted a brief conversation in the tongue she had known from childhood, Brad grimaced, then announced that she wasn't speaking any version of French that *he* knew of. She started to explain her position but for some reason stopped partway through.

"Well, I guess your teachers would know best."

They had more luck in their discussions of history and geography, certainly in the flush of mutual excitement during those first few months when Lily packed him a lunch and walked with him to the trolley. She waited by the window in the gathering dusk till she spied his slim figure among the crowd of returning workers and put their kettle on. She listened to his tales of the English kings – the wicked and the sublime – and of the odysseys of the mad, foolish, wonderful seafarers who sailed straight off any horizon. Cautiously she would interrupt him, trying to keep the countries and oceans in their place, baffled by the flat maps in his textbook and by his abrupt expositions. He himself worshipped England, her sanguinary pageant and her heroic verse, and felt irked by Lily's persistent questions about Ireland and where this or that minor country might be, as if it mattered to anyone. When she reminded him that his grandfather and grandmother came from there, he looked puzzled, then hurt.

"This is history, Ma, not family." Then that soft and engaging side of his nature, the side that needed to be loved, re-emerged, and he would curl up beside her on the chesterfield and read aloud from *The Idylls of the King*.

By the winter term these happier sessions were fewer and further apart. He seemed more and more to prefer studying alone, drawing the curtain around his bed, or when Robbie clumped through, wrapping himself in a shawl and disappearing into the drafty shed. Several times in January he came home late for supper without explanation and picked at his food. Finally, he confessed he was going out with school chums to have a coffee at a restaurant where they read the newspapers and talked, and occasionally bought supper. He said how sorry he was for worrying her and that it would not happen again, he was sure. The fellows had all treated him so many times he just couldn't throw himself on their hospitality any more. Next morning, Lily gave him a silver dollar.

"You ain't a beggar," she said. "You need money to treat your friends. Just tell me when you plan to stay late down there." He made a solemn promise, and most of the time remembered to honour it.

In June, Lily received a letter from Mr. Axelrod, the principal and read it with wonder and trepidation. In a formal style and script, it informed her that her son was at the head of the class and reported to be one of the most brilliant students his teachers had ever seen. She was exhorted not to reveal such appraisal to her son for fear of unpredictable consequences in the orderly development of his moral character. It was important for his mother to realize the depth of his talent that still lay untapped by enlightened instruction and to make preparations for her son's potentially long and fruitful academic career. In short, it was never too soon to start saving money, as even with the scholarships Brad was sure to obtain, a university education in a capital city was expensive. That much Lily already knew, and her intuition about her son's precocity was now confirmed. She went immediately to the jar under her bed, next to Sounder's pouch, and counted out sixty-nine dollars – two year's savings. She would have to find more, but there were three years still to worry about that. Robbie was paying her a little board money whenever he got work at the sheds. Violet often refused to take the salary Lily gave her, but Lily put it aside in a separate cache – it wasn't her money. We'll make out, she said to Tom, like we always do.

In March, she had wondered if that sentiment were true when Brad, studying in the shed to punish his boorish brother, caught a chest cold which rapidly turned into pneumonia.

"It ain't my fault, Ma," Robbie pleaded, and Lily absolved him with a touch and together they once again nursed Brad through his fever and delirium.

In so doing, Robbie expended some small part of affection and faith that was afterwards irrecoverable. He pitched in and helped Violet with the laundering, swearing the household to secrecy, while Lily sat by Brad's bed reading aloud to him (in a cadence almost as good as Miss Kingman's) his current favourite, *The Lady of Shallot*. When at last he was strong enough to speak, the first words he said were: "I love you, Ma. I'll never leave you. Never." He began to shake, not from the fever but its devastating aftermath. Tears slipped unannounced down his livid cheeks, and though Lily brushed them aside with a soft cloth, they continued to fall. He *knows* already, she thought. One way or another, I will lose him.

As soon as she had finished counting out the precious savings, Lily went fishing for Brad's Easter report card. She didn't know why but she wanted to look at it and admire the scarlet A's printed there, shimmering like heraldic gules; to hold them up to the light for Tom to see. It wasn't in the apple-box beside the bookcase so she pulled out the drawer under Brad's bed where he kept his papers and notes from school. It was there, but she didn't pick it up. A notebook, half-open, caught her eye. She leafed through it, scanning the crabbed printing that was unmistakably her son's. Each page contained a poem, scribbled over and copied out and altered and finally printed in immalleable block capitals. They were Brad's own poems. From the fading of the ink, she concluded that some of them had been written many months ago. She could not read them. She closed up the secret book and put it back in its rightful place. She sat down at the kitchen table, shaken, unable to think a single mitigating thought.

"Hey, Ma, I'm cleanin' two cottontails out here, you want 'em for supper?" Robbie called, and then came in from the shed to see if she was all right. "I'll get the fire goin'," he said.

With the depression showing no sign of being able to discriminate between *bleu* and *rouge*, Robbie had been able to find only occasional work at the freight sheds, lugging barrels and crates much as Tom had done in the full heat of the summer. Redmond continued to give him three half-days delivering grocers in the township, plodding along at the mercy of Rocket whose swayback and irregular trot amused children and roused the derisive instincts of the young toughs about town. Robbie never complained, and although naturally taciturn, he often sank into a black silence that Lily noticed immediately and gave a wide berth to. When Brad blundered into one of them, a brief flare-up ensued with Brad snapping out something elegant and barbed and Robbie stammering an unoriginal curse before stomping off to the woods.

The woods he loved still – to walk in, hunt in, do whatever private ruminating he needed to do when the world flummoxed him as it so often did. He was like a gentle bull with its horns growing inward. One day on his return from hunting in Second Bush, he said to Lily, "I stopped over at the old place."

"You did?"

"I looked in the barn. Nothin's been touched. There's a bed in there an' Ti-Jeans rocker. I almost forgot about that old place."

"It's still ours," Lily said, looking for some defense.

A week later Robbie did not come home all night; Lily didn't notice until she called out to the pup-tent where he often slept in the spring and discovered it was empty. He arrived shortly after breakfast and said, with a hint of badgering pride, "I slept over at the old place. It's real cozy. You get a fresh breeze out there, all night."

During June, he seemed to spend more and more of his spare time 'out there'. When she questioned him about this, he grew silent, then morose. She stopped asking. One day, when she and Violet were out for their Sunday walk, they found themselves coming out of First Bush by a new path and crossing Michigan Ave. towards the town-line not a stone's throw from Bridie's place. Sensing where they were destined, Violet drew Lily into a direct route and they came upon their ruined homesteads through the rotting stumps of the windbreak. What they saw surprised and then astonished them. A fully developed vegetable garden had arisen like a materialized dream image exactly where the old one had always been: leaf and vine and tuber and wrinkled blossom. Robbie came out of the barn, blinking. "It's real good ground," he said.

Nothing was said about it, but when Lily felt up to it, she slipped over to 'Rob's place' (as it was now called) in the early June evenings of 1878 and stepped into stride beside her son, hoe in hand, as of old. She offered no advice and none was asked for. He can't make a living out of this patch, she thought, fertile as it is, but he loves it. It allows him to give something of himself completely without the fear of hurting or being hurt. When the August blights spoiled half of his crop, he was undaunted. He gathered his harvest, sold it at the Sarnia Market every Saturday during the season, and gave his mother ten dollars of his earnings. She put it in the schooling fund. When Brad whined and pleaded and threatened over the question of his boarding in Sarnia during his Grade 10 year, Lily was able to hold fast and say no. The trust fund had taken on an aura of something sacred between them. Someday Brad would understand it all. For the time being, though, he retaliated by staying away more to squander his money and time with school friends she was never to meet.

Just before the elections and the fuss over property title, Robbie received a letter with an exotic stamp on it. He had never before received a letter of any kind. Somewhat guiltily he slunk away to his tent and read it. Lily heard him jerk his shotgun off the shed wall and tramp towards the bush. The letter was floating, abandoned, in the breeze near the tent. Lily rescued it and read it as she knew she was meant to. It was from Fred Potts (Blub) and contained a thrilling account of his adventures with the circus. There were lurid descriptions of the southern American towns and backwaters they visited each year, including a narrative of his rise from stable boy to midway helper to full-scale barker for the girly show. He hinted that the circus would be coming next spring at least as far as London, and that a world of unimaginable wonder awaited the ruthless and the brave.

When Lily and Rob finished piling the last of the pumpkins onto the barrow, they sat on the bench outside the barn and sipped tea made over the open fieldstone fireplace Rob had built nearby. Lil was thinking of past pleasures and sadnesses so she was startled when Rob said to her in his blunt, unprefaced manner, "I'll never leave you, Ma."

4

It was close to Halloween with a frail bloom of Indian summer on the village-to-be when news reached the Alleyfolk that the council-elect had voted, unofficially, three to two in favour of accepting their suit. Nor was their joy dampened by the provisos to the original request: that the lots be resurveyed as far as possible to conform with the accepted geometric principles; that the winding lane in consequence be 'straightened' into two tolerable curves; that the latter be attached to Prince Street at the tracks and adopt *that* nomination for all time to come; and finally, that a settlement stipend of fifty dollars per property, regardless of size or length of tenure, be paid within three years. This would cover back taxes, the cost of the survey and the necessary legal fees and convince the legitimate citizens once and for all that the Alleyfolk intended to be ratepaying members of this community. The celebration, fueled by John the Baptist's new still, went on for days.

Lily took no part in it. She was not ready yet to celebrate. She had more than the necessary fifty dollars, and could raise that much again in three years if need be. In the back of her mind she had thought all along that she would sell Bridie's legacy and with it invest in something of her own choosing. The appropriateness of taking possession of this property seemed foreordained. She owed ten or twelve dollars in back taxes on the old place, which the township, noting the rekindled interest in the land, had decided to press for. But even in the currently depressed market, almost two acres of cultivated land with a barn would sell for forty dollars or more. Bridie's place was now Rob's place. No thought of selling it could enter her mind. It's his, she thought; he's made it his. I'll pay the taxes and sign the deed over to him. What else have I to give my firstborn son? Even so, enough cash remained to buy back her birthright, as she now thought of it. Of course, she would have no reserve money of any kind. Brad needed a new suit; the two she'd bought him last year had shrunk around his sprouting frame. He was going to be tall and slim and handsome.

The warning in the principal's letter and the burden of her own responsibility weighted heavily upon her. More immediately, she was worried about Brad's increasing truancy, and though his grades remained high, he was drifting away from her control and into habits that could be ruinous. She knew she must let him board in Sarnia under the supervision of a respectable family whose influence, though not her own, would be essential to his progress. Painful as it might be, she would have to make the move after Christmas. For that, she needed cash, all she could earn slaving six days a week.

When Sophie heard, she was shocked, then enraged, then consoling. She offered to give Lily every dollar she could "squeeze out of Mr. Flintskin, esquire, when he comes home." The only form of assistance she contributed, though, was to tell Lily's story to Hap Withers, Dowling's factory foreman and father of ten. Hap came to Lily's place the next day and made the offer in that quiet, direct way of his that had endeared him to both sides of the village tracks. His own house lay on Prince Street, a hundred feet from the Alley. He proposed to pay her fifty-dollar fee to the council himself, take temporary ownership of the property, and rent it back to her for a dollar a year and taxes.

"I'll have a contract drawn up," he said, "to say that you have a right to buy me out for fifty dollars anytime over the next five years – and of course I won't be able to sell the land. If you don't want or need the place by then, I'll buy your house and give it to one of my sons."

Well, Lily mused, watching Hap whistling down the lane, I've got half a root down, and five years to grow the rest of it. There's lots in this world who've got less than that. By Halloween, Rob had a deed and Lily became a tenant.

29

1

Stoker arrived home unexpectedly at the end of the first week of November. His ship had run aground near Goderich and limped into dry dock there. With only three weeks left in the season, it was possible the crew would not be asked to make another trip. He usually headed north to the Bruce lumber camp on the first of December. So it was three weeks at home – with Sophie. Lily did not go over, but she kept a wary eye on the Potts' place and at night slept lightly, listening for the telltale sounds.

After a snowy Halloween, Indian summer had returned more perfect than ever – a thin, sweet stratosphere distilled of all impurities. Lily and Violet went for long strolls across the river flats and the blanched, silent marshes. They gathered bulrushes and feathered cattails and milkweed pods whose silk parachutes sailed anywhere the wind swivelled them. Coming home from Hazel's late one afternoon, Lily saw Stoker and Sophie with Bricky between them (Wee Sue had gone 'into service' in September), ambling towards the flats at the back of their property with a slow ease that bespoke comfort, familiarity and trust. Against the setting sun they were a single-etched silhouette. Lily hurried on, repressing a pang of envy or regret. She woke with a start at the slap of a screen door the next morning, stumbling to the window in time to see Stoker and Bricky walking northeast towards First bush, their claret hunting caps winking in the early sun.

Later in the morning, after her first wash was complete, she saw Sophie flopped in her rocking chair on the verandah, fanning herself languorously. She had somehow squeezed into her orange print dress, the effort leaving her strapped for breath. She waved at Lily. Lily waved back then rejoined Violet in the steaming laundry room. At dusk, she heard singing and looked out to see Stoker and Bricky cavorting around a huge bonfire onto which they tossed armfuls of stubble, husks and other refuse of the spent harvest. Sophie watched them as the hens eddied about her feet and the sow sighed a few yards away among her sucklings.

The next day Bricky went off with Rob to sleep overnight in "the little barn" and join in a squirrel shoot organized by the McCourt boys. Stoker had given him a new .410 gauge with instructions that he was to use it only under Rob's supervision. To Lily's surprise, Rob walked over to Potts' and spent several hours with Stoker ("shooting the breeze, he's a great guy, Ma, he's got a million stories") before leading Bricky off on his first all-male expedition. Even though Brad was staying over with one of his Sarnia chums and the house was empty, Lily fell into the first deep sleep she'd had in some time.

She was wakened, not ungently, by the twang of a banjo, a quarter-note chord. tart and sensual. Sophie's laughter could be heard in the rich calliope of its range from skirring giggle to braying chortle— rude, skeptical, and embracing. After a long quiet came the crash of flung glass followed by a tittering hysteria rescued at the brink by the banjo's bawdy accompaniment. This lewd invitation reached Lily's ears intact and aflame, until Sophie crushed it with a stuttering guffaw. Words now: Sophie's taunting mockery above the lumbering accusation beneath it. Lily was half-way across her yard and flinging a kimono over her shift when she heard the clatter of struck furniture and Sophie's gloating whoop. Then she heard Stoker grunt and the smack of flesh on flesh. Lily flung open the door and barged straight into the Potts' kitchen.

Two lamps had been smashed and lay smouldering in corners. Only one small oil-flame illumined the faces which froze before Lily's intrusion. Sophie sat on the table where she'd landed after being struck by Stoker, a frying pan distended from her right hand. The left side of her face still bore the livid imprint of his fingers, her eyes braced for the coming shock of pain but still able to bring a glance of dismay to Lily's presence. Stoker had raised his fist again in such a way as to strike a backhand blow on Sophie's other cheek. At the sound of the door opening he stopped it long enough to stare down anyone foolhardy enough to enter this territory. He turned the alcoholic jet of his gaze upon the interloper.

"*Who the fuck are you?*"

Lily edged into the pool of light. "You know who I am, Stoker Potts," she said as if they were at tea together.

"Go home, Lil, go home," Sophie said in a ghastly whisper, and she crumpled to the floor, tipping over the table.

"No good layin' there like a whimperin' pig," Stoker said, turning away from Lily and advancing towards Sophie. "Get your fat ass off the floor an' take your lumps." An egg-size bump wobbled at the base of his skull.

Sophie put up a hand, not to protect herself but to soothe the stinging welts on the left side of her face. She began shuffling backwards like a paraplegic tortoise, whimpering and all the while attempting to find a way to get herself upright. Lily stepped between Stoker and Sophie. She looked into Stoker's eyes, less than a foot away from him.

They were infernos, not merely of the rage and outrage and brute animosity she expected to see but also of self-loathing and frantic, contending appetites. "Get outta my way, you interferin' bitch, or I'll bash your face in, too."

Behind her Sophie was scrabbling to her feet. "Do what he says. It's none of your business."

"Hear the woman, eh? She wants you to butt outta our business." Despite the slurring of his voice, Lily could see that he wasn't stupid drunk, that he probably *never* was, since he appeared to use alcohol as a fiery fuel which he rapidly consumed.

"Get outta here, Lily Marshall," Sophie cried from the narrow hallway behind them, her words sandwiched between choking sobs. "What right've you got pokin' your nose in here?"

Stoker was trying to peer around Lily to see where Sophie was going, but Lily wouldn't release him from her gaze.

"You hear me, Lily? Get the fuck otta here!"

"Don't you try runnin' off, woman!" Stoker shouted, his spittle sizzling on Lily's cheek. But he didn't move an inch. He was trapped between the sideboard and the overturned table, with Lily ahead and a coward's retreat in back of him. His quarry's sobs were fading down the hallway towards safety.

"You gonna move, bitch, or do I beat the shit outta you, then outta her, an' then come back here an' give you somethin' you been needin' for years!"

"Go ahead," Lily said, "beat up a woman half your size an' brag about it all over the Alley."

Stoker went back on his heels.

"You don't think I'd keep my mouth shut like that poor creature back there?" Lily said.

For a second nothing moved, or spoke. Then a door rattled, squeaked open, slammed shut, and a latch dropped into a slot.

"Well, you bitch, she's safe now."

"I ain't leavin' here till you promise not to touch her," Lily said.

Stoker turned upon Lily the full blaze of the bottled fury in his eyes. They burned like bitterroot. They scalded the tears that assaulted them.

"Have a drink with me," Stoker said, tilted forward in the chair with his head in his hands. "Please."

Lily drew up a stool beside him and steadied his grip as he poured out two glasses of whiskey from a jug. Lily sipped at hers while Stoker downed his in two gulps.

"I need to talk."

"People've told me I'm a good listener," Lily said.

Stoker dredged up a smile for her but it did little for his face which, drained of its prevailing animus, was a hollow, devastated mask. The voice he chose came from a person deep inside and hidden, unaided by external expression. Lily stared into the moon shadows around the stove and listened.

"Nobody on this Alley would believe it, but I love that woman. I never meant to hurt her, not once. We been together a long, long time, ever since we was kids ourselves, and I only hit her a few times. I love her; I never, never meant to hurt her." He took Lily's silence as reassurance.

"We got married real young, an' God we was happy. We lived in Sarnia for a long while an' we took some boat trips together an' when Burton an' Marlene was born, I was the happiest soul alive. Sophie was beautiful then. I know you find that hard to believe, but she was, and I worshipped the ground she walked on."

He paused while they both contemplated such an improbability, and Lily poured herself a half a glass of whiskey.

"Everybody on this lane thinks I'm a wife-beatin' bastard, and I guess I am, but they don't know what I been through. It was her idea to move here when I first went stokin' on the boats, an' she promised on her grandmother's grave we'd move into a nice house for the kids' sake just as soon as we got the money. And I made plenty of money, slavin' in the boiler rooms of a dozen stinkin' tubs an' cuttin' timber in the township before we cut all the trees down. But she would spend it, every penny of it. I'd leave her with the money an' by the time I got back she'd squandered it, spoilin' the kids or givin' it away to her poor relations up in Huron an' havin' buggerall to show for it. It drove me *mad*, so I started hidin' some of it an' savin' up to move out of this, this *pig sty!*"

He assumed Lily was assessing the room they were in, its smell of unwashed dishes and vegetable rot. "At first I tried to keep it lookin' respectable, 'cause I could see the older kids was gettin' ashamed of it; I built the verandah an' the back sheds an' shingled the roof an' put a coat of gray paint on the outside. Then she took up midwifin' an' things got worse. She was never home night or day, the house turned into a garbage dump. I was desperate to move so I told her about the money I'd hidden away an' it was then I knew she would never move from this place. She actually *liked* it here. I bought the seven kids we had then some new boots an' clothes and I went off for the winter to the bush up north." He located the whiskey glass and drank. *"I ran away from it all."*

Lily listened for any sound from the back room.

"I know I'm to blame, that's what drives me crazy sometimes. I should've come home an' grabbed her an' carted her off to a nice home in Sarnia an' laid down the law an' took care of my kids. But you don't know how Sophie can be. She'd see me thinkin' that way an' she'd start to sweet-talk me an' get 'round me like she's done since she was sixteen. Even now, as fat an' ugly as she seems to other people, she's got a way with me. Till I get mad."

"Sophie has a way with folks," Lily said.

Stoker finally looked up. He continued to speak calmly but his words were blurred by the aftertaste of rage. "She drove my children away. All but Bricky. She spoiled them an' beat them an' doted on them an' left them to fend for themselves. She was a slob and a heathen. But they loved her, every last one of them, an' yet every time I come home, she's driven another one away."

"An' Marlene?"

Stoker stared at Lily as if realizing for certain what he had assumed all along: she might be made to understand. "Every hypocrite on this lane knows I slapped Marlene an' that she left an' ain't never spoken to either of us since. But none of 'em knows why. Only me. An' Soph." He went on with a menacing, whispered vehemence. "That *hooer* in there did it right in front of her own children! Can you imagine that? Hardly a curtain between her an' Marlene lyin' there in the next room, listenin' to such disgust an' filth." His hands shook on his knees and he started to rock back and forth in the chair.

"Lily, as God is my witness – and I've never stopped believin' since I was a kid – I've never been with another woman since I married Sophie

MacGregor thirty years ago. All those weeks an' months on the boats and in the bush, an' not one woman, though the squaws an' hooers was lyin' all around us – quarter a throw. Not one goddamn time. Then I got to find out from my own daughter that her mother's no better than those pitiful hooers on the streets of Port Arthur. Only worse. An' worse than that, I go an' slap my daughter around – the child I loved the most in the world – 'cause I know she's lyin'. Every time I come home that summer I slap her again, for nothin' at all, 'cause I'm ragin' inside. An' so she leaves, an' then I find out she's been tellin' the truth. That girl ain't spoken to us in ten years. We don't even know where she lives 'cause Burton won't tell." After a while he added, as if it were essential, "We was so happy once, but nothin' turned out the way we planned it."

Lily leaned over and touched the back of Stoker's hand. "Most of the time it don't."

A sharp groan from the other room broke the deep silence that had fallen between them. "I got to go to her," Lily said.

"It's all right."

As she hurried towards Sophie, Lily heard the front door open and then the sound of Stoker's heavy body slumping into the wooden rocker.

•

The left side of Sophie's face was blue and so swollen she couldn't see out of that eye and her speech was slurred. For a while, seated on the edge of Bricky's bed, she pretended not to notice Lily's presence beside her. She let the moonlight bathe her bruised flesh and breathed through a slit in her mouth. She paid for every breath with measured pain then added the sting of words. Against the ear, they were gentle and evocative. Lily was not prepared for what she was about to hear from the woman she felt she knew so well.

"When I was Sophie MacGregor, I was the cat's meow an' gloried in it. We lived in a brick house in Goderich overlookin' the river. My Dad was a lowland Scot who dabbled in land an' was sometimes rich an' sometimes broke. He had a laugh that would crack granite. Mother was half Irish an' half Chippewa, though she did everythin' possible to hide that honour. I spent every summer on the Kettle Point Reserve with my Grandma, a daughter of Chief Wawanosh, soakin' up the wild ways my mother hoped a lot of schoolin' would soon cure. Funny though, I liked school. I read every book in the common school an' every tome in my dad's library. So when I was twelve, it was decided I ought to be shipped off to a proper school where there'd be enough books an' smart teachers to keep me from gettin' too uppity. My dad's maiden sister, Aunt Harriet, lived in London, so that's where I landed, on Princess Street a few blocks from a private grammar an' continuation school for would-be ladies.

"Soon I became their star pupil, every teacher's pet, and I played it to the hilt. When I complained of being lonely, my mother sent me a new dress or money to have one made. I still managed to get a couple more wild summers in before Grandma died, but by then I'd decided to like both city life and education. I sailed into my third year with straight A's an' dotin' teachers an' jealous schoolmates. My head was bulgin' with math an' literature, but so were certain curious parts of my body. I was sixteen but whenever I started to take public notice of my best parts, I got frowns an' horrified stares from my elders. So I plunged into my studies. I had it in mind to sit the normal-school exams an' become a teacher. I fancied a country school of my own where I'd be a queen bee and empress an' lady saint all rolled into one.

"In March of 1847, when I was just a year from graduatin' an' was headin' for another semester of honours, I met Morton Potts. He'd come up from Windsor to cut timber for the proposed railroad; I'd seen the wagons one mornin' pickin' up the men at the end of Princess Street. Mort was boardin' with a great aunt a few blocks away. He spotted me right off. On wet days when their work was cancelled, he'd follow me home from school, and I pretended I was too good to pay any attention to the likes of him. Aunt Harriet saw him talkin' to me at the corner an' threatened him with the constable. He laughed in her face, and I loved him from that second onwards."

Lily wanted to say something, touch some part of her friend's sorrow, but she dare not.

"Oh, he was a handsome, clever, devil-take-the-hindmost man. When he kissed me behind the bushes or against a snowbank, the promises I made to my Aunt turned to water. He loved every part of me, it seemed, and especially those parts I was so shy about an' so curious to know the meaning of. He made me laugh an' he made me talk a blue streak an' he made me feel good all over. I felt like Lochinvar's bride. Of course, I didn't know as much about love an' life as I thought I did, so when Mort cooked up a scheme to get us alone for a whole weekend, I said yes right off. I told my Aunt I was goin' home for a few days to visit a sick friend, and I *did* plan to do that but not for the five days I told Aunt Harriet about.

"When the stagecoach reached Lucan, I got off an' practically fell into Mort's arms. He put me in a cutter an' we whisked off into the nearby woods to a cabin that belonged to a chum of his. We stayed there two whole days before I got back on the stage for Goderich. It snowed all the time and Mort kept a glorious blaze goin' in the stone fireplace and it was warm as toast. Which was a good thing because we didn't spend much time in our clothes. I can close my eyes this very minute an' see an' hear an' feel every speck of them days. It's as if it was snowin' outside right now, and I was as round an' innocent an' clear-skinned as I was at sixteen, when my lover's eyes popped like mulberries every time I let his hand find a new surprise. We loved an' talked an' made eternal promises an' loved some more. We gloried in our bodies an' we cared for nothin' that didn't agree with the feelings we could only make when we were together. We pledged our faith."

Lily wanted to tell Sophie something of her own, but again, held back. After this, she knew, there would be lots time.

"Of course, my mother and Aunt soon compared recipes an' found us out. My God, what a row there was! I was locked up an' chaperoned an' tuttutted over day an' night. If I hadn't been the star pupil I'd've been thrown outta school as 'damaged goods' sure to corrupt on touch. For a while I may have believed, that they were right – that I was seduced an' drugged an' led astray by an accomplice of the archfiend himself. But not for long."

Lily heard the wince of a chuckle and stinted breathing.

"Stoker never gave up for a minute. He knew what kinda passion he'd stirred up in that snowy cabin. They'd got a judge's warrant to keep him away from me. They'd have charged him with rape if they thought they could've survived the scandal. We managed to meet within a few weeks when I ran off from an Arbour Day outing, an' we made wild love in the clover that was scarcely green enough to smudge our bare bottoms. Stoker was big enough an' strong enough to beat the world off if he had to. I was hooked – on sex and all the wonderful sideways feelings it sent bubblin' through me. Lily, I loved that thing between his legs so much and I wanted it so bad, I'd have kissed a parson's arse for it. I would."

Lily felt the jiggling of Sophie's mirth up through her tears, the hurting purge of her unique laughter.

"I gave it all up – my books, my family, the life I dreamt ahead of myself. I cut them off like a turnip top and I never looked back. So that oughta tell you why I'm the way I am."

2

By the time Lily dragged herself out of bed and back into the laundry shed, Violet was starting the second round of washing. The first was flapping in the last breeze of Indian summer. Lily had slept well once she had reached her bed shortly before dawn. Though she was still groggy and somewhat enervated by the trauma of the night, she found it easy to smile for the faithful Violet and pick up the rhythms of the workday with fresh buoyancy. By noon, she was humming and tattling away to Violet about the crazy time Maman LaRouche set about baking a gingerbread man for her and little Guy, convincing them she had put one of the Millar boys inside the dough for being *un bébé fou*. Guy had started crying and Maman laughed and cuddled him, soothing him with *Ah, Ti-Guy, mon pauvre bébé* then accidentally saying *mon bébé fou*, which sent him into hysterics. He let Lil eat the entire cookie with Billie Millar baked alive inside. They laughed about this through their brief lunch at the outdoor table.

They were stopped by a loud, clear voice that could only have been Stoker Potts'. "Don't you ever throw Marlene up to me again, you hear!"

Nothing audible had preceded it and nothing followed, though the women sat deathly still for a long minute. Lily got up and peered around the corner of the house. She could detect no sound or movement over there. After a bit, Stoker waltzed out of the woodshed, a bundle of trash under his arm and, whistling a sea-shanty of sorts, headed for the refuse fire out by the flats.

Lily and Violet worked extra hard that afternoon to take advantage of the good drying weather. Lily was pegging the last of the sheets from The Queen's onto the line when she heard the thud of running footsteps. A heavy body crashed through the dead stalk and wizened burdock leaves. She whirled in time to meet Stoker Potts as he plunged into the yard. He appeared dishevelled, his face smeared with soot as if he had just crawled out of his engine-room, his look deranged and feral. But the voice was a little boy's – pleading and frightened beyond guilt or reason.

"I didn't mean to, Lily, I didn't mean to, oh Christ in Heaven I didn't mean to, it was an accident!" He spoke in a singsong cadence wholly out of tune with his flailing arms that begged someone, *anyone,* to come and help.

"Where is she?"

"Hurry, please."

"Where is she?"

"Out back, oh Christ, we gotta hurry."

"What've you done?"

"Nothin', she just fell, I didn't mean for anythin' to happen," he babbled after Lily as she raced across the lane towards the river flats.

He screamed wildly up and down the Alley till his legs gave out and he sank to his knees, choking on his own sobs. *"I love her!"* he shouted at Violet as she ran past him. *"I love her!"*

"Get back, Vi!" Lily yelled as she neared the trash fire and spotted something grotesque twisting in the dead grass. "Go get a doctor, *anybody!"* But Vi stood frozen in her own fear a few feet away.

Sophie's huge body lay in the weeds, which still smouldered from the impact of her blazing flesh. Charred swatches of orange cloth had welded to the jellied muscle of her back and buttocks. Lily could see where the pink skin had shrivelled, then puffed, then dissolved, leaving the raw red flesh to thicken in the air. The body seemed shake from within as if the bones had just felt the shock. Lily heard what sounded like a prolonged sigh on a single note, as if that one sound would have to make do in expressing grief or rage or goodbye. She shuddered at its intensity, this pelvic hiss that might in other circumstances have been taken for a woman's cry of elucidation at the apex of love. With a gasp of greasy smoke and a stench of singed flesh, the body rolled partway over and slid bonelessly into the cradle of the grass. Lily looked for one horrified second at the dead face. Stoker's bruises were still visible on the skin of both cheeks now swollen into two ghastly sacs about to burst. Between them the mouth was rigidly ajar, lips stretched back over the lunging teeth, the tongue bloated and immobile. The last grimace of lockjaw—the death grin she had seen so often on the faces of muskrat or beaver caught alive in one of Papa's traps. Sophie's eyes, buried in the flesh that had never been able to contain them, said nothing, not even for Lily.

30

1

It was the largest funeral the village had ever seen. Not that it was meant to be, for none of the local ministers would consent to give Sophie Potts, infidel and blasphemer, a Christian burial in the non-denominational cemetery. Most gentlemen of public esteem (and ambition) announced their support for the clergy's stand. Still, the son of the Methodist minister who had baptized Sophie and ferried her through Sabbath School in Goderich, agreed to come down and hold a service in the Potts' home and to superintend the interment. Good weather prevailed, and luckily so, for the several hundred mourners who drifted in one by one from the township, hamlets, backwaters and (thinly disguised) from the respectable avenues of the village, were pleased to stand in the sunshine and hear the sacred homilies tolled for one amongst them so rudely taken away. Reeve-elect Dowling was there and even walked behind the horse-drawn hearse all the way to the gravesite where the closed coffin was lowered with earnest gentility into the wide earth. It was noted that there was a large number of women in attendance. Notice was also taken of the native people, who, although not appearing at the service, did show up at the cemetery where they stood quietly among the fallen leaves, and watched.

As Lily was led away between Hazel and Winnie, she looked back long enough to see the Chippewa men, gray-haired and austere, slip out of the shadows and across the grass to form a ring about the grave. She was sure their lips were moving, as in song.

•

All the Potts' children were present except for Fred, whose whereabouts were unknown, and Marlene. What rearrangement of loyalties and patterns of retribution were to take place among them over the coming months Lily knew little about and could not bring herself to care. At the inquest a few weeks later, Sophie's death was ruled accidental. Stoker was the only witness called since he was the only one who had seen the unfortunate fall. If I *had* been called, Lily said to herself, what difference would it have made if I'd told what I thought I knew? Stoker went off to the bush as usual, but did not return in the spring.

Back at Hazel's the evening after the funeral, the Alleyfolk decided to hold a proper wake. Baptiste Cartier brought in a supply of newly-minted hooch, Stewie and John carted up a batch of Sophie's own homemade beer, and Angus Shawyer was kept sober long enough to play his fiddle. They might as well have hauled in a dirge drum and pounded it sepulchrally, for no one danced. No one sang for fear they would weep. The mourners collected in clusters about the haunted rooms where Sophie had presided so often and whispered into the gathering gloom stories that had once evoked irrepressible laughter.

"God damn it to hell," Hazel blurted to staunch her pain. "What a shame, what a rotten shame. All her life she lives on this Alley, she slaps half the kids in this town on the bottom before they're a second old, she works an' slaves to make a home for her family, an' just a month before that home is about to become her own for keeps, she up an' dies. Not only that but she's the one with the gumption an' the brains to give us all a chance at owning what's ours. Now where's the justice in all that, I wanna know?"

"The Lord moves in mysterious ways," offered Stumpy.

"Fuck the Lord!" Hazel snapped.

Hazel's lament set off a wave of grumbling and apostasy and boozy self-pity.

"A year from now an' she'll be a nobody, forgot like all of us are the second we're outta mind," said Winnie. She snuffled and made a fuss over the silent, tearless Violet.

"Damn shame."

"But true."

"It don't have to be."

The parlour went quiet, as if the corpse had slipped in and just been noticed. Lily Marshall had spoken, and the mourners were not listening so much as watching.

"I said it don't have to be true about Sophie. There's one way to make sure the town remembers an' to make sure nobody on this Alley ever forgets what she done for us."

"What're you talking about, Lily?" Stumpy asked.

"You all know the council is gonna change the name of Prince Street to Prince Edward Boulevard in January when we get to be a village. Then they're gonna hook it up with the Alley. I say we oughta suggest to the Reeve that the whole street be called Potts' Lane."

The rightness of the suggestion struck home. Murmurs of assent rose from all quarters, and one or two defiantly whispered a call to arms.

"You think the Reeve'll go for this?" Stumpy said. "After the pressure we used on him to get the land title? I'm afraid we've used up all our tokens."

"We oughta try," Lily said. "We're only askin' for what's fair."

•

Stumpy was appointed sole legate for the task of broaching the question to the Reeve-elect. He returned to inform a grim afternoon session of the rump parliament that their request had not merely been denied but ridiculed. Dowling's words, as reported, were: "What in the name of Satan makes you think this town would name its most sacred street after a whoring, whiskey-peddling tub of blubber?" Or metaphors to that effect.

Honeyman offered to stuff the Reeve-elect down a suitable sinkhole and Spartacus brandished a set of pliers capable of transforming him into a capon. When such displays of resolution and solidarity ended, Lily asked if she might speak. Violet came and stood beside her and squeezed her arm.

"We'll get him to change his mind," Lily said, and no one doubted her word. They waited for her proposal.

"Once the Reeve's made up his mind, he'll get the council to do what he wants. Now, I want Shadrack to write down the main points of a story I know an' then Stumpy'll go to the Reeve an' tell it to him. When he hears it, he'll change his mind."

•

Hazel and Stumpy had urged Lily to do the talking when they went to Dowling's house, but she refused. "I can't talk fancy," she said, and held her ground. The notes outlining the story were tucked into Stumpy's coat pocket. The story was one that Tom had told to Lily during the first winter of their marriage as the hearth fire blazed and her lover did all things possible to make her laugh and see the world through his eyes. Like all Tom's anecdotes, she recalled this one word for word. The northeast wind blew a dusty snow in their faces as they trooped up Victoria Street that Tuesday morning. Stumpy led with his sailor's amble, followed by Hazel in her best hat, Maggie Shawyer, Honeyman Belcher and Lily. Dowling must have spied them before his maid did because he was on his verandah just as they wheeled through the gap in the hedge, a white silk scarf tossed about his exposed throat.

"I've heard the last petition from you gang of rascals that I intend to hear," he shouted against the wind. "Take your causes henceforth to the council and its official meetings. Be off before I call a constable!"

This latter remark was flung into the ear of Honeyman Belcher as his two-hundred-pound bulk brushed Dowling aside and barged through the front door. The others followed, and by the time they had removed their galoshes and coats in the vestibule, the shivering Reeve had decided to join them.

"Five minutes," he snapped with his back to them, warming his hands by the fire and absorbing most of its welcome. "Then it's the constable."

"This won't take five minutes," Stumpy said. "We come to ask you to change your mind about namin' Potts' Lane."

"Don't call it that!" he roared. "It'll never have a name like that as long as I'm reeve of this town. You're wasting your breath. Go home to your seedy little hovels. At least you *own* them, thanks to me."

Stumpy didn't reply. He pulled two sheets of paper out of his pocket, and when Dowling's curiosity was piqued, he said, "I brought along a story to help you change your mind."

A flicker of fear or animal wariness passed across Dowling's face but was erased by a belligerent ruffling of feathers. "What in hell are you talking about?"

His hands shaking, Stumpy started to recite the story as best he could from memory and blurred notes. Nineteen years ago this month, the Great Western Railway held a gala ball in the London armouries. The well-known and beautiful wife of the railroad's vice-president was seen to dance more than once with a handsome, young, dark-haired gentleman, also an officer of that company. The lady returned to the watch of her husband as the dancing ended. Several hours later, she was observed, poorly disguised in a coachman's cape, entering a nearby hotel and slipping up to the second floor and into a gentleman's room without a knock. At six in the morning, she was spotted by a drayman skipping down the alley behind the hotel.

From the first mention of the month and year, Dowling dropped his bully's stance and started to listen. By the time Stumpy had finished, Dowling's face was an impassive mask, closed to all secrets. He looked past Stumpy and speared each of the others with a questing glance, but found nothing he needed to know. He recognized several of the faces but could attach no certain name to them, make no connection between the narrative and this crew of outcasts.

"A droll story, I'm sure," he said at last. "And a nasty one as well. Good enough to smear the reputations of a dozen honest men."

Stumpy's jaw dropped, and he heard the sag of confidence behind him. He wanted desperately to turn to Lily. He was both shocked and relieved to hear Hazel's voice, clear and cold.

"London House, October 31, 1859, room 218, the lady's name reminds one of a flower, her husband was . . . "

Dowling stared incredulously at Hazel when he cut her off. "That's enough."

"What you did back then ain't none of our concern," Hazel said, "and won't ever be anybody else's. We only come to ask you for what we think's fair."

The Reeve-elect smiled at her as if she were Dame Justice herself and he a lifelong servant of the helpless blind. "Just so," he said.

•

On January 1, 1879, Point Edward was incorporated as a village, and without fanfare or the world's notice quietly gave birth to itself.

2

The first act of the inaugurated village council was to pass a resolution declaring the third Saturday of that month "Point Edward Day", a motion that was declared unanimous (until the principal form of celebration turned out to be a dance, at which juncture there was a Methodist retraction). The second motion, as Lily had predicted, was passed with much grumbling dissent but no audible *nays*. The extended street facing the river along its whole meandering length was officially denominated "Potts' Lane." Even the Prince might have approved, Lily thought.

The dance was held in the newly constructed Oddfellows' Hall, an imperial edifice of brick and mortar and mitred glass. It stood at the edge of the sprawling marsh below and beyond, as solid and respectable as a redoubt or a medieval keep. Inside, though, it had been transformed into a miniature, temporary Camelot. Against the starred January dark that stiffened the myriad mercurial panes, crystal light splashed from chandeliers or blazed defiance from ceremonial rushes clamped to the north wall. That afternoon a soft snow had fallen, and then the skies had been brushed clear of configuring cloud by some moon-impelled wind just in time for evening's ascension. Anyone gazing down from that perspective would have seen a village unmarked by tread or traffic of any kind, as if its streets and alleys and byways had been reinvented for the occasion. By seven o'clock, there was not a path or passage of any sort which did not bear the imprint of some one of its citizens. Not one of these pointed anywhere but towards the momentary heart of the village itself, and its communal, celebratory beat.

The band was makeshift: two fiddles, a squeeze-box, a battered army bugle and matching drum, a lone asthmatic harmonica, undermined by assorted, improvised percussives. It was of local genesis and propelled by an imperturbable optimism. Unfettered by sheet-music or conductor's baton, it poured out the latest waltz from old Vienna, the jazziest lancers from the Buckingham Guard, the airiest jig from Londonderry. At first, the Alleyfolk, awed by the garish ostentation of cutaway coat and puffed silk, and ever chary of releasing even the smallest atom of their secret selves to public scrutiny, huddled in clumps under the fiery rushes along the windowless wall. Not one of them, despite the heat and press and sweat, inched towards the crystal bowl beneath the main arch where Reeve Dowling's personal tangerine punch winked and rippled its welcome. Then, without warning, during one of the intermittent reels, the druggist's son crooked an errant arm into the waiting loop of Miss Shawyer's elbow and swept her out of her flock out of the Alley and into the ages-old anonymity of the reel itself. If it was a signal, it worked. If not, it worked anyway. As the fiddles sizzled and sang their ancient solipsisms, one by two and two by three, the choruses in the wings of the great hall emptied into its epicentre of sets and squares.

Enthused by a music bereft of word and sign and the tautology of time, they convened, divorced, colloquied, parted forever, resumed at once, met and kissed goodbye, remembered and forgot their names: Shawyer with Redmond, McCourt with Durham, burgher with rag-picker. Only the character of the sexes remained constant and preserved and happily at odds.

•

Lily stood alone at the open door; behind her, the music and the fragmentary revels. She peered west towards the evening star, just risen; towards the river, iced tight, its winter's-long stream cached and pulsing black fathoms beneath all hearing; towards the ragamuffin boys skating out some ritual game on the frozen pond a few rods below her. She listened to the crisp snub of their blades against any resistance, the boasts and yelps and elbowing affection of their careless buffoonery. She knew that Rob and Brad somehow were among them—Brad, most likely crouched in a moon's halo and watching, weighing, reading the shadows and the shapes under them. Rob would be buffered headfirst into whatever shoulder offered its challenge, and whooping, with the others, the last and the loudest of their boyhood salvoes.

What would become of them, fatherless as they were? And now growing more out of their own stock than out of hers. And out of this place, too. There was something here that could not be got round. And we've made it better, Sophie, she whispered into the pure dark ahead of her. We made it more real, anyways. *You* did. But how can we believe in it now that you've left us? It seems like just as soon as I get to know something, it goes and dies on me.

Strange, but just before she had decided, for Sophie's sake, that she ought to come here, Lily had surprised herself by digging out Sounder's pouch where it had lain, dust-covered, for the longest time. Had she given up on the aboriginal promise of magic in this world? Trembling, she'd drawn open the leather sachet and one by one fingered the contents: Mama's crucifix with its forlorn sheen under the muted winter-light; Papa's Testament still unread and the Lady Fairchild of its inscription having long ago relinquished her titles; the cameo pendant with the ivory profile someone once said might have been a grandmother undiminished by seas or eons. For a second she had wanted to weep, not at her irreconcilable loss but at the absence of feeling itself. Just then Rob had called from the lane, "C'mon Ma, everybody's leavin'!" She put the pouch aside, and flung her scarf resolutely about her throat. The Alleyfolk cheered as the night chill struck the warmth of her greeting.

Lily laughed then glanced around to make sure none of the buskers had seen her smiling through the tears congealed on her cheeks. She remembered something Sophie had said only a few months ago. Hazel had asked her if she was interested in having her picture taken by one of those daguerreotype men who came around to the Heaven every once in a while.

"Christ, no," Sophie snapped. "I don't need no picture of myself to be remembered by. Who'd ever forget *this* shape once they laid their unsuspectin' eyeballs on it? Stoke calls me the pink poppy with the purple dropsy, an' he ain't far afield on that one!"

The skaters had started a bonfire near the rink. Its avid orange flame tongued the black penumbras above it. It twisted and grew fabulous as she watched, unleafing its fragile intensities in scrolls ever widening, brightening, taunting the very edges of expiry. Lily shuddered, blood-deep in her being. I am still here, she thought. I don't know why and I never have. I am carried along by urges I can feel but not describe, not even to myself. Perhaps they were the same urgencies sweeping these dancers into the music and the moment. Perhaps not. Hers might be her own, after all.

Yet how indifferent the world's imperatives must be to have passed so many with barely a sideways glance, their primal promptings devoid of pity or humanity or even acknowledgement. How little comfort they had been to Solomon in his sea-coffin, to Maman and Mama in their frozen loneliness, to Aunt Bridie or Uncle Chester or Papa in their grave grounds as alien as the moonscape above her now. How much time had she herself been given to mourn her lover, wild and brave and cold as the snows that held his faithfulness forever from the true earth? Who had decided then that she should go on? And how often had she yearned to hear the voices of the gods – the ones Old Samuels had promised her if she could only find the shaman's ground they worshipped from in the midst of their fear and helplessness. They would have something to say to her, here, now, not an arrow's toss from the hallowed mounds where he and Southener lay in perpetual something-or-other.

I am here. And Sophie is already become another of those I can weep for only because they are absent. Not so. Not true. The dead drive us forward, onward, headlong towards the dark heart of what haunts them. They ache in their knowing.

Without realizing it, Lily had drifted back into the quick heat of the ballroom. She felt the blush of it across the nape of her neck, and instinctively removed her coat. Something whisked it away to her right. Her scarf unwound itself and slithered off. She registered only mild puzzlement. The music rose up to meet her sudden attention. It filled her ears like harp's wind through a seashell, its echoes infinitesimal.

"It's a waltz. Would you like to dance?"

"Yes. I think so."

A muscled hand, her own gently crushed within it.

"A tad off-key, but our own, eh?"

Eager, masculine voice. Accustomed to command?

She must have told him her name, for it graced his lips as often as he dare allow between the suave stint-and-glide of the waltz they were now so engaged in. Then she did hear her own voice, witty and demure. The music took them both into the sweet morphia of its all encompassment, and she felt her body detach itself from something ugly and abiding, and swing free, at last, of its own longing.

Who cared that such music was a prisoning bliss? And not once did she deign to glance down at her partner to confirm what she already knew: that it was Tom on that miraculous night of the Great Western?/ arms like oars under the pavilion's perfect light. She was, after all, here. She was alive. She was Lily. She was dancing.

BOOK TWO

Shaman's Ground

PART ONE

Granny

31

1

Granny Coote was dreaming she was awake again – but she wouldn't be fooled this time. No fool like an old one, she thought, especially one who has learned so little for the effort spent. She was having more trouble keeping her dreams and her reveries apart. Yesterday afternoon, she had sat down at the kitchen table with the fresh tomatoes left by the well-meaning Mrs. Buchan, and was about to slice the ripest one with a shaky right hand, when the room went dark. She was positive she had not closed her eyes nor fallen asleep. But the sun had gone down without notice and the tomato lay carved on the breadboard in those little wedges she had been fashioning for more than seventy years. The knife still lay in her hand.

Arthur and Eddie had been visiting again: Arthur at the piano, Eddie tapping his toes and letting the juice from the tomatoes squirt down his chin. His blue eyes – replica of his father's – never left his Granny—teasing, tempting, full of the wondering beneficence of the happy child.

"Eat your supper, then sing," she had told him.

"He's singing for his supper!" Arthur called from his dais, and broke into a verse from 'A Wandering Minstrel' just to annoy her.

"Let the boy finish his supper, you old coot!" Both the boy and the baritone broke into unchastened laughter.

"He's just teasing, Granny," Eddie said. And she wanted to reach across the table and hug him with her bony arms. Arthur wailed out his parody of Katashaw's song, his grin as sunlit as the meadows of Titi-pu.

But there was no music here. There had been none since Eddie went away so many years ago. And Arthur, bless him, slept near his wife in the village cemetery beyond First Bush. She had continued her meal as if she had not lost three hours somewhere, glad to sit in the dark where it didn't matter if she were asleep or not. Still, it worried her, this lapsing, this forgetting in the middle of an action – cutting flowers, mending the old chesterfield

Arthur loved so much, where they had made their last, startling love. Arthur had closed his eyes so she wouldn't see his treachery as his hand stiffened forever in hers. She would wake to find herself away off in the sunflowers or squatting beside the hedge that kept the street at bay. So this is what it is to be senile, she thought. I already know what it is to be old; I've had lots of practice chewing on my gums and getting out of bed piecemeal with every joint cracking like a rusted block and tackle. But this is trouble. They'll finally have an excuse to put me out of this place, and lord knows they've been looking for one ever since Arthur died and that thing happened with Eddie. The Ladies Auxiliary suggested a 'good home' in the city where she had spent her life fighting. But then the tragedy of 'eighteen had struck like the foul afterbreath of the Great War itself, and she had given them something else to think about.

I'm not senile, she thought, refusing to open her eyes to acknowledge the supremacy of the dream and the incursions of the night world. I may be a bit 'barmy' as the Alleyfolk used to say, but then I have cause. When that thing happened to her throat after the news came, she had been unable to tell them it was all right, that she understood exactly why and how it had happened. She saw her neighbours turn away, their fright a reflection of her own. It was the same stunned stare she had seen in the eyes of the bereft: widows, mothers, betrothed, most of whom had lost a loved one and a god also. They, too, were speechless in their dumbfounding.

The rattle of pebbles across the glass of the front window confirmed it: she was asleep and about to awake. Her eyes opened to the richness of mid-morning August, 1921. She was fully clothed; her flower-print housedress was soaked with sweat and wrinkled beyond redemption. They'd love to come in and catch me like this, she thought, easing her brittle body off the cot – still slim but no longer muscled, her breasts about as lively as a couple of fallen cupcakes ("The trouble with old age," Sophie used to say, "is your arse gets too tight an' your cunny too loose"). She got seated upright, steadied herself on the edge of the cot for a moment, then let the sun pour across her bare feet from the vivifying east. As the circulation pushed fretfully through her warming bones, she felt the rheumatic ache subside to its daytime level. She flexed her legs and stood up. The blood rushed back to her head and she grabbed the dressing table just in time.

Stupid old woman, she muttered to herself. Mrs. Buchan'd love to come in here this aft and find me sprawled on the rug with a broken hip and lolling like a mute. It would be Sunset Glades for sure. The village'd be rid of the last of its eyesores, and the council would get its house back and the urchins'd have to go all the way to Potts' Lane for their amusement.

She felt just a touch woozy, most likely because she had fantasized having supper as the wincing of her stomach reminded her. She glanced about the single room. It had been her home for five years, ever since she had shut the last of the two little bedrooms Arthur had added to the far side of the place. Coote's shack, as it was known in the village. It was a large room, with the kitchen area facing the south sun and the parlour with its spacious east window and two 'port-holes' in the north wall over Arthur's piano. The rug was bleached erratically by the sun and stained where the roof had leaked before the Reeve had come over to fix it for her.

Yes, her supper – vegetables from her garden (and Mrs. Buchan's) and some lumpish bread she'd made one cool morning in the stove she'd picked up from the Lane. Eddie had squealed with delight when old Badger Coombs had let him take the reins for a while and pouted all afternoon till she baked him his red-currant tarts. Her blood flowed again, her muscles loosened in the warmth of the room, the rheumatism in temporary retreat. Granny felt strong enough to face the day – whichever one it was – as surprised as ever at the resilience of her body's flesh and nerve. Uwilled potency gathered its wits each night and surged forth to greet each anonymous morning. In spring, summer and fall, there was the garden to occupy her body's self-renewing restlessness, the passage of people before her parlour window. She could hear the cries of children from the fields and swamps below her yard, the bleat and harrumphing of lake steamers half a mile away on the St. Clair, the clatter of the city-line streetcar on Michigan Ave., and the periodic fart of Gassy Peter's flivver jostling with the gravelled lanes of the village. She needed them all. She had not left her property – except for the epidemic – since that black day in September.

It was the winter that frightened her most: the stark stretches of space between house and trees, the icy desert of ragged swamp all the way down to the St. Clair and the distant snow-shrouded freight sheds. Birds fled or vowed silence. The children emerged to test the air or the ice. On Sunday afternoons, their cheers and angel gliding over the improvised rinks of the marsh saved her from whatever darkness threatened the domestic and habitable variety she had known for over eighty years. Though her ancient bones invariably found some fresh and independent source for hope, she was not sure she could survive another winter. Why don't you just pack it in, she often said to her complaining flesh. After all, I've given you a good run. There's nothing you haven't tried or survived; no muscle, no gland has gone unflexed or untitillated; no appetite untempted or unappeased. I'm as sick and tired of your whining as you are of mine. I've been ready for a long time. What sort of bribe will you consider? Think about it, because I'm about to embarrass us both.

•

She remembered the clatter of stones that had roused her. She went to the only door, on the south side near the sink, and pushed on the sagging screen. On the plank stoop sat a glass bowl covered by a dishcloth. She reached down and lifted it up. Inside the kitchen again, she removed the cover and saw half a dozen sweetcakes and a small loaf of raisin bread, signature of the handiwork of Leila Savage across the street. She went to the front window and peered about for any sign of the Savage twins or the McCourt bullies who often led them by the nose. The roadway was deserted; the men all off to work in the city, their wives toiling in the back kitchens or leftover victory gardens. Liberated children played at the beach or roamed the dunes and bushland with the eyes of aborigines. Over on the main street, she knew, the post office and market provided a hub of activity for the women to shop, gossip and exchange complaints – at least for those who could still talk.

There you go again, old woman, she thought, feeling sorry for yourself. It does you no good and you know it. Believe me, nobody's listening.

The McCourt cousins – five of them from three strands of the same freckled stock – spent much of their time mimicking their elders by plotting ambushes against the offspring of the village's half-dozen Catholic families. They picked fights at random or on principle to keep their prejudices tuned and generally misled the susceptible youth of the Point. When things were particularly quiet or unpromising on a summer's night, they would skulk into Granny's garden from the marsh and, under cover of the shrubs and a beclouded moon, begin their repeated, increasingly cantatory verses:

Granny Coote is a witch
Granny Coote is a bitch
Granny Coote hitched a
Ride on a broomstick…

and the broom bit back!

This latter retort was unfailingly followed by disintegrating laughter before the charm was again wound up in the moon-filtered dark. What they were hoping for, naturally, was that the witch herself should materialize, shaking with righteous anger to the point where she would start to rail at them and they would hear – as they had only once before – the unalloyed, chilling, magic-babble of wizardry itself. Then could they scatter in gleeful terror to the four winds. Once last summer, from her gladioli beds in the front yard, she had heard two little girls a block away skipping rope and chanting as if the words had no meaning beyond their dance of innocence:

Granny Coote has no teeth
Granny Coote eats roast beef
with her
gum gums!
Granny Coote has no toes
Granny Coote counts by twos
on her
bum bum!

She heard the rope accelerate at the end, and pictured the wild fandango of the elfin feet. She too had danced to that irreverent beat, once, when the lily of her name had hung like a bell in her child's heart.

•

Lately, the McCourts and occasional camp followers like the Savage twins had become bolder. They would appear behind the house at dusk – taunting, daring the village with the sounds of their illicit bravery. Still, the victim did not appear. But one evening last week after a particularly callous variation of their rhyme, the side door swung open and into the twilight floated a caped figure. Its legless silhouette appeared welded to a large whisker broom, its arms extended more like wings set to try the wind over the hushed garden. The shadows seemed to hide all trace of human visage except for the yellow pricks of eyes and the toothless hollow of a mouth – beef-blooded in hue and emitting a shrill thread of sound like a scream being squeezed to death. The Savage twins were trampled by the precipitate retreat of the Ulster vigilantes.

Back inside the house, Granny Coote shook with laughter and aftershock, amazed that she had once again taken up the cudgel. She had hauled the cape, mask and whistle out of Arthur's ancient theatrical trunk in order and lay in wait for the pranksters as she had so many times. In her eighty-odd years, she was often on the wrong side of respectability and had suffered, or abetted, the consequences.

"You chose to be an outsider," Cap had told her.

"None of us chooses anything except the form of our reprisals," she had shot back. How she could talk then?

As the thumping of the routed platoon through the bushes reached her ears, she removed the mask and smiled to herself. This one is for you, Arthur, who showed me the gentle half of men's dominion and gave me a name and a house to carry me through these final years more to be endured than understood. But then, when had she understood anything even in the midst of love, of commitment to those whose youth or vulnerability bound her to a future she never believed in? Anyway, sweet Arthur, I shall wear your name, surrogate though it may be, till they chisel it on the granite beside yours.

2

After nibbling at one of Leila Savage's cakes – a touch too much vanilla in the overbeaten batter – Granny Coote went into her garden as she had done for seventy-odd summers without fail. It was, as she herself termed it, a little old lady's vanity patch. Showy English-style perennials on the perimeter, a neat elevated vegetable section in the middle divided off by Grand Trunk ties Arthur had brought here when the railway left and the town went bust. Arthur's wife's hands had been bred to coddle a bassoon, not a hoe handle, so it was with relish that Granny had undertaken the familiar task of resurrecting a moribund garden. Arthur had been pleased, amazed even, as city folk often are at the vigour and dexterity of country labours. It was vanity now, pure and simple. She could not eat a quarter of what bulged and fletched here in the summer heat, nor could she give much away to the thrifty, war-wary householders with well-stocked victory gardens of their own.

Once a week, young Wilf Underhill would stop by to collect several packets of peppers or carrots to take to the destitute beyond Potts' Lane. He had not forgotten her 'service' during the terrible fall of 'eighteen. Shy though he was, he often sat and had a cup of tea with her, content to let the silence ferry its own meaning back and forth between them. He told her a bit about his life in the old country because he could see from the shifting light in her eyes that she enjoyed his company. And now that their baby boy had arrived, there was more joy to share. At times like that she was not unhappy about what had happened to her throat. She would not have to tell him what anguish the world might yet bring to those who dared poach on its prerogatives.

Still, the flowers and shrubs were beautiful; they gave pleasure to the eye and to the village heart shaken by doubt. With every root that delved thumbs down into this patch of ground, and with every corona of colour that took majestic possession of this air, Granny felt she was establishing her right to belong. The council wanted this land back as vacant as the lot they had conceded in their haste to Arthur and his bride. They would not get it. It was never theirs, she thought. It is only mine in trust.

She was hoeing the cauliflower, the instrument perfectly tuned to her intricate gymnastic – learned and repeated and refined and remembered. No thought was required. She could close her eyes after sighting down a row and carry on without missing a plantain or chokeweed. These motions evoked neither pleasure nor pain, satisfaction nor ennui. They were as effortless as breathing, and as necessary.

She stopped to enjoy the shade of the only tree left on her lot by the Grand Trunk choppers seventy years ago. It soared above the marsh below it and the neighbouring houses with their prearranged maples. Don't boast, she whispered to it, you're here because you're lucky, not invincible. She waved to Ethel Carpenter working in her tomatoes. She recalled their former intimacies, shared tragedies and the desperate confusion on that good woman's face when Granny's mouth contorted and the air was chilled by its alien vowel. Now she just waved, exchanging remembrances.

Granny heard the child's step in the hedge before she saw Flora, Ethel's six-year-old, tiptoe into the dazzling light – head tilted to dart away. Elfin, blond, the blue eyes star fed, she edged into the yard then stopped. One eye was on the old woman rigid under the hickory tree, the other on the harlequinade of iceland poppies at her feet.

Granny felt a rush of emotion, a surge of recognition, but she made not the slightest move. Without stepping towards the child, she indicated in pantomime that Flora should go ahead and pick the flowers her fancy had claimed. The meaning was instantly comprehended. The girl's quick fingers one by one gathered in a fragile bouquet. She took one step towards the old woman, hesitated, saw what she hoped for, and came up to her with a sidling skip and shuffle. The shade encompassed them. A breeze tufted the girl's hair, the poppies aflutter. The aged hand swept upward to accept the gift offered.

Bless you, she said with her eyes, and the girl smiled a shy acknowledgement.

"Can I bring you some cheese, Granny? My uncle brung some in from the farm."

Granny Coote felt the words of response shape themselves in her lower throat. The consonants coiled and stretch across the rampant vowels, the inchoate syllables rose towards articulation up the hollow nave to the threshing, trapped tongue gonging in its belfry. The consonants froze in their chambers while the vowels twisted and howled in anguished release. The shock of them against the open air stunned even her ears. She reeled backwards and fell. The child's cry was soundless but complete. Her fleeing form was swallowed by the hedge. In Granny's fist, the poppies shed a garish blood.

•

Bless you, child, she was thinking. Bless you for being. I held you in my arms days after your birth; I held the wasted body of your dying brother in these hands and tried to invent some comfort. These hands that have pulled many a ruby-skinned pollyw1og kicking and squalling into this world. And to what end? In hopes that one or two of my own would live to soften my dying? Well, where are they? Only a neighbour's child to bring me a bouquet of flowers, a nosegay for the old girl – may she soon pop off and leave us in peace.

She opened her eyes. The sun had burned her arm right through its leathery tan. When she rolled sideways to see how far the sun had moved, she was jolted by a pain in her right leg. A scab was already congealing on her elbow. How long have I been here? Panic stabbed at her more sharply than her bruised thigh. She touched the dried tears on her cheek. My lord, have I been bawling and jabbering out here all afternoon? They'll be coming to get me, just like they tried that time with old Malloney. She started to get up but the grass swayed and she hung on, closing her eyes to let her breath catch up with her heart.

•

When she opened them – feeling once again the regular, sturdy beat of her pulse – it was almost dark. She felt cold, but the ache in her leg was gone and she was able to totter to her feet. No broken bones anyway, she thought. You stupid old woman, letting yourself forget that thing in your throat, scaring little Flora half to death then falling down and snivelling your way through the afternoon. Almost broke a hip and an arm in the process. "Get your arse in harness and giddyup!" Sophie always said when things looked bleakest.

Monitoring each step, Granny walked through the hazy twilight towards Arthur's house. At the corner of the front hedge she spotted Flora, her nimbus of golden hair still ablaze in the fading light. A pale face like a moon's satellite peered out of the shadowed honeysuckle. She stopped breathing. The figure was in view now; it was not Flora. The hair was too native, too radiant; the dress simple and unadorned; the posture questioning.

It was *her*. There was no doubt. She had seen the face, the stance, the elemental flame of the hair too many times not to know it. She had dreamt this tableau of Madonna and lost child many times over.

The child's eyes materialized in the otherwise blank face: *save me, save me* they cried for all to hear. Granny heard her own feet hitting the earth, her heart ricocheting in its prison, her breath catch against her gums. She ran towards the figure that had beckoned to her in a dream they had shared for decades. The name of the child fought at the torque of her tongue. She hit the crushed stone with both knees – snapping her body forward onto her splayed palms and silencing for the moment the tremor of her hyena howl. Those who heard it afterwards declared it to be as much the laughter of the mad as the grief of the inconsolable.

•

"It's a miracle there's nothin' broken."

I'm all right, I'm all right: she was trying to make the words with her lips, fighting the treachery of tears and trying to get up.

"Don't worry, Cora," the voice soothed. "It's me, Bob Denfield. I'll take care of you."

Yes, Cora thought, the Reeve is a man of his word. Like Arthur.

But my name is Lily, she remembered thinking – just before the blackness struck again. At least it was, once.

32

1

It was a January without thaws that first month of 1922 in the village between the Lake and the River. The snows were Russian deep. In their Arctic grip, the memories of Ypres, Passchendaele and the Somme were permitted a momentary absence. The streetcar from the city squealed on its icy rails, and the smoke from the war-inspired foundry billowed and froze. Despite the vagaries of season, commerce or *réalpolitik*, the public business of a municipality must proceed.

Council meetings were held twice a month on Thursdays in the small room that housed the library. Below it laid the four jail cells unoccupied till the weekend. Next door sat the newly purchased scarlet fire engine, close to its crew. If ever there should have been a fire on a Thursday evening during a week of any month, the council chamber would have been instantly cleared. When special meetings of wider public interest were held, as they often had been during the Great War and its dreadful aftermath, the tiny library was given over in favour of the more spacious Oddfellows' Hall next to the old Coote shack. In the opinion of Reeve Denfield, looking at the agenda, the time was fast approaching when such a 'town-meeting', as their Yankee neighbours termed it, would have to be called. Tonight, for the time being, the library-cum-jail would suffice.

•

"No one is more sensitive than I," Councillor Stokes was proclaiming from his pulpit, "as a minister of the Church of England and servant among you now for these eighteen years, to the plight of this wretched woman. It would take a heart of stone not to bleed with pity at the thought of her living out her last days in utter squalor and loneliness. Our Lord said 'blessed are the poor in spirit for theirs is the Kingdom of Heaven'. But shall we stand by while Mrs. Coote suffers in her long wait for that Light to shine at last upon her? I appeal to your conscience as Christians." He gestured dramatically to the far pews.

What did he know about her long wait? the Reeve wondered. About the poor in spirit? He, too, wanted her out of sight and out of mind, tucked away in a cubicle in an old people's home, condemned to silence. He fingered the smooth, pink scald that was the left side of his face. Behind him he felt the whisper of snow against the window like the breath of a child.

•

Councillor Garnet Fielding –"Choppy" to his cohorts – was on the counter atttack, barking orders against the odds to his shell-shocked gunnery. "I mean no disrespect to the cloth when I say we've got no right to treat the widows and homeguard who stood by us so well in such a manner. I was born in this village more than forty years ago, and I was raised to respect and revere my elders. This woman who you youngsters call Granny Coote has been a citizen of the Point for most of her life. I recall my parents talking about her heroic actions in the 'seventies, and everyone in this room knows what she did for us during the terrible autumn of 'eighteen." Choppy was surprising everyone, even himself. He was a laconic man despite his high-school education and his sergeant's stripes, clerk's job in the city and the Distinguished Service Medal riveted over his heart. His speech was somewhat impeded by the prosthesis which formed the major part of his jaw. "Took my breath an' half my chin away," he always said when recounting the explosion that had kept him out of action for several months.

"Some citizen!" huffed Councillor Harold Hitchcock –'Half-Hitch' to his wife and other detractors. "Thirty years an Alleywoman before old man Coote went senile an' rescued her." He waved his gloved, wooden hand like a pointer.

"Would you like the floor, Hitch?" the Reeve asked icily.

•

"Everyone in this room's been through the hell of war," Half-Hitch informed the multitude. He brandished a legal-looking document tweezered between his mechanical thumb and forefinger. "Except one," he added. He looked away from young Horrie MacIntosh who somehow – lacking credentials, battle-experience, and years – had got himself elected to council at the age of twenty-four. "We can't be accused of callousness. We've suffered and lost too much," he cried through his oscillating glove. "But the facts're clear; so is our duty. Accordin' to this record in my hand, the village council granted Arthur Coote back in 1888 a lease on the village lot number 82 at one dollar a year for as long as he remain organist of the Methodist Church, and thereafter, if he retire in good standing, unto his death." He had spent hours memorizing the heady lingo of the document and found the words in actual presentation satisfying. "My point here is this: we've let this woman stay illegally on municipal land for ten years. We've shown mercy and pity for the wretched soul. But enough is enough. Her contributions to the community are well known. But everyone here knows what an eyesore that shack's turned into. All of us know the stories of how Granny Coote has scared the Sam Hill out of children an' babies with her crazy babble. An' last fall you all know she was ridin' on a broom in her back yard. How much more can we take?"

"Hitch is right," said Lorne 'Sandy' Redmond, the elderly grocer. "Olive's asked me to remind the council that the City car goes right by that shanty every hour. She says she can't hardly go to a WCTU meetin' down there without some gossip or other comin' up about Granny Coote. How can those of us who're older," and here he fixed the victims of his jab, "forget she was a shanty woman, a crony of bootleggers and scarlet women. An' she was a boozer and a heathen to boot." Murmurs of assent suffused the room.

"I am prepared," said the Reverend Stokes, "to suggest that a public collection be taken up for the perpetual support of this ancient citizen who, though she has fallen on sad times, seems worthy of our forgiveness and charity."

And we could cast a bronze medal for her, the Reeve mused, to hang in her miserable vestibule at Sunset Glades.

More enthusiastic yea-saying followed. Young MacIntosh had not yet spoken. It was three for and one against. Sunny Denfield's views were well known. If Horrie were to follow his own feelings, the best that could be achieved was a tie. Grant Griffiths, the sixth Councillor, was down at the 'hospital' in London being treated for recurring shell shock and wouldn't be back till God knew when. Still, he held back.

"An' what's your opinion, Horrie?" said the Reeve.

•

Reeve Denfield was on his feet. "The legal aspect of the matter's clear," he said quietly. "The lease to Arthur Coote, accordin' to our lawyer in the city, was to last until his death. If his wife was still livin', she was to be allowed to buy the property at market value. When Arthur died, nobody gave a damn about another vacant lot. Nothin' was done. Till now."

He paused and stared out at the falling snow as if counting individual flakes in the general mass curling over the sill. Then he spoke into the shuffle of embarrassment. "So we haven't any case, one way or the other. But I'd like to say to you, my friends and fellow soldiers, that I see a strong link between this discussion and items two an' three on the agenda. The buildin' of the cenotaph is the most important thing we've ever done as a village. In 1914, we had fifteen hundred souls livin' here, just over three hundred families. Two hundred an' fifty boys an' men went off to France in 1915 – almost one per family. A hundred of them were casualties, half of 'em maimed or dead. I've got the two lists here. Most of you could read the names off by heart. We fought for different reasons but all of us were proud to be from the Point. When I came here from the biggest city in 1901, I was eighteen years old. I saw vacant lots where the houses had been pulled up by the roots an' carted off. It was a ghost town. We built it back up board by board. An' the War tried to do us in again, killin' an' maimin' the best of our men. We owe them a monument."

The councillors sat stunned, as shocked as they might have been when the words of a dull sermon suddenly jelled into meaning.

"So what are we doin'? We're sitting around this table jawin' away about our most senior citizen who's fought as hard as any of us to keep the political chisellers and city types out of here. We're thinkin' of pullin' her out of the house she's lived in for twenty years an' dumpin' her in a poorhouse run by the riff-raff of Sarnia. We're behavin' just like the people we've despised an' battled against all our lives. Don't you see the connection?"

If they didn't, none of the municipal legislators was prepared to admit it in this public forum. Young MacIntosh wished he had followed his heart. Occasionally it paid off.

•

The remainder of the meeting progressed smoothly. With luck, the third period of the hockey match would not be out of reach. When the door was opened to let the starch out of the steam heat, the councillors could hear the drum of wood on wood and the choric encouragement of the village crowd.

The members fell over one another suggesting ways in which the unfortunate Mrs. Coote could be aided in her final days. It was agreed unanimously that someone should approach her to explain her legal position and assure her that no precipitate action would be taken. Reeve Denfield volunteered, but the Reverend Stokes pointed out that as a long-time friend and semi-regular visitor to the house, the Reeve might be perceived by the befuddled old soul to be a biased report. What was needed was someone of probity and evident neutrality seen by Mrs. Coote to represent the will of the council and the village. While the Reeve failed to see the logic of this sophistry, he reluctantly agreed. But when the council nominated the good Anglican pastor for the task, he revealed his humility by refusing the proffered honour. In his place, he suggested the Reverend Buchan whose Methodism and common touch were suited to the delicate venture. He himself would speak to that man of God on the morrow. The amended motion was passed.

Sandy Redmond then reported that the finance committee for the cenotaph now had sufficient monies – in pledges and cash – to allow the project to move forward to the next stage. He outlined a series of benefit hockey games, bazaars and government promises which would enable the village to erect a glorious monument. New committees could now be struck to search for a designer builder and a suitable site.

On a wave of optimism and good cheer, they swept out into the snowy night and managed to see the hometown Flyers wallop the hapless Wanderers of Landsend 9-2. The auguries were in place, and they were smiling.

33

1

It had snowed again in the night and in her dream. It must be almost February, Granny thought. She lifted the kettle from the stove and stared across the unblemished tundra as far as the eye could travel to the northwest. She had no calendar except the one over the sink with the bleached buffoon's visage of King George grinning down at his faceless subjects. It had been left unchanged since that terrible September day. But more than eighty years of superintending the passage of the seasons had left her with a clock more subtle than almanacs or Swiss watches. She had heard the shout of school children passing by and knew the Christmas holiday had begun. The church bells rang from the trinity of God's Houses in the village, and so she counted the Sundays as they held fast in spite of sleet, thaw and squall. The silence of Christmas Day was as awe inspiring and as puzzling as it had always been. No one came; the snow lay uncreased over her yard and dormant gardens. Next day, though, Sunny Denfield and his boy, Boots, came around with a dish of turkey and dressing and fruitcake. She nodded her gratitude at the door, and they felt thankful that she didn't motion them inside. Forewarned, Boots tried hard to smile and not stare too long but managed only the latter. The boy had the inerasable kindness of his father's eyes. He will be another one who suffers, she thought, watching them leave their prints in Saturday's drift.

From time to time, parcels of food – clothing even – appeared on her porch, the tiny trails in the snow betraying the identity of the secret heralds. Bless the children, she thought; they're afraid but they don't hate easily. To some of them Granny Coote's a witch from the Lane, but at least they think of me as somebody, a creature with her own peculiar power, magic, and brand of terror. What am I to the others? Something that *was*, and got left over.

The snow was comforting. Without it she knew she wouldn't survive another winter intact. Not die, of course. That was out of the question given this body of sinew, gristle, bones of oak. Once the arthritis unstiffened in the morning, and the blood honeyed the desiccated veins one more time, her body went about its daily exercises and evacuations. Pain she was accustomed to; it was relegated to some lower order of response, and forgotten. You don't die of pain, she thought, or we'd all be soon dead. Nor loneliness.

The snow re-established its beauty like a goose ruffling its plumage. It created spaces between the trees, houses and hedges. Into these blank meadows she poured her thoughts – half-memory and half-feeling. Memories she would never run out of. They returned as whole sequences of events – tragedies, comedies, farce, melodrama – or as a single moment of action. Some remained fresh and uncorrupted, some coloured by intruding events that enriched or mitigated, others redeemed or crushed by the perspective of eighty years of remembering. But I can still think, and I still know a foolish sentiment when I feel one even if the damn tear ducts don't. I remember so I can stay alive, so I can be myself, whoever that is. But then you don't want to stay alive, do you, old woman with the sagging breasts and brindled hair? You close your eyes every night and hope that something will stop the nightmare machine. Yes. But I won't go before my body does. I am not my body, though enough people have thought so over the years.

The winter nights were eternal and terrifying. Dream was not memory, though it brewed its maelstrom from the remnants thereof. Nor was dream prophecy, though its phantasmic imagery sometimes held out the illusion of augury. There had been magic in the world, and she had had those dreams which touch upon its tenderest mystery. No more. In these present nightmares the same tale was told and retold, a masquerade of her life parading as the truth, begging her to accept its mutant reconstruction of reality. In the daylight she could dream or doze or resurrect and defend herself against such depredations. In February, the nights were longest. And if the night dreams began to eclipse those of the day, it would be over. Then I'll be as batty as people think. They'll cart me off to London in a cattle car, and I won't even care. You can't have a nightmare if you're *in one*.

Even if she should ever talk again and people didn't think she was loony, it wouldn't make too much difference. Who would she talk to? There was nobody left from her generation. Old Duckface Malloney's still alive, she recalled, innkeeping at the Sunset Glades.He'd had four strokes, none kind enough to do him in. Half the people she had known left after the tunnel fiasco of 1890; the Boer War got a few more. Several had died from the pressures of the Great War – losing sons and grandsons and staring at the gray months stretching ahead, and just giving up. As she should have.

All the original Alleyfolk older than she were long dead. She had watched them, in sorrow and in envy, enter the earth one by one. The Potts' Lane crew began to move away and drift off – as she had done – because no one arrived to renew their naïve faith in that perverse community. Even the kids found jobs, respectability and excuses not to visit. After the War and the epidemic had wiped out the last of the Laners along with almost everybody else over seventy-five, the European refugees had begun to discover the shacks and improvised abodes. I wish I could go there, she thought. I want to hear their stories. I've heard them since I was six. I would know what comfort, if any, to give them. You don't need a war to make you an outcast, though I've seen four of them if they care to swap miseries.

Not only was there no one left here, few of the second and third generation knew her or anything about her. She had lived in and around this spot for seven decades and she knew every family who'd ever put down roots here. She knew their relatives, connections, feudal histories, pretensions and genial follies. "You've made yourself an outsider," Cap used to say with that arching smirk. "You enjoy watching and judging. You're afraid deep down to take part in the rituals that sustain their daily lives for fear they'll swallow you up. You've judged these values before you've had the courage to try them. I tried them and with a little help from Dame Misfortune gave them up. I may be a bum, but I know who I was, and what I am."

Not true. She found herself arguing with him again – between the hedge and shriven hickory tree. You don't know what I've lived through before I was even an adolescent. You couldn't have survived for one night without a quart of brandy. What is more to the point, you were not a woman. To be woman is to be consumed by ritual. If I forget, my nightmares remind me.

Many of the basic stock of the village – Brightons, Barbers, McCourts, Carpenters, Savages – had been here since the beginning. The children of these pioneers would know her only through the stories told by their churchgoing parents. She had heard them all in their embroidered forms; that was the price – one of many – she had paid for living on the fringe. She had never complained then and wasn't about to start now. Sophie's yarns and epic jokes about the citizens in good standing gave back more than they'd received. "That old mister Redmond, if you stuck a turnip up his arse, he'd ask you the price per pound!" Or, after an Easter Sunday promenade: "By the Judas, did ya see the riggin' on the Reverend Missus? Four corsets wrapped in a mainsail. One fart an' she'd've blown us all to Kingdom Come!" To the children she was just Granny Coote. To their elders, she was queer old Arthur's second folly. To others still older, she was Cora Burgher, the cleaning woman. Before that there was no one to remember she had once been Lily. Or care.

2

The Reeve cared. After Limpy Jenkinson (shrapnel at St. Eloi) and his retarded son Wally (Walleye to the kids) delivered a cord of wood in November and again in February, Sunny Denfield would come over after work at the Foundry and split enough kindling to last her through. When it got real cold he would lug a scuttle of soft coal over for the Quebec heater. Granny would smile her thanks, but shake her head when he left. Like so many others her age she had been raised in drafty cabins and shacks. She knew how to keep warm.

Last week following Limpy's delivery, the Reeve arrived and began splitting wood in the tiny shed off the kitchen area. She lay on the chesterfield where she often slept since Arthur died and listened to the two-step cadence of the axe on wood. There was comfort in it, and reassurance.

"That should carry you through to the spring, Cora," he said, a vee of sweat on his shirt-front. "Goin' to be an early one, they say."

He always called her Cora. She had been that when he arrived in Sarnia to take advantage of the boom created by the tunnel under the River. Something, lord knows what, prompted him to take up residence in the Point where Prudie KcKay espied him and persuaded him to make the move permanent.

"Good mornin', Mrs. Burgher," he would say to her – dropping into the local accent. He met her each day outside the Queen's Hotel in his brief bachelor period: he heading for the streetcar stop at the end of Potts' Lane and she trudging up the steps towards another day of housecleaning.

Instead of saying good night and returning to his family, the Reeve went over to the stove and put the kettle on.

"Don't budge, Cora. I know where everything is. I'm goin' to make us a cup of tea, an' then I've got somethin' important to tell you."

She was awake now.

"It's good news," he said immediately.

I'll believe it when I taste it, she thought.

•

When he had poured the tea, Reeve Denfield sat beside her on the chesterfield and began talking. For some reason he was the only person besides Wilf Underhill who did not stiffen before her silence. He realized she was not at all silent, that her nods, looks, minute shades of gesture and quick touches of the hand represented a fierce desire to communicate. She always felt he was talking *with her*. Over the years, he had come to know by trial and error not only every nuance of her response to his questions but also what subjects she liked him to talk about, what village tales she wished to be told and retold. He was her lifeline to that part of the world – small as it was – which she had marked out for her own. It wasn't a matter of keeping up with the gossip – she'd lost the passion for that when Sophie had died so horribly – but as the Reeve himself discovered, a question of maintaining the continuity of one's being.

Lucien's bride, Cora the cleaning woman, Eddie's granny, Mrs. Arthur Coote, Granny Coote, these lives were kept coherent and drew meaning only if the person she now was also moved in time. If not, the web of memories sustaining her would be loosened from all anchorage and set adrift.

"Don't look so sceptical," the Reeve smiled knowingly. "It *is* good news of a sort."

I told you so.

"You've heard that up-and-comin' types like Harold Hitchcock are keen to get this property back. Yes, I know he's a phoney, but he's also cunning. He's playin' to certain prejudices an' sentiments in town, as you know so well. I was hopin' that the spirit of cooperation brought on by the War and the epidemic would carry on. I think it can, Cora, really, I do." Her stare had almost stopped him.

"We're goin' to need that spirit, as I've told you before. This town's in rough shape. No one knows better than you what the village went through during the railroad years an' the tunnel scandal and the wholesale depopulation."

Did he know what had happened? The details? Were they written down somewhere? She hadn't considered that possibility.

"When I came here, there were fifty vacant lots and a dozen houses rottin' where they sat. The Anglican Church was boarded up. Even the Lane was half-empty."

I left it, too. A deserter, like the rest.

"You stuck it out as long as you could. Don't deny it now."

She did, emphatically.

"You know how hard we struggled to get the stone works and the Foundry in here. Then the War and all those men, our neighbours, gone. An' the fever attackin' the young an' the helpless." He paused, seeing the pain in her face, but she urged him on.

I need to cry she said to him, I need to feel.

"Well, times are boomin' again. But just stand at the car stop any mornin' at seven an' watch three-quarters of our men leavin' town to work at the refinery or the railroad shops. How long can that go on before they start feelin' like city people? An' how long before Sarnia decides to make another move to fulfil the dream they've had for forty years? The War came close to breakin' us. Unless we get back our sense of bein' a community, we'll go under."

She nodded her agreement.

"That's why the monument means so much to us. It's goin' to be bigger an' nobler an' more lastin' than the one in the city. I need to keep the council together, and this business of your property has to be settled. Oh, don't be alarmed. You know where I stand. I told them last week that our lawyer said you have the right to buy the lot before any other move can be made."

Her eyes filled with tears. Oh damn, she thought, there you go, acting like a senile old woman, snivelling at every turn of emotion. But the tears fell.

"I've had the property assessed, without the council's knowledge. What I have to know is, do you have any money? Did Arthur provide for you?"

She nodded.

"Three hundred dollars?" he asked with hesitation.

She was comforted by the concern in his voice. Her smile was all he needed.

"In the bank?"

No. In a much safer place.

"Don't tell me," he laughed, much relieved. "I'll make all the arrangements. The council meets again next week. I'll have the deed, if we can find one, in your hands by then. That is, if you *want* to stay here."

There was little doubt about that. She got up and went to the steamer-trunk next to the locked door of Arthur's room. She pulled out a small slate, the one Eddie used before she got him into school. A piece of used chalk lay on the ledge at the bottom. The Reeve watched with intense curiosity.

She came back and sat beside him. She laid the slate on her knees and took the chalk in her left hand. He saw the concentration in the furrows of her brow and the tendons mount on her wrist. Her hand flexed, and she began to write in shaking, tentative curls across the slate. When she finished she smiled grimly and gave him the board. "Tell the council I wish to die in this house."

3

She was thinking back to New Years. Outside, the snow fell as gently as confetti on a bride's veil, as it had on that night. She had perched herself on the arm of the Morris chair – Arthur's own – to survey the couples entering the Oddfellows' Hall next door. The electric lights inside stretched every quadrangle of glass to the limit (she still preferred the hominess of coal oil or the dazzle of gas). Soon the orchestra struck up the welcoming number. The horns dominated the strings in the modern style. She closed her eyes and pictured them dancing – a whole village in cadenced, concentric motion in the arms of the music, palpable and reassuring. Through the transmuting snow she detected variations of fox trot and waltz, and somewhat later, as a gift to the elders, the polka and a solitary, fiddle-driven reel. No jig, no fling, no hornpipe. No galop or lancers. Then something strange, something novel: horns and drums only, the beat fevered, truant, edging towards chaos, held fast by some primitive fulcrum between beat and cadence, sound and melody. She could not imagine what sort of dance they would be doing to such rhythms, such raw choristry. She sensed it would go well before a fire in the dark under starlight. The snow sizzled and she was asleep.

4

Could it be that after all these years of searching and effort she would have a home of her own? I'll believe it when I've got the deed in my hands – in triplicate with the king's spit on it. Not that she hadn't lived in places where she had felt at home. A home is something no one can take away from you. That's the reason her forebears and thousands after them had come here: to find a place, build a house, and be at home. This shack, as the villagers called it, with its leaking roof, tarpaper skin, sloping porch and rambunctious gardens was Arthur's gift to her. Thirty-six years ago – installed in the honeymoon suite of the St. Clair Inn – she would not have dreamt such a finale as this.

"Life is mainly what happens to you," she had said to Cap.

"Nonsense," he had replied. "I built my own chamber in Hell. And so did you."

34

1

It was snowing again, like slow-motion shrapnel, and thick enough to asphyxiate the streetlamps in front of the library. No wind ruffled this February evening. The snow fell with the absolute illusion of innocence upon the sills, the eaves, and upon the nervous domesticity of a post-war winter village.

"An' so to wrap it all up," the Reeve was saying to the assembled councillors, "she's an old lady who's lived here for three generations. She's got legal entitlement to the property if she's willin' to pay fair market value, an' she definitely wants to live out her days in peace in that shanty. I already asked our lawyers to find out a proper price. Any questions on item one?"

The worshipping hand of the junior Miss Robertson came to a breathless halt at the end of the Reeve's remarks. She took advantage of the pause in her note taking to tilt her calf's eye upward in hopeless adoration. She did not, as the Reeve did, notice that although there were no questions on the issue, the room was electric with anticipation on the brink of disclosure. Neither the heat undulating from the floor register nor the imperturbable silence of the snowfall against the night could distract the council from the matters of state before it.

"Then I'll ask Sandy to speak to item two."

The village grocer, whose father had come to the Point with the railroad in 1862 and stayed to found a dynasty of shopkeepers, rose and presented the report of the subcommittee for selecting a designer and builder for the proposed war memorial. As luck would have it, they had been able to locate a man who could both design and build a monument to meet any specifications they wished. It turned out that he had done just that for three villages in Grey, two in Huron and one each in Middlesex and Kent Counties. His specialty, verified by references, was erecting impressive monuments – simple and noble in design – in small towns at reasonable rates. If the stories told were true, he had a grudge against big cities and 'government' types, and had devoted the last three years to building cenotaphs in underfunded villages that would outshine those overpriced calamities indulged in by senior municipalities. The man's name was Sam Stradler. He hailed from a hamlet near London. He had been a stonemason and tombstone carver before serving overseas. Once a site was chosen and the ice broken up, he would begin work – about mid-March or early April – and finish in six to eight weeks.

Approval was audible and unanimous. Miss Robertson recorded the verdict with a proud flourish. A feeling that something significant and abiding had been done suffused the meeting place. The snow emptied itself into the darkness outside.

Half-Hitch clicked his hickory thumb and forefinger and rose to speak to item three. Stubby Fielding and young MacIntosh, who had fidgeted and looked embarrassed during the earlier presentation by the Reeve, resumed their fidgeting. Stubby preferred the direct statement of an artillery barrage to all this oblique conniving. But he had been convinced by the devious Hitchcock of the necessity for secrecy. There were times, he allowed, when battle plans had to be kept under wraps if the strategy itself was not to be jeopardized and the humane goals forever compromised. Stubby had grunted assent. Horrie MacIntosh, on the other hand, was in no position to argue any side of the matter: he was the recruit, the cadet untested by battle and not yet sanctified by its scarring.

"Our committee's reached a unanimous decision," Hitchcock said from memory. "We explored every angle of the issue at hand, and we found only one spot – site – that meets all the requirements." He fished the requirements out of the recall-box: "(1) central location, (2) flat land of at least one-quarter acre in size, (3) property owned by the village or available at nominal cost, and (4) ah –" He flipped the stuck card in his head. "Presence of shade trees."

"Get on with it, Hitch!" barked the Boer veteran. "This ain't church! No offense, Mort."

The Reverend Mort, unaware that high drama was ravelling its sinuous subplots around him, took neither offense nor heed.

Half-Hitch had now irreparably lost his place. He plunged ahead recklessly. "We all agreed, all three of us, there was only one spot to fit the needs we set out here last meetin'. The spot we chose is in the dead centre of town. It's on a main street where the city trolley passes every hour. It's got a marvellous big shade tree, an' shrubs an' hedges to boot. You can see across the marsh to the docks an' up to the dunes by the Lake. An' best of all, it's almost owned by the village."

The Reeve leaned forward in his chair. He now understood the edgy quiet during his earlier speech. His anger, alas, was tempered by the force of the logic in Hitchcock's report. The only other vacant lot in the middle of town was the one beside them; but it was the last of the railroad properties: a memorial on its ground would be the ultimate betrayal. He had assumed they would choose the original site of the old Anglican Church where the cub scouts pitched their tents. He'd underestimated the opposition.

"I move," Half-Hitch said through his smug smile, "we agree on the Coote property as a site for the monument, an' begin legal proceedin's to take back title."

The motion passed.

2

Granny liked the snow the way it was tonight. Once, with Eddie on her knee and nothing but dark days ahead and only two small presents under the tree, she had watched the Christmas Eve snowfall through the child's eye. She called it the snow of remembrance. Back then, she had thought, 'someday I'll be sitting in another place with times as bad as these and I'll remember the wonderful gentleness of this falling'. And here I am.

This could be any of the snowfalls upon any of the spruces she had lived beside, or under, in the seasons of her childhood, girlhood, womanhood, dotage, deathwatch. "Who wants to live to be old?" Cap said to her many times, his flesh wan and shivering after a bad bout. "What would you do with a useless body and all that time on your hands? Sit and remember when your elements used to work and your brain could count to three? How many good times can you relive anyway before they're worn out and you come to despise them?"

She had no answer, then; neither of them had been old enough to speak from experience. I'll tell you now, she thought. It's not the way you imagined. Yes, I live on my memories, but they are not summoned up like individual pearl buttons to be turned over in the hand and admired till the eyes water. It doesn't work that way, Cap. Not for me. Some moments do come back almost whole, like Eddie and me watching the Christmas snow of 1897 with different versions of hope in our hearts. Like the snowy night of 1886 that was like this one except for the wind that blew through it like an invisible beam when Lucien and I rode out to find heaven on a one-horse sled. Or any of a dozen more – from parts of my life you never surmised – full of sweetness and pain, but more often marked by the exquisite surge of innocence against experience. You would be astonished, Cap, to hear me talk like this, use words in such a way. Then again perhaps you wouldn't. Still, you must take the blame for some of it. You maintained that the world wouldn't be a safe or sane place to live in if ever women were taught to read and write. But then you didn't know Eddie, or his father. They taught me that poetry can be gossip made glorious by language. Sophie knew so; she lived it and died for it. You saw in her only what your prejudices allowed.

And you've got no prejudices of course. She laughed to herself. You see, old darling, that is how memory works. That is how I fill these hours before I'm overtaken by exhaustion and the dread of the night dream. Forgive me if I failed to acknowledge your anguish. You see how the mind refuses to accept the denial of a present or future. I think of Eddie, of snow, of you, of Lucien Burgher, of Sophie's battered face, of sweet Arthur. They have voices, you know, like you; they can be talked to. They can speak with one another in the special existence I lend them, here on a February evening in 1922 with a snow falling. You gave it all up too soon, old pessimist. I am ready for death's surprises, if he has any. But I am not lonely. I am still, after all these years, waiting for something to happen.

Like the stove going out, you day-dreaming old fart, she thought, shivering and shuffling over to the Quebec heater. It stared at her, one-eyed and glum. Against the protest of her rheumatism, she shook the grates as vigorously as she could manage. Several intractable clinkers had lodged between the flanges. She'd have to get Sunny to clean out the firebox when he came over to tell her about the meeting. He had left her a fine white notepad on which to write out requests and things she needed. She was grateful, though it was difficult at first to scrawl anything legible. It wasn't just the arthritis. Whatever had afflicted her throat had spread to her writing hand. But it was easier now to list the few supplies she needed for either Sunny or Wilf Underhill to take to Redmond's or Turnbull's. It made her feel better about possessing Arthur's house, at last. They won't think I'm completely batty. Just old. Maybe I'll be allowed to die with a little dignity.

She tried to recall anyone she loved who had.

Now the good burghers of the town would be able to pity her with a clear conscience. But what if they'd been able to observe her wrestling with the paper and kindling in a plugged stove with smoke polluting the chill of her front room? "Poor old soul, used to be strong as an ox, scrubbed floors in The Queen's for years. Then age and arthritis gets the best of us all, don't it. And she never did take care of herself, livin' in that drafty shack in the Lane all those years. Never settin' foot in a church or a decent body's house." I prefer the children, she thought. They only think I'm a witch, an outcast – with status.

She felt pain firing through both her knees. She was on the floor among the spilled cinders and ash. The kindling had burned itself, the smoke had escaped with the brief heat through the cracks in the walls. Had she blacked out? A tumour? Tiny strokes? She winced at the bruising in her knees and the scalding of tears. Get up. Get up. The room spun on the axis of a single candle flame in the front window. Lie down. Let it be.

•

The temporary blaze was taking the chill off, and the hot tea warmed wherever it went. Granny pulled the kimono more snugly around her throat and continued her vigil at the snowy window overseeing the street. Arthur was a sweet man, so different from the others. He loved to walk, as she did, with no aim or purpose other than the pleasures of being in motion—in the woods or along the beaches or among the cattails or under the parliament of stars. Often they would pull Eddie on his sled through snows like this over to the dunes. He would fling himself into semi-flight down their slick slopes to the borderless prairie of the beach below. When they got home, after a brisk fire and mulled wine – with Eddie snug in his cocoon – she would make slow, mutinous love to Arthur. He was always too shy, too untrusting of the tender impulses that throve in him to initiate lovemaking. She would think of him, though she never told him so, as an instrument that she would rub and thrum till its music wakened and overwhelmed. "We shouldn't, love, we're too old, too ridiculous," he'd murmur, and she'd say, "Keep your eyes closed, sweet; it's beautiful, it's beautiful in here."

So rare in a man was that refined reticence, that rare combination of resignation and engagement, gentility and passion, that she – Cora Burgher –

would have scoffed at the very notion. Cap would have laughed out loud, and Sophie offered some devastating quip. "I know he's sweet and kind and does the dishes, dearie, but has he got a dick or a doily down there?"

In a letter she wrote but never sent to Eddie, she said about Arthur: 'He was the kind of man every woman should marry. As lovers only should we take the adventurers, the wanderers, the plunderers. When we've taken our pleasure, we'll turn them loose again to waste themselves upon the world'.

I've had my share of the other kind, she thought. And their children. They're dead and gone, all of them—willing victims of whatever demons drive the male flesh to annihilation. And the innocents along with them. Eddie. I can't even say your name out loud. The gods that could have helped us are still in hiding. When Arthur left he took some of the earth's music with him, but you were my last cause for hope. What am I doing here now? The gods won't answer from their skulking places. Even death has passed me by. Cap was right. Waiting is not living.

You're waiting for something to happen. Yes, of course. That's it. I almost forgot.

She heard a commotion in her front yard and turned to see the blurred outline of Sunny Denfield, the puffing portliness of Mortimer Stokes and the loping strut of Harry Hitchcock. From the gait and bearing of these harbingers, she recognized, from long and repeated experience, the peculiar footfall of officialdom. And the news it bore, she knew, was never good.

3

Granny again dreaming Lily, dreaming the long-ago as if it had actually happened or could happen again, only differently, so everything would be changed in the wake-up world. She was eight and alone under the moon. The shadows around her blurred into smoke when she touched them, and the night air was jarred and riven by a music that had no sound. There was no melody, only cadence and verberation. She was aware that the smoke wreaths and shadow substances were other souls twisting in the same silence, driven by the same yearnings towards the bliss of oblivion. They shared a simultaneous cry of release and not a single regret. She awoke to find herself sleeping upon the shoulder of the Southener, the last of the Shawnees from the legendary battles of the war with the States. In the clearing among the Pottawatomie wigwams around them, they watched with separate intensities the midnight ceremony repeating itself before them. When all the chanting was done and all the transformations had taken place within their spheres, she was able to smile into the moon-varnished dark with the face of her new name. She was no longer White Blossom but Seed of the Snow Apple, and all that was promised therein if summer should ever come, or the darkness imbedded above the moon ever lifted from the dreamer's eye...

35

1

On such a night as this – with the stars frozen in place, the quarter moon windless with wonder, – did Lucien, the locomotive man, thirty-six years ago to the month, baptize his bride "Mrs. Cora Burgher". To the astonishment of the other burghers of the village, no doubt. But nothing fazed them concerning the behaviour of any former inmate of Mushroom Alley. Being one of its superannuated denizens, Granny thought, granted one a comforting sense of immunity, a licence to commit extravagant social irreverencies. Not that being made an honest woman by Lucien Burgher was all that irreverent. Lucien, with his great grappling hands and a titanic laugh recognized over the competition of a steam whistle and the wail of wind through the open windows of the cab. With a heart as hot and propulsive as the firebox he fed each night with lozenges of beach and elm. You were the only one willing to take me away, out of myself, take me sailing on the white wave that sweeps us clear of our body's weight. We made our secret pact and kept it without compromise. Less than three months. And, Lucien, my love, the gods of either hue were watching – in trepidation and delight. Yes, all that *did* happen.

Even when you left, I thought to keep your name. I braved the taunting and snobbery to make them say it long enough to forget I'd ever had another. You'd have been proud of me, but pride, as we both knew, was never a substitute for the meshing of our brief nights together. You would have roared with laughter, or cried, to overhear – as I did at The Queen's while scrubbing out a room – the wheezing and whimpering next door, or off-key giggle. Sadness like an aftersmell no scouring could efface. Only the memory of our love and your courage not to be kept me going in that black year.

I kept your name—it grew around me in the Lane and in the village. The graft took. When Eddie came, he needed something to call me. Granny. I resisted, gently. The child needed a surname. I gave him yours, and mine. When sweet Arthur carried us off together, I surrendered it with reluctance. You know that. We talked it over at the time, remember? I told you what a sacrifice Arthur Coote was making, offering his widower's hand to a woman thrice fallen, risking all for love as one of his theatrical publicists might have put it. Don't laugh. Driving down to the Sarnia Court House in a borrowed butcher's cart to be "hitched" by a judge was one of the most courageous acts I've seen any man perform. I told him to pretend he was on stage and he did, and I gave him rave reviews for a week. You would have come to like the Arthur I was privileged to see. Don't forget, he was an actor, an entertainer. He played The Royal in Victoria and the Lyceum in San Francisco. Being organist and choir director at the Methodist Church was his greatest role, though you wouldn't like me saying that.

She thought of that night a few weeks after the ceremony. Arthur sat over there at his piano and began to play, in slow time, the opening bars of "I am a model of a modern major-general." Young Eddie, barely ten and wide-eyed with wonder, picked up Arthur's baton, tucked it under his chin like a swagger stick and started marching up to the music. Arthur, his shyness finally easing, began to speed up towards the song's regular triphammer gallop; Eddie's legs hopped in rapid synchronization, his arm jerking up and down in perfect parody. His eyes danced in accelerating cadence till they left the safety of his granny's. When the cups on the shelf ceased to rattle from the final chord, he scooted past her waiting arms and flung himself at Arthur, who hugged the child so tightly he could feel the diminuendo of music still humming in the tiny bones.

2

The front room was as warm and cozy as it had ever been. Sunny Denfield had removed the clinkers and cinders and built a fast, hot maplewood fire to take off the chill. He stayed for tea even though he knew Prudie would get that hurt, puzzled look in her eye, certain there was some sinister explanation for long visits with a strange soul who sat without speech, winter after winter, cheating death. Charity had its limits. God would not credit such excess.

"I didn't tell you, did I," he was saying, "that I got another letter from my

cousin, Ruth-Anne, in Toronto. Yes, it's true. Seems like the hoity-toity side
of the family has decided to acknowledge its black sheep." He was aware of
her acknowledgement, reflected in her face. He observed, as he spoke, the
slightest quiver of her lip or brow, assessing each shift of light in her eyes.

"You remember, of course, the callow bachelor who set up shop in The
Queen's back in the fall of 'nineteen-one. I was only eighteen. I didn't tell my
parents where I was till after I got settled in the job at the sheds and was
pretty certain Prudie McKay would say yes. What few people know even
today is that I ran away from private school. My family was, an' still is, high
mucky-muck."

She acknowledged the accuracy of the term.

"My grandfather was a minister in the old Union government of
Baldwin-Lafontaine. My father was a fancy city solicitor in Toronto. He died
during the war. Lucky for me, I stopped to see him on my way overseas in
'fifteen. He knew he was dying, I think, because he made a great show of
forgivin' me. I was sure I'd die before him, an' maybe he thought so too."

She pushed another of Mrs. Savage's cookies in his direction.

"Anyway, it seems my Aunt Grace, my mother's sister, who died a year
ago, got interested in her family tree. She'd married Bramwell Beattie, a sort
of junior tycoon, a guy I hated all my life. But Aunt Grace was a pet, the
sweetest, kindest soul there was. Since my own mother died havin' me, Aunt
Grace was the closest thing to a mother I ever had. I wrote to her all along.
I'm sure she understood my rebellion. At any rate, she kept my secret. I
wrote to her a lot during the war."

Her eyes narrowed.

"Well, anyway, accordin' to my cousin, Ruth-Anne MacEnroe – that's
her married name – who was Aunt Grace's only child, we've got some
distant relatives on my Aunt's side of the family who lived in Lambton
County at one time. Trouble is, they seem to have moved away an' nobody
can now locate them. Since her mother died, Ruth-Anne's been like a fanatic
about tracing her roots. You'd think with cabinet ministers an' lawyers an'
tycoons on your family tree, you'd be satisfied an' leave well enough alone."

She underlined the irony in the remark and Sunny smiled broadly.
Draining the cold tea from his cup, he rose to go.

"That stove should behave till spring," he said, pulling on his mackinaw.
She watched every move he made. He reached into his tool kit and pulled
out a notepad, the brown wrapper still on it. He placed it over on the kitchen

table then looked across the room at her.

"The mass meetin's tomorrow night," he said. "Right next door. I want you to write out on this paper whatever you want to say to the people of the Point. I'll read it aloud to them. You have some rights in all this, you know."

Her eyes said neither yes nor no.

At the door, with his scarf tucked in, he said, "I think you should be there. "I'll come for you around eight."

An icy draft from the open door struck her a sideways blow before the heat of the cleansed stove replenished itself.

36

By seven-forty-five the Oddfellows' Hall was almost full. More than half the town's six hundred adults gathered to hear confirmation of the facts which were already public knowledge and spice for the rumour mill. The infirm, of whom there were more than the usual numbers, sat on wooden benches arranged especially for the occasion. Everyone else stood in clusters, or leaned elbows on sills and wainscoting, happy to observe and judge. On the dais at the north end, the councillors peered down at their constituents, secure behind the trestle table now littered with official looking papers that were shuffled more than necessary. The Reeve's chair remained unoccupied.

Just before eight o'clock, the door opened and Reeve Denfield entered. Granny Coote was beside him. A stunned hush gripped the assembled. No rumour of this sort had tested the village breeze. What they saw through their surprise was a tiny old woman, barely five-feet tall, with mottled gray hair pulled back into an uncustomary bun and tamed with a frayed blue ribbon. The Irish-white skin was blotched with liver-spots and yellowed from too much indoor light, but the eyes incandesced in their shrinking flesh, like two jets set in a shaman's mask. She allowed herself to be guided by the Reeve's arm, although it was plain she wasn't feeble. It was her bearing that arrested the viewers' attention. She walked with an autonomous, erect grace that reminded the hunters in the hall of the way a whitetail lopes through a maze of brushwood, never once condescending to take a sideways glance.

To the further surprise of the gathering and to the councillors themselves, Sunny Denfield escorted 'mad Granny' to a place beside him at the table. There they removed their coats and sat downstage centre. Needless to say, the subsequent proceedings were scrutinized with more than usual interest.

•

The Reeve announced that for reasons which would become clear later on, he was turning the chair over to the Reverend Stokes. He and Granny

moved down to a less ostentatious position at the west end of the table. She
did not flinch under the obsessive watch of the assembly, nor did she take the
Reeve's arm. The impression she left was one of determined fragility.
Throughout the speeches that followed, she sat straight up in the wooden
chair and looked out at the townspeople she had lived amongst for decades.
Her eyes shone with a sanity that shamed them.

There's not a face I don't recognize, she thought. That would surprise
most of them. I can't put a name to everyone, but I know the family stamp:
big noses, weak chins, sallow eye, the unmistakable hybrid smile. She could
rhyme off their lineage – public and suppressed. She knew whom their
second cousins married in Goderich or Petrolia. She remembered the high
hopes their parents once had for them. All these years the good citizens
figured it was they who watched the sideshow of Mushroom Alley and the
Lane. Who did they think we talked about? Whose rebels and strays kept our
blind pigs fed and our whorehouses wholesome? We took in rumours like
transfusions. We invented the last laugh.

The chairman pro tem had begun. He called on Sandy Redmond, who
repeated the stale news about the selection of Sam Stadler to design and build
the monument. The gathering added its applause to the speaker's own.

Redmond continued when the last clap had exhausted its echo, "I must
tell you the buildin' fund will still need to be added to, as the cost of the
landscapin' hasn't been figured in. So we're askin' you to dig as deep as you
can. I think it's fair to say your council's stretched a dollar as far as it can go."

Like your wife stretches them behind the counter, Granny mused. You've got a
grin and a handshake and a gift for the gab, but it's Olive who keeps the
business afloat. Any woman who's been president of the WCTU knows how
to dot the 'i' and cross the 't's' in temptation. But does she know you used to
slip down to the Lane just like your Dad for a quick snort? I liked your Dad.
He had doe's eyes.

"Harry Hitchcock will now give us his report on the selection of the site,"
said Chairman Stokes. "But before he does, I want to take this opportunity –"

And every opportunity you get.

"– to say a special word about those who have sacrificed, in silence and
humility, their time and energy, and in one case more than that, for a cause
which we are all agreed is a noble one, even a divinely inspired one."

Oh no, he's about to make a platitude out of a beatitude.

"Our Lord said, 'Blessed are the meek, for they shall inherit the earth',"

and he bent to acknowledge the frail being at the end of the table, blessing
her with his roast-beef smile.

And blessed are the obese for they shall batten on the pastures of heaven. Sunny
Denfield touched her hand but she stared straight ahead.

•

Half-Hitch was on his feet and sailing through his set piece, which he
managed to complete. Into the sea of puzzled faces he then said, "Of course,
you now see the special sacrifice the good pastor was referrin' to. We need to
have back the lot where Mrs. Coote now lives. Her house'll have to come
down to make way for the monument. We're all dreadful sorry about that.
But I'm sure we all know that progress has its price. And there'll be
compensation for Mrs. Coote beside the reward of the Almighty Himself.
We're gonna decide on it at our meetin' next week. We won't bore you with
the complicated details now, but I was asked by council to tell you that Mrs.
Coote's generosity will not be overlooked or ever forgotten. After all, a war
memorial's all about sacrifice an' rememberin'." He executed a little
semaphore motion with his wooden souvenir.

*That's some remembrance you're waving. You don't know that I know how you
lost that hand, and it wasn't in the trenches. I got a full description from Eddie of you
toppling off that barstool in some bordello at Givenchy during an air-raid and getting
your arm crushed between two barrels of beer.*

The stingy applause for Half-Hitch was cut even shorter by the Reeve's
rising and holding up his hand. Half-Hitch sulked for a moment, but like the
others surrendered to curiosity and waited for the chief councillor to speak.

"I stepped out of the chair," he said quietly, "because I was the only
member of council not to vote in favour of the Coote property as a site for
the monument. I didn't want to influence the decision before you all had a
chance to hear the explanations. Even though the vote of council is legal, I'm
sure nobody wants to do anythin' that would go against the conscience of
the village. So I feel duty-bound to present to you Mrs. Coote's side of the
story."

He waved before them what looked like a handwritten letter. All eyes
followed it.

"As most of you know, Mrs. Coote can't speak for herself because she's
got an affliction of the throat that stops her from talkin'. But I want to tell

you, Cora Coote is as bright an' sharp of mind as she ever was, and I have here her feelings on this matter, which she wrote down for me last night. I'd like to read these words if the chairman and council will let me."

There was consternation among council but the assembly made the decision for them. "Agreed," seconded chairman Stokes.

The Reeve then read. "Dear members of council: I wish you to know that I wholeheartedly agree with your selection of a site for the monument. You have chosen wisely and with good reason. I wish you to know also that I will do nothing to stand in the way of your plans. My house and land are yours. They are sacred to me for reasons no one but myself could understand, but then so is the village. I was here when the railroads arrived. I saw the townsite grow, block by block, house by home. I cheered when it was proclaimed a village. In a small way, I helped to name one of its streets. In all those years, the house I now live in was the only one I could call mine. My hope was to die in it. What I ask of the council is not compensation in dollars, which are of no value to me, but compensation in kind. I want to live out my days here in the village. I do not wish to be cast into a home for the wretched. The property is yours, in any event. I ask only that you think of me as you would any true citizen of the Point. Yours respectfully, Mrs. Cora Coote."

The Reform party in council was devastated. No ploy, no plea or manoeuvre of any kind could have been as effective as these words. The old dame's a long ways from being bonkers, Half-Hitch thought. She was giving up her property but throwing her eighty-year-old-frail-pathetic-hard-done-by body upon the mercy of a boastfully Christian community. Even Reverend Stokes was able to discern the sheer cunning behind the move. What could be done? There was no public property to trade for hers, outside of unimproved fringe lots near the dunes, the dump or the swamp. Any solution that appeared in the least to be mean-spirited would crush the communal joy in whose spirit the monument was to be erected.

In the midst of these hushed mutterings, few people noticed young MacIntosh rise and ask for the floor. The Reeve, resuming command, rapped his gavel on the table.

"There is a solution to the problem," said the junior member of council, his voice quavering. "A solution that's fair an' workable."

"Go ahead, Horrie," said the Reeve.

"Well, I been thinkin' about fair compensation for Mrs. Coote all week, and I did some askin' around an' some fishin' in the County Court records. You all know the old lane that used to run between the Savage house and the Waggoner's place right across from Coote's? Hasn't been used as a lane I find for more than thirty years. The Savages now grow potatoes on it, an' Murray lets his grass grow over his half. Well, it seems the actual allowance there is thirty feet, twice the size of the lane. What I'm sayin' is, there's more than enough property to build a small cottage on. My suggestion is that we get together as a community, pool our skills, an' with the help of donations and any money Mrs. Coote can spare, build her a cottage to live in an' give her a deed to the property. When that's done, we can knock down the Coote house an' start to build the monument."

As one, the village turned to Granny Coote. She fought back tears with limited success. She looked towards Sunny Denfield and imperceptibly nodded.

37

1

March of 1922 was one of those late winter months which people remember as part of a past not only better but more connected with God's grace. His grand scheduling of events for the world's good remained in place – before the rude intercession of wars, pestilence, and apostasy. Even God was growing nostalgic.

Here before the villagers' immediate eye was proof of a larger beneficence, a firm hand on the throttle of natural progress. The snow continued to fall but only at night. Each morning, it surprised and delighted anew; fostering the hope it had not fallen from an empty sieve of the universe, but rather had grown from the essence of limb, eave and chimney pot. By day, the thermometer held steady at thirty degrees under a velvet sun, coaxing icicles out of warmed gables. Rinks glistened by noon but froze tight again overnight. Snowballs packed as neat as baseballs yet struck like puffs of childish laughter. The meanest shanty, suffering neglect brought on by war and the failure of hope, was transformed by the architecture of ice and snow into a glittering edifice.

Some folk conceded that the old Coote shack was 'almost presentable', though the latter sentiment may have been prompted equally by the thought that, come spring, it would no longer grace the village landscape in any of its transformations. During this brief interregnum of the seasons, passersby could not help but notice the small, alert face of Granny Coote in her front window. She seemed, to all her newly-hatched well-wishers, to be staring across the street where, despite the weather, several burly young men were seen, at noon or after work, clearing the snow and chopping out a rectangular trench. When winter had yielded to necessity, this would hold the concrete footing of a new house. Around them were piled several sections of 'material' – two-by-fours, joists, cedar siding – purchased out of the public purse and the charity of the citizenry. They were covered with several tarpaulins, all turned outward to expose the donor's identity: McKeough Fishery, Point Edward, Canada.

Though her attention was from time to time drawn towards the intermittent construction activity, she noted with appreciation (and the pure pleasure of memory) the presence of Charlie Brighton, old Mike's boy, out of work, his nerves still bad from the war. There was also Wilf Underhill, taking precious time from his new son, Stu Macdonald and young MacIntosh, and Sunny Denfield who always came over afterward. She was more likely to be thinking back to other days of renewal, to the remembrance of those few, joyous months with Lucien Burgher, and those years afterward. She bore his name through some of the darkest times of her life. *Cora. Cora Burgher. Cora Coote. Cora the Cleaning Woman.* She was all of them and none of them. Before that, through a haze of memories deliberately obliterated, she remembered being Lily – of Mushroom Alley, of Potts' Lane…

2

The years between 1879 and 1885 saw the new nation regain the confidence it had lost during the great depression. For a few shameful moments, some citizens had suffered a lapse of faith in the ineluctability of their own progress. Aided by crop failures and a cattle epidemic in England, and sanguinary adventures in Egypt and the Sudan, the local economy turned pink with health. If good works were a sign of election, who could doubt the divine rightness of Sir John A's national hope, fulfilled at last in 1885. A three-thousand-mile band of iron welded the faintheart provinces and empty territories together in a singular purpose. Add to this a thousand breathtaking bridges and trestles, mathematically graded inclines, brooding watchtowers, suspended steel arcs and ballooning grain elevators stretching between Montreal and Vancouver. The Canadian Pacific Railway swept all before it, the juggernaut of the transcendentalist dream. By happy coincidence, in 1882, the Grand Trunk succeeded in swallowing whole its ancient rival, the Great Western. Within a year, rumours of a magical underwater tunnel began to circulate. This was an engineering miracle that would not only confirm God's allegiance to His chosen creatures but link the Canadian transcontinental grid with the spidering network of iron and affluence south of the border.

In 1884, the world adopted Sir Sandford Fleming's scheme for standard time, made necessary throughout the civilized world if rational and efficient train schedules were to be realized. Who could doubt that the railways, and the foundries forging their steel nervous system, carried with them the aspirations of mankind and the sanction of the Almighty? Malcontents and Luddites (who preferred to set local time by the local sun) wrote strident letters to newspapers complaining of "railroad tyranny" and accusing our noble men of science of "tampering with God's time". But such pusillanimous voices were silenced by the last spike driven home at Craigalachie.

3

For Lily the first two years following the incorporation of Point Edward as a village were deceptively peaceful. She mourned the death of Sophie, as she did all those she had lost. Around her the seasons and the lives within them changed and throve. The surveys along Potts' Lane were carried out. The new half of the street was a little less rambling than before but not as straight as the town's other ones were (having been drawn on a map with a ruler in some official's study). Except for Lily and her secret arrangement with Hap Withers, no one on the Lane was unable to scrape together fifty dollars to make their quietus with the council and the railway. The surveyors 'squared up' the wandering lot lines, driving red stakes into the ground to prove their point. The resulting deeds were registered, fixed for all time. But if the village worthies expected fences and hedges to spring up along these fresh definitions of ownership, they were disappointed. Nor was there a rush on paint and plaster at Lockwood's Hardware by the citizenry of Potts' Lane.

Over a period of months, signs of proprietorship did become visible to the discerning eye: a shingled roof (one side only), a single, sparkling pane of glass, a thrust of perennials along a barren wall permitted to bloom if they were persistent enough, a stone fireplace that didn't get finished but was used and admired nonetheless.

Mushroom Alley evolved in the Lane in other ways, no more dramatic but much more important to Lily and her life there. People moved away and were replaced, one or two at a time. At first, little difference was felt: a brief break, a hiatus, some memories, and you could reassure yourself that the Lane was still the alley with a better name and that the requisite essentials for one's continuance remained in place. Then one morning you wake up and realize that everything has changed. It had been changed for some time, and people around you are looking at you as if you're the only thing that hasn't. How did it happen?

That Stoker Potts didn't come back from the Bruce was no surprise to anybody on the Lane. The house stood empty all that winter, the screen door slamming in the wind till Rob finally went over and nailed it shut. Next to Hazel's it was the biggest and best-built house among them. Rumours flew that some entrepreneurial stranger was about to buy it with a view to gobbling up the neighbouring properties to make room for a hotel larger than The Queen's. The depression was giving way to prosperity and financial adventure.

It was soon confirmed that the fifty dollars had been paid and a deed transferred. There was considerable relief when Peg Potts (now Granger) and her husband moved in, bringing their own child, and her young brother, Bricky, with them. But Peg, though she still had Sophie's devilish eyes and hair-trigger laugh, had got religion and was quite reserved, 'standoffish' according to Betsy and Winnie. Her husband was a sober man who worked in Sarnia and tried to build a fireplace to please his wife. "Still," Hazel philosophized, "they're not *the other kind*." Bricky spent a lot of time with Rob, and when Rob was away, with Lily.

One windy autumn day in 1880, Cap Whittle leaned too far out on his topsail yardarm and tumbled into the billows below. He cracked three ribs and jarred another dime loose in his overworked imagination. His lot was sold to the eldest McCourt boy and his girlfriend, who proceeded to live in splendid sin in the neat clapboard cottage they erected and painted pale blue. Despite the impudence of the paint, they were deemed to be genuine Alleyfolk (the girl being a cousin of the Shawyers from Bosanquet Township). Lily had known Pippy McCourt for years, and she waved to him every day as he passed on his way to the freight sheds. He always gave her a big smile. I wonder why, Lily thought then chided herself for such foolish introspection.

In the bitter winter of 1881-82, Honeyman Belcher caught pneumonia and died alone in his shack. The frozen body was discovered three days later by his friend, Stumpy. Honeyman's business was taken over by a man from Sarnia. Hazel organized a campaign to raise money so that one of the Shawyer girls and her husband could afford to buy the lot and make the place habitable. It was something Sophie might have done – they all thought but did not say. Another property had been preserved from contamination, it seemed, but no one was willing yet to admit that each change put the whole enterprise – if indeed there was one – in jeopardy. No one dared to even think that with Sophie's death something vital and irreplaceable had gone out of their collective life. In some mysterious way, Sophie Potts had *been* the Alley and that the Lane in which they had immortalized her name was already something else.

In May of 1881, without warning or explanation, John the Baptist capped his still, chivvied Aquinas the boar onto a wagon with his furniture, and moved to another shack in the south end near the recently constructed racetrack and fairgrounds. "Got some French woman hot for his product," Hazel opined , but nobody laughed. A few nights later, a gang of hooligans put the torch to his shanty when they found he still without sustenance. "I don't believe in signs!" Hazel snapped at Betsy to shut her up.

As it turned out, Stumpy and Lily were the last of the hard-core Laners to survive there. In the fall of 1882, Spartacus, complaining of "too damn much noise an' interferin' in a body's business", moved in with John the Baptist. Both lived and carried on their work into the 'nineties and were missed when they passed on. They never returned to the Lane. Poor Stumpy, whose supply of derelicts was not diminished by Sir John's 'economic miracle', continued his good deeds until December of 1884 when one of his boarders stabbed him to death, mistaking him in the dark for an avenging Beelzebub whom he had seen leaping from the evening express moments before. The assassin was shipped off to the asylum in London.

●

Several weeks after Baptiste Cartier's place burned down, Violet arrived at Lily's in tears.

"What's wrong?" Lily asked.

"Betsy an' Shad are gettin' married."

"What *else*?"

"We're all gonna move."

To a rambling brick house in Forest, twenty miles to the north-east. "We're goin' legitimate again, Lil," Hazel explained, "in a town where we can start over. Shad an' my girls – Winnie an' Betsy an' dear Vi – we're gonna fix it up an' start a boardin' house. I mean it, Lil, a genuine boardin' house. I'm goin' back to cookin' again. This here's been fun but we're all too old for it. Winnie almost died with her last abortion an' Betsy's insistin' on keepin' the one she's got in her now – at forty-six years of age. She's sure it belongs to Shad. So I headed off for Forest on the train one day last week, and I just up an' bought this old place."

"Who'll get *this* house?" Lily asked.

"Hap Withers has already bought it – for his eldest."

"When're you leavin', then?"

"Next week, after the holiday. Ain't it excitin'? You can hop on the Day Express an' come up an' visit us any time. Any time you please."

"Yes," Lily said, "it's not even an hour, I'm told."

Hazel, almost white-haired now, let her eyes mist over. "I remember when you was a red-haired beauty with the shyest smile in the County an' your little pony Benjamin pullin' you up Front Street every Saturday mornin'. Betsy an' Winnie were the worst teases ever."

"I remember, Char."

"Christ in Heaven, Lily," she cried, "what's to become of us?"

•

Violet came into the laundry shed to say goodbye. When Lily had gathered enough courage to ask her why she wanted to go with Hazel, and to assure her that she could stay here and live and work and be happy as long as she lived, Violet looked at the floor. "I got to go with Hazel. She's been good to me." Like the mother you never had, Lily was thinking when Violet's words stunned her. "She needs me, Lil."

The two women embraced, and it was Lily who let go first.

"I got somethin' for you," she said.

Violet glanced at the carpetbag in which Lily had packed some of the clothes and trinkets Violet had left over the years. Lily had secretly tucked into it the one hundred and fifty dollars of unclaimed income that Bachelor Bill's 'retarded' daughter had earned as her helper and her friend.

"Not that," Lily said. "Something my mother gave me I'd like you to have to remember me by."

"Hazel says you'll come up to see us on the train."

"Of course I will." Lily drew the gold crucifix and chain from her apron pocket and as Violet leaned forward, Lily placed it around her throat.

"Remember me," Lily whispered.

•

Lily always intended to visit Hazel and Violet and did receive one letter months later indicating that all was well: Betsy's baby was robust and black, Winnie's health had improved, Hazel was practically running the village, and oh yes, Violet had found herself a gentleman friend and specially asked after Lily. With Brad's help, Lily composed a stilted letter wishing them all well and promising once again to climb on the train and visit. She couldn't, of course, tell them what sort of chaos her own life was sliding into.

4

In the belly of the night dream again from which there was no remembrance, only the aftertaste of ash and self-loathing. Birdsky's child called Rabbit danced around her again on his jackrabbit legs. His chestnut face looked burnished by the summer's sun; his slim, undulant boy's arms waved them backwards towards the forbidden dark beyond the spot of sunlight reserved for Mama's grave. Its heat poured onto her neck and shoulders and cast a nine-year-old Lily shadow upon the ghost of her mother's cold breath. But Rabbit's happy dance was hopping in the bell chambers of her little girl's heart. He led her away from the hearth where death dwelt unabashed in the daylight where Papa committed his treacheries upon the copper woman who cried out like a nightjar. Her baby Rabbit danced his two-foot/four-foot Indian jig into the sweated crotch of ancient branch and Cambrian bole. Somewhere in the black interior the sound of music drifted out of brass and violin and tympani. Rabbit's hand grew firmer, and in the glow of hoarded moonlight, she could see he had sprung taller and light of hair. His smile was Tom's smile, a first lover's smile. "Come on, come on," it crooned, waltzing into the intricate distance till it drew her at last into his dancer's grip. She saw that his eyes were pebble blue, iced amethysts agleam like the stiffened orbs of the long-drowned, staring starward as the seasons' rivers wash mockingly over them...

38

1

Bradley, as he was now called, continued to do well in school. Studying was as effortless as breathing to him, and no amount of dereliction interfered with the steady flow of A's on his report cards. In January of 1879, Lily agreed to let him stay at Mrs. Tideman's boarding house, a block from the high school in Sarnia. She talked for an hour with that good lady and concluded that she was a sober-minded, conscientious Christian who specialized in haltering the headstrong youth of the town. "He'll keep his nose to the grindstone here, and it's lights out at nine-thirty!" She did her best. So did Lily, but Bradley was rapidly turning into an impetuous, brooding young man. He stood taller than his father by a head at age sixteen, with an effeminate handsomeness that both attracted and repelled the young women in whose company he was seen. He cultivated the tubercular look of a romantic poet, letting his blond curls droop over a pale brow and wan cheek. He was supposed to spend his weekends at home, and did so until he entered Grade 11 and took up with the likes of Paul Chambers, the solicitor's son.

Even when Bradley was at home, Lily often found herself at her wits' end. Whenever she would cut short his swaggering arrogance with a stare or a retort he was unable to handle, he would sulk for hours, often ending up in a fit of remorse. He wept until Lily wrapped her arms around him and let him feel how deep and unqualified her forgiveness was. For days on end he would be a model son, provoking a smoky fire at dawn and serving her tea and toast in bed, or sitting with her and explaining who the Tudors were or how the United Empire Loyalists came to be and why they were hailed as the founding pillars of Canadian society. He even helped with her writing which, he insisted, was coming along famously. But even when Bradley was in one of his rare good moods, Rob would not stay at the house nor in his backyard tent. He headed for solitude on his own place – where she had lived so long ago with Bridie and Uncle Chester, when she had been – it seemed forever – Lily Ramsbottom. When Bradley left for Sarnia, Rob would arrive home for supper and be so ill-tempered for days that Lily found herself taking out her anger and frustration on the innocent one. With the depression ending at last, Rob was working three days a week at the sheds all year round. Whatever resentment he felt towards Bradley was swallowed for Lily's sake; she knew this and tried her best to be fair to him. But Rob was not a talker. She could feel the currents reverberating deep in his body as she sat in the same room with him, but they were rarely expressed in words. I wish I knew what he wanted for his life, she often thought. Then I would give it to him tenfold.

"He's living out there in that shack with some tramp," Bradley pouted. "Why don't you do something about him?"

"With Sue Potts, you mean," Lily said, and Bradley went white, then silent.

But in the fall of Bradley's entry into Grade 11, Wee Sue eloped with the baker's son.

•

Paul Chambers was bright and ambitious and rich. Mrs. Tideman, throwing up her hands, declared him "a bad influence" capable of leading "the Virgin Mary astray". But vexed and puzzled as she was by the whole affair, Lily was inclined to believe he was a kindred spirit that Bradley, for reasons she could not yet define, had sought out and bonded himself to. His head is full of words he hasn't found things to pin them to, was one way she thought of the restless, tethered creature he kept inside him. If he stays here he'll suffocate; he'll tear his own brains out. She watched and hoped and kept putting money into the crockery jar under the bed. There's love inside him, too, she consoled herself when the rheumatism started up. Words are a way of feeling and Bradley's only got to get them aimed away from himself and towards something bigger and more wonderful *out there*.

In Paul Chambers he found a purpose for poetry and politics. Canada First was the frenzied ultra-nationalist club of writers and apprentice thinkers that was sweeping the salons and tearooms of the confederation. Chambers had founded a local chapter of the society, used his father's money to rent a club room at the St. Clair Inn every Tuesday and Thursday evenings, and gathered about him a group of like-minded believers. It was reported they smoked cigars and drank French wine. Most of the adherents were between seventeen and twenty-two years of age, youthful, idealistic, bent on literary careers and affecting (without achieving) the Byronic form of ascetic Hedonism. Only Bradley was successful in getting a poem accepted for publication in the society's national organ, *Rose-Belford's Canadian Monthly*. For a time the legendary Goldwyn Smith was their idol and mentor.

On rare weekends when Bradley came home during his senior year, Lily was made an honorary inductee and subjected to lengthy expositions of the Canada First manifesto. His eyes would flash with righteousness and confidence of youth, and there was in them a purity of purpose that frightened her, but also amazed and gratified her. Mostly, though, she was inundated. It seemed that people like her were representative of the provincialism, the homespun timidity that was keeping Canada from taking her place among the senior cultures of the world. They held back the natural development of a larger national spirit, a more capacious transcontinental loyalty and a more transcendent view of citizenhood. That, moreover, sabotaged the politically independent forms of literature and philosophy which were necessary to the growth of civility itself.

When Lily protested that she failed to see how she was at fault in these matters, he grew more vehement and repeated his arguments with an increasing number of polysyllabic words. And when she had the temerity to ask him how much of the Maritimes and Prairies and Rockies he had seen, or questioned the sincerity of 'St. John' Macdonald, he threw a tantrum then retreated into his morose/remorse routine. She soon realized she was not meant to comment or defend or reprove but to listen as the lava of his words hardened in the clear air around them. As she had once done long ago when he had been afraid to sing to the dark, she would be the trustee of his secret self. And so she came to accept in silence his elocutionary harangues until tears shattered and regrouped behind her eyes and he slumped exhausted on the table. Once, Rob was in the shed chopping wood during one of these gruelling sessions and came in at the finish. Bradley glowered and went out, slamming the door. Lily released her tears more in annoyance than hurt. She felt Rob watching her, axe in hand. She looked up at him for some gesture of help, comfort, understanding – anything. He flung the axe-blade into the floor and stomped out the back way.

•

When Bradley graduated *magna cum laude* in June of 1881, Lily was fussed over by Hazel, Betsy and Winnie until they could declare her 'a regular town lady'. Hazel contributed a fancy hat and Betsy a parasol, both of which Lily politely refused. But she did allow them to stitch and tuck the dress they'd created cloth until she was respectable enough to pass muster. She did not want her son to be embarrassed on the most important occasion of his life. Bradley seemed surprised and not altogether pleased by the bearing of his mother during the ceremony and the apparent ease with which she made polite conversation with her betters at the reception. "I bet she could joke with the old Queen and get away with it," Paul Chambers burbled. "Where *have* you been hiding your mother, you rascal?" Bradley was not amused, though he too was unable to take his eyes off his mother. When Counsellor Chambers himself asked her to dance, Bradley blushed from half a dozen contending emotions. Rob did not come.

The following week, just after the news of Hazel's decision to leave reached her, Lily was buoyed by word from Mr. Axelrod that Bradley's application to University College in Toronto had been accepted and that a modest scholarship of twenty-five dollars was proffered with the promise of much more down the line. That night as an early summer storm raged around them, Lily and Bradley sat down to map out the details of his future. He held the principal's letter in his hand as if it were an executioner's telegram. All the blush and bravado had drained from his face. In his trapped blue eyes Lily watched a boy's fear of the crooked dark, sly moonlight, bat shadows under eaves, the giant's fee-fi-fo-fum. She braced herself, but he would not say it.

"You must go," she said.

"I will, I will," he said, "but I can't. Not yet."

"When?"

"As soon as I have enough money. I was expecting a much bigger scholarship. Twenty-five dollars is an insult."

"How much do you need?"

"Paul says at least four hundred dollars over the four years."

"But I got two hundred an' fifty already in the crockery jar. An' the principal says you can expect more scholarship money by second year."

"What in hell does he know? He's never been east of London."

"Okay, then, tell me when."

"I need a year off. I've talked it over with Paul and his father. He has agreed to take me on as a clerk for a year; I'll earn enough money to put myself right through, and we won't have to be beholden to anyone."

"Is Paul going?"

Bradley paused before he answered, scanning his mother's face with anger and amazement. "No," he said almost inaudibly. "Paul's going to tour Europe for a year, and he'll register at University College after that."

•

When Violet left, Lily tried to carry on alone with her business. But the summer was exceptionally hot and she soon became exhausted. Rob found her one day in a faint, seated beside the mangle as if she were taking a snooze. She couldn't remember where she was or how she'd got there, and when Rob clasped her arm to raise her up, she screamed with pain. She spent three weeks in bed exorcising the fever. Rob was at her side much of the time. Bradley came on weekends.

"You don't need to do this, you know," Rob said in exasperation as she tottered back to the shed and surveyed the accumulated laundry Rob himself had not been able to clear away. "There's only yourself to take care of."

"I'll get a couple of the McLeod girls to help me. They need the money." And she did.

2

Frieda and Mitsy proved to be good workers and kind, grateful neighbours. But nothing could replace the loss of Violet and the others. Cap Whittle's fall and Honeyman's death made Lily feel much older and very tired. Rob lugged freight full-time and talked about adding some animals to 'his place' in the spring. Bradley worked diligently in the law office. He started to talk again with enthusiasm about university, Lily noted, after the arrival of a letter from Paul with a postmark from Rome or Paris. So she wrapped herself in sweaters and plunged each morning into the frost and singe of the laundry shed in winter. Frieda and Mitsy sang off-key in shy, tin-whistle voices, but sing they must, and laugh – as everyone around Lily eventually did.

Paul Chambers arrived home on the first of May for a month's visit before touring New York, Baltimore, Chicago and the far west by train. Bradley informed Lily that he and Paul were going to Toronto for a few days to inspect the campus and make preliminary arrangements for their entrance in the autumn. "We're going to stay at the Royal York, and see the sights," he said. His guilt at the twenty dollars he would spend drowned in his excitement. When he left, with an extra five dollars from Lily to buy some new clothes, she sat by herself and drank a slow cup of tea. It's going to happen at last, she allowed herself to think.

When he returned five days later with his tweed jacket torn and a bruised carnation in his lapel, Lily heard little talk of the university. The subject was Mr. Oscar Wilde, whom they had heard lecture twice at the Botanical Gardens and spied up close in the flesh during one of his 'progresses' up York Street.

Bradley's eyes blazed with something hard and radium and irreducible. They held Lily in their spell while he paced back and forth across the kitchen like a frantic Socrates, gesticulating and querulous.

"We've been wrong, Paul and me, all along. Not completely wrong, because we've been trying to expand our sense of the world, to cut all the ties that bind us here, and to reach for something larger and more wondrous and unknowable. Something beautiful and sacred, like the spirit of a nation, because it is *bigger* than the miserable little lives that combine to make it up—wretched lives that have no poetry in them unless they're broken and consumed by the *idea* of nationhood. Not blind, stupid patriotism, but the noble conception of a collective consciousness, an invisible Over-soul that moves and directs a country's destiny, just as Emerson has said. You know how passionately Paul and I have held to this notion, and how we've begun to put our poetry and schoolboy philosophy at its service. But then, to have heard Oscar Wilde speak to us as he did from that dais, and tell us in words I shall never forget – I shall take them to my grave – that we were only partly right, that Beauty, and the arts that create Her, are valuable *for their own sake*. There's a magic, universal truth that inspires beauty and goes beyond the spirit of nation-states, German philosophies and pious moralities. Don't you see, Ma, we were headed in the right direction. We were trying to learn more about the world out there, about the unseen powers that regulate its fate, ideals that would allow us to transcend our petty day-to-day lives, the forces of poetry and art and history. We just didn't go far enough. There are universal truths we can't begin to grasp until we've disentangled ourselves from politics and moralizing, and until we are ready to devote our lives to the pure contemplation of what is beautiful."

Lily picked up the carnation that had fallen on the table and brushed it partly back to life. "This was Mr. Wilde's?" she said.

Bradley nodded, then sat down, still shaking, and let Lily pin it back onto his lapel. "I'll stitch your jacket up before you leave."

Bradley caught her hand in flight. "You *do* see, Ma, why I've got to go to Toronto. There's so much I have to know. There's so much out there to see. There's so much buzzing around inside my head I think someday it will just explode and that'll be the end of me. I got to keep going, Ma. I got to find out what I am."

•

Rob was actually the one who found the note on the table and the smashed crockery jar beside the bed. Lily had been over at Peg's helping her nurse the babe through the whooping cough. Frieda, terrified by the look that Rob had given her, came dashing across the Lane to fetch her. Lily and Rob read the note:

Dear Ma and Rob:

I love you both more than my life. I'm sorry I have never been able to show it or prove it to you. But I must make the break now and for a while it must be complete. I've got to have a look at the world out there. When I do, I'll be back.

In the meantime, please don't try to find me. Take good care of her, Rob.

Bradley

3

Lily waited only a few weeks before she walked down to Hap Withers' cottage and told him he could have her house as well as the property. He moved the last of his numerous brood into the place and, being a widower and now alone, asked Lily if she would like the use of his two front rooms in return for a few housekeeping duties. Since they were already furnished, she brought nothing with her but a laundry bag full of clothes, a bookcase, a few trinkets and keepsakes the boys had given her as gifts over the years, and Sounder's pouch with Papa's Testament, the talisman, and the cameo pendant with her grandmother's face on it. She put the pouch under her bed and left it there.

Rob was good to her. He stopped by often for tea or supper with her and Hap Withers. He took her down to Sarnia on the trolley for supper at a fancy English tearoom on Christina Street. He urged her to come over and help with his garden. He was full of plans for expanding the operation. He fixed up the little barn so that it was comfortable in a rustic way, shingled and shuttered, with white-pine floorboards and a split-log table he had built. Nearby he had constructed a pigeon cote full of homers and tumblers, each with a name and pedigree. Below it, his pet angoras lived in luxurious innocence. He'd adopted a stray dog who slept with him at night and guarded the premises by day. He seemed content most of the time, but still she knew there was restlessness in him, inarticulate but deep. Only when he got a letter from his friend, Fred Potts, (who had run away with the circus and was now in charge of all the animals and had just married one of the bareback riders in Texas) did he let his regret and helplessness show. She left him alone, with his pigeons and his dog.

Lily went to Duckface Malloney at The Queen's, who agreed to let her do the hotel's wash in the new sheds he'd just added at the back. Her other customers she let go, though she decided that since she was now alone she ought to get out and around more. She was often seen during the next couple of years working in the households of Mrs. Durham, Mrs. Saltman, Mrs. Blakely and others – washing, ironing and most of all minding the children. Three mornings a week, she toiled at The Queen's where there was company if you wanted it and solitude if you needed it.

She went out to Rob's place two or three times a week during the growing seasons, working away in the garden with Rob at her side whenever he could be. She heard at The Queen's that he was seeing a young lady at Camlachie up the lakeshore a bit. On many a summer evening it would be almost dark when he got home, and he'd pitch in beside her, chopping away at the offending weeds. Still, despite their joint efforts, the garden seemed always in a state of imminent disorder. One day, when she came over in the afternoon while Rob was at the freight sheds, she was surprised to see a bedraggled young woman and her three children pulling up beets and tearing off tomatoes, trampling as much as they were retrieving. "Rob told us to come an' help ourselves, mum. Sorry if we give you a scare."

When she mentioned the event a few days later, Rob grunted. "Yeah, I said they could take what they wanted. Her husband died last winter up in Camlachie." He got up. "I gotta go out for a while. Don't go fussin' too much over the cabbage patch, eh." She didn't. She sat on the bench beside the cooing pigeons and let some of the realities of her life sweep over her. One was the fact, now irrefutable, that Rob had kept this miserable patch going for her sake alone. He had come to despise the sight of it.

•

Since Lily never went up to the Post Office for her mail, the postmaster decided it was his duty to deliver the letter to her door. She thanked him then stared at the florid, feminine calligraphy on the envelope. She could barely recognize her own name as she unwrapped the vellum paper.

Toronto, October 10, 1884

Dear Mrs. Marshall:

You do not know me. My name is Sarah Crawford. I am a good friend of Bradley, your son. I met him last year here in Toronto, and we shared the same boarding house. Before he went to Montreal, we belonged to the same literary circle. He was the most promising poet among us. A few months ago he wrote me from England, where he was staying with Paul Chambers, who was there for the summer break. He told me he was on the verge of something great and important in his life, and that he would write again soon. He never did. But I did get a letter from Paul Chambers. He too had decided to give up school and make his way in England. He never mentioned Bradley until the letter that came yesterday morning. Oh Mrs. Marshall, I cannot write this without weeping. Paul told me that Bradley took his own life a short while ago. He left a note begging Paul to tell no one, and just walked into the Thames. Paul arrived in time to see him go under and disappear forever. Paul does not know that I found your name and address in Bradley's room after he left for Montreal. I felt it my sad duty to write you immediately. I loved your son, Mrs. Marshall. I tried to save him. I hope that someday we shall meet.

Yours respectfully,
    Sarah Crawford

I tried too, Lily thought. And I loved him.

4

The second Riel Rebellion was in every way different from the first. Where it
had taken a ragtaggle, improvised militia almost three months to traverse the
northern wilderness by paddle and portage, the modern Canadian army
boarded trains all along the old Intercolonial line and embarked on a three-
day excursion to the Saskatchewan River courtesy of the Canadian Pacific
Railway Company. Militia or regulars, this was a pan-Canadian force of crack
troops under seasoned leadership. At the other end, the rebellious natives
and half-castes were better organized and armed than their forebears had
been along the Red and Assiniboine. But muskets and religious fanaticism
were no match for rifles, the drill of discipline and the new Gatling gun on
loan from the U.S. Army, who was anxious to test the latest 'improved feed'
model in legitimate combat. It performed splendidly, spitting out a record
twelve hundred bullets per minute and scaring crows for miles around. The
major battle at Batoche was won in less than a day. The hillsides where the
Métis had dug themselves into the earth were littered with their dead. The
log cabins behind them where their women and children crouched were
razed by the efficiency of 6-pounders, and the mad secessionists were silenced
for all time. It was a clear victory for mechanized order in the service of
benevolent civility. The integrity of the fledgling nation had been breeched,
and that breech was not healed with blood. Only seven citizen-soldiers died
in the cause. If this first great national military action was not on the same
scale as the American Civil War – with its million dead and million maimed –
it was nonetheless a landmark victory for the universal cause of nation-
making. It was also, in miniature, a curtain raiser for the horrors to come less
than thirty years later.

    There would have to be a little political fence-mending in the squalid
aftermath of the shooting, but nothing Sir John could not accomplish over
time. Few loyal citizens wished to see the publication of those letters sent
home by militiamen who, upon seeing the pathetic conditions their

adversaries had been forced to live in, decided they had more in common with the Métis than with Mr. Macdonald. Such naive emotional lapses are to be expected under duress, and a generous victor can afford to be forgiving. Louis Riel was hanged.

•

Rob surprised Lily in the pantry of The Queen's where she was fetching a jar of marmalade for the cook.

"Hap Withers said you'd be here," he said.

She saw the blue of his uniform, nothing else.

"I got to go, Ma."

"Yes", she said.

"I'm not Brad. I'll be back. I swear."

She had heard those very words before.

•

The night before the battle of Batoche, Lily dreamt she was the angel of innocence, floating over the battleground with the folds of her shift swept upward into wings as warm as a swan's throat. In the grassy shadows below here, scythed here and there by a quartering moon, lay the corpses of the seven who died. One by one she settled over them and the winnowing of her angel arms awoke in them some instinct sharper than death. Each in his turn rolled over, yawned, and opened his eyes abruptly. The seventh figure did not respond to the angel's wing breath no matter how fervently it was offered. Sadly, the kindly seraphim eased the body over into the moonlight. The face was dead. It was Robbie's.

5

And Granny—again, or still, in the sea-warmth of the night dream where all that was precious had to be remembered with its pristine pain intact or be claimed by oblivion. She was in the Lambton swamp once more and still called Lil, only eleven and very much alone. The river of light poured past her like some maddened tributary of the Styx. She was chilled to the marrow, drifting towards the sleep where death's welcome seemed a comfort and waking in the presence of the stranger from the lost south, the Shawnee, or Southener as he was known. When she reached to touch the warmth his kindness had brought, the robes over his ancient flesh weakened and thinned in the pre-dawn radiance around them. When she tried to speak in one of the ancient tongues she knew, his gentle face cringed and clenched, the lips crying no, no, before they began to fade, the face with them. Only the wrinkled outlines were preserved and the old eyes grew larger till they filled the smoky space with their sad brilliance. It must have been the eyes that spoke to her; there was no longer a mouth to utter its oracles. A hand, no bigger than a father's lovingly in his daughter's, floated in the immeasurable distance between them, and on its upturned palm, there glowed the jasper talisman. Scarlet as a hummingbird's throat, the voice shimmered in its carnal incandescence. She remembered the words in their alien consonance because all that was precious must be remembered, bruising and fresh. "This will bring you luck all your days, it will help you find a home here and in the hereafter. I received this magic stone on a sacred ground, long known by generation upon generation of tribes who have dwelt in these woods and waters and passed on. The days of its guardianship are almost over. There is little magic left in the forests and the streams, older now than our legends. The locomotives of the white man's soul are on their way, and when you have no more use for the stone's power, I ask that you return it to the sacred grove whence it came. You will know when you are standing on it because it resides beneath the protecting branches of a giant hickory on a knoll where the forest begins. When you look west and north, you will see, at the commencement of summer, the joining of the lake and the river, set on a line to the North Star we call the eye of Wendigo." The words of the Southener echoed and re-echoed in her long dream until daylight came to quench them...

39

1

It was bitterly cold when Lily left the hotel after her shift. Normally, the fresh December wind, sweeping across the open water of the lake and slashing at the village, would have blown her north-eastward towards the shacks along the Lane. Instead, she walked west towards the river. There was no hurry in her walking, no evident purpose. The river was frozen tight, its rage arrested. Locomotives languished on sidings, their armour plate complaining in the cold. One or two lamps glowed feebly in the dockside hotel to her left. Nor was her walking aimless, though she soon left the road that wound its way to the freight sheds and seemed to drift into the frozen verges of the marsh. It was as if she were walking towards some end about to reveal itself ahead of her, or that lay curled inside her near the heart ready to declaim its desires when this ritual walking was complete.

She felt no windburn on her face, her exposed throat, her ungloved hands. Her eyes blurred in the keen chill of the night air, but she had no difficulty seeing what she had to see. Her heart pumped in her chest like a featherless bird beating its bony wings against invisible ramparts of ice. But she felt no emotion flow from its exertion. It was connected only to her legs and to its own mechanical instincts. The heart that had once stored her feelings and stoked them out of memory on command was now dead. Numbed then drained, then irreconcilably dead. Considering what had happened to her over these last months, these last years, the death of feeling was no surprise. Only so much could be borne, lived through, and accommodated to the adjusting heart. To bear more after such pain and loss was not to expand the borders of her humanity, but to deny any of its elements was essential, unshakeable, or rooted in necessities like love and steadfastness. *I will not live because my flesh yearns to continue, and this flap of muscle in my chest convulses in its own selfishness. I am more than flesh and gulping blood. I can feel the pain everywhere, I can hear it running backwards all the way to my youth, my childhood, the moment of birth.*

What was surprising was that she had carried on at all. She knew her daily trek to The Queen's to repeat the labours of a thousand days was not the automatic motions of a body not knowing how to do anything different nor the trust of a numbed will in the therapy of familiar routine. 'Busy hands and the seasons will mend the fractured heart' was the village cliché. Well, she had lived enough to know the worth of such homilies. The next day, after the dreadful news about Robbie had been confirmed, she arrived for work on time. It was on the same day that she began this nightly ritual of wandering the village paths and byways in search of something, lost or promised.

Tonight there was more urgency. She felt it somewhere between her frost-bitten cheeks and the haemorrhaging of her heart. She did not notice the snow begin to fall just as the wind died. She failed to hear the shale ice crumble underfoot. The dark dissolved before her. The air was lit by snow, by moving and motionless bits of the universe, by the arctic friction at the heart of the snow's design. Uninvited, individual flakes touched her cheeks without regret, and made their own tears. Something incorruptible was melting, gaining radiance.

For a moment the snow lifted and the night sprang back. She was lost – in the marshlands that lay on the peninsula between the river and the lake. She was not frightened. She felt nothing but a vague edge of urgency. Set out against the shadowy blur of houses and gardens on the rise where the village began, she saw the outline of a fantastic, multi-limbed figure stretched upward through the veil of snow, the etch of its gesture between yearning and defiance. The snow closed in again. Her walking recommenced. She was moving towards the figure no longer visible. She touched its shadow falling through a white daze and heard its breath as she neared. She felt encompassed, kindled, amnesiac, at home. Her back rested against its rooted bole. At last, she saw the snow as it was: dancing its intricate, hopscotch, hornpipe fling for her eyes only. *This is it. The reason.* She sat down and let her eyes close themselves. She let the last magic take her.

•

"You give us quite a scare," Malloney said. He looked uncomfortable, not certain whether to sit on the captain's chair that could barely contain his bulk or to stand above her with no place to plant his hands. They were alone, in his room at the right front of the hotel. She cleaned it twice a week.

"It's lucky for us all," he said, glancing around, "we was havin' our Oddfellows' meetin' down there tonight."

She coughed, and he sprang forward with a cup of hot tea in his grip. She saw that it was half consumed.

"You'll need some more of this," he said, then looked away.

She was crying.

Poor Duckface, she thought. That is what everyone called Kevin P. Malloney, some to his face, others out of earshot. The epithet was descriptive of his large, fleshly face that was pushed inward along the centre, resembling a ruffled duck's tail, as if his mother, in shock or despair, had struck her infant with an angle iron. As a result, his beady eyes had been squeezed closer together and his mouth, longing to be spacious, pursed and dilated. It was difficult for him to convey emotion, the range of overt expression being limited from the outset. Most people were content to assume and accept that he was, as his face forewarned the world, a saturnine, obtuse, uncaring sloth of a man. It was reported that his Irish eyes only danced to the jig of a cash register.

She saw that her hands were shaking as she sipped at the tea.

"Almost froze to death, you did," Malloney said. He drew one of the shawls about her shoulders with a shy hand. "I saw this bunch of clothin' through the snow, scrunched under that big tree back of the Hall, and I says to old Redmond, I think somebody's fallen over, sick or somethin'. Just your imagination, he says. But I goes over anyways. Thank the Lord."

She felt nothing but the fierce scald – on her tongue, on her cheeks – and a mocking pulse somewhere below her throat. Malloney tried to catch the cup before it toppled off the bed but he missed, burnt his finger, and stifled a curse. The mutant angles of his face grimaced inward to corral the giant's breath behind it. "Owww," he squeaked, and, pitched sideways by the congested pressure. He crushed the china cup.

She giggled. My word, she thought, I'm alive.

•

"Nobody's got more right than you to think about endin' it all. There comes a time when everybody, churchgoer or not, thinks about it. Few people in this town have gone through what you have: your husband, your kids, not to speak of poor ol' Sophie goin' up in –". Malloney was clearing away the supper plate he'd brought into her. It appeared to her that he was intent on preserving his reputation for toughness. He was aware that *she* had no reputation worth saving. She had never heard him string so many sentences together before, but it didn't surprise her in the least. She'd lived long enough to know that even the most taciturn being had inside him whole pages and chapters of the unspoken: lamentations, indictments, confessions, recantations, fervent manifestoes, poems of the beleaguered heart. She had heard them all.

"What you need most is to get out of here, away from this place. You been here too long. You've had too much grief. There's ghosts on every street. You been in most of the houses in this dump, so you can't shut out what you know they're sayin', even now. Every one of them cheered when Riel was strung up, you could hear them on the docks. Don't matter to them what the Rebellion did to you an' Rob."

Later, when it was dark in the room, he returned. He lit the small lamp by the bed. His face was scavenged by shadow and lurid light, but the eyes shone out at her, their message clear and unmistakable. Don't do this to me, she shouted, but his was the only voice in the room.

"You've got no hold here anymore," he said. "No kin, no land. What you had is all gone. Wiped clean. No reason to stay. You've got to start fresh. You ain't fifty years old yet. You're as healthy as a yearling."

Stop, please.

"I got a friend in Sarnia, works on the railroad there. They need a janitor, a woman. I can arrange for you to have the job, right away. About two blocks from the station there's a boarding house run by the Widow Jarvis, a former lady friend of mine. She'll take you in. You'll be a long, long ways from this place," he said, "from this, this *shit*."

"Could I have more tea," she said.

2

Malloney had been right about the job. She was taken on immediately. Her duties were simple, repetitive and comfortably numbing. She felt no twinge of irony or resentment at being, after all these years, an employee of the Grand Trunk Western. She was employed. She walked two blocks to a boarding house made up with ferns, doilies, lace curtains, carpets and comforters to resemble a home. She ate, tolerated the chit chat of the resident ladies, slept without dreaming, walked to work again. The only change in routine occurred when she switched on alternate weeks from day shift to afternoons when she worked from four till midnight. The tasks were much the same. She assisted the male janitors in scrubbing and dusting the waiting room of the huge, refurbished station. There were six passenger trains a day between Chicago and Toronto and dozens of local and highball freights. She kept the ladies' toilets clean by herself. On the afternoon shift, at seven o'clock, she walked down the platform and across the yard to the new bunkhouse complex where she worked alone for an hour or so, washing dishes and tidying up. Twice a week (she worked six days with Sundays off) she stayed longer, moving to the attached laundry room where she 'did' the dirty sheets and pillowcases accumulated from the men's bunks. In the damp steam chill of that room, arms up to elbow in boiling water, hands like flails against the washboard, punching into resistant shape these cotton sheets, she felt bone and body take full possession of her being. Why did I fight it so long...

•

The bunkhouse was relatively new and comfortable, having been built only two years previously, following the merger of the Grand Trunk and the Great Western. Being a woman, Lily was not allowed into the bunk rooms, which formed a separate section of the complex. She was expected to be at ease in the kitchen and laundry room, set on the side of the building opposite the bunks. Between these exclusively male and female demesnes lay the sprawling comfort of the 'parlour', replete with tables and chairs (for eating, poker play, solitaire) and several chesterfield suites of chewed leather (for snoozing, contending, yarn spinning). Its hallmark was tobacco smoke and the afterbite of spittoons. As a woman, she was allowed in to clear the tables of dishes, to empty ashtrays, flush out cuspidors, and when no one was present, scrub out a week's soil and smudge.

The bunkhouse was frequented by engineers, brakemen and conductors whose homes, when they had any, were not in Sarnia. Since most of the passenger and freight trains plied between Sarnia and Toronto, these men were likely to be from the capital city, using the new facility to 'lay over' until they were due to make a return run, usually the next day. Railroaders from Sarnia likewise 'lay over' in Toronto. Many of them, bachelors or *de facto* bachelors, lived in boarding houses near the station here (or in Point Edward), where they waited to be called. She had on occasion been asked to sweep out the Yard Office, where she had seen the huge call boards listing the names of the running crews and yard gangs. When a train was 'made up' and ready to go, elfin messengers would scatter from here across the south end of the city to 'call' the men to their labour. Sometimes, of course, they had only to dash to the bunkhouse or, as one of the regulars dubbed it, 'Palaver Palace'. Some of the grizzled veterans among the engineers and conductors had routine schedules. Most of the running crew led semi-nomadic lives with sudden wake-ups, cold breakfasts, chilling dashes to overheated cabooses or blazing furnace rooms where even the iron stanchions froze as the arctic night whistled by.

"I just ignore 'em. I barge right in there; after all's said, I got my work to do," Big Meg had explained to her. "Most of them's gentlemen, long as you ignore their cussin', which they can't help, and don't want to help when it comes right down to it." She chortled, and her forearms shook. "If you don't barge right in there, you'll never get the chores done." She winked. "Besides, they tell a juicy story or two."

But she did not take Big Meg's advice. She figured out when the peak periods of use occurred and when the parlour would be empty or occupied by a solitary derelict snoozing away a hangover or sulking with a cigar in a far corner. During the latter times she whisked in and out – tiny, unnoted, anonymous. In the kitchen, with its own stove and gingham curtains and lamplight on the copper pans, she felt able to breathe again. Because the parlour was separated from the kitchen only by a heavy velvet curtain (the original door having been kicked in by a drunken fireman under the misapprehension that his young wife lay thrashing behind it with her secret lover) she could hardly help but hear the muffled grit of railroader talk and its blend of scuttlebutt and tall tale. She could rattle the dishes in their warm suds or hum too loud for comfort, but not forever. Whenever there were three or more men in there, they gabbed between hands at poker, slumped on smoky leather, or floated on a whiskey edge.

One voice in particular insisted on separating itself from the others, not because it was loud (they were all loud) or colloquial (earthiness of speech was endemic). There was something in it that was at once hearty, spare, generous, withholding. When this one spun a yarn, the room would be restless at first as some of the uninitiates, or the odd interloper would spar with the teller. These exchanges gave way to rapt attention as the voice took control and the story itself grew larger and grander (though many had told it before) and the laughter at the end not quite as predictable. She heard him laugh too – at the story, at the teller, at the trapped parishioners. His guffaw would have embarrassed a bull moose.

"You remember the Guffer? Stuffy McGuffin we called him when he first come brakin' on the late-great Western. 'Course the son of a bitch was near fifty even then. Married the leanest of the superintendent's three daughters. Hell of a way to break into railroadin." A pause for laughter. "She turned out to be a bit too tart for him to ever call her sweetheart, but he always claimed if he caught her downwind on a Saturday night, she give him more bumps an' thrills than a gravel train to Cayuga. Mind you, these trips didn't happen too often, least not as often as Guffer would've liked. The poor bugger got to draggin' his caboose into every 'waterin' trough' between Trenton and Ing-arse-hole. Drinkin' was harmless as long as he was brakin', and even when he fell into stokin', it wasn't too bad. Though you all remember the story, denied by everybody but the Guffer himself, about him pissin' his pants in the cab of 1546 on the old Barrie run in the middle of February an' the air cold enough to crack walnuts an' other precious jewels. And' old Fartsy Farmer cursin' beside him an' tryin' to see through the snow comin' as thick as the Governor-General's undies. 'Jesus McJesus, you stupid son of a bitch, do somethin' about that stink or I'll pitch you onto the first siding I can see.' 'Course, it's the ice formin' round his balls that's interestin' Guffer the most. So, driven by the thought of no more gravel runs to Cayuga, he yanks open the firebox door, drops his pants, turns round, and *sits down*."

"Horseshit!"

Gales of horse laughter.

"I'm only repeatin' what I know to be the gospel truth. The Guffer soft boiled his eggs so beautifully that night near Barrie, he went straight home and at the tender age of fifty-nine started to assemble his own way freight. It's true. The son of a bitch had five kids before he retired."

Skeptical, gelding laughter.

"I thought you was gonna tell us a new one, you prevaricatin' bastard!" Hoots, steam whistles, derisive applause.

"Where was I? Ah, yes. I got the Guffer up to –"

"Up to his arse in bullshit!"

"– Up to his last fateful year of the Festerin' Western. To save a dyin' enterprise, they promoted the old fart to engineer. Christ, he was like a kid with a hay rake. An' they give him one of the new 2160's, runnin' highballs between here and Toronto. One day in the middle of July, he gets all tanked up on his stopover in London. He's so pissed his eyes are settin' fire to the tablecloth, an' he churns up old '62 an' starts to let her loose around Mandaumin, an' by this time he's got her up to eighty miles an hour an' climbin'. His fireman's hanging onto the tender for dear life and a high wailin' sound can be heard from the caboose a hundred yards behind. But the Guffer he's laughin' an' singin' away like one of them Eye-talian bassoes with a pinched prick, an' suddenly they're five minutes outside Sarnia Yard. Wouldn't you know, on the main-line track of this here station was sittin' the doodlebug from Stratford waitin' to take on passengers. The platform was jammed with people. At first they was all intent on gettin' their tickets an' baggage in order. Then they heard this god-forsaken screech-a-comin' at them from the east an' their hearts froze. It was the Guffer's song ridin' along in front of old '62, now doin' ninety-five miles an hour an' scatterin' car men, oilers, yard crew an' jiggers in all directions. Mercifully, the Guffer brought her untouched an' unscathed – there wasn't a mark on him – clean through to the station. Some say he was pullin' on the throttle 'cause he thought it was the brake, but we'll never know. What we do know is that the engineer, fireman an' conductor on the doodlebug jumped left an' right an' that the Guffer stopped singin' about two seconds before the collision."

"To take breath, relight a pipe?

"As luck would have it –"

Raucous response, checked only by the anticipation of something further.

"As luck would have it, the doodlebug was not bashed to one side or the other – which would have resulted in the grisly deaths of numerous bystanders or the sudden slaughter of a corral full of steers. She was knocked

straight an' clean ahead. She popped up into the air an' did a series of back
flips down the main line as tidy as a tumbler across a mat. About a hundred
yards from the end of line near the old dock, it hopped sideways an' settled
into an alfalfa field. Which was a good thing, too, 'cause Guffer an' number
62 was followin' it real close, rippin' up track all the way but stickin' to its
line like a trouper. Then, boom, she hits the block an' flicks it aside like a flea
on your collar, an'*n she went.*"

A gulf of speechlessness. "In the river?"

"Christ no, into the river *bank*, an' deflectin' downward so she starts to
plough forward, an' the stoker an' crew jump just before she disappears
completely into the ground, tossin' back whole gopher towns of dirt risin' up
like a huge sandstorm that covers all Sarnia. Some of the passengers on the
platform think its Armageddon. The last we ever saw of old '62 was the
thrashin' of the caboose before she was sucked underground."

"And the Guffer?"

"Oh, *him*. Why, he come up face first on the other side of the River,
smilin' and fartin' and assumin' he was in paradise. Yessir, he done the Great
Western a genuine favour. He gouged a *tunnel* straight under the St. Clair
from the Dominion of Canada to the U.S. of A. Now all we gotta do is figure
out how to get the son of a bitchin' *train* out of the hole!"

Uproarious approbation. A spell had been wound up, held, and released.
She heard the conversation break up into its customary blurred elements.
The dishes had got themselves washed and dried. From the shuffling behind
her she knew the men were about to leave. She edged over to the curtained
doorway, drew the velvet apart, and watched. They were every shape, size
and age. They lumbered, sauntered, hurried, only their faces exposed above
mackinaws and denim as they turned from the cozy brotherhood of their
room to the blizzard outside.

She could not fit the voice to a body.

•

Most of the times they played cards – poker – and the yarn spinning was
given over to sporadic jokes and ritual teasing. Even then, though less often,
that grained, seasoned voice prevailed. No amount of compulsory bluff and
blarney could completely disguise the grit of authenticity at the core of it.

"Hear the one about the brewer who couldn't swim?"

"Are you in or out?"

"In."

"What'd he do, Luce?"

"Fell into a vat of his own beer. Raise you two."

"See ya'. Did he drown or what?"

"Not right away. He had to crawl out twice an' take a piss."

Belly laugh as big as moose country.

"Jesus Murphy, but who laughs louder at his own shit?"

"C'mon Luce, stop laughin' an tell us what ya' got."

"Three aces. Sorry."

"You son of a bitch!"

All the coins seesawed in one direction.

•

When they were all gone, clumping into the snowy dark, she waited fifteen minutes then entered the parlour to clean up. She emptied the ashtrays into a can and was brushing the crumbs off the table when she noticed one of the overstuffed chairs at the back was occupied. A coal-oil lamp, singed and smoking, threw a shadowed light across the face turned towards the door. A smouldering briar pipe sat discarded on the low table beside the chair. Near it, as if flung aside in the same gesture, laid a puffed, weary hand. At the sound of falling glass, the face swung numbly towards her, failed to focus on the source of irritation and swung back.

In that instant she knew who it was. She had an impression of size – of bulk and crag and underpracticed muscle – and a rumpled dignity of dress and demeanour. But it was only the face that registered. The grooved laugh lines sagged and fleshed around the mouth and the coal-black eyes used to dancing for reasons the heart behind them kept to itself. They slackened in their oversize sockets like exhausted gavottes. They saw nothing.

She fought to regain her breath, turning to go.

"Don't, please. You're not disturbin' me."

It was him. She left.

•

The tenor of the talk in the parlour of the Widow Jarvis had shifted several quarters as December of 1885 drew to a close.

"Herbert insists I go straight to Walker's an' order up the fanciest dress in the store."

"It's only New Years once a year," said the Widow generously.

"And it is the biggest ball in town, sponsored by the railroad an' all."

"How'd you come by that invitation again?" Miss Spence asked.

"All the veterans was given one, as is only right considerin'. Herbert risked his life for all of us."

"Usually only the bigwigs an' some railroad people's invited," said Miss Spence in awe.

"I don't suppose anybody knows this, but my dear Harold was a fightin' man, a grenadier he was. An' left me a widow almost twenty-two years ago, battlin' them nigger people over there somewhere near Egypt."

They did know.

"Niggers, Indians, Frenchies, what's the difference?" asked Miss Spence. Her eyes stayed pinned to the last row of Senior Book Four. "Can't stop 'em from fightin', they love it. It's born in them."

"Poor Harold."

•

She was doing the laundry, well away from the boisterous revels in the parlour. It was snowing again and the heat from the kitchen stove could not cut the damp cold that hung everywhere, stiffening the sheets and forcing her to fetch fresh pails of boiling water. Twice she scalded her left wrist. The sudden steam rushed over her face with its illusory warmth, and soaked her hair. She thrashed the scrub board to beat the blood to the surface of her skin and back again to the chill in her leg bones. The sheets froze solid against the clothes horse like opaque window glass. The rollers nipped her right forefinger, but she didn't feel the pain. Till later.

Long after she heard them clatter out of doors, she slipped back into the kitchen, pulled a stool in front of the stove and sat there motionless, without thought, without the compunction to commit a single redemptive act. Her tresses thawed, tattered, dripped. The fire swallowed its lone sound.

"Excuse me, ma'am."

She turned around.

"Pardon me for interruptin', but I assumed you was finished your work."

She felt her hand in her hair.

"My name's Burgher. Lucien Burgher. The fellas call me Luce." His smile carried his mouth, his eyes and some further part of him with it.

She felt beads of sweat in the tiny hollow of her throat.

"Of course my mother wouldn't approve. She prefers Lucien. I tell them that, but they don't pay no attention to me. No respect."

"I thought you had –" she began.

"I waited for you," he laughed, flashing his grin full upon her then dropping his glance for a moment.

She watched his hands. They seemed shy but strong, as if they could commandeer the world. One of them reached into the pocket of his engineer's tunic.

"Would you like to dance?" he said.

She backed up a step, the heat surging behind her.

"What I mean is, could I have the pleasure of escorting you to the New Year's dance?"

She let his eyes, at last, have hers.

"I can't tell you exactly how I come by it, but this here's an official invitation to the Grand Trunk Ball tomorrow night. I've tried on occasion, but I don't dance too good by myself."

She reached out with her left hand, exposing the scalded wrist, now blistering painfully. Confused, he pushed the white card into it.

"What's your name," he asked gently.

She hesitated for a long moment, the invitation poised between them. "Cora," she replied."

It was at the very moment of his asking that she discovered what it was she had been trying to quit forever. A picture had sprung into her mind. She lay in Southener's arms and the Pottawatomie tom-toms sounded through the smoke as the girl named White Blossom was transformed, by the dance of her elders and the dance inside her, into her new being: Seed of the Snow Apple. The seed core. *Cora*. Beginning again.

"Cora," he repeated. "Beautiful name. An old and sacred name. And?"

"Does a last name matter?"

"Not to me," he grinned. "You'll go then?"

She nodded.

PART TWO

Cora

40

By mid-April there was barely a trace of snow to be found in the village. The sun thawed, stirred, reminisced with the earth. In the memorable warmth of the afternoons, workmen of every shape and ilk came to help with the making of Granny Coote's cottage: a mason, a joiner, a sawyer, several carpenters, a lather and plasterer, two roofers, assorted painters and paperers, a clandestine electrician, a legitimate plumber, and countless helpers, apprentices, and sidewalk foremen. Each one, novice or seasoned hand, was watched over by the still figure outlined in the front window of the miserable shack across the street. A pale, disinterested ghost looking for new ground to haunt. Not once did she wave, nod, or otherwise break her silent superintendence.

The workmen might have been relieved to learn that the supervising wraith behind the glass did not spend all her watching time observing their amateur, though enthusiastic, performance. She never left her post, but on most days, shortly after noon, she would cast an eye up or down the street to catch the stride of the young men en route to the site and trace its advance until a moment of recognition occurred. Ah, that's young Mike, Maggie Hare's lad—Bunny, they used to call him. He'd come running home bawling and quivering with hurt, too tiny to fight back, to cast off the name that would dog him all his days. But I would always put down my mop and make sure Maggie was out of earshot. I would let him fling his eight-year-old arms around me and butt me in the stomach as hard as he wanted till he'd slow down real gradual and just hug me. I'd reach into my apron, as if I'd thought of something special, and pull out a peppermint – like a prize for a clever, strong boy who would never again let the bullies call him Bunny. He doesn't remember that anymore. It was a long time ago and she and Maggie did have a falling out shortly after. She had been, after all, a lifelong Alleywoman. By the time Granny looked up from such thoughts, the studding for a bedroom wall or a new doorway would have mysteriously come into being across the street. For Sunny's sake, she did try to watch, but it was hard.

There's Slowboat Saunders, Eliza's youngest. She was too old to have any more and she paid for it. Slowboat could drive a nail through his thumb and then wonder why he couldn't pick his nose. Poor dear soul.

I've wiped that nose many a time after Alf got his leg crushed in a coal-tender's bogies and Eliza went back to school teaching. He waves at me and grins, but I'm sure he can't connect what he sees here behind glass with those days before Arthur, before Eddie, before the catastrophes of age. Even the Army wouldn't take Slowboat – flat feet, they said. To her surprise, the last of the roof boards had already been put in place. She could no longer see inside. I didn't even hear the hammering, she thought.

Moments later, she saw Sunny Denfield climb down from the roof, stand with his arm on Slowboat's shoulder, then detach himself and walk across the street towards her gate.

•

"I guess you remember the day when my father came lookin' for me. He got the police out by tellin' them I was under eighteen an' pullin' some strings in the government. They expected that bein' a young lad accustomed to money and pleasure, I would run off to the fleshpots of Montreal or Detroit. It never occurred to them that I might be runnin' *away* from those very things. To be honest, I didn't know what I was doin' except findin' some room to breathe an' think an' sort out my life. I suppose if I'd had a mother, I'd have stayed away just long enough to give them all a good scare, but I didn't. To this day I haven't a clue as to who tipped off my father that I might be livin' in some little dump of a railroad town called Point Edward. Probably one of the big shots stayin' at The Queen's where I had that room near the back annex. Unfortunately, I'm the spittin' image of my father. Anyway, as you'll recall, it was only a month after I'd settled in at the sheds – in September of 'ought-one – when he comes scoutin' after his lost son." He dunked one of Mrs. Carpenter's cookies in his tea. "The whole village knew somethin' was afoot," he laughed.

Granny had written on her slate. She held it up: 'We all heard him'.

"So did everyone in Port Huron and Sarnia. Imagine, comin' to fetch a runaway back home in a horseless carriage, firin' off sparks an' fartin' bedlam in every direction, deafenin' dogs an' spookin' horses an' givin' old Mrs. Farrow a case of the hiccups she claimed took her ten years to get over."

The sun now shone through the west window over the sink. She felt its warmth around her ankles. Soon, in her garden, it would be tempting bulb and tuber.

"He left it sittin' in front of The Queen's, surrounded by townsfolk, an' walked by himself across the fields towards our work gang. We were cuttin' ragweed or somethin', between boats, with our shirts stripped off showin' our muscles an' tan to the whole world. He didn't know I saw him, but he stood near a little hawthorn, watchin' us work an' horse around as we always did. By that time I was feelin' like one of the gang, with all my blisters toughened up, an' real *earned*money in my pocket. He never said a word, and I never let on I saw him. He just turned an' walked away. We heard the poppin' and jumpin' of the automobile all the way across the marsh, and I remember one of the fellas sayin': 'Christ, it's like ridin' a Gatling Gun!'"

Arthur built that little cupboard beside the sink, she was thinking. He let Eddie cut out the scrolls and curlicues with his coping saw. He was so patient, Arthur, with his hands on the piano. We were always going to fix up the outside, but there was never enough money and the property was not ours. But the inside was always cozy and full of music, and the nimbleness of Arthur's fingers never did transfer from piano hammers to a carpenter's, though he could never figure out why, staring up at her for absolution.

"You would have liked my Aunt Grace, Cora," Sunny was saying. "I never could understand how she came to marry such a stuffed shirt as my Uncle Bramwell. You couldn't picture two more opposite types. She cared nothing for money or fancy things. She loved people. Especially children, an' she regretted bein' able to have but one child. She almost died havin' Ruth-Anne, I was told. I'm hopin' you'll get a chance to meet Ruth-Anne soon. I've been tryin' to help her with her pursuit of her family tree. She insists her mother had relatives livin' in this county and is threatenin' to come down here an' prove it to herself. I hope she does. You'll like her. She's got her mother's spunk."

Granny smiled as best she could. She wrote a word on her slate. 'When?'

"Two weeks," he said. "The plaster an' paint won't take long. It's gonna look real nice, Cora. Just the way you an' me sketched it out. We'd like you to move in by the first of May. The monument man's comin' from London about then. We're plannin' a little ceremony for you. I know you don't approve but it's to make the council feel good about it all, if you wouldn't mind. That won't be till later because the lawyers are still sortin' out the legal stuff. But I promise you, you'll have a *bona fide*deed in your hand by June. You'll own that piece of land an' that cottage outright. Nobody'll ever be able to take it away from you. It's the least we owe you."

She was listening and not listening. She got up and walked to the west window. She looked out over her dozing gardens. Sunny Denfield was at her side. "I'm sorry," he said, his voice breaking. Her hand on his wrist said, *I know.*

A stranger, walking by, might have caught them in their window – glazed by a westering glow – and mistaken them for mother and son.

41

1

The Grand Trunk Ball was the social event of the winter season. For twenty years – years marked by unparalleled human progress (one or two depressions and the odd insurrection notwithstanding) – the affair had been held in the largest, most resplendent ballroom of western Ontario, the G.T.R. Station Hotel on the docks of Point Edward. Burned to the ground by revisionist forces of nature in 1871, it had been immediately resurrected, more capacious and vainglorious than ever. Three dozen Venetian chandeliers were a testament to the depth and longing of the mercantilist fancy that confected them. Though the edifice herself was imperceptibly aging, about to be sacrificed to such commercial inevitabilities as mergers and corporate restructuring, she had fitted herself out for this annual ceremonial with no intimation that the cracks at the edges of her smile might one day be irremediable. Whether by coincidence or design, the last evening of 1885 – a year which had seen the young nation riven by dissent, racial antagonism and rebellion – turned out to be clear, crisp and star spangled.

Gliding along in their railroad-provided open sleighs, the celebrants could lean back against their nuzzling furs and behold the earth commanded by the night sky, so dark and eons deep that the stars appeared as tiny semaphores chilled forever in bas-relief. Around the carollers, the snow had flattened and blanched an unresisting landscape. The black, unseamed horizon folded over the verges of their little world, and it seemed as if they were afloat on a bone-white saucer. When their Clydes or Percherons puffed towards the confluence of river and lake, the grand old dowager loomed ahead like a bejewelled atoll, garish and preposterous against the asperity of those panarctic constellations. Unperturbed, an ambidextrous footman, mustered in gold and vermillion, hopped down before the evergreen welcome arch and raised a dainty mitt to the first descending lady. The festivities were underway.

•

The orchestra had been imported all the way from London. It remembered the fading courtly dances – gavotte, lancers, galop – and paid them due respect. Under the steadfast blaze of the chandeliers, the sets and squares whirled to their ancient, magic geometry. Speed, intricacy, the levitation of brass and fiddle, all conspired to project the illusion of momentary anonymity. But it was a modern age and the sophisticates from Middlesex could bedazzle the country folk with waltz, polka, schottische, and once, jovially, they unleashed an exotic fandango. Even the most jaded romantic could borrow the energy of the sweeping violins, the tympanis, the peremptory surge of coronet and horn, and sail into the sweet amnesia of the music.

The performance was non-stop. Sets broke apart but quickly reconfigured; couples clung or recomposed. Though the critical complement was never threatened, individual participants would slip away to the north section, where uniformed waiters filled crystal goblets with champagne chilled in snow. At the south end stood the powder rooms and several improvised salons where a gentleman could find relief and a reassuring cigar. But the music drew them back, out of themselves and the petty gravitation of their lives.

•

At five minutes to midnight, the orchestra ceased on a pre-arranged downbeat and the indefatigable conductor stepped aside. The dais was occupied by three distinguished guests: the Honourable Halpenny Peebles, deputy premier of the province, on loan for the occasion; Mr. Margison Dilworth, first vice-president of the Grand Trunk Western (who invited himself); and Mr. Stanley R. 'Cap' Dowling, reeve of the village since its incorporation back in 1878, present by divine right. This trio of luminaries, further distinguished by a pair of arc lights, proceeded to lead the assembly now formed into a huge circle of interlocked hands in a singing of Auld Lang Syne. There was much toasting, and as soon as the choir directors could be urged off stage, more dancing.

•

Lucien and Cora danced. They sipped champagne and anticipated dancing. During the eventful evening, they exchanged no conversation other than the requisite formalities of greeting, thanksgiving and good manners. On the sleigh ride from town (they met at the Sarnia depot), they clasped furred appendages, warmed a common shoulder, and let the stars look at them with their loveliness. Whatever pretence each had chosen for this extraordinary courting, it was accorded the unquestioned blessing of the other. No single note jarred the harmony of their shared narrative. They danced, sometimes alone and sometimes together, each happy to confer upon the other the prize of simple presence, however fleeting. In the dance, with all motion foreordained, they were released to their own fictions.

Lucien laughed and glided and marshalled his companion with large, commodious gestures, driven it seemed by some inward, transparent, uncalculating reservoir of locomotion. Cora smiled, choreographed her partner's laughter, and curtsied to the universe in three-quarter time. She danced as if the world cared, or mattered. She believed, for now, in the eyes that beheld her as if she had just been born.

•

A caress of powdered snow greeted them as they stepped outside. Still, there were no clouds and the stars glittered overhead. It was blissfully cold.

"I didn't tell you," Lucien said as he helped her onto the back of the sleigh, "but I been livin' here in Sarnia for almost a month."

"You left Toronto?"

He hopped aboard. "Uh huh. I hang around the bunkhouse, of course, for obvious reasons."

She smiled and let him wrap his heavy arm about her. She snuggled in, not thinking of any moment before here, content with this.

"I been livin' down by the River. On Front Street." He squeezed against her, testing. "At the St. Clair." He waited for some part of her body to reply. Then, softly so as not to disturb the sleepy revellers on either side of them, he said: "I got a suite. Two rooms."

2

"I started watchin' you the second I spotted you in the waiting room. I found out from Big Meg when you was due to work in the bunkhouse." He poured her a tumbler of champagne from a bottle that had been cooling on the window ledge, catching her eye so she could nod to tell him when to stop.

"There wasn't much to see," she said. She took the glass, tipped it in his direction, and sat on the edge of the settee in the 'sitting area'. He stood – tie askew, shirt adrift – leaning on a balky commode.

"That depends on how experienced an eye is lookin'," he said. "An' this pair's seen plenty. I'm no yearling, you know." He patted his paunch reverentially. "You tried to fool me, I suspect, with those aprons an' bandanas an' steam-bath hairdos. You might've tricked a few of the greenhorns 'round the Yard, but not a veteran like me. I know beauty when I see it."

"And I know blarney when I hear it," she said, glancing past him to the other room, the wink of a brass bed visible.

"But you love it just the same?" His face, flushed from cold and drink, lit up in a broad grin. Only the creases there and the bitumous glow behind the dancing eyes belied the boyishness of the attempt. Somehow, unlike most men of his vintage and temperament, he did not look ridiculous when he allowed his high spirits to overwhelm his fatigued, resisting flesh. Always, there remained a residue of dignity.

"I used to," she replied. "Quite a long time ago."

His face teetered on the verge of collapse, then brightened: "You weren't thinkin' of long ago tonight."

"I don't think either of us was," she said, holding out her glass as he refilled it.

"Happy New Year," he said.

"So you left home," she said.

"Uh huh. Just packed up an' packed it in. Nothin' to it," he said, "once you make up your mind."

"I guess you could say I left home, too," she said. "Though I didn't come as far."

"Point Edward?"

"You knew."

"The miles make no difference," he said, sitting down beside her, but not close. "The truth is I saw something in you I can't explain. When I asked you to the dance, I'd never done anything like that before in my life. I didn't even know what I wanted to do – talk, have some laughs, feel a woman dancin' near me again, turn a caterpillar into a butterfly –"

"No need to talk." She unlocked the tumbler from his grip one finger at a time. "It mostly spoils things."

"I know."

"Promise me one thing," she said, blowing out the lamp and letting the snow-brushed starlight in. "No talk of what's gone before. None."

He followed her – amazed – to the inner chamber.

•

Neither of them made a move to light a bedside lamp. They undressed, apart in the shadows, and slipped under the nearest half of the comforter. Their bodies met, without ceremony and gave way to their individual hungers.

Cora and Lucien were past middle age. They felt no urgency to have their flesh explored nor to be reminded – by an accidental touch or a gesture of forgiveness – of scar, stretch mark, crease, sag, weathered muscle. Cora needed to know if the dead thing in her belly could be revived long enough to die with her consent. Lucien needed to know that he could waken, with the vestige of his lust, some flesh more drugged than his own.

He was hard in seconds, and she guided him in. Aware of his own craggy weight, his angular need against her seeming frailty, he hunched, catapulted elbows first, lanced, withheld, thrashed, and crushed two pillows. She winced joyfully at the pain then tried to right his lopsided fervour and find some balance or rhythm one of them could use, some pressure point that would trigger *something* they could ride out together. Nothing worked. Unwilling to call up those memories that might have established some sort of order, however bogus, and not yet knowing enough of each other to improvise the event, they staggered to separate states of incompletion. Nor was there the impetus of youth to rally them to a further attempt. They had contended in good faith, and discovered nothing but their age and the extent of their weariness.

But the Druid moon, almost full, had risen in the east and was tilting over the west edge of the room's window, flooding it with light borrowed from defunct suns. Side by side they lay. No word was exchanged – of apology, consolation, promise, regret. Into a silence fed only by moonlight and across the long hour before dawn, they reached accommodation and more. A hand that bruised and commanded, settled like a wing upon a thigh. A whisper lingered in the ear like a long, shy kiss. Someone's lips plucked a tear from a cheek.

Much later, it might have been in a common dream or in a fantasy shared with the moonless dark, they made love that was both violent and tender that threatened to touch the ache abiding deep inside them.

When they woke, it was January.

42

1

Throughout the winter of 1886 Lucien and Cora lived together in the St. Clair Inn on Front Street. Their love, if that term be at all appropriate to their curious co-existential relationship, was founded upon a strict set of covenants, unspoken but observed. They did not speak of their own past even when – secure in the embrace of a lover or vulnerable in the sinking aftermath of passion – they were tempted. They asked no question that might carry them beyond the moment of their meeting. They took their dark time alone, suffering through it as best they could. When they came back together to make love or talk about the long January afternoons, there was no camouflaging of that private pain, that burden from their night dreaming. They did not use their passion nor any of its incidental pleasures to ease or soothe or sedate. Their lovemaking – frequent, intermittent, unpremeditated – was a way of transmitting not the detail of sufferings lived and defined but rather their gravity, the sudden echo all the ruptured joy that once had been. Such surprise was enough. They accepted the blunt physicality of their comingling almost if it were a phenomenon outside their instigation or control. Each was content to let the other translate the results in his own way.

Their cohabitation caused a stir and a buzzing abroad. Since they were both strangers in a sense, the radius of the gossip was limited to the fringes of the beverage rooms, the quiet corners of the foyer, and the lively but closed network of fancy that followed the main-line of the amalgamated Grand Trunk Western. Percy O'Boyle – Suds to his customers – who clerked behind the registry desk by day and slung beer by night, blushed a deeper red than his hair whenever Cora came down to breakfast sometime before noon and smiled her ingenuous 'good morning'. "Mornin', ma'am – missus uh – ma'am." His eyes rose up on their own to trail her figure through the doorway to the dining room. Except for Mulligan, the owner and principal waiter, she found herself anonymous among the carpetbaggers, drummers and occasional couples who drifted in and out – off the boats, ferries or trains, and always en route to somewhere else. Sarnia, like the place she had left, was a stopover town, all bustle and hubbub. But seated at her regular table near the west window, she could sip tea shyly (she never got used to being waited on, ever startled by Mulligan's shadow at her elbow, embarrassed by his incessant hand-wringing) and look over the traffic along Front Street. She would keep her eyes fixed upon that blue pulse, its tiny ventricle breath as whispered and hesitant as her own.

"Would Madam like some more toast?" Mulligan would say with his blend of sarcasm and hope.

"Madam don't wish no toast at the moment." She watched his puzzlement, certain that he never quite managed to penetrate the ironies proffered.

•

The arrangements were simple. And for two people who had led entangled and encumbered lives, they were made with speed and no touch of regret. Yes, Cora would be pleased to quit her job. No, she didn't mind taking up residence in a second-class hostel. Nor did she object in the least to a lover who would be away more than at home. Lucien was a senior engineer with a regular highball run from Sarnia to Toronto. Leaving Sarnia at noon on Monday, Wednesday and Friday; return from Toronto by three on Tuesday, Thursday and Saturday. Which meant overnight in a cold Toronto bunkhouse three nights a week and four warm ones in a specially heated bower in the St. Clair Inn. After which, a leisurely breakfast for two, an abrupt departure, farewells nursed till again the sudden arrival, the brisk, physical greeting of flesh in its loneliness.

Only Saturday and Sunday were exceptional. When Lucien arrived early in the afternoon, tired from the six-hour trip and the layover in London, they would not make love. Instead, she would draw him a bath in the room at the end of the hall and languidly cleanse his rumpled, gray flesh. The sensual flapping of water and the murmurs of their give-and-take would drive Suds O'Boyle's blush down to the tips of his torso, so that he had to rattle the papers on his desk or bang the bell with his elbow for relief. Refreshed, the couple would stroll down to the Christina Tea Room for supper, and then it was time to prepare for the dance at the Armouries. Though the dances were different – guest orchestras coming from as far off as Windsor – they were both aware that each was a vital re-enactment of the first one. They did not speak, they merely danced and lived to dance. They rode the three blocks home in a hired cutter. They drank a tumbler of champagne from a bottle cooling in the snow on the sill. She took his hand and led him into the sanctum, where they made love, now, alas, coordinated though no less lacking than before in tough, sweaty, buckling urgence. It seemed, to Cora at least, that they contributed to this fiction of re-enactment more to assure themselves that they *had* a shared past of some sort rather than as a refusal to accept the inroads of time on their relationship.

The enforced absences were crucial to their feelings for each other and the tilting equilibrium they had established. On Sundays, for example – their only full day together – they rented a cutter and drove south or east of the town, down the back side roads of the township plump with farms and settled prosperity. They laughed or sang some improvised ditty as the bells on the Clydes jingled an icicle tune of their own and their big breath left a fading print on the air. Then after a dinner at three, they would relax on the chesterfield (she'd had it exchanged for the spartan settee) with a mug of coffee, and talk. Lucien entertained her with slightly bowdlerized versions of his folk tales, stringing a story out till it seemed to float over the gloaming of their Sunday communion. Embellished for her ears alone, they made her laugh and re-see the world made over by this man who inexplicably loved her, or wished to cast whatever love he had left upon some image of her she was not about to question.

"Now let me tell you about one of the funniest characters ever to throttle an engine or puke up in the back seat of a caboose. Old Pokey Burdette. One time when I was workin' in the Yard Office, long before I went on the road, Pokey comes into the place about four in the mornin' an' there's half a dozen fellas there smokin' an' warmin' their thumbs by the heater. They see right away by the whites of his eyes that he's as mad as a plucked gander. He's just come in from Montreal on a passenger – six hours late! 'Stuck in a snowbank as big as a buffalo's arse,' he cries, 'somewheres between Cornwall an' Trenton. An' you know who went an' put it there?' Nobody could guess, so Pokey swats his cap down on the nearest desk an' yells, 'George McPherson, the president of this here railway, that's who!' Then when everybody's real quiet, he says, 'Well, the son of a bitch goes off on his New Years' toot, gets himself gassed up, goes outside to take a piss in the wind, jerks the wrong lever and accidently lets a fart fly, which starts a fuckin' avalanche rollin' down the main line all the way from here to Port aux Basques!"

Cora herself had little to offer to this exchange beyond her enthusiastic response to Lucien's efforts. Under his encouragement, she was persuaded to tell him about the odd ducks she'd seen in the dining room or about her running series of *contre temps* with Mulligan:

"Top of the mornin' to you, Mrs...Burgher. A menu?"

"The usual, I'm afraid."

"Oh, I do hope you haven't gone an' lost your wedding ring," – staring hard at her left hand exposed upon a soiled napkin.

"Not at all. As a matter of fact, my *husband* keeps it..."

Pause—the silence delicate.

"*...in his nose.*"

To which Lucien would applaud with a bray of guffaws loud enough to make the clerk's bell jump with alarm in the lobby below them.

But there was mainly the long Sunday to fill and a few scattered hours over meals and after naps during the week. There would not have been enough stories to plug the silences that a day to day, hour to hour relationship would have demanded. Nor could they have sustained the bruising-healing quality of their lovemaking outside of regulated absence and joyous re-acquaintance. When they were separated, and alone, though, the hours were hard won. Cora walked, made polite conversation with young Suds and several of the benchwarmers in the lobby, and waited for the black moments to engulf her. When they did, she tried to muffle her sobbing with the comforter—Lucien's smell lingering there. But sometimes, she forgot and woke up in a daze in the sitting room with a broken glass at her side and the window wide open to let the wind howl through.

She supposed that he too suffered such relapses, though she saw only the wreckage in his fatigued flesh as he slumped into sleep after a difficult shift. He works it out, though, she thought. He rides that locomotive through the dark. I can hear its singing whistle in the words of his stories. But I am alone, without work, without recourse. I am mad, with little islands of sanity bubbling up and mocking me several times a week. Then Lucien would come back – needing her to need him. I am sane, she concluded. When I go mad, I won't know it. That's a comfort.

"You need a story," Lucien said, "even though it ain't Sunday yet. A Pokey Burdette story by the look of ya'."

So Lucien spun another one of his tall tales. Cora laughed in all the right places, reassured once more by the unaffected ease of her response and the certain knowledge that Pokey Burdette had never had any existence beyond the confines of this room.

2

Early in February, Lucien arrived from Toronto bearing under his arm a cardboard carton tied up with string. "For you," he announced, grinning and wary. She sensed something forced in his voice.

"Nice wrapping," she said.

"Did it myself."

"A shame."

"Go on, silly woman, open it."

She did. Inside were a dozen or so very large books, several of them uncut, their calf bindings unsmudged.

She stared.

"From my mother's old place. She liked to read."

"They're beautiful."

"Dickens, Trollope, some fella named Hardy. A Yankee called Fenimore Cooper; *Uncle Tom's Cabin*. She liked them all."

"They must've cost an awful lot."

"They're for you – to read on the days when I'm on the road."

She was holding the largest book in her hands, as if guessing its weight.

"You *do* like to read?"

"Yes. I do. Really." She seemed strangely touched, and he knew enough to say nothing more, though words of all sorts ached for release. She saw the desperate reconnaissance of his eyes.

•

The books remained on the little mahogany table where they had been opened, and the weekday routine continued as before. The next morning, Lucien left for the Yard earlier than usual. She felt the extra tension in his shoulders as he held her.

"When you hold my arm like that," she said once, "I get the feeling you're squeezin' a throttle."

"My hands never leave it," he said, trying to grin.

"You can't set still for long."

"Had St. Vitus dance when I was a kid."

"I'm serious."

"It's not so much that I like bein' on the road," he said at last. "After all, I don't get anywhere. It's just that I can't stand bein' cooped up. Makes me feel like a badger in a hutch."

So he was off again, to ride down whatever demons had chosen him long ago. As usual, though she still felt bad sometimes, she was relieved. The rooms were hers. They were sanctuary. And now there were the books. She went right to them.

At first she treated them like sacred texts, circling them, easing them open and glancing at the black type as if it were a set of shimmering runes about to divulge something clandestine. Gradually, her anxieties diminished and though she was not ready to tackle an entire book, she would flip open one of them to a random page and sit reading and re-reading a single paragraph. An hour might go by before she looked up long enough to realize the sun had moved above the sash.

"I see you been readin' a bit," Lucien remarked as soon as he got in. She caught the strained casualness of his tone right away.

"A little bit. They're beautiful books. Your mother must've been a beautiful person."

The book froze in his hand.

"I'm sorry," she said. "I really am. I didn't mean –"

"These were her favourites," he whispered.

"I'll read them, Luce," she said. "All of them."

First, she had to read one of them. It had been a little while since she had read anything, and while the trick of it came back quickly, the associations it brought with it were not pleasant. After an hour or so of trying to decipher the opening of *Bleak House* (she was drawn to the title), she found herself dizzy and faint. She went to lie down on the bed. She did not remember reaching it, though she was evidently asleep for the black dream was now upon her. Its pestilential winds swept her along while she lay begging that other half of herself – the one that would not speak – to succumb, to let the greater will have its way. When she opened her eyes, she realized with dread that she was lying on the carpet in the hallway outside Mr. Stewart's room. The hall table was tipped beside her, its little genie-lamp shattered.

"Are you all right, Missus – uh – ma'am?"

Waves of nausea rolled up into her throat. She blinked at the young clerk. His hand was very gently upon her arm, about to lift then jerked back abruptly as if stung. He crabwalked away from her down the hall, stumbling, reaching wildly behind him for the railing. Stamped on the *tabula rasa* of his boy's face, she saw the insignia of her misery.

"I'll g-get some help," he called hoarsely and disappeared.

Where? she thought, and was sick on the wool roses.

•

"Tell me, Mr. O'Boyle," she said to him in the lobby the next week, "what does the word 'chancery' mean?"

"Don't know, ma'am," he said warily. "Somethin' to do with courts and b-bigwigs, I think."

"Did you go to school?"

He looked for help. "Yes, m-ma'am. We all did, I got my l-leavin' certificate. Did real good, my m-mum says. She don't approve of m-me slingin' beer."

"Do you have one of them books that explains all the words?"

"A dictionary, you mean? No, I don't. But Mr. M-Mulligan's got one in the office b-back there. Belonged to his wife, b-before she run off." Then as if he felt the latter remark demanded exposition, he said, "That was all she l-left him."

It was heavy sledding, decoding *Bleak House* with the aid of Noah Webster's Dictionary and her own mother wit. It wasn't that the words were long and the sentences interminable, but so much of the world being described therein was itself foreign. The strange speech; the courts and alleys and traffic of an imperial metropolis; the exotic manners and customs – all had to be learned part by part in a vain effort to get some sense of the whole society, some feel for the meaning she was certain lay locked in the words. Sometimes, as she used to do, she read quickly, letting her instincts catch at the flutter of truth sweeping past her. Gradually, she felt the grip of the story, the particulars fading the moment their impression was made. She felt the loneliness and the spirit of the motherless heroine. Her heart went out to the

poor and the abused, but most of all she was drawn to Jo. She read the
chapters about the abandoned street urchin many times over; struck by the
pathos of a soul so orphaned by the world he had less than half a name to call
his own.

"You're gonna wear that one out," Lucien said.

"I *will* get to the others," she replied, and seeing that look in his face, she
brightened and said, "but let's get the cutter and go into the country. I feel
like a little travellin' today."

The air was clear and cold. The sun shone on them. Across the fields the
wind blew soft snow upon the week's bruising. The runners sang in the
horses' wake.

"You ain't travelled much, have you," Lucien said, turning for home.

A bit later, Cora opened her eyes, her lashes laced with frost. "This is far
enough for me."

"Someday soon, I'll take you for a real ride," he said. "We'll get on the
C.P.R. an' cruise all the way over the prairies and up the backside of the
Rocky Mountains an' slide down to the ocean out there past Vancouver an'
hop the first whale we see an' sail the blue sea to China."

This was a voice she hadn't heard before. Still looking ahead she reached
across and touched his hand, tight on the reins. "An' have a decent cup of
tea," she said.

When they pulled up in front of McPeck's livery, Lucien gave her a furry
bear hug in full view of the astonished grooms.

"You were right," he whispered. "She *was* beautiful."

•

And she did get to the other books. For five weeks on alternate days she read
and absorbed and puzzled and thought more than she ever had in her whole
life. She began to get some sense of that 'old country' she knew only through
what she had heard and been told. That old old land where her own parents
and the parents of almost everyone she knew had begun their lives. They had
given, through their stories and speech, a temporary credence to exotic
landscapes: gardens, hedgerows, wobbly lanes, ancient abbeys among the
meadow-growth, and peculiar notions of town and village and dialect as
indigenous as the local loam or limestone. In some ways, thinking as she did
about the mighty river and the freshwater sea of the Hurons and the vast

prairie the scarlet soldiers had crossed, the old world was as exotic as ancient China or some far Hindustan. Somehow, she thought, alone in her brown study, I am one of them, yet not a part of them. Then, like most of her thoughts, it wouldn't stay still long enough for her to grasp and she would be left frustrated and aching with a great emptiness.

When she began browsing through the other books, she noticed a peculiar thing: the flyleaf page had been cut out of each, probably with a razor, so neat was the incision. She became aware of this only because in the copy of *Uncle Tom's Cabin* the page had been crudely removed, as if in anger, leaving jagged edges despite a subsequent attempt to disguise the initial violence. It was the moment she realized that every book was supposed to have such a page and began examining the others. She said nothing to Lucien. He seemed more tense and absorbed, though at times he could be garrulously happy in the usual manner. She would catch him staring at her at odd angles, the mask of his face dissolved, leaving only his eyes to carry the burden of whatever he could not feel or say. So she found herself beginning to fill some of the more frequent silences by recounting for him the stories, as she heard them, from the great tomes he had brought her.

"We'll make a story-teller out of you yet," he said.

She put on a brave front. This cannot last, she thought. We've tried, but it can't be done. Whatever has happened to him, he's needed me in the same way I've needed him – to get through enough days with some feeling, some pretense of caring, some ritual repeated enough to seem necessary. Just until we can decide whether there's anything left worth salvaging. But I don't want this to stop and neither does he, I think. Why, then, should we not keep it going? Who is to tell us it can't be done? It was we ourselves who decided to make the night we met the first day of our lives. But it can't last. Love, whatever it's been, has never been enough.

She leafed through *The Last of the Mohicans*, a novel she had started but left, for some reason, till now. A page fell out. It was blank. A flyleaf ripped. From *Uncle Tom's Cabin*. She turned it over. She saw the handwriting there, but it was several minutes before she could disentangle it enough to be sure of the sense. 'To my beloved Mary, to while away the lonesome nights, from your devoted wanderer, Luce. Christmas 1875'.

•

When he arrived home that afternoon, early in March of 1886, Lucien was all smiles. She'd heard him humming to the banisters. "Get your bonnet on, Susie Q," he said. "We got business at the Court House."

They did. They were married by a drowsy judge in cold chambers with a scrubwoman and a janitor gaping on. They hurried home to a warm bed and made love as if it were New Year's Eve.

"You went an' made an honest woman outta me," she said, watching him smoke.

"Too late for that."

"Too late long ago. An' more than once."

"That wasn't the main reason, though," he said.

"Oh?"

He grinned. "Somebody had to do somethin' about young Sudsy's stutter."

43

1

All across the reunited Confederation it had been a heartless, unrelenting winter. Snow clogged the Laurentian trench, inundated the fields and fallow of the southwest, blew without purpose across the vacant prairielands, and settled like a bride's veil over the graves at Batoche and Duck Lake. In March, a week after the wedding of Cora and Lucien Burgher, came the great thaw. The world around them sagged, glistened, and hummed with the promise of heat. Then the unforgettable blizzard of 1886 struck home in the middle of the night, howling from the northwest.

For three citizens of the Province, such a dramatic shift in the weather was an act of divine intervention, a pope's blessing on the deed about to be accomplished. Their meeting, if somewhat unorthodox, was nonetheless predestined. Sometime just before or after, the trio's singing of Auld Lang Syne at the Grand Trunk Ball, the initial commitment had been made. The Honourable Halpenny Peebles, Mr. Margison Dilworth, Q.C., and Stanley R. Dowling, reeve of the village, whispered the same word together and decided, after due time for consultation and soul-searching, they should meet again, in utmost secrecy, to put their particular seals upon these first covenants. The word they whispered was 'tunnel'.

It was a word heard before in these parts. Both the Great Western and the Grand Trunk had boasted of blasting a channel below the St. Clair River to link the destinies, common ideals and profit margins of two great nations so unhappily divided by the inconvenience of a natural border. It was all bluff. No one in Sarnia or the Point took it seriously; before the merger of 1882, that is. With a combined strength and an unabated capacity to plunder the public purse at will, the Grand Trunk Western's boasting about a tunnel was henceforth received with joy in the village and muted applause in the town.

Any such tunnel would be built across the narrowest strip between the

Republic and the Dominion: where the GTR reached the very edge of Canada: Point Edward. This meant some of the advantages gained by Sarnia at the original merger – main passenger terminus on the principal line between Sarnia-London-Brantford-Toronto, expanded switching yards and car shops – might well be stunted or wiped out by the inevitable surge of power westward towards the heartland of America via a *Point Edward* tunnel. Little talk of any kind regarding such an engineering miracle had been heard for more than a year. To those in the know, – boardroom bullies, intimates of the disbanded Compact, the Scottish moneylenders – such silence signalled that the most feverish plans were afoot. Only the most trusted insiders, the directors of the railway, the premier's own Privy Council, and one outsider, knew that the issue was no longer financial or even technological. If the fittest were to survive, then the survivors of this Dominion would be the fittest. The dynamite and the air compressors were ready. What was holding up the orderly advancement of the nation was something more pivotal than money or technique: politics. Though a village, the Point had become a symbol to many another small Ontario community that had invested in railway promises only to be left holding worthless debentures and their assigned mortgages. The government of the day was vulnerable in the villages and hamlets. If Point Edward were seen to have been 'done dirty' by the railway or by a government in collusion with a railway, the upcoming election itself might be lost with the resultant chaos and inestimable human calamity. Word had just come from Montreal by coded message: Hobson, the world-renowned Canadian engineer, had completed his feasibility study. His news was unequivocal and without prejudice. The geology of the terrain at Point Edward precluded a tunnel ever being built there; the ideal spot lay five miles to the south, near Sarnia.

Enter Reeve Dowling, politician and former railway executive. The trick, he announced, was to get the population of the village to actually want the tunnel built at Sarnia. Vague promises were to be made, *quid pro quo*. The town gets the dirty, noisy, hazardous tube, but the village keeps its lucrative car shops, roundhouse, freight sheds, and will certainly have its port facilities expanded at public expense and the almost certain possibility that a large steamship company – beholden to the present government – would set up house at dockside. *Et cetera*. And who better to present such a package of delights to wary constituents than the Reeve himself. For his part in the melodrama, the Reeve would be offered – without contest – a safe provincial seat to the north, from which redoubt he might well eventually storm the gates of Queen's Park itself. The key to success lay in the Reeve's gradual and delicate revelation of details so that neither collusion nor predetermination be apparent. The timing was all.

The blizzard of March 15 was both a blessing and a sign. No one except a sleepy yardmaster noticed, through the haze of snow, the arrival, around suppertime, of a 'special way freight' consisting of locomotive, tender, three empty box-cars and a caboose. The sole occupant of the caboose was Deputy-Premier Peebles. The conductor had sat shivering in the engine cab with the driver and fireman all the way from Toronto. This 'ghost train' was turned around then backed onto a far siding. Its crew, following prearranged orders, left the locomotive primed and running, and headed for the comforts of the bunkhouse. They had been commanded to return at precisely seven o'clock and without a by your leave head back to Toronto.

A few minutes after they had left the train deserted, the doodlebug from Stratford arrived and debouched a handful of well-chilled passengers. The heating apparatus, clogged with snow and striations of ice, gave up in Ailsa Craig. One of these, distinguished in black, did not enter the faint warmth of the waiting room but, instead, turned, and pausing to confirm his anonymity, slipped through the snow towards the mystery locomotive. The male figure – at ease even in a blizzard as if he might at any second command it to cease – glanced up at the deserted engine cab and nodded with satisfaction. He walked casually down past the three box-cars to the caboose. A single lamp flickered bravely outward. Vice-President Margison Dilworth hopped aboard, shutting the caboose door behind him, disdainful of the privy councillor's teeth-chattering 'hello'.

A second pair of prints, suffering a like fate, fast approached along the tracks from the north where they curved and ran down Front Street towards the outskirts of Point Edward.

2

By six o'clock the snow was deep enough to impede all walking. So Lucien and Cora decided to celebrate the first week's anniversary of their marriage in the dining room of the St. Clair. After a light supper they began toasting one another (and several recruits from nearby tables) with champagne and heartiness only partially forced. There was in Lucien's eye a manic twinkle that had taken spark sometime before his arrival home early in the afternoon, not in the least assuaged by their fiery coupling nor its amber aftermath that prospered with each tumbler of elixir he lavished upon it.

"Tonight," he said, "I'm gonna take you on that ride I been promisin'."

"In this?" she said lightly, scanning his eyes for some sign of what the fire shielded with its glint.

"Snow never stopped a train," he said.

When they stepped outside, Cora could discern the outlines of a horse and cutter. Lucien silenced the muttering of the driver with a silver dollar and swept his beloved onto the snowy seat. "To the station, my good fellow. And hurry. We've got a train to catch!"

Cora snuggled against him. His heart drummed through layers of wool. The sound of the horse's hooves never reached them. It was hard to believe that somewhere behind the muffling veil around them there was a night full of darkness punctured by stars. No lights blinked at their passing along Front to Cromwell. The driver closed his eyes, sagged forward, and gave up the reins. Only the instinct of beasts brought them at last before the looming shadow of the former Great Western depot.

The waiting room was deserted, its gas lamps blazing. Brushing the snow from his coat, Lucien said, "You wait here. Scrubby Parsons said we could hop on his way freight down to the Point. About seven o'clock. I'll see if he's in the bunkhouse."

Cora spotted Big Meg in the doorway of the Ladies and pulled her scarf further up across her face. She felt a twinge of shame. Meg didn't see her. "It'll be just an hour's run to the Point an' back," Lucien had explained, "but you'll get the feel of it. There's nothin' on this earth like it."

His hand touched her shoulder. "Can't find him anywheres. One of the boys thinks the run might've been cancelled." She saw in his face the deep disappointment, the souring of the champagne's sheen and beneath it the germ of something black and combustible. "I'll just check the back sidings. They may be out there waitin' for us."

"I'll come with you," Cora said.

"Okay, but wait on the platform," he said. "You can't tell a tie from a T-bar out there."

She followed him outside and stood in the passenger area beside the main-line as Lucien headed across the half acre of tracks normally visible to the southeast. Within seconds he was gone. The snow beat against her face like the frayed wings of winter sparrows. She shivered but was not cold.

Lucien reappeared, flushed. "I found it," he puffed. "Six tracks over behind the car man's shed. She's primed an' ready to go."

Cora hesitated, her head tilted to one side. She listened for some sound in the mute threshing about her – a warning perhaps, an all-clear, a starter's gun.

"Come on," he said, no longer able to mask the desperation behind his excitement.

Above them the clock hanging over the platform, if it had been unobscured, would have read five minutes to seven.

Hand in hand they crossed the tracks they could not see.

•

The locomotive stood rigid in its berth, huffing and sighing to itself. The snow sizzled on its hot metal and, dripping downward, froze instantly into stalactites, which lent an illusion of immobility. The great gulping steam chambers, hissing inside it, said otherwise. Lucien pulled her into the cab with a gentleman's grace and slid the flap closed behind them. They were alone.

"Where's Scrubby? An' the crew?"

His broad shoulders were turned towards the dials and levers in front of him. "Sleepin' it off in the caboose, I reckon. We'll do them a big favour, takin' it down there on our own."

Any response she may have been contemplating was cut short by the shriek of the steam whistle – two short blasts, repeated. "She's steamed up an' ready to go," he shouted back. "All set?" He hopped over to a leather bench on the right, slid open the window, leaned out and with his left hand grasped a lever and slowly eased it towards him.

Everything metallic around them shivered and creaked and strained against gravity. The creature lurched, skidded, lurched again. A tremor of motion hummed through their bones and shook its way back through the coal tender, box-cars and caboose. Safe in this cab, surrounded by steel, Cora could sense the power of the released steam as it crashed into the cylinders like stunted thunder and poured its dissipating energies into the pleasures of motion and speed. Lucien pointed to the stoker's seat under the left-hand window. She looked out in time to see several blotched shadows below her. They appeared to be waving. She waved back.

●

"I got her up to thirty," he called across, peering at a smoky gauge an inch beneath his nose. "She was well primed."

The only light was cast by two fixed lamps above the benches that shivered and threatened to jump ship with every jerk and skid of the locomotive over the drifted, erratic roadbed. The slitted firebox, near Cora's side, glowed with radiant, welcoming heat but cast over wall and ceiling scraps of fretting shadow that reminded her of moths caught in a coal-oil lamp.

"Feels like we're curvin' to the left," she said. "Shouldn't we have veered right by now?"

He slipped open his window a little ways, pushing his face into a white flail. "Yup, we would've," he said, "if we was goin' towards Point Edward."

Cora looked out her side. She was certain she could see a ragged horizon line bouncing just beyond the storm's fury. "I see the bush," she said. "We're headin' for London!"

"We were, old sweetheart, until this second!" As he spoke the cab jumped sideways, spilling Cora onto the stippled steel floor and pinning Lucien to his perch. The screech of iron rebelling against iron pierced the ear, stunning them both. As each of three box-cars and the caboose met the crossover switch behind them, they were struck again. The whole train tilted wildly to the right, yearning to roll over into the battened ditches beside it.

Lucien's powerful throttle hand was under her. He helped her back to her bench, mouthing endearments and apologies then starting to laugh uncontrollably. Without the least notion why, she joined him. Whatever direction the beast had chosen, it seemed content to travel on its own. Lucien's lips closed her eyes. After a time, he drew back. They could hear again the steady, imperturbable cadence of Pegasus en route to anywhere.

●

"I don't know why we got turned east," he said. "We hit the main-line just past the bunkhouse. I figured we'd spend the night in London, but somebody left 'number-three switch north' where it was an' now we're aimed up the spur line that don't end till Woodston. Up in Huron County."

"Are they expectin' us?"

"Ain't got much of a choice!" He was laughing and trying to holler over from his side where he scrutinized the steam-gauges. "There's nothin' between us an' them an' we sure ain't gonna park out here tonight. In fact, we got a straight run in there. Oughta make it in about forty-five minutes."

"I know someone in Woodston," Cora said. "I'm sure she'd let us stay overnight."

Lucien didn't hear her. He had his window wide open. The blizzard poured into the cab and spent itself in miniature frenzies. "Hang on, sweetheart! Woodston, here we come, and if you don't like it, we'll shove somethin' hot up your ante room!" He pushed his head outside and wailed: "*Ya-hoooo!*"

The whistle skirled in unison with the engineer's taunt. Cora was astonished to find the cord in her own grasp.

•

"She's losin' pressure! You'll have to take over while I stoke her." He motioned Cora over to him. He took her hand and placed it on the throttle beside his. Then he eased away. "Hold her steady an' keep an eye on the pressure gauge," he said, starting to strip off his coat.

Cora felt the lever seize her hand. It throbbed in her grip and she felt through it the monumental trembling of the whole apparatus – furnace, boiler, cylinders, pistons, driver wheels, the cold ignition of metal on metal, its hair-trigger touch.

As Lucien flipped open the firebox door, a jet of flame shot across the cab, scalding the walls. He was bare to the waist. His torso gleamed with sweat and the wash of infrared. She saw the crevasses between muscle and muscle, tendon and bone, as he leaned back towards the opened chute, scooped up a huge shovelful of coals as if they were beans on a spoon, and in unbroken arc of motion and strength hurled them into the furnace. At first, his pace was slow and methodical; soon it accelerated, gaining momentum and urgency. The firebox roared, then howled, and frothed into a white, wordless delirium. The stoker's motions became blurred, no one part distinguishable from another. Suddenly, the motion ceased and the stoker leaped sideways, kicked the door shut, and punched a knob below the pressure gauge. A cloud of steam burst from each of the creature's nostrils. They heard its death scream and the hail of melted snow and ice crystals flung against the windows.

"Can't have her blowin' on us, can we?" His cheeks were as scarlet as a berry harrowed in Hades, his grin was as wide as Beelzebub's. *"Open her up! Let's make her fly!"*

Cora pulled back on the throttle. All the needles on all the gauges flinched.

"Use these," Lucien shouted.

She slipped on the goggles, slid open her window and peered out, not letting go of the throttle, the microscopic valve that somehow enflamed the steaming heartstrokes of this leviathan on a toot. She had to see what her lover saw, what he felt. She peered ahead.

The storm had tapered off to intermittent squalls. Between sieges, she was able to see the glint of the piston levers, the patina of exertion along the bevelled boiler plates, the thrust of the stack with its charred smoke blanched and flattened by the wind, the headlamp pinpointing a thousand discrete snowflakes for the quarter second it took them to self-destruct. She could see no sign of the track. Somewhere below and beyond must be a meridian, however thin or obscure, guiding them across a landscape blown featureless by the blizzard and past the reach of star or sextant.

Lucien was at her side. His warmth enveloped her. She lay her cheek beside his along the ledge. She was aware of her eyes closing with his. They took their breath together. Wherever they were pointed became their destination. In them the snow dazzled, deepened, blossomed with crystal flowers untouched by grief. Without moving, with not a whisper of expended passion, hurtling at seventy miles an hour through a blinding snowstorm in an iron box alternately freezing and searing, dumbfounded by cacophony and inviolate silence – Lucien and Cora made patient, memorial love.

•

Lucien was talking. She had screamed a tacit, unending *no* and he had frozen his lips with her kiss. She yanked the throttle lever as far back as it could go until the struts and bolts of the beast rattled like coffin bones in an earthquake. But no ground can hold a voice whose words must be spoken.

"Her name was Mary. I met her through her sister, who was married to a friend of mine, a fireman like me on the Great Western. I was no longer young but rich, as I thought, an' footloose. I let her charm me, an' she did. But she said she knew from her sister's experience how much hell was in store for the wife of an engineer. I hadn't had a chance to ask, but she'd already said no. Of course, I kept seein' her, an' she was always unattached, so I begun to wonder. Besides, I was getting a bit tired of stokin' an' cattin' around in Detroit an' them places. So I told her if she'd marry me I'd settle down an' become a respectable family man. When she doubted me, I quit the Great Western an' joined the Grand Trunk, breakin' all my old ties. For two years, though, I stayed on the road, but when Mary became pregnant, I gave in. I hired on as a clerk in the Yard Office. So that's what I became at age thirty-five. I hated it as much as I loved my wife. It was like workin' in a rabbit's den. You couldn't breathe, you sucked in the stink of everybody's body, you had no place to run or feel free in when you needed to. But I did it, for five years I loved an' hated.

"We had two beautiful children, a girl first, then a boy. But my salary wasn't a third of what I made stokin' on the road. We rented a house in the east and down near the river mouth by the lake. It was a shantytown, though we painted the place, an' put a fence round it an' planted ourselves a garden. But it was swampy down there and in the winter the snow piled up, thawed an' froze, an' the dampness went right through the wood. You couldn't keep enough paint or pine tar on it to stop it from rottin' under you. In the daytime the bugs devoured the vegetables in the heat, an' the mosquitoes come out at night to torment us. I begged Mary to let me go back on the road. She said she would get a job as soon as the kids were older – she had a high school certificate. So I went off one mornin' an' hopped on a freight an' never went back to that stinkin' clerk's den. I took only short day runs. I lied every day to my wife an' kids until my punishment was revealed to me in all its horror.

"My little girl complained of a headache after supper one day. It got worse by bedtime. By the middle of the night she was screaming in agony an' bewilderment. When the fever hit the next day, we knew it was typhoid. We'd seen it in summers past. An' shuddered, an' prayed. Her little body was burnin' an' tremblin' at the same time. The diarrhea weakened her. Like a thief, I stole away. I took the money I'd secretly earned an' went for a doctor.

Not many would come down to our slum for any sort of money. But I found one who would; he told us it was typhoid fever. That only one of us should stay in the house as nurse, that we should boil our water, an' so on. He gave us some laudanum for the pain an' suggested we pray. He wasn't gone an hour when my boy, barely a year old, was struck down with it. Mary and I did what we could. We knew full well only the strongest survived. We needed more medicine. Mary hadn't slept in three nights but she said I must go back to work to get some money for the kids, an' to keep my job which I could lose at any moment for being absent. So I did. I took a way freight to Jackson's Point. When I got back that night I was stopped about a block before my house by Mrs. Putnam, our neighbour. 'Don't go there,' she said. 'Come to my place. It's best.' But I tore away from her. I ran down that muddy street like a madman. I saw the crowd gathered 'round the spot where my house had been.

"There was nothin' left but cinders an' charred bits of wood an' bone. 'Just as the sun was settin',' Mrs. Putnam said, 'she come out the front door carryin' a lantern an' wavin' it frantically all about. *They're dead!* she hollered. *They're gone!* An' before we could stop her, she ran back inside, an' seconds later smoke poured out the cracks in the sidin' an' then flames shot into the air, an' we never heard a single sound come from inside the house. Not one.' She died alone, my Mary, without leavin' me a word. Everythin' was gone, burned to ashes. Later I found out she'd loaned her sister the books I'd bought her over the years. They're all that's left. That was eight years ago. I been on the move ever since."

•

Lucien's hand was on the throttle once more. Cora clung to him—to the terror and exhilaration in him. Every needle on every dial had peaked then snapped, the glass restraining them shattered. The firebox door throbbed like a fevered eye. Welding scars on the engine's joints stiffened, brittle as ice. One more revolution and the whole contraption would fly apart in a welter of primal steam and lava. We'll die together, was Cora's thought as she heard the shriek of rending boiler plate, the shudder of disconnecting wheels. She waited out the silence that preceded the impact, holding her breath and Lucien's hand.

But there was no crash, no clatter of wheels on pig iron, no surge of piston in its chamber. No sound but the rushing of the wind behind the snow. They had left the track, the invisible meridian, the groove of all gravity. They flew weightless and triumphant through the spaces between the snow that rose with them. They soared through its black immaculateness towards the polestar whose belly was the Milky Way and whose jasper eye would draw them beyond any calculus of the frozen heart.

•

Most of the population of the hamlet of Woodston heard the ghost train of 'eighty-six as its shadow hummed past the Grand Trunk passenger station. They heard the muted screech of its futile braking. They flinched as one at the abrupt thud of cast-iron on drifted snow. In fact, despite the blizzard and dire storm warnings, the good people of Woodston came out in force to christen their brand-new depot, just completed mere days ago and ready to receive its first passengers on the morrow. The unscheduled arrival of the ceremonial train was more than a shock. Woodston's reeve was in the midst of a passionate toast to the eternal glory of railways in general and the Grand Trunk in particular. The wine goblets glistened beneath the gas lamps. The room burbled with the good cheer that comes from unearned contentment and free booze. So concentrated was the assembly's attention on the latter exigency that no one noticed, shortly after the meal began about six-thirty, the rumble and roar of a nearby avalanche. Not more than fifty yards from the station where the spur line itself came to an end, there stood on one side of the tracks a mountain of stored coal, ready to be used as soon as the connecting spur to the northern trunk line was completed in the spring. Opposite was another mountain, this one of crushed stone to be likewise deployed in the expansion project. Over the preceding two days local squalls off the lake dumped acres of fresh snow onto these man-made peaks. Somewhere between the roast beef and the baked apple, a huge ledge of packed snow gave way and rolled unimpeded into the valley below. This fracture awakened the trolls in the mountain opposite and it too sent an avalanche bevelling down upon the first. The result was that the end of line was now defined by a trapezoid of snow thirty feet high, twenty feet across and a hundred yards in length.

Into this welcome – decelerating at sixty miles per hour – the purloined locomotive erupted.

•

What the reeve and the press in the doorway behind him saw as they peered into the haze left them speechless. The rear end of a caboose had burrowed into what appeared to be an improvised dune of snow where the tracks used to be. The caboose door had been knocked by the plundering impact and was giggling on one hinge. Nothing else moved or was visible. Further along, a thread of steam or frost began to uncoil from the mountain ridge. Something under there was breathing. Then like a blue whale blowing in a fairy-tale sea, a spume of spittle and geysering breath stunned the onlookers.

The noise seemed to rouse whatever life lay cowering within the caboose. At that same instant the reeve detected several shadows emerging from the ruptured doorway. Through a scrim of snow he could distinguish them only in silhouette, but it was clear there were three men who occupied various stations of suffering. The forward shadow was taller and more erect, striding so as to disguise a twisted knee and wrestling manfully with the impossible task of repositioning his crushed bowler. A yard behind him a second shadow essayed to keep pace with abrupt, paralytic steps. Further back, a hunched, crabbed figure advanced with painful slowness, as if its thighs were glued together. On the platform, no one moved or spoke. The figures came silently towards them, close enough at last so that they were seen, despite the snow, to have human faces. They appeared dazed, tentative, and slackened by incredulity as if they had just stepped onto the dark side of Pluto's moon.

"Mr. Dilworth!" gasped the reeve.

"Where in hell's *this*!"

"Woodston, sir. But what are you doin' here this time of day?"

"Never mind that," boomed the voice that made boardrooms tremble and second vice-presidents quake in their sweat. He swivelled and pointed at the crippled creature behind them. "Get the deputy premier to a toilet." The reeve leaped forward. "He's shit his pants." And leaped back.

"Then round up your strongest men and dig that son of a bitch out of there!" He aimed a gloved finger at the far end of the avalanche where the smoke stack of a locomotive was materializing out of snow, steam and the night air. "I want that renegade's balls broiled for breakfast!"

3

There are many ways in which a conspiracy may be accidentally disclosed, but one no more public than when the railway executive, the privy councillor and the ambitious reeve staggered into the Woodston station – dazed, malodorous, trembling with the aftershock of an hour's journey into terror - under the scrutiny of two hundred well-dressed guests of every political stripe. Nor was it convenient to keep from popular view the speculation of the presence of a runaway train embedded in an impromptu ski slope. The celebratory dinner had attracted several gentlemen of the press and one keen photographer, who, between them, managed to immortalize the train of events in bold face and daguerreotype. Nonetheless, both governments and railroads are wont to survive such momentary embarrassments, as they did in this instance.

The tunnel was built where God had ordained it, and the ruling clique clung to power for one more term, though the railway lost a faithful servant. The federal senate was fleshed out with another retiring member of cabinet. The most evident victim of these unfortunate and unpredicted violations of the natural order was Stanley R. Dowling. Two weeks after the catastrophe, with eighteen months left in his term, he resigned as reeve of Point Edward, a position he had held by acclamation since the birth of the village itself. In total disgrace, he faded from the printed page of local history.

•

Cora remembered the soft surreality of the crash, the sensation of falling into a cushion of cloud, then being pitched forward. That was all. When she woke up, she was in the infirmary of the Woodston doctor. It was noon. The sun shone in a blue sky. Where is Lucien? she asked. The railroad police had already taken him away to London, to jail. It was assumed since she was a woman that she had been abducted and was as much a victim as the wretched trio who had bounced about in the lampless caboose. Much solicitude was shown her. She said as little as possible, mostly because she could do nothing but think of Lucien. She wanted to go immediately to London, but two days later, when her head stopped spinning, she was taken to the train (the inaugural one having arrived late) and accompanied by an official back to Sarnia. She was left, alone at last, in Lucien's rooms.

The next train for London left at five-thirty. She started to pack, her hands shaking uncontrollably. One image above all others floated in front of her: a badger in a wire cage swallowing its own fury.

When the knock came at the door, she jumped up. It was young O'Boyle, his face ashen. He had a telegram in his hand.

"I'm sorry, Mrs. Burgher," he said.

"He's dead," she said, as if telling him the news he already knew.

"Yes, ma'am. Word come along the railroad 'vine' about noon. It's all over town."

"How?"

"Hung himself, ma'am. In his cell."

•

Ten minutes later, Mr. Mulligan opened the door a notch, paused then came in. Cora was seated on the chesterfield, holding a book bigger than a Bible. When she finally looked up, after his third cough, he said: "I want you outta this place by noon tomorrow, bag an' baggage."

There was little commiseration in his Irish grin.

44

The arrangements were now complete. In the morning they would come and move her things across the street into the cottage they had built for her. Sunny asked her to come and have a gander at it before the trauma of moving day, but she had refused. I'll see it when I get there, she thought. At my age, I may not wake up in the morning, and then I won't get there anyway, so what's the point of seeing something first and getting all stirred up for nothing? I fussed about the future many times, in the nine lives I've had before this one, and where did it get me? All the way to Grief Street, that's where. For Sunny's sake, she had feigned interest in choosing wallpaper from the assorted bundles he lugged over. None of the ghostly roses, dumpling flags or haplessly cheerful urchins he unrolled for her held any appeal. In the end, she selected the plainest and least offensive. What did it matter? She was not interested in a house which she herself had been tempted to help confect. Houses ought to grow, she had always thought. They should express the lives lived there. They should be surprised, dreamed, mercurial, beautiful to the beholder. I guess that's why I loved the Lane, and why I never could explain it, not to Cap and not even to Arthur, who tried hard and whose own handiwork was, despite his good-natured disclaimers, done in the same spirit. 'Only the temptations of the church saved you from bein' a Laner,' she used to tease him. 'And only *you* saved *me* from the church,' he'd laugh back.

I'll ask them to move your trunk last, Arthur, she promised. I'll walk beside it. That way we'll keep the ghosties inside. You realize they aren't going to be too happy with the sudden transfer. Being theatrical ghosts, though, they ought to be used to being on the move. They told me you were almost fifty before you settled in one pew. She wished now that she could have seen Arthur in his prime, treading the boards of the great stages of the West, warbling away like his own favourite – the bluebird – with not a touch of winter in his song.

It was May now and unseasonably warm. Her crocuses had bloomed in their usual profusion. The tulips along the house bulged in the trapped sunlight. The vegetable beds lay spaded and expectant. "We'll leave the border flowers an' shrubs, for a while," Sunny had assured her. "But the garden'll be turned into grass. The whole area will be landscaped in some manner suited to a cenotaph. It'll be a kind of special ground. There's a bit of land behind your new place. We may have to clear some trees, though, to get enough sun in there."

Granny felt the need to get out for a while, out of Arthur's house, out of the gardens they had planted together, out of the vegetable patch she would never tend again. As far as she could recall, she had not been off her own property since the terrible autumn of 1918. I'll go out there and have a look at this town one more time before I settle in somewhere to die. If these wobbly old legs will carry me. And if I happen to topple into the River, I'll save the council the price of a ceremony.

She felt surprisingly sturdy. She walked north along her own street towards Michigan Ave. She recognized every house she passed, found familiar every gable, stoop, gate, half-finished dormer, or coppery window with one blank eye unpatched since the War. Each house sent its voices wafting out to her – grown faint with the years but still unappeased, still desperate for attention, the need for a story to be told in full. Too late for all that now, she whispered as she hurried past.

She passed the houses of the respectable, some fallen since to disrepute, and heard no apologies for the treatment received there by Cora the cleaning woman, or before that, 'that washerwoman Lily from the Lane'. Houses where she had been good enough to wash clothes, scrub floors, cook a meal, wipe up the children's snot and shit, love them without premeditation, but not to share a meal or carry a confidence. 'But did you ever try to *talk* to them? See life from their point of view?' Cap had asked her many times. 'You kept yourself aloof. You expected the world to come to you. You were a loner by choice. It was your chosen philosophy.' Perhaps there was more to Cap's accusations than she had ever acknowledged during their long hours of reciprocal interrogation. But what did it matter now? They were all dead. Several of them she had walked with to the edge, helping them across when the props of their respectability cracked asunder, when death dared them to enter his chamber unattended, and they couldn't.

'But you'll be glad to know,' she said to Cap now, 'I felt no satisfaction.'

Some, of course, like Eliza Sanders, had been kind, slipping her an extra dollar when a husband wasn't looking, giving hand -me-downs she was too proud to take home to her boys but others along the Lane were happy to receive.

She passed Redmond's Grocery, the Post Office, the new hotel, the pool room – feeling heads turn in shop windows – and crossed the street to the Lane where The Queen's had stood for fifty years. It was a rooming house now, she had heard, but the spirits that poured out of its bowers, anterooms, closets, pantries and wine cellars stopped her in her tracks, overwhelmed her with their babble. She felt dizzy. Don't faint, you stupid old fool, she thought, not right here on the main street with the sun shining.

She didn't, though she couldn't be certain because when she opened her eyes she was not in front of The Queen's or any other building. Nor was she on any of the village sidewalks. She was in some sort of field. In the summer, it would be covered with sawgrass and sandburs, but at the moment, it was soft and fern like. Her legs carried her, not willy-nilly through it, but along a wide path that was, for a short time in this young half of spring, plainly visible. This had been a road once—a winding, sauntering one. On either side of her, she noticed clumps of concrete or the shell of what had been a porch or chicken run, some of its wire rusted as thin as fish nets in the drying sun. To her left, a window, its glass intact, stood rooted to the ground where it had slumped and stuck while all else around it had rotted away. She almost tripped over the frail skeleton of a child's sled. An icy breeze from the lake reminded her of more than she was prepared to remember.

She looked unbelieving to the northeast. She saw the backyards, sheds, coops and rambling pitches of the houses built along the 'official' Lane, straightened by statute. I helped to do this, she thought, long ago, in another name. Now the air was filled with human sounds, voices skewed and thinned by the breeze. Her body propelled itself towards them. She saw the crazed outline of chicken wire, caught the thick stink of swine too long in their stys, heard the domestic singsong of women's conversation as they laboured. Her eyes strained ahead to see them, to know who these inheritors were, whether they knew what ground, what tradition, what demons they had promised to possess. No one was in sight. She stumbled. The voices arrived, loud and clear: a foreign tongue. She listened, ignoring the burn in her knees. It was no language she knew, or had ever heard. The syllables stabbed at her eyes, raced unconnected through her head like bat's echoes in a belfry. She couldn't hear the last beats of her heart or the bounce of her kneecaps on the stiff earth.

•

When the sounds stopped ringing in her head, she was still walking. It was getting dark or misty, or both. She was in a sort of hollow, for though she could hear the lake breeze high in the distant trees, she felt no wind at all on her face. She was lost, her legs had gone numb, but she was not afraid. At any moment of her choosing, she could lie down on one of those sandy mounds, close her eyes and sleep the longest, deepest, sunniest sleep of her life. The air around her trembled with invitation. There were voices in it but they spoke to the weariness of her bones. They carried the news of consolation. It's time to lie down, she thought.

A shadow flicked, off to her right. A bird, returned from its journey? A mourning dove? Something bright and shifting caught the last of the daylight and transformed it. It's alive, she thought.

Then, a sound, the last quarter of a whimper. She forced her legs towards it, gritting with pain. Don't worry, she cried, I'm coming.

The sun froze in the entanglement of a child's hair—glinting as it twisted in the grip of something perilous. It was a cry. A little girl's cry. The sun turned blood red. It jerked the blond tresses of the lost girl upward into a scarlet, lungless scream.

"Mom-mee! Mom-mee! Mom-mee!"

The child's face caught fire. The features blurred and congealed. The hair flared like a halo and cindered. The lips alone remained to surround their one word, emptying it again and again into the empty air.

Granny felt her heart burst. Her knees hit the sidewalk, then her elbows, then her chin. She looked up. The sun grinned down at her. She read the faded letters of the Queen's Hotel on a yellow brick wall. This is not Heaven, she thought, just before the pain blinded her.

45

1

Granny Coote lay in her new house and listened to the warm wind stirring against gables. She heard every errant sound that the house contrived to interrupt her sleep: the complaint of green lumber along the eaves, the slap of an ill-fitted shutter, the rattle of windows not yet settled into their glaze, the fluting of air across the chimney pot, the exotic tick of the pendulum clock in the strange space. I must not be ungrateful, she told herself a dozen times a day. There was a time when this is what I wanted most, foolish as that notion might seem now. We all want a moorage of some kind, though the space it takes to launch us out of this world is not nearly so large as we would suppose. The day after Wilf Underhill, Sam Brighton, Limpy Jenkinson and the others had moved her furniture and belongings – baggage of many decades – across the street to this house, she had begun to undo their patient work. They had put the table and chairs in the kitchen at the back with the queer gas stove and ice box; the chesterfield and piano went into the front room, Arthur's bed and her cot into the bedroom at the back. They set up her Quebec heater near the tiny vestibule next to the bay window overlooking the street. Arthur's theatre trunk went into the bedroom. Out back was a neat woodshed with a privy off it so she would never have to brave the elements again. She regarded the electric lamps – donated by the Methodist Auxiliary – with a mixture of suspicion and wonder. But none of this could be. As soon as they were gone, she dragged the cot into the front room, marvelling at her frailty as she struggled to move it a few inches at a time. She set it up across from the heater. She managed to get the table and one chair out of the kitchen and into a spot near the cot. Perhaps when she had a chance to get a garden in, she would eat in the strange, closed kitchen and look out the window at the dense greenery. For now she felt she needed only this solitary room, surrounded by these few necessities and comforted by them. From here she could gaze westward, at a moment's notice, through the bay window where the empty rectangle stared blankly back at her from across the street, where the familiar side hedges flourished, where the stems of tulips combed the rim of the sky at the edge of the marsh, where the arching hickory allowed its thick, gnarled limbs to fringe the breeze with its maidenhair green. "They'll take the front hedges out but not the side ones, and they'll leave the flowers as is for this year," Sunny assured her. "The builder an' his helpers'll be comin' in next week. You got a front-row seat."

She tried to get Arthur's trunk into its proper place. She wished she'd just had the courage to tell them she wanted everything in this room, but she didn't want to hurt their feelings. Besides, she thought, they think I'm queer enough as it is. By sitting on it and pushing off with her feet, she managed to get the trunk as far as the doorway where it wedged itself in permanently. Sunny arrived just as she was trying to lever it up with a stick of kindling.

"I'll do that for you," he said. After a cup of tea and a scone (Anglican Auxiliary), he said: "And if you want to go walkin' again, you just let me or Purdie know. No need to go off by yourself."

And fall on your face, she added, in front of The Queen's and suffer the double mortification of a bloody nose and having been rescued by Half-Hitch Hitchcock, who promptly assured the whole town that he had told her so but what can you do with doddering old ladies who don't know enough to die when they have the chance.

"The deed should be ready in two or three weeks," Sunny said. "But you know lawyers, don't you, Cora?"

She did indeed.

2

Cora Burgher surprised the village in a number of ways when she returned a few days after Lucien's death. Her coming back to live there was itself a surprise, considering what happened to her, what painful memories must have lain all about her. Second, she did not return to the Lane though the meagre room she rented again in old Hap Withers' cottage was as close as you could get to the Lane without actually being a citizen of that nether town. Third, she not only brought her new name with her but flaunted it all over the place, despite the fact that it had had only a few months itself to settle in. She seemed obsessed with having herself addressed as Mrs. Burgher or, worse, Mrs. Cora Burgher. Even by the gang at The Queen's who had known her best, she appeared not to hear or became distracted. But then she *had* suffered more than a body could be expected to bear without the sustenance and solace of religion, poor thing. What surprised no one who bothered to notice was that she returned to her job at the Queen's Hotel and to that itinerant society still regarded by the villages with disdain and raw envy. For a few months, then, Mrs. Cora Burgher was discussed litigiously then taken for granted then forgotten.

Cora herself was so numbed by Lucien's death that she recalled little of those early weeks back in the Point. She did not know why she was here, why she was even living, except that any decision not to be required more effort than merely going through some deadening ritual dredged up from the past and substituted for existence. Happy Withers found her wandering in front of The Queen's and took her in again, as if she were an orphan dropped on his doorstep a second time. What else could he do? When she became coherent, he fetched her things from the St. Clair Inn and then took her down to Malloney. Within hours she was back at work.

When Malloney or Gertie Flounder called her Lily or Mrs. Marshall, she flinched and said automatically in a low, thin voice: "I'm Cora Burgher, Mrs. Cora Burgher," and kept repeating it till Malloney, bewildered as he always was face to face with any feeling he couldn't count, would say "Yes, *Mrs. Burgher*," startling the benchwarmers in the lobby. It took Gertie quite a while to say "It's all right, Cora, we know." It was soon 'Mrs. Cora Burgher' almost everywhere. When some of the numbness turned to mere pain, to the slow singe of grief she recognized and welcomed, she carried that name in her heart like a gift, a legacy of their brief love. For a while it would be her reason for being.

Gertie, of course, had been promoted in her absence, so Cora was content to clean the lobby, beverage room, Malloney's suite and the kitchen area out back. This meant more scrubbing on hands and knees, emptying spittoons, scraping up grease and crushed cigars, and scrubbing out the foul toilets near the bar. Gertie was the upstairs maid, making the beds and tidying up the half-dozen suites on the second and third floors. When there was extra scrubbing to be done – clogged fireplaces, debauched carpets and duvets – Cora was called upstairs to assist. She didn't seem to mind. She arrived shortly after seven, had a bit of breakfast with the cook, and worked until six or seven in the evening, when she would take a cold supper and trudge the single block back to Hap's cottage.

At first Cora preferred to work alone in the back corners of the place but gradually came to like those moments when she could slip into the lobby, a large front room with a double door and scenic window overlooking the flats leading to the river and the lake. She dusted or emptied the brass ashtrays while the commerce of a busy railway village passed before her. The three suites on the third floor were still advertised as elegant and often played host to smartly attired executives, officious politicians or blustering entrepreneurs, all of whom were in themselves worth observing and who provided fodder for days of follow-up analysis and commentary by those seated on the sidelines. For the lobby, with its hospitable stove, drew to its domain an unchanging cast of locals: a half-dozen or so elderly denizens who spent half the day in the barbershop up the street and the other on these benches (and the two stools given to those with seniority). They called themselves the Smokehouse Gang, comprised of whey-faced pensioners, discarded elderly uncles and a pair of defrocked patriarchs, all from the respectable part of town and all with much to say about the decline and fall of the human race. Some of them Cora knew from earlier days – when they were unwrinkled and God-fearing – Pudge Grogan, Tubby Trout, Ballroom Baker. Others she knew only by their trade names: Wart, Dicer, Shotgun. Through some pact worked out years ago, they were never to arrive before two o'clock nor stay later than five-thirty. And though they would always be certain to arrive one at a time to establish their independent worth, the benches were full by three-fifteen and deserted by five-forty. Soon Cora was organizing her chores so that the lobby required her presence in the late afternoon. Malloney seemed relieved, though he never said anything to Cora about that night in his room and made no overture that might be misconstrued as friendship.

More than a year passed. If the great world around her were moving, Cora didn't notice.

•

"Tunnel don't matter a fig's tit," opined the Wart. "Railroad ain't gonna move the shops an' sheds outta here till the day before doomsday."

"How d'ya figure it?" Shotgun asked.

"They still own half of this here town, that's why. A crow don't shit in its own nest."

"Just in everybody else's," Shotgun said. He sat back to bask in the stringy laughter of his easily amused colleagues.

"Never get her built anyways," said Pudge Grogan, who used to build things.

"Why's that?"

"Gravity, that's why. Never heard of Newt's first law of gravitations?"

Before the next riposte could be delivered all eyes turned in silent appraisal upon two figures coming through the double doors. Both were dressed in expensive business suits. The young one, a bright-looking chap with a scrubbed face and soft eyes, supported almost the full weight of the older man who stumbled on the doorjamb, uttered a ghastly cough and fell to his knees. Duckface Malloney stood at his ledger behind the desk counter, grimaced, but did not look up. None of the onlookers made a move or sound. The young man reached down, and as gently as he could, raised the older one to his feet. "He had one too many at the meeting," the fellow said. A dozen heads nodded *we know*. "I'll need some help getting him up to his room."

"Elmer, get out here!" Malloney shouted without looking up. A skinny lad appeared from the barroom and helped gather the drunk into a manageable lump to be carried upstairs.

Cora came in just in time to hear them clumping onto the second-floor landing. Someone up there let out an elongated retching noise. Elmer cursed, and the clumping resumed. Cora went for her mop and pail.

•

Over the course of the winter, it became evident that there was one spot she was never asked to clean: the spacious bed-sitter on the northwest corner of the third floor, the one with the view of both river and lake. When she asked Gertie about it, all she got was a blush and a forefinger laid against the lip. Gertie herself, as far as Cora could tell, went in there intermittently. "He don't go out much," she confided, "an' till he does, I got orders to stay outta there."

One day early in July, Gertie was off sick and Cora was told to do the third-floor rooms. "Stay away from 3A though," Duckface said and Cora detected more fatherly admonition than command in his voice. When she searched his face for more, he swung abruptly away. It was stifling up there, even in the morning with the hall windows wide open and a hot breeze wafting the curtains. When she had finished the other two suites, Cora came down the hall to do the water closet. As she passed the mysterious bed-sitter, she thought she heard a groan, as if someone were in extreme pain. She eased over to the heavy door and put her ear against it. Nothing. She was about to leave when it came again, a breathy groan as if someone were being punched, followed a half-second later by the tight whine of a second voice, descant and linked to the pain of the other. A staggered cadence and vocal accompaniment which she had heard inadvertently many times before from these rooms around her – unmistakably sexual. As she headed back towards the stairway, wondering vaguely who the lovers might be, she was pursued by the coupled climactic cry, and there was something alien in it, chilled and yearning, not even close to pleasure. She shivered and descended.

•

Gertie returned the next day and Cora forgot about everything except surviving in the swelter of that summer. She took to walking down to the river in the cool of the mornings and evenings, catching the wind off the water before the parched fields heated it up for distribution over the village. Malloney suggested she and Gertie lie down in one of the empty rooms during the blaze of the afternoons and finish up their chores after supper. So it was that Cora happened to be scrubbing out the pantry one evening about seven o'clock when she heard a commotion in the lobby. She put her pail down, got up and walked along the hall in the direction of the noise: men's voices raised in anger and the thump of bony flesh on wood. She hurried into the front room.

She was surprised to see four or five of the Smokehouse gang seated in place. Then she remembered they too had taken to coming in after the heat – with Malloney's grudging permission. The Wart, Shotgun, Dicer and several others were all staring towards the stairs near Malloney's desk. Their eyes were popping as if they'd all just inherited the same goiter. Cora stepped further into the lobby until she could see the stairway itself. She went no further.

Malloney, his duckface squeezed in rage, had a huge hand on the collar of a man he was dragging down the stairs and across the carpet towards the door. The man resisted by flailing his arms and digging his black leather oxfords into the rug. His considerable bulk was in Malloney's fierce grip.

"Get on your feet you, fat-assed bum an' haul yourself outta here," Malloney shouted into his ear.

The victim's gray hair was askew, covering a good portion of his face, but Cora could see the flush of humiliation and amazement there. His arms flopped about him, as if he felt he ought to be striking out though all the time knowing it was hopeless.

"You're lucky I don't call the constables to come down here an' kick the livin' shit outta you!" Duckface opened his fist and the man dropped to the floor. The crack of his elbows shot through the room like a whiskey glass on a bar top. The Smokehousers flinched en masse, their mouths agape.

Cora watched the man. He rubbed at the smudges on his worsted trousers, got himself seated upright then peered out to see where the next attack might come from.

"Get on your feet, you drunken deadbeat. You got thirty seconds to haul your ass outta here." For the first time Malloney seemed aware that he was not alone. He whirled towards the benches, his beady eyes defiant and daring. The old men rocked back onto their seats, appalled and thrilled. Their collective rheumy eye swept the room with the instincts of a gunsight. Malloney did not see Cora.

The man was now up to a crouching position. His sweaty hair had fallen away from his eyes. She could see him trying to garner some fury, some outrage, some word of reprisal. Nothing could penetrate his amazement.

With no warning, Malloney kicked out his foot and caught him in the lower back. He teetered towards uprightness, paused at the suddenness of his ascent then canted forward onto his face. For the first time he let out a cry, high-pitched, a little boy's stunned by undeserved pain. When he rolled over onto one side, blood spurted from his smashed nose.

Malloney, who had his foot raised for another blow, froze. The man whimpered, caught sight of the onlookers and said in a whisper, "Please help me."

Dicer rose from his stool. "What's he done?" he said to Malloney.

"Ain't paid me a fuckin' cent of rent for three weeks. Nor his bar bill of eighteen dollars. So out he goes. You got trouble with that?" He put a threatening edge to the last comment but it was unnecessary. In truth, he had gone as far as he intended to go.

"You fellas want to help me assist this gentleman to the exit," he said in what he assumed was a jocular tone.

The man had finally managed to get to his feet. He pinched his nostrils to staunch the blood. He was shaking all over. "I can pay, I can pay," he said from under his hand, staggered, and fell again. The blood sailed in a wet sheet down his white shirt, his skewed tie, his ripped morning coat.

"Leave him alone," Cora said, coming towards Malloney.

Malloney wheeled around, surprised. His eyes narrowed to shut out any indecision. "Stay outta this, Mrs. Burgher," he said. "Ain't your business."

"He needs a doctor," Cora said.

"He can get a doctor after he's well an' gone from here. The deadbeat owes me three weeks' rent and a bar bill an' he ain't got a farthing to stuff up his nose." He turned to his supporters. "I'm out thirty-nine dollars an' he's got a bloody nose!"

Malloney, his outrage re-stoked, moved menacingly towards the man, who slithered backwards, sobbing and uttering a slurred jumble of words. Malloney reached him a yard from the door. He raised his fist; the elderly chorus behind him gasped and hung onto their breath. Then Malloney gave a quick, clandestine glance towards Cora, winked, and opened the double-door.

"Go tell your troubles to your pals up at the station. See if *they'll* let you get into them for thirty-nine dollars."

"You tell him," Dicer said, delighted to have recovered his voice.

"We don't take to deadbeats an' traitors in this town."

"You had your chance here, fella, an' you blew it."

"There's not a spit of pity left for the likes of you."

"An' when you hit the town line just keep on goin'."

Malloney lifted the target of his abuse to his feet and pointed him towards the sun they could all see sinking below the west bank of the river. Behind it, darkness beckoned.

"Let him be," Cora said.

"Stay outta this, woman, if you want to keep on workin' here."

In the air Cora could taste the stale, desiccated breath of these old men and their ancient, jovial hatreds.

"Let him stay."

"What are you sayin'?" Malloney's eyes widened in disbelief.

"I'll give you the money," Cora said.

•

No one offered to help her get the man back up the two flights of stairs he had just been dragged down. She didn't ask. The cook, Mrs. Suitor, kept Cora's money for her in a little safe in the pantry. Malloney went there to get the cash he was owed only after he had ordered the pillars of the community out of his hotel. He glared at the victim, and muttered brave homilies to Cora about the fate of women stupid enough to squander their money on hopeless cases. In the midst of this petulant tirade, it was clear to Cora that Malloney would regard her in a new light, observing her with sidelong scrutiny, his natural wariness deepened and yet undercut by doubt and something akin to wonder.

When Cora got the man to his room – number 3A – she washed the blood off his face, got his shirt and shoes off, and tipped him onto his bed. His eyes were glazed with fatigue. He had said nothing to her; she wasn't certain he knew what had happened. As she wiped away the blood and pushed his hair back into place, his features – the nose puffed – came into Cora's view. She stepped back at the shock of recognition. He spoke drowsily but in his normal deep voice. She remembered it. "Thank you for helping. You were...glorious."

"I'm Cora Burgher," she said, not ready yet to believe her eyes.

"Glad to meet you, Cora." He spoke now in a threadbare, weary whisper. "My name's Stan Dowling. People used to call me Cap."

46

1

"I told that pinch-faced marmot down there I was no deadbeat. People like that, with no education and less breeding, assume that because a man gives up his worldly goods and vain ambitions in favour of a quiet and contemplative life, he must be impoverished, a fool, and a cheat. I told that creature a dozen times my great aunt would not survive this heat wave, that if he showed the slightest scintilla of patience he would get his money back threefold. If I were a vindictive man, or if I still cared for such normal pleasures as spit and vengeance, I'd have my lawyers on him. But then I've had my fill of lawyers, haven't I?"

Cora, dusting off the crystal decanters and watching boys on the flats in a ritual tag game, nodded in agreement. Cap sat in his plush chair beside the narrow north window and looked across the room at her as she worked.

"There's just enough in dear Auntie's legacy to keep me comfortably here for as long as I wish to stay, and not near enough to tempt me back into those ways I renounced with such flourish and finality." He waved his solicitor's letter at her as if it were a flag. "And of course I shall write my first cheque in your name, with a few extra dollars for you and your loved ones."

Cora finished dusting the sill, sweeping the shrivelled flies into her dustpan. "No hurry," she said. "I don't need the money."

"But your family –?"

"Got no use for it," Cora said at the door.

"Just a minute!"

She waited.

"Ah, Mrs. Burgher, would you tell Malloney not to send Gertie up here any more?"

•

Cora loved the view from here—high enough to see both banks of the river where they stretched into the lake. At eye level, the herring gulls or bullied the breeze over the soft shoreline. Way below her a fisherman swung his net through the current to the rhythm of slow music inside him.

"I was the son of a struggling merchant in London. My father sold hardware, but he wanted a lot more than that for me. He got religion just so I could attend the right church and study law in Toronto. There I learned a lot about gambling, the fast track, and how money is made to ensure that such luxuries are maintained throughout one's life. In short, I met and was liked by the right people. I started collecting that useless pile of haberdashery you try to straighten out every afternoon."

He flicked a finger at the wardrobe with its doors jammed irreversibly open – suitcoats, vests, silk shirts, trousers stuffed in and threatening to abscond. Cora would reorganize these habillements at least once a week, but when he'd had a brandy or two, he'd go fishing for some poignant moment of his past. He was always successful. She'd find him the next afternoon slumped in a flawlessly matched outfit for dinner, dancing, or a royal audience, with a bib of vomit down his vest. But he left the haberdashery in chaos. Sometimes he even managed to get into one of his three dozen pairs of shoes.

"Why don't you give some of these things away to people who could use them?"

"They are reminders of what I have repudiated. I don't believe you could understand."

"You don't keep them just in case?"

He began to cough as he often did this late in the day after a dozen cigars. He would go limp and let the coughing shake him this way and that then peek over at Cora. "There's no help for this, you know," his look seemed to say. But a cup of hot tea with lemon and honey was rarely refused.

"I cut quite a figure in Toronto and London society when I returned there in 1852. It was a small pond and I was, to put it as modestly as possible, a glittering gander in their midst. With a little help from my friends in government, I bought and sold some property that made me at the age of twenty-five independent of my father's influence. In short, I enjoyed myself. I explored each of the seven deadly sins with a Franciscan zeal. You may not guess but I was as slim and trim as a birch in those days. The ladies were, as they say, drawn to my company."

Little of that glamorous figure had survived the rigours of middle age. He was now a gray, greasy-haired, obese man with pink, deflated flesh, side whiskers long ago left to their own vices (Cora shaved him twice a week but was not allowed to trim or cut), a gourmand's paunch, skinny legs that complained of the burden they bore, and milky, shapeless fingers that spent too much time coddling brandy snifters, fondling Cuban cigars, and coaxing dollar bills into or out of wallets. Only his eyes gave any sign that a life had been lived and remained to tell the sad story. When he wasn't drinking, or when he had slept a full night, or when Cora found him as she occasionally did in his chair by the north window with a book open on his lap and his face turned to the sky, his eyes seemed grotesquely out of place. But to Cora, they looked beautiful, shining with the intensity of a life lived and only partly regretted.

Most afternoons when she came up after finishing her duties, she found him snoring in his chair, half dressed, cigar ash littering his paunch, a snifter overturned and bleeding on the table. His snores scattered the sparrows on the sills of the west window. She would wash his face and torso and wrestle him into a clean shirt. As he muttered his way grumpily towards consciousness, she tidied the room, humming to herself and giving the decanter an extra clink.

"Stop that racket!" he'd holler, stung by his own voice. After waking, he would often ignore her presence for upwards of an hour. He sat in a sort of stupor as if he were trying to recall and identify the various parts of his quisling anatomy. Sometimes he pretended to read the book before him as if he'd accidentally dozed off and now resuming his onerous intellectual responsibilities. Or he'd reach for his toppled brandy glass and appear surprised that it had disappeared without his permission. She would continue her work, tidying the pillaged wardrobe, taking fouled garments down to the water closet where she washed them in the tub, and finally curling up on the bay window ledge to watch the autumn afternoon linger in the fields.

"I'd like some tea now," a small voice would say from a farther part of the room.

Cora would bring up their supper. Cap had the lamps lit and their evening began.

•

"The real power and money lay in the railroads. And the glamour. Contrary to what most people assumed, I was never that fond of money. I could have made a hell of a lot more in real estate. It was the sheer excitement of being in a position of power or being close to its centre. It has a glamour unknown to those who've never reached for it." His eyes glinted in the winter light of the late afternoon.

"You got to meet the Prince of Wales and all that."

"Exactly. That's exactly my point. I not only got to shake his hand among the self-professed dignitaries of London, but as an investor and young executive for the Great Western, and then the Grand Trunk, I got to chat with him over dinner in the presence of Lady Marigold and Mr. Dunbar Cruickshank at the inaugural luncheon of that very palazzo you spend so much of your time admiring from this distance."

"It burned down," Cora said.

"Pardon me, you're right, and the barons of steel from Threadneedle Street built it back up in a wink. *That's* power. And believe me, glamour and romance flow directly from it. You couldn't imagine, I'm sure, how it feels to ride out into that lake on a fragile craft bearing you and the future king of an empire, to share a brandy and cigar with him. Imagine, the prince-in-waiting was mine for an afternoon and for years to come. I saw it in the eyes of others as they envied me and curried their pathetic little favours. For a time, Cora, I was afire, ablaze, one of the elect."

"I hear you give all that up," Cora said from her window-seat.

•

"I shocked everyone, especially those who thought they knew me," Cap said, shivering in his velvet robe. Cora had the west window raised so she could put the remnants of the supper he hadn't eaten out on the ledge for the sparrows.

"With Lady Marigold, you mean?"

He looked startled. "Close the damn window, woman, I'll shake my teeth loose!" The room was as stuffy and warm as always. He had been off the booze for two days, having ordered Cora to hide the supply then yelling at her and cursing her perfidy when she refused to change the rules of his game. Finally, he just shivered and sulked.

"Everybody around here knew all about you an' Lady Marigold."

"Oh, that. Sure. That was another part of the glamour – we felt like equals, we could admire or hate one another as we chose. There wasn't much else going on there. Not as much as the *hoi poloi* imagined, anyway, though we enjoyed their envy and rancour."

She brought a blanket over and laid it across his shoulders. He smiled wanly at her. "It's time," he said.

"You said you didn't really need it."

"I say a lot of things."

She poured him a snifter of his medicine. He sipped it slowly, breathing the restorative fumes. The late winter darkness seeped into the room. "Don't," he said when she started to light the lamp.

She left him earlier than usual, walked home under the March moon and slept alone, as she always did.

•

"Quit fussing with those damn clothes and come here."

She continued her work. Every jacket had its sleeves pulled inside out, like skinned muskrats.

"What I was referring to the other day when I said people were shocked was my sudden switch from the Great Western to the Grand Trunk. But my motive was simple. I could smell a rotting carp at twenty paces. I decided to put my money on a winner –"

"Money you didn't care about."

"– so to speak. Again, you see how wrong you can get things from your restricted vantage point. The Grand Trunk was bigger, grander, more ambitious than the Great Western. It had plans to build from sea to sea. It had a lion's heart and lion's pride."

"An' teeth."

"Naturally. But it's what I wanted. And I did well, as you know. I suppose if I'd known I would have jumped again to the C.P.R., but by the mid-seventies I was over forty years of age and much of the romance was beginning to pall. It was clear we were going to crush the Great Western, but the C.P.R. had usurped our place in the royal sun, and there seemed little left for a man of my temperament. When I sucked caviar through champagne all

I tasted was ashes." He drew in a lungful of his Havana and held it in defiantly.

"Must've been terrible," Cora said, tossing clean sheets onto his huge canopied bed.

"But I had a dream of my own, one nobody knew about but me. My parents, who'd long ago disowned me, were now dead, and I felt the weight of some indefinable obligation descending upon me. It filled me with unnameable regret and remorse."

"We call it a bad conscience."

He persevered. "I quit my directorship. I gathered my life's savings and came to Point Edward, a place I hadn't seen for years but whose beauty had impressed itself upon me in a way I could never forget. I decided to give back to the world some of the things I'd robbed it of. You'll recall much of the rest yourself: my little factory down on the flats – still operated of course, by others – my meteoric rise to the reeveship in return for my influence in persuading the Grand Trunk to let this village *be*."

Cora nodded.

Cap began coughing. When his defiance had subsided, he said, "What a waste."

"I can see the smoke comin' from your factory," Cora said. When she came over to help him into bed and fluff up his goose-down pillows, he propped her chin on his soft fingers and said: "Why do you do this?"

Grasping his fingers, she said, "For the money."

As she let herself out, she heard his coughing start up, loose and wayward, as if he were about to embarrass himself by crying.

•

"I should have stayed there in the factory. Hap Withers was a great manager. I'm glad he's got it now. But you see in this experience how the vanities of life have to be renounced completely. They have to be expunged from the tablet of memory, cauterized from the flesh they've preyed upon. After the glamorous life of civilized debauchery I'd led heretofore, you'd think the temptations of reeveship and regional politics would have seemed petty or beneath my considerable talents."

"Maybe you had more in mind?"

He examined her shrewdly, his teacup at half-mast. "I'm glad you decided you were good enough to share my table," he said with heavy irony, pleased at the power he still held over words. Throughout the winter, Cora had served his supper on the silver tray and then retreated to the bay window. She ate her own meal in a silence he ignored with particular satisfaction. A week ago – through Gertie – orders had been given to have a single meal for two prepared and sent up at precisely six o'clock, winter or summer, sunshine or gloom. Cora now sat opposite him on the stool he used to launch himself back into bed.

She poured herself a second cup of tea.

"I'm sure I did at that," he said. "I guess all along I knew this was not the United States or whatever name we chose to call ourselves by. In my heart I knew the corridors of power and the chambers of decision lay in Toronto and in Ottawa, in the legislatures and in the sanctum of the Privy Council. I was getting old, Cora; I know you can understand that. I had only one more chance for the genuine thing, a run at the crown itself. Better men than me have been o'er-thrown by such ambitions."

"Then you took a train ride," Cora said, watching his face for signs and portents.

He sat back. His side whiskers quivered like a tomcat's in front of the master's cheese. His thin lips tightened, causing the jowl to ripple and rebel. But his eyes danced with the kind of joy a ballerina might feel pirouetting on a sprained ankle. "What a way of putting it," he said, snarling out a laugh. "I took a train ride I didn't buy a ticket for. And derailed. What a spectacular fall that was! Wolsey would have been envious."

"Who's Wolsey?"

"A fat man who couldn't swim."

"Tell me, I'd really like to know."

Elmer knocked at the door and she took the tray over to him. She felt Cap's eyes on her. She didn't turn around right away. It was still light. The summer wind floated in, bringing with it the swallow's song, Queen Anne's Lace and other intimations.

Next day when Cora came into the room she discovered it was as tidy as a monk's study. Cap was seated in his chair with a gray tome open on his knees. He was turned so that he could observe the motions of the sky to the north. A pleasant breeze lifted the brushed hair back from his strong brow and a bowl of mints rested at his side. He pretended not to hear her. It was only when she let out a cry of surprise that he could bear to turn and face her.

"It's for you. Go ahead. Sit."

Cora put her mop down and stared at the chair he had ordered Elmer to bring up. It was placed opposite his on the other side of a walnut gate-leg table he'd also ordered from the collection he recalled seeing in one of the 'luxury' suites on the second floor. The table was covered with a lace cloth and graced with a silver tea setting. The new chair was high-backed, cushioned and beautiful. The mahogany legs shone.

"Please, sit."

She did,

"It's time we had a proper tea and conversation."

•

After their meal, Cap poured himself a brandy and lit up a cigar. He kept his eyes on Cora, as if he thought she might bolt at any minute.

"Now that you've heard my life story," he said, "it's time for you to tell me something about yourself." When he saw that she was going to say something, he averted his gaze, slouched back into his comfort, and listened.

Cora soon found herself responding to his request. She realized that she had not talked for a very long time. Not merely aloud, to others – for that was only a minor form of talking. But not even to herself in those dream monologues she could detach herself from and listen to her own thoughts as clear and necessary as her heartbeat. She didn't tell him much. Much he would be unable to understand; some would be too strong for a man in his condition; some would not ever be told.

She had come, by a circuitous route, to Lucien. She hesitated. She felt the strange security of this chamber she had seen only in the late afternoon and early evenings of four full seasons. We are exchanging our voices only, she thought. We do not know or even want to know each other outside the safety of this collaboration. For now, that is enough. It is a kind of miracle. When Lucien's name left her lips, she felt at once like a traitor and glanced across to see how much she'd given away, how much was irretrievable.

Cap was sound asleep.

2

The sparrow lay unresponsive in her cupped hands. She waited for the heart's flutter, the spasm of blood in the misted eye.

"Leave go, Cora," Cap said from the hutch of his bed. "You can't save them all, you know."

Several of the dead bird's cousins flapped against the pane then settled into the snow on the sill, where they pecked away at the crusts left there by the same providence that caused one's blood occasionally to congeal.

"Bring me the Schopenhauer," he called. "The one with the gray cover."

"I can read," Cora said.

"Pardon me, but I forget little things like that."

She brought him the book.

"You don't expect me to read in *this* light?"

•

"Sometimes, Cora, I think you deliberately try to misunderstand me. Is it your way of getting back at me, pretending to be stupid because you never had the benefit of an education?"

"I'm a woman, remember?"

"That is an unforgettable verity. But my point, to get back to it, was that I, by choice, by an act of the invisible personal will repudiated my life of vanity and power seeking. Only I know what went on inside my head during those weeks after the calamity up in Woodston. Just because the world around us assumes that a combination of x and y conspired to undo us, to turn us along a certain path, does not mean we followed that course for those reasons. What people think is never the sufficient cause. If you'd been listening to what I told you about Schopenhauer's statement on the issue, you'd understand that."

"And if you'd given it all up one minute before the train left the Sarnia station, more people would be ready to believe you."

"But quantity is irrelevant here. Only what I do and know is significant. Look at it this way – just because the society I sought to exploit decides to strip me of opportunity and honour – dump me down the shit-hole, so to speak – does not mean that I, at the same moment, cannot have a sudden insight into the hollowness of that society – both its rewards *and* its so-called punishments. The fact is, I did. Long before they defrocked me and cast me out like a leper, I had decided to renounce both the pleasures and the pains of that community of hypocrites. That was my way of coping with their petty retributions and with the horror of my own past. I decided to retire from social intercourse of all kinds, to follow Schopenhauer's path of ascetic withdrawal to the life of contemplation shorn of vanity and pretension. I would devote the rest of my allotted days to studying the great thinkers of our age. Over there you see the expanding fruits of the labour." He waved towards the glassed-in bookcase already filled with volumes which arrived weekly from a bookseller's on King Street in Toronto. Elmer carried them in reverently, as if they were Bibles fresh from Caxton's press. Cora had to dust them daily in spite of the glass parapet.

"Seems to me," she said, "most of them saints you talk about had themselves a fair old time before they saw the light."

"Woman, there are times when I'm sure you're a hopeless case!"

She jumped up and Cap jerked back against his pillow, spilling his tonic. "Look, I'm sorry –" he said.

"It's alive," Cora cried. She drew the fluttering creature out of her apron pocket, lifted it to the window and let it beat its way into the blackness of a winter sky. Her thigh still tingled where the bird had made the decision to live.

•

"I don't need no raise," Cora said.

"That's not the point. You're the best worker that sleazy leprechaun's ever had slaving for him. I told him to give you more money or I'd hire a gang of thugs from the Alley to break his knees and then his Irish mouth. He seemed impressed by my logic."

"I thought you was supposed to have 'renounced' the things of this world?"

"I have." He gave her one of his philosopher's looks – bristling with protective ambiguities. "By the way, did you get me those cigars?"

•

Every evening about ten o'clock, Cora walked to her room in Hap Withers'
cottage. She missed the outdoors, the pleasant walks along Canatara beach, a
sleigh ride to Little Lake to watch the skaters in the winter, flower-hunting
expeditions into First and Second Bush. The odd time, in the month of June
when the sun stayed until almost ten o'clock, Cap would fall into a brandy
doze and she would slip out – sometimes as early as eight o'clock – and walk
briskly in any direction, drinking in whatever Nature offered the senses. Most
of the time she arrived home by ten, fell into a dreamless sleep, and rose
early enough to help Mrs. Suitor with the breakfast and chat amiably with
Elmer or one of the new girls Malloney had not yet frightened out of a job.
At four o'clock sharp she went up to the third floor – her duties for Malloney
completed – and entered Cap's retreat. How he survived his night or what he
did during the morning to recuperate and justify his existence she could only
guess from the detritus he left about, or read in the scavenged slag of his face.

"The salient point in all of this, then, is not *when* you discover the truth
but the fact that you *have* accepted it into your life to the extent that all your
subsequent actions are consonant with it. That is pure Schopenhauer. I read
that only after I had come to similar conclusions myself. My disgrace, if you
will, was merely one of the means which prompted me to see what was
there all along: that as long as one persists in pursuing one's own desires,
which means working against the world's will, one will never be in the
position of making a choice. It's strange, I know, but the more you try to be
yourself by desiring the things of the world and lusting for dominion over
them, the more you play right into the hands of a universe that cares nothing
for such vanities or will-o'-the-wisps. The only choice we can make is to
renounce all vanities, all desires except the pursuit of truth through
contemplation. One can choose to do that."

"When you tempt fate, it gets you."

"Well, that's oversimplifying a grand notion, but yes, that's part of it.
Sooner or later one of the world's accidents will drop its careless hammer on
your hopes – which you thought you could direct and manage to some
personal conclusion. Certainly you would concede that an impromptu train
ride at the hands of a drunken suicide was one of the world's more bizarre
examples of happenstance?"

"Maybe the German fella was in love," Cora said.

For a second Cap caught the edge in her voice, waited, but when she added nothing more, he said, "Love has nothing to do with it. Love is one of those desires we must purge ourselves of. I speak, as Schopenhauer does, of Eros, not Caritas or Agape. These latter await those who can approach the best in themselves, and thereby come close to the spirit of the World's Will, which is suffused with sympathy and the kind of knowledge that cannot help but issue in the complete affection of Agape. When we know fully, then we sympathize, then we love with utter acceptance. That's the hope that Schopenhauer offers us."

"He had no vanity?"

"None."

"Why did he choose to lecture at the same hour as the great Hegel at the University of Berlin?"

"You've been reading these books," he said, astonished and not a little befuddled.

"Only when you're asleep. I don't take them out of the room."

"How long?"

"Just a little while. You seem to be snoozin' more these days."

"It's the damn soft coal," he said.

"But I can only read some parts. Usually the part about their lives. The rest is too hard."

His gaze narrowed. "What else do you know about Schopenhauer?"

"He saw the world as a dark place, full of horrors, from a lonely room. Maybe he needed to get out more."

Cap's face relaxed visibly. He flashed an indulgent smile and surveyed his pupil as from a great height. "You think his magnum opus, *The World as Will and Idea*, was coloured by an unhappy, friendless existence?"

"Some of it, yes."

"That's why women aren't encouraged to study philosophy," he said, fumbling for his silver lighter. "The man *chose* to be alone. To think. As I have."

Cora took the lighter from under his napkin and handed it to him. She waited until he had his cigar lit and was sucking greedily on its adrenalin. "He kept a dog with him. All his life."

•

That second spring Cap had a bad time with his cough. Cora would wrap him in blankets and get Elmer to help her carry him to the bathroom, where she would fill the air with steam from the water, and sit with him till be could breathe again. She begged to be able to stay with him through the night but he insisted she leave. "You're a respectable widow," he would say, winking. "I'll survive. Or I won't," he added with Schopenhaueran resignation. But Cora knew the look in a doubter's eye. She'd seen it more often than she'd wanted to, seated at many a sick bed with the smell of camphor in the air like a gruesome incense. But she went. Malloney followed her footsteps down the block from his bedroom vigil. Cap survived. He went back to the cigars.

"Can't give them up," he said. "They fuel the gray matter up here. And I don't mean my hair. But I'm giving up the brandy. You were right. It is a desire, a vestige of my former vainglories. More symbolic than real, but significant all the same. It goes."

The day after these resolutions, Cora arrived to find a pad of lined paper set on the table in front of her chair. There were notes made in a neat, printed hand.

"They're for you. I'm summarizing the main points of Schopenhauer so you can read and study them and ask me questions."

She stared at the notes, wary and elated. "Can I ask *him* questions, too?"

He smiled shakily, and she could see he had both hands tucked into his trousers. His flesh was the colour of grass along the flats in November. "Only if he'll let me answer for him."

•

When Cora came in she knew immediately that something was wrong. The room was frigid, the charred coke lifeless in the grate. Her eye caught the snow beating against the narrow north window. His chair was empty.

"Cap?"

The bedding had been tossed aside as if in anger, the white sheets glowed eerily in the winter dusk fast descending. Sparrow wings flapped against glass, begging entry. Cap's moan answered from somewhere behind the bedstead. Cora strode to the end of the bed and peered around it into the shadows that hovered between it and the west wall. He had fallen out of bed, the covers had gone one way, their tormentor the other. Automatically she lit the bedside lamp and knelt down to him.

"Go away. Let me die in peace."

He was sitting where he had landed, propped obliquely on one bruised elbow, his brittle spindle legs flopped to either side of the fattened toadstool of his belly. His free hand pawed compulsively at the fringes of the mattress the way a gutted woodchuck might claw at his burrow wall. The only visible wound was the fractured brandy decanter, forlorn against the wainscotting.

"You people got nothing better to do than sit and stare at me? I'm no traitor. I'm just a man, just like you. So leave me be."

His eyes peered out of their devastated flesh but did not see her, even as she bent and kissed them and her arm slipped under his numbed shoulder to begin easing him up. "It's only me," she said.

"Let me die in peace."

His face came up into the lamplight. The flesh was sallow yet as puffed as if he'd been beaten with a cuckold's fists. His beard and hair were matted with vomit from some previous misadventure, and his speech, his pleading whine, squeezed through his stunned lips without once jarring them.

Later, scrubbed and remorseful, he said to Cora: "Whatever I said to you, I didn't mean it. I've been told I'm a mean drunk."

"And a sweetheart when you're not."

"Be kind. I fell three bloody feet off the bed."

"An' the wagon."

•

Cora paused, drew the razor back and seemed to be contemplating her unfinished handiwork. Either that or the opium of the lilacs drifting in from the four quarters of the town had induced a reverie of its own. "You didn't tell me that German fella said there was more than one way to give up thinkin' about the world."

"*Schopen – hauer.*"

"Don't put me off."

She finished his left cheek, wiped the blade and sat back. He reached over and touched her wrist. "A day like this and I'm almost tempted to venture into the chaos out there just to see the trees again."

"Almost."

"Schopenhauer, as you well know and are pretending not to, suggests that although the ascetic life of contemplation is the only permanent way to avoid the wrath of the universal Will, one can indeed obtain temporary relief and insight into the more benign, spiritual side of the life force by studying and appreciating works of art."

She sat back again. His hand lay where it had fallen.

"Have I got it right?" he said.

"But why can't it last? He don't seem to say much about that."

"I didn't write that part out, I guess."

After a moment she said, "Why?"

He feigned annoyance. "Because it's deductible from the system as a whole. Too much exposure to, or an obsession with, art constitutes yet another form of desire and egocentrism and becomes, therefore, self-defeating. Now would you fetch me my cigars?"

"I don't know what you mean."

He lit his cigar without removing his eye from her. She could see the effort it took for him to concentrate, to keep his fingers steady, to let some of the pleasures so rigidly curtailed simmer again in a glance that once held salons and boardrooms in thrall, had skewered the witless and charmed the unwary, that had never quite become reconciled to its own delight.

"I think you'd give Socrates a hard time."

"Who's Socrates?"

"See what I mean?" he said theatrically, peeking back over his shoulder. Then he sighed deeply, coughed through his teeth without jolting loose his cheroot, and said: "I'll use an example, an *exemplum*, to illustrate. So listen carefully. In England there has developed over the past few years a school of esthetics which promulgates the notion of art for art's sake. To a degree, Schopenhauer would have approved. They believe in the creation and contemplation of beauty for its own sake – no other. You see how that view of art precludes the world out there with its phoney social and moral values. Beauty is to be loved for her beauty and that beauty as loved gives the beholder a momentary insight into the One Will whose expressive breath activates the heart of the universe."

"The way I like lilacs or you like them cigars?"

He made a brief effort at filtering out the ironies, sighed, and continued. "In a homelier sense, yes, though art – in painting or music – is created by an act of the individual will, and is not merely nature."

"Oh."

"But you're getting me sidetracked. The point I'm making is that *that* school itself, in practice, has become perverted to the sorts of desire we must renounce – the kinds of the things I have given up to live as I do in this hermitage."

Elmer arrived with hot water and Cora made the tea.

"I'm speaking of young Oscar Wilde of whom you might have heard."

"So I have." The memories stirred by the mention of that name lapped and stung.

"Came here in 'eighty-two. I met him in Toronto, showed him the sights. He was marvellous. He gave a speech in the botanical gardens about making your house itself a work of art. Impressive. He told me he planned to actually *live* the esthetic credo, to be a breathing, walking *objet d'art*. You'll recall I was in Toronto at that time to help with the merger of the railways. My genius had not been forgotten. What few people know is that I was asked by the Grand Trunk in 'eighty-five to go to England and help sell the idea of the tunnel to the British owners. They thought a little charm might help. What they were worried about, of course, was that Joseph Hobson, the only engineer bold enough to attempt the feat was, alas, a native Canadian."

"You saw Wilde again?"

"Yes. I went to Paris and Rome and when I returned to London I discovered that he was still notorious and that he had indeed tried to live out the purely esthetic life. I was invited to his house on Tite Street, the most infamous household in the Empire. I saw for myself the results of a philosophy based solely on the exigencies of beauty."

His eyes drooped and glazed, as they often did when he talked too lengthily. Sometimes he would just drift into sleep, waking minutes or hours later, not remembering what had driven him to repose and occasionally getting irritated when Cora tried to renew the lapsed discussion. It seemed that as long as he was talking, uninterrupted, his thought was coherent and edged, but if he tired or was distracted, the coherence faltered and could not be recovered. The thought itself might well be lost for days or weeks, sometimes resurfacing in unexpected intervals as whole as before, yet as unconnected as ever to any of the other sequences that emerged in their own time. It was a mind, Cora thought, in brilliant disarray.

"This life – of Wilde's – it didn't work," Cora said, gently.

He thrust his lidded gaze at her. "Desire," he rasped. "All desire."

She waited. His breathing slowed. He was asleep.

•

"It looks like another one of them days, almost beautiful enough to tempt you into walkin'," Cora said at the bay window. "There's no shade of purple quite like the milkweed flower. I used to walk out on those marshes every fall as long as I can remember. With my kids, too. I like to see the pods shrivel an' dry out an' then surprise everybody when they crack and all that white silk floats into the air, not carin' very much that winter's almost on it."

Cap watched her from his chair, saying nothing, afraid to cough or breathe too hastily. He watched her slim form and the strength it never telegraphed while at rest: chin set in expectation; hands folded peacefully in her lap; eyes moving in a meditative sweep over the landscape of their attention. In the autumnal silence, her still-life composed itself for contemplation.

•

"Of course, not all the arts are equal. Mr. Wilde was perhaps too overzealous concerning the visual. Schopenhauer suggests that music is the highest of the art forms, closest to the sublime, less tainted by the coarseness of individual life. In short, more universal, more in tune with the circulation of the spheres, so to speak."

"You like music?"

For a while he appeared to ignore the question; then: "When I was in Europe I heard the most sublime music, the kind that must have moved Schopenhauer to advance such a claim for it. You have to hear it played by orchestras so grand and stirring that no one in this province could even imagine. Sometimes I lie in that ugly bed and try to recall it. I can't. No one can. The old German fella was right."

Cora helped him into bed. He had talked for almost two hours in bursts interrupted only by brief forays into the brandy or more lengthy appraisals of his audience. She didn't know which manoeuvre discomfited her more. He was pallid, palsied in his attempts to get his nightshirt over his mountainous stomach, and yet as she guided him onto the sheets she could feel a strange resolve in him.

"I wish you could have heard it," he said, turning with great difficulty and balancing, egg-like, on the precipice of the bed. "I wish we could leave this place sometime and go there and hear it. Where else could we come as close to the transcendent?"

He patted a spot beside him and Cora, wary, joined him. She felt light-headed. It was past ten o'clock.

"What kind of music do you people around here have, eh? The bugle band?" He draped his hand over hers. She sensed the fear in it.

"I dance." Cora said.

•

"Don't go, please."

"You seem awful tired."

She allowed her hand to curl up inside his, sweated and blood-warm.

"I watched you all afternoon. In that window."

Gently – afraid, unafraid – she tugged against the pull of his hand, the room, the momentum of the seasons behind them.

"You don't even know how beautiful you are. That is the wonder of it. That's what takes my breath away, my shrivelled old-man's breath away. Still..." With his free hand – the other clasped to hers – he reached over and staring steadily at the vee of her throat, he tried to unbutton her blouse. She let him fumble there just long enough to let him know she didn't mind then raised her hands so she now held both of his in front of her.

"Cap," she said, "I love you in a way I've loved nobody else. That's the truth."

She saw his eyes moisten, his lip quiver, his fingers tensed to overpower or take flight.

"But there's no need. Please understand. You don't have to"

He peeled her hands back, startled at his own strength, and with a prisoning tenderness he took her breasts beneath the thin cotton. She wore no corset; they came willingly into the shape he imagined for them. Then with a sort of forced, grotesque humour, he closed his eyes and whispered. "I must. You've been walking home every night for more than two years now with every lecherous eye on the street pursuing you. Not once have you stayed till morning. People will begin to think you're a respectable woman."

His grip slackened; she felt the shuddering through him, and knew it was not desire.

Softly, she planted a kiss on his brow, easing herself out of his limp embrace. "It's all right, Cap. My dearest. I know. I've known all this time."

"Know what?" he said, but it was not really a question, for already he was scanning her face for the ill-disguised signs of disgust and repudiation. There were none.

"You always liked the young men," she said.

3

The night dream had pursued her here, as she knew it must. Its abode was in the bone's blood and in the mind that imagined it into being. She lay in its icy grip and felt its absolute breath against the last tenderness and heard it whisper sinuously of treacheries and mocked promises. She was Lily once again, squeezed tiny and tight into the last of the long-ago scenes. The branched dark was still vivid after seventy-one years, the ether of mosses and sweating fern and marooned violets awash in the nostrils and shut eyes. Papa's voice, clear and unquenchable, mouthed its sweet prevarication : "To my dearest princess, the Lady Fairchild, from your Papa who loves you forever." Forever was less than a night, less than the time it took her to dream of a father with arms like brass buttresses and breath as warm as wool and a stare as strong as Sampson's and truer than Troilus under the Trojan wall. She woke to find Papa gone and the gift of the Testament with its perjured inscription forlorn in her hand. Her heart froze, not caring one whit that the greenwood around her was weeping for all its lost children and crying out against the perfidy of a world cursed with the fickle seasons and tides of propagation.

47

1

Most days now Cap did not get out of bed until Cora arrived. Elmer came in early in the morning to help him to the water-closet and prop him up in his chair or help him back to bed. Cora never entered before the designated hour, though she often sneaked up to his door during her chores and listened to the wheezing cough that had replaced his breathing – asleep or awake.

"You're like an old trout gulping air," she teased.

"A sturgeon, amusing the caviar."

He never dressed now. When Cora closed and locked the wardrobe for good, he applauded like a seal behind her. Instead, he wore a silk dressing gown trimmed with ermine that Cora had been ordered to retrieve from a musty trunk. "To remind me of my past sins," he explained.

One day in late September, she arrived to find him sitting by the window. A book lay open in his lap, several more were scattered nearby.

"I do love that goldenrod along the river," he said. "It seems so pleased with itself."

Cora pulled her chair close, and fussed at his robe.

"I read all these books," he said, "long before I came to that German fella. I guess what I found in them – though it was better than the mess I'd made of the world – was not to my liking. Nonetheless, there's both truth and illusion in them in their pure forms."

She squeezed his hand and looked out across the prospect they had marked out as their own: marsh, river, lake, dune.

"Terrifying. Mr. Darwin got most of it right. There's more order and more chaos out there than we've yet dreamed of. What he didn't know – or didn't care to say – was that man has already freed himself from those laws. He has loosed the bonds of evolution, he has exorcized the ghost of god; he's inventing his own future. I've seen some of it already, but it's just begun. We've got the steam engine, the Gatling gun, the screw-prop battleship, we've got the power *up here* to unravel the laws that've governed our behavior and held it in check for thousands of years. It's wonderful and terrifying. A part of me wants to live longer just to see the outcome. But I'm terribly afraid, Cora. I look into the blackness where my heart used to be wonder what will become of us when we have invented everything? How much of our being human depends wholly upon our need to be a part of the mystery itself?"

•

"So you see now that all those flirtations I was notorious for, even my flamboyant escapades with Lady Marigold, served a very special purpose. When one is known everywhere as a roué, it is much easier to indulge one's illicit proclivities. You'd be surprised how many lonesome young men the army produces and how much comfort an older, wiser, more licentious gentleman can provide in times of stress."

Cora was curled in the bay-window seat – reading, half-listening, mildly annoyed at his attempts to shock, to keep the attention flowing his way.

"I knew that pervert of a Calvinist Dane would get to you," he said. He started to cough, *in extremis.*

"Your medicine's three inches from your ring finger," she said without looking up.

"I choose, therefore I am."

"I like that."

The coughing wound down to a feeble nickering sound: "Cora, come over and talk to me."

She did. "This Danish fella is sayin' that we have to know who we are by makin' up our own minds about what we do, an' being strong enough to take the consequences. The key to it, as you've written out for me, is makin' choices."

Cap shook his head ruefully. "Cora, you've told me more about your life and your travails than any one man ought to know, and I'll be damned if I can see where you had much choice. Like most women, you've been devastated by wars you never started, diseases you can't cure, and children who die on you or run off to lead their own lives without a pennyworth of gratitude. The world cares only for the species, and women bear the brunt of that reality."

She mulled that over for a while. "May be," she said. "But I chose somethin'. Every time."

"And what would that be?"

"I chose to love."

•

Cora entered the room as quietly as she dare. The morning brightness of Indian summer suffused the air, coming from no discernible direction, like altar light in a sunny cathedral. Cap was seated in his philosopher's chair, the familiar German tome, covers closed, on his knee. His gaze was aimed outward, his white beard radiantly professional. His right forearm was raised above the chair, its forefinger pointing out an error or an omission. Cora moved to his side. She looked at him for a long, commemorative second, then reached over and closed both of his eyes.

2

A cold, uncalled-for wind with the bite of December swept down from the lake over the dunes and through the shanties along the Lane and around the cozy homes of the town-site. It brushed past the little windbreak of firs at the north edge of the village cemetery, rippling the late-summer grass at Cora's feet. She shivered. The singsong intonations of the Reverend Baddeley sailed past her, warped by the wind. She kept her eyes on a tiny corner of the coffin – red cedar, all she could afford – and the ridge of soil near it. According to the worthies, she should have been grateful that the good parson, placing Christian compassion above Anglican orthodoxy, had offered to render the burial service to such an apostate. Conspicuously unrepentant to the end, cohabiting in squalid sin with a woman who changed her name more often than her address. She didn't care, though it occurred to her, despite the rector's graveside drone, that Cap might well be savouring the ironies of the situation. This ground won't hold you long, she thought. You need an audience.

Man that is born of woman hath but a short time to live, and is full of misery. He cometh up and is cut down like a flower; he fleeth as it were a shadow and never continueth in one stay…

A brief service had been held in the lobby of The Queen's. Duckface
Malloney was there, Elmer, Gertie and Mrs. Baddeley, who sang a sad hymn
in a high sunny soprano. Only Elmer accompanied the undertaker, the
parson and Cora as they clopped up Michigan Ave., barely noticed, though
several workmen doffed their caps. No church bells offered their petition to
the autumn air. The crunch of box-cars coupling echoed past them into First
Bush and beyond.

...we therefore commit his body to the ground,
earth to earth, ashes to ashes, dust to dust...

Cora glanced around her, once, to see if anyone else had come in behind
them. With solemn gaze, the undertaker, Josiah Smiley from Sarnia, kindly
remained beside the minister as he intoned the familiar words of intercession
and false comfort. Elmer stood nearby, watching Cora. She half expected the
two cousins from Toronto to show up, sooner or later, to claim what was left
of Cap's fortune. When she had suggested he make a will, he scoffed at the
notion. "I've never been able to will anything while alive, how could I
manage it when I'm dead? Besides, what would the old German think?" But
no one had followed them in.

When she had asked Malloney if they could use the lobby for the service,
he said yes immediately though without enthusiasm or apparent feeling of
any kind. Cap was never discussed between them. That Malloney must have
been under pressure from the community to purge it of this pariah whose
treacheries were even now felt throughout the village, Cora had little doubt.
How or why he resisted it, she did not know, though she suspected that he,
like her, had chosen to come to accept a life on the periphery. Were you right
after all? she wanted to shout to Cap.

The minister's orthodox lamentation was challenged by a stifled sob then
several unstifled ones more or less in unison. All eyes sidled right. Two
elderly, arthritic ladies – adorned in mourning clothes – had slipped into the
quietude unremarked to observe the ceremony from a short distance.
Overwrought by the holy litany and the sadness of the situation, they had
given vent to their sorrow. The cousins from Toronto, Cora thought, and
fought against a strange feeling of resentment. Their cries and lyric
whimperings seemed heartfelt. She tried to block them out. At least they're
weeping. You deserved that, at least. I'm glad they're here.

Reverend Baddeley carried on, doubling both volume and tempo.

...in sure and certain hope of the Resurrection to eternal life through our

Lord Jesus Christ who shall change our corruptible body…

The cross he had nervously essayed with the sand through his fingers looked more like a crooked question-mark waiting for someone to 'dot' it. Brushing past Cora, he strode over to the strangers and waited for them to receive his outstretched hands. She heard the ritual exchange, the timbre of inconsolability in the voices of the women.

"We're only second cousins," she heard one say, "but we grew up with him, we went to school together and you never forget that sort of experience, being so young and attached."

"Never, indeed," said the good parson, his relief both obvious and immense. He was back on home ground. "And you haven't seen him in some time, I assume?"

"Years and years," said the thinner, more aggrieved voice. "But once you knew Emery, you never forgot him. He was a sweet, sweet man."

"Emery?"

"We always called him by his middle name. He wanted us to call him Stan when he got older, but we never would. We always were a bit of a tease with him." She interrupted her encomium with several more sobs that left even Mr. Smiley discomfited. He began mumbling endearments to his horse.

"May the blessings of Our Lord ease your sorrow in the days to come," said the Reverend Baddeley.

"We come all the way down from Owen Sound and then up from London on the train. It was late. The taxi brought us right here from the station."

The taxi man's mare, obscured by the cedar hedge near the road, whinnied in the direction of the undertaker's gelding.

"Emery was from Owen Sound, you know," said the stronger cousin. "The whole family, what's left of us."

Her sister added a sniffle for emphasis.

"But I understood Mr. Dowling was born and raised in London."

A silence deeper than death seized the cemetery and its grieving occupants. The gelding's tail whisked an imaginary fly. Cora turned to look. Mr. Smiley, as shocked as if one of his cadavers had sat up and saluted him, came over to the ladies, who looked pathetically about them for some explanation.

"Your cab driver's gone an' made a terrible mistake," he said, hat in hand.

"But we told him, didn't we sis, we was late, we'd missed the church service but would he please take us as fast as he could to the interment of Stanfield E. Dowler."

"And he brought us here."

"Saints preserve us," said the minister.

•

They were all gone: even Elmer, his sad moon face turning away down Michigan Ave., the cousins, poor souls, to grieve again at another site; the minister and undertaker to the call of their respective professions. Later, under the cloak of darkness, the sexton would come with his boy to lower the coffin and seal it off, with dirt and grass-seed, from the morning sun. For the moment, she and Cap were alone once again. The chill wind sent some of the fallen leaves chattering across the grass. The limbs of a maple stretched and complained, but Cora was no longer cold. She thought of the cousins jouncing and breathless in the taxi, afraid they would be too late to expend their grief loyally husbanded all the way down from Owen Sound and all the way up to Sarnia on the Grand Trunk, late as usual. And Reverend Baddeley trying to retract his hasty, misdirected condolences, saving them for a more appropriate occasion. She felt a bubble of laughter disrupt the numbness around her heart, then the tears intercepting it.

•

As soon as she got back, Cora went to the pantry to continue the cleaning she had started the day before. Malloney came to the door and called her out into the hall.

"You don't have to work today, Mrs. Burgher. Why don't you go home, or just find a place to rest around here. You been through a lot."

"I'd like to work," she said, "if it's all right."

He seemed uncomfortable, the wrinkles in his face tensed against some certain ambush. Suddenly they relaxed, and his eyes doubled their size, gripping everything in their ken. "Cora," he said, "you been hearin' the same rumours I've been, about the Grand Trunk packin' up an' desertin' this place after thirty years. Well, even the rumours, which I don't for one second believe, are keepin' people away. Business is real slow right now. You can work if you like, but I suggest you take a few weeks off. Go somewhere. See somebody. Get the hell outta this place."

"I got no other place to go," she said.

His face twisted in preparation for some kind of speech or gambit, his eyes shrivelled in their casing, but nothing came out. His drayman's hands swung at his side, and finally he slouched towards the lobby.

"Mr. Malloney."

He looked back over his shoulder then came fully around. "Kevin," he said.

"You may be hearin' from some cousins Cap had in Toronto, once they read about his funeral in the papers."

He came close to her, alert.

"His aunt left him some money, not a lot, but all the same I expect they'll be comin' down to find out."

Malloney looked straight at her. "Dowling's got no money to leave to nobody."

"I thought –"

"His aunt's money run out. He's bust."

She could barely get the next words out. "How long?"

"A year ago."

•

The wind blew harder and colder that night, the last one of September, 1892 – the date some stranger's hand had chiseled on Cap Dowling's tombstone. Doors were locked and shutters tightened. There was talk of a tornado, of gales on the lake wild enough to send tremors through the sailors' wives alone in their beds, through the captain's helpmate measuring the minutes along her widow's walk. On nights like this, the Point was all maritime. Later on, foghorns wailed against the driving sleet, proclaiming loneliness and fear in the cold tongue below the gut. Cora made a pot of tea and sat by herself in the gloom. Hap was at the factory helping his sons batten the hatches. Above the clatter of rain on the windows, she heard the Grand Trunk Express roaring around the bend by the river and steaming towards the station. She thought of the hoboes in their encampment beyond the Lane, rain dancing on the tin of their lean-tos and dripping into the hot, flameless fires below. She thought of the outcasts, the exiles, the forsaken, the unforgivable. She pulled the comforter off her bed and sat down in Hap's rocker. Let it rain, she thought. Let it not rain. I am here.

•

The rap on the door jolted her upright and awake in one motion. Hap never knocked. The rapping came again, magnified by the dark. Loud but not regular enough to be official. As she started for the door, candle in hand, it came again, rattling the hinges in its urgency. One of Hap's boys was her only thought. She lifted the latch and let the door swing inward.

A man stood blinking at the flame and the wash of interior heat. He was a hobo, no doubt just off the Express. The rain had smeared soot into grotesque shapes over his face. He wore a battered fedora and a wool overcoat three sizes too large and soaked through. He held a rumpled package in his hands and stared at her as if he ought to know her.

As she started instinctively back, he stepped forward and pulled up the canvas flap shielding the gift in his arms "It's me, Mama. Bradley." He spoke in a consumptive whisper. "I've come home."

She fell back as if struck.

"And this is Eddie." He lifted the baby's face into view.

PART THREE

Eddie

48

1

Granny Coote sat by the window looking at the altered landscape to the west, wondering when Mr. Stadler would arrive to begin the transformation, and finally drifting into a doze. "After wars, pestilence," Cap had told her many times. You were right, for once, she thought. She let the events of that extraordinary month in 1918 pass before her for Cap's skeptical appraisal.

•

Sometime in the middle of the night of October 1, Oliver Fletcher sneezed. Just a cold but worrisome nonetheless because Ollie had been gassed at Ypres and returned home with half a lung. Young boys stopped him on the street and asked to hear him breathe. By midday he was running a fever. Five-year-old Barbie Savage, who'd survived scarlet fever and whooping cough, stopped playing with her china-head doll and asked to be put down for her nap an hour early. Chuck Simmers, delivering bread, felt a stab of pain in his lower back: lumbago. He headed for the Richmond House and some afternoon solace.

There was considerable unease along Charles Street at the sight of young Dr. Simon, black bag in hand, hurrying up to the Fletcher house and entering without a knock or by your leave. By suppertime everyone knew that Ollie had died: poison gas. A hero.

Still, no one was seen going in or out of the stricken house. It was morning before the undertaker arrived from Sarnia. Mrs. Carpenter, a lifelong friend, was observed about noon on her way to Mrs. Fletcher's with a soup tureen still steaming. Barbie Savage refused to get up from her nap. A fever took hold of her in the early hours. Dr. Simon rushed in. Neither of the Savage twins was seen on the streets that evening. Chuck Simmers had to be carried home from the hotel in his wagon. He swore he'd only had two drafts. By morning, his wife had covered him with three blankets and he was calling for more. By the time Dr. Simon arrived, his lips were beginning to turn blue, a deep lassitude had taken possession, and he mistook the doctor for his horse. Mrs. Simmers locked the children in their rooms.

Some sort of collective distemper seemed to have struck the village. Sailors just off the boats were ordered to stay on the docks. Two who slipped undetected into the Mens at the Richmond House found themselves in a scuffle, then a punch-up in the alley, and finally were dragged to the wharf and dumped. Any stranger on the street was eyed with suspicion, rudely dealt with by junior clerks, welcomed out of town. Among friends, customers and neighbours, tempers were short: a lifelong word misunderstood, newly resented. "The war's been goin' on too long," grocer Redmond said to his wife before bed, "people are gettin' squirrely."

"Too many false stories about an armistice," Maxie Wise opined to his wife already in bed. "You can't keep raisin' people's hopes like that."

Next day while the hearse carrying Ollie Fletcher's body to the cemetery passed by a weeping crowd of mourners along Michigan Ave., news arrived of the deaths of little Barbie and Chuck Simmers. Turned blue an' died, both of 'em, the rumour rippled west to east following the black caisson of the fallen soldier. *Flu.*

•

Granny heard the church bells tolling their dark news. She saw the hearses from Sarnia passing her house en route to one of the three churches on the main street. She saw the toy coffin being carried from the Savage's house. She saw the white wreath on the door. She tried to make room in her heart for the grief of a child's death.

•

For days no one seemed to pass her window, at least not while she was looking. The recess bell from the school stopped ringing in mid-morning. Twice more that week she was roused by a carillon of death – all three belfries lamenting in unison. Dr. Simon went into the Savage house again. He wore a surgical mask. That Sunday, no bells proclaimed heaven to the faithful. Two figures in white – masked – hurried past and into Mrs.

Carpenter's next door. A mother's cry scattered the eerie Sunday silence. For two years now Granny had not ventured beyond the front gate or the back hedge. Her tongue had paralyzed itself. She had nothing to say.

On Monday morning she went out to look at the village.

•

The sun was bright, the air dry and warm. She was alone on St. Clair Street. Not a soul stirred on verandah or waved from hedge or fence. Not a single door or window stood open to the breeze, to the rare sweetness of autumn. As she passed familiar doorways, she felt curtains part and fall behind her. Leila Savage, eyes red-rimmed above her gauze mask, kept her glassy stare aimed straight ahead as she went by. She was carrying a crockery pot wrapped in a towel. On Michigan Ave. several figures, heads down, walked briskly towards some overweening imperative, as if any contact with the streets themselves were irrelevant, hazardous even. Several women came out of the back entrance of the Anglican Church, not saying a word, reached the sidewalk and parted company, pretending their momentary meeting was accidental. The town gossips, she thought, amazed. She turned into the churchyard. Alien ground. She was walking on the moon, the back side.

In the vestibule she heard the minister's wife say that they had more food than they could use, wasn't it wonderful how generous people were in a crisis, and so on. But they needed volunteers to take it into the worst houses, some of which, like the McLeod clan farther down the Lane, had not been checked at all. Perhaps they were all dead. She felt the astonishment of the Anglican ladies upon her as she reached out for a tureen of soup. Mrs. Stokes handed her a mask. She shook her head no. It had begun. Without a word.

•

On this part of the Lane noise was usually continuous and varied. Babies cried in several keys of displeasure, there were shouts of unincarcerated children, the bawl of a calf or pig or battered wife. At this moment not even the chickens flicked an eyelid. Silence had become something positive, not an absence but an embodiment of something foul oozing out of the cracks in the house, under the doors, and settling over the styes and coops and hutches where animals squeezed into the darkest corners and watched.

She walked briskly, stepping over the debris in the yard of Jessie McLeod's shack, wishing she could call out some warning, some comforting salutation. She banged the tureen, still steaming, against the door. No sound from within. She turned the knob and leaned inward. Then she glanced down and saw the jamb that had been wedged against the world. She waited. She heard breathing on the other side of the door, shallow but quick. A child's. She fought the urge to speak, knowing what chaos that would bring. Instead she began to hum, searching for a tune and keeping her voice soft and lullaby low. Something ticked – weakly – at the shim. It popped loose. Seconds later, still humming, she felt the door drawn backwards into whatever fear had seized the interior and its inhabitants. She saw a black-haired McLeod child - a girl about five-years-old.

Granny smiled or thought she did because the child did too. Granny edged into the gloomy 'front room' of the shack.

"Mommy won't wake up," the child said. "We're hungry but Pa says he'll whip us if we go out." She began to weep, not in the sobbing, physical manner of children but in the quiet, foreknowing way of stricken adults.

Granny put her hand on the little girl's shoulder. She strode to a table, put the food down, and went through some curtains into a bedroom. Jessie – barely thirty, one of Eddie's playmates – lay propped up on two filthy pillows, her eyes closed, feigning sleep, feigning peace – for the children's sake. Beside the bed was a homemade cradle. Granny reached down to grasp the baby's hand. It was as stiff as a doll's. Closing the curtains, she went into the next room. Three mattresses, salvaged from the dump, had been laid out on the floor. Sam McLeod – Jessie's second cousin, sweetheart, then husband – lay naked on one of them, shivering and moving his lips in soundless, misshapen moans. His three boys were huddled under covers nearby, alive but unable to acknowledge her presence, their eyes glazed, all their weeklong aching passed into painless languor. She felt for fever and there was none. The youngest boy let his eyes try to take her in. Through his puffed lips she heard him whisper: "Are you an angel?"

Granny set about her work, little 'Claire' at her heels. Pillows were improvised so the boys could be propped up, washed and fed a drop or two of soup. Sam was made warm and as comfortable as possible. He couldn't take any food. Claire ate ravenously, and turned chatty. Granny sent her in to cheer up her brothers while she washed and wrapped the bodies in the other room. Then she went next door to Katie McLeod's. Katie's face appeared in the window. "We're all right," she mouthed. "Go away, please." Granny gestured and pointed towards her sister-in-law's place, trying to convey with her eyes the dread news. The curtain was whipped shut. Moments later a male voice said: "Get out of here, old woman, an' leave us alone!"

She walked all the way back to young Dr. Simon's house on Alfred Street and sat on the stoop, waiting for him to return. His nurse glanced out of the surgery window from time to time, not unkindly. Young Dr. Simon, the first physician ever to have his residence in the village, pale and solemn, followed her to the Lane. When he had finished inside, he said to her, "We need you very much, Mrs. Coote. You come to my office in the mornings if you can, and I'll tell you where to go and how to help." He touched her hand, the way Eddie used to when he needed her approval.

•

Mrs. Stokes had everything ready for her at the Church each morning, afternoon and evening: food, aspirin, quinine, clean bedding. Dr. Simon was too busy now. He left instructions and disappeared. He looked sixty-years-old and haunted. One by one, the volunteers themselves went down. More were needed; few could be found. Neighbours lived in fear not only of the pestilence – now spread to every street and lane – but of the cry from the door or a child with a name on the verandah begging help, the dreadful and unretractable decision to be made in an instant. Mrs. Carpenter walked down to her sister's with a bundle of food and stood for ten minutes on the front porch before entering the diseased rooms within. The next day her whole body went numb. She lay helpless while six-year-old David and the three-year-old peered at her with puzzled faces. Eventually, David started to cry; Flora wandered into the shed and began to play with her doll. It was still light when Granny came by – her day spent in ceaseless walking, washing the living and the dead, holding the children in her arms, and bearing the useless medicines of the day – unable to utter a single word of comfort or goodbye. Flora's face was pressed against the front window. Granny turned and went in.

•

Ethel Carpenter was moving into the fever stage. Granny went for the doctor who was out. The nurse, glassy-eyed herself, said he was near collapse. Granny was back at the Carpenter's gate when she heard the bell over the Presbyterian church begin its sombre tolling, joined shortly by its sister muses. Flora sat on her mother's bed. Ethel was in a deep sleep. Granny lifted the child away and after much difficulty succeeded in getting her off to sleep as well. Then she went in to the boy. Fever and aches were upon him. When she tried to get the medicine down, he vomited all over her. She had just got clean sheets on the bed and the shivering lad covered when the nosebleed struck. Granny shuddered. It took over an hour to get it stopped. Blood sprayed over her and the bedding and the boy as if someone had cracked a fire hydrant. David sobbed and went silent with terror. He slumped back into an incredulous semi-coma, his eyes wide open, taking in every tick and rustle of movement in the room and in his rebellious body. He'll die of the fear, she thought. Like the others. She moved about as if she knew exactly what she was doing and every move were calculated to bring about instant recovery. She held his hand, stroked his brow, set some kind of hope in her face, and tried to forestall the exhaustion and the bone-deep ache threatening to overwhelm her.

When she woke it was dawn. She felt feverish. Flora was tugging at her sleeve. The boy seemed to be resting. She went across to Ethel who slept peacefully. She's dreaming of her husband, and the promised armistice and reunion. Granny went back to check on David. His fever had ebbed, but she could not get the boy to open his eyes. Whenever she touched him, he cried out in a hollow voice, moaned, and went still.

Granny went again for the doctor. He was exhausted and resting for the first time in days. At the church, Mrs. Stokes begged her to take some soup to the McLeod's then quinine and camphor to three other families – with all members stricken – along Albert Street. She stayed on there to cook meals, stepping over dazed or delirious victims who had selected any convenient spot to lie down and rest and refuse to move. They ogled her like a ghost whose presence was deemed not a little malign. Their arms floated towards a soup bowl then drowned in its weight. Eyeballs bulged, tightened, braced for the siege. Eyes pleaded, called out for explanation, justice, expiation. The children clung to their skirts, and put their fingers against her lips' refusal.

When she got back to the Carpenters' it was almost dark. David's lips were swollen shut, his skin scorched, and his eyes were squeezed tight against all the terrors the night would bring but one. He opened them once, saw the dark angel bending down then closed them for good. When the sun nudged her awake in the morning, Granny looked upon the dead boy and then his mother. Ethel Carpenter stared not at her son but at Granny. Her look said: what right have you to save me and not him? Who are you, anyway? When Flora came skipping up behind her and grabbed her mother's skirts in play, Ethel whirled and slapped her across the face. Granny started towards the stunned child, and Ethel glared at her again. *There, you see, you don't have it all to yourself.* The child's scream was piercing enough to startle the dead.

•

On the third Saturday in October the pestilence reached right into the heart of the village. Within an hour everyone who could listen heard the news that young Dr. Simon had succumbed to the disease he had helped so many to survive. The funeral was held on a Sunday, an unprecedented event. The cortege included most of those who could still walk, had already recovered, or brave enough to venture out at any cost. The Methodist bell tolled for an hour. The other two bells had been struck dumb by the plague.

Granny did not attend the graveside ceremony. She was busy nursing Rose Underhill through the critical period of her delirium.

•

"The plagues that followed a war," Cap said, "were not unlike the year-long sieges of an enemy castle in the late Middle Ages. The shells or missiles or fireballs or arrows fell at random in no fixed sequence. People died under them regardless of the precautions they took, the prayers they incanted, or their own self-evident worthiness. In such cases over a prolonged period of time, the random marauding of Master Death often cause the victims to blame themselves and prompt the survivors to look for new configurations of the heavens or new canons of blessedness to explain their own good fortune. A plague is a devilishly unsettling affair."

Rose Underhill got well. Flora searched in the garden for her brother.

The bells tolled twelve times in all during that month. Five of the souls were Anglican.

•

Granny returned to the sanctuary of Arthur's shack. But not before she overheard, on her final trip to the church kitchen a one-sided 'conversation' between the Reverend Stokes and several senior churchwomen.

"She may be a bit queer – who isn't at her age – but I tell you, ladies, she's a candidate for sainthood, if you'll pardon the expression. You saw the way she worked throughout this dreadful month. A hundred times she risked her own life, going right into the dens of disease where no one else but dear Dr. Simon would venture. It was as if she knew that God Himself had chosen her for this mission of mercy and would offer her all the protection she needed. Rarely have I seen such an example of God's love and the spirit of Christianity 'bodied forth' in the actions of a single parishioner. My own feeling is that the dear soul, even though she's not attended service these many years, decided that during the few months remaining before her own imminent entry into paradise, she would bear witness in a way that would atone for a lifetime of neglect or perhaps even rejection. We must find a way of honouring such valour, such selflessness, such preeminent charity."

•

Safe in her own kitchen, Granny curled her hands around a cup of tea and said softly into the glow behind the stove: "I'm sorry, Arthur. I'm still here. You'll have to wait a little while yet."

•

With more than three-hundred-fifty thousand German troops incapacitated by the Spanish influenza that had already killed more than twenty million people world-wide, a halt was called to the mutual slaughter in Europe. On November 11, shortly after noon, Granny heard the bells ringing out the news.

2

Across the street a battered, lime-encrusted pick-up farted and coughed to a standstill in front of the vacant lot. A middle-aged fellow, swarthy and lithe, jumped from the open cab and, hands on hips, surveyed the site for the monument. Out of the passenger's seat hopped an old man who scuttled over to the younger man's side. They were both smiling.

The stonemasons, come at last.

49

1

The hardest thing Cora had ever done in her fifty-some years on this earth was to start walking up the Lane a few doors to tell Peg Granger that she couldn't keep the baby. She'd have to give him up. Peg had been looking after him while Cora nursed Bradley; she had not set eyes on the thin, quaking thing since. Ten years ago, any decision not to accept the responsibility of rearing an orphaned creature – especially one with her own blood in its veins – would have been unthinkable. Those ten intervening years had brought her to *this* pass: where, for two nights following Bradley's interment in the Point Edward cemetery (not many yards from Cap's resting place), she had lain awake rehearsing the speech she would deliver to Peg explaining why the child ought to be placed in the Sarnia orphanage. That Peg herself might offer to raise it with her own large brood – two of them almost grown – had not figured into her stream of excuses and pleas. I am old, she had thought, not in years but in experience, in the expenditure of human feeling. After all, there was only so much pity or remorse or hurt, only so many tiny jolts of joy or vacant acres of grieving loss that any one set of flesh-and-bones could be expected to endure. Something had to be kept in reserve, for oneself, for the last days. It took energy to die, as Bradley had just shown her, and reserves of feeling.

With Cap, she had known this from the moment she had interceded to prolong his life. There would be no redemption for either of them, but at their age and in their circumstance something more vital and prized: a rich living-through of select hours, one by one. That she was there in his room to shepherd him towards death and towards some version of dying he could accept as appropriate was never in question. But it had been only towards the end that she had come to the realization that Cap himself began to understand how much it was she who needed him. And when he died, she did not feel the stabbing sense of loss and dismemberment that followed the

other deaths small and large, expected and sudden. She missed him and
would have to reorient her remaining days to exclude their daily
collaborations. But Cap's voice persisted inside her – not as a lapsing memory
or object of endearment (as the others were still) but as part of her own
speech and the thoughts it shaped. You will never be anybody's memory, she
said. Not like Brad, she thought sadly. Resurrected—for what? To die again?
To let me play out once again the mockeries of nurse and angel?

But a child, six-months old, who deserved to grow and breathe the wide
air and become something in a world partly of his own making – that was
asking more than she was capable of giving. That the dark gods were
heartless she had known since she was eight or nine, and ever since had
gathered evidence for the case against them. That they were capable of such
a cruel jest as this, that their laughter was a joker's guffaw, she was now
certain. In her own view, she was a tired, worn-out, benumbed creature,
disenfranchised of the earth's aboriginal blessings. She desired now only the
small comfort of a quiet, brief old age, a little time to dream backwards.
Then, out of the jester's joke book – or the world's will as Cap might say –
presto: the return of the prodigal son, dead twice already, and the babe, the
boy – Eddie.

How can I play the mother again? My fingers are arthritic, the skin
droops from my cheeks, I've lost a tooth, my breasts are withered pods. I am
a parody of motherhood; I haven't smiled with any semblance of innocence
in ten years. The little tad will shriek when he sees me, as he did the first
night in his fever. And what if I should dredge up, somewhere, some
facsimile of mother's love, some fissure of untapped affection from which to
nurture that miniature being – what then? I might die when he's four or eight
or twelve – where will be he then? Who would care for him enough to
embrace his orphaned heart? I am alone. I have no one. I rent two rooms in
an old man's house. I have nothing to give but the derelict self. And what if
some perverse miracle should occur and we both survive? When he's twenty
and a man, I will be over seventy years – a creaking, babbling buffoon of a
woman with cataracts and a weak bladder and the temper of a nanny goat. It
can't be done, she concluded. It would defy reason and nature.

So when she had left her place that bright morning in October, she had
irrevocably decided to have Peg carry the babe straight to the orphanage. She
wouldn't even ask to see it. But in the few minutes it took her to reach the
tracks and cross them, she changed her mind. She decided to take Eddie back

with her. Reasons were never enough. Don't you dare laugh, Cap Dowling, she said, swinging her arms to work out the kinks.

•

"He's an angel," Peg Granger said. "Good as gold; you won't ever be sorry for keepin' him."

Cora had steeled herself against the worst: nights of fretful crying, daytime tantrums, numb suffering under the fever of measles, chicken-pox, mumps, whooping cough or worse. She had seen it all, survived and not survived, and if she must do it again. She'd take the bit as far forward in her teeth as she could and smile through the grimace. Eddie soon let her down. He was a joy, a child with happiness and good humour born in him. He slept right through most nights, and the few occasions when the colic struck, he needed only to feel her arms around him and the rhythm of the rocker to be soothed again. And just before he'd drift back to sleep, without fail he would grasp her by one of her thumbs and squeeze it. When he did get the measles, at two, he whimpered with the pain in his sunless room till she thought she'd go mad. The moment the fever subsided, he cast the pale, blue gratitude of his eyes upon her and begged for a story. Even then he never took advantage of an illness, as most children do. Whenever he complained, Cora was certain he was hurting somewhere. Whenever he had a choice, he chose joy.

Where did such feeling originate? she often wondered. I loved all my own children as much, doted on them more than I do Eddie because I was then young and vigorous and foolhardy. During the first winter she left him on his own more than she should have – when the arthritis or the black mood would come upon her and leave her frozen to the bed for hours on end while the fire took its chill from the room. Once, in February, when he was starting to crawl everywhere, and she lay in a daze dreaming of snow and fiery locomotion, she was brought back from the brink of something wondrous and lethal by a tug on her left thumb. She opened her eyes. Eddie was pulling himself upright so that his face was parallel with hers. He grinned in delight at his triumph and her sharing of it. He pushed his nose against her stiff cheek and made his 'choo-choo' sound, and laughed. She let him pretend he was drawing her upright by the thumbs out of her delirium.

•

Hap Withers, now over seventy, went up to the Lane to live with his son and family. He told Cora she could have all four rooms of the cottage if she wanted, for a dollar a year. All he needed to know was that the couch in his old room would be available on those few occasions when he felt like "coming home for a spell". He never did, and that room became Eddie's when he was ready for it.

When the decline of the village began in earnest, Cora found herself working only two days a week at The Queen's. She bundled Eddie up, tucked him in a wicker basket and hauled him on a sled down there with her. The staff did their best to disrupt his even disposition. With her savings over the years she didn't need to work full-time, but she found it helped to get out and around and see familiar faces and places, though many of them jarred old griefs. By spring, Eddie was beginning to toddle and say his first words, and she could see he deserved better than staying cooped up day and night with an old crone. On sunny days while she revived her vegetable patch, she tied Eddie onto a long rope so he could roam a bit and get the feel of unfettered walking. Still, he had little company except the maids at The Queen's. She watched his eyes perk up at the animal calls of the urchin boys back in the dunes.

She went out and arranged to do some housecleaning for Elizabeth Sanders, the schoolteacher and helped mind her retarded son, Sammy (Slowboat to the kids). She was recommended in turn to Maggie Hare, wife of the manager of the freight-sheds. From time to time she worked for Agnes Farrow and Mrs. Thibeault, scrubbing or ironing or helping with a meal on special family occasions. "She's quick and quiet," Mrs. Thibeault said all over town, "and what's more, she keeps her mouth shut. For some queer reason, the kids go for her."

She brought Eddie along, on a sled in winter and a wagon in summer. He spent much of his second year of life sitting on a pile of laundry, playing second or third fiddle to the household children and enjoying the constant shift of scene and character. His cheerfulness was so infectious it often obstructed the premeditated whining of the little brats abandoned to her care. If Sammy lunged after a toy of his, Eddie would look hurt for a second, weigh the effects of a piteous glance at Cora then pick up a less-prized object and begin to play with it. Sammy, who was a year older than Eddie but spoke

with a slurred stutter, soon started to call her 'Gran-nee', despite repeated
warnings from his mother. When Eddie's words began to arrive – fresh and
tumbling over each other – the one he chose for her was Granny. And
Granny she became, even at The Queen's among the staff and old-timers in
the lobby, several of whom remembered most of the names she had
accepted as her own in the years past.

Granny decided to give Lucien's name to young Eddie. Eddie Burgher.
Why not? she thought. I have been Mrs. Cora Burgher for eight years. It is
the name I will take to my grave. All she ever told Eddie about his real
parents was that his mother died having him in Toronto (which was almost
the truth) and that his father had been an engineer on the Grand Trunk,
whose locomotives still roared by their back window several times a day.
"When you're grown up, I'll tell you all I know about them," she promised
after he'd endured teasing it in the schoolyard. Trusting her with a naive
faith which afterwards led her to weep in her room, Eddie never raised the
subject again.

•

Still, many days were spent at the little cottage Hap Withers provided for
them. Sometimes Hap could be persuaded to leave his own clan and join
them for a Saturday supper. Eddie, normally shy around males, took to him
immediately. Hap whittled him a tiny flute out of willow and showed him
how to tease a skidding, dizzy music out of it. The neighbourhood near the
tracks was populated not only by Hap's grandchildren but by second and
third generations of Shawyers, McCourts and McLeods. Gangs of ruffian
boys combed the shadows at dusk with their signal cries, and bruited danger
in the long afternoons of summer. One day, when Eddie was three, they
came for him, and she could no longer hold him back.

"We're just gonna play hide-and-go-seek," he begged her. "I won't go
near the water."

From her place in the garden, she scanned the flats and the blotches of
bush, detecting the telltale signs of his running, the teasing crouch behind a
shrub or sandbank, the soar of his little-boy voice *Home free!* against the
surrounding derision and mockery. When he came home, he had a scrape
and a bruise on his cheek. "I fell down chasing Jimmy Shawyer," he lied.
Though he never became part of the residential gangs, he joined them for

games or swimming at the beach, content to take what the moment offered and always making up his own mind about what he wished to do or how far he would venture into their tribal rites. Oddly enough, they could not cope with his cheerful outlook and irrepressible goodwill. When one of the bullies jerked his prize apple out of his hand and chomped into it, Eddie grabbed him so quickly by the wrists the bully's back was against a tree trunk with his dignity collapsing before he could bleat out a protest. With the entire retinue watching (Granny from behind her raspberry canes), Eddie glared at his tormentor, threatened him with a devastating knee. He let a smile overtake his countenance, his laugh gently coaxing a guarded one out of the bully till they both laughed. Eddie relaxed his grip and turned around to let the others know that it had all been in good fun.

He's going to be all right, Granny thought. Whenever he can, he'll choose happiness.

2

The effects upon Point Edward of the new tunnel under the St. Clair River were not immediate. People in the Point at first joined in the bubbling of self-congratulation over having one of the century's great engineering achievements. 'Let the Yankees top that one' was a common sentiment. The first cheer echoed when the passenger service from London – despite the skeptics and doomsayers – continued right through to the Point Edward wharf. The car shops and roundhouse and the freight sheds to service the steamships remained intact and thriving in the last boom years before the depression of the early 'nineties.

But when strangers arrived one morning in 1893 and began chipping away at the grand station as if it were a temple abandoned to the conquerors, people began to talk – on corners, in the barbershop, over tea, in smoky taverns. When the wrecking crew came shortly thereafter and proceeded to demolish the roundhouse without a care to what they smashed or burnt in the fields, the talk turned to whispers, half-hearted jokes, and jittery silences. Everyone and no one knew what blow would next strike or from what quarter. Half the town either worked in or supplied the wants of the car shops where every damaged coach or hopper in western Ontario was hauled. A small local car shop had been constructed in Sarnia near the new roundhouse, which was near the new tunnel. A few men were transferred there. No one panicked yet. The transferees stayed put, taking the trolley to work every morning. They were lauded from three pulpits.

•

In the spring of 1894, Harmon Hayman, the milkman, and his wife, Billie, returned home from a weekend visit with relatives in Wyoming. Harmon was unhitching the horse by the barn at the edge of Alexandra Avenue when he heard Billie shout from the raspberry patch—a sharp 'yip' as if she'd been stabbed with tines. When he reached her side and was relieved to discover no blood or bruises, he looked across in the direction of his wife's trembling forefinger. Jeb Stuart's house was gone, as was his chicken coop and tool shed. Posts, fencing, everything that was portable was gone. The vegetable patch was stripped clean. On Friday, when the Haymans had waved goodbye, everything had been in its customary place, though as Billie remarked later, the Missus had been a 'mite teary-eyed'. The Haymans stood silently together, staring at an absence, a failure of permanency they could not accept. The Stuart house may have been the first of the Point Edward homes to be dismantled and removed overnight to the more favourable climes of Sarnia, but it was not the last. Between 1893 and 1901, the village population dwindled from well over two thousand to seven hundred and eighty. Two of the churches closed for a year because they could not muster enough souls to pray for the town's survival. Folks kept a wary watch on their neighbours, searching for early signs of faithlessness as they invigilated the quarantined homes that carried pestilence enough to undo them all.

Entire streets disappeared, ragweed and wild carrot rioted on the wounds, and boys flew kites over the grassy graves in the autumn. A gaggle of wagons was a common sight during these years. Tumbrils and overpacked drays moved up St. Clair Street towards Sarnia through the mist of a spring morning. Bricks and mortar and salvageable boards of lives lay stacked beside chesterfields and weeping children. Forlorn dogs, foolish in their faith, trailed in the dust behind. 'Gotta go where the work is' was the universal plea of exculpation. It was a sad truth no villager could deny.

The thriving hotel trade, the verve of boarding-house life, the cosmopolitan flux of sailor, bagman, bigwig, drummer, carny and capitalist: all followed the romance of the rails elsewhere. As one of The Queen's philosophers said: "We rolled to riches an' glory on the wheels of progress, an' now they just up an' run over us."

•

Eddie loved to sing, and though he remained shy with strangers, he announced that he would take part in the Methodist Christmas concert. He had agreed to be one of the three kings. "I get to give the gold," he said, "and I get to sing 'We Three Kings of Orient Are'." Granny showed commendable enthusiasm. It would be good for him to get on stage, get over a little of his shyness, or more accurately, his natural reticence to put himself forward.

"What are Kings of Orient?" he asked.

"I don't think it matters," she said.

"You're gonna come?" he asked. There was no answer but "Yes."

•

Thus it happened that Granny found herself in the basement hall of the Methodist Church on the twenty-third of December, 1899. Eddie, a few weeks short of his eighth birthday, took his place on a makeshift stage. He appeared draped in ersatz gold lamé with a cardboard crown on his temple and Mrs. Sanders' jewel box in his hands. Granny nodded politely to several of the older women she recognized, brushing aside their stares and resisting any of the droll rejoinders that echoed in her head. Mercifully, Eddie's number – shared with two other regal personages whose soprano was suspiciously high – came early in the programme. His voice was pure tone, like the A-note struck on the unvarnished oak of a xylophone. It sweetened all the air it sailed through. Granny felt irked that several boorish women in front of her began mumbling before the last chord of the piece had faded.

For the remainder of the pageant Eddie stood at the back of the stage and placed his kingly gaze upon the manger and a host of other late arrivals. Only once did he allow his eye to meet his Granny's and return stalwartly to his duties. Long before the pageant ended with a multi-sided rendition of 'Joy to the World', Granny had ceased observing the drama before her. The music began to make an impression upon her, in particular the robust yet nimble choreography of the piano accompaniment. She was drawn again and again to the instrument, and to the fingers that hopped and sprang and babied and ambushed the high-strung keys. The ancient carols and roundelays shook the cornerstones and belfry beams of the Lord's edifice. She dared to peek up at the eyes fathering such divine mayhem, and discovered them in search of her own.

●

One of the odd jobs Granny had taken on to supplement her diminished savings was sweeping out the Oddfellows' Hall each Thursday morning after the regular meeting the evening before. Beside the Hall sat the 'Coote shack' as it was known around town. It had not always been so. When Arthur Coote arrived in 1888 with his bride, Helen, to take up his duties as organist and choir director for the Methodist Church, a grateful congregation talked the village council into leasing them a town lot beside the Oddfellows' Hall. They built with their own hands a pleasant cottage suitable for a childless couple. Granny herself recalled the whitewashed siding, blue shutters and scrolled flower-boxes straining with geraniums. But when Helen Coote died suddenly around 1894, the place 'went to pot' by degrees. No more paint touched its outer walls, the shutters dangled, rotted, retreated into the weeds and stuck up through the winter snows like mangled thumbs. The geraniums had thinned, grown emaciated, sucked at the summer air, and suffocated just before the bottom fell out of the boxes. Ragamuffin boys ripped the sides off to make weapons. But Arthur remained inside with his piano and memorabilia. He continued to rouse congregations with unrehearsed Bach or Schubert, patiently assembled the wayward voices of his choir, and found time to give piano lessons to several village prodigies. "I think your grandson may have musical talent," he said to Granny at tea after the concert. "I'd be happy to have him come over. Free of charge, of course." She didn't mention anything to Eddie.

On New Year's Eve, the last day of the nineteenth century, an appropriately grand and progressive ball was held at the Oddfellows' Hall. Four blocks away, seated in a wooden rocker reading the 'Tale of the Sleeping Beauty' to a drowsing Eddie, Granny could hear the brass and drums and wild shenanigans. Long into the night and the first dawn of the new age, her sleep was disturbed by whoops and fireworks and the casual discharge of rusty carbines.

When she arrived in the morning to clean up, she was not dismayed by

the mess left by the celebrants. Eddie was safe in the hands of one of the
Granger girls, so the whole day lay before her. She surveyed the debris and
wreckage around her, mentally plotting a path through it towards a
semblance of order. Humming to herself, she started to work.

At some point the hum in her head began to match the tune on the piano
coming from afar. She thought she might be imagining it, but when she
stopped and arched an ear towards the high windows on the south side, the
lilt of the Londonderry Air was unmistakable. It was coming from Arthur
Coote's shack. At the tea after the concert she remembered his words. "They
tell me I'm a very good teacher. I wouldn't know about that, but I do get
along well with children. You should come over some time and let me play
for you". He had glanced down to include Eddie in his invitation, but before
he could continue, he was spirited away by an anxious looking Mrs. Sanders.

When Granny stopped to eat her bread and cheese at noon, she heard
the piano start up again. The song was a strenuous marching version of 'John
Brown's Body'. She mouthed the words, and tapped her toe on the dance
floor.

Come over some time and let me play for you.

Now was as good a time as any.

50

Every Thursday afternoon at three o'clock, Cora Burgher, the cleaning woman, left her job at the Oddfellows' Hall and joined Mr. Arthur Coote, the Methodist choir director and church organist, for tea in his salon next door. Every afternoon for two hours during the months of January through April. Tongues wagged without charity. On his sixty-fifth birthday, Arthur Coote retired, and at the May 1st dinner to honour his twelve years of faithful service, he delivered a touching valediction. His remarks concluded with the announcement of his engagement to "the lady who has been the subject of your most heartfelt concern these past months, dear Mrs. Burgher." In the respectful silence that attended his sitting down, a teacup shrieked.

•

When Granny explained she could not be married in the Methodist Church, Arthur smiled. "Well, then, how about the Anglican? I was raised C of E and didn't mind it." When she told him she meant no church of any kind, he said cheerily, "Then it will be the judge's chambers for us, luv; just like my first time."

Though she didn't know him well then, she knew enough to realize how difficult a decision he had just made. While he was no religious zealot, Arthur Coote had given many years of faithful service to his church, and he continued to be loyal to it until his death. She felt it was his passionate commitment to certain ideals and principles which enabled him to understand without explanation her own position on the issue. He accepted her wishes as worthy of his own unquestioned support, and once he made up his mind, he was not one to glance back with a moment's regret. Although he loved to regale her with tales of his legendary and shady past on the frontier, he was not one to dwell there. Those events, sad or comic, had been lived through. She often wondered what he dreamt about in his deep unhaunted sleep, or if he dreamt at all. "I certainly *do* dream," he'd proclaim, feigning umbrage. "Why, last night I dreamt of sweet LuLu Sweet," and then he'd wink his all-purpose wink.

With her, and later with Eddie, Arthur felt lively and at ease, talkative and thoughtful, ever alert to the tones under and between their words. With strangers he was still diffident despite his years on the stage, and with those he knew casually – like his acquaintances in the Church and town – he was courtly and reserved. It was only when he got *en rôle*, as he was when she first saw him at the Christmas concert, that the hobgoblins and minor demons were allowed into the light, and only when there was enough music to animate and camouflage. The sparkle in his eye came from something so clear and aboriginal in his childhood; it was unquenchable. He reminded her of someone she'd known fifty years ago.

"Just because we're gonna get 'hitched' in the judge's broom closet doesn't mean we can't do this thing in style," Arthur said. And he meant it.

•

On the first Saturday of June, labouring men traipsed home from the sheds and docks through the afternoon sun. Their women gathered on street corners or under the main street shop awnings and children roamed loose about the alleys and vacant lots. A buggy conspicuously decamped from the livery behind the Queen's Hotel and headed, without shame, up Michigan towards St. Clair, where it turned and in a sedate jog moved towards Sarnia. Everyone looked and recognized the vehicle at once. It was the butcher's cart—actually, a two-wheeled touring buggy of vintage descent with scuffed leather seats and applewood doors and a garish tin box improvised behind the passengers section big enough to hold 'on ice' a morning's delivery of steaks and roasts. Bobbin, the buckskin mare, was in her accustomed pace with a pertness in the arch of her mane and the carriage of her tail. Someone had tossed a sprig of lilac over her withers.

In the buggy sat three odd figures: an old woman dressed simply in blue with no bonnet to shield her silver locks or dampen the audacity of the single plum-blossom adorning them; an old gentleman dolled up in his Sunday suit with boots polished and a gray top hat to crown his snowy hair; and between them, a small boy with eyes bigger than his face. The mare's rein lay curled in the glee of his grip. Many of the bystanders stood open-mouthed, some waved reflexively, a few waved purposefully, but if the occupants were aware of such accolades, they acknowledged them only with their eyes. When several young defenders of the public faith offered them a choice of catcalls, they responded to none, choosing silence and the dignity of their own company. As the wedding-carriage made the turn towards Bayview Park and the county seat beyond, three smudged urchins raced behind it, caterwauling and hurling ill-rhymed taunts. Bobbin kept to her course and soon the boys fell back, winded and unrepentant. One of them, half-heartedly, flung a stone.

Arthur turned, doffed his hat, and said without raising his voice, "Thank you, ladies and gentleman, for those good wishes". And the carriage rocked with laughter.

•

Granny and Eddie moved from the cottage near the Lane to Arthur's house on St. Clair Street near the geographical centre of the village. He put a fresh coat of whitewash on the siding and managed to get one of the shutters to hang straight before losing heart. The only hammers he could use without injury were part of a piano. Granny got busy planting perennials and a bulb garden and vegetable patch in the rich soil of the yard. Often the three of them ate lunch or supper on a checkered cloth spread under the giant hickory tree where gray squirrels convened and robins made their seasonal stand. Inside, the house was warm and cozy, with Arthur's piano to brighten the winter evening gloom and his stage trunk crammed with the props and memorabilia of a lifetime. He insisted that his wife would not work, as his savings and small pension would carry them as far as they could ever wish to go. But Granny decided to keep on working her two days a week at The Queen's, partly because Eddie was doing well enough at school to be a candidate for high school and perhaps even university. Extra money would be needed, partly because she still enjoyed working somewhere and mostly because Duckface Malloney needed her. With the decline of his business in the 1890's, Malloney had seen the bustling, polyglot clientele of the boom years turn into a trickle of tired drummers and advance men. The aged chorus had long ago deserted the lobby in favour of the barbershop and the livery stable near the racetrack. Just after the new century dawned and the last Grand Trunk car man transferred to the Sarnia shops, Malloney had a mild stroke that left him with a shuffle and blurred speech. The only person he would speak to was "Mrs. Burgher", as he still called her. Granny relayed his weekly instructions to the rest of the bewildered staff. When Duckface moved to Sunset Glades in 1908, Granny's life of formal labour came to an end. So did The Queen's.

•

Arthur Coote was born in England in 1835 and raised to be an Englishman, a not inconsiderable challenge for his parents who emigrated to Montreal when he was only nine. He retained much of the tripping cadence of his upper-middle-class London upbringing and all the courtly manners. His father was a furrier, his mother a lady of the lesser aristocracy who, if she had not had the misfortune of being overbred, would have spent her life on the illegitimate music-hall stage . Even in colonial, bourgeois Montreal, she managed to find music teachers for her only son. And a boarding school that ranked good manners above mere academic attainments. He was such a deft *improvisateur*at the piano that the amateur theatrical groups among the better class vied for his services as accompanist to their farces and burlesques. At eighteen, he entered McGill to prepare for law or commerce or some useful adjunct profession his father could deploy in the fur trade. In 1858, at the age of twenty-three, he left his father's second-best desk and headed for Chicago and thence to the gold fields of the Fraser Valley in New Caledonia.

"I wanted to get away, anywhere that wasn't my family and their transplanted version of what life was. More truthfully, I still had a lot of the Old Nick in me. I was young and frisky. But I'll tell you, luv, I didn't last two weeks in the mining camps along the Fraser where we froze at night and burned all day and nine out of ten 'panners' hailed from 'Californy' and spoke no English. I was bashful in those days and though I wasn't afraid, I didn't know how to obtain the least bit of information useful in becoming a successful millionaire in the gold business. I broke my left thumb driving in my first claim stake, and I was so worried I wouldn't be able to play the piano again I ran all the way to New Westminster, got a splint put on it by a horse doctor, and resumed running till I hit Victoria and the Pacific Ocean."

Once there he got a job in a bank counting other people's gold. To his surprise and delight, this frontier town – concocted to stand as a cultural redoubt against a riptide of Yankee pollutants – was alive with theatrical and musical enterprise. "I started out playing in the local orchestras and bands brought in to support the professional troupes from California. When the Chapman family started their stock company and built the Colonial Theatre, I joined them, playing violin, squeeze-box and piano, and getting a chance to act in bit parts. We travelled back to New Westminster and followed the gold fields as far north as Caribou County. But when we got back to Victoria, the company folded, the winter set in, most of the Yankees went back to sunnier climates for the season, and I slipped back into the safer world of gentleman's theatricals. As no gentlewoman would ever be seen on a stage, younger men like myself played the female parts. I discovered that I enjoyed these excursions. I did not creep out of my shyness—I burst out of it with a patter song or a frenzied rhetorical flourish in one of the melodramas, or in the wee voice of the female I found way inside me. Occasionally, several of the 'commercial' actresses would be asked to join us and that was great because then we could act out the tragedies, even some Shakespeare. Such fallen women were excluded from the respectable dances and balls that always followed the play."

But when the good weather brought a new crop of American speculators and entrepreneurs, Arthur was drawn back into the greasier, tinsel world of the troupes. In 1861, he joined for a spell the John S. Potter Dramatic Troupe, quitting his job so he could travel with them to the Lyceum in San Francisco. "And there I fell madly in love with our resident *ingénue*, Miss Lulu Sweet, seventeen years old with a figure like Aphrodite's daughter and the lilt of a Siren. We billed her as 'Juvenile Actress, Songstress and Danseuse', and she was all those and more."

"Do go on," Granny prompted.

"When I asked her to marry me, I was thunderstruck when she said yes. We eloped with half the San Francisco police force on our trail, but not before we'd tasted enough bliss to make our trespass unforgivable."

"How long did it last?"

"Longer than you might imagine. About two months, the first month being a disaster and the second a total disaster. The only thing sweet about Lulu was her voice."

The bank, short on men of probity, gave him his job back, and for a while he drifted again into the 'English set' of Victoria society where his soaring tenor voice and his engaging piano were in steady demand. By the mid 1860's, though, the Colonial Theatre had become a music-hall—American style with minstrel shows, and seedy burlesques. He regaled Eddie and

Granny with stories of sneaking out of his respectable boarding house, incognito, and joining the banal drollery of the 'box-house'. Vaudeville sketches and routines were added to the minstrels in the late 1860's and Arthur's versatile pianoforte was judged one of the wonders of the age. "Once I even put on a blackface when one of the regulars took ill, and I forgot to wash it off before coming down to breakfast at Mrs. Tiffen's. She went white and green, and before I could think up a plausible excuse – like having fallen down in the mud of Governor Street – one of the young rams around the table quipped, 'Why don't y'all sing us a chorus of Massa's in de col' col' ground?'"

He was quick at arithmetic and helped Eddie almost every night during the long winters. Granny and Arthur took turns reading aloud to him. Between or after, there was music and treble singing and the sizzle of the coal fire. Many hours passed in silent reading, Arthur in his chair, Granny in the rocker, Eddie curled on the chesterfield. Arthur loved romance novels and devoured the latest works of W. D. Lighthall and Sir Gilbert Parker and a newcomer from the States named Zane Grey. He would go on at length about a book like Lighthall's *The Young Seigneur* or *Nation-Making*, amplifying its idealism and its plea for a belief in essential goodness till his eyes glistened and even little Eddie stopped reading to watch. When Eddie brought some of his high-school chums to the house, Granny would cajole Arthur out of his reserve. He would begin with a song at the piano, a vaudeville classic:

I saw Esau kissing Kate
And in fact we all saw three
For I saw Esau, he saw me
And she saw I saw Esau.

Warming up, he would burst into the role as the Lord High Executioner, at which point the lads would join in and whole scenes would spin out, impromptu and cavalier and self-engaging, and the mood set for one or more of Arthur's true-life tales. When he finished and Granny served the tea or mulberry wine, he reverted to his courtly, gentle self.

•

Arthur subscribed to all the papers and read them avidly. He tried to engage Granny in political discussion, which turned into harmless jousts of words. He never did learn how she could dismantle one of his arguments,developed from the latest hard data and editorial disquisition, without recourse to similar foundations of fact and opinion. He tried to catch her reading anything but the local pages of *The Observer* but never did.

"How can you be so critical of the Tories when you haven't looked at one blessed statement they've made since Laurier got in?"

"I've known about Tories for a long time, since I was a child. I don't need to hear their latest lines."

"No wonder they don't consider giving women the vote."

"I ain't heard no one proposin' it."

"Well then, if you don't approve of Tory policies, then you must be a Grit, deep down."

"Worse than the Tories by half, they are."

"But in Canada you have to be one or the other. If you're not a Liberal then you've got to be a Conservative. Red or blue, it's an axiom."

"I'd put the axe to both of 'em."

"Don't be impertinent, Granny Coote."

•

Though he admired Laurier and his optimism about the Dominion's place in the twentieth century, Arthur was a worshipper of the late Sir John A. Macdonald and his 'national policy'.

"The greatest man North America has ever produced, and that includes Lincoln. The epitome of the nineteenth century. Out in British Columbia where he was hated and loved, we called him the Old War Horse. He brought us the railroad and saved us from the Visigoths of California. He had a dream bigger than all of us."

"Never cared much for the man," Granny said.

Arthur peered out of his reveries long enough to say, "Oh, why is that?"

"He was a Scotchman through and through." And I know, she wanted to say aloud, I met the gentleman once with his promises down.

Arthur seemed more puzzled than hurt by this odd remark. He winked and said, "With a Frenchman's liver, eh?"

"Don't be impertinent."

•

Granny told Arthur only those few facts of her own life which she felt he could withstand. How much he guessed or she gave away, she never knew. The great advantage, she thought, of *not* having shared the same past at our advanced age is that we can choose to reinvent those parts that please us or offer the best chance for hope. What we dream in private must remain our own. There is not time nor words enough to begin the whole retelling, and that is a blessing in itself. On his side, Arthur tried many devices to get her talking, particularly about the 'pioneer days' as he called them. One day, he left *The Observer* open at the local page where she would be sure to see the lead story—a feature interview with one Bessie Sycamore: Pioneer of Warwick Township. Through a series of adroit questions, the cub reporter was able to elicit from ninety-year-old Bessie the fact that she had borne fifteen children in a log cabin snug in the back bush, eight of whom, she was proud to say, lived to adulthood. Moreover, she spent six happy, unscathed decades cooking for the survivors and caring for two husbands, thirty-one grandchildren and uncounted great-grandchildren. She was now distressed because this year for the first time she had been unable to bake her two dozen blueberry pies for the church bazaar. Arthritis, you know. And the secret of her long life? Hard work and prayer twice a day.

When Arthur came in from the shed, Granny gave him such a look of malevolence he thought he must have inadvertently poisoned her tea. Later, alone, she realized that the article had dismayed her as much as it had angered her. *Did* such people exist? Were there ever *lives* like that? Was it possible to watch seven children perish – who had ripped their way out of your flesh and seized the air you offered them in hope and trust – could anyone suffer that and still go on baking blueberry pies as if God and not the world mattered? Someone, she thought bitterly, has a lot to answer for.

•

"You might say I squandered my youth leading a double life," Arthur said, recovering from his nap and trusting that she was awake in the chair next to him. "I couldn't stay away from the minstrels or the 'Free and Easies' as we called them back then. When Charles and Ellen Kean came to Victoria, I was in the front row of the Theatre Royal. I could hear the echo of the illustrious

Edmund Kean himself, and I vowed ever after to hold my appetites in check and feed only on a steady diet of *Hamlet* and *Richelieu*. I offered my services to one of the Anglican churches and rediscovered the organ. Still, I'm ashamed to admit I was not only present in 1875 when Charles McDonald's 'Occidentals' performed *Black-Eyed Susan* and pranced about the stage like trained bears, I was in the wings supplying some of the traitorous music. That night marked a turning point in my life, for I saw a side of the theatre I had refused to acknowledge before. This American impresario had gathered together from each of the tribes of British Columbia nine native people whom he billed as 'the Occidentals' and described on his posters as 'four squaws and five men...the best specimens of the children of the forest'. Besides a repertoire of hideous farces in which he'd trained them to mime a grotesque self-parody, these wretches performed nightly an Indian War Dance, contorted their bodies into 'sixteen different pyramids' and concluded the evening's spectacle with the Indian Feast of Fire. This so-called aboriginal ceremony consisted, as the playbill proclaimed in bold type, of 'eating fire, drinking burning naptha, devouring burning torches, breathing smoke and fire, and pulling long poles from their mouths'. And this travesty played at the Theatre Royal before a cheering Governor Douglas and the local, highborn poohbahs."

Arthur sighed deeply. Granny shifted audibly in her chair.

"Later on, I heard this monstrous troupe was feted in Philadelphia and Washington during the 1876 celebrations, and then went abroad to the Crystal Palace in England to be gawked at by thousands of foreigners. In Paris they were booed off the stage because they failed to resemble the inhabitants of the Punjab. Shortly after that night, a new customer came into our bank, and a few months later I was engaged."

As Arthur was fond of saying in jest, it was the longest engagement in recorded matrimonial history – eleven years and twenty-nine days. Helen Driscoll had come out to Victoria with her father, a Methodist preacher, and although the old man liked Arthur a great deal, he forbade his daughter to marry an Anglican, even a lapsed one. In desperation Arthur embraced the Methodist faith but after too much doubt and reflection. When the old bigot finally died in 1887, they married. By this time Arthur was a full-fledged communicant and part-time organist of his bride's church. When a position as full-time organist back in Helen's hometown became available, the newlyweds returned east to London, Ontario. A year later, internal politics and factional rivalries in the London parish prompted Arthur and Helen to accept the offer of the Point Edward Methodists, who were more than happy to have in their midst a musician of Arthur Coote's standing.

"But you still love the old ditties and the drumrolls," Granny said. "How did you hide them all those years?"

"I only disguised them a little," he laughed. "I don't think there was a soul who didn't notice."

She waited a while until some tone in the shuttered room had imperceptibly shifted. "Why did you really give it up?"

He let the question get comfortable before responding. "I wanted something...*authentic*in my life."

Granny murmured reassurance.

"I wanted, after a lot of wandering about, to come home."

They listened to the tic toc of the rocker through the room.

"I'm still here," Granny said.

51

1

When Eddie went off to Victoria College in Toronto to study philosophy and literature in the mellow autumn of 1910, the house was a lot quieter. And they were getting old – Arthur and Granny – overtaken by sudden naps, drifting into snoozes in the sunlight through the window, into lapses of thought or purpose, bickering pleasantly over the imperfections of memory. Whatever the season, Granny went out every day to check the mail for letters from Eddie, to buy the few groceries they pretended to need each day. She nodded to the few souls she still knew and listened from shy corners to the buzz of gossip among the young who barely remembered her. She was touched by their enthusiasm and sense of having inherited this time and place whole and without obligation. In the winter, she pulled Eddie's sled to Redmond's – where Sandy now presided – or up to the coal dock for a bushel of coke. Sometimes she stood on the wharf and looked at the Great Lake till the chill took her. A brisk walk home warmed her up again. Arthur's gout kept him indoors much of the time, though he came out once a day in the growing seasons to offer editorial comment on the flowers or vegetables or the trimming of the hedges. Before he was allowed to go back inside, they would promenade arm in arm around the perimeter of their land, admiring the view over the marsh clear to the River before turning homeward. Once, Granny overheard young Ethel Carpenter, who assumed all old people were deaf, whisper to her husband: "Now ain't they a cute pair!" Granny winced then smiled all the way to the stoop.

•

Eddie wrote them every week while he was in college. In the summers he worked for the Sarnia newspaper, *The Observer*, and lived at home. He had many friends in Toronto and in Lambton. He assumed there was good in the

world and spent much of his time searching it out, though Granny could see
that the books he studied and the sights he'd seen in the big city had left him
with little doubt of the magnitude of his quest. But he was not one to flinch
from its pain. He had courage and a winning heart. Friends flocked to him,
and many of them, she thought, would remain steadfast in the causes he had
persuaded them to undertake with him. Already he was talking about
graduate studies, of being a professor or lawyer or someone who could move
the earth an inch or two just by being in it. Arthur and Granny would sit at
the kitchen table in the lamplight and compose letters to him. Arthur's
English-schoolboy hand flowed across the white page carrying thought and
feeling into elegance and a permanence he only vaguely comprehended. She
was the one – always – to read back what they had written in a sober cadence
that made Arthur laugh till she swatted him with the letter and started over.
When the return letter arrived faithfully within the week, they sat on the
chesterfield taking turns presenting it, re-enacting the best moments many
times, constructing in their minds the unfolding biography and pageant of
their grandson's life. You won't believe me, Cap Dowling, Granny said to
him one day, but I am happy.

•

Arthur died at 1:00 a.m. in the morning of April 3, 1912, a month shy of his
seventy-seventh birthday. Granny was beside him on the chesterfield where
he'd been resting close to the stove. His recurrent pleurisy had turned to
pneumonia. He died peacefully in an interval between dreams. Just before he
closed his eyes for the last time around midnight, he smiled at the companion
of his latter years and asked her to hold his hand. When she did she found his
grip resolute. He was too weak to say anything more but as his lids came
down, she saw something in his eyes she interpreted as 'forgive me' before a
twinkle extinguished it. About one o'clock his breathing stopped. She
permitted his hand to grow cold in hers.

•

Of all the deaths and departures she had endured in her seven decades of
living, Arthur's was the most simple and most touching. For the first time in
her life Granny found she could mourn with a pure and biding sadness

uncomplicated by guilt, remorse, rage, helplessness. Arthur lived a long and eventful time on earth, taking little and giving much. Near the end he could talk of heaven as if he believed it was waiting for him. He was one of the lucky ones.

•

Eddie felt terrible about having to go straight back to college to write his exams, but he felt reassured by the steady look Granny gave him that said, 'You *have* to; I'll be all right'. Though not unexpected, Arthur's death had dealt Eddie a sideways blow. He was bearing up well, but when he came home again for the summer, she would have to keep a close watch on him.

Arthur's funeral was attended by most of the village and the outpouring of sorrow was genuine. Granny noted that many of the young people, students and choir members under Arthur, who came over to offer their condolences did not seem sure who she was, other than Granny Coote. It was an odd sensation and one that disquieted her more than the tedious eulogy by the recently arrived Methodist minister. Arthur's tombstone stood in a sunny spot on the southwest side of the little cemetery. Granny noted how much it had filled with graves since the lonely day when Cap was put under the horse chestnut in the northeast corner. She recognized too many of the names cut in stone. After the interment, she stood apart with Eddie and gazed at the ground that now possessed her husband – body and spirit – thinking that this was a fitting spot for him and most of all for her. I'll lie right here, Arthur, she whispered to him, not a yard away. In the meantime, you behave yourself.

As they turned to leave, Granny took a step towards Cap's grave, acknowledged it then swept her eyes across the plain tablet a few feet to the south. The strange syllables of Bradley's name hovered on her lips. She moved into the silence and dropped the flowers she had been holding. She felt Eddie's stare and for a moment dared not turn to face him. In the carriage all the way back to the reception hall, she waited for his question. If he asks, she thought, I'll have to tell him. I have no choice.

Eddie said goodbye at the station, clinging to her as he used to with the blind trust of the child he no longer was.

2

In the spring of 1914, Eddie graduated with honours from the University of Toronto. He desperately wanted her to come to the convocation and arranged for Ralph Sifton to accompany her on the train. But she took ill a few days before the event – the doctor diagnosed it as severe grippe – and she had to send Ralph off alone. She was furious with herself. Even now nearing seventy-four, she was rarely sick except for her rheumatism, and that was never disabling. When Eddie came home, there was no hint of disappointment in his face. He modelled his cap and gown for her, hung his framed baccalaureate next to the tintype of Arthur at the piano of the Theatre Royal, and then brought out the photographs Ralph had taken of the ceremony with *The Observer's* best camera. He escorted her to supper at the Colonial Hotel in Sarnia, still bustling with its own celebrations as the nation's newest city, and told her of his plans.

Using the money Arthur had set aside for him in his will, Eddie said he was going to return to Toronto in July to begin studying for his master's degree in comparative literature. That would take him about eighteen months, after which he would look for a job teaching in one of the small Maritime colleges or right here in Ontario where there was talk of expanding the university in London. He hoped to continue his studies, but for the near future he wanted to find a place where he could be useful and self-supporting. A small town where he could put down roots and bring his granny to live out her days with him.

"You can't say no, Gran. Arthur would have wanted it to be that way."

What could she say?

•

Eddie began to write to her as soon as he had returned to school, every two weeks as he had done since Arthur's death. But Arthur was no longer here to write out the words or tease and cajole in his special way so that what she ended up saying to Eddie was lively, witty and charged with good humour. Seated alone at their table, with a shaky pen unaccustomed to writing let alone the free fall of her inner speech, she found she could not recapture the verve of those joint letters. She had little to narrate in the way of current events. As she told Eddie in one letter that first winter, "the word 'current' and your granny aren't to be seen in the same dictionary." She had lots of thoughts – she'd never been short on that score – but discovered it took so long to scratch and blot them on paper they soon tumbled over one another and came up nonsense. "Try to picture yourself talking to someone," Eddie wrote back, "Arthur or me or a friend on the street corner." She had some success when Cap was in the room visiting, until he started to chip in too many of his own silly ideas. Gradually, the task got easier, and though her stilted replies were not newsy enough, she did manage her four pages a month.

In fact, during the unusual quiet of the summer of 1914, she came to the realization that what remained of her life was in Eddie's hands. Less and less did she attend to the daily traffic of human affairs she had spent a lifetime observing. The great events of the world beyond her own township – elections and reciprocity fights and skirmishes in Africa and the Sea of Japan, which had never been able to hold her attention for long – now receded almost completely from the foreground of her existence. She lived for Eddie's letters and for the essence of him they conveyed for her appraisal and concern. We have lived past our three-score-and-ten, old man, she said to Arthur. And we haven't got a lot to show for it. We tried. I know I did. I bore four children. I stayed put for seventy years, hoping to have planted in this barren place something permanent. Nothing took hold. Nothing but Eddie out of all that. Eddie was a gift of the near-sighted gods, an oversight perhaps in the frenzy of their careless blundering – but we took him and fostered him and let him be. I am learning to live through his eyes. May he prosper, may he love and marry and father a dozen children, each of them obsessed with living. May the roots of that tree be numerous and strong and deep as the underground rivers that feed them.

There, Arthur. Now, if only you could write that down for me.

•

In October, Eddie wrote to say he had decided to 'join up' and that he hoped to complete his course work before going overseas.He would start his dissertation as soon as he got back, and that he would come home for a few days before leaving. She wrote and begged him not to come home. But this time he could not bring himself to do what she wished.

52

1

Granny Coote sat at the window of her new house and kept a faithful watch on the workmen across the street. Mr. Stadler had brought along two helpers to assist him in unloading the rough slabs of limestone he would smooth and shape into a memorial pillar over the weeks to come. Sunny Denfield had shown her the drawings so she was able to speculate about how these raw-cut stones might be teased into the elegant promise she'd seen on paper. The stones were heavy and had to be eased down ramps from the back of the truck then skidded over to a spot near the site. The young men appeared to be sons or nephews of the builder; they were as lithe and wiry as he, and moved with animal ease. Their skin was tanned and roughened, the mark of men who spend much of their life outdoors. The old man, who came almost every day, was a delight to watch. He hopped about like a rabbit on a griddle, firing off instructions that were respectfully ignored. He lent a hand when it was least required then lapsed into a state of deep repose from which he observed and blessed the intricate actions of his son (surely he must be Stadler's father). When they sat down on one of the stone for a brief rest, the old fellow seemed to dominate the conversation, speaking in a low voice and gesturing as if he were telling long, weathered stories. There is something familiar about the Stadler family, Granny thought, but then I've lived so long and seen so much around these parts, everything looks familiar.

2

Eddie began writing to her as soon as the troops reached Valcartier camp for the second phase of their training. He had joined up in the new year when recruiting for the Second Canadian Division began in earnest. Five of his college friends joined with him as part of one of the university companies who would form replacements for Princess Patricia's Canadian Light Infantry already overseas and in combat. Such students received permission to carry on with their studies during the local training period, which ended in March, after which they entrained for Valcartier. Granny knew Ralph Sifton well and though she had not met them, she felt she knew the other four since they had been part of Eddie's conversation for two or three summers. As she read over each name of 'the Vic platoon' in Eddie's letter, a picture of past exploits – derring-do and hijinks and irresistible good humour – formed in her mind. Besides young Ralph from Sarnia (studying law as his father had), the platoon included Cliff Strangways from British Columbia (graduate history); Sandy Lecker from Waterloo County (biological science), the first of his family ever to attend university; Bart Ramsay (graduate philosophy) whose Toronto family had enough money to protect him from the temptations of academia, but couldn't; and Henry Potter, raw-boned prairie lad who was studying French in hopes of joining the foreign service and seeing parts of the world that weren't flat. Although they didn't all get into the same platoon, they were part of a single company, an inseparable fraternity.

In April, Eddie started writing once a week, his letter arriving Tuesday morning while she waited in the Post Office on Michigan Ave. to pick it up. She never opened one before she got back home, nodding to friendly or anxious faces on the street. Once there, she made herself a cup of tea to sip as she read the words aloud at first, then silently.

"Valcartier is a pleasant surprise considering the rumours we were foolish enough to believe in advance. It's a huge complex of barracks, drilling grounds, rifle ranges and mock battlefields – all cut right out of primeval bush. I get the strangest sensation firing my Ross .303 at a painted target two hundred yards across a scraped pasture and looking up at the evergreens behind them which roll unbroken for a thousand miles north of anywhere. Do you know what I mean?

Yes, Eddie, I do, though I haven't got the words you have to describe it.

"Bart, our city boy, went for a stroll in the woods last night, as if he were off to High Park in pursuit of pretty girls – of which there are none, pretty or girlish, within twenty miles – and got himself lost. The Vic platoon volunteered for the search party, and it was Cliff, who grew up in the Kootenays, who found him on the second tallest branch of a spruce tree, where he claimed a black bear had driven him out of spite. Cliff is of the opinion that it was a Sasquatch, abetted by the shadows and on overheated imagination."

Granny found it a daunting task to respond to these weekly outpourings. Four or five pages of elegant script captured a side of Eddie she knew she would not see if he were at home – closer, safer. There was nothing else to do but sit at the kitchen table in the afternoon sun or the evening lamplight and try to make the pen say the thousand things racing through her. By the time the Second Division was ready to embark for England in May of 1915, she was able to write several pages of stilted prose, sweating over it for two days. Eddie made it easier by asking questions about his chums in the village or about local events she herself had long ago excluded from her sphere of concern: "Who's joined up lately? Did they finally get Hitch? Or Sandy Redmond? Who's to replace MacPherson on the council? Will you be sure to clip the theatre items from *The Observer*?" And so on. Though replying to these and making an occasional comment herself helped to fill up the weekly quota of two pages, she was not pleased with the results. Her first letters were choppy, disconnected pieces; she felt she was not conveying anything of herself in them. Every instinct she possessed told her that Eddie was waiting out there, listening with his heart for some force behind her words more tender and compelling than the voices he heard daily inside him and all around. I can't do it, Eddie. I never learned. I'm too old, too stubborn, too stupid.

In desperation, as he prepared to sail for England and foreign battlefields thousands of miles away, she began to tell a few of the simple follies that peppered everyday life in the village and upon which she had begun to cast an ironic eye. To her surprise she found the effort much easier than she thought it would be – closing her eyes and recapitulating a scene or a conversation overheard. "The fellows want to hear more of your stories about the village. I assure them you're not making them up, but they're not inclined to believe me. Bart wants to know if Bomber had to share the purse with his master."

Granny found herself in turn asking more and more about the fellows. "How did Bart make out with the nurses at the camp dance? Was Henry too shy to ask anyone?"

"Bart appropriated the prettiest girl among the two dozen allotted to our battalion and danced with her the whole evening. Unfortunately for the course of true romance, she was the worst dancer, stomping on his feet so often he had to be carried to the barracks and soaked up to his ankles in ice for three days. He claims he purloined a kiss behind the packing cases. As you surmised, Henry was too shy to ask for a dance, so Cliff did it for him. I don't think Henry had ever seen anything but a square dance (*you* remember them, I reckon), but he adapted well. I danced with a girl from London and one from Fredericton. How odd to be holding, as intimately as sweethearts, two complete strangers from different parts of the continent coming together in a Quebec bush camp for the sole purpose, we hear, of shooting to death a million Germans."

Granny waited a week for Eddie's next letter.

"We are to complete our basic training here in Shorncliffe in the picturesque county of Kent. What a relief after the stories told about First Division's autumn and winter in the rains and muck of Salisbury Plain. Here it is dry and warm, we are surrounded by tropical green and curious, anachronistic villages with quaint names like Dibgate, Otterpool and New Inn Green (very old). Our own bell tents are pitched on St. Martin's Plain. Among the trees and shrubbery on every side we can see church steeples shining in the sun, and hear medieval bells tolling the hours. Ralph sprained his ankle during a bayonet drill. He didn't take kindly to suggestions that he engage the services of his prominent daddy in a lawsuit against the inventor of the Ross Rifle. By the way, Cliff has just learned of the death of his grandfather and is feeling remorseful about not going to see him before embarkation. It seems Cliff is interested in the history of the region and had promised that he would record the old tales his grandfather often told about the pioneer days in New Westminster. I told Cliff about Arthur, and it turns out that his grandfather knew Arthur quite well. This was confirmed recently by Cliff's mother. Cliff would like to hear from you about any of those great yarns Arthur used to tell us. He won't believe my versions, and I don't blame him. Henry is terribly homesick. Any advice?"

So it was that Granny came to add into her letters whole paragraphs addressed to individual members of the Vic platoon. "This is for Henry only" she would print in teasing caps, for she knew they sat around and read her letter together and began to pen postscripts of increasing length to Eddie's own accounts. She found herself spending entire days composing responses, part of the time spent in reflection on past events in reference to the questions and requests raised. Cliff could not get enough detail about Arthur's days in the theatre of the 1860s, and she found herself rummaging through Arthur's trunk, sometimes parting with a cherished playbill – the names receding but still legible – for the boy's sake. She was quite certain nothing would ever assuage the sense of regret he was suffering so far away. Minor detail elicited from Cliff's mother would be relayed back to Granny and in some cases half-told stories from each side were dovetailed to make a complete one, so that Arthur himself, through the eyes of the deceased Mr. Strangways, was enabled to speak to her with fresh and vicarious verve. When Sandy Lecker asked about farming techniques in the pioneer days, she found herself talking about events she had not even dreamt about in more than twenty years. Sandy was a farm boy and he was willing to brave the gentle derision of the others.

Soon they were on their way to France on the seventeenth of September. In his last letter before leaving Shorncliffe, Ralph made light of the impending event. "We went on manoeuvres yesterday for the sole purpose of proving that Sir Sam Hughes' secretary was right after all, that the 'MacAdam shovel' which bears her name (and many unofficial ones provided free of charge) will not only defy German bullets but dig a six-foot trench with the aid of the human hand. Sir Sam refuses to believe reports, spread by the envious Brits, that the shield won't stop a BB at thirty yards and, lacking a handle, the spade is useless as a delving device. Bart suggests the whole thing is a Canadian plot to have the Kaiser's army laugh itself to death."

Several of the boys now wrote to her separately in the packet-sized letters that left the postmistress puzzled and not a little suspicious. Granny in turn continued to compose equally impressive omnibus editions in addition to the smaller, private confidences to 'her boys'.

"There are no words to describe the battleground," Eddie wrote. "Nothing could have been done to prepare us for it. Our training over here was cut short when we were sent to the front as part of the newly organized Canadian Corps (chalk up one for the colonies!). They tell us we're in Flanders near the Belgian village of Vierstraat, south of Ypres. Some of the ground we occupy has changed hands several times already and the devastation here is complete. I expected to see battered houses and charred barns and rotting orchards, but there are no such human signposts anywhere. Between our trenches and the German's a few hundred yards away, and behind us for over a mile, there is not one distinguishing landmark. The outbuildings have been flattened, pulverized by repeated shelling and then tramped upon by marching feet so thoroughly into the mud there is not the slightest hint of a farm ever having been. Occasionally, you step on something firm underfoot, and if it isn't a corpse, it's likely to be the submerged stump of a tree, blasted then buried, with its roots still gripping something grim that lurks below us everywhere. As we approach our frontline position, or as we're returning to billets for our stint in reserve, we can see the shattered orchards or half-burned rooves of hay barns, enough to remind us of what we must have ruined. I peer ahead of me over the sandbag parapet, searching for prey with my sniper's eye and cannot see any sign of where the ground itself was. It is moon ground, the erg-desert of my nightmares. Sorry to be so depressing, but I do need someone to unburden this on; among the fellows I have to be careful about each word, each gesture, each well-intended jibe. The feelings we have for one another are as fragile as they are deep. That is one thing I am learning about the war, even before we've gone into battle."

"Tell me your feelings, Eddie, all of them. Let me know how the boys are *really* doing, I can't trust the stories they invent to make me feel less anxious. Let me know what they need to hear."

"Some of the Canadians were involved a few days ago in the fighting around Loos, part of a larger offensive at Artois and Champagne. A fiasco, we suspect, from the endless lines of walking wounded filing past with their faces gray as paste, the whites of their eyes the brightest colour visible against the backdrop of mud, the wan uniforms, darkening bandages, and dirt-streaked faces. They remind me of blackface minstrels minus the smiles, music and hypocrisy. Eddie's next letter was worryingly short. "Write soon.""

"They always used axes to cut down the big trees because usually only one man started the process, or the bush was too thick to wield a two-man saw, or you couldn't control the drop spot. Then hundreds of small branches had to be trimmed with an expert axe hand so that only the trunk remained. You must remember that in Lambton County we are talking about pines and plane trees and walnut that soared a hundred and fifty feet in the air and often ran six or eight feet across at the bole. It took a trained ox team to move these trunks and get them into a pile where they could be burned. Only the best-looking limbs were sawn up for cordwood. Everything else was burned into powdery ash."

"Gran, we've discovered a virtue in the rain and mud that permeates our daily routine. Only humans can live in it. The rats, without barns or granaries, have retreated to the billet areas behind us. The field mice can find neither fields nor fodder, and their burrows are washed out faster than they can tunnel them. No birds fly overhead, except the tidy cormorants, because there is no tree to light on, no grass for a nest, no water that is not stinking. Even the earthworms have drowned. We are the only living things for miles. But enough of my dark philosophizing. Bart tells me to inform you that we also have mechanized ravens here, called aeroplanes, but they don't talk dirty like Mrs. Finch's crow and aren't half as much fun. The German version is called a Fokker, and Bart says it gets garbled in the translation."

"Mrs. Finch's crow has learned a new trick. He hops along the clothes-line behind her and picks off the pegs as she pins them then slips into the apple tree before she can figure out what ill-wind keeps blowing her sheets away. I'm tempted to tell her, but the crow is known to have a vengeful streak in him."

"We've begun a series of what are called 'night-raids', our first real action in the two months we've been here. We blacken our faces and hands with burnt cork, and then when the moon goes under, our platoon slips over the parapet and pads through the muck of No Man's Land with only the point of a dark ridge to our north to act as a guide. The idea is to drop into the German's foremost trench, yell and stab and create havoc for ten mad minutes, then retreat in the darkness before they can warm up their field guns or counterattack. This manoeuvre is designed to keep the enemy scared – as if that were difficult. Our group went 'over the top' last week, and we got all the way to the Bosch trenches without incident. I heard Cliff Strangways give the attack cry and we leaped into the gap at our feet. It was eerie beyond description, like jumping off the edge of the world. We didn't know whether we'd land on a soldier's stomach or a keg of Bavarian beer or a parked bayonet. We sang out our banshee howls and jumped, swivelling our spear guns like the Turkish infidel and waiting for the wince of human flesh at the end of the blow. Nothing happened. We landed askew in the dark, shouting and stabbing, but no one shouted back. Our sergeant barked a 'cease attack' that brought us all to a quivering halt. No sound of the dying or the terrified. A torch was lit and we gazed in horror at the sight around us. An hour before, during one of the periodic artillery duels staged by mutual consent, one of our batteries must have misfired several 'short' rounds meant for the front-line ridge beyond. Those shells had made a perfect, if unintentional, strike on this isolated part of the trench. Thirty or forty corpses, still warm and oozing, stared out at us with death's eyes. We had been told in the silly propaganda paper circulating here that the Germans were troll-like creatures who devoured their own babies when angered, who drank blood for breakfast, and so on. But I can tell you, Gran, all of us have looked on the faces of our enemy. They are just men who die as men everywhere in the futility of battle."

We burned wood for fuel heat and cooking fire. We made flutes out of softwood sticks to make the music to carry us through the long winter. We walked over the snow – five feet deep – on wooden snowshoes. Our world was made of wood. We loved and hated it."

"Bart was killed in one of the raids two nights ago. We were almost back from a *mêlée* in the enemy trench when their artillery opened fire. We'd stayed a minute too long. I landed among some piles of equipment and slashed my way through it without encountering a soldier until the cry went up to retreat. Just as I dropped into our own trench, the first shell exploded, and Cliff and I heard Bart scream as if a cat had raked his flesh. Despite the noise and panic all around us, we heard it as clear as if he'd spoken to us across a quiet room. He'd fallen about ten yards away, and Cliff and I went out after him, shells breaking up everywhere. I was as scared as I'll ever get. I had thought under these circumstances that I would think of my past life or my life to come or of you and Arthur shielding me against the wind along the river flats. But I thought of nothing, nothing – there was nothing in my brain but a gray numbness, the way death itself may be. We got Bart's body back into the trench, but he was already dead. We drew lots to see who should write home to his parents. Ralph lost."

"Please do not give me any of the details of the boys' deaths or injuries, Eddie. My heart recoils at the thought of what you must bear alone. Tell Sandy he can prevent trench feet by taking grease from the cook's skillet and rubbing it all over the inside of his boots. The Indians, they tell me, used to have much success with the method."

The Vic platoon saw little action as the winter dragged on in Flanders where record rainfalls turned the mud into a quagmire. "Henry says he may be the only one here who isn't affected by the muck and slime. He claims the gumbo south of Winnipeg is twice as sloppy and has four times the sticking power. Some of the fellows are suffering terribly from the grippe and dysentery and trench feet, which can become gangrenous. They wish they could get into battle, thinking it would be a form of relief. We try to assure them it is not so, though the wet and the waiting are hellish in themselves – with the din of distant siege guns reminding us that some people out there are fighting and dying and maybe winning the war. Morale is high, I hasten to add, likely because we feel a powerful camaraderie more important than the so-called reasons we're given for our sacrifices – the defense of the Empire and the freedoms it stands for, as if the two notions were connected or even compatible. Most of us volunteered in one form or another, and here we're going to stay to see this thing through. A strange rationale for fighting, isn't it? But what can you say in defense of General Haig who refers to our combat casualties as 'tolerable levels of wastage'. We had a good laugh about that one, the five of us."

Granny was now writing as many as four letters a week. No longer did her left hand balk at the glare of a page; it skittered across with a nervous energy of its own, sensitive now to every eddy of the mind and emotion that propelled it. The words flowed – now guarded, now brazen, delicate, all thumbs, scrolled, jagged. They carried their share of the burden and in them she was able at last to see those reflections of herself she had not thought possible in seventy-six years of living. She began to compose with inordinate speed, with a soft fury of phrasing – the words tumbling out, jelling in the cold squeeze of ink against the page. She felt and she wrote. She thought and she wrote. She read and she wrote. Her room was full of voices and urgencies. The letters accumulated in huge piles in the corner beside the table. She re-read them at intervals. She put a rubber band around Bart Ramsay's, and one day she sat down and began writing a letter to Mrs. Ramsay in Toronto, the first of many. By March, she was so weary she often woke in the dark with her head on the table and a sentence half-finished on a page she couldn't recall writing.

At the end of April, the Canadian Corps, now three divisions strong, went into full-scale battle. Although Eddie's description of the combat and of trench life itself became more circumspect – he had sensed the alarm perhaps in her letters – she was able to reconstruct the horrific events surrounding the St. Eloi craters and the battles of Mount Sorrel with enough clarity to comprehend their impact on him. On April 29th, he reported they had slogged through slime up to their waists while under constant fire. "But we achieved our objectives, according to the C.O. That is no news at all to Henry. He left us yesterday at five o'clock. I am to write soon to his father. He was the only child of a widower. What do I say?"

For ten full days there was no letter from Eddie or any of the remaining boys. The papers boasted of the recent successful offensives and mentioned the spearhead towards Mount Sorrel. A few days later, three letters arrived, one of them from Eddie. They were all lengthy. Sandy Lecker went on about tracing his family tree back through the Lowlands to the broken clans of 1845. Cliff Strangways had written out several comic songs his mother had found in grandpa's theatre-trunk – did she happen to know the music that might go with them? Eddie described the feelings he had when he first went skating on the pond ice of Little Lake. He quoted from a poem by Wordsworth, the English fellow he was writing part of his thesis on. Eddie's words were more beautiful than the poet's. At the end of a long letter he said, "We've just come back from Sorrel. Ralph did not come back with us. I've written to his mother."

Granny could not write for a week. For a while she thought that her arthritis had decided to stall her efforts. A second letter arrived from Eddie. Was she all right? Perhaps it would be better if he only wrote once a month, perhaps she should not hear, right off, about the fellows leaving them. He was terribly sorry, for placing such a burden on her—he had no right to do so. She wrote him back that afternoon, taking the letter down to the post office herself.

Eddie, Cliff and Sandy all wrote cheering notes to her that week, each describing in his own way the arrival of the Dumbells' troupe for a weekend of performance before their fellow soldiers. "The spirit of 1860 and the old Colonial Theatre," Cliff enthused. "You should have been there to see it. Arthur should have been there to take a bow." Near the end of his letter, Sandy let it be known that rumours were flying about a "big push to end the war" coming up soon, so that if they stopped writing, she was not, repeat *not*, to worry. Eddie's letter was forcibly cheerful and newsy. "Don't worry, Gran," it concluded, "we're certain it will be over soon."

She dropped the letter on the table and went immediately to Arthur's trunk. Under posters and playbills she found what she was looking for: a vellum envelope. From it she drew a sheet of ordinary writing paper on which, in Bradley's crabbed hand, were written several stanzas of poetry. The title over them read: "Colloquy, for Sarah." When she had finished writing to Eddie, she copied the poem out in her own hand then tucked the original in with the letter. This is all your father brought home to me from the wreckage of his life, she said to herself. It's time you knew the truth about that, and about the gifts you have to carry you into the future he refused to face. You have an obligation to live. Please, Eddie.

•

On the evening of July 1, 1916, Granny was wakened from a restless sleep by a thunderclap that brought her upright into the silence of her living room. She felt a stabbing at her heart as if an icicle had been plunged there by the Bogeyman. My heart, she thought right away, and braced herself for the next blow. Several peremptory 'pops' from the direction of Bayview Park broke the momentary quiet, and she peered in puzzlement at the night-sky visible from her window. Three skyrockets, celebrating the forty-ninth birthday of the Dominion, burst against the velvet backdrop, obliterating the stars and fanning out like irradiated metallic flowers.

53

1

Granny had not heard from Eddie – nor Cliff or Sandy – for more than a month. She knew why. The papers couldn't be avoided. News of the 'big push' to end the war and bring the boys home for Christmas was in the air and some believed it. Without letters, the hours were empty and would not be filled. Ralph's mother came to see her and stayed the afternoon. She wrote a long letter to Henry's father, and reluctantly, put all of Henry's notes and cards in the envelope. Except one. Bart's parents wanted her to visit them in Toronto. She felt touched by the gesture.

Just before midnight on the fourteenth of September, Granny awoke with a start. She was dressed and in her chair by the back window where she had watched the sun set behind the great hickory tree. The stars shone in the moonless dark. Something outside had drawn her awake. She got up, shook the sleep out of her left arm, and went out into the back yard. It was so dark she could only make out the curve of the treetop where it blackened the skein of stars above it. She entered the arc of the shadow under the tree; let its dark radiance possess her. The North Star brightened to the left of the point where lake and river conjoined. Then it widened like the lens of a prophet's eye. Somewhere five or six hours away to the east, the sun was rising over the Somme and the Ancre.

•

Zero hour for the move on the village of Courcelette was 6:20 a.m. The Canadian Corps was to attack with two divisions on a 2200-yard front. In a single bound they were to advance 1000 yards and strike at the defences in front of Courcelette: Candy Trench, the fortified ruins of a sugar factory, and 1500 yards of Sugar Trench. The siege guns in Sausage Valley behind Pozieres opened up in a furious bombardment as mile upon mile of batteries of every calibre joined in. Then came the grinding mechanical roar of tanks entering combat for the first time. The frontline German trenches, blown apart by the artillery barrage, were taken in fifteen minutes. On the right, three assaulting battalions of the 4th Brigade were on their objectives by 7:00 a.m. On the left near Monquet Farm, the 8th Brigade had done its duty with despatch. General Turner directed the 4th and 6th Brigades to establish posts on the south side of Courcelette.

...Eddie was sitting on his heels in the trench, a piece of paper that might have been a page from a letter tucked into the pocket over his heart. The five or six recruits squatting near him were not looking in his direction, yet the angle and arrangement of their figures took as their fulcrum the solemn calm of their corporal's face. Shreds of the night's shadows washed about their feet, more comforting than the yawn of light at the parapet's edge. Eddie glanced at his watch then touched with a reassuring eye each member of his platoon. A few yards away to his left Cliff Strangways stood smoking a tailor-made. He risked a glance at Eddie. To Cliff's right, Sandy Lecker checked and rechecked the bolt on his Lee-Enfield, the clicking noise jarring stomachs all the way down the mile-long trench. Reaching for his cigarettes, Cliff grazed the back of Sandy's hand, and the silence of the early morning resumed. Then the ground trembled as if there were anguish inside it, and the bastinado of cannon fire roared once before it deafened them all. The seventeen-year-old huddled next to Eddie was sobbing, his trousers wet and steaming. No one looked. The veterans counted the seconds by distinguishing the howitzer's screech from the whump of eighteen-pounders or the popping of trench mortars. The thunder ceased on some anonymous command. In its wake, the livid scream of silence in the heart's hollow. A minute later, the first wave went over the top. Rifles cracked, cries schismed, smoke and cordite careened on the imperceptible breeze. Eddie counted to twenty and rose to his feet. He couldn't feel them. He put an arm on the boy beside him. He saw the sergeant's battle cry before its tremor struck him. Eddie's lips were moving. He may have been shouting 'go', but the word *no* sallied in his head. He leapt up and over. The sunlight grooved him with all its strength. He released the boy, and watched him fall away, bowels blown out.

•

The second Canadian assault of that day was carried out in broad daylight. After ten minutes of 'smart bayonet fighting', the 22nd and 25th Battalions advanced right through the village. The 26th Battalion was left to mop up. In front of Courcelette, the Canadians came under severe German counterattacks, suffering numerous casualties. There was also trouble on the right. The Princess Pats lost their bearings over the broken ground where every distinguishing landmark had been obliterated. They struggled forward through shell holes while being raked by repeated rifle and machine-gun fire.

Within a minute the second wave had overtaken the first. Eddie tripped on a body and went down, instinctively thrusting his rifle upwards at an angle as his elbows hit the muck. His face pitched into a patch of slime. He tasted urine and shit. His eyes burned. He could see nothing but a blurred echo of sun behind a shroud of smoke, like a Turner sunset. Then shadows jerking forward, lumpish puppets unstrung, running on their own courage. When he got up, there was blood smudged on his right sleeve. Not his own. He ran forward, dodging the bodies tipped and askew everywhere. Some seemed to be crying out, but he could hear no human sound, not even his own frantic breathing. The crack of rifle and machine gun was so continuous it was a single blank roar; only the quaking of the earth under the earth told him the big guns were mailing their javelins to the enemy's throat. He could sense comrades running beside him, faceless, trusting in kinship, in collective valour, in the numbers of death's lottery. No one was ahead. Through the smear of air before him he could make out the chasm of the German trench, the cordite puffs from their rifles drifting like wispy pipe smoke. He dropped to his elbows, aimed and began firing. Something heavy and unprepared flopped on his legs. He twisted around, keeping low, and rolled the wounded soldier as tenderly as he could into a small depression. A bullet had ripped the right arm almost completely away from the shoulder. Muscle, bone and blood gaped at the sudden air. Cliff tried to speak but shock still gripped him. In a moment pain would annihilate speech. Eddie tore off a shirt sleeve, already bloodied, and strapped the limb to the torso. Cliff blinked as if he were staring down an eclipse. "It's okay, old chap, you're gonna get a pass home. Lie low and wait for a stretcher." Either Cliff smiled or the pain creased his lower face, but Eddie was already up and plunging ahead towards the ragged outrunners of his platoon no more than thirty yards from the enemy trench. The ground jumped under him and a vertical wall of granite straightened him to his full height, flattened him and rolled on. He felt the ooze from his punctured eardrum as he scrambled to his knees, dizzy and sick. He had dropped his rifle somewhere. A shell. Trench mortars. From the German second line behind the village. He was facing west. The morning sun warmed the skin on his exposed back. Cliff was gone. Where he had lain, the shell had made a crater, unblemished by blood, pus or excrement.

•

....The barbed wire and breastworks of Fabeck Graben were now visible through the pall of smoke that clung to the windless air. This time the Germans were ready. The ground Eddie was running over had no flat plane anywhere. Where the noon hour artillery duel had accidentally focussed, it was oozing rubble. Sandy had disappeared behind a hummock of dirt on top of which the trunk of a corpse lay – which side it had belonged to was impossible to say. Eddie could hear, with his good ear, pounding feet everywhere, yet he seemed to be alone. Ahead, the terrain levelled somewhat, pools of liquid phosphorous under the haze. He waited, crouched – the animal panic in him stunting then stirring. Sandy's familiar figure uncurled in the light and charged across the open ground. A tear-gas shell burst behind him like a smashed sunflower. The ground bevelled and shivered. Eddie couldn't hear the shrieks of Sandy's platoon behind him, protesting dismemberment. He sprinted forward, dropped, fired with a crazed instinct, rose and charged. As he dropped again, another shell exploded to his left. For a second, he saw nothing. The searing pain in his eyes drove him to his knees, his arms flapping like a grounded gull's wings. He felt the din of battle and dying in the tremble of his skin, through the sting of his ruptured eardrum, along the taut veins of his strummed throat, in the tuning fork of his long leg bones. The stutter of mortar shells, the screech of shrapnel, the wail of the maimed, the hiss of gas, the bark of futile commands, the ululation of the terror-struck – he heard each one as though he had ears and a heart that had survived dumbfounding.

The thirty-foot rolls of barbed wire darkly ahead. To the left, some of his comrades had found breaks in the wire and their bayonets flashed silver and then red. Eddie sighted and fired, a green coat stiffened in the act of straightening, and folded. Dead ahead, Sandy ran alone towards the bristling parapet, zigzagging like a soccer player, dancing amidst the bullets, his rifle floating in his hand as if he were carrying a flag on the end of it. Aiming his body like a missile, he dropped the rifle, flew over the remaining terrain with the grace of a five-minute miler, and while the astonished enemy gaped in disbelief, sailed into the barbed wire as if he had not seen it or else disdained its petty intercession. As a result he lifted, flattened and hung there, stunned. With some regret, a machine-gun barrel swivelled around, locked into place and chattered. Eddie saw the steel-jacket bullets rip out of Sandy's back, the helmet snap off and clatter to the ground, the head loll giddily from side to side saying no, no, no. But the body remained on the wire.

What was left of Eddie's platoon came up behind him. Their sergeant and company captain were dead. The soldiers raised their rifles and fired at the nameless targets. Bolts jammed. Barrels blushed and seized. Cartridge chambers exploded. Eddie took the rife from the corpse beside him, a scarlet welt where the face should have been. He inched forward. The dirt sizzled in front, this side, that side. Bullets hummed like maddened worms. Eddie continued to crawl forward, alone now, close enough to throw his grenade. It landed short. The barbed wire unsprung, jangling. But nothing they could do over the next two hours, *nothing* could stop the Germans – standing in the ruins of Fabeck Graben on balustrades of their own dead – from blasting to shreds, one bullet at a time, the pinioned flesh and bones of Sandy Lecker, the farmboy from Waterloo County.

•

...Eddie was alone. In the din and pall he recognized no one. There were no units, no officers, no direction. Twice out of the mist of smoke and steam of opened flesh, greenish limbs blundered into the rage of light around him, and he had fired or stabbed, stepped over the crumpled baggage and tried to find a place to run towards. Once, he stood up stock still and tried to squeeze his eyes shut against his own death, but the cordite tears flushed them wide and searing with absolute sight. Everywhere he put his foot down it skidded on blood, rubbed against bone, slithered on living intestine.

Through a fissure in the maelstrom, his glance caught the blank bullseye of a machine gun. He felt himself launched towards it. It stuttered and jammed. His rifle jumped and the youth behind the gun gasped as the bullet sliced through his throat and cut off his cry. Eddie turned in time to see the wayward shell – it could have been from either side – complete its mile-long random arc no more than a handspan from his next step.

He was flung sunward with the slow-motion ease of a levitation dream, blood stretched to the fingertips, toes, the whites of the eyes. The joints unhinged. The bones disengaged – legs, arms, scapula, skull spun out of the disintegrated skin towards the compass points of some unimagined gravity. The centrifuge of the heart at last gives way and releases with it from time's cradle these fragments: snatches of a Celtic lullaby; a telltale bubble of healing laughter; the perfect stanza of an unfinished poem; phrases of affection shaped but not uttered; three flawless lines from 'Tintern Abbey'; cherished moments of child bravery, fright, longing, devotion, steadfastness, the courage to be; memories as green as the hours that nurtured them one by one in all the afternoons and evenings and mornings it takes to bring the man out of the boy; dreams that run deeper than memory.

•

The Battle of the Somme began on July 1, 1916 and ended on November 28 of that year. The Germans lost 582,919 men. The Allied Forces counted 623,907 casualties. Of these, Canadian losses were 24,029 killed, wounded, and maimed.

Every one of them was Eddie.

2

Granny came out of the house into the austere light of the September morning. She might have been on her way to tend the chrysanthemums or the cucumber beds or the tomatoes that had survived the first frost. She carried her trowel but no hamper. Her left hand tightened into a fist, and her walk a little less spontaneous than usual. She moved slowly but without hesitation towards the big tree at the end of the property. The wind which had risen with the sun filled the yellowing leaves with sibilant motion. She stood under its shade, the breeze from the lake on her face and tried to imagine what this place – the knoll east of the marshes below and the great hickory above – was like when Southener's forefathers had first come seen it – as Lily had so long ago – from the water's edge staring eastward into the rising sun. Were they drawn to its sibylline whispers? Its promise of shade and renewal? Its bounteous strength bridging four seasons? Even now, with the magic of the talisman gone, she recalled the words Southener had spoken to her, in trust, more than sixty-five years before: "I received this magic stone on a sacred ground, long known as such by generations of tribes who have dwelt in these woods and waters and passed on, as we all do. The days of its guardianship are almost over; there is little magic left in the forests and the streams, older now than our legends. So when you have no more use for the stone's powers, I ask that you return it to the sacred grove whence it came, to the gods of that place who lent their spirit to it."

She opened her left hand. The jasper amulet lay in the palm as cold as when she had removed it a minute ago from the leather sachet she had carried out of the bush in another century. Only two of the treasures now remained there: the Testament with Papa's inscription inside the cover and the cameo pendant bearing the face of the woman who may have been her grandmother. Transferring the stone to her right hand, she dug a small hole in the ground between the two largest roots of the tree. She placed the jasper in the hole and for several minutes watched it. Then she brushed the soil over it. Under that seal of earth lay the dead amulet, Lil Corcoran, Lady Fairchild, Lily Ramsbottom, Lily Marshall, Cora Burgher, Granny Coote and what remained of whoever she was now.

•

Mrs. Carpenter, who had just heard the terrible news, came through the hedge and spotted Granny coming towards her from the garden.

"Oh Cora, we just heard. It's all over town. You poor, dear thing." She was wringing her apron and putting on the bravest face she could muster. "What *can* we do to help?"

Granny opened her mouth to reply but nothing came out – not a vowel, not a spent breath. From that day forward, not a single intelligible word passed her lips.

PART FOUR

The Return

54

1

The work of the monument proceeded apace. Sam Stadler brought his sons along only on those days when there was lifting or manoeuvring to be done. Otherwise he laboured alone under the vigilant supervision of the old man now rumoured to be his uncle. When the grand-nephews were about, the old fellow gambolled and chided and offered copious instruction. When they were not, he sat on one of the unprepared stone slabs and rarely took his eyes off the movements of the artisan's hands. Neither did Granny from her own watchtower across the street.

The monument was to consist of a double-pedastalled base of polished alabaster sandstone guarded by eight newel-posts linked with black iron chain. Surmounting this elegant base was a cube of rough-cut limestone with projecting cornice. On each facet of this cube was set a smooth tablet in which Sam Stadler had patiently inscribed the scroll of the dead. Normally these tablets would have been prepared in a workshop and transported to the site for installation, but Sam Stadler was no ordinary builder of memorials-in-stone. Every cut and gesture of his craft was executed on the grounds in the open air. When it rained, as it did often that April and May of 1922, he drew a tarpaulin over the unfinished pieces and sat in his truck smoking and smiling at respectable intervals as the old fellow chattered beside him. Sometimes if the rain were warm and misty, they sat silently in its midst, the droplets beading on the brims of their crumpled fedoras, cigarettes cupped lovingly in hand. Often several hours would pass before they moved – to return to the task or climb contentedly into the battered truck to go home.

On sunny days Sam Stadler sat on a stool and chipped into stone the strangers' names written on the sheet of paper spread out before him on the ground. Though hammer and chisel and file were his instruments, the play of his fingers across the grooved tablet reminded Granny of a pianist's fingers, Arthur's fingers – with their supple strength, their easy precision, their effortless acceptance of art's tyranny. Letter by letter she watched him chisel into continuance the names of the children of the village, and something in the tenderness of his gestures and in the deep resignation behind the quick smile he gave to the curious attending silently from the sidewalk, told her that to him these were more than yet another set of sad anonyms. He was, she thought, a calligrapher spelling out the letters of his first born in the reverence and awe and regret we feel for all things cherished and mortal.

On top of the pedestal and memorial facets was to be erected a twenty-foot obelisk of cut limestone interspersed with inscribed tablets to record the names of the battles wherein the sons and fathers had fallen or whatever cause had driven them hence: Ypres, St. Eloi, Vimy, Passchendaele, Hill Seventy – names that would enter the village vernacular like the names of those diseases which had struck and departed: diphtheria, typhus, small pox, Spanish influenza. They would be forever the whispered words of quarantine, of taboos only partially exorcized, of cold subcutaneous fear. The obelisk was constructed in five-foot sections to be fitted in place at the end of the work. On top of the last section a stone bust of the unknown soldier was to be erected. It was uncrated from a box delivered from the freight-sheds. Somewhere, Granny thought, there was a factory that turned these out from a single mold and shipped them to the hinterland. Against the wishes of Sam Stadler and of Reeve Denfield, the council had insisted on this necessary fillip, perhaps to offset the uncompromising idiosyncrasy of the rest of the piece, perhaps to ensure, for some, the military character of the memorial which the words alone, in their ambiguous solitude, could not do. "It's ugly and says nothing," was all Sunny said to her about the figure, and she nodded in agreement.

What was especially charming during the construction was the way in which people came to observe, almost always alone (even the children), in silence on the nearby walk, watching for long moments when you were certain they had not breathed and waiting as a faithful terrier does for recognition – a tip of the mason's hat or a wink (for the kids) or a cornerwise smile for the regulars. Granny observed many of these brief exchanges, no two of them quite the same though generated from similar sources and needs. She marvelled once again how much could be conveyed without the sweet contamination of language. One day just after the base was completed, Granny walked across the street with a thermos of tea. She stood and watched the three men sweating in the smooth sun, aware of the old fellow's stare. When the men had finished the task they were engrossed in, Sam Stadler acknowledged her presence with a grin.

"You been keepin' a good eye on us for some time now," he said pleasantly. "Denfield tells me it was your house they took down to make room for this."

Granny nodded and pointed to her lips.

"It's okay," Sam Stadler said. "I know." He turned to his sons. "I'm Sam and this here's Harry and Pat, my boys. The old wood-grouse there in the corner is my Uncle Jack but everybody calls him Old Jack for short."

Old Jack murmured an indistinct but not unfriendly greeting and kept his owl's eye fixed upon her in happy puzzlement. "He don't talk neither," Sam said and laughed good-naturedly as his sons and uncle joined in. "But that's never stopped him from gettin' his point across."

"If that's hot tea you got in there," Old Jack said with a superfluous wink in the direction of the boys, "we'd sure like some."

Sam Stadler spread the tea-towel in which he had wrapped their lunch over one of the slabs of stone."If you'd like to sit for a while, please do," he said. Granny sat down in the sun.

A little while later the boys drove off in the truck, and Old Jack, after some strenuous bantering over lunch, ambled to the back of the lot and fell asleep under the hickory tree. Sam Stadler picked up several chisels and awls, sat on his stool before one of the partly finished memorial tablets, and began chipping out the letters of a name. The sun warmed his fingers and mellowed the stone that gave way smoothly under their insistence. The shadow of his face fell over the name. When he sat back to roll himself a smoke, Granny read the letters he had just etched there: EDWARD ARTHUR BURGHER. Sam Stadler lit his cigarette, turned towards her, caught his smile in time, and said quietly, "You knew him."

After a deep draught of smoke he went on. "I didn't know him, of course, or any of these others. But four of my sons were there, and only two come home." She reached out and placed a hand over his. He didn't move. Not an eyelash.

•

Towards the end of April with only the base completed and part of the memorial section, the town council proudly announced that the Governor-General, Lord Byng, and his wife, Baroness Byng, would take time out of their busy schedule to visit the Point and consecrate a cornerstone of the cenotaph. Sam Stadler was hastily contracted to make a suitably engraved tablet, which became the first stone to be set in place upon the pedestal. The whole town went into a flutter of anticipation. And even though their Excellencys would spend less than an hour in the village – the rest of their hectic day to be apportioned among the various functions devised by the Sarnia-city elite – the visit was generally held to be a matter of civic pride. The veterans were to escort Lord Byng of Vimy from Bayview Park to the site of the cenotaph where patriotic speeches would be delivered, a bouquet of flowers presented to the Baroness by Harry Hitchcock's little girl, Susie, and a blessing uttered over the sacred cornerstone.

Granny heard the blare of bugles bent by the wind, and the tramp of military boots on pavement. The shadows of the restless throng around the site (some of them crowded back onto her lawn) flickered on the far wall. Although the words of the speeches – by Deputy Reeve Hitchcock and the Commanding Officer himself – were inaudible, Granny knew what platitudes they would employ, what pauses would be made so that the visiting press could capture each cliché intact and uncorrupted by novelty. Somewhere in the middle of an invocation by one of the innumerable local reverends, Granny drifted far enough into unconsciousness to enter the world of her own thought. She was thinking of Eddie and the time just after Arthur died when they went for a Sunday drive in Ralph's father's automobile, down into Moore Township.

•

Eddie was being especially cheerful, regaling her with stories of Bart's outrageous behavior last semester and showing off his driving prowess whenever the road widened sufficiently. They were taking the gravel highway that hugged the River south all the way to the county's end. The water lolled by them, midsummer blue. Iron-clad lake-steamers churned upstream or coasted down, no more than a hundred feet away. They looked for a schooner's sail but did not see one. To the east of the road the farms ran back from the riverfront for several miles, all neatly fenced; the forest was shaved clean around them except for a few anomalous spinneys, wispy on the far horizon. Wheat and oats and corn and green fallow gave proof of unremitting labour, steady progress and certain prosperity. Whatever the people in these clapboard or brick houses with the tall barns believed in, it was beneficent. They stopped for tea in Courtright. When Granny asked the elderly proprietress if she knew where 'Millar's Corners' might be, Eddie was surprised but asked no questions. Instead, he listened carefully as the woman, after recovering from her own surprise, gave them brief instructions.

"Do you know if there are any of the Partridge family still livin' in this area?" Granny asked as they were about to leave.

The woman peered at her as if she were a ghost likely to tell indecent stories on its return. Then she smiled dubiously. "I'm a Partridge. By marriage."

Eddie's cheeriness was replaced by respectful silence. Two concessions south of Courtright he turned east. The rectangular farms continued on either side. They passed a sugar bush. In one of the pastures Holsteins grazed as if in a dream of themselves. Metal mailboxes greeted the road at every gate. The houses, tidy and spare, were set back from the gates at a daunting distance, and spaced evenly apart every half mile or so. The heat shimmered, untouched, in the vacancy between. A boy, no more than ten, sat on a split-rail with his bare legs tucked under and stared at their passing. Nothing else moved.

The first time they went right past the sign and Eddie stopped the car about a mile to the east of it. He shut off the engine, and they sat in the sharpened silence of the afternoon heat and just listened for a long while. A song sparrow, two meadowlarks and a chorale of grasshoppers identified themselves. Eddie touched the back of Granny's hand on the seat beside him. "I think we passed it back there," he said.

Engrimed with seasons of dust and grit, the sign had been kicked over into a shallow ditch, and, unheeded by anyone anymore, had not been re-erected. If Millar's Corners had had hopes of expanding beyond a postal drop and a family's ambition, they had not been seriously entertained for many decades. Nevertheless, the castaway sign did mark one of the oldest crossroads in the township, and the side road that ran south of it was itself of ancient origin.

"Well," Eddie said, pointing to the mailboxes as they passed by, *"some* of the Millars stuck around."

"They were like that," Granny said, but did not elaborate.

Nothing was recognizable. Not a single memory could be reconstructed from these ruins, so complete was the transformation. The sickly clumps of trees were all second growth. The road itself was as straight as the ruler used to draw all the lines and side roads on the flat map of the county. She scanned the names on mailboxes, and gave up. She tried to imagine a small girl walking along the shoulder all the way home from the big cabin of the Millars. She counted trees, steps, invisible minutes.

"Stop here, Eddie."

He shut off the engine but did not follow her as she waded across the grassy ditch, slipped through a rail fence and walked towards a brick farmhouse situated on a slight rise to the east. Somewhere behind it, a creek lapped against low stones. She went up into the shade on the north side of the house, newly built, she could see, on some old site. A barn rose proudly on her left and she walked past it, measuring something in her mind, sealing her eyes now and then, ears alert for the sound of water. She did not go right up to the creek, knowing it would not resemble anything she would remember, but stood thirty or forty feet from it, listening to the timbre of its midsummer lament. Then she turned and stared at the knoll on which the house stood.

Sometime later a voice said: "You all right, missus?"

Granny looked up to see a red-cheeked farmer smiling uncertainly at her. "Where that new house of yours is," she said," was there ever anyone buried there?"

"You sure you're all right?"

"I used to live here, a long while back."

"We been here an awful long time ourselves," he said. "And yes, there was a couple of gravestones just about where our kitchen would be now. I remember them still bein' there when I was a kid and we had the old house further down the lane. Relatives of yours?"

"What happened to them?"

"Well now, I couldn't tell you exactly when, but they was dug up an' moved off here about 1880 or so, when the township started to collect all those kind of graves an' put them in proper cemeteries. You know."

"Where did they take them?"

"More than likely up to the public cemetery near Corunna. Just off the highway."

"Do you remember the names on them?"

He paused. "That's a long ways back, but I do remember because when the county men came to fetch them, they couldn't read a word on either of the stones. The names weren't scraped on there too good, you see, an' by the time they got here there wasn't a letter you could recognize. So they took the bodies up to Corunna an' buried 'em all with the others that didn't have names." Unable to read the look on her face, he added, "They're real nice graves up there."

When Granny came back across the field towards the car, Eddie waved to her.

3

Work had started again on the monument. The immanence of the royal visitation had begun to fade and wax fantastical. Sam Stadler took up his tasks as if nothing much had happened. He was pleased when Granny herself returned in a few days, with tea and Mrs. Savage's muffins.

Old Jack was at the boys again, sensing a coeval and possibly sympathetic ear nearby and wishing she could speak on his behalf as eloquently as her eyes intimated she wished to.

"You can't change your blood, you know. Blood is kin and those bonds are unbreakable. They're written on the inside of your bones

"That's enough, old man," Sam Stadler said sharply, jarring the two boys awake.

Uncle Jack snapped something back at him. It was not English. Sam Stadler returned the compliment in kind. The argument may well have continued had not Granny got up from her place, walked between the two men, both of them now standing, and placed her hand on the old fellow's shoulder. He stayed bone-still as she scrutinized every line in his face, every crevice of light in his expressive, aged eyes. Then his jaw began to drop as he heard her straining towards speech, a throttled gargle bulging up and jamming its coherence against her teeth, her stubborn tongue.

"Waupoore." The double-syllable entered the air, released from its dumbfounding. The old man reeled back as if struck by his mother's fist; he sat down on a stone slab and tried to catch his breath. He looked to Sam Stadler for help, but Sam was peering in disbelief at the old woman, at the contortions of her mouth out of which no subsequent word could be uttered to qualify or explain. The hoarse expulsion of enjambed sounds from her throat had reduced both boys to a silent stare as they sat fixed to the ground. After a minute or so, the rattle eased and Sam Stadler took Granny's arm in a reassuring grip.

Uncle Jack had recovered. In the language that was not English he cried, "Yes, I'm Waupoore, the Rabbit!" He was hopping up and down and looking beseechingly at Sam Stadler and then at Granny, and finally at the boys who were staring with detached fascination at the scene.

•

Sam Stadler sat beside Granny while she sipped her tea and they both waited for Rabbit to settle down long enough for her to write on the pad in front of her these words: Rabbit, Birdsky, Michael Corcoran, Lil, Old Samuels. Rabbit seized on them singly, holding up his hand to slow their effect, and after each he gave out a wincing smile as, somewhere within, a bulb of memory burst into dim bloom. As Granny watched him, she remembered the shy dance he had perfected for the world, amazed at how little it had diminished with age and heartbreak.

"You're Lily," he said. "Oh, how I worshipped the ground you walked on."

Yes, I was Lily – once.

•

While Sam Stadler measured with his jeweller's squint the wedges of stone to fit the tapering column and cut them with his watchmaker's touch, while he whetted and polished the flat tablets on which the names of the battlegrounds appeared one letter at a time as if some mist-of-dawn were lifting to reveal the spellbound runes of a legendless people, while Sam Stadler's sturdy sons erected the scaffolding from which the separate parts of the obelisk would be successively fitted into place and he was free to sip tea in the shade of the great hickory and saviour the blue wind over the far bay –

Granny gathered the pieces of Rabbit's story.

When Birdsky realized that Papa had left for good, she took up with a former lover, a Chippewa man who persuaded her, when the squatters' camp broke up, to come to the Muncey Reserve near London, where it was rumoured there was plenty of land and lots of work in the bush. Old Samuels and his family went north to the Sarnia Reserve, and Rabbit never saw them again. Old Samuels was very sick with a cough which he blamed entirely on the inferior quality of the 'White Mens' black tobacco. Soon after they settled at Muncey, Birdsky's man died under a felled tree, and within a month she married an Oneida named Doxtader. Rabbit took his name but resisted for a long time the imposition of 'Jack' which his step-father demanded when they moved to London and entered the white man's domain. Since his native name covered both cottontails and jackrabbits, Birdsky always laughed and said that 'Jack' was at least half-rabbit. For many years they lived in the nether-world below the white man's, completely cut off from the Reserve and its native traditions, attenuated though they might be. They drifted. Of the numerous brothers and sisters born after him, only one boy survived, Joe, ten years his junior. With Rabbit and Joe and their sisters, Birdsky returned to Muncey after her husband died. They made a great effort to recapture whatever it was they thought they had lost. But too much had passed by them. Joe, black-haired and brown-skinned, his full-blooded hatchet-face the envy of Rabbit with his suspiciously brown hair and light skin, was wretchedly discontent. Though he retained some of the Ojibwa language his mother had preserved for him, the English words were more tailored to his lips and more native to his deepest feelings. Joe left the Reserve when we was sixteen and never returned. He married a white woman and got a job as a bricklayer. Sam was their firstborn. When he was only two or three, about 1880, Birdsky died, and for a time Rabbit clung to the Reserve where he had no relatives and few friends. Finally he was persuaded to live in London, first with one of his sisters and finally with his brother Joe. After a while he even got used to being called Uncle Jack by his nephews and nieces. He embarrassed himself by telling stories better in English than he had rehearsed them in Ojibwa in his head, though only Birdsky who never left his right shoulder really noticed, and she adored him too much to scold. Young Sam was good with his hands. He made bows and arrows under his uncle's tutelage, he carved out the emblems of Michebou, the Great Hare. He had a good ear and Rabbit whispered into it enough of the sacred words to keep his spirit afloat until it could be claimed. Later when Sam got back from the war in South Africa, he took up the craft of masonry and tombstone sculpture. He drew white men's angels on their monuments. He changed his name to Stadler. When Rabbit's brother Joe died, it hurt Rabbit very much. It hurt even worse to have to move in with Sam and be treated as if he mattered.

•

One day towards the middle of June, Sam and his sons hoisted the last section of the obelisk into place and fitted the bust of the unknown soldier on top of it. It had rained all morning, keeping the curious villagers at bay. When the weather unexpectedly brightened in mid-afternoon, Sam got up from his nap under the hickory and signalled for the work to begin immediately. Thus it was that Granny was the only observer that day when the monument was completed. While his boys dismantled the rough scaffolding which still marred any appropriate view of the finished object, Sam and Granny walked across the street and stood in the yard of her new house. He did not speak, and there was no need. They were both looking west, and waiting. Young Pat pulled the last timber away from the base and dragged it to the edge of the lot. He peered over at them, grinning. Harry was on the other side. Rabbit was still asleep in the shade.

The four o'clock sun was just visible above the roof of the hickory, burning down over its steaming green and striking with glorious force the upthrust altars of the village memorial, its elegant pedestals as pure and sudden as Athenian light, the limestone obelisk with the weight of the village dead on its facades soared aloft into the vivid air as if it had been carved whole from a pictographic-cliff high above Superior and anchored to the granite of the earth.

"I wanted to see it from here, with the trees behind it and the sun along the solstice line. It will be beautiful in the mornings as well. The shadow of the column will fall along the trunk of the tree."

Granny wanted to touch his arm but she dare not.

"Uncle Jack thinks we've sold out our heritage," Sam Stadler said in a voice that was clearly meant to have her remain within the ambience of the wonder they were sharing. "But that happened a long time ago, before Rabbit himself was born. When I came here, I knew right away this place had once been a magic ground. I felt the ghosts all around me. When I was a boy, Rabbit told me that magic was the hardest thing in the world to kill. Well, the old ways are gone for good. But that don't mean we have to forget them, do we?"

55

It's goin' to look beautiful for the opening ceremonies, now isn't it," Sunny
Denfield said. Granny tilted her head slightly in agreement. "By then the
sod'll be somewhat stitched together, an' your delphinium an' poppies'll be
in their glory back there."

She accepted the compliment, knowing it was well-meant, and she was,
she had to admit, secretly pleased that most of the flower-beds she had
planted for Arthur had been left in their natural state, at least until next year.
All the hedges except the one adjoining the Carpenter property had been dug
up and the whole area around the monument turned into lawn and park. By
autumn both monument and greenery would have taken hold, and who
would there be to remember that they did not always belong to this place?

"We've set the date," he said. She held her teacup rigid. "The first of July
at eleven o'clock."

She swallowed her tea but did not look up.

"For Dominion Day," he explained hastily. *And butchery along the Somme.*

She flashed him an ironic smile he pretended to miss.

"The unanimous choice of the council, though I suspect we didn't all
vote for the same reasons. The vets will form up at Bayview, they'll be led by
our own small drum-and-bugle corps down St. Clair to the monument.
We've covered the Honour Roll with a flag, as you can see, and at precisely
11 A.M. I'll unveil the memorial plaque an' the first wreath of
remembrance'll be laid."

He paused. She was listening intently.

"Could I have a bit more tea?"

She reached for the pot, stopped and peered over at him with a gesture
which clearly said, 'Tell me what's really on your mind, I can take it'.

"The council – recognizin' all you've done an' meant to this community
for sixty years, an' seein' that you're now a deed-holdin' landowner,"– he
was unable to complete the smile here –"would like you to lay the wreath. It
was unanimous. Even Hitch. The rightness of the choice was self-evident.
They – that is, I don't see how anyone else could possibly do." Finally he

turned to face her. The burn-scar on his left cheek glowed softly in the muted sunlight of the room. Unconsciously he drew his fingers over its numbness.

"Look, Cora, I know how much we're askin' of you. And I have a pretty fair idea of what you think of the War an' politicians an' pooh-bahs. But that part of it's over, you see. We let Lord Byng an' his Lady an' his entourage of party hacks come here an' have their say back in April. You can't keep them away from a thing like this. So we invited the whole shebang includin' a brass band. They come an' they said their piece an' they went. Not a one of them will ever remember again where Point Edward is without checkin' a map first. What we're plannin' for July is goin' to be our own. Sure, we couldn't say no to the local M.P. an' his cell-mate from the Legislature, but that's all. Not even His Worship from the City will be here. Just us. The people who suffered an' the people who sacrificed. The people who wanted this monument built, an' know, each one of them, what it means."

The flies along the window-ledge buzzed in the local sun.

"I think you know, Cora, that in some ways you've been almost a mother to me. Sometimes Prudie gets annoyed with me comin' over here so much, and I'm at a loss to give her an explanation she can believe." He paused, drew a deep breath, and said more quickly, "This monument'll mean different things to different people, but let me tell you what I think, an' what I believe many others in the village think deep down inside. This monument isn't a memorial to war or the so-called triumph of good over evil. There's nothin' glorious about war whether you win or lose. We know that for ourselves. There's not a man between twenty-five an' forty in this town who isn't limpin' or half blind or wakin' up screamin' in the middle of the night from the shrapnel that ain't come out yet or the nightmares of shell-shock. An' the women know even better than we do – they suffered here at home for four years, they looked into the grim faces of the bereaved, an' most of them felt that pain themselves before it was over." He swallowed hard. "No one felt it deeper than you did."

She tried to deny it but her eyes failed her.

"I'll tell you what I think that monument means to most of us when we walk past it by ourselves, when we're sure no one is watchin' or listenin'. You've seen them already, haven't you, from this window? To them it's not a fancy pillar to the glorious dead. It's a memorial to those of our own who left us for a cause we thought to be right. They died, and I know that some of them found courage before they died and others didn't. That don't matter.

They were ours, they left us, and if we don't remember them no one else will, no one but us will really care. We want our grandchildren to know, years an' years from now, whenever they see this column an' the names on it, that once there was a village here, with people who were brave an' foolish an' caring. This is goin' to be a monument to ourselves as a village, what we been through in the past, how much we can be together in the future. This is only one of the wars we've already been through. Who knows that better than you?" He got up and stood at the window looking across to the cenotaph and the ancient tree behind it.

"So you see why it has to be you to lay the wreath."

When he found the courage to face her, she gave a reluctant consent.

"The council also asked me to give the dedication address," he said. "I agreed, of course. And I will. But I'd like you to write out the words for me."

Granny made no attempt to brush away the tears that would do as they pleased anyway. When Sunny started towards her, she held up her hand, and smiled. As he watched in a sort of anguished awe, she got up, joints creaking a bit, went over to Arthur's trunk on top of which she kept her writing tablet, and wrote something on it in slow, stiff surges. He waited as she brought the paper across to him.

It read: 'Not necessary, you already have'.

•

Sunny Denfield wrote out for her a detailed description of the ceremonies and her small role in them. "By the way, my cousin Ruth-Anne is comin' down for the occasion. She hasn't had any luck in tracin' her mother's relatives, but I guess she's heard so much about this fabulous town lately, she decided she had to come an' see it for herself. I'm delighted. I haven't seen her in eight years. We ain't been much of a family, I guess, and I'm anxious to make amends. I think you'll like her."

As he was about to leave, Granny wrote on her pad: 'I wish to give you a gift, something personal, for all you have done'. While he was energetically refusing such undeserved kindness, she reached into Arthur's trunk and brought out a leather pouch. She loosened the drawstring and he saw two objects inside: a pendant with what appeared to be a cameo portrait of some kind and a calf-bound book, perhaps a miniature Bible. He could tell from the way she fingered them that these objects were heirlooms of great value.

Again he demurred, but she held out the book until he took it, gently, into his hands. On her tablet she wrote: 'This belonged to my father and he got it from his mother. He inscribed it for me and asked me to keep it until I could pass it along to my own children'.

56

1

Three days before the ceremony Prudie Denfield came over. She insisted on showing Granny how to use the new-fangled gas range in the kitchen, and after a brief one-sided tea, the two women went through the dusty trunks in the uninhabited bedroom until a presentable dress was unearthed. It was the black one she had worn to Arthur's funeral. How thin she had become since that time, ten years ago almost to the month. I thought I'd be with you long before now, she said quietly to him when Prudie's back was turned. But then I never was lucky at planning anything for long.

Prudie fussed over her, pinning the dress with elaborate care for the alterations she was threatening to carry out. She even promised to bring over a boxful of vintage hats – representing all sizes and generations – from which a choice eventually could be made. Before she left, she sat Granny down in her padded rocker and began brushing her hair with long, rhythmic, drowsing strokes. When her eyes opened, the room was dark. She let her dream continue. She was dreaming of Bradley and the night he came back from the dead...

•

Bradley had no sooner stepped into Hap Withers' cottage that night when he staggered and collapsed on the linoleum. The swaddled child struck the floor before she could catch it, and began crying. Holding it in her arms, she forced the door shut with her body, already soaked from the wind-driven, icy rain pouring in on them. She stripped off the wet rags and wrapped the baby in an old quilt, its cries shuddering through her, its tiny face wizening as if it were trying to squeeze all the blood out with whatever pain or terror was twisting inside. Bradley groaned and heaved onto his side. Something black and oily dripped from his mouth. The baby shrieked. She hurried back to the kitchen, but the stove was cold. She lay the baby down on her bed and returned to the front room. Somehow with the child wailing and the storm lashing about the eaves and sills, she managed to haul Bradley's unconscious form onto Hap's bed. She could not get more than his jacket off because each time she pulled at his clothes he jerked back as if he'd been jabbed by a cattle-prod. She pulled the large comforter over him, tucked it firmly in all around, and went back for the baby. Covering it with her own coat, she ran into the fury of the storm towards Peg's house, just across the tracks.

Despite her good marriage and religious conversion, Peg Potts Granger was still an Alleywoman. She asked no questions; the desperation in Lily's face was all the testimony she required. Two of her boys were dispatched to rouse the doctor in Sarnia. She herself took charge of the baby, and while Lily – Peg called her Mrs. Burgher because she could not bring herself to call her mother's lifelong friend 'Cora' even though most of the village had grown accustomed to the change – while Lily stood shivering in uncharacteristic helplessness, Peg dug out an old bottle, warmed some milk and soon had the baby's wailing damped down for the night. "Go back to Bradley, missus. I won't say a word till you tell me. The baby'll be here when you're ready for him."

After satisfying herself that Bradley was still breathing, Lily went into the kitchen and got a roaring fire started. Then she walked grimly back to her son. She was not even sure just how she had come to recognize him, something in the eyes perhaps that no metamorphosis however savage could disguise. The once-thin, ascetic face was monstrously bloated, his skin had the pallor and touch of gray-white mushrooms too long in the rain. The top of the head was bald but not smooth – as if the hair had been pulled out in frenzied tufts. What hair remained – on the sides and back of the head – was a weathered, colourless fungus no amount of scrubbing would ever make blond again, or curly. As she pulled away the vest and shirt, she saw that the body flesh was similarly puffed and shapeless. Under her touch, it oozed. As she drew his trousers down, she caught sight of the swollen, lopsided protuberance stretching out below his right ribs – like a blooded liverwort. His breathing came in short, gasping seizures followed by a death-like quiescence – equally frightening.

It was dawn when the rain stopped and Dr. Dollard arrived, white-haired and exhausted after a night in the township. He accepted Lily's offer of a cup of hot coffee and a biscuit, and they sat in a grateful silence for a while –

though there was much that lay between them. Finally he said to Lily in a grave tone: "I'm afraid he's come home to die."

"How much time?" Lily said.

"A few days, a week. No one can say for sure. He's slipping in and out of hepatic coma, and it appears from his breathing as if pneumonia's setting in. His liver's finished."

"Drink?"

"I'm afraid so."

"Did you recognize him?"

"To be honest, no. I've seen a lot but I didn't think a young man could change that much in so short a time. I'm sorry, Mrs. Burgher."

"What do I do?"

"Keep him warm or cool as his temperature varies, get some liquid into him if you can. I must warn you, he may go into *delirium tremens* if the pneumonia don't work fast enough. If he does, get some help quick. And call me."

"Thank you."

At the door he said, "You take care, Lily."

•

Bradley had his first seizure before noon. Asleep on the chesterfield, Lily was brought upright by some loud muttering from the bedroom. When she went in, he was still unconscious and shouting violently at some antagonist in his dream and thrashing his arms about as if warding off savage blows. The comforter was knocked askew, and suddenly both of his knees shot up, flinging it to the floor. With a fierce cry he rose up and began flailing at his invisible assailants; she could distinguish only 'no, no, no' as he fell back in a crumpled ball, knees up and against the belly like a monstrous foetus. Then everything began to quiver, then tremble, then quake – skin, puffed flesh, the elastic bone, the pale lids of the eyes. She heard the scraping of his clenched teeth and the embowelled groan trapped behind it. The force of it unbent his body and popped his eyes wide open.

•

Hap Withers, bless him, promised to stay close, but Lily assured him there was no need. She was not frightened. After one of his brief seizures, Bradley was calm and perfectly lucid, as if some kind of exorcism had occurred without his blessing. Although his voice was thin and without colour, it was one she remembered, and from the ruined housing of that flesh it was Bradley's eyes that looked at her. On these occasions he was usually able to speak for half an hour or so before he tired and slipped into a sleep which was both shallow and fathomless. In the seven days that he lived – during which she left his side for brief moments only, trying to sleep when he did, eating with him, suffering with him as she had so many times before when the fever and the fever-dream chose to strike – they never really had a conversation. If he were quiet but alert, she would speak for a while, telling him what she thought he ought to know or just letting him hear the strength of her voice. He would dip his chin slightly or move his eyes in a certain way to let her know she was to continue, and sometimes, though rarely, he would murmur in assent or acceptance. At other times she would find him awake and before she could utter his name, he would begin talking in his whispered monotone. When this happened, she had to sit close to him to catch every word; if she moved an inch to loosen the crick in her neck, his eyes would widen with a childish terror and he would start to speed up his speech towards a frantic blur until she moved in close enough, once more. At times she felt he was talking right past her to some more unconvinced ear beyond this room – the words, the jumble of ideas, the arcane references, the assumed knowledge – all tending to puzzle and estrange. Yet even when the flow of his talk became trancelike or confessional, she had only to turn her head to one side before he seized upon the gesture as a betrayal. Every word that he uttered during the last week of his life was something he needed to say, and, in a way she never fully understood, something he needed to say to her or in her presence. Though all of it was obviously not meant for her, every word and every deed behind it required a sanction only she could give. She made it her business to cherish each syllable.

2

Bradley said that when he and Paul Chambers went to Toronto in 1892, they quickly fell into the Bohemian life they both so desired. They frequented the coffee houses and literary salons, such as they were in a backwater like Toronto. It was at one of the latter that he met Sarah Crawford, the daughter of Isabella Valancy Crawford, a person who could call herself a legitimate poet. Bradley admitted he was soon in love. The highlight of the year, however, was the visit to Toronto of Oscar Wilde during his North American tour. He spoke eloquently of Art for Art's sake, a credo that Bradley and Paul took instantly to heart.

Soon after, Bradley moved into a cold-water flat with Sarah and her mother. Inspired by Isabella, he soon began to write poetry, and the form he chose was the epic. He began work on what was to be his first poem and a masterpiece: *The Ruins of Arcady*. Paul's wealthy father supported his son, and Paul made sure that Bradley did not want for anything. But Toronto began to close in on them, a city of Philistines in Wilde's view. Paul suggested they move to Montreal. There they found a more literary community, and work on the epic continued apace. About this time, his father, concerned for Paul's dissolute life, decided to finance both young men on a long trip to England, where, it was hoped, Paul would eventually take up studies at the University of London. They sailed the next week.

Once in London, they immediately started to visit the haunts of Whistler and Wilde, hoping that *The Ruins of Arcady*, at last completed, could be shown to the great men. Initially they found it impossible to get near Wilde and his set, but Wilde's current lover was a Canadian, Robbie Baldwin, and through his auspices, they were able to arrange a short visit to Tite House. They were in awe of Wilde, who entertained them with his wit and panache. When the poem was finally proffered, Wilde took it in both hands and told Bradley to come back in a week. The time went slowly by, but they mustered up their courage and went to hear the verdict. Wilde handed back the thick envelope and pronounced the epic "American drivel." Bradley said he felt crushed and suicidal. Paul kept a close watch on him, and it was fortunate that he did so because Bradley, thinking he was alone, flung himself into the Thames, and Paul came in after him. When they got home, drenched and shivering, Paul listened to his friend say that his life was essentially over. He implored Paul to write to Sarah and say he had drowned.

That news would soon reach his mother and she would have to accept that her son was dead. Paul, fearing for Bradley's health and state of mind, reluctantly did so.

For the next seven years the two men stayed in the flat, still financed by Paul's father. Paul went out often, making friends and carousing, while Bradley stayed in and drank, still fretting about his epic but lacking the heart to destroy it. The drinking got so bad he fell victim to a case of DTs and had to be resuscitated in hospital.

"It's time to go home," Paul said, and he bought a single passage to New York the next day. Bradley insisted he had dried out and remained sober during the voyage. The only thing of note on board occurred when he stood on the stern deck and, one by one, tossed the leaves of *The Ruins of Arcady* into the icy waves of the Atlantic.

To his surprise and delight, Sarah (who thought him dead) was there when he arrived at her doorstep. She was shocked to see him both alive and in desperate health. Her mother had died and she herself was working in a garment factory. Bradley moved in, and despite his avowals started to drink again. Eventually, she asked him to leave.

He spent the next sixteen months in taverns and dives, suffering a second bout of DTs. The doctor told him it would be his last. When he was sober enough, he crawled back to Sarah. She smiled and handed him Eddy. Seven months old. Whole. Then she told him that she had tuberculosis.

Bradley took a deep and exhaustive breath and uttered the last of his million words:

"It was hard but I didn't take another drink. I knew full well that I couldn't build another life for myself. There was nothing left. But I thought I could perhaps borrow whatever of me remained in Sarah and the boy and hang on as long as I could. I owed the world something. As soon as I was better, I planned to bring Sarah and Eddie here for a while. At long last I realized what I could never admit all those years, whether I was up or down. It was you I must see – not to reconcile or expiate, but merely to release. Though less merciful, love is more binding than death."

"A few weeks ago, I began writing poems, scraps of verse, lines only but powerful ones, expunging ones, untranslatable, with images so stark they seemed to have been drawn with the ink of dreams. Every one of them was about Sarah. I finished only one. It's in my satchel. I want you to have it. It's not much, but it's all that's left of me. I read it to Sarah in the evening before she died."

3

Granny woke up with the sun on her back, streaming through the kitchen window and the open doorway behind her. Stiffly she rose and went in to put the kettle on. She fidgeted with the new-fangled gas range until it popped into flame. Well, well, she thought, that wasn't too difficult, was it? Maybe I'll even get used to it.

At least you came home, Brad. That's something.

57

1

Knowing she would not sleep much the night before the ceremony, Granny switched off the electric lights in the front room, lit the coal-oil lamp and placed it on the table beside Arthur's trunk. She sat down and began leafing through the memorabilia of a lifetime. Each of the playbills recalled the story Arthur had associated with it, something bizarre in event or character, something that always ended with a chuckle or a wink in her direction that said 'the world's a funny place if you don't die laughing'. The lingering twilight – they were just past the high solstice – had just succumbed to the deep darkness of the summer night when she reached into Bradley's satchel and drew out the loose scraps of paper on which he had scrawled his last words. Among their blotted, unfinished number she found the copy of his poem to Sarah, the one she had made before sending the original off to Eddie. Had he read it before he died? Did it make any difference?

She stared at the five stanzas – not quite filling a single page with lines that touched neither margin. So this is it, she thought, this is what all the pain of birth and loss and absence and wishing-to-be has come down to? A few lines of shrunken verse. This is where all the joy of foolish affection and helpless love and desire under the dark has finally landed? In this let's-pretend house confected out of pity, with a worn-out skin-and-bones scarecrow of a crone who can't even say hello or goodbye or it's time to go. All that energy of genesis, all that procreative hope, all that suffering smothered in the mouth and held in and mined against the future. For this. For nothing.

After Mama's death Old Samuels, wise in his blindness, had said to her, "We must listen to the good gods and keep them on our side; they will help those who listen for them. But we must also help the gods. Sometimes the demons are strong and the good gods go into hiding." Well, she had done her share of listening and she had tried her best to help. So had the others. Old Samuels assured her she was one of those chosen to hear their special music and dance it for the world's sake. Well, she had danced in her time, but not enough perhaps, perhaps without the purity of purpose the music needed to prevail.

A series of images passed before her eyes. Maman LaRouche kneading fat buttocks of dough before the outdoor oven and sliding them into its wombing heat where they would pop into being like fairy-tale babies, and Maman LaRouche lying ever so quietly in her bed of ice afraid of waking the robins before spring arrived, and the Frenchman dead with the clench of a curse unuttered against the malign spirits of that place he could never recognize as home and knowing with his last breath his children would scatter before his flesh was cold and not a kinsman left even to tend a grave or whisper a purgatorial prayer, and her own Mama rocking to the rhythms of the brushstrokes through her hair as the sun mellowed in the little room she was preparing to enter alone, and Papa's voice above the embers telling of ocean voyages and rescue at sea and brave departures and love broken by effort and fatigue and failure against the deities of the bush and Papa's arm about her at last shepherding her into sleep, and Old Samuels' pipe smoke and the words that came through it and lifted some feeling/some hope that floated in her all the years and even now, and the dances she did to resurrect the twinkle in the old sagamore's eye, and the mask of Southener's face in the stillest of dawns and the sad auguries breaking there like raw light through ancient mist, and the graveyard of the lost and the dispossessed not a mile away where some of the benevolent spirits still crouched in anxious wait and where the wind-tossed grasses took root in that more ample quietude, and Aunt Bridie at twenty wrapped in her mother's shawl against the sea-wind, standing alone on the foredeck and staring ahead where some land was supposed to be in which even orphans could find love, and Uncle Chester among the workshop shavings coaxing wood into toy shapes his son would never see, and Tom dancing at the Great Western Ball happy and handsome and unaware that across the room an eye had caught him in its prophecy, and Tom's arms and Tom's laugh and Tom's touch in the near-dark and the mutual yearning that gave them Robbie and Brad and sent them off to cultivate the minor gods of this ground they hoped at last to be able to call home – but you left me, Tom, you left me and I don't know why and I never will and I've missed you every day since, even those days when I refused to say your name aloud and banished your treachery from all thought, and I think of you haunting some barren-ground above Superior with a ghost who can't find his way back, just as Uncle Chester lies among Baptists and do-gooders in a town he never saw and would have hated, as Aunt Bridie lies caged in some Yankee mausoleum with her emigré soul battering forever at the cold bars, as Solomon lies in his underwater coffin staring up at the chilling sun, as Mama and the La Rouches lie unvisited under nameless markers in a stranger's cemetery even the bees are ashamed to attend, as Lucien lies reclaimed by the territory he spent a lifetime fleeing from, as Sophie lies in the grief of the deep, cool earth and dreams of fire and air, as Robbie lies in his soldier's tomb at Batoche where the curious come to cluck and wonder, as Papa lies in a Negro churchyard worshipped in anonymity by puzzled blacks, as Eddie lies nowhere and everywhere in the charnel-house of Europe.

You, Eddie, you were the reason for it all, the reason the world held out to us in derision. You came like a son of Lazarus, conceived in a moment of miraculous randomness. You had the mark of redemption on you from the beginning. You redeemed the wastrel who fathered you and passed along to you the gift of speech and its poetries. You brought me back to the best part of myself, you reminded me that the benevolent gods Old Samuels talked about – always under siege – could in the midst of their powerlessness make subversive music, you showed me again what I had always known: that belief is a hard flame to extinguish; you brought me back to the words Cap had nourished me with before he could die, you brought me to Arthur and together we pledged allegiance to the future you promised just by your being.

It had come to naught. There was no meaning after all in events, in words, in the sufferings of the human heart. They were random and terrible. Cap was right: history is a fiction, a weak disguise for our disordered desires.

She was looking at Bradley's poem. Though she knew it by heart, she went through the motions of reading it.

COLLOQUY, FOR SARAH

MAN:
December's grasped my soul, stark, leaf-bereft of all but spite
at autumn's fall –
from the infidel dark I curse you'

for having loved.
Alone, in your grave you sing with the
strength for two
of olives and January light
WOMAN:
Across the winter's width a cruising wind, brute sun, a
lecherous petal
licking light.
In your distress
you rake the
bruised map
of my face with a
treacherous kiss
I draw down
towards the dappled acre of my
tenderness.
We go under
and wait.

Not enough to keep Eddie alive, she thought. But it was, without question, beautiful.

•

Just before she drifted into a clear, dreamless sleep, a single image asserted itself – without preface or prologue: she was five years old, she was in the woods, she was watching a tiny head squeeze out of some fleshly crevice like a water-logged chestnut, until its gleaming skull burst forth in a halo of blood whose petals spun at her feet, whose medallions dripped from the slow leafage. As the scene faded, she distinctly heard the sound of Rabbit's boyish laugh.

2

When she woke it was mid-morning, and she felt surprisingly rested. Moments later Prudie Denfield arrived, all smiles and about to make a to-do over getting her 'frumped up' for the grand occasion. Prudie noted with

some satisfaction that Granny had been using the gas range. Prudie heated
lots of water and helped her bathe and powder her wrinkles and ease her
angles into the deceiving curves of the dress. A scarecrow in a tux is still a
scarecrow, she thought, suddenly wishing she could speak – to murmur all
the pleasantries and reassuring simplicities of woman's casual conversation.
Prudie, bless her, gabbed on as if Granny were holding up her end of the
bargain. There was perhaps something odd in that effusiveness, some special
feeling of affection behind it that was not carried at all in the words or even
the tone. Also, she caught Prudie more than once staring at her when she
thought she was unnoticed, with a sort of wondering appraisal, the way one
searches the face and gestures of a person you've just been told is a friend
you haven't seen for thirty years. When she was caught out, Prudie blushed
briefly, then began to talk with even greater urgency about the trivia of dress
and protocol. Something strange was afoot.

About ten o'clock, an hour before the ceremony, as Prudie was putting
the final touches on her stitchery, Granny saw three figures coming along the
sidewalk towards her house. Prudie spotted them, too, and dropped her pins,
said, "Oh my, Cora, it's time for me to go and get ready. I'll just let myself
out the back way." And she did.

Sunny Denfield turned into her yard, resplendent in his uniform. Beside
him, keeping pace, was a young woman of medium height whose brown
hair, straight nose and curious dark eyes suggested close kinship with the
Reeve. Ruth-Anne, she thought, the cousin from Toronto. The tailored
clothing and confident bearing at once bespoke a woman from the city, with
breeding and inherited urbanity. Between them, and struggling to keep pace
with a sort of dancing skip-and-a-jump, was a waif of a creature, blond as a
Viking water-sprite, with freckles as big as her blue eyes, in a flounced yellow
dress as bold as a butterfly wing, out of which the narrow, tapered little-girl
limbs sashayed with all the awkward grace of an apprentice ballerina.

•

Granny let them in, unable to take her eyes off the little girl. When she
finally met Sunny Denfield's gaze, she knew something had happened since
his last visit three days before, something more profound and unsettling than
the arrival of a cousin and her daughter. He was in turn staring at her in a
way which suggested that some long-suspected truth had been confirmed,

though not unattended by surprise. The young woman was also staring at her with a mixture of curiosity and awe. The little girl hopped up and down on the spot between them. She couldn't have been more than six years of age.

These exchanges took seconds only, and Sunny said, "Mornin'. I brought you someone I know you've been anxious to meet."

She nodded to indicate that she knew who they were and was happy to receive them. When Sunny paused mysteriously, like a bad tragedian before a soliloquy, his cousin made as if to speak on her own behalf and he cut in quickly. "I'd like you to meet my first cousin, Ruth-Anne MacEnroe. Ruth-Anne, this is Mrs. Coote, my longtime friend, an' your long-lost grandmother."

Ruth-Anne opened her mouth to speak, but could not. What she had already seen, whatever form it had taken, had confirmed the impossible, and she let several unladylike tears escape through her astonished smile.

Sunny pressed ahead. He put his hand on the little girl's shoulder and she looked up at the old woman. "An' this is –" he said, his own voice on the verge of breaking...*Victoria*, Granny said to herself in a rush before Sunny said, "Victoria, your great granddaughter."

•

At fifteen minutes before eleven, just as the first strains of the drum-and-bugle corps were carried southward on the soft breeze of that special day, four figures emerged from the new house and crossed the street to join the host of villagers already assembled before the monument.

3

Over the next two weeks, and before Ruth-Anne and Victoria had to return to Toronto, the stories on both sides were gradually and lovingly told. Granny wrote out her responses to the questions of her granddaughter and her 'foster nephew' – as Sunny now called himself – in a cramped hand that only gradually began to flow and curve with the urgency and excitement of the impossible narrative.

When Mrs. Edgeworth in the spring of 1861 had written down 'Lily

Fairchild' on a calling card and given it to the government man who had come to repossess the Prince's daughter, no one had any idea of the consequences of the act. Apparently the card accompanied the child, whom Lily had secretly named Victoria, to her new home in Toronto with Olive and Parker Macdonnell. Macdonnell was a busy minister in the Baldwin-LaFontaine cabinet and thus left the raising of their adopted daughter mainly to his wife. The little girl was christened Grace and a year later, as often happens in such cases, a natural daughter was born to the Macdonnells, and called Faith. Faith and Grace were raised together, without prejudice. Both married, Faith to a barrister named Harvey Denfield and Grace to an entrepreneur named Bramwell Beattie. Just before she died in 1890, Olive Macdonnell summoned Grace to her bedside and told her that she was an adopted child, and that even though she had promised on her husband's grave not to break her vow of silence, she felt compelled to do so now that she faced her own death. She gave to Grace, who was pregnant with Ruth-Anne at the time, the note revealing her true mother's name – Lily Fairchild. She added that she had been able to discover only two other facts about her identity: she had aristocratic – perhaps even royal – blood in her veins and her mother came from Lambton County, probably Sarnia. While Grace was shocked by the revelation, her life was too crowded with feeling and activity to do much about it. For a long time, watching over her own daughter and her orphling nephew, Sunny, kept her thoughts entirely away from her royal lineage, but as she neared the end of her own life, just as her stepmother had done, she called her daughter to her and passed along the only scraps of information in her possession. Ruth-Anne had asked for Sunny's help in tracing any existing Fairchilds in the County. Mitch Strong, the postmaster, and a librarian friend of his in Sarnia, got hold of several old directories and gazetteers, and Sunny himself searched the registry records. No Fairchild of any sort had ever lived in Lambton. There were, of course, a thousand Lilys. The search came to an abrupt end.

Then only three days before the memorial ceremony, Granny had given Sunny Denfield a gift, a Testament with an inscription made by her father: 'To my dearest princess, the Lady Fairchild'. Excited but hardly knowing what to make of the discovery, Sunny tried to think of someone still alive who might have known Granny Coote or Cora Burgher in the distant past. Prudie suggested Duckface Malloney down at the Sunset Glades in Sarnia. Sunny went to see him and after several hours of frustrating interrogation, he learned conclusively that Cora had once been Mrs. Lily Marshall and before that Miss Lily Ramsbottom, and what-is-more she had lived on a farm near Sarnia about the time of the strange events of 1861. He didn't know why or how yet, but he knew. When Ruth-Anne arrived and he took a good long look at his 'niece', he had no more doubt. After all, blood was blood.

•

Reeve Denfield was about to speak. Moments before, the MLA for Lambton West, awed by the monumental stillness and the hushed crowd, had spoken briefly and from the heart, his prepared speech untouched in his pocket. Granny stood with the wreath in her hand, haloed by the perfume of uprooted flowers, and listened.

The Reeve spoke quietly with a gentle earnestness, the way people do in the sunshine after Sunday service. He reminded them of the things that had gone before: the days when the Attawandarons had roamed freely over territory still unmapped, when the land they were now standing on had been some sort of sacred grave or shaman's ground where prayers and incantations and holy relics had been offered in a language now lost to time and history. He recalled the days when the village site was a mere ordnance ground before the great railroad adventure began. He talked of the coming of the Grand Trunk and the first labourers who hacked a right-of-way through the bush, laid their cross-ties, slept in shacks and stayed on to found a community. He spoke of high hopes, the building of churches and schools, the passion for politics and nation-making, the movement towards villagehood. His tone darkened as he recalled the treacheries of railroad amalgamation, tunnel-construction, the removal of the car-shops. Many in the audience would remember the wagons with their human cargo moving sadly through the secretive mists of early morning, and the vacant neighbourhoods and boarded-up churches. The Reeve went on to talk about the long recovery, the heroic contributions of specific citizens, the struggles against annexation, the new pride of place at last gathering momentum as they faced the second decade of a new century. Sunny's voice continued on as she had heard it so many times over the years and he spoke those sentiments about the War and what it meant in the way he had inadvertently rehearsed them for her.

She too would remember all of these things. But what she would remember most, in whatever years remained to her, was placing around the neck of the little girl now clutching her hand the silver pendant and its cameo sketch of one said to have been a grandmother of her own blood in a far country. Something squeezed her hand. She glanced down. The cameo turned tenderly on the child's tiny fingers, and as the sunlight struck the ivory profile from a momentary quartering angle, it might have been taken for a replica of her own. The child's touch trembled on the silhouette, circled some memory hidden there, and took possession

Bibliography

- Abels, Jules. *Man on Fire: John Brown and the Cause of Liberty.*New York: Macmillan, 1971.

- *Adventures on the Great Lakes.* Coles Canadiana Reprint, Toronto: 1980.

- Beasley, David H. *The Canadian Don Quixote: The Life and Works of Major John Richardson, Canada's First Novelist.* Erin, Ontario: The Porcupine's Quill, 1977.

- *Canada in the Great World War,* 7 vols. Toronto: United Publishers, 1920.

- Careless, J. M. S. *The Pioneers: An Illustrated History of Early Settlement in Canada.*Toronto: McClelland and Stewart, 1968.

- Careless, J. M. S. *The Union of Canadas. 1841-1857,* Toronto: McClelland and Stewart, 1968.

- Cellem, Robert. *Visit of HRH The Prince of Wales to the British American Provinces and the United States in the Year 1860.*Toronto: Henry Rowsell, 1861.

- Chapman, L.J. and Putnam, D.F. *The Physiography of Southern Ontario,* 2nd ed. Toronto: University of Toronto Press, 1966.

- Copleston, Frederick, S. J. *A History of Philosophy: Fitche to Nietzsche,* (vol. 7). Westminster, Maryland: Newman Press, 1965.

- *County of Lambton Gazetteer and General Business Directory for 1864-65.*Ingersoll: Sutherland Brothers, 1864.

- Craig, G.M. *Upper Canada: The Formative Years.* Toronto: McClelland and Stewart, 1963.

- Creighton, D. G. *John A. Macdonald: The Young Politician.*Toronto: Macmillan, 1952.

- Creighton, D. G. *John A. Macdonald: The Old Chieftain.*Toronto:

Macmillan, 1955.

- Currie, A.W. *The Grand Trunk Railway of Canada*. Toronto: University of Toronto Press, 1957.

- Drew, Benjamin. *The Narratives of Fugitive Slaves in Canada*.Boston: John P. Jewitt, 1956.

- Edwards, Murray D. *A Stage in Our Past*. Toronto: University of Toronto Press, 1968.

- Elford, Jean Turnbull. *A History of Lambton County*. Sarnia: Lambton County Historical Society, 1967.

- Evans, Chad. *Frontier Theatre*. Victoria: Sono Nis Press, 1983.

- Fowke, Edith. *The Penguin Book of Canadian Folk Songs*.London: Penguin, 1973.

- Goodspeed, D.J. *The Road Past Vimy: The Canadian Corps, 1914-1918*.Toronto: Macmillan, 1969.

- Guillet, Edwin C. *Early Life in Upper Canada*. Toronto: University of Toronto Press, 1933.

- Henry, J. T. *Early and Later History of Petroleum*. New York: Augustus Kelley, 1970.

- Higgins, Frank G. *A Physical and Cultural Atlas of Lambton County*. Sarnia: Lambton Historical Society, 1969.

- Hill, Daniel G. *The Freedom-Seekers: Blacks in Early Canada*. Toronto: Book Society, 1981.

- Howard, John Kinsey. *Strange Empire: The Story of Louis Riel*. Toronto: Swan Publishing, 1965.

- *Illustrated London, Ontario, Canada*, 2nd ed. London, Ontario: London Printing Company, 1900.

- Judd, Denis. *Edward VII: A Pictorial Bibliography*. London: Macdonald and Jane's, 1975.

- Jury, Elsie McLeod. *The Neutral Indians of South-Western Ontario*. London, Ontario: The University of Western Ontario, 1974.

- Landon, Fred. *Western Ontario and the American Frontier*. Toronto: McClelland and Stewart, 1967.

- Lauriston, Victor. *Lambton's Hundred Years: 1849-1949*. Sarnia: Corporation for the City of Sarnia, 1949.

- Lauriston, Victor. *Romantic Kent*. Chatham: Corporation for the County of Kent, 1952.

- *The London Free Press: 1849-1922*. Canadian Microfilms.

- *The London Advertiser: 1863-1922*. Canadian Microfilms.

- *McGuffey's Fourth Eclectic Reader*. New York: Van Antwerp Bragg, 1979.

- Miller, Orlo. *The Point: The History of the Village of Point Edward*. Point Edward: Corporation for the Village of Point Edward, 1978.

- Morley, Sheridan. *Oscar Wilde*. London: Wiedenfeld and Nicolson, 1976.

- Morton, W. L. *The Critical Years: 1857-1873, The Union of British North America*. Toronto: McClelland and Stewart, 1964.

- Morton, W. L. *The Kingdom of Canada*, 2nd ed. Toronto: McClelland and Stewart, 1969.

- Mulvaney, Charles P. *The History of the North-West Rebellion*. Toronto: A. H. Hovey, 1885.

- Nicholson, G. W. L. *Canadian Expeditionary Force, 1914-1919*. Ottawa: Queen's Printer, 1962.

- Nock, O. S. *Railways of Canada*. London: Adam and Charles Black, 1973.

- O'Brien, Kevin. *Oscar Wilde in Canada*. Toronto: Personal Library, 1982.

- *Pen Pictures of Early Pioneer Life in Upper Canada by 'A Canuck'*. Toronto: William Briggs, 1905.

- Pettigrew, Eileen. *The Silent Enemy: Canada and the Deadly Flu of 1918*. Saskatoon: Western Producer Prairie Books, 1983.

- Phelps, Edward and Whipp, Charles. *Petrolia: 1866-1966*. Petrolia: The

Petrolia Advertiser-Topic, 1966.

- Phillips, C. E. *The Development of Education in Canada*. Toronto: Gage, 1957.

- Richardson, John. "A Trip to Walpole Island and Port Sarnia" in *Tecumseh and Richardson*. A. H. U. Colquhoun, ed., Toronto: Ontario Book Company, 1924.

- *The Sarnia Observer: 1853-1922*. Canadian Microfilms.

- Siebert, William H. *The Underground Railroad from Slavery to Freedom*. New York: Arno Press, 1968.

- Smith, W. H. *Canada: Past, Present and Future*, 2 vols. Toronto: Thomas MacLear, 1850.

- *Smith's Canadian Gazetteer: 1846*. Toronto: William H. Smith, 1846.

- Stamp, Robert M. *The Schools of Ontario 1876-1976*. Toronto: University of Toronto Press, 1982.

- Stanley, George F. *Canada's Soldiers 1604-1954*. Toronto: Macmillan, 1954.

- Stevens, G. R. *Canadian National Railways: Sixty Years of Trial and Error*(vol. 1). Toronto: Clarke Irwin, 1960.

- Still, William. *The Underground Railroad*. New York: Arno Press, 1968.

- Thomson, Colin. *Blacks in Deep Snow: Black Pioneers in Canada*. Toronto: J. M. Dent, 1979.

- *The Tour of HRH The Prince of Wales Through British America and the United States*. Montreal: John Lovell, 1860.

- *Trading and Shipping on the Great Lakes*. Coles Canadiana Reprint, Toronto: 1980.

- Waite, P. B. *Arduous Destiny: Canada, 1874-1896*. Toronto: McClelland and Stewart, 1971.

- Walsh, Henry H. *The Christian Church in Canada*. Toronto: Ryerson Press, 1966.

- Wilgus, W. J. *The Railway Interrelations of the United States and Canada*. Toronto: Ryerson Press, 1937.

Lightning Source UK Ltd.
Milton Keynes UK
UKHW040952220720
366958UK00001B/168